Zuckerman Bound

A TRILOGY AND EPILOGUE

BOOKS BY PHILIP ROTH

Philip Roth

Zuckerman Bound

THE GHOST WRITER

ZUCKERMAN UNBOUND

THE ANATOMY LESSON

EPILOGUE:
THE PRAGUE ORGY

FARRAR STRAUS GIROUX / NEW YORK

First printing, 1985

The text of *The Ghost Writer* first appeared
in *The New Yorker*. In slightly different form,
sections of *Zuckerman Unbound* appeared in
The Atlantic, The New Yorker, and *Playboy*,
and sections of *The Anatomy Lesson* appeared in
Esquire, Vanity Fair, and *Vogue*.

The quotation from James Cyriax's *Textbook
of Orthopaedic Medicine*,
copyright © 1978 by Ballière Tindall,
is reprinted with the
kind permission of Ballière Tindall,
1 St. Anne's Road, Eastbourne, East Sussex, England

Library of Congress Cataloging in Publication Data
Roth, Philip.
Zuckerman bound.
"A trilogy consisting of The ghost writer, Zuckerman
unbound, The anatomy lesson, Epilogue."
I. Title.
PS3568.O855Z45 1985   813'.54   84-23265

Contents

The Ghost Writer

1 Maestro

It was the last daylight hour of a December afternoon more than twenty years ago—I was twenty-three, writing and publishing my first short stories, and like many a *Bildungsroman* hero before me, already contemplating my own massive *Bildungsroman*—when I arrived at his hideaway to meet the great man. The clapboard farmhouse was at the end of an unpaved road twelve hundred feet up in the Berkshires, yet the figure who emerged from the study to bestow a ceremonious greeting wore a gabardine suit, a knitted blue tie clipped to a white shirt by an unadorned silver clasp, and well-brushed ministerial black shoes that made me think of him stepping down from a shoeshine stand rather than from the high altar of art. Before I had composure enough to notice the commanding, autocratic angle at which he held his chin, or the regal, meticulous, rather dainty care he took to arrange his clothes before sitting—to notice anything, really, other than that I had miraculously made it from my unliterary origins to here, to him—my impression was that E. I. Lonoff looked more like the local superintendent of schools than the region's most original storyteller since Melville and Hawthorne.

Not that the New York gossip about him should have led me to expect anything more grand. When I had recently raised his name before the jury at my first Manhattan publishing party—I'd arrived, excited as a starlet, on the arm of an elderly editor—Lonoff was almost immediately disposed of by the wits on hand as though it were comical that a Jew of his generation, an immigrant child to begin with, should have married the scion of an old New England family and lived all these years "in the country"—that is to say, in the *goyish* wilderness of birds and trees where America began and long ago had ended. However, since everybody else of renown I mentioned at the party also seemed slightly amusing to those in the know, I had been skeptical about their satiric description of the famous rural recluse. In fact, from what I saw at that party, I could begin to understand why hiding out twelve hundred feet up in the mountains with just the birds and the trees might not be a bad idea for a writer, Jewish or not.

The living room he took me into was neat, cozy, and plain: a large circular hooked rug, some slipcovered easy chairs, a worn sofa, a long wall of books, a piano, a phonograph, an oak library table systematically stacked with journals and magazines. Above the white wainscoting, the pale-yellow walls were bare but for half a dozen amateur watercolors of the old farmhouse in different seasons. Beyond the cushioned windowseats and the colorless cotton curtains tied primly back I could see the bare limbs of big dark maple trees and fields of driven snow. Purity. Serenity. Simplicity. Seclusion. All one's concentration and flamboyance and originality reserved for the grueling, exalted, transcendent calling. I looked around and I thought, This is how I will live.

After directing me to one of a pair of easy chairs beside the fireplace, Lonoff removed the fire screen and peered in to be sure the draft was open. With a wooden match he lighted the kindling that apparently had been laid there in anticipation of our meeting. Then he placed the fire screen back into position as precisely as though it were being fitted into a groove in the hearth. Certain that the logs had caught—satisfied that he had successfully ignited a fire without endangering the two-hundred-year-old house or its inhabitants—he was ready at last to join me. With hands that were almost ladylike in the swiftness and delicacy of their movements, he hiked the crease in each trouser leg and took his seat. He moved with a notable lightness for such a large, heavyset man.

"How would you prefer to be addressed?" asked Emanuel Isidore Lonoff. "As Nathan, Nate, or Nat? Or have you another preference entirely?" Friends and acquaintances called him Manny, he informed me, and I should do the same. "That will make conversation easier."

I doubted that, but I smiled to indicate that no matter how light-headed it was bound to leave me, I would obey. The master then proceeded to undo me further by asking to hear something from me about my life. Needless to say, there wasn't much to report about my life in 1956—certainly not, as I saw it, to someone so knowing and deep. I had been raised by doting parents in a Newark neighborhood neither rich nor poor; I had a younger brother who was said to idolize me; at a good local high school and an excellent college I had performed as generations of my forebears had expected me to; subsequently I had served in the Army, stationed just an hour from home, writing public-information handouts for a Fort Dix major, even while the massacre for which my carcass had been drafted was being bloodily concluded in Korea. Since my discharge I had been living and writing in a five-flight walk-up off lower Broadway, characterized by my girl friend, when she came to share the place and fix it up a little, as the home of an unchaste monk.

To support myself I crossed the river to New Jersey three days a week to a job I'd held on and off since my first summer in college, when I'd answered an ad promising high commissions to aggressive salesmen. At eight each morning our crew was driven to some New Jersey mill town to sell magazine subscriptions door-to-door, and at six we were picked up outside a designated saloon and driven back to downtown Newark by the overseer, McElroy. He was a spiffy rummy with a hairline mustache who never tired of warning us—two high-minded boys who were putting away their earnings for an education, and three listless old-timers, pale, puffy men wrecked by every conceivable misfortune—not to fool with the housewives we found alone at home in their curlers: you could get your neck broken by an irate husband, you could be set up for walloping blackmail, you could catch any one of fifty leprous varieties of clap, and what was more, there were only so many hours in the day. "Either get laid," he coldly advised us, "or sell *Silver Screen*. Take your pick." "Mammon's Moses" we two college boys called him. Since no housewife ever indicated a desire to invite me into the hallway to so much as rest my feet—and I was vigilantly on the lookout for lasciviousness flaring up in any woman of any age who seemed even half willing to listen to me from behind her screen door—I of necessity chose perfection of the work rather than the life, and by the end of each long day of canvassing had ten to twenty dollars in commissions to my credit and an unblemished future still before me. It was only a matter of weeks since I had relinquished this un-hallowed life—and the girl friend in the five-flight walk-up, whom I no longer loved—and, with the help of the dis-tinguished New York editor, had been welcomed for the winter months as a communicant at the Quahsay Colony, the rural artists' retreat across the state line from Lonoff's mountain.

From Quahsay I had sent Lonoff the literary quarter-lies that had published my stories—four so far—along with a letter telling him how much he had meant to me when I came upon his work "some years ago" in college. In the same breath I mentioned coming upon his "kinsmen" Chekhov and Gogol, and went on to reveal in other unmistakable ways just how serious a literary fel-low I was—and, hand in hand with that, how young. But then nothing I had ever written put me in such a sweat as that letter. Everything undeniably true struck me as transparently false as soon as I wrote it down, and the greater the effort to be sincere, the worse it went. I finally sent him the tenth draft and then tried to stick my arm down the throat of the mailbox to extract it.

I wasn't doing any better in the plain and cozy living room with my autobiography. Because I could not bring myself to utter even the mildest obscenity in front of

Lonoff's early American mantelpiece, my imitation of Mr. McElroy—a great favorite among my friends—didn't really have much to recommend it. Nor could I speak easily of all McElroy had warned us against, or begin to mention how tempted I would have been to yield, if opportunity had only knocked. You would have thought, listening to my bowdlerized version of what was a tepid enough little life history, that rather than having received a warm and gracious letter from the famous writer inviting me to come and spend a pleasant evening in his house, I had made this journey to plead a matter of utmost personal urgency before the most stringent of inquisitors, and that if I made one wrong move, something of immeasurable value to me would be lost forever.

Which was pretty much the case, even if I didn't completely understand as yet how desperate I was for his recognition, and why. Far from being nonplused by my bashful, breathless delivery—out of character though it was for me in those confident years—I should have been surprised to find that I wasn't down on the hooked rug, supplicating at his feet. For I had come, you see, to submit myself for candidacy as nothing less than E. I. Lonoff's spiritual son, to petition for his moral sponsorship and to win, if I could, the magical protection of his advocacy and his love. Of course, I had a loving father of my own, whom I could ask the world of any day of the week, but my father was a foot doctor and not an artist, and lately we had been having serious trouble in the

family because of a new story of mine. He was so bewildered by what I had written that he had gone running
to *his* moral mentor, a certain Judge Leopold Wapter,
to get the judge to get his son to see the light. As a result,
after two decades of a more or less unbroken amiable
conversation, we had not been speaking for nearly five
weeks now, and I was off and away seeking patriarchal
validation elsewhere.

And not just from a father who was an artist instead of
a foot doctor, but from the most famous literary ascetic in America, that giant of patience and fortitude and
selflessness who, in the twenty-five years between his first
book and his sixth (for which he was given a National
Book Award that he quietly declined to accept), had
virtually no readership or recognition, and invariably
would be dismissed, if and when he was even mentioned,
as some quaint remnant of the Old World ghetto, an out-
of-step folklorist pathetically oblivious of the major cur-
rents of literature and society. Hardly anyone knew who
he was or where actually he lived, and for a quarter of a
century almost nobody cared. Even among his readers
there had been some who thought that E. I. Lonoff's
fantasies about Americans had been written in Yiddish
somewhere inside czarist Russia before he supposedly
died there (as, in fact, his father had nearly perished)
from injuries suffered in a pogrom. What was so admirable to me was not only the tenacity that had kept him
writing his own kind of stories all that time but that hav-

ing been "discovered" and popularized, he refused all awards and degrees, declined membership in all honorary institutions, granted no public interviews, and chose not to be photographed, as though to associate his face with his fiction were a ridiculous irrelevancy.

The only photograph anyone in the reading public had ever seen was the watery sepia portrait which had appeared in 1927 on an inside jacket flap of *It's Your Funeral*: the handsome young artist with the lyrical almond eyes and the dark prow of a paramour's pompadour and the kissable, expressive underlip. So different was he now, not just because of jowls and a belly and the white-fringed, bald cranium but as a human type altogether, that I thought (once I began to be able to think) it had to be something more ruthless than time that accounted for the metamorphosis: it would have to be Lonoff himself. Other than the full, glossy eyebrows and the vaguely heavenward tilt of the willful chin, there was really nothing at all to identify him, at fifty-six, with the photo of the passionate, forlorn, shy Valentino who, in the decade lorded over by the young Hemingway and Fitzgerald, had written a collection of short stories about wandering Jews unlike anything written before by any Jew who had wandered into America.

In fact, my own first reading through Lonoff's canon —as an orthodox college atheist and highbrow-in-training—had done more to make me realize how much I was still my family's Jewish offspring than anything I had carried forward to the University of Chicago from childhood Hebrew lessons, or mother's kitchen, or the discussions I used to hear among my parents and our relatives about the perils of intermarriage, the problem of Santa Claus, and the injustice of medical-school quotas (quotas that, as I understood early on, accounted for my father's career in chiropody and his ardent lifelong support of the B'nai B'rith Anti-Defamation League). As a grade-school kid I could already debate these intricate issues with anyone (and did, when called upon); by the time I left for Chicago, however, my passion had been pretty well spent and I was as ready as an adolescent could be to fall headlong for Robert Hutchins' Humanities One. But then, along with tens of thousands of others, I discovered E. I. Lonoff, whose fiction seemed to me a response to the same burden of exclusion and confinement that still weighed upon the lives of those who had raised me, and that had informed our relentless household obsession with the status of the Jews. The pride inspired in my parents by the establishment in 1948 of a homeland in Palestine that would gather in the unmurdered remnant of European Jewry was, in fact, not so unlike what welled up in me when I first came upon Lonoff's thwarted, secretive, imprisoned souls, and realized that out of everything humbling from which my own striving, troubled father had labored to elevate us all, a literature of such dour wit and poignancy could be shamelessly conceived. To me it was as though the hallucinatory strains in Gogol had been filtered through the humane skepticism of Chekhov to nourish the country's first "Russian" writer. Or so I argued in the college essay where I "analyzed" Lonoff's style but kept to myself an explication of the feelings of kinship that his stories had revived in me for our own largely Americanized clan, moneyless immigrant shopkeepers to begin with, who'd carried on a shtetl life ten minutes' walk from the pillared banks and gargoyled insurance cathedrals of downtown Newark; and what is more, feelings of kinship for our pious, unknown ancestors, whose Galician tribulations had been only a little less foreign to me, while growing up securely in New Jersey, than Abraham's in the Land of Canaan. With his vaudevillian's feel for legend and landscape (a Chaplin, I said of Lonoff in my senior paper, who seized upon just the right prop to bring an entire society and its outlook to life); with his "translated" English to lend a mildly ironic flavor to even the most commonplace expression; with his cryptic, muted, dreamy resonance, the sense given by such little stories of saying so much—well, I had proclaimed, who in American literature was like him?

The typical hero of a Lonoff story—the hero who came to mean so much to bookish Americans in the mid-fifties, the hero who, some ten years after Hitler, seemed to say something new and wrenching to Gentiles about Jews, and to Jews about themselves, and to readers and writers of that recuperative decade generally about the ambiguities of prudence and the anxieties of disorder, about life-hunger, life-bargains, and life-terror in their most elementary manifestations—Lonoff's hero is more often than not a nobody from nowhere, away from a home where he is not missed, yet to which he must return without delay. His celebrated blend of sympathy and pitilessness (monumentalized as "Lonovian" by *Time*—after decades of ignoring him completely) is nowhere more stunning than in the stories where the bemused isolate steels himself to be carried away, only to discover that his meticulous thoughtfulness has caused him to wait a little too long to do anyone any good, or that acting with bold and uncharacteristic impetuosity, he has totally misjudged what had somehow managed to entice him out of his manageable existence, and as a result has made everything worse.

The grimmest, funniest, and most unsettling stories of all, where the pitiless author seems to me to teeter just at the edge of self-impalement, were written during the brief period of his literary glory (for he died in 1961 of a bone-marrow disease; and when Oswald shot Kennedy and the straitlaced bulwark gave way to the Gargantuan banana republic, his fiction, and the authority it granted to all that is prohibitive in life, began rapidly losing "relevance" for a new generation of readers). Rather than cheering him up, Lonoff's eminence seemed to strengthen his dourest imaginings, confirming for him visions of terminal restraint that might have seemed insufficiently supported by personal experience had the world denied him its rewards right down to the end. Only when a little of the coveted bounty was finally his for the asking—only when it became altogether clear just how stupefyingly unsuited he was to have and to hold anything other than his art—was he inspired to write that brilliant cycle of comic parables (the stories "Revenge," "Lice," "Indiana," "Eppes Essen," and "Adman") in which the tantalized hero does not move to act *at all*—the tiniest impulse toward amplitude or self-surrender, let alone intrigue or adventure, peremptorily extinguished by the ruling triumvirate of Sanity, Responsibility, and Self-Respect, assisted handily by their devoted underlings: the timetable, the rainstorm, the headache, the busy signal, the traffic jam, and, most loyal of all, the last-minute doubt.

Did I sell any magazines other than *Photoplay* and *Silver Screen*? Did I use the same line at every door or adapt my sales pitch to the customer? How did I account for my success as a salesman? What did I think people were after who subscribed to these insipid magazines? Was the work boring? Did anything unusual ever happen while I was prowling neighborhoods I knew nothing about? How many crews like Mr. McElroy's were there in New Jersey? How could the company afford to pay me three dollars for each subscription I sold? Had I ever been to Hackensack? What was it like?

It was difficult to believe that what I was doing merely

to support myself until I might begin to live as he did could possibly be of interest to E. I. Lonoff. He was a courteous man, obviously, and he was trying his best to put me at ease, but I was thinking, even as I gave my all to his cross-examination, that it wasn't going to be long before he came up with a way of getting rid of me before dinner.

"I wish I knew that much about selling magazines," he said.

To indicate that it was all right with me if I was being condescended to and that I would understand if I was soon asked to leave, I went red.

"I wish," he said, "I knew that much about anything. I've written fantasy for thirty years. Nothing happens to me."

It was here that the striking girl-woman appeared before me—just as he had aired, in faintly discernible tones of self-disgust, this incredible lament and I was trying to grasp it. Nothing happened to him? Why, genius had happened to him, art had happened to him, the man was a visionary!

Lonoff's wife, the white-haired woman who had instantly removed herself after letting me into the house, had pushed open the door of the study across the foyer from the living room, and there she was, hair dark and profuse, eyes pale—gray or green—and with a high prominent oval forehead that looked like Shakespeare's. She was seated on the carpet amid a pile of papers and folders, swathed in a "New Look" tweed skirt—by now a very old, outmoded look in Manhattan—and a large, loose-fitting, white wool sweater; her legs were drawn demurely up beneath the expanse of skirt and her gaze was fixed on something that was clearly elsewhere. Where had I seen that severe dark beauty before? Where but in a portrait by Velázquez? I remembered the 1927 photograph of Lonoff—"Spanish" too in its way—and immediately I assumed that she was his daughter. Immediately I assumed more than that. Mrs. Lonoff had not even set the tray down on the carpet beside her before I saw myself married to the *infanta* and living in a little farmhouse of our own not that far away. Only how old was she if Mama was feeding her cookies while she finished her homework on Daddy's floor? With that face, whose strong bones looked to me to have been worked into alignment by a less guileless sculptor than nature— with that face she *must* be more than twelve. Though if not, I could wait. That idea appealed to me even more than the prospect of a marriage here in the living room in spring. Showed strength of character, I thought. But what would the famous father think? He of course wouldn't need to be reminded of the solid Old Testament precedent for waiting seven years before making Miss Lonoff my bride; on the other hand, how would he take it when he saw me hanging around outside her high school in my car?

Meanwhile, he was saying to me, "I turn sentences around. That's my life. I write a sentence and then I turn it around. Then I look at it and I turn it around again. Then I have lunch. Then I come back in and write another sentence. Then I have tea and turn the new sentence around. Then I read the two sentences over and turn them both around. Then I lie down on my sofa and think. Then I get up and throw them out and start from the beginning. And if I knock off from this routine for as long as a day, I'm frantic with boredom and a sense of waste. Sundays I have breakfast late and read the papers with Hope. Then we go for a walk in the hills, and I'm haunted by the loss of all that good time. I wake up Sunday mornings and I'm nearly crazy at the prospect of all those unusable hours. I'm restless, I'm bad-tempered, but she's a human being too, you see, so I go. To avoid trouble she makes me leave my watch at home. The result is that I look at my wrist instead. We're walking, she's talking, then I look at my wrist—and that generally does it, if my foul mood hasn't already. She throws in the sponge and we come home. And at home what is there to distinguish Sunday from Thursday? I sit back down at my little Olivetti and start looking at sentences and turning them around. And I ask myself, Why is there no way but this for me to fill my hours?"

By now Hope Lonoff had closed the study door and returned to her chores. Together Lonoff and I listened to her Mixmaster whirling in the kitchen. I didn't know what to say. The life he described sounded like paradise to me; that he could think to do nothing better with his time than turn sentences around seemed to me a blessing bestowed not only upon him but upon world literature. I wondered if perhaps I was supposed to be laughing, despite the deadpan delivery, at his description of his day, if it wasn't intended as mordant Lonovian comedy; though then again, if he meant it and was as depressed as he sounded, oughtn't I to remind him just who he was and how much he mattered to literate mankind? But how could he not know that?

The Mixmaster whirled and the fire popped and the wind blew and the trees groaned while I tried, at twenty-three, to think of how to dispel his gloom. His openness about himself, so at odds with his formal attire and his pedantic manner, had me as unnerved as anything else; it was hardly what I was accustomed to getting from people more than twice my age, even if what he said about himself was tinged with self-satire. Especially if it was tinged with self-satire.

"I wouldn't even try to write after my tea any more if I knew what to do with myself for the rest of the afternoon." He explained to me that by three o'clock he no longer had the strength or the determination or even the desire to go on. But what else was there? If he played the violin or the piano, then he might have had some serious activity other than reading to occupy him when he was not writing. The problem with just listening to music was that if he sat alone with a record in the afternoon, he soon found himself turning the sentences around in his head and eventually wound up back at his desk again, skeptically looking at his day's work. Of course, to his great good fortune, there was Athene College. He spoke with devotion of the students in the two classes that he taught there. The little Stockbridge school had made a place for him on the faculty some twenty years before the rest of the academic world suddenly became interested, and for that he would always be grateful. But in truth, after so many years of teaching these bright and lively young women, both he and they, he found, had begun to repeat themselves a little.

"Why not take a sabbatical?" I was not a little thrilled, after all I had been through in my first fifteen minutes, to hear myself telling E. I. Lonoff how to live.

"I took a sabbatical. It was worse. We rented a flat in London for a year. Then I had every day to write. Plus Hope being miserable because I wouldn't stop to go around with her to look at the buildings. No—no more sabbaticals. This way, at least two afternoons a week I have to stop, no questions asked. Besides, going to the college is the high point of my week. I carry a briefcase. I wear a hat. I nod hello to people on the stairway. I use a public toilet. Ask Hope. I come home reeling from the pandemonium."

"Are there no children—of your own?"

The phone began ringing in the kitchen. Ignoring it, he informed me that the youngest of their three children had graduated from Wellesley several years before; he and his wife had been alone together now for more than six years.

So the girl isn't his daughter. Who is she then, being served snacks by his wife on the floor of his study? His concubine? Ridiculous, the word, the very idea, but there it was obscuring all other reasonable and worthy thoughts. Among the rewards you got for being a great artist was the concubinage of Velázquez princesses and the awe of young men like me. I felt at a loss again, having such ignoble expectations in the presence of my literary conscience—though weren't they just the kind of ignoble expectations that troubled the masters of renunciation in so many of Lonoff's short stories? Really, who knew better than E. I. Lonoff that it is not our high purposes alone that make us moving creatures, but our humble needs and cravings? Nonetheless, it seemed to me a good idea to keep my humble needs and cravings to myself.

The kitchen door opened a few inches and his wife said softly, "For you."

"Who is it? Not the genius again."

"Would I have said you were here?"

"You have to learn to tell people no. People like that make fifty calls a day. Inspiration strikes and they go for the phone."

"It's not him."

"He has the right wrong opinion on everything. A head full of ideas, every one of them stupid. Why does he hit me when he talks? Why must he understand everything? Stop fixing me up with intellectuals. I don't think fast enough."

"I've said I was sorry. And it's not him."

"Who is it?"

"Willis."

"Hope, I'm talking to Nathan here."

"I'm sorry. I'll tell him you're working."

"Don't use work as an excuse. I don't buy that."

"I can tell him you have a guest."

"Please," I said, meaning I was no one, not even a guest.

"All that wonder," said Lonoff to his wife. "Always so greatly moved. Always on the brink of tears. What is he so compassionate about all the time?"

"You," she said.

"All that sensitivity. Why does anybody want to be so sensitive?"

"He admires you," she said.

Buttoning his jacket, Lonoff rose to take the unwanted call. "Either it's the professional innocents," he explained to me, "or the deep thinkers."

I extended my sympathy with a shrug, wondering, of course, if my letter hadn't qualified me in both categories. Then I wondered again about the girl behind the study door. Does she live at the college or is she here with the Lonoffs on a visit from Spain? Would she ever be coming out of that study? If not, how do I go in? If not, how can I arrange to see her again by myself?

I must see you again.

I opened a magazine, the better to dispel my insidious daydreams and wait there like a thoughtful man of letters. Leafing through the pages, I came across an article about the Algerian political situation and another about the television industry, both of which had been underlined throughout. Read in sequence, the underlinings formed a perfect precis of each piece and would have served a schoolchild as excellent preparation for a report to his current-events class.

When Lonoff emerged—in under a minute—from the kitchen, he immediately undertook to explain about the *Harper's* in my hand. "My mind strays," he told me, rather as though I were a physician who had stopped by to ask about his strange and troubling new symptoms. "At the end of the page I try to summarize to myself what I've read and my mind is a blank—I've been sitting in my chair doing nothing. Of course, I have always read books with pen in hand, but now I find that if I don't, even while reading magazines, my attention is not on what's in front of me."

Here she appeared again. But what had seemed from a distance like beauty, pure and severe and simple, was more of a puzzle up close. When she crossed the foyer into the living room—entering just as Lonoff had ended his fastidious description of the disquieting affliction that came over him when he read magazines—I saw that the striking head had been conceived on a much grander and more ambitious scale than the torso. The bulky sweater and the pounds and pounds of tweed skirt did much, of course, to obscure the little of her there was, but mostly it was the drama of that face, combined with the softness and intelligence in her large pale eyes, that rendered all other physical attributes (excluding the heavy, curling hair) blurry and inconsequential. Admittedly, the rich calm of those eyes would have been enough to make me wilt with shyness, but that I couldn't return her gaze directly had also to do with this unharmonious relation between body and skull, and its implication, to me, of some early misfortune, of something vital lost or beaten down, and, by way of compensation, something vastly overdone. I thought of a trapped chick that could not get more than its beaked skull out of the encircling shell. I thought of those macrocephalic boulders the Easter Island heads. I thought of febrile patients on the verandas of Swiss sanatoria imbibing the magic-mountain air. But let me not exaggerate the pathos and originality of my impressions, especially as they were subsumed soon enough in my unoriginal and irrepressible preoccupation: mostly I thought of the triumph it would be to kiss that face, and the excitement of her kissing me back.

"Done," she announced to Lonoff, "for now."

His look of wistful solicitude made me wonder if she could be his *grand*daughter. All at once he seemed the most approachable of men, relieved of every care and burden. Perhaps, I thought—still trying to explain some oddness in her that I couldn't identify—she is the child of a daughter of his own who is dead.

"This is Mr. Zuckerman, the short-story writer," he said, teasing sweetly, like *my* grandfather now. "I gave you his collected works to read."

I rose and shook her hand.

"This is Miss Bellette. She was once a student here. She has been staying with us for a few days, and has taken it upon herself to begin sorting through my manuscripts. There is a movement afoot to persuade me to deposit with Harvard University the pieces of paper on which I turn my sentences around. Amy works for the Harvard library. The Athene library has just extended her an exceptional offer, but she tells us she is tied to her life in Cambridge. Meanwhile, she has cunningly been using the visit to try to persuade me—"

"No, no, no," she said emphatically. "If you see it that way, my cause is doomed." As if she hadn't charm enough, Miss Bellette's speech was made melodious by a faint foreign accent. "The maestro," she explained, turning my way, "is by temperament counter-suggestible."

"And counter that," he moaned, registering a mild protest against the psychological lingo.

"I've just found twenty-seven drafts of a single short story," she told me.

"Which story?" I asked eagerly.

" 'Life Is Embarrassing.' "

"To get it wrong," said Lonoff, "so many times."

"They ought to construct a monument to your patience," she told him.

He gestured vaguely toward the crescent of plumpness buttoned in beneath his jacket. "They have."

"In class," she said, "he used to tell the writing students, 'There is no life without patience.' None of us knew what he was talking about."

"You knew. You had to know. My dear young lady, I learned that from watching you."

"But I can't wait for anything," she said.

"But you do."

"Bursting with frustration all the while."

"If you weren't bursting," her teacher informed her, "you wouldn't need patience."

At the hall closet she stepped out of the loafers she'd worn into the living room and slipped on white woolen socks and a pair of red snow boots. Then from a hanger she took down a plaid hooded jacket, into whose sleeve was tucked a white wool cap with a long tassel that ended in a fluffy white ball. Having seen her only seconds before banter so easily with the celebrated writer—having myself felt ever so slightly drawn into the inner circle by her easy, confident way with him—I was surprised by the childish hat. The costume, now that she had it on, seemed like a little girl's. That she could act so wise and dress up so young mystified me.

Along with Lonoff I stood in the open doorway waving goodbye. I was now in awe of two people in this house.

There was still more wind than snow, but in Lonoff's orchard the light had all but seeped away, and the sound of what was on its way was menacing. Two dozen wild old apple trees stood as first barrier between the bleak unpaved road and the farmhouse. Next came a thick green growth of rhododendron, then a wide stone wall fallen in like a worn molar at the center, then some fifty feet of snow-crusted lawn, and finally, drawn up close to the house and protectively overhanging the shingles, three maples that looked from their size to be as old as New England. In back, the house gave way to unprotected fields, drifted over since the first December blizzards. From there the wooded hills began their impressive rise, undulating forest swells that just kept climbing into the next state. My guess was that it would take even the fiercest Hun the better part of a winter to cross the glacial waterfalls and wind-blasted woods of those mountain wilds before he was able to reach the open edge of Lonoff's hayfields, rush the rear storm door of the house, crash through into the study, and, with spiked bludgeon wheeling high in the air above the little Olivetti, cry out in a roaring voice to the writer tapping out his twenty-seventh draft, "You must change your life!" And even he might lose heart and turn back to the bosom of his barbarian family should he approach those black Massachusetts hills on a night like this, with the cocktail hour at hand and yet another snowstorm arriving from Ultima Thule. No, for the moment, at least, Lonoff seemed really to have nothing to worry about from the outside world.

We watched from the front step until Lonoff was sure that she had cleared both the windshield and rear window; snow had already begun adhering to the icy glass. "Drive very slowly," he called. To get into the diminutive green Renault she had to hike up a handful of long skirt. Above the snow boots I saw an inch of flesh, and quickly looked elsewhere so as not to be found out.

"Yes, be careful," I called to her, in the guise of Mr. Zuckerman the short-story writer. "It's slippery, it's deceptive."

"She has a remarkable prose style," Lonoff said to me when we were back inside the house. "The best student writing I've ever read. Wonderful clarity. Wonderful comedy. Tremendous intelligence. She wrote stories about the college which capture the place in a sentence. Everything she sees, she takes hold of. And a lovely pianist. She can play Chopin with great charm. She used to practice on our daughter's piano when she first came to Athene. That was something I looked forward to at the end of the day."

"She seems to be quite a girl," I said thoughtfully. "Where is she from originally?"

"She came to us from England."

"But the accent . . . ?"

"That," he allowed, "is from the country of Fetching."

"I agree," I dared to say, and thought: Enough shyness then, enough boyish uncertainty and tongue-tied deference. This, after all, is the author of "Life Is Embarrassing"—if he doesn't know the score, who does?

Standing by the fire, the two of us warming ourselves, I turned to Lonoff and said, "I don't think I could keep my wits about me, teaching at a school with such beautiful and gifted and fetching girls."

To which he replied flatly, "Then you shouldn't do it."

A surprise—yes, yet another—awaited me when we sat down to dinner. Lonoff uncorked a bottle of Chianti that had been waiting for us on the table and proposed a toast. Signaling his wife to raise her glass along with his, he said, "To a wonderful new writer."

Well, *that* loosened me up. Excitedly, I began talking about my month at Quahsay, how much I loved the serenity and beauty of the place, how I loved walking the trails there at the end of the day and reading in my room at night—rereading Lonoff of late, but that I kept to myself. From his toast it was obvious that I had not lost as much ground as I feared by confessing to the lure of clever, pretty college girls, and I did not want to risk offending him anew by seeming to fawn. The fawning, supersensitive Willis, I remembered, had been given less than sixty seconds on the phone.

I told the Lonoffs about the joy of awakening each

morning knowing there were all those empty hours ahead to be filled only with work. Never as a student or a soldier or a door-to-door salesman did I have regular stretches of uninterrupted time to devote to writing, nor had I ever lived before in such quiet and seclusion, or with my few basic needs so unobtrusively satisfied as they were by the Quahsay housekeeping staff. It all seemed to me a marvelous, a miraculous gift. Just a few evenings before, after a day-long snowstorm, I had accompanied the Colony handyman when he set out after dinner on the snowplow to clear the trails that twisted for miles through the Quahsay woods. I described for the Lonoffs my exhilaration at watching the snow crest in the headlights of the truck and then fall away into the forest; the bite of the cold and the smack of the tire chains had seemed to me all I could ever want at the end of a long day at *my* Olivetti. I supposed I was being professionally innocent despite myself, but I couldn't stop going on about my hours on the snowplow after the hours at my desk: it wasn't just that I wanted to convince Lonoff of my pure and incorruptible spirit—my problem was that I wanted to believe it myself. My problem was that I wanted to be wholly worthy of his thrilling toast. "I could live like that forever," I announced.

"Don't try it," he said. "If your life consists of reading and writing and looking at the snow, you'll wind up like me. Fantasy for thirty years."

Lonoff made "Fantasy" sound like a breakfast cereal.

Here for the first time his wife spoke up—though given the self-effacing delivery, "spoke down" would be more exact. She was a smallish woman with gentle gray eyes and soft white hair and a multitude of fine lines criss-crossing her pale skin. Though she could well have been, as the amused literati had it, Lonoff's "high-born Yankee heiress"—and an excellent example of the species at its most maidenly—what she looked like now was some frontier survivor, the wife of a New England farmer who long ago rode out of these mountains to make a new start in the West. To me the lined face and the shadowy, timorous manner bore witness to a grinding history of agonized childbearing and escapes from the Indians, of famine and fevers and wagon-train austerities—I just couldn't believe that she could look so worn down from living alongside E. I. Lonoff while he wrote short stories for thirty years. I was to learn later that aside from two terms at a Boston art school and a few months in New York—and the year in London trying to get Lonoff to Westminster Abbey— Hope had strayed no farther than had the locally prominent lawyers and clergymen who were her forebears, and whose legacy by now came to nothing more tangible than one of the Berkshires' "best" names and the house that went with it.

She had met Lonoff when he came at the age of seventeen to work for a chicken farmer in Lenox. He himself had been raised just outside Boston, though until he was five lived in Russia. After his father, a jeweler, nearly died from injuries suffered in the Zhitomir pogrom, Lonoff's parents emigrated to primitive Palestine. There typhus carried them both away, and their son was cared for by family friends in a Jewish farming settlement. At seven he was shipped alone from Jaffa to wealthy relatives of his father's in Brookline; at seventeen he chose vagabondage over college at the relatives' expense; and then at twenty he chose Hope—the rootless Levantine Valentino taking as his mate a cultivated young provincial woman, bound to the finer things by breeding and temperament, and to a settled place by old granite gravestones, church-meetinghouse plaques, and a long mountain road bearing the name Whittlesey: somebody from somewhere, for all the good that was to do him.

Despite everything that gave Hope Lonoff the obedient air of an aging geisha when she dared to speak or to move, I still wondered if she was not going to remind him that his life had consisted of something more than reading and writing and looking at snow: it had also consisted of her and the children. But there was not the hint of a reprimand in her unchallenging voice when she said, "You shouldn't express such a low opinion of your achievement. It's not becoming." Even more delicately, she added, "And it's not true."

Lonoff lifted his chin. "I was not measuring my achievement. I have neither too high nor too low an estimate of my work. I believe I know exactly wherein my value and originality lie. I know where I can go and just how far, without making a mockery of the thing we all love. I was only suggesting—surmising is more like it—that an unruly personal life will probably better serve a writer like Nathan than walking in the woods and startling the deer. His work has turbulence—that should be nourished, and not in the woods. All I was trying to say is that he oughtn't to stifle what is clearly his gift."

"I'm sorry," replied his wife. "I didn't understand. I thought you were expressing distaste for your own work." "Work" she pronounced in the accent of her region, without the "r."

"I was expressing distaste," said Lonoff, employing that pedantic tone he'd taken with Amy on the subject of her patience, and with me, describing his light-reading problem, "but not for the work. I was expressing distaste for the range of my imagination."

With a self-effacing smile designed to atone on the spot for her audacity, Hope said, "Your imagination or your experience?"

"I long ago gave up illusions about myself and experience."

She pretended to be brushing the crumbs from around the bread board, that and no more—while with unforeseen, somewhat inexplicable insistence, she softly confessed, "I never quite know what that means."

"It means I know who I am. I know the kind of man I am and the kind of writer. I have my own kind of bravery, and please, let's leave it at that."

She decided to. I remembered my food and began to eat again.

"Do you have a girl friend?" Lonoff asked me.

I explained the situation—to the extent that I was willing to.

Betsy had found out about me and a girl she had known since ballet school. The two of us had kissed over a glass of Gallo in the kitchen, playfully she had shown me the tip of her wine-stained tongue, and I, quick to take heart, had pulled her out of her chair and down beside the sink. This took place one evening when Betsy was off dancing at the City Center and the friend had stopped by to pick up a record and investigate a flirtation we'd begun some months earlier, when Betsy was away touring with the company. On my knees, I struggled to unclothe her; not resisting all that strenuously, she, on her knees, told me what a bastard I was to be doing this to Betsy. I refrained from suggesting that she might be less than honorable herself; trading insults while in heat wasn't my brand of aphrodisia, and I was afraid of a fiasco if I should try it and get carried away. So, shouldering the burden of perfidy for two, I pinned her pelvis to the kitchen linoleum, while she continued, through moist smiling lips, to inform me of my character flaws. I was then at the stage of my erotic development when nothing excited *me* as much as having intercourse on the floor.

Betsy was a romantic, excitable, high-strung girl who could be left quivering by the backfire of a car—so when the friend intimated over the phone to her a few days later that I wasn't to be trusted, it nearly destroyed her. It was a bad time for her, anyway. Yet another of her rivals had been cast as a cygnet in *Swan Lake*, and so, four years after having been enlisted by Balanchine as a seventeen-year-old of great promise, she had yet to rise out of the corps and it didn't look to her now as though she ever would. And how she worked to be the best! Her art was everything, a point of view no less beguiling to me than the large painted gypsy-girl eyes and the small unpainted she-monkey face, and those elegant, charming tableaux she could achieve, even when engaged in something so aesthetically unpromising as, half asleep in the middle of the night, taking a lonely pee in my bathroom. When we were first introduced in New York, I knew nothing about ballet and had never seen a real dancer on the stage, let alone off. An Army friend who'd grown up next door to Betsy in Riverdale had gotten us tickets for a Tchaikovsky extravaganza and then arranged for a girl who was dancing in it to have coffee with us around the corner from the City Center that afternoon. Fresh from rehearsal and enchantingly full of herself, Betsy amused us by recounting the horrors of her self-sacrificing vocation—a cross, as she described it, between the life of a boxer and the life of a nun. And the worrying! She had begun studying at the age of eight and had been worrying ever since about her height and her weight and her ears and her rivals and her injuries and her chances—right now she was in absolute terror about tonight. I myself couldn't see that she had reason to be anxious about anything (least of all those ears), so entranced was I already by the dedication and the glamour. At the theater I unfortunately couldn't remember—once the music had begun and dozens of dancers rushed on stage—whether earlier she had told us that she was one of the girls in lavender with a pink flower in their hair or one of the girls in pink with a lavender flower in their hair, and so I spent most of the evening just trying to find her. Each time I thought that the legs and arms I was watching were Betsy's, I became so elated I wanted to cheer—but then another pack of ten came streaking across the stage and I thought, No, there, *that's* her.

"You were wonderful," I told her afterward. "Yes? Did you like my little solo? It's not actually a solo—it lasts only about fifteen seconds. But I do think it's awfully charming." "Oh, I thought it was terrific," I said, "it seemed like more than fifteen seconds to me."

A year later our artistic and amatory alliance came to an end when I confessed that the mutual friend had not been the first girl to be dragged onto the floor while Betsy was safely off dancing her heart out and I had nighttime hours with nothing to do and nobody to stop me. I had been at this for some time now and, I admitted, it was no way to be treating her. Bold honesty, of course, produced far more terrible results than if I had only confessed to seducing the wily seductress and left it at that;

nobody had asked me about anybody else. But carried away by the idea that if I were a perfidious brute, I at least would be a truthful perfidious brute, I was crueler than was either necessary or intended. In a fit of penitential gloom, I fled from New York to Quahsay, where eventually I managed to absolve myself of the sin of lust and the crime of betrayal by watching from behind the blade of the snowplow as it cleared the Colony roads for my solitary and euphoric walks—walks during which I did not hesitate to embrace trees and kneel down and kiss the glistening snow, so bursting was I with a sense of gratitude and freedom and renewal.

Of all this, I told the Lonoffs only the charming part about how we had met and also that now, sadly, my girl friend and I were trying a temporary separation. Otherwise, I portrayed her in such uxorious detail that, along with the unnerving sense that I might be laying it on a little thick for this old married couple, I wound up in wonder at the idiot I had been to relinquish her love. Describing all her sterling qualities, I had, in fact, brought myself nearly to the point of grief, as though instead of wailing with pain and telling me to leave and never come back, the unhappy dancer had died in my arms on our wedding day.

Hope Lonoff said, "I knew that she was a dancer from the *Saturday Review*."

The *Saturday Review* had published an article on America's young, unknown writers, photographs and thumbnail sketches of "A Dozen to Keep Your Eye On," selected by the editors of the major literary quarterlies. I had been photographed playing with Nijinsky, our cat. I had confessed to the interviewer that my "friend" was with the New York City Ballet, and when asked to name the three living writers I admired most, I had listed E. I. Lonoff first.

I was disturbed now to think that this must have been the first Lonoff had heard of me—though, admittedly, while answering the interviewer's impossible questions, I had been hoping that my comment might bring my work to his attention. The morning the magazine appeared on the newsstands I must have read the bit about "N. Zuckerman" fifty times over. I tried to put in my self-prescribed six hours at the typewriter but got nowhere, what with picking up the article and looking at my picture every five minutes. I don't know what I expected to see revealed there—the future probably, the titles of my first ten books—but I do remember thinking that this photograph of an intense and serious young writer playing so gently with a kitty cat, and said to be living in a five-flight Village walk-up with a young ballerina, might inspire any number of thrilling women to want to try to take her place.

"I would never have allowed that to appear," I said, "if I had realized how it was all going to come out. They interviewed me for an hour and then what they used of what I said was nonsense."

"Don't apologize," said Lonoff.

"Don't indeed," said his wife, smiling at me. "What's wrong with having your picture in the paper?"

"I didn't mean the picture—though that, too. I never knew they were going to use the one of me with the cat. I expected they'd use the one at the typewriter. I should have realized they couldn't show everybody at a typewriter. The girl who came around to take the pictures"— and whom I had tried unsuccessfully to throw onto the floor—"said she'd just take the picture of the cat for Betsy and me."

"Don't apologize," Lonoff repeated, "unless you know for sure you're not going to do it again next time. Otherwise, just do it and forget it. Don't make a production out of it."

Hope said, "He only means he understands, Nathan. He has the highest respect for what you are. We don't have visitors unless they're people Manny respects. He has no tolerance for people without substance."

"Enough," said Lonoff.

"I just don't want Nathan to resent you for superiority feelings you don't have."

"My wife would have been happier with a less exacting companion."

"But you *are* less exacting," she said, "with everyone but yourself. Nathan, you don't have to defend yourself. Why shouldn't you enjoy your first bit of recognition? Who deserves it more than a gifted young man like yourself? Think of all the worthless people held up for our esteem every day: movie stars, politicians, athletes. Because you happen to be a writer doesn't mean you have to deny yourself the ordinary human pleasure of being praised and applauded."

"Ordinary human pleasures have nothing to do with it. Ordinary human pleasures be damned. The young man wants to be an artist."

"Sweetheart," she replied, "you must sound to Nathan so—so unyielding. And you're really not that way at all. You're the most forgiving and understanding and modest person I have ever known. Too modest."

"Let's forget how I sound and have dessert."

"But you are the kindest person. He is, Nathan. You've met Amy, haven't you?"

"Miss Bellette?"

"Do you know all he's done for her? She wrote him a letter when she was sixteen years old. In care of his publisher. The most charming, lively letter—so daring, so brash. She told him her story, and instead of forgetting it, he wrote her back. He has always written people back—a polite note even to the fools."

"What was her story?" I asked.

"Displaced," said Lonoff. "Refugee." That seemed to him to suffice, though not to the wagon-train wife, who surprised me now by the way that she pressed on. Was it the little bit of wine that had gone to her head? Or was there not something seething in her?

"She said she was a highly intelligent, creative, and charming sixteen-year-old who was now living with a not very intelligent, creative, or charming family in Bristol, England. She even included her IQ," Hope said. "No, no, that was the second letter. Anyway, she said she wanted a new start in life and she thought the man whose wonderful story she'd read in her school anthology—"

"It wasn't an anthology, but you might as well keep going."

Hope tried her luck with a self-effacing smile, but the wattage was awfully dim. "I think I can talk about this without help. I'm only relating the facts, and calmly enough, I had thought. Because the story was in a magazine, and not in an anthology, doesn't mean that I have lost control of myself. Furthermore, Amy is not the subject, not by any means. The subject is your extraordinary kindness and charity. Your concern for anyone in need —anyone except yourself, and your needs."

"Only my 'self,' as you like to call it, happens not to exist in the everyday sense of the word. Consequently, you may stop lavishing praise upon it. And worrying about its 'needs.' "

"But your self *does* exist. It has a perfect *right* to exist—and in the everyday sense!"

"Enough," he suggested again.

With that, she rose to begin to clear the dishes for dessert, and all at once a wineglass struck the wall. Hope had thrown it. "Chuck me out," she cried, "I want you to chuck me out. Don't tell me you can't, because you must! I want you to! I'll finish the dishes, then chuck me out, tonight! I beg of you—I'd rather live and die alone, I'd rather endure that than another moment of your bravery! I cannot take any more moral fiber in the face of life's disappointments! Not yours and not mine! I cannot bear having a loyal, dignified husband who has no illusions about himself *one second more!*"

My heart, of course, was pounding away, though not entirely because the sound of glass breaking and the sight of a disappointed woman, miserably weeping, was new to me. It was about a month old. On our last morning together Betsy had broken every dish of the pretty little Bloomingdale's set that we owned in common, and then, while I hesitated about leaving my apartment without making my position clear, she started in on the glassware. The hatred for me I had inspired by telling the whole truth had me particularly confused. If only I had lied, I thought—if only I had said that the friend who had intimated I might not be trustworthy was a troublemaking bitch, jealous of Betsy's success and not a little crazy, none of this would be happening. But then, if I had lied to her, I would have *lied* to her. Except that what I would have said about the friend would in essence have been true! I didn't get it. Nor did Betsy when I tried to calm her down and explain what a swell fellow I actually was to have been so candid about it all. It was here, in fact, that she set about destroying the slender drinking glasses, a set of six from Sweden that we had bought to replace the jelly jars on a joyous quasi-connubial outing some months earlier at Bonniers (bought along with the handsome Scandinavian throw rug onto which, in due course, I had tried to drag the photographer from the *Saturday Review*).

Hope Lonoff had now slumped back into her chair, the better to plead with her husband across the table. Her face was patched with blotches where she had been digging at the soft, creased skin in a fit of self-abasement. The frantic, agitated movement of her fingers alarmed me more even than the misery in her voice, and I wondered if I shouldn't reach over and pick up the serving fork from the table before she turned the prongs into her bosom and gave Lonoff's "self" the freedom to pursue what she thought it needed. But as I was only a guest—as I was "only" just about anything you could think of—I left all cutlery where it was and waited for the worst.

"Take her, Manny. If you want her, take her," she cried, "and then you won't be so miserable, and everything in the world won't be so bleak. She's not a student any more—she's a woman! You are *entitled* to her—you rescued her from oblivion, you are more than entitled: it's the only thing that makes sense! Tell her to accept that job, tell her to stay! She should! And I'll move away! Because I cannot live another moment as your jailer! Your nobility is eating away the last thing that is left! You are a monument and can take it and take it—but I'm down to nothing, darling, and I can't. Chuck me out! Please, now, before your goodness and your wisdom kill us both!"

Lonoff and I sat talking together in the living room after dinner, each sipping with admirable temperance at the tablespoonful of cognac he had divided between two large snifters. I had so far experienced brandy only as a stopgap household remedy for toothache: a piece of absorbent cotton, soaked in the stuff, would be pressed against my throbbing gum until my parents could get me to the dentist. I accepted Lonoff's offer, however, as though it accorded with my oldest post-prandial custom. The comedy thickened when my host, another big drinker, went to look for the right glasses. After a systematic search he finally found them at the rear of the bottom cabinet in the foyer breakfront. "A gift," he explained, "I thought they were still in the box," and took two into the kitchen to wash away dust that seemed to have been accumulating since the time of Napoleon, whose name was on the sealed brandy bottle. While he was at it he decided to wash the four other glasses in the set, and put them back in hiding in the breakfront before rejoining me to begin our merrymaking at the hearth.

Not much later—in all, maybe twenty minutes after he had refused to respond in any way to her plea to be replaced by Amy Bellette—Hope could be heard in the kitchen, washing the dishes that Lonoff and I had silently cleared from the table following her departure. She seemed to have gotten down from their bedroom by a back stairway—probably so as not to disturb our conversation.

While helping him to clear up, I had not known what to do about her broken wineglass or about the saucer she inadvertently had knocked to the floor when she rushed from the table. My duty as ingenue was clearly to spare the stout man in the business suit from bending over, especially as he was E. I. Lonoff; on the other hand, I was still trying to get through by pretending that nothing shocking had happened in my presence. To keep the tantrum in perspective, he might even prefer that the broken bits be left where they were for Hope to clean up later, provided she did not first commit suicide in their room.

Even as my sense of moral niceties and my youthful cowardice battled it out with my naïveté, Lonoff, groaning slightly from the effort, brushed the glass into a dustpan and retrieved the saucer from beneath the dining table. It had broken neatly in two, and after inspecting the edges he observed, "She can glue it."

In the kitchen he left the dish for her to repair on a long wooden counter where pink and white geraniums were growing in clay pots beneath the windows. The kitchen was a bright, pretty room, a little cheerier and livelier looking than the rest of the house. Besides the geraniums flowering abundantly here even in winter, tall reeds and dried flowers were stuck all about in pitchers and vases and little odd-shaped bottles. The windowed wall cupboards were bright and homey and reassuring:

food staples labeled with unimpeachable brand names—
enough Bumble Bee tuna for an Eskimo family to survive
on in their igloo till spring—and jars of tomatoes, beans,
pears, crabapples, and the like, which seemed to have been
put up by Hope herself. Pots and pans with shining cop-
per bottoms hung in rows from a pegboard beside the
stove, and along the wall above the breakfast table were
half a dozen pictures in plain wooden frames, which
turned out to be short nature poems signed "H.L.," copied
in delicate calligraphy and decorated with watercolor de-
signs. It did indeed look to be the headquarters of a
woman who, in her own unostentatious way, could glue
anything and do anything, except figure out how to make
her husband happy.

We talked about literature and I was in heaven—also
in a sweat from the spotlight he was giving me to bask in.
Every book new to me I was sure he must have annotated with his reading pen long ago, yet his interest
was pointedly in hearing my thoughts, not his own. The
effect of his concentrated attention was to make me heap
insight onto precocious insight, and then to hang upon his
every sigh and grimace, investing what was only a little
bout of after-dinner dyspepsia with the direst implications
about my taste and my intelligence. Though I worried
that I was trying too hard to sound like the kind of deep
thinker for whom he had no love, I still couldn't stop myself, under the spell now not just of the man and his accomplishment but of the warm wood fire, of the brandy

snifter balanced in my hand (if not yet the brandy), and of the snow falling heavily beyond the cushioned window-seats, as dependably beautiful and mystifying as ever. Then there were the great novelists, whose spellbinding names I chanted as I laid my cross-cultural comparisons and brand-new eclectic enthusiasms at his feet—Zuckerman, with Lonoff, discussing Kafka: I couldn't quite get it, let alone get over it. And then there was his dinner-table toast. It still gave me a temperature of a hundred and five each time I remembered it. To myself I swore that I would struggle for the rest of my life to deserve it. And wasn't that why he'd proposed it, this pitiless new master of mine?

"I've just finished reading Isaac Babel," I told him.

He considered this, impassively.

"I was thinking, for sport more or less, that he is the missing link; those stories are what connect you, if you don't mind my mentioning your work—"

He crossed his hands on his belly and rested them there, movement enough to make me say, "I'm sorry."

"Go ahead. Connected to Babel. How?"

"Well, 'connected' of course isn't the right word. Neither is 'influence.' It's family resemblance that I'm talking about. It's as though, as I see it, you are Babel's American cousin—and Felix Abravanel is the other. You through 'The Sin of Jesus' and something in *Red Cavalry*, through the ironical dreaming and the blunt reporting, and, of course, through the writing itself. Do you see what I mean? There's a sentence in one of his war stories: 'Voroshilov combed his horse's mane with his Mauser.' Well, that's just the kind of thing that you do, a stunning little picture in every line. Babel said that if he ever wrote his autobiography he'd call it *The Story of an Adjective*. Well, if it were possible to imagine you writing your autobiography—if such a thing were even imaginable—you might come up with that title too. No?"

"And Abravanel?"

"Oh, with Abravanel it's Benya Krik and the Odessa mob: the gloating, the gangsters, all those gigantic types. It isn't that he throws in his sympathy with the brutes—it isn't that in Babel, either. It's their awe of them. Even when they're appalled, they're in awe. Deep reflective Jews a little lovesick at the sound of all that un-Talmudic bone crunching. Sensitive Jewish sages, as Babel says, dying to climb trees."

" 'In my childhood I led the life of a sage, when I grew up I started climbing trees.' "

"Yes, that's the line," said I, expecting no less but still impressed. On I went. "Look at Abravanel's *Properly Scalded*. Movie moguls, union moguls, racketeer moguls, women who are moguls just with their breasts—even the down and out bums who used to be moguls, talking like moguls of the down and out. It's Babel's fascination with big-time Jews, with conscienceless Cossacks, with everybody who has it his own way. The Will as the Big Idea. Except Babel doesn't come off so lovable and enormous himself. That's not how he sees things. He is a sort of Abravanel with the self-absorption drained away. And if you drain away enough, well, in the end you arrive at Lonoff."

"And what about you?"

"Me?"

"Yes. You haven't finished. Aren't you a New World cousin in the Babel clan, too? What is Zuckerman in all of this?"

"Why—nothing. I've only published the four stories that I sent you. My relationship is nonexistent. I think I'm still at the point where my relationship to my *own* work is practically nonexistent."

So I said, and quickly reached for my glass so as to duck my disingenuous face and take a bitter drop of brandy on my tongue. But Lonoff had read my designing mind, all right; for when I came upon Babel's description of the Jewish writer as a man with autumn in his heart and spectacles on his nose, I had been inspired to add, "and blood in his penis," and had then recorded the words like a challenge—a flaming Dedalian formula to ignite *my* soul's smithy.

"What else?" Lonoff asked. "Come on, don't get bashful. This is enjoyable. Talk, please."

"About—?"

"All these books you read."

"Your books included or excluded?" I asked him.

"Suit yourself."

I said, "I think of you as the Jew who got away."

"And does that help?"

"There's *some* truth in it, isn't there? You got away from Russia and the pogroms. You got away from the purges—and Babel didn't. You got away from Palestine and the homeland. You got away from Brookline and the relatives. You got away from New York—"

"And all of this is recorded where? Hedda Hopper?"

"Some there. The rest I pieced together myself."

"To what end?"

"When you admire a writer you become curious. You look for his secret. The clues to his puzzle."

"But New York—I was there for three months over twenty years ago. Who told you I got away from New York?"

"Some of the Jews down there you got away from."

"I was there for three months and I think I got a word in only once. What word I don't remember, but suddenly I belonged to a faction."

"That's why you left?"

"Also, there was the girl I'd fallen in love with and married. She wasn't happy."

"Why not?"

"Same as me. Those were terrifying intellectual personalities even back then. Real ideological Benya Kriks, even in their diapers. I didn't have enough strong opinions to last me down there through a year. My Hope had even fewer."

"So you came back here, you got away for good."

"From Jews? Not altogether. The game warden tells me there are some more up in these woods besides me. But you're more or less right. It's the deer in their fields that drive the farmers crazy, not the few of us they see around here in caftans. But where's the secret, Nathan? What's the puzzle?"

"Away from all the Jews, and a story by you without a Jew in it is unthinkable. The deer, the farmers, the game warden—"

"And don't forget Hope. And my fair-haired children."

"And still all you write about are Jews."

"Proving what?"

"That," I said, cautiously, "is what I'd like to ask you."

He thought about it for a moment. "It proves why the young rabbi in Pittsfield can't live with the idea that I won't be 'active.' "

I waited for more, but in vain.

"Do you know Abravanel?" I asked.

"Nathan, surely by now you get the picture."

"What picture?"

"I don't know anybody. I turn sentences around, and that's it. Why would Abravanel want to know me? I put him to sleep. He spoke at Amherst last spring. An invitation arrived so we drove over to hear him. But that's the only time we've ever met. Before the lecture he came down the aisle to where I was sitting and introduced himself. He was very flattering. My respectful younger colleague. Afterward we had a drink with him and his actress. A very polished fellow. The satirist you don't really see till you catch the commedia dell'arte profile. There's where the derision lives. Head-on he's something of a heartthrob. Bombay black eyes, and so on. And the young Israeli wife is like lava. The Gentile dream of the melon-breasted Jewess. And the black head of coarse, curly hair—the long female version of his. You could polish a pot with it. They tell me that when she played in the big movie of the Bible she stole the show from the Creation. So there were those two, and there was I with Hope. And with this," he said, once more lightly laying his hands on his belly. "I understand he does a humorous imitation of me for his friends. No harm intended. One of my former students ran into him in Paris. He'd just addressed a full house at the Sorbonne. I'm told that upon hearing my name he referred to me as 'the complete man—as unimpressive as he is unimpressed.'"

"You don't like him much."

"I'm not in the business. 'Liking people' is often just another racket. But you're right to think well of his books. Not up my alley maybe, all that vanity face to face, but when he writes he's not just a little Houyhnhnm tapping out his superiority with his hooves. More like a Dr. Johnson eating opium—the disease of his life makes Abravanel fly. I admire the man, actually. I admire what he puts his nervous system through. I admire his passion for the front-row seat. Beautiful wives, beautiful mistresses, alimony the size of the national debt, polar expeditions, war-front reportage, famous friends, famous enemies, breakdowns, public lectures, five-hundred-page novels every third year, and still, as you said before, time and energy left over for all that self-absorption. The gigantic types in the books *have* to be that big to give him something to think about to rival himself. Like him? No. But impressed, oh yes. Absolutely. It's no picnic up there in the egosphere. I don't know when the man sleeps, or if he has ever slept, aside from those few minutes when he had that drink with me."

Outside, it was like a silent-film studio, where they made snowstorms by hurling mattress wadding into a wind machine. Large, ragged snowclots raced across the window, and when I heard their icy edges nicking at the glass—and the sounds of someone puttering in the kitchen—I remembered Lonoff's wife begging to be discarded, and wondered if the plea would have been quite so thoroughgoing on a sunny spring day. "I think I better get the taxi," I said, pointing to my watch, "so as to catch the last bus back."

Of course, I wanted never to leave. True, while Hope was falling apart at the dinner table I had momentarily found myself wishing for my cabin at Quahsay; now, however, the way the crisis seemed magically to have resolved itself served only to intensify my awe of Lonoff, particularly for what he unblushingly had called *my own kind of bravery*. If only I had thought to take his approach when *Betsy* had gone wild; if only I had kept my mouth shut until she finished berating me, then swept up the broken crockery and settled into my chair to read another book! Now, why didn't I? Because I was twenty-three and he was fifty-six? Or because I was guilty and he was innocent? Yes, his authority, and the rapid restoration of household sanity and order, might well owe something to that. "Take her! It's the only thing that makes sense!" cried Hope, and Lonoff's easy victory seemed to reside in never even having wanted to.

I also hated calling a taxi because of Amy Bellette. I was hoping, a little crazily, that when she came back from dinner with the college librarian, she would offer to drive me through the storm to my bus. Earlier, while Lonoff was measuring out the brandy—concentrating like a bartender who'd trained at Los Alamos with fissionable fifths—I had asked where she went. I hadn't the nerve to inquire about her status as a displaced person. But at the table, when he'd said that she had come to Athene as a refugee, I was reminded of "the children starving in Europe" whom we had heard so much about when we were children eating in New Jersey. If Amy had been one of them, perhaps that explained the something in her that seemed to me thwarted and underdeveloped, despite the dazzling maturity and severe good looks. I wondered if the dark refugee girl with the curious name Bellette could be Jewish, and in Europe had suffered from worse than starvation.

"Yes," said Lonoff, "you'd better call the taxi."

Reluctantly I stood to go.

"Or, if you like," he said, "you can stay over and sleep in the study."

"No, I think I really have to be off," I said, and cursed the upbringing that had taught me never to be greedy about second helpings. How much better if I had been raised in the gutter! Only how would I have gotten from the gutter to here?

"Suit yourself," Lonoff told me.

"I wouldn't want to inconvenience your wife."

"I think it will disturb her more if you leave than if you stay. She might hold herself responsible. I'm certain she would."

I pretended I had taken my dinner on the moon. "But why?"

"Sit down. Stay for breakfast, Nathan."

"I'd better not. I shouldn't."

"You know who Jimmy Durante is?"

"Of course."

"Do you know the old Durante number 'Did you ever have the feeling that you wanted to go, still have the feeling that you wanted to stay'?"

"Yes."

"Sit."

I sat—suiting myself, as the man said.

"Besides," he told me, "if you go now, you'll leave most of your cognac."

"If I go, so will you."

"Well, the Jew who got away didn't get away altogether." He smiled at me. "You don't have to finish it, just because you're staying. That's not part of the deal."

"No, no, I want to," I said, and took my biggest sip of the night. Saluting me with his glass, he followed suit.

"Hope will be pleased," he said. "She misses people. She misses the children and their friends. She went to art school in Boston before I brought her back here, sixteen versts to the nearest railway station. Manhattan terrified her, but Boston's her Moscow, she'd move there tomorrow. She thinks I would enjoy it in Cambridge. But all I need are those dinner parties. I'd rather talk to the horse."

"You have a horse?"

"No."

I loved him! Yes, nothing less than love for this man with no illusions: love for the bluntness, the scrupulosity, the severity, the estrangement; love for the relentless winnowing out of the babyish, preening, insatiable self; love for the artistic mulishness and the suspicion of nearly everything else; and love for the buried charm, of which he'd just given me a glimpse. Yes, all Lonoff had to say was that he did not even have the horse to talk to and somehow that did it, released in me a son's girlish love for the man of splendid virtue and high achievement who understands life, and who understands the son, and who approves.

I should mention here that some three years earlier, after several hours in the presence of Felix Abravanel, I had been no less overcome. But if I did not fall at his feet straightaway, it was because even a college senior as writer-worshipping as myself could see that with Abravanel such boundless adoration—at least if offered up by a youthful male admirer—was doomed to go unrequited. The ardor of those books, composed in the sunny stillness of his California canyon and seething with unbuttoned and aggressive innocence, seemed to have little to do with the author himself when he came coolly out into the fallen world he'd been so ardent about down in the canyon. In fact, the writer who found irresistible all vital and dubious types, not excluding the swindlers of both sexes who trampled upon the large hearts of his optimistic, undone heroes; the writer who could locate the hypnotic core in the most devious American self-seeker and lead him to disclose, in spirited locutions all his own, the depths of his conniving soul; the writer whose absorption with "the grand human discord" made his every paragraph a little novel in itself, every page packed as tight as Dickens or Dostoevsky with the latest news of manias, temptations, passions, and dreams, with mankind aflame with feeling —well, in the flesh he gave the impression of being out to lunch.

Which isn't to suggest that Felix Abravanel lacked charm. On the contrary, the charm was like a moat so oceanic that you could not even see the great turreted and buttressed thing it had been dug to protect. You couldn't even find the drawbridge. He was like California itself—to get there you had to take a plane. There were moments during his public lecture—this was at Chicago, my last year there—when Abravanel had to pause at the lectern, seemingly to suppress saying something off the cuff that would have been just too charming for his audience to bear. And he was right. We might have charged the stage to eat him up alive if he had been any more sly and enchanting and wise. Poor marvelous Abravanel (I mean this without satire)—even what was intended to guard the great rose window of his inner brilliance was itself so damn beautiful that the ungifted multitudes and art lovers of the world could not but find him all the more alluring. On the other hand, maybe he wanted it that way. There is obviously no simple way to be great, or so I was beginning to find out.

After the lecture I had been invited to come along to a faculty-club reception by the professor whose protégé I was. When we were able at last to break through the rings of admirers, I was introduced as the student whose story would be discussed the next morning in the class Abravanel had consented to visit. From the dash of imperiousness in the photographed face I had never envisioned him quite so guarded-looking, or with a head a good size and a half too small for the six-foot plank that supported it. He reminded me, amid all those who would flatter and adore him, of a radio tower with its tiny red light burning high up to warn off low-flying aircraft. He wore a five-hundred-dollar shantung suit, a burgundy silk tie, and gleaming narrow black tasseled loafers, but everything that counted, all that made for the charm and the laughs and the books and the breakdowns, was stored compactly right up there at the top—at the edge of a precipice. It was a head that the Japanese technicians, with their in-genuity for miniaturizing, might have designed, and then given over to the Jews to adorn with the rug dealer's thinning dark hair, the guarded appraising black eyes, and a tropical bird's curving bill. A fully Semiticized little transistor on top, terrific clothes down below—and still the overall impression was of somebody's stand-in.

I thought, In the novels nothing ever seems to get by him, so how come when he's here, he's not? Perhaps so much assails him that he has to close down ninety per-cent of himself to phenomena in order not to explode. Though then again, I thought, maybe he's just out to lunch.

Abravanel shook my hand obligingly and was about to turn away to shake another obligingly when the professor repeated my name. "Of course," said Abravanel, "N. Zuckerman." He had read a mimeographed copy of my story on the plane from the Coast; so had Andrea read it. "Sweetheart," he said, "this is Zuckerman."

Well, where to begin? Andrea had maybe only five years on me, but five years put to good use. After graduating from Sarah Lawrence, she had evidently continued her education at Elizabeth Arden and Henri Bendel. As we all knew—her fame having preceded her—Andrea's father had been a dollar-a-year man in the first Roosevelt Administration, and Mother was Carla Peterson Rumbough, the loquacious liberal congresswoman from Oregon. While still a college student she had written the first of her portraits of "Men in Power" for *The Saturday Evening Post*, the series eventually collected in her best-selling book. Undoubtedly (as the envious were quick enough to point out), family contacts had got her going, but clearly what encouraged those busy and powerful men to keep on talking was the proximity of Andrea herself, for Andrea was a most juicy girl. Truly, you felt that if you pressed her, you could drink a glassful of refreshing, healthy Andrea for breakfast.

At the time, she was in residence with Abravanel at his Pacific Palisades retreat, a few miles from the home of his friend and mentor, Thomas Mann. ("The grand human discord" was how Mann had perceived Abravanel's subject in the elevating preface with which he had consecrated the German edition of *Properly Scalded*.) After Abravanel's latest divorce (and rumored emotional collapse), Andrea had come to interview him for the *Post* series and, as transcontinental literary legend had it, had never left. Legend also had it that Abravanel was not only the first man of letters to be named a man of power in America but the first man of power to whose advances Andrea had yielded. I myself wondered if maybe Andrea wasn't the first journalist to whose advances Abravanel had yielded. He looked more like the one who would have had to be seduced.

"How terrific finally to meet you," Andrea said, briskly shaking my hand. The briskness of the handshake was in disarming contrast with the soft voluptuous appearance. The face was heart-shaped and gentle, but the handshake said, "Have no doubts, I am the girl who has everything." Not that I was about to argue. I was already convinced a month before laying eyes on her, when we had exchanged letters about hotel accommodations. As student representative of the University Lecture Committee, I had, per her instructions, reserved a room in their two names at the Windermere, the closest the neighborhood had to a grand hotel. "Mr. Abravanel and Miss Rumbough?" the desk clerk had asked. "Are they husband and wife, sir?" This question was put to me, mind you, in March of 1953, and so when I answered with the lie that I had devised to shelter a hero from scandal—"Mrs. Abravanel is the well-known journalist; that of course is her professional name" —I was sure that the end result of Miss A. Rumbough's bohemian daring would be my expulsion from college without a degree.

"I loved your story," she said. "It's *so* funny."

Grimly I acknowledged the compliment tendered my

wit by the bosomy girl with the heart-shaped face and the milkmaid complexion and the soldierly self-assured grip. In the meantime, having passed me on to Andrea to dispose of, Abravanel found himself being exhibited by another of our professors to a huddle of graduate students waiting shyly beside their teacher to ask the writer serious questions. "Oh, well," I heard him say, with a light annihilating laugh, "I don't have the time these days to think about 'influences'—Andrea keeps me pretty much on the run." "Felix," she was telling me, "is nuts about the story, too. You should have seen him on the plane. He just kept throwing back his head and laughing. Where are you going to publish it? Maybe Felix ought to talk to—" She mentioned a name. It was Knebel, but for one whose stories had appeared previously only in the college literary quarterly, the effect would have been no more stunning if she had said, "After the reception I have to get back to the hotel to interview Marshal Tito in the bar—but while I do, Felix can rise unto Heaven from the lobby and discuss your funny little mimeographed story with the author of *The Brothers Karamazov*. We all met in Siberia when Felix and I did the prison tour." Somewhere behind me I heard Abravanel applying himself to another serious question from the graduate division. "Alienation? Oh," he said, with that light laugh, "let the other guy be alienated." Simultaneously Andrea informed me, "He's seeing Sy tomorrow night in New York—" (Sy being Knebel, the editor for twenty years of the New York intellectual quarterly that I had been devouring for the past two).

The next day Abravanel visited our advanced-writing class, accompanied—to the surprise of those ready to live only for art—by the bold Andrea. Her luminous, shameless presence in the very front row (and her white jersey dress; and her golden hair, out of some rustic paradise) led me to recall October afternoons half a lifetime ago when I sat like a seething prisoner, practicing my penmanship at my sloping school desk while the World Series was being broadcast live to dinky radios in every gas station in America. It was then that I learned what tore at the hearts of the delinquents and the dummies who loathed the classroom and the teacher and wished the whole place would burn down.

Hands plunged into his pockets, and angled casually against the professor's desk, Abravanel spoke of my story with oblique admiration, defending it, largely with his laugh, from criticism brought by the orthodox Forsterites that my narrator was "two-dimensional" instead of being "round" like the characters they'd read about in *Aspects of the Novel*. But that day to all carping I was immune. *Andrea*, I thought, whenever one of those fools said "round."

Afterward I was invited by Abravanel for a cup of coffee at a local luncheonette, along with Andrea, my professor, and a member of the sociology department, an old friend from Abravanel's youth who had been waiting outside the classroom door to give Abravanel a nostalgic hug (which the author managed graciously to accept even while backing away). Abravanel had extended the invitation personally (as I was to write my parents) and with what sounded for the first time like real sympathy: "They're a rough bunch, Zuckerman. You better come along for a transfusion." I figured he would tell me over the cup of coffee that he was taking his copy of my story to New York to show to Seymour Knebel. For a hundred reasons I was in ecstasy. When he told me to come along for my transfusion, I could not remember having *myself* ever felt like such a round character before. What Mann had done for him he was about to do for me. Literary history in the making. Good thing Andrea was there to get it all down for posterity.

But over his coffee Abravanel said not a word: just leaned his long demi-emaciated frame back in his chair, looking smooth and strokable as a cat in his teaching attire of soft gray flannel slacks, a light mauve pullover, and a cashmere sports coat. With hands and ankles elegantly crossed, he left it to his buoyant young companion to do the talking—lively, funny stories, mostly, about Felix's old father, an L.A. housepainter, and the winning remarks he made to her in his homely mix of two languages. Even the sociology professor was bowled over, though from campus gossip I knew he was a dear friend of Abravanel's litigious first wife and disapproved of the writer's treatment of her, first in the flesh, then in fiction. Moreover, he was said to disapprove of Abravanel's way with women generally and, on top of that, believed that a novelist of his stature oughtn't to have articles about himself in *The Saturday Evening Post*. Yet now the sociology professor began lifting his voice so as to get Andrea to hear him. As a boy, he also had been a great fan of Felix's father's malapropisms, and he wanted it known. " 'That fellow,' " shouted the sociologist, imitating the elder Abravanel, " 'he ain't here no more—poor guy committed suitcase.' " If Abravanel thought the retired housepainter was so impressive for speaking cockeyed English all his life, he didn't let on. So genteel and assured and courtly was the posture he'd assumed to listen to Andrea tell her stories that I found myself doubting it. Out in the open, Abravanel's cup did not spill over with sentiment for the old days in L.A.; such effusions he left to readers of his novels who had come to love the super-charged emotional world of his childhood as though it had been their own. He himself seemed to prefer to look down at us from a long way off, like a llama or a camel.

"Good luck" was what he said to me when they got up to catch the New York train—and Andrea said even less. This time, because we knew each other, she took my hand in five soft fingers, but the touch of the fairy princess seemed to mean much the same to me as the garrison handshake at the faculty-club reception. She's forgotten, I thought, about Knebel. Or maybe she's told Abravanel and figured he'd take care of it, and he's forgotten. Or maybe she's told him and he said, "Forget it." Watching her leave the luncheonette on Abravanel's arm— seeing her hair brush his shoulder as out on the street she rose on her toes to whisper something into his ear—I realized that they'd had other things than my story to think about when they got back to the Windermere the night before.

All of this was why, from Quahsay, I had mailed my four published stories to Lonoff. Felix Abravanel was clearly not in the market for a twenty-three-year-old son.

Just before nine, having checked the time on his watch, Lonoff drank up his last drop of brandy, which had sat thirty minutes at the bottom of the glass. He said that though he must be off, I might stay in the living room and listen to music, or, if I preferred, I could retire to his study, where I would be sleeping. Beneath the corduroy cover I would find that the study daybed was already made up with fresh linen. Blankets and an extra pillow were in the closet there, on the bottom shelf, and fresh towels were in the downstairs-bathroom cupboard—please, I mustn't hesitate to use the striped ones, they were the least worn and best for a shower—and also in the cupboard, at the rear of the second shelf, I would find a toothbrush in its original unopened plastic case, and a small new tube of Ipana. Any questions?

"No."

Was there anything else that I would need?

"Thank you, this is all perfect."

He winced when he stood—lumbago, he explained, from turning one too many sentences around that day— and said that he still had his evening's reading. He did not do justice to a writer unless he read him on consecutive days and for no less than three hours at a sitting. Other- wise, despite his notetaking and underlining, he lost touch with a book's inner life and might as well not have begun. Sometimes, when he unavoidably had to miss a day, he would go back and begin all over again, rather than be nagged by his sense that he was wronging a serious author.

He told me all this in the same fastidious way he had described the location of the toothpaste and towels: a blunt, colloquial, pointedly ungrandiloquent Lonoff seemed to take turns with a finicky floorwalker Lonoff as official representative to the unwritten world.

"My wife considers this a grave affliction," he added. "I don't know how to relax. Soon she'll be telling me to go out and have a good time."

"Not that soon," I said.

"It's only as it should be," he said, "for somebody else to think I'm a fool. But I can't afford the luxury myself. How else am I supposed to read a book of real depth? For 'enjoyment'? For the hell of it—to put me to sleep?" Wearily—more ready for bed, I would have thought from the tired, irascible tone, than for one hundred and eighty

minutes concentrating on the inner life of a deep book
by a serious author—he asked, "How else am I to conduct
my life?"

"How else would you like to?"

Well, I had done it, escaped at last from wooden self-
consciousness and egregious overearnestness—and sporadic
attempts to be witty in the Lonovian mode—and put to him
a direct, simple question, the answer to which I wanted
very much to hear.

"How else might I like to?"

It thrilled me to see him standing there taking altogether seriously what I had asked. "Yes. How would you
live now, if you had your way?"

Rubbing at the small of his back, he replied, "I would
live in a villa outside Florence."

"Yes? With whom?"

"A woman, of course." He answered without hesita-
tion, as though I were another grown man.

So, as though I were one, I went ahead and asked,
"How old would she be, this woman?"

He smiled down at me. "We have both had too
much to drink."

I showed him that there was brandy enough still to
swirl around in my snifter.

"For us," he added, and not bothering this time to
catch the trouser crease in his fingers, sat back down
somewhat gracelessly in his chair.

"Please," I said, "I don't mean to keep you from reading. I'll be fine alone."

"Sometimes," he said, "I like to imagine I've read my last book. And looked for the last time at my watch. How old would you think she should be?" he asked. "The woman in Florence. As a writer, what would be your guess?"

"I think you'll have to ask me to guess that thirty years from now. I don't know."

"I say thirty-five. How does that strike you?"

"As right, if you say so."

"She would be thirty-five and she would make life beautiful for me. She would make life comfortable and beautiful and new. She would drive me in the afternoon to San Gimignano, to the Uffizi, to Siena. In Siena we would visit the cathedral and drink coffee in the square. At the breakfast table she would wear long feminine nightgowns under her pretty robe. They would be things I had bought for her in a shop by the Ponte Vecchio. I would work in a cool stone room with French windows. There would be flowers in a vase. She would cut them and put them there. And so on, Nathan, in this vein."

Most men want to be children again, or kings, or quarterbacks, or multimillionaires. All Lonoff seemed to want was a thirty-five-year-old woman and a year abroad. I thought of Abravanel, that fruit gatherer, and the Israeli actress—"like lava"—who was Abravanel's third wife. And of that rounded character Andrea Rumbough. In whose sea did Andrea bob now? "If that's all . . ." I said.

"Go on. We're having a drunken conversation."

"If that's all, it doesn't sound too hard to arrange," I heard myself telling him.

"Oh, yes? What young woman that you know is out looking for a fifty-six-year-old bald man to accompany to Italy?"

"You're not the stereotypical bald man of fifty-six. Italy with you wouldn't be Italy with anyone."

"What does that mean? I'm supposed to cash in the seven books for a piece of ass?"

The unforeseen plunge into street talk made *me* feel momentarily like the boutonniered floorwalker. "That isn't what I meant. Though of course that happens, such things are done . . ."

"Yes, in New York you must see a lot of it."

"No one with seven books in New York City settles for one piece of ass. That's what you get for a couplet." I had spoken as though I knew what I was talking about. "All I meant was that you're not exactly asking for a harem."

"Like the fat lady said about the polka-dot dress, 'It's nice, but it's not Lonoff.' "

"Why not?"

"Why not?" he repeated, a little scornfully.

"I meant—why couldn't it be?"

"Why should it be?"

"Because—you want it."

His answer: "Not a good enough reason."

I lacked the courage to ask "Why not?" again. If drunk, still only drunk Jews. So far and no further, I was sure. And I was right.

"No," he said, "you don't chuck a woman out after thirty-five years because you'd prefer to see a new face over your fruit juice."

Thinking of his fiction, I had to wonder if he had ever let her in, or the children either, who, he had told me earlier, had provided him with diversion and brought a certain gaiety into his world for so long as they lived at home. In his seven volumes of stories I could not think of a single hero who was not a bachelor, a widower, an orphan, a foundling, or a reluctant fiancé.

"But there's more to it than that," I said. "More to it than the new face . . . isn't there?"

"What, the bed? I had the bed. I know my singularity," said Lonoff, "and what I owe to it." Here, abruptly, he concluded our drunken conversation. "I've got my reading. Let me show you before I go how to work the phonograph. We have an excellent classical record collection. You know about wiping the records? There is a cloth—"

He came heavily to his feet; slowly and heavily, like an elephant. All the obstinacy seemed to have gone out of him, whether owing to our exchange or to the pain in his back—or exhaustion with his singularity—I didn't know. Maybe every day ended like this.

"Mr. Lonoff—Manny," I said, "may I ask you something before you go, while we're alone—about my stories? I don't know if I entirely understood what you meant by 'turbulence.' At dinner. I don't mean to hang on to one word, but any word from you—well, I'd like to be sure I understand it. That is, I'm thrilled just that you read them, and I'm still amazed even to have been invited, and now staying over—all that should be enough. It is enough. And the toast you made"—I felt my emotions getting out of hand, as I had, to my astonishment, while receiving my college diploma with my parents looking on—"I hope I can live up to it. I don't take those words lightly. But about the stories themselves, what I'd like to know is what you think is wrong with them, what you think I might do—to be better?"

How benign was his smile! Even while kneading the lumbago. "Wrong?"

"Yes."

"Look, I told Hope this morning: Zuckerman has the most compelling voice I've encountered in years, certainly for somebody starting out."

"Do I?"

"I don't mean style"—raising a finger to make the distinction. "I mean voice: something that begins at around the back of the knees and reaches well above the head. Don't worry too much about 'wrong.' Just keep going. You'll get there."

There. I tried to envision it, but couldn't. It was more than I could take being *here*.

I told Hope this morning.

Meanwhile, buttoning his jacket and smoothing down his tie—and checking his watch with the glance that ruined his wife's every Sunday—he attended to the last item of business on the agenda. Working the record player. I had interrupted his train of thought.

"I want to show you what happens if the arm doesn't go all the way back at the end of the record."

"Sure," I said, "absolutely."

"It's been acting up lately and nobody is able to fix it. Some days it somehow fixes itself, and then out of the blue it's on the blink again."

I followed him over to the turntable, thinking less about his classical record collection than about my voice starting back of my knees.

"This is the volume, of course. This is the start button. This is the reject, you push it—"

And this, I realized, is the excruciating scrupulosity, the same maddening, meticulous attention to every last detail that makes you great, that keeps you going and got you through and now is dragging you down. Standing with E. I. Lonoff over the disobedient arm of his record player, I understood the celebrated phenomenon for the first time: a man, his destiny, and his work—all one. What a terrible triumph!

"And," he reminded me, "it would be best for the records, and for your own pleasure, if you remember to wipe them first."

Oh, the fussiness, the fastidiousness! The floorwalker incarnate! To wrestle the blessing of his fiction out of that misfortune—"triumph" didn't begin to describe it.

Suddenly I wanted to kiss him. I know this happens to men more often than is reported, but I was new to manhood (about five minutes into it, actually) and was bewildered by the strength of a feeling that I had rarely had toward my own father once I'd begun to shave. It seemed, at the moment, even stronger than what invariably came over me when I was left alone with those long-necked aerial friends of Betsy's, who walked with their feet turned charmingly outward and looked (just like Betsy!) so appetizingly wan and light and liftable. But in this house of forbearance I was better at suppressing my amorous impulses than I had been lately, unchained in Manhattan.

2 Nathan Dedalus

Who could sleep after that? I didn't even turn the lamp off to try. For the longest time I just stared at E. I. Lonoff's tidy desk: neat piles of typing paper, each stack a different pale color—for different drafts, I assumed. Finally I got up and, sacrilege though it surely was, sat on his typing chair in my undershorts. No wonder his back hurt. It wasn't a chair made for relaxing in, not if you were his size. Lightly I touched my fingers to his portable typewriter keys. Why a portable for a man who went nowhere? Why not a machine on the order of a cannonball, black and big and built to write for all time? Why not a comfortable padded executive's chair to lean back in and think? Why not indeed.

Pinned to the bulletin board beside his desk—the cell's only real embellishments—were a little wall calendar from the local bank and two annotated index cards. One card bore a fragmentary sentence ascribed to "Schumann, on Chopin's Scherzo No. 2 in B flat minor, Op. 31." It read, ". . . so overflowing with tenderness, boldness, love, and contempt that it may be compared, not inappropriately, to a poem by Byron." I didn't know what to make of it there, or rather, what Lonoff made of it, until I remembered that Amy Bellette could play Chopin with great charm. Maybe it was she who had typed it out for him, scrupulous attribution and all—enclosing it, perhaps, with the gift of a record so that in the late afternoons he could listen to Chopin even when she was no longer around. Perhaps it was this very line she'd been musing upon when I first saw her on the study floor: musing because the description seemed as pertinent to herself as to the music . . .

If displaced, what had become of her family? Murdered? Did that explain her "contempt"? But for whom the overflowing love, then? Him? If so, the contempt might well be for Hope. If so, if so.

It required no ingenuity to guess the appeal of the quotation typed on the other card. After what Lonoff had been telling me all evening, I could understand why he might want these three sentences hanging over his head while beneath them he sat turning his own sentences around. "We work in the dark—we do what we can—we give what we have. Our doubt is our passion and our passion is our task. The rest is the madness of art." Sentiments ascribed to a story I did not know by Henry James called "The Middle Years." But "the madness of art"? I would have thought the madness of everything but art. The art was what was sane, no? Or was I missing something? Before the night was over I was to read "The Middle Years" twice through, as though preparing to be examined on it in the morning. But that was canon law to me then: ready to write a thousand words on "What does Henry James mean by 'the madness of art'?" if the question should happen to turn up on my paper napkin at breakfast.

Photographs of Lonoff's children were set out on a bookshelf behind the typing chair: one male, two females, not a trace of the paternal genes in any of their bones. One of the girls, a fair, freckled maiden in horn-rimmed glasses, looked, in fact, much as her shy, studious mother probably did back in her art-school days. Beside her photo in the twin frame was a postcard that had been mailed from Scotland to Massachusetts one August day nine years earlier, addressed to the writer alone. This perhaps accounted for its status as a memento to be preserved under glass. Much about his life indicated that communicating with his children had been no easier for him than having enough opinions for Manhattan in the thirties. "Dear Pop, We are now in Banffshire (Highlands) and I am standing amidst the wreck of Balvenie Castle, Dufftown, where Mary Stuart once stayed. Yesterday we biked to Cawdor (Thane of Cawdor, *ca.* 1050, Shakespeare's Macbeth), where Duncan was murdered. See you soon, Love, Becky."

Also directly behind his desk were several shelves of his works in foreign translation. Seating myself on the floor I tried translating from French and German sentences that I had read first in Lonoff's English. With the more exotic tongues the most I could do was try to spot his characters' names in the hundreds of indecipherable pages. Pechter. Marcus. Littman. Winkler. There they were, surrounded on all sides by Finnish.

And which language was hers? Portuguese? Italian? Hungarian? In which did she overflow like a poem by Byron?

On a large lined pad that I took from my briefcase, a bulging *Bildungsroman* briefcase—ten pounds of books, five obscure magazines, and easily enough paper to write the whole of my first novel if it should happen to come to me while riding back and forth on the bus—I began methodically to list everything on his bookshelves I had not read. There was more German philosophy than I had been expecting, and only halfway down the page I already seemed to have sentenced myself to a lifetime at hard labor. But, worthily, I kept going—to the accompaniment of the words with which he had commended me before going up to his reading. That, and the toast, had been echoing in my head for an hour. On a clean sheet of paper I finally wrote down what he'd said so as to see exactly what he'd meant. All he'd meant.

As it turned out, I wanted someone else to see as well, for soon I had forgotten the forthcoming ordeal with Heidegger and Wittgenstein, and was seated with my pad at Lonoff's desk, struggling to explain to my father—the foot-doctor father, the first of my fathers—the "voice" that, according to no less a vocalist than E. I. Lonoff, started back of my knees and reached above my head. The letter was overdue. Three weeks now he had been waiting for some enlightened sign of contrition for the offenses I had begun to commit against my greatest supporters. And for three weeks I had let him stew, if that is how you describe being yourself unable to think of little else upon awakening from bad dreams at 4 a.m.

Our trouble had begun when I gave my father the manuscript of a story based on an old family feud in which he had played peacemaker for nearly two years before the opponents ended up shouting in court. The story was the most ambitious I had written—some fifteen thousand words—and, as I saw it, my motives for sending it to him were no less benign than those I'd had in college, when I mailed home poems for the family to read even before they appeared in the student verse magazine. It wasn't trouble I was looking for but admiration and praise. Out of the oldest and most ingrained of habits, I wanted to please them and make them proud.

That wasn't hard either. For years I had been making him proud just by sending along clippings for his "files," a voluminous accumulation of magazine and newspaper articles—including an unbroken series of transcripts of "America's Town Meeting of the Air"—on what he called "vital issues." Whenever I was home on a visit, my mother, who could repeat herself, would invariably remind me— with her own deeply satisfied look—of the thrill it gave him to say to his patients (after working them around to the vital issue on his mind), "I just got something in the mail this morning on that subject. My son Nathan saw it at college. He's out at the University of Chicago. Straight A's in everything. Went out there when he was sixteen—special program. Well, he saw it in one of the Chicago papers and sent it on for my files."

Oh, what sitting ducks I had for parents! A son of theirs would have had to be a half-wit or a sadist *not* to make them proud. And I was neither; I was dutiful and thoughtful, and too excited with myself in flight to be ungrateful for the boost I'd begun with. Despite the flaming wrangles of my adolescence—weekend night hours, fashions in footwear, the unhygienic high-school hangout, my alleged but ceaselessly disavowed penchant for the last word—we had emerged from our fifty textbook scenes of domestic schism much the same close family bound by the same strong feelings. I'd slammed a lot of doors and declared a few wars, but still I loved them like their child. And whether or not I wholly knew just how extensive the addiction, I was much in need of their love for me, of which I assumed there was an inexhaustible supply. That I couldn't—wouldn't?—assume otherwise goes a long way toward explaining why I was naïve enough to expect nothing more than the usual encouragement for a story that borrowed from our family history instances of what my exemplary father took to be the most shameful and disreputable transgressions of family decency and trust.

The facts I had begun my story with were these:

A great-aunt of mine, Meema Chaya, had left for the education of two fatherless grandsons the pot of money she had diligently hoarded away as a seamstress to Newark's upper crust. When Essie, the widowed mother of the twin boys, attempted to invade the trust to send them from college to medical school, her younger brother, Sidney, who was to inherit the money remaining in Meema Chaya's estate upon conclusion of the boys' higher education, had sued to stop her. For four years Sidney had been waiting for Richard and Robert to graduate from Rutgers —waiting mostly in pool rooms and saloons, to hear the family tell it—so he could buy a downtown parking lot with his legacy. Loudly—his way—Sidney proclaimed that he was not about to postpone the good life just so there could be two more fancy doctors driving Caddies around South Orange. Those in the family who detested Sidney's womanizing and his shady friends immediately

lined up in support of the boys and their dignified aspira-
tions, leaving Sidney with a phalanx consisting of his ill-
used, timid wife Jenny, and his mysterious Polish tootsie
Annie, whose scandalously florid *shmatas* were much discussed, if never once seen, at family weddings, funerals,
etc. Also in the phalanx, for all it was worth to him, was
me. My admiration was long-standing, dating back to
Sidney's Navy days, when he had won four thousand
dollars on the homeward journey of the battleship *Kansas*,
and was said to have thrown into the South Pacific, for the
sharks to dispose of, a Mississippi sore loser who at the end
of an all-night poker game had referred to the big winner
as a dirty Jew. The lawsuit, whose outcome hinged on
how exhaustive Meema Chaya had meant to be in her will
with the ringing words "higher education," was eventually
decided by the judge—a *goy*—in Sidney's favor, though
within only a few years the Raymond Boulevard parking
lot bought with his inheritance became such a hot piece
of real estate that it was nationalized out from under him
by the Mob. For his trouble they gave Sidney a tenth of
what it was worth, and shortly thereafter his heart broke
like a balloon in the bed of yet another overdressed bimbo
not of our persuasion. My cousins Richard and Robert
were meanwhile being put through medical school by
their iron-willed mother. After she lost the lawsuit, Essie
quit her job at a downtown department store and for the
next ten years went to work on the road selling shingles
and siding. So iron-willed was she that by the time she

had finally bought carpeting and venetians for the new offices leased for Richard and Robert in suburban North Jersey, there was hardly a working-class neighborhood in the state that she hadn't left encased in asphalt. Out canvassing one hot afternoon during the twins' internship, Essie had decided to spend an hour in an air-cooled Passaic movie theater. In her thousands of days and nights finding leads and closing deals, this was said to be the first time ever that she stopped to do anything other than eat and call the boys. But now residencies in orthopedics and dermatology were only just around the corner, and the thought of their advent, combined with the August heat, made her just a little light-headed. In the dark movie theater, however, Essie hadn't even time to mop her brow before a fellow in the next seat put his hand on her knee. He must have been a very lonely fellow—it was a very stout knee; nonetheless, she broke the hand for him, at the wrist, with the hammer carried in her purse all these years to protect herself and the future of two fatherless sons. My story, entitled "Higher Education," concluded with Essie taking aim.

"Well, you certainly didn't leave anything out, did you?"

Thus began my father's critique on the Sunday I'd come to say goodbye before leaving for the winter at Quahsay. Earlier in the day, along with a favorite aunt and uncle and a childless neighbor couple—also called "Aunt" and "Uncle" by me since the cradle—I had partaken of our family's traditional Sunday brunch. Fifty-two Sundays a year, for most of my lifetime, my father went out to the corner for the smoked fish and the warm rolls, my brother and I set the table and squeezed the juice, and for three hours my mother was unemployed in her own house. "Like a queen" was how she described the predicament. Then, after my parents had read the Newark Sunday papers and listened on the radio to "The Eternal Light"— great moments from Jewish history in weekly half-hour dramatizations—we two boys were rounded up and the four of us set off in the car to visit relatives. My father, long in contention with an opinionated older brother for the vacant position of family patriarch, generally delivered a hortatory sermon somewhere along the way to somebody who seemed to him to need it, and then we drove home. And always at dusk, before we reassembled around the kitchen table to observe the Sunday-evening rites—to partake of the sacred delicatessen supper, washed down with sacramental soda pop; to await together the visitation from heaven of Jack Benny, Rochester, and Phil Harris— the "men," as my mother called us, went off for their brisk walk to the nearby park. "Hi, Doc—how are you?" So the neighbors we passed along the way always greeted my popular and talkative father, and though he seemed never to be bothered by it, for a time his class-conscious little boy used to think that if only there had been no quotas and he'd become a *real* physician, they would have greeted him as "Doctor Zuckerman." "Doc" was what they called the pharmacist who made milk shakes and sold cough drops.

"Well, Nathan," began my father, "you certainly didn't leave anything out, did you?"

I was by then a little weary from doing my duty and anxious to leave for New York to pack for Quahsay. My brunch-time visit had now lasted the entire day and, to my surprise, had been marked by the comings and goings of numerous relatives and old family friends dropping by seemingly just to see me. Kibitzing, reminiscing, swapping dialect jokes, and munching too much fruit, I had hung around until the company began to leave, and then had stayed on, at my father's request, so that he could give me his thoughts on my story. Portentously he said he wanted an hour with me alone.

At four that afternoon, in our coats and scarves, the two of us set out for the park. Every half hour a New York bus stopped just by the park gateway on Elizabeth Avenue, and my plan was to catch one after he'd had his say.

"I left a lot of things out." I pretended to be innocent of what he meant—as innocent as when I'd sent him the story, though the moment he'd spoken in the house of giving me his "thoughts" (rather than his pat on the head), I realized immediately how mindless I had been. Why hadn't I waited to see if I could even get it published, and then shown him the story already in print? Or would that only have made it worse? "Things had to be left out—it's only fifty pages."

"I mean," he said sadly, "you didn't leave anything disgusting out."

"Did I? Didn't I? I wasn't thinking along those lines, exactly."

"You make everybody seem awfully greedy, Nathan."

"But everybody was."

"That's one way of looking at it, of course."

"That's the way you looked at it yourself. That's why you were so upset that they wouldn't compromise."

"The point is, there is far more to our family than this. And you know that. I hope that today reminded you of the kind of people we are. In case in New York you've forgotten."

"Dad, I had a good time seeing everybody. But you didn't have to give me a refresher course in the family's charms."

But on he went. "And people who are crazy about you. Is there anybody who came into the house today whose face didn't light up when they laid eyes on you? And you couldn't have been kinder, you couldn't have been a sweeter boy. I watched you with your family and with all our old dear friends, and I thought to myself, Then what is this story all about? Why is he going on like this about ancient history?"

"It wasn't ancient history when it happened."

"No, then it was nonsense."

"You didn't seem to think so. You were running from Essie to Sidney for over a year."

"The fact remains, son, there is more to the family, much much more, than is in this story. Your great-aunt was as kind and loving and hard-working a woman as you could ever meet in this world. Your grandmother and all her sisters were, every last one of them. They were women who thought only of others."

"But the story is not about them."

"But they are *part* of the story. They are the *whole* story as far as I'm concerned. Without them there would be no story at all! Who the hell was Sidney? Does anybody in his right mind even think about him any longer? To you, as a boy, I suppose he was an amusing character, somebody to get a kick out of, who came and went. I can understand how that would be: a big six-foot ape in bell-bottom trousers, clanking his I.D. bracelet and talking a mile a minute as though he was Admiral Nimitz and not just the nobody who swabbed the deck. Which is all he ever was, of course. I remember how he came to the house and got down on the floor and taught you and your little brother to roll dice. As a joke. I wanted to throw the lummox out on his ear."

"I don't even remember that."

"Well, I do. I remember plenty. I remember it all. To Meema Chaya, Sidney was never anything but heart-ache. Little children don't realize that underneath the big blowhard who rolls on the floor and makes them laugh there can be somebody who makes other people cry. And he made your great-aunt cry plenty, and from the time he was old enough to go into the street, looking for grief to give her. And still, *still*, that woman left him that chunk of her hard-earned dough, and prayed that somehow it would help. She rose above all the misery and the shame he had caused her—just like the wonderful woman that she was. 'Chaya' means life, and that is what she had in her to give to everybody. But that you leave out."

"I didn't leave it out. I suggest as much about her on the first page. But you're right—I don't go into Meema Chaya's life."

"Well, that would be some story."

"Well, that isn't this story."

"And do you fully understand what a story like this story, when it's published, will mean to people who don't know us?"

We had by now descended the long incline of our street and reached Elizabeth Avenue. No lawn we passed, no driveway, no garage, no lamppost, no little brick stoop was without its power over me. Here I had practiced my sidearm curve, here on my sled I'd broken a tooth, here I had copped my first feel, here for teasing a friend I had been slapped by my mother, here I had learned that my grandfather was dead. There was no end to all I could remember happening to me on this street of one-family brick houses more or less like ours, owned by Jews more or less like us, to whom six rooms with a "finished" basement and a screened-in porch on a street with shade trees was something never to be taken for granted, given the side of the city where they'd started out.

Across the wide thoroughfare was the entrance to the park. There my father used to seat himself—each Sunday the same bench—to watch my brother and me play tag, yelling our heads off after hours of good behavior with grandparents, great-aunts and great-uncles, ordinary aunts and uncles—sometimes it seemed to me that there were more Zuckermans in Newark than Negroes. I wouldn't see as many of them in a year as I saw cousins on an ordinary Sunday driving around the city with my father. "Oh," he used to say, "how you boys love to shout" and with one hand for each son's head would smooth back our damp hair as we started out of the park and back up the familiar hill where we lived. "Any game with shouting in it," he would tell our mother, "and these two are in seventh heaven." Now my younger brother was knuckling under to the tedium of a pre-dental course, having surrendered (to my father's better judgment) a halfhearted dream of a career as an actor, and I—? I apparently was shouting again.

I said, "I think maybe I'll just get the bus. Maybe we

should skip the park. It's been a long day, and I have to go home and get ready to leave for Quahsay tomorrow."

"You haven't answered my question."

"It wouldn't be useful, Dad. The best thing now is to put the story in the mail and send it back to me—and try to forget it."

My suggestion triggered a light sardonic laugh from my father.

"All right," I said sharply, "then don't forget it."

"Calm down," he replied. "I'll walk you to the bus. I'll wait with you."

"You really ought to go home. It's getting cold."

"I'm plenty warm," he informed me.

We waited in silence at the bus stop.

"They take their time on Sundays," he finally said. "Maybe you should come home and have dinner. You could catch one first thing in the morning."

"I've got to go to Quahsay first thing in the morning."

"They can't wait?"

"I can't," I said.

I stepped out into the street to watch for the bus.

"You're going to get yourself killed out there."

"Perhaps."

"So," he said, when at last, in my own sweet time, I came back up on the curb, "what do you do with the story now? Send it to a magazine?"

"It's long for a magazine. Probably no magazine will publish it."

"Oh, they'll publish it. The *Saturday Review* has put you on the map. That was a wonderful write-up, a terrific honor to be chosen like that at your age."

"Well, we'll see."

"No, no. You're on your way. The *Saturday Review* never sold so many copies in North Jersey as when your picture was in it. Why do you think everybody came by today, Frieda and Dave, Aunt Tessie, Birdie, Murray, the Edelmans? Because they saw your picture and they're proud."

"They all told me."

"Look, Nathan, let me have my say. Then you can go, and up there at the artists' colony maybe you'll think over in peace and quiet what I'm trying to get you to understand. If you were going to turn out to be nobody, I wouldn't be taking this seriously. But I do take you seriously—and you have to take yourself seriously, and what you are doing. Stop looking for that goddam bus and listen to me, *please*. You can catch the *next* bus! Nathan, you are not in school any more. You are the older brother and you are out in the world and I am treating you accordingly."

"I understand that. But that doesn't mean that we can't disagree. That's what it *does* mean."

"But from a lifetime of experience I happen to know what ordinary people will think when they read something like this story. And you don't. You can't. You have been sheltered from it all your life. You were raised here in this neighborhood where you went to school with Jewish children. When we went to the shore and had the house with the Edelmans, you were always among Jews, even in the summertime. At Chicago your best friends who you brought home were Jewish boys, always. It's not your fault that you don't know what Gentiles think when they read something like this. But I can tell you. They don't think about how it's a great work of art. They don't know about art. Maybe I don't know about art myself. Maybe none of our family does, not the way that you do. But that's my point. People don't read art—they read about *people*. And they judge them as such. And how do you think they will judge the people in your story, what conclusions do you think they will reach? Have you thought about that?"

"Yes."

"And what have you concluded?"

"Oh, I can't put it into one word, not out here in the street. I didn't write fifteen thousand words so as now to put it into one word."

"Well, I can. And the street isn't a bad place for it. Because I know the word. I wonder if you fully understand just how very little love there is in this world for Jewish people. I don't mean in Germany, either, under the Nazis. I mean in run-of-the-mill Americans, Mr. and Mrs. Nice Guy, who otherwise you and I consider perfectly harmless. Nathan, it is there. I guarantee you it is there. I *know* it is there. I have seen it, I have felt it, even when they do not express it in so many words."

"But I'm not *denying* that. Why did Sidney throw that redneck off his ship—?"

"Sidney," he said furiously, "never threw any redneck off any ship! Sidney threw the bull, Nathan! Sidney was a petty hoodlum who cared about nobody and nothing in this world but the good of Sidney!"

"And who actually existed, Dad—and no better than I depict him!"

"Better? He was worse! How rotten he was you don't *begin* to know. I could tell you stories about that bastard that would make your hair stand on end."

"Then where *are* we? If he was *worse*— Oh, look, we're not getting anywhere. Please, it's getting dark, it's going to snow—*go home*. I'll write when I get up there. But there is no more to say on this subject. We just disagree, period."

"All right!" he said crisply, "all right!" But only, I knew, to defuse me for the moment.

"Dad, go home, please."

"It won't hurt if I wait with you. I don't like you waiting out here by yourself."

"I can manage perfectly well out here by myself. I have for years now."

Some five minutes later, blocks away, we saw what looked like the lights of the New York bus.

"Well," I said, "I'll be back down in a few months. I'll keep in touch—I'll phone—"

"Nathan, your story, as far as Gentiles are concerned, is about one thing and one thing only. Listen to me, before you go. It is about kikes. Kikes and their love of money. That is all our good Christian friends will see, I guarantee you. It is not about the scientists and teachers and lawyers they become and the things such people accomplish for others. It is not about the immigrants like Chaya who worked and saved and sacrificed to get a decent footing in America. It is not about the wonderful peaceful days and nights you spent growing up in our house. It is not about the lovely friends you always had. No, it's about Essie and her hammer, and Sidney and his chorus girls, and that shyster of Essie's and his filthy mouth, and, as best I can see, about what a jerk I was begging them to reach a decent compromise before the whole family had to be dragged up in front of a *goyisher* judge."

"I didn't depict you as a jerk. Christ, far from it. I thought," I said angrily, "I was administering a bear hug, to tell you the truth."

"Oh, did you? Well, it didn't come out that way. Look, son, maybe I *was* a jerk, trying to talk sense to such people. I don't mind being made a little fun of—that couldn't bother me less. I've been around in life. But what I can't accept is what you don't see—what you don't *want* to see. This story isn't us, and what is worse, it isn't even *you*. You are a loving boy. I watched you like a hawk all day. I've watched you all your life. You are a good and kind and considerate young man. You are not somebody who writes this kind of story and then pretends it's the truth."

"But I *did* write it." The light changed, the New York bus started toward us across the intersection—and he threw his arms onto my shoulders. Making me all the more belligerent. "I *am* the kind of person who writes this kind of story!"

"You're not," he pleaded, shaking me just a little.

But I hopped up onto the bus, and then behind me the pneumatic door, with its hard rubber edge, swung shut with what I took to be an overly appropriate thump, a symbol of the kind you leave out of fiction. It was a sound that suddenly brought back to me the prize fights at the Laurel Garden, where once a year my brother and I used to wager our pennies with one another, each of us alternately backing the white fighter or the colored fighter, while Doc Zuckerman waved hello to his few acquaintances in the sporting crowd, among them, on one occasion, Meyer Ellenstein, the dentist who became the city's first Jewish mayor. What I heard was the heartrending thud that follows the roundhouse knockout punch, the sound of the stupefied heavyweight hitting the canvas floor. And what I saw, when I looked out to wave goodbye for the winter, was my smallish, smartly dressed father—turned out for my visit in a new "fingertip" car coat that matched the coffee-toned slacks and the check-ered peaked cap, and wearing, of course, the same silver-rimmed spectacles, the same trim little mustache that I had grabbed at from the crib; what I saw was my bewildered father, alone on the darkening street-corner by the park that used to be our paradise, thinking himself and all of Jewry gratuitously disgraced and jeopardized by my inexplicable betrayal.

Nor was that the end. So troubled was he that several days later, against the counsel of my mother, and after an unpleasant phone conversation with my younger brother, who warned him from Ithaca that I wasn't going to like it when I found out, he decided to seek an audience with Judge Leopold Wapter, after Ellenstein and Rabbi Jo-achim Prinz perhaps the city's most admired Jew.

Wapter had been born of Galician Jews in the slums adjacent to the city's sweatshops and mills some ten years before our family arrived there from Eastern Europe in 1900. My father still remembered having been rescued by one of the Wapter brothers—it could have been the future jurist himself—when a gang of Irish hooligans were having some fun throwing the seven-year-old mocky up into the air in a game of catch. I had heard this story more than once in my childhood, usually when we drove by the landscaped gardens and turreted stone house on Clinton Avenue where Wapter lived with a spinster daughter—one of the first Jewish students at Vassar College to earn the esteem of her Christian teachers—and his wife, the department-store heiress, whose philanthropic activities had given her family name the renown among the Jews of Essex County that it was said to have in her native Charleston. Because the Wapters occupied a position of prestige and authority rather like that accorded in our household to President and Mrs. Roosevelt, I used to imagine her, when I was a small boy, going around wearing Mrs. Roosevelt's dowager hats and dresses, and, oddly for a Jewish woman, speaking in the First Lady's awesome Anglified tones. It did not seem to me that, coming from South Carolina, she could really *be* Jewish. Which was exactly what she thought about me, after reading my story.

To approach the judge, my father had first to contact a lofty cousin of ours—an attorney, a suburbanite, and a former Army colonel who had been president for several years of the judge's Newark temple. Cousin Teddy had already helped him to the judge once before, back when my father had gotten it into his head that I should be one of the five youngsters for whom each year Wapter wrote letters of recommendation to college-admissions officers which—it was said—never failed to do the trick. To go up before Judge Wapter I had to wear a blue suit on a bus in broad daylight and then, from where the bus left me off at the Four Corners (our Times Square), to walk all the way up Market Street through throngs of shoppers, whom I imagined dropping in their tracks at the sight of me out in my only dress suit at that hour. I was to be interviewed at the Essex County Courthouse, in his "chambers," a word that had been intoned to relatives on the phone so frequently and with such reverence by my mother during the preceding week that it may well have accounted for the seven visits I made to our bathroom before I could get myself buttoned for good into the blue suit.

Teddy had telephoned the night before to give me some tips on how to conduct myself. This explained the suit and my father's black silk socks, which I was wearing held up with a pair of his garters, and also the initialed briefcase, a grade-school graduation present that I had never removed from the back of my closet. In the gleaming briefcase I carried ten typewritten pages I had written for International Relations the year before on the Balfour Declaration.

As instructed, I "spoke up" right away and offered to show the judge the essay. To my relief, his chambers had turned out to be one room, not ten—and a room no more grand than the principal's office in our high school. Nor did the tanned, plumpish, cheery judge have the shock of white hair I had been expecting. And though not as small as my father, he still was easily a foot shorter than Abraham Lincoln, whose bronze statue you pass coming into the courthouse. He actually looked years younger than my own anxious father, and not half as serious. Reputedly an excellent golfer, he was probably either on his way to or from a game; that's how I later came to terms with his argyle socks. But when I first noticed them—as he leaned back in his leather chair to flip through my essay—I was shocked. It was as though he were the callow, unworldly applicant, and I, with my father's garters pulled tight as a tourniquet, were the judge. "May I keep this for now, Nathan?" he asked, turning with a smile through my pages of *op. cits* and *ibids*. "I'd like to take it home for my wife to see." Then began the inquiry. I had prepared myself the night before (at Teddy's suggestion) by reading through the Constitution of the United States, the Declaration of Independence, and the editorial page of the Newark *Evening News*. The members of Truman's Cabinet and the majority and minority leaders of both Houses of Congress I of course knew already by heart, though before bed I had gone over them out loud with my mother just to help her relax.

To the judge's questions I gave the following answers:

Journalist. The University of Chicago. Ernie Pyle. One brother, younger. Reading—and sports. The Giants in the National League and the Tigers in the American. Mel Ott and Hank Greenberg. Li'l Abner. Thomas Wolfe. Canada; Washington, D.C.; Rye, New York; New York City itself; Philadelphia; and the Jersey shore. No, sir, never to Florida.

When the judge's secretary made public the names of Newark's five Jewish boys and girls whose college applications Wapter would endorse, mine was one.

I never saw the judge again, though to please my father I had sent my sponsor a letter from the University of Chicago during orientation week of my freshman year, thanking him again for all he had done on my behalf. The letter I received from Wapter some seven years later, during my second week as a guest at Quahsay, was the first I knew of their meeting to talk about "Higher Education."

Dear Nathan:

My familiarity with your fine family goes back, as you must know, to the turn of the century on Prince Street, where we were all poor people in a new land, struggling for our basic needs, our social and civil rights, and our spiritual dignity. I still remember you as one of the outstanding Jewish graduates of our Newark public-school system. I was most pleased to hear from your father that your college record was at the same high level of achievement that you had maintained throughout your school career here, and that you are already beginning to gain recognition in the field of short-story writing. Since there is nothing a judge likes better than to be right from time to time, I was delighted to know that my confidence in you as a high-school senior has already been substantiated in the larger world. I expect that your family and your community can look forward to great achievements from you in the not too distant future.

Your father, knowing of my interest in the development of our outstanding young people, recently asked if I would take time out from my judicial duties to write you with my candid opinion of one of your short stories. He in-

formed me that you are soon to submit the short story entitled "Higher Education" to a leading national magazine,
and he wanted to know whether I thought the story contained material suitable for such a publication.

In our lengthy and interesting conversation here in
my chambers, I informed him that classically, down
through the ages and in all countries, the artist has always
considered himself beyond the mores of the community
in which he lived. Great artists, as history reveals, have
been harshly persecuted time and again by the frightened
and ill-educated, who do not understand that the artist is
a special individual with a unique contribution to make
to mankind. Socrates was considered an enemy of the
people and a corrupter of the young. The Norwegian
playwright and Nobel Prize winner, Henrik Ibsen, was
forced into exile because his countrymen failed to understand the profound truth of his great dramas. I explained
to your father that I for one would never want to be
allied with the intolerance shown by the Greeks towards
Socrates, or by the Norwegians towards Ibsen. On the
other hand, I do believe that, like all men, the artist has
a responsibility to his fellow man, to the society in which
he lives, and to the cause of truth and justice. With that
responsibility and that alone as my criterion, I would
attempt to give him an opinion on the suitability for publication in a national magazine of your latest fictional
effort.

Attached you will find a questionnaire about your story,
prepared jointly by my wife and myself. Because of Mrs.
Wapter's interest in literature and the arts—and because

I did not think it fair to rely solely upon my reading—I
have taken the liberty of securing her opinion. These are
serious and difficult questions to which Mrs. Wapter and
I would like you to give just one hour of your time. We
don't want you to answer them to our satisfaction—we
want you to answer them to your own. You are a young
man of great promise and, we all think, of potentially
great talent. But with great talent come great responsibilities, and an obligation to those who have stood behind you
in the early days so that your talent might come to frui-
tion. I would like to think that if and when the day should
dawn that you receive *your* invitation to Stockholm to
accept a Nobel Prize, we will have had some small share
in awakening your conscience to the responsibilities of
your calling.

> Sincerely yours,
> Leopold Wapter

P.S. If you have not yet seen the Broadway production
of *The Diary of Anne Frank*, I strongly advise that you
do so. Mrs. Wapter and I were in the audience on opening
night; we wish that Nathan Zuckerman could have been
with us to benefit from that unforgettable experience.

The sheet of questions prepared for me by the Wapters
read as follows:

TEN QUESTIONS FOR NATHAN ZUCKERMAN
1. If you had been living in Nazi Germany in the thirties,
   would you have written such a story?
2. Do you believe Shakespeare's Shylock and Dickens's

Fagin have been of no use to anti-Semites?

3. Do you practice Judaism? If so, how? If not, what credentials qualify you for writing about Jewish life for national magazines?

4. Would you claim that the characters in your story represent a fair sample of the kinds of people that make up a typical contemporary community of Jews?

5. In a story with a Jewish background, what reason is there for a description of physical intimacy between a married Jewish man and an unmarried Christian woman? Why in a story with a Jewish background must there be (a) adultery; (b) incessant fighting within a family over money; (c) warped human behavior in general?

6. What set of aesthetic values makes you think that the cheap is more valid than the noble and the slimy is more truthful than the sublime?

7. What in your character makes you associate so much of life's ugliness with Jewish people?

8. Can you explain why in your story, in which a rabbi appears, there is nowhere the grandeur of oratory with which Stephen S. Wise and Abba Hillel Silver and Zvi Masliansky have stirred and touched their audiences?

9. Aside from the financial gain to yourself, what benefit do you think publishing this story in a national magazine will have for (a) your family; (b) your community; (c) the Jewish religion; (d) the well-being of the Jewish people?

10. Can you honestly say that there is anything in your

short story that would not warm the heart of a Julius Streicher or a Joseph Goebbels?

Three weeks after hearing from the judge and Mrs. Wapter, and only days before my visit to Lonoff, I was interrupted around noon by the Colony secretary. She had come out to my cabin in her coat, apologizing for the disturbance, but saying that I had a long-distance phone call that had been described by the other party as an emergency.

When my mother heard my voice she began to cry. "I know it's wrong to bother you," she said, "but I can't take any more. I can't take another night of it. I can't sit through another meal."

"What is it? What's the matter?"

"Nathan, did you or didn't you get a letter from Judge Wapter?"

"Oh, I got it all right."

"But"—she was flabbergasted—"then why didn't you answer it?"

"He should not have gone to Wapter with that story, Mother."

"Oh, darling, maybe he shouldn't. But he did. He did because he knows you respect the judge—"

"I don't even *know* the judge."

"That's not *true*. He did so much for you when you were ready for college. He gave you such a wonderful boost. It turns out that in his files he still had the essay you wrote on the Balfour Declaration in high school. His secretary took out the files and there it was. Daddy saw it, right in his chambers. Why you haven't given him the courtesy of a reply . . . Daddy is beside himself. He can't believe it."

"He'll have to."

"But all he wanted was for you not to bring yourself harm. You know that."

"I thought it was the harm I was going to do the Jews that you're all worried about."

"Darling, please, for my sake, why won't you answer Judge Wapter? Why won't you give him the hour he asks for? Surely you have an hour where you are to write a letter. Because you cannot, at the age of twenty-three, ignore such a person. You cannot make enemies at twenty-three of people who are so admired and loved, and by Gentiles, too."

"Is that what my father says?"

"He says so much, Nathan. It's been three *weeks* now."

"And how does he even know I haven't answered?"

"From Teddy. He didn't hear from you, so finally he called him. You can well imagine. Teddy is a little fit to be tied. He's not used to this treatment, either. After all, he also extended himself on our behalf when you wanted to go to Chicago."

"Ma, I hate to suggest this, but it could be that the judge's famous letter, procured after great ass-kissing all around, had about as much effect on the University of

Chicago as a letter about my qualifications from Rocky Graziano."

"Oh, Nathan, where's your humility, where's your modesty—where's the courtesy you have always had?"

"Where are my father's *brains!*"

"He only wants to *save* you."

"From what?"

"Mistakes."

"Too late, Mother. Didn't you read the Ten Questions for Nathan Zuckerman?"

"Dear, I did. He sent us a copy—and the letter, too."

"The Big Three, Mama! Streicher, Goebbels, and your son! What about the *judge's* humility? Where's *his* modesty?"

"He only meant that what happened to the Jews—"

"In Europe—not in Newark! We are not the wretched of Belsen! We were not the victims of that crime!"

"But we *could* be—in their place we *would* be. Nathan, violence is nothing new to Jews, you *know* that!"

"Ma, you want to see physical violence done to the Jews of Newark, go to the office of the plastic surgeon where the girls get their noses fixed. That's where the Jewish blood flows in Essex County, that's where the blow is delivered—with a mallet! To their bones—and to their pride!"

"Please don't shout at me. I'm not up to all of this, please—that's why I'm calling. Judge Wapter did not mean *you* were Goebbels. God forbid. He was only a little shocked still from reading your story. We all were, you can understand that."

"Oh, maybe then you all shock a little too easily. Jews are heirs to greater shocks than I can possibly deliver with a story that has a sharpie in it like Sidney. Or Essie's hammer. Or Essie's lawyer. You know as much yourself. You just *said* as much."

"Oh, darling, then tell the judge that. Just tell him that, the way you told it to me, and that'll do it. Your father will be happy. Write him *something*. You can write such wonderful and beautiful letters. When Grandma was dying, you wrote her a letter that was like a poem. It was like—like listening to French, it was so beautiful. What you wrote about the Balfour Declaration was so beautiful when you were only fifteen years old. The judge gave it back to Daddy and said he still remembered how much it had impressed him. He's not against you, Nathan. But if you get your back up and show disrespect, then he will be. And Teddy too, who could be such a help."

"Nothing I could write Wapter would convince him of anything. Or his wife."

"You could tell him you went to see *The Diary of Anne Frank*. You could at least do that."

"I didn't see it. I read the book. *Everybody* read the book."

"But you liked it, didn't you?"

"That's not the issue. How can you *dis*like it? Mother, I will not prate in platitudes to please the adults!"

"But if you just said that, about reading the book, and liking it . . . Because Teddy told Daddy—well, Nathan, is this true?—that to him it looks like you don't really like Jews very much."

"No, Teddy's got it confused. It's him I don't like very much."

"Oh, darling, don't be clever. Don't start that last-word business, please. Just answer me, I'm so confused in the middle of all this. Nathan, tell me something."

"What?"

"I'm only quoting Teddy. Darling . . ."

"What is it, Ma?"

"Are you really anti-Semitic?"

"I'll leave it to you. What do you think?"

"Me? I never heard of such a thing. But Teddy . . ."

"I know, he's a college graduate and lives with wall-to-wall carpeting in Millburn. But they come pretty stupid too."

"Nathan!"

"Sorry, but that's my opinion."

"Oh, I don't know anything any more—all this from that story! Please, if you will not do anything else I ask, at least phone your father. He's been waiting for something for three whole weeks now. And he's a doer, your father, he's not a man who knows how to wait. Darling, phone him at his office. Phone him now. For me."

"No."

"I beg of you."

"No."

"Oh, I can't believe this is you."

"It *is* me!"

"But—what about your father's love?"

"I am on my own!"

In Lonoff's study that night I began letter after letter explaining myself to my father, but each time I got to the point of repeating E. I. Lonoff's praise for my work, I tore the thing up in a rage. I owed no explanations, and he wouldn't buy those I offered anyway, if he even understood them. Because my voice started back of my knees and reached above my head wasn't going to make him any happier about my informing on those unsavory family miscreants who were nobody's business but our own. Nor would it help to argue that Essie wielding her hammer came off in my story as something more impressive than an embarrassment; that wasn't what other people were going to say about a woman who behaved like that, and then expressed herself in a court of law like a man in a barroom brawl. Nor would a spin through the waxworks of my literary museum—from Babel's Odessa gangsters to Abravanel's Los Angeles worldlings—convince him that I was upholding the responsibilities placed on me by his hero, the judge. Odessa? Why not Mars? He was talking about what people would say when they read that story in North Jersey, where we happened to come from. He was talking about the *goyim*, who looked down on us with enough unearned contempt already, and who would be only too pleased to call us all kikes because of what I had written for the whole world to read about Jews fighting over money. It was not for me to leak the news that such a thing could possibly happen. That was worse than informing—that was collaborating.

Oh, this is useless, I thought, this is idiotic—and tore up yet another half-finished letter in my defense. That the situation between us had deteriorated so rapidly—by his going to Wapter with my story, and by my refusal to justify myself to my elders—was as it had to be, sooner or later. Hadn't Joyce, hadn't Flaubert, hadn't Thomas Wolfe, the romantic genius of my high-school reading list, all been condemned for disloyalty or treachery or immorality by those who saw themselves as slandered in their works? As even the judge knew, literary history was in part the history of novelists infuriating fellow countrymen, family, and friends. To be sure, our dispute hadn't achieved the luster of literary history quite yet, but still, writers weren't writers, I told myself, if they didn't have the strength to face the insolubility of that conflict and go on.

But what about sons? It wasn't Flaubert's father or Joyce's father who had impugned me for my recklessness —it was my own. Nor was it the Irish he claimed I had maligned and misrepresented, but the Jews. Of which I was one. Of which, only some five thousand days past, there had been millions more.

Yet each time I tried again to explain my motives, the angrier with him I became. It's you who humiliated yourself—now live with it, you moralizing ass! Wapter, that know-nothing windbag! That dopey pillar! And the pious belle with her love for the arts! Worth ten million and she chides *me* about "financial gain"! And Abba Hillel Silver on top of that! Oh, don't waste time on prodigal me about Rabbi Silver's grandeur, lady, tell my late cousin Sidney and his friends in the Mob—quote Zvi Masliansky to them, like you do at the country club on the eighteenth hole!

At around eleven I heard the town snowplow clearing the unpaved road beyond the apple orchard. Later a pickup truck with a snowblade clamped to the front end charged into the driveway and shoved the evening's snowfall into the orchard atop the snowfall of the previous thirty nights. The little Renault arrived last, swerving slowly into the driveway about half an hour later, one beam on high, the other dim, and with half-dead windshield wipers.

At the first sound of her car returning, I had flipped off all my lights and crawled to the study window on my knees so as to watch her make her way toward the house. For I had not stayed awake simply because I couldn't forget my father's disapproval or E. I. Lonoff's toast—I also had no intention of being unconscious when the enchanting and mysterious houseguest (all the more alluring, of course, as Hope's imagined erotic rival) got back to change into her nightdress on the floor above me. What I would be able to do about this, I had no idea. However, just to be awake and unclothed in one bed while she was awake and nearly unclothed in another was better than nothing. It was a start.

But predictably, it was worse than nothing and the start of little that was new. The lantern on the half-buried lamppost between the house and the car shed went dark, and then, from where I was kneeling beside the study door, I heard her enter the house. She moved through the hallway and up the carpeted stairs—and that was the last of her that I saw or heard until about an hour later, when I was privileged to audit another astounding course, this one in the adult evening division of the Lonoff School of the Arts. The rest of what I'd been waiting up for I had, of course, to imagine. But that is easier work by far than making things up at the typewriter. For that kind of imagining you don't have to have your picture in the *Saturday Review*. You don't even have to know the alphabet. Being young will usually get a fellow through with flying colors. You don't even have to be young. You don't have to be anything.

Virtuous reader, if you think that after intercourse all animals are sad, try masturbating on the daybed in E. I. Lonoff's study and see how you feel when it's over. To expiate my sense of utter shabbiness, I immediately took to the high road and drew from Lonoff's bookshelves the volume of Henry James stories containing "The Middle Years," the source of one of the two quotations pinned to the bulletin board. And there where I had indulged myself in this most un-Jamesian lapse from the amenities, I read the story two times through, looking to discover what I could about the doubt that's the writer's passion, the passion that's his task, and the madness of—of all things— art.

Dencombe, a novelist "who had a reputation," is convalescing from a debilitating ailment at an English health resort when a copy of his latest book, *The Middle Years*, arrives from his publisher. Seated alone on a bench looking out to sea, Dencombe reluctantly opens the book —to discover what he believes is the artistic distinction that had always evaded him. His genius has flowered, however, just when he no longer has the strength to develop a "'last manner' . . . to which his real treasure would be gathered." That would require a second existence, and everything tells him that the first one is nearly over.

While fearfully contemplating the end of his life, Dencombe is joined on the bench by a garrulous young stranger carrying his own copy of *The Middle Years*. He begins to speak ardently of Dencombe's achievement to the mild gentleman who he finds has also been reading the new novel. The admirer—"the greatest admirer . . . whom it was supposable he might boast"—is Dr. Hugh, physician to a rich, eccentric English countess who is at the hotel, like Dencombe, to recover from some grave illness. Inflamed with passion for *The Middle Years,* Dr. Hugh opens the book to read aloud a particularly beautiful passage; but, having mistakenly seized Dencombe's copy rather than his own, he discovers that the printed text has been altered in a dozen places by a pencil. With this, the anonymous and ailing author on the brink of being discovered—"a passionate corrector" never able to arrive at a final form—feels his sickness sweeping over him and loses consciousness.

In the days that follow, Dencombe, bedridden, hopes that some remedy miraculously concocted by the attentive young physician will restore his strength. However, when he learns that the countess plans to disinherit Dr. Hugh of a magnificent fortune if he continues to neglect her for the novelist, Dencombe encourages Dr. Hugh to follow her to London. But Dr. Hugh cannot overcome his passionate idolatry, and by the time he acts on Dencombe's advice to hurry to his employer, he has already suffered "a terrible injury" for which Dencombe almost believes himself to be responsible: the countess has died, in a relapse brought on by her jealousy, bequeathing to the young physician not a penny. Says Dr. Hugh, returning from her grave to the dying soul whom he adores, "I had to choose."

"You chose to let a fortune go?"

"I chose to accept, whatever they might be, the consequences of my infatuation," smiled Doctor Hugh. Then, as a larger pleasantry: "The fortune be hanged! It's your own fault if I can't get your things out of my head."

A thin black line had been drawn beneath the "pleasantry" in Lonoff's book. In script so tiny it was almost unreadable, the writer had noted beside it a droll pleasantry of his own: "And also your fault if I can."

From there on, down both margins of the final page describing Dencombe's death, Lonoff had penned three vertical lines. Nothing resembling drollery here. Rather, the six surgically precise black lines seemed to simulate the succession of fine impressions that James's insidious narrative about the novelist's dubious wizardry had scored upon Lonoff's undeluded brain.

After Dencombe has learned the consequences of the young man's infatuation—consequences so utterly irreconcilable with his own honorable convictions that, upon hearing of his place in it all, Dencombe utters "a long bewildered moan"—he lies "for many hours, many days . . . motionless and absent."

At the last he signed to Doctor Hugh to listen and, when he was down on his knees by the pillow, brought him very near. "You've made me think it all a delusion."

"Not your glory, my dear friend," stammered the young man.

"Not my glory—what there is of it! It *is* glory—to have been tested, to have had our little quality and cast our little spell. The thing is to have made somebody care. You happen to be crazy of course, but that doesn't affect the law."

"You're a great success!" said Doctor Hugh, putting into his young voice the ring of a marriage-bell.

Dencombe lay taking this in; then he gathered strength to speak once more. "A second chance—*that's* the delusion. There never was to be but one. We work in the dark—we do what we can—we give what we have. Our doubt is our passion and our passion is our task. The rest is the madness of art."

"If you've doubted, if you've despaired, you've always 'done' it," his visitor subtly argued.

"We've done something or other," Dencombe conceded.

"Something or other is everything. It's the feasible. It's *you*!"

"Comforter!" poor Dencombe ironically sighed.

"But it's true," insisted his friend.

"It's true. It's frustration that doesn't count."

"Frustration's only life," said Doctor Hugh.

"Yes, it's what passes." Poor Dencombe was barely audible, but he had marked with the words the virtual end of his first and only chance.

Within moments of hearing muffled voices coming from above my head, I stood up on the daybed—my finger still holding my place in the book—and, stretching to my full height, tried to make out what was being said up there and by whom. When that didn't help, I thought of climbing onto Lonoff's desk; it was easily a foot or so higher than the daybed and would put my ear only inches from the room's low ceiling. But if I should fall, if I should alter by a millimeter the placement of his typing paper, if somehow I should leave footprints—no, I couldn't risk it and shouldn't even have been thinking of it. I had gone far enough already by expropriating the corner of the desk to compose my half dozen unfinished letters home. My sense of propriety, not to mention the author's gracious hospitality, required me to restrain myself from committing such a sordid, callow little indecency.

But in the meantime I had done it.

A woman was crying. Which one, over what, who was there comforting her—or causing the tears? Just a little higher and maybe I could find out. A thick dictionary would have been perfect, but Lonoff's Webster's was down on a shelf of fat reference books level with the typing chair, and the best I could manage under pressure was to gain another couple of inches by kneeling to insert between the desk and my feet the volume of stories by Henry James.

Ah, the unreckoned consequences, the unaccountable uses of art! Dencombe would understand. James would understand. But would Lonoff? *Don't fall.*

"Now you're being sensible." Lonoff was the speaker. "You had to see for yourself, and so you saw."

A light thud directly overhead. Someone had dropped into a chair. The weary writer? In his bathrobe now, or still in suit and tie and polished shoes?

Then I heard Amy Bellette. And what was *she* wearing at this hour? "I saw nothing—only more misery either way. Of course I can't live here—but I can't keep living there, either. I can't live anywhere. I can't *live*."

"Quiet down. She's had it for today. Let her rest, now that she's asleep."

"She's ruining everyone's life."

"Don't blame her for what you hold against me. I'm the one who says no around here. Now *you* go to sleep."

"I can't. I don't want to. We can talk."

"We've talked."

Silence. Were they down on their knees listening through the old floorboards for *me?* Then they had long since heard my drumming heart.

Bedsprings! Lonoff climbing in beside her!

But it was Amy getting out of bed I heard, not Lonoff climbing in. Her feet lightly crossed the floor only inches above my lips.

"I love you. I love you so, Dad-da. There's no one else like you. They're all such dopes."

"You're a good girl."

"Let me sit on your lap. Just hold me a little and I'll be fine."

"You're fine now. You're always fine in the end. You're the great survivor."

"No, just the world's strongest weakling. Oh, tell me a story. Sing me a song. Oh, imitate the great Durante, I really need it tonight."

At first it sounded like somebody coughing. But then I

could hear that, yes, he was singing to her, very quietly, in the manner of Jimmy Durante—"So I ups to him, and he ups to me"— I could catch just the one line, but that was enough for me to recall the song itself being sung by Durante on his radio show, in the celebrated raffish voice, and with the hoarse, endearing simplehearted delivery that the famous author was now impersonating overhead.

"More," said Amy.

Was she now on his lap? Amy in her nightie and Lonoff in his suit?

"You go to sleep," he told her.

"More. Sing 'I Can Do Without Broadway.' "

" 'Oh, I know don well I can do widout Broadway— *but* . . . can Broadway do widout meeeee? . . .' "

"Oh, Manny, we could be so happy—in Florence, my sweetest, we could come out of hiding."

"We're not in hiding. We never have been."

"No, not when it's like this. But otherwise it's all so false and wrong and lonely. We could make each other so happy. I wouldn't be your little girl over there. I would when we played, but otherwise I'd be your wife."

"We'd be what we've always been. Stop dreaming."

"No, not so. Without her—"

"You want a corpse on your conscience? She would be dead in a year."

"But I have a corpse on my conscience." The floor creaked where her two feet had suddenly landed. So she *had* been on his lap! "Look!"

"Cover yourself."

"My corpse."

Scuffling on the floorboards. The heavy tread of Lonoff on the move.

"Good night."

"Look at it."

"Melodrama, Amy. Cover up."

"You prefer tragedy?"

"Don't wallow. You're not convincing. Decide not to lose hold—and then don't."

"But I'm going crazy! I cannot live apart from you! I don't know how. Oh, why didn't I take that job—and move back! And the hell with her!"

"You did the right thing. You know just what to do."

"Yes, give things up!"

"Dreamy things, correct."

"Oh, Manny, would it kill you just to kiss my breasts? Is that dreamy, too? Would it cause the death of anyone if you just did that?"

"You cover yourself now."

"Dad-da, *please*."

But next I heard Lonoff's carpet slippers—yes, he was out of his suit, dressed for bed—padding through the upstairs corridor. Soundlessly as I could, I slipped down from the desk and made my way on my toes to the daybed, where, from the sheer physical effort that had gone into my acrobatic eavesdropping, I collapsed: My astonishment at what I'd overheard, my shame at the unpardonable breach of his trust, my relief at having escaped undiscovered—all that turned out to be nothing, really, beside the frustration I soon began to feel over the thinness of my imagination and what that promised for the future. Dad-da, Florence, the great Durante; her babyishness and desire, his mad, heroic restraint— Oh, if only I could have imagined the scene I'd overheard! If only I could invent as presumptuously as real life! If one day I could just *approach* the originality and excitement of what actually goes on! But if I ever did, what then would they think of me, my father and his judge? How would my elders hold up against that? And if they couldn't, if the blow to their sentiments was finally too wounding, just how well would I hold up against being hated and reviled and disowned?

3 Femme Fatale

It was only a year earlier that Amy had told Lonoff her whole story. Weeping hysterically, she had phoned him one night from the Biltmore Hotel in New York; as best he could understand, that morning she had come down alone on a train from Boston to see the matinee performance of a play, intending to return home again by train in the evening. Instead, after coming out of the theater she had taken a hotel room, where ever since she had been "in hiding."

At midnight, having only just finished his evening's

reading and gone up to bed, Lonoff got into his car and drove south. By four he had reached the city, by six she had told him that it was the dramatization of Anne Frank's diary she had come to New York to see, but it was midmorning before she could explain even somewhat coherently her connection with this new Broadway play.

"It wasn't the play—I could have watched that easily enough if I had been alone. It was the people watching with me. Carloads of women kept pulling up to the theater, women wearing fur coats, with expensive shoes and handbags. I thought, This isn't for me. The billboards, the photographs, the marquee, I could take all that. But it was the women who frightened me—and their families and their children and their homes. Go to a movie, I told myself, go instead to a museum. But I showed my ticket, I went in with them, and of course it happened. It had to happen. It's what happens there. The women cried. Everyone around me was in tears. Then at the end, in the row behind me, a woman screamed, 'Oh, no.' That's why I came running here. I wanted a room with a telephone in it where I could stay until I'd found my father. But all I did once I was here was sit in the bathroom thinking that if he knew, if I told him, then they would have to come out on the stage after each performance and announce, 'But she is really alive. You needn't worry, she survived, she is twenty-six now, and doing very well.' I would say to him, 'You must keep this our secret—no one but you must ever know.' But suppose he was found out? What if we both were? Manny, I couldn't call him. And I knew I couldn't when I heard that woman scream 'Oh, no.' I knew then what's been true all along: I'll never see him again. I have to be dead to everyone."

Amy lay on the rumpled bed, wrapped tightly in a blanket, while Lonoff listened in silence from a chair by the window. Upon entering the unlocked room, he had found her sitting in the empty bathtub, still wearing her best dress and her best coat: the coat because she could not stop trembling, in the tub because it was the farthest she could get from the window, which was twenty floors above the street.

"How pathetic, you must think. What a joke," she said.

"A joke? On whom? I don't see the joke."

"My telling this to you."

"I still don't get it."

"Because it's like one of your stories. An E. I. Lonoff story . . . called . . . oh, you'd know what to call it. You'd know how to tell it in three pages. A homeless girl comes from Europe, sits in the professor's class being clever, listens to his records, plays his daughter's piano, virtually grows up in his house, and then one day, when the waif is a woman and out on her own, one fine day in the Biltmore Hotel, she casually announces . . ."

He left his chair and came to sit beside her on the bed while she went to pieces again. "Yes," he said, "quite casually."

"Manny, I'm not a lunatic, I'm not a crackpot, I'm not

some girl—you must believe me—trying to be interesting and imitate your art!"

"My dear friend," he replied, his arms around her now and rocking her like a child, "if this is all so—"

"Oh, Dad-da, I'm afraid it really is."

"Well, then, you have left my poor art far behind."

This is the tale that Amy told the morning after she had gone alone to the Cort Theatre to sit amid the weeping and inconsolable audience at the famous New York production of *The Diary of Anne Frank*. This is the story that the twenty-six-year-old young woman with the striking face and the fetching accent and the felicitous prose style and the patience, according to Lonoff, of a Lonoff, expected him to believe was true.

After the war she had become Amy Bellette. She had not taken the new name to disguise her identity—as yet there was no need—but, as she imagined at the time, to forget her life. She had been in a coma for weeks, first in the filthy barracks with the other ailing and starving inmates, and then in the squalid makeshift "infirmary." A dozen dying children had been rounded up by the SS and placed beneath blankets in a room with twelve beds in order to impress the Allied armies advancing upon Belsen with the amenities of concentration-camp living. Those of the twelve still alive when the British got there had been moved to an army field hospital. It was here that she finally came around. She understood sometimes less and sometimes more than the nurses explained to her, but she would not speak. Instead, without howling or hallucinating, she tried to find a way to believe that she was somewhere in Germany, that she was not yet sixteen, and that her family was dead. Those were the facts; now to grasp them.

"Little Beauty" the nurses called her—a silent, dark, emaciated girl—and so, one morning, ready to talk, she told them that the surname was Bellette. Amy she got from an American book she had sobbed over as a child, *Little Women*. She had decided, during her long silence, to finish growing up in America now that there was nobody left to live with in Amsterdam. After Belsen she figured it might be best to put an ocean the size of the Atlantic between herself and what she needed to forget.

She learned of her father's survival while waiting to get her teeth examined by the Lonoffs' family dentist in Stockbridge. She had been three years with foster families in England, and almost a year as a freshman at Athene College, when she picked an old copy of *Time* out of the pile in the waiting room and, just turning pages, saw a photograph of a Jewish businessman named Otto Frank. In July of 1942, some two years after the beginning of the Nazi occupation, he had taken his wife and his two young daughters into hiding. Along with another Jewish family, the Franks lived safely for twenty-five months in a rear upper story of the Amsterdam building where he used to have his business offices. Then, in August 1944, their

whereabouts were apparently betrayed by one of the workers in the warehouse below, and the hideout was uncov-
ered by the police. Of the eight who'd been together in the
sealed-off attic rooms, only Otto Frank survived the concentration camps. When he came back to Amsterdam
after the war, the Dutch family who had been their pro-
tectors gave him the notebooks that had been kept in hiding by his younger daughter, a girl of fifteen when she
died in Belsen: a diary, some ledgers she wrote in, and a
sheaf of papers emptied out of her briefcase when the
Nazis were ransacking the place for valuables. Frank
printed and circulated the diary only privately at first, as
a memorial to his family, but in 1947 it was published in a
regular edition under the title *Het Achterhuis*—"The
House Behind." Dutch readers, *Time* said, were greatly
affected by the young teenager's record of how the hunted
Jews tried to carry on a civilized life despite their depriva-
tions and the terror of discovery.

Alongside the article—"A Survivor's Sorrows"—was
the photograph of the diarist's father, "now sixty." He
stood alone in his coat and hat in front of the building on
the Prinsengracht Canal where his late family had im-
provised a last home.

Next came the part of her story that Lonoff was bound
to think improbable. She herself, however, could not consider it all that strange that she should be thought dead
when in fact she was alive; nobody who knew the chaos
of those final months—the Allies bombing everywhere,

the SS in flight—would call that improbable. Whoever claimed to have seen her dead of typhus in Belsen had either confused her with her older sister, Margot, or had figured that she was dead after seeing her so long in a coma, or had watched her being carted away, as good as dead, by the Kapos.

"Belsen was the third camp," Amy told him. "We were sent first to Westerbork, north of Amsterdam. There were other children around to talk to, we were back in the open air—aside from being frightened it really wasn't that awful. Daddy lived in the men's barracks, but when I got sick he managed somehow to get into the women's camp at night and to come to my bed and hold my hand. We were there a month, then we were shipped to Auschwitz. Three days and three nights in the freight cars. Then they opened the doors and that was the last I saw of him. The men were pushed in one direction, we were pushed in the other. That was early September. I saw my mother last at the end of October. She could hardly speak by then. When Margot and I were shipped from Auschwitz, I don't even know if she understood."

She told him about Belsen. Those who had survived the cattle cars lived at first in tents on the heath. They slept on the bare ground in rags. Days went by without food or fresh water, and after the autumn storms tore the tents from their moorings, they slept exposed to the wind and rain. When at last they were being moved into barracks, they saw ditches beyond the camp enclosure piled high with bodies—the people who had died on the heath from typhus and starvation. By the time winter came, it seemed as if everyone still alive was either sick or half mad. And then, while watching her sister slowly dying, she grew sick herself. After Margot's death, she could hardly remember the women in the barracks who had helped her, and knew nothing of what happened to them.

It was not so improbable either that after her long hospital convalescence she had not made her way to the address in Switzerland where the family had agreed to meet if they should ever lose touch with one another. Would a weak sixteen-year-old girl undertake a journey requiring money, visas—requiring hope—only to learn at the other end that she was as lost and alone as she feared?

No, no, the improbable part was this: that instead of telephoning *Time* and saying, "I'm the one who wrote the diary—find Otto Frank!" she jotted down in her notebook the date on the magazine's cover and, after a tooth had been filled, went off with her school books to the library. What was improbable—inexplicable, indefensible, a torment still to her conscience—was that, calm and studious as ever, she checked *The New York Times Index* and the *Readers' Guide to Periodical Literature* for "Frank, Anne" and "Frank, Otto" and "*Het Achterhuis*," and, when she found nothing, went down to the library's lowest stacks, where the periodicals were shelved. There she spent the remaining hour before dinner rereading the article in *Time*. She read it until she knew it by heart. She studied her father's photograph. Now sixty. And those were the words that did it—made of her once again the daughter who cut his hair for him in the attic, the daughter who did her lessons there with him as her tutor, the daughter who would run to his bed and cling to him under the covers when she heard the Allied bombers flying over Amsterdam: suddenly she was the daughter for whom he had taken the place of everything she could no longer have. She cried for a very long time. But when she went to dinner in the dormitory, she pretended that nothing catastrophic had once again happened to Otto Frank's Anne.

But then right from the beginning she had resolved not to speak about what she had been through. Resolutions were her strong point as a young girl on her own. How else could she have lasted on her own? One of the thousand reasons she could not bear Uncle Daniel, the first of her foster fathers in England, was that sooner or later he wound up telling whoever walked into the house about all that had happened to Amy during the war. And then there was Miss Giddings, the young teacher in the school north of London who was always giving the orphaned little Jewess tender glances during history class. One day after school Miss Giddings took her for a lemon-curd tart at the local tearoom and asked her questions about the concentration camps. Her eyes filled with tears as Amy, who felt obliged to answer, confirmed the stories she had heard but could never quite believe. "Terrible," Miss

Giddings said, "so terrible." Amy silently drank her tea and ate her lovely tart, while Miss Giddings, like one of her own history students, tried in vain to understand the past. "Why is it," the unhappy teacher finally asked, "that for centuries people have hated you Jews?" Amy rose to her feet. She was stunned. "Don't ask me that!" the girl said—"ask the madmen who hate us!" And she had nothing further to do with Miss Giddings as a friend—or with anyone else who asked her anything about what they couldn't possibly understand.

One Saturday only a few months after her arrival in England, vowing that if she heard another plaintive "Belsen" out of Uncle Daniel's mouth she would run off to Southampton and stow away on an American ship—and having had about enough of the snooty brand of sympathy the pure-bred English teachers offered at school—she burned her arm while ironing a blouse. The neighbors came running at the sound of her screams and rushed her to the hospital emergency room. When the bandage was removed, there was a patch of purple scar tissue about half the size of an egg instead of her camp number.

After the accident, as her foster parents called it, Uncle Daniel informed the Jewish Welfare Board that his wife's ill health made it impossible for them to continue to have Amy in their home. The foster child moved on to another family—and then another. She told whoever asked that she had been evacuated from Holland with a group of Jewish schoolchildren the week before the Nazis invaded. Some-

times she did not even say that the schoolchildren were
Jewish, an omission for which she was mildly rebuked by
the Jewish families who had accepted responsibility for
her and were troubled by her lying. But she could not
bear them all laying their helpful hands upon her shoulders
because of Auschwitz and Belsen. If she was going to be
thought exceptional, it would not be because of Auschwitz
and Belsen but because of what she had made of herself
since.

They were kind and thoughtful people, and they tried
to get her to understand that she was not in danger in
England. "You needn't feel frightened or threatened in
any way," they assured her. "Or ashamed of anything."
"I'm not ashamed. That's the point." "Well, that isn't
always the point when young people try to hide their
Jewish origins." "Maybe it isn't with others," she told
them, "but it is with me."

On the Saturday after discovering her father's photograph in *Time*, she took the morning bus to Boston,
and in every foreign bookstore looked in vain for a copy
of *Het Achterhuis*. Two weeks later she traveled the three
hours to Boston again, this time to the main post office to
rent a box. She paid for it in cash, then mailed the letter
she was carrying in her handbag, along with a money
order for fifteen dollars, to Contact Publishers in Amsterdam, requesting them to send, postage paid, to Pilgrim
International Bookshop, P.O. Box 152, Boston, Mass.,

U.S.A., as many copies as fifteen dollars would buy of *Het Achterhuis* by Anne Frank.

She had been dead for him some four years; believing her dead for another month or two would not really hurt much more. Curiously she did not hurt more either, except in bed at night when she cried and begged forgiveness for the cruelty she was practicing on her perfect father, now sixty.

Nearly three months after she had sent the order off to her Amsterdam publisher, on a warm, sunny day at the beginning of August, there was a package too large for the Pilgrim Bookshop post-office box waiting to be picked up in Boston. She was wearing a beige linen skirt and a fresh white cotton blouse, both ironed the night before. Her hair, cut in pageboy style that spring, had been washed and set the previous night, and her skin was evenly tanned. She was swimming a mile every morning and playing tennis every afternoon and, all in all, was as fit and energetic as a twenty-year-old could be. Maybe that was why, when the postal clerk handed her the parcel, she did not tear at the string with her teeth or faint straightaway onto the marble floor. Instead, she walked over to the Common—the package mailed from Holland swinging idly from one hand—and wandered along until she found an unoccupied bench. She sat first on a bench in the shade, but then got up and walked on until she found a perfect spot in the sunshine.

After thoroughly studying the Dutch stamps—postwar issues new to her—and contemplating the postmark, she set about to see how carefully she could undo the package. It was a preposterous display of unruffled patience and she meant it to be. She was feeling at once triumphant and giddy. Forbearance, she thought. Patience. Without patience there is no life. When she had finally untied the string and unfolded, without tearing, the layers of thick brown paper, it seemed to her that what she had so meticulously removed from the wrappings and placed onto the lap of her clean and pretty American girl's beige linen skirt was her survival itself.

Van Anne Frank. Her book. Hers.

She had begun keeping a diary less than three weeks before Pim told her that they were going into hiding. Until she ran out of pages and had to carry over onto office ledgers, she made the entries in a cardboard-covered notebook that he'd given her for her thirteenth birthday. She still remembered most of what happened to her in the achterhuis, some of it down to the most minute detail, but of the fifty thousand words recording it all, she couldn't remember writing one. Nor could she remember anything much of what she'd confided there about her personal problems to the phantom confidante she'd named Kitty— whole pages of her tribulations as new and strange to her as her native tongue.

Perhaps because *Het Achterhuis* was the first Dutch book she'd read since she'd written it, her first thought when she finished was of her childhood friends in Amsterdam, the boys and girls from the Montessori school where she'd learned to read and write. She tried to remember the names of the Christian children, who would have survived the war. She tried to recall the names of her teachers, going all the way back to kindergarten. She pictured the faces of the shopkeepers, the postman, the milk deliveryman who had known her as a child. She imagined their neighbors in the houses on Merwedeplein. And when she had, she saw each of them closing her book and thinking, Who realized she was so gifted? Who realized we had such a writer in our midst?

The first passage she reread was dated over a year before the birth of Amy Bellette. The first time round she'd bent back the corner of the page; the second time, with a pen from her purse, she drew a dark meaningful line in the margin and beside it wrote—in English, of course— "uncanny." (Everything she marked she was marking for him, or made the mark actually pretending to be him.) *I have an odd way of sometimes, as it were, being able to see myself through someone else's eyes. Then I view the affairs of a certain "Anne" at my ease, and browse through the pages of her life as if she were a stranger. Before we came here, when I didn't think about things as much as I do now, I used at times to have the feeling that I didn't belong to Mansa, Pim, and Margot, and that I would always be a bit of an outsider. Sometimes I used to pretend I was an orphan ...*

Then she read the whole thing from the start again,

making a small marginal notation—and a small grimace—whenever she came upon anything she was sure he would consider "decorative" or "imprecise" or "unclear." But mostly she marked passages she couldn't believe that she had written as little more than a child. Why, what eloquence, Anne—it gave her gooseflesh, whispering her own name in Boston—what deftness, what wit! How nice, she thought, if I could write like this for Mr. Lonoff's English 12. "It's good," she heard him saying, "it's the best thing you've ever done, Miss Bellette."

But of course it was—she'd had a "great subject," as the girls said in English class. Her family's affinity with what families were suffering everywhere had been clear to her right from the beginning. *There is nothing we can do but wait as calmly as we can till the misery comes to an end. Jews and Christians wait, the whole earth waits; and there are many who wait for death.* But while writing these lines ("Quiet, emphatic feeling—that's the idea. E.I.L.") she had had no grandiose delusions about her little achterhuis diary's ever standing as part of the record of the misery. It wasn't to educate anybody other than herself—out of her great expectations—that she kept track of how trying it all was. Recording it was enduring it; the diary kept her company and it kept her sane, and whenever being her parents' child seemed to her as harrowing as the war itself, it was where she went to confess. Only to Kitty was she able to speak freely about the hopelessness of trying to satisfy her mother the way Margot did; only to Kitty could she openly bewail her inability even to pronounce the word "Mumsie" to her aloud—and to concede the depth of her feeling for Pim, a father she wanted to want her to the exclusion of all others, *not only as his child, but for me—Anne, myself.*

Of course it had eventually to occur to any child so *mad on books and reading* that for all she knew she was writing a book of her own. But most of the time it was her morale that she was sustaining not, at fourteen, literary ambition. As for developing into a writer—she owed that not to any decision to sit down each day and try to be one but to their stifling life. That, of all things, seemed to have nurtured her talent! Truly, without the terror and the claustrophobia of the achterhuis, as a *chatterbox* surrounded by friends and *rollicking with laughter*, free to come and go, free to clown around, free to pursue her every last expectation, would she ever have written sentences so deft and so eloquent and so witty? She thought, Now maybe that's the problem in English 12—not the absence of the great subject but the presence of the lake and the tennis courts and Tanglewood. The perfect tan, the linen skirts, my emerging reputation as the Pallas Athene of Athene College—maybe that's what's doing me in. Maybe if I were locked up again in a room somewhere and fed on rotten potatoes and clothed in rags and terrified out of my wits, maybe then I could write a decent story for Mr. Lonoff!

It was only with the euphoria of *invasion fever*, with

the prospect of the Allied landings and the German collapse and the coming of that golden age known around the achterhuis as *after the war*, that she was able to announce to Kitty that the diary had perhaps done more than just assuage her adolescent loneliness. After two years of honing her prose, she felt herself ready for the great undertaking: *my greatest wish is to become a journalist someday and later on a famous writer*. But that was in May of 1944, when to be famous someday seemed to her no more or less extraordinary than to be going back to school in September. Oh, that May of marvelous expectations! Never again another winter in the achterhuis. Another winter and she would have gone crazy.

The first year there it hadn't been that bad; they'd all been so busy settling in that she didn't have time to feel desperate. In fact, so diligently had they all worked to transform the attic into a *superpractical* home that her father had gotten everybody to agree to subdivide the space still further and take in another Jew. But once the Allied bombing started, the superpractical home became her torture chamber. During the day the two families squabbled over everything, and then at night she couldn't sleep, sure that the Gestapo was going to come in the dark to take them away. In bed she began to have horrifying visions of Lies, her schoolfriend, reproaching her for being safe in bed in Amsterdam and not in a concentration camp, like all her Jewish friends: *"Oh, Anne, why have you deserted me? Help, oh, help me, rescue me from this hell!"* She would see herself *in a dungeon, without Mummy and Daddy*—and worse. Right down to the final hours of 1943 she was dreaming and thinking *the most terrible things.* But then all at once it was over. Miraculously. "And what did it, Professor Lonoff? See *Anna Karenina.* See *Madame Bovary.* See half the literature of the Western world." The miracle: desire. She would be back to school in September, but she would not be returning to class the same girl. She was no longer a girl. Tears would roll down her cheeks at the thought of a naked woman. Her unpleasant menstrual periods became a source of the strangest pleasure. At night in bed she was excited by her breasts. Just these sensations—but all at once forebodings of her miserable death were replaced with a craze for life. One day she was completely recovered, and the next she was, of course, in love. Their troubles had made her her own woman, at fourteen. She began going off on private visits to the secluded corner of the topmost floor, which was occupied exclusively by Peter, the Van Daans' seventeen-year-old son. That she might be stealing him away from Margot didn't stop her, and neither did her scandalized parents: first just teatime visits, then evening assignations —then the defiant letter to the disappointed father. On May 3rd of that marvelous May: *I am young and I possess many buried qualities; I am young and strong and am living a great adventure.* And two days later, to the father who had saved her from the hell that had swallowed up Lies, to the Pim whose favorite living creature she had always longed to be, a declaration of her independence, *in mind and body*, as she bluntly put it: *I have now reached the stage that I can live entirely on my own, without Mummy's support or anyone else's for that matter . . . I don't feel in the least bit responsible to any of you . . . I don't have to give an account of my deeds to anyone but myself . . .*

Well, the strength of a woman on her own wasn't all she'd imagined it to be. Neither was the strength of a loving father. He told her it was the most unpleasant letter he'd ever received, and when she began to cry with shame for having been *too low for words*, he wept along with her. He burned the letter in the fire, the weeks passed, and she found herself growing disenchanted with Peter. In fact, by July she was wondering how it would be possible, in their circumstances, to *shake him off*, a problem resolved for her on a sunny August Friday, when in the middle of the morning, as Pim was helping Peter with his English lessons and she was off studying by herself, the Dutch Green Police arrived and dissolved forever the secret household still heedful of propriety, obedience, discretion, self-improvement, and mutual respect. The Franks, as a family, came to an end, and, fittingly enough, thought the diarist, so did her chronicle of their effort to go sensibly on as themselves, in spite of everything.

The third time she read the book through was on the way back to Stockbridge that evening. Would she ever read another book again? How, if she couldn't put this one down? On the bus she began to speculate in the most immodest way about what she had written—had "wrought." Perhaps what got her going was the rumbling, boundless, electrified, indigo sky that had been stalking the bus down the highway since Boston: outside the window the most outlandish El Greco stage effects, outside a Biblical thunderstorm complete with baroque trimmings, and inside Amy curled up with her book—and with the lingering sense of tragic grandeur she'd soaked up from the real El Grecos that afternoon in the Boston Museum of Fine Arts. And she was exhausted, which probably doesn't hurt fantastical thinking, either. Still spellbound by her first two readings of *Het Achterhuis*, she had rushed on to the Gardner and the Fogg, where, to top off the day, the self-intoxicated girl with the deep tan and the animated walk had been followed by easily a dozen Harvard Summer School students eager to learn her name. Three museums because back at Athene she preferred to tell everyone the truth, more or less, about the big day in Boston. To Mr. Lonoff she planned to speak at length about all the new exhibitions she'd gone to see at his wife's suggestion.

The storm, the paintings, her exhaustion—none of it was really necessary, however, to inspire the sort of expectations that resulted from reading her published diary three times through in the same day. Towering egotism would probably have been sufficient. Perhaps she was only a very young writer on a bus dreaming a very young writer's dreams.

All her reasoning, all her fantastical thinking about the ordained mission of her book followed from this: neither she nor her parents came through in the diary as anything like representative of religious or observant Jews. Her mother lit candles on Friday night and that was about the extent of it. As for celebrations, she had found St. Nicholas's Day, once she'd been introduced to it in hiding, much more fun than Chanukah, and along with Pim made all kinds of clever gifts and even written a Santa Claus poem to enliven the festivities. When Pim settled upon a children's Bible as her present for the holiday—so she might learn something about the New Testament—Margot hadn't approved. Margot's ambition was to be a midwife in Palestine. She was the only one of them who seemed to have given serious thought to religion. The diary that Margot kept, had it ever been found, would not have been quite so sparing as hers in curiosity about Judaism, or plans for leading a Jewish life. Certainly it was impossible for her to imagine Margot thinking, let alone writing with longing in her diary, *the time will come when we are people again, and not just Jews.*

She had written these words, to be sure, still suffering the aftereffects of a nighttime burglary in the downstairs warehouse. The burglary had seemed certain to precipitate their discovery by the police, and for days afterward everyone was weak with terror. And for her, along with the residue of fear and the dubious sense of relief, there was, of course, the guilt-tinged bafflement when she realized that, unlike Lies, she had again been spared. In the aftermath of that gruesome night, she went around and around trying to understand the meaning of their persecution, one moment writing about the misery of being Jews and only Jews to their enemies, and then in the next airily wondering if *it might even be our religion from which the world and all peoples learn good. . . . We can never become just Netherlanders*, she reminded Kitty, *we will always remain Jews, but we want to, too*—only to close out the argument with an announcement one most assuredly would not have come upon in "The Diary of Margot Frank": *I've been saved again, now my first wish after the war is that I may become Dutch! I love the Dutch, I love this country, I love the language and want to work here. And even if I have to write to the Queen myself, I will not give up until I have reached my goal.*

No, that wasn't mother's Margot talking, that was father's Anne. To London to learn English, to Paris to look at clothes and study art, to Hollywood, California, to interview the stars as someone named "Anne Franklin"—while self-sacrificing Margot delivered babies in the desert. To be truthful, while Margot was thinking about God and the homeland, the only deities she ever seemed to contemplate at any length were to be found in the mythology of

Greece and Rome, which she studied all the time in hiding, and adored. To be truthful, the young girl of her diary was, compared to Margot, only dimly Jewish, though in that entirely the daughter of the father who calmed her fears by reading aloud to her at night not the Bible but Goethe in German and Dickens in English.

But that was the point—that was what gave her diary the power to make the nightmare real. To expect the great callous and indifferent world to care about the child of a pious, bearded father living under the sway of the rabbis and the rituals—that was pure folly. To the ordinary person with no great gift for tolerating even the smallest of differences the plight of that family wouldn't mean a thing. To ordinary people it probably would seem that they had invited disaster by stubbornly repudiating everything modern and European—not to say Christian. But the family of Otto Frank, that would be another matter! How could even the most obtuse of the ordinary ignore what had been done to the Jews *just for being Jews*, how could even the most benighted of the Gentiles fail to get the idea when they read in *Het Achterhuis* that once a year the Franks sang a harmless Chanukah song, said some Hebrew words, lighted some candles, exchanged some presents—a ceremony lasting about ten minutes— and that was all it took to make them the enemy. It did not even take that much. It took nothing—that was the horror. And that was the truth. And that was the power of her book. The Franks could gather together by the radio to listen to concerts of Mozart, Brahms, and Beethoven; they could entertain themselves with Goethe and Dickens and Schiller; she could look night after night through the genealogical tables of all of Europe's royal families for suitable mates for Princess Elizabeth and Princess Margaret Rose; she could write passionately in her diary of her love for Queen Wilhelmina and her desire for Holland to be her fatherland—and none of it made any difference. Europe was not theirs nor were they Europe's, not even her Europeanized family. Instead, three flights up from a pretty Amsterdam canal, they lived crammed into a hundred square feet with the Van Daans, as isolated and despised as any ghetto Jews. First expulsion, next confinement, and then, in cattle cars and camps and ovens, obliteration. And why? Because the Jewish problem to be solved, the degenerates whose contamination civilized people could no longer abide, were they themselves, Otto and Edith Frank, and their daughters, Margot and Anne.

This was the lesson that on the journey home she came to believe she had the power to teach. But only if she were believed to be dead. Were *Het Achterhuis* known to be the work of a living writer, it would never be more than it was: a young teenager's diary of her trying years in hiding during the German occupation of Holland, something boys and girls could read in bed at night along with the adventures of the Swiss Family Robinson. But dead she had something more to offer than amusement for ages 10–15; dead she had written, without meaning to or trying to, a book with the force of a masterpiece to make people finally see.

And when people had finally seen? When they had learned what she had the power to teach them, what then? Would suffering come to mean something new to them? Could she actually make them humane creatures for any longer than the few hours it would take to read her diary through? In her room at Athene—after hiding in her dresser the three copies of *Het Achterhuis*—she thought more calmly about her readers-to-be than she had while pretending to be one of them on the stirring bus ride through the lightning storm. She was not, after all, the fifteen-year-old who could, while hiding from a holocaust, tell Kitty, *I still believe that people are really good at heart.* Her youthful ideals had suffered no less than she had in the windowless freight car from Westerbork and in the barracks at Auschwitz and on the Belsen heath. She had not come to hate the human race for what it was— what could it be but what it was?—but she did not feel seemly any more singing its praises.

What would happen when people had finally seen? The only realistic answer was Nothing. To believe anything else was only to yield to longings which even she, the great longer, had a right to question by now. To keep her existence a secret from her father so as to help improve mankind . . . no, not at this late date. The improvement of the living was their business, not hers; they could improve themselves, if they should ever be so disposed;

and if not, not. Her responsibility was to the dead, if to anyone—to her sister, to her mother, to all the slaughtered schoolchildren who had been her friends. There was her diary's purpose, there was her ordained mission: to restore in print their status as flesh and blood . . . for all the good that would do them. An ax was what she really wanted, not print. On the stairwell at the end of her corridor in the dormitory there was a large ax with an enormous red handle, to be used in case of fire. But what about in case of hatred—what about murderous rage? She stared at it often enough, but never found the nerve to take it down from the wall. Besides, once she had it in her hands, whose head would she split open? Whom could she kill in Stockbridge to avenge the ashes and the skulls? If she even could wield it. No, what she had been given to wield was *Het Achterhuis, van Anne Frank*. And to draw blood with it she would have to vanish again into another achterhuis, this time fatherless and all on her own.

So she renewed her belief in the power of her less than three hundred pages, and with it the resolve to keep from her father, sixty, the secret of her survival. "For them," she cried, "for them," meaning all who had met the fate that she had been spared and was now pretending to. "For Margot, for my mother, for Lies."

Now every day she went to the library to read *The New York Times*. Each week she read carefully through the newsmagazines. On Sundays she read about all the new books being published in America: novels said to be "notable" and "significant," none of which could possibly be more notable and more significant than her posthumously published diary; insipid best-sellers from which real people learned about fake people who could not exist and would not matter if they did. She read praise for historians and biographers whose books, whatever their merit, couldn't possibly be as worthy of recognition as hers. And in every column in every periodical she found in the library—American, French, German, English—she looked for her own real name. It could not end with just a few thousand Dutch readers shaking their heads and going about their business—it was too important for that! "For them, for them"—over and over, week after week, "for them"—until at last she began to wonder if having survived in the achterhuis, if having outlived the death camps, if masquerading here in New England as somebody other than herself did not make something very suspect—and a little mad—of this seething passion to "come back" as the avenging ghost. She began to fear that she was succumbing to having not succumbed.

And why should she! Who was she pretending to be but who she would have been anyway if no achterhuis and no death camps had intervened? Amy was not somebody else. The Amy who had rescued her from her memories and restored her to life—beguiling, commonsensical, brave, and realistic Amy—was herself. Who she had every right to be! Responsibility to the dead? Rhetoric for the pious! There was nothing to give the dead—they were dead. "Exactly. The importance, so-called, of this book is a morbid illusion. And playing dead is melodramatic and disgusting. And hiding from Daddy is worse. No atonement is required," said Amy to Anne. "Just get on the phone and tell Pim you're alive. He is sixty."

Her longing for him now exceeded even what it had been in childhood, when she wanted more than anything to be his only love. But she was young and strong and she was living a great adventure, and she did nothing to inform him or anyone that she was still alive; and then one day it was just too late. No one would have believed her; no one other than her father would have wanted to. Now people came every day to visit their secret hideaway and to look at the photographs of the movie stars that she'd pinned to the wall beside her bed. They came to see the tub she had bathed in and the table where she'd studied. They looked out of the loft window where Peter and she had cuddled together watching the stars. They stared at the cupboard camouflaging the door the police had come through to take them away. They looked at the open pages of her secret diary. That was her handwriting, they whispered, those are her words. They stayed to look at everything in the achterhuis that she had ever touched. The plain passageways and serviceable little rooms that she had, like a good composition student, dutifully laid out for Kitty in orderly, accurate, workaday Dutch—the superpractical achterhuis was now a holy shrine, a Wailing Wall. They went away from it in silence, as bereft as though she had been their own.

But it was they who were hers. "They weep for me," said Amy; "they pity me; they pray for me; they beg my forgiveness. I am the incarnation of the millions of unlived years robbed from the murdered Jews. It is too late to be alive now. I am a saint."

That was her story. And what did Lonoff think of it when she was finished? That she meant every word and that not a word was true.

After Amy had showered and dressed, she checked out of the hotel and he took her to eat some lunch. He phoned Hope from the restaurant and explained that he was bringing Amy home. She could walk in the woods, look at the foliage, sleep safely in Becky's bed; over a few days' time she would be able to collect herself, and then she could return to Cambridge. All he explained about her collapse was that she appeared to him to be suffering from exhaustion. He had promised Amy that he would say no more.

On the ride back to the Berkshires, while Amy told him what it had been like for her during the years when she was being read in twenty different languages by twenty million people, he made plans to consult Dr. Boyce. Boyce was at Riggs, the Stockbridge psychiatric hospital. Whenever a new book appeared, Dr. Boyce would send a charming note asking the author if he would kindly sign the doctor's copy, and once a year the Lonoffs were invited to the Boyces' big barbecue. At Dr. Boyce's request, Lonoff once reluctantly consented to meet with a staff study group from the hospital to discuss "the creative personality." He didn't want to offend the psychiatrist, and it might for a while pacify his wife, who liked to believe that if he got out and mixed more with people things would be better at home.

The study group turned out to have ideas about writing that were too imaginative for his taste, but he made no effort to tell them they were wrong. Nor did he think that he was necessarily right. They saw it their way, he saw it like Lonoff. Period. He had no desire to change anyone's mind. Fiction made people say all kinds of strange things —so be it.

The meeting with the psychiatrists had been underway for only an hour when Lonoff said it had been an enjoyable evening but he had to be getting home. "I have the evening's reading still ahead of me. Without my reading I'm not myself. However, you must feel free to talk about my personality when I'm gone." Boyce, smiling warmly, replied, "I hope we've amused you at least a little with our naïve speculations." "I would have liked to amuse *you*. I apologize for being boring." "No, no," said Boyce, "passivity in a man of stature has a charm and mystery all its own." "Yes?" said Lonoff. "I must tell my wife."

But an hour wasted some five years ago was hardly to the point. He trusted Boyce and knew that the psychiatrist would not betray his confidence when he went the next day to talk with him about his former student and quasi daughter, a young woman of twenty-six, who had disclosed to him that of all the Jewish writers, from Franz Kafka to E. I. Lonoff, she was the most famous. As for his own betrayal of the quasi daughter's confidence, it did not count for much as Amy elaborated further upon her consuming delusion.

"Do you know why I took this sweet name? It wasn't to protect me from my memories. I wasn't hiding the past from myself or myself from the past. I was hiding from hatred, from hating people the way people hate spiders and rats. Manny, I felt flayed. I felt as though the skin had been peeled away from half my body. Half my face had been peeled away, and everybody would stare in horror for the rest of my life. Or they would stare at the other half, at the half still intact; I could see them smiling, pretending that the flayed half wasn't there, and talking to the half that was. And I could hear myself screaming at them, I could see myself thrusting my hideous side right up into their unmarred faces to make them properly horrified. 'I was pretty! I was whole! I was a sunny, lively little girl! Look, look at what they did to me!' But whatever side they looked at, I would always be screaming, 'Look at the other! Why don't you look at the other!' That's what I thought about in the hospital at night. However they look at me, however they talk to me, however they try to comfort me, I will always be this half-flayed thing.

I will never be young, I will never be kind or at peace or in love, and I will hate them all my life.

"So I took the sweet name—to impersonate everything that I wasn't. And a very good pretender I was, too. After a while I could imagine that I wasn't pretending at all, that I had become what I would have been anyway. Until the book. The package came from Amsterdam, I opened it, and there it was: my past, myself, my name, *my face intact*—and all I wanted was revenge. It wasn't for the dead—it had nothing to do with bringing back the dead or scourging the living. It wasn't corpses I was avenging— it was the motherless, fatherless, sisterless, venge-filled, hate-filled, shame-filled, half-flayed, seething thing. It was myself. I wanted tears, I wanted their Christian tears to run like Jewish blood, for me. I wanted their pity—and in the most pitiless way. And I wanted love, to be loved mercilessly and endlessly, just the way I'd been debased. I wanted my fresh life and my fresh body, cleansed and unpolluted. And it needed twenty million people for that. Twenty million ten times over.

"Oh, Manny, I want to live with you! That's what I need! The millions won't do it—it's you! I want to go home to Europe with you. Listen to me, don't say no, not yet. This summer I saw a small house for rent, a stone villa up on a hillside. It was outside Florence. It had a pink tile roof and a garden. I got the phone number and I wrote it down. I still have it. Oh, everything beautiful that

I saw in Italy made me think of how happy you could be there—how happy I would be there, looking after you. I thought of the trips we'd take. I thought of the afternoons in the museums and having coffee later by the river. I thought of listening to music together at night. I thought of making your meals. I thought of wearing lovely night-gowns to bed. Oh, Manny, their Anne Frank is theirs; I want to be *your* Anne Frank. I'd like at last to be my own. Child Martyr and Holy Saint isn't a position I'm really qualified for any more. They wouldn't even have me, not as I am, longing for somebody else's husband, begging him to leave his loyal wife to run off with a girl half his age. Manny, does it matter that I'm your daughter's age and you're my father's? Of course I love the Dad-da in you, how could I not? And if you love the child in me, why shouldn't you? There's nothing strange in that—so does half the world. Love has to start somewhere, and that's where it starts in us. And as for who I am—well," said Amy, in a voice as sweet and winning as any he'd ever heard, "you've got to be somebody, don't you? There's no way around that."

At home they put her to bed. In the kitchen Lonoff sat with his wife drinking the coffee she'd made him. Every time he pictured Amy at the dentist's office reading about Otto Frank in *Time* magazine, or in the library stacks searching for her "real" name, every time he imagined her on Boston Common addressing to her writing teacher an intimate disquisition on "her" book, he wanted to let go and cry. He had never suffered so over the suffering of another human being.

Of course he told Hope nothing about who Amy thought she was. But he didn't have to, he could guess what she would say if he did: it was for him, the great writer, that Amy had chosen to become Anne Frank; that explained it all, no psychiatrist required. For him, as a consequence of her infatuation: to enchant him, to bewitch him, to break through the scrupulosity and the wisdom and the virtue into his imagination, and there, as Anne Frank, to become E. I. Lonoff's *femme fatale*.

4 Married to Tolstoy

The next morning we all ate breakfast together like a happy family of four. The woman whom Lonoff could not throw out after thirty years just because he might prefer to see a new face over his fruit juice proudly told us —over our fruit juice—of the accomplishments of the children whose chairs Amy and I occupied. She showed us recent photographs of them, all with their own children. Lonoff had not mentioned to me the night before that he was a grandfather several times over. But why would he?

Hope seemed overnight to have been transformed from his aging, aggrieved, lonely wife into somebody rather more like the happy author of the sweet nature poems framed on the kitchen wall, the tender of the geraniums, the woman of whom Lonoff had said over the broken saucer, "She can glue it." Nor did Lonoff seem quite the same man; whether deliberately or not, he was humming "My Blue Heaven" when he came to the breakfast table. And almost immediately began the mordant clowning, also designed to make Hope all the happier.

And why the change? Because Amy would return to Cambridge after breakfast.

But I could not really think of her as Amy any longer. Instead I was continually drawn back into the fiction I had evolved about her and the Lonoffs while I lay in the dark study, transported by his praise and throbbing with resentment of my disapproving father—and, of course, overcome by what had passed between my idol and the marvelous young woman before he had manfully gone back to bed with his wife.

Throughout breakfast, my father, my mother, the judge and Mrs. Wapter were never out of my thoughts. I'd gone the whole night without sleep, and now I couldn't think straight about them or myself, or about Amy, as she was called. I kept seeing myself coming back to New Jersey and saying to my family, "I met a marvelous young woman while I was up in New England. I love her and she loves me. We are going to be married." "Married? But so fast? Nathan, is she Jewish?" "Yes, she is." "But who is she?" "Anne Frank."

"I eat too much," said Lonoff, as Hope poured the water for his tea.

"It's exercise you need," Hope said. "It's more walking. You gave up your afternoon walk and so you began to gain weight. You actually eat almost nothing. Certainly nothing that's fattening. It's sitting at the desk that does it. And staying in the house."

"I can't face another walk. I can't face those trees again."

"Then walk in the other direction."

"For ten years I walked in the other direction. That's why I started walking in this direction. Besides, I'm not even walking when I'm walking. The truth is, I don't even see the trees."

"That's not so," Hope said. "He loves nature," she informed me. "He knows the name of everything that grows."

"I'm cutting down on my food," said Lonoff. "Who wants to split an egg with me?"

Hope said, happily, "You can treat yourself to a whole egg this morning."

"Amy, you want to split an egg with me?"

His invitation for her to speak gave me my first opportunity to turn her way without embarrassment. It was so. It *could* be. The same look of unarmored and unimpaired intelligence, the same musing look of serene anticipation ... The forehead wasn't Shakespeare's—it was *hers*.

She was smiling, as though she too were in the best of spirits and his refusal to kiss her breasts the night before had never happened. "Couldn't do it," she said to him.

"Not even half?" asked Lonoff.

"Not even a sixteenth."

This is my Aunt Tessie, this is Frieda and Dave, this is Birdie, this is Murray ... as you see, we are an enormous family. This is my wife, everyone. She is all I have ever wanted. If you doubt me, just look at her smile, listen to her laugh. Remember the shadowed eyes innocently uplifted in the clever little face? Remember the dark hair clipped back with a barrette? Well, this is she. . . . Anne, says my father—the Anne? Oh, how I have misunderstood my son. How mistaken we have been!

"Scramble an egg, Hope," said Lonoff. "I'll eat half if you'll eat half."

"You can eat the whole thing," she replied. "Just start taking your walks again."

He looked at me, imploringly. "Nathan, eat half."

"No, no," said his wife and, turning to the stove, announced triumphantly, "You'll eat the whole egg!"

Beaten, Lonoff said, "And to top things off, I threw out my razor blade this morning."

"And why," said Amy, pretending still to be in her blue heaven too, "did you do a thing like that?"

"I thought it through. My children are finished with college. My house is paid for. I have Blue Cross and Major Medical protection. I have a '56 Ford. Yesterday I got a check for forty-five dollars in royalties from Brazil— money out of the blue. Throw it out, I told myself, and have a fresh shave with a new blade. Then I thought: No, there's at least one shave left in this blade, maybe even two. Why be wasteful? But then I thought it through further: I have seven books on the paperback racks, I have publishers in twenty countries, there's a new shingle roof on the house, there's a quiet new furnace in the basement, there's brand-new plumbing in Hope's little bathroom. The bills are all paid, and what is more, there is money left over in the bank that is earning three percent interest for our old age. The hell with it, I thought, enough thinking—and I put in a new blade. And look how I butchered myself. I almost took my ear off."

Amy: "Proves you shouldn't be impulsive."

"I only wanted to see what it was like living like everybody else."

"And?" asked Hope, back at the table now, frying pan in hand.

"I told you. I almost took my ear off."

"Here's your egg."

"I only want half."

"Darling, feast for once," said Hope, kissing his head.

Dear Mom and Dad: We have been with Anne's father

for three days now. They have both been in the most moving state of exaltation since our arrival ...

"And here's your mail," said Hope.

"I never used to look at this stuff until the end of the day," he explained to me.

"He wouldn't even look at the newspaper headlines," said Hope. "He wouldn't even eat breakfast with us until a few years ago. But when the children were all gone, I refused to sit here by myself."

"But I wouldn't let you talk to me, would I? That's new."

"Let me make you another egg," she said.

He pushed aside his empty plate. "No, darling, no. I'm full."

Dear Folks: Anne is pregnant, and happier, she says, than she ever thought possible again ...

He was sorting now through the half dozen letters in his hand. He said to me, "This is what gets forwarded from a publisher. One in a hundred is worth opening. In five hundred."

"What about a secretary to open them?" I asked.

"He's too conscientious," Hope explained. "He can't do it that way. Besides, a secretary is another person. We can't turn the house into Grand Central Station."

"A secretary is six other people," he informed her.

"What is it this time?" she asked Lonoff as he turned over the penciled sheets in his hand. "Read it, Manny."

"You read it." He handed the letter across to his wife.

"Let Nathan see what it is to be lifted from obscurity. Let him not come hammering at our door to tell us that he wasn't warned."

She wiped her hands on her apron and took the letter. It was quite a morning she was having, a new life altogether. And why? Because Amy was on her way.

" 'Dear Mr. Lonoff,' " she read. " 'I suggest that you with your talent write a story with the following plot. A non-Jew comes from the West to New York City and meets Jews for the first time. Being a good-natured person he does them favors. When he gives up part of his lunch hour at work to help them, they act like pigs in getting as much of his time as possible. When he helps his co-workers by getting them ball-point pens wholesale, the same happens. They try to get him to buy some for strangers by saying, "A man I know wants to buy a dozen pens," and saying later, "I didn't tell you to, I didn't ask you to buy them for him, I only told you I wanted two dozen and you can't tell me I told you to buy him two dozen." Consequently he develops a dislike for Jews. Later he finds out that non-Jews who don't try to impose are trying to put him out of a job while the Jews take his side when the boss wants to fire him. When he gets sick, the Jews donate blood for him. At the end he has a conversation with a person in which he learns how the history of the Jews led to their habit of opportunism. Yours truly, Ray W. Oliver. P.S. I am also a writer of short stories. I am willing to collaborate with you on a story using that plot.' "

"Me too," said Amy.

"The consequences of his infatuation," I said. A line out of "The Middle Years," but not even Lonoff seemed to remember it. "From Henry James," I added, flushing. " 'The rest is the madness of art.' "

"Aha," said Lonoff.

Ass! Idiot! I had been caught—while showing off my erudition! *Aha.* He knew everything.

But rather than asking me to get up and go because of the way I had behaved in his study, he opened a second letter and removed the small index card inside. He read it and handed it to Hope.

"Oh, these," she said. "They make me so angry."

"Has style, however," said Lonoff. "I like the absence of the salutation. Just puts out the line and hangs up the wash. Read it, Hopie."

"I hate these so."

"Go on. For Nathan's edification."

Then he *didn't* know. Or knew and forgave me.

" 'I have just finished your brilliant story, "Indiana," ' " Hope read. " 'What do you know about the Middle West, you little Jewish shit? Your Jew omniscience is about as agreeable to the average person as is your kike sense of "art." Sally M., Fort Wayne.' "

Lonoff, meanwhile, had been carefully slicing open a blue overseas air letter.

"New Delhi," he announced.

"You've been made a Brahman," said Amy.

Hope smiled at the girl who would be gone now in less than an hour. "He won't accept."

"Well," replied Amy, "maybe he's in luck and they made him an Untouchable."

"Or less," said Lonoff, and handed the letter to Hope.

"You can't have everything," Amy told him.

Hope read, this time without being prompted. " 'Dear Sir, I am a twenty-two-year-old youth from India. I introduce myself as there is no other way to make your acquaintance. Perhaps you may not relish the idea of being acquainted with a stranger who is bent on exploiting you.' " Here, suddenly, her confidence seemed shaken, and she looked up at Lonoff, confused as to what to do next.

He told her. "Go on."

"—'bent on exploiting you. I beg your assistance fully aware of the barriers like caste, creed, etc., that divide us. As I am just a beggar in different garb I will put forward my request rather impetuously. My desire is to settle down in America. Will you please take me out of my country by some means? If my educational qualification disqualifies me from entering America as a student, and if all other means fail, will you just adopt me as the last resort? I am quite ashamed to write such a request for I am so old and I have parents who depend upon me to provide for them during their old age. I shall do any kind of work and I will try my best to be of some use to you. Sir, by now you would have formed in your mind the unimpressive figure of a short, dark, ambitious Indian guy whose character is sprinkled with a generous amount of jealousy. If you have thought in the above manner you are in for a surprise. For the above description suits me to the core. I want to escape from the harsh realities and live with some peace and pursue part-time education. Sir, please let me know whether it is possible for you to assist your humble servant—' "

Hope brought the letter to her chest—she saw that Amy had pushed back her chair and was standing. "I'm sorry," Hope said to her.

"Why?" asked Amy, forcing a smile.

Hope's hands began to tremble.

I glanced toward Lonoff, but he was saying nothing.

With just a tinge of exasperation, Amy said, "I don't understand why you should be sorry."

Hope undertook to fold the letter from India, though not with any method I could discern. Her eyes went to the geraniums when she said, "I didn't mean to embarrass you."

"But I'm not embarrassed," said Amy, innocently.

"I didn't *say* you were," Hope conceded. "I said I didn't *mean* to."

Amy didn't follow—that was the act. She waited for Hope to explain herself further.

"Forget it, please," said Hope.

"It's forgotten," Lonoff said softly.

"I'm going now," Amy said to him.

"Must you," asked Lonoff, "without finishing the coffee?"

"You're half an hour behind schedule already," Amy said. "What with all this promiscuous socializing over your egg, it could take you the rest of the morning to recover."

"Yes," I said, jumping up, "and I have to be off, too."

"There's no bus this early," Lonoff informed me. "The first bus north arrives at eleven-twenty."

"Still, if she could drop me in town, I'll just walk around—if that's not out of your way," I added, and looked as shyly as I had the day before at the girl I had veiled in so many imaginings, and whom *still* I couldn't see plain.

"Suit yourself," said Lonoff.

He rose and came around the table to kiss Amy on her cheek. "Stay in touch," he told her. "And thanks for the help."

"I think I at least got each of the books separated out. At least that's in order."

"Fine. The rest I have to see to myself. And think about. I'm not sure it's for me, my friend."

"Please," she said, "I beseech you, don't destroy anything."

A charade it may have been, but still I understood her to be entreating him about the worksheets of his old stories that she had been sorting for the Harvard manuscript collection. But to Hope the girl's request clearly had a less innocent intention. Before either of them could speak another double entendre in her presence, Hope was out of the room.

We heard her mount the stairs, and then the bedroom door slammed shut overhead.

"Excuse me one moment," said Lonoff, and buttoning his jacket, he followed after his wife.

Silently Amy and I took our things from the hall closet and got dressed for the snow. Then we stood there trying to decide what to do next. I had all I could do not to say, "Did you ever have the feeling that you wanted to go, still have the feeling that you wanted to stay?"

What I came up with was not much better. "Last night at dinner he told me about the letter that you sent him from England."

She took this in and went back to waiting. On her head was the white wool cap with the long tassel that ended in a fluffy white ball. Of course! He had given it to her, her first winter here in the Berkshires; and now she could not part with it, no more than she could part with him, her second Pim.

"When was that?" I asked. "When were you living in England?"

"Oh, my." She closed her eyes and pressed one hand to her forehead. I saw then how very tired she was. Neither of us had slept the night before, she thinking of who she might become living in Florence with Lonoff, and I thinking of who she might have been. When the sleeve of her coat fell back, I of course saw that there was no scar on her forearm. No scar; no book; no Pim. No, the loving father who must be relinquished for the sake of his child's art was not hers; he was mine. "I was short, dark, ambitious—and sixteen. Eleven years ago," she said.

Making her Anne Frank's age exactly, had she survived.

"Where had you been before England?"

"That's a long story."

"You'd been through the war?"

"I missed the war."

"How so?"

She smiled politely. I was getting on her nerves. "Luck."

"I suppose that's how I missed it too," I replied.

"And what did you have instead?" she asked me.

"My childhood. What did *you* have instead?"

Dryly she said, "Somebody else's. I think perhaps we should go, Mr. Zuckerman. I have to be off. It's a long drive."

"I'd rather not leave without saying goodbye."

"I'd rather not, either, but we better."

"I'm sure he wanted us to wait."

"Oh, did he?" she said strangely, and I followed her into the living room, where we sat in the easy chairs beside the fireplace. She had taken Lonoff's chair and I took my place in the other. Angrily she removed the hat.

"He's been awfully generous to me," I explained. "It's been quite a visit. For me," I added.

"He's a generous man."

"He helped you to come to America."

"Yes."

"From England."

She picked up the magazine that I'd leafed through the evening before while Lonoff spoke on the phone.

I said, "Pardon me, for insisting . . ."

She smiled vaguely at me and began turning pages.

"It's just—that you bear some resemblance to Anne Frank."

A shiver went down my body when she replied, "I've been told that before."

"You *have?*"

"But," she said, bringing her intelligent eyes directly up to mine, "I'm afraid I'm not she."

Silence.

"You've read her book, however."

"Not really," she said. "I looked at it."

"Oh, but it's quite a book."

"Is it?"

"Oh, yes. She was a marvelous young writer. She was something for thirteen. It's like watching an accelerated film of a fetus sprouting a face, watching her mastering things. You must read it. Suddenly she's discovering reflection, suddenly there's portraiture, character sketches, suddenly there's a long intricate eventful happening so beautifully recounted it seems to have gone through a dozen drafts. And no poisonous notion of being *interesting* or *serious*. She just *is*." My whole body was damp from the effort of compressing my thoughts and presenting them to her before Lonoff returned to inhibit me. "The ardor in her, the spirit in her—always on the move, always starting things, being boring as unbearable to her as being bored—a terrific writer, really. And an enormously appealing child. I was thinking"—the thought had only just occurred to me, of course, in the rapture of praising Anne Frank to one who might even be her—"she's like some impassioned little sister of Kafka's, his lost little daughter—a kinship is even there in the face. I think. Kafka's garrets and closets, the hidden attics where they hand down the indictments, the camouflaged doors—everything he dreamed in Prague was, to her, real Amsterdam life. What he invented, she suffered. Do you remember the first sentence of *The Trial*? We were talking about it last night, Mr. Lonoff and myself. It could be the epigraph for her book. 'Someone must have falsely traduced Anne F., because one morning without having done anything wrong, she was placed under arrest.' "

However, despite *my* ardor, Amy's mind was elsewhere. But then so was mine, really—back in New Jersey, where the lucky childhood had been spent. To be wed somehow to you, I thought, my unassailable advocate, my invulnerable ally, my shield against their charges of defection and betrayal and reckless, heinous informing! Oh, marry me, Anne Frank, exonerate me before my outraged elders of this idiotic indictment! Heedless of Jewish feeling? Indifferent to Jewish survival? Brutish about their well-being? Who dares to accuse of such unthinking crimes the husband of Anne Frank!

But, alas, I could not lift her out of her sacred book and make her a character in this life. Instead, I was confronted by Amy Bellette (whoever *she* might be), turning the pages of Lonoff's magazine, and, while she savored his every underlining, waiting to see if at the last minute he would not change his life, and hers with it. The rest was so much fiction, the unchallengeable answer to their questionnaire that I proposed to offer the Wapters. And far from being unchallengeable, far from acquitting me of their charges and restoring to me my cherished blamelessness, a fiction that of course would seem to them a desecration even more vile than the one they had read.

Hope was coming down the stairs, dressed for the outdoors in a hooded green loden coat and wearing snow boots pulled over her wool trousers. She held firmly to the banister with one hand—to prevent herself from falling—and in the other carried a small overnight bag.

Lonoff spoke to her from the top of the stairs. "This won't do," he said softly. "This is pure—"

"Let's all have what we want, please." She spoke without looking back at him; in her emotional state she had all she could do to negotiate the stairs.

"This is hardly what you want."

She stopped—"It is what I have wanted for *years*"—then proceeded once more with leaving home.

"Come back up here. You don't know what you're saying."

"You're just frightened," she said, from between her teeth, "of losing your boredom."

"I can't hear you, Hope."

Safely now at the bottom landing, the little woman turned and looked up the stairs. "You're just worried about how you will get all your writing done and all your reading done and all your brooding done without the boredom of me. Well, let someone else be boring for you from now on! Let someone else be no trouble!"

"Please come back up here."

Rather than doing as he asked, she picked up her bag and came into the living room. I alone stood to receive her.

"Take off your coat," she said to Amy. "Now *you're* going to have thirty-five years of it!" And with that she began to shake with sobs.

Lonoff was now making the cautious trek down the stairs. "Hope, this is playacting. And pure indulgence."

"*I am going*," she told him.

"You're not going anywhere. Put the bag down."

"No! I am going to Boston! But don't worry—she knows where everything is. It's practically home to her already. No precious time will be lost. She can hang her things back in the closet and be ready to begin boring you as soon as I'm out the door. You won't even notice the difference."

Amy, unable to watch any longer, looked down into

her lap, prompting Hope to say, "Oh, she thinks otherwise. Of course she does. I've seen her fondling each sheet
of each draft of each story. She thinks with her it will all
be the religion of art up here. Oh, will it ever! Let her try
to please you, Manny! Let her serve as the backdrop for
your thoughts for thirty-five years. Let her see how noble
and heroic you are by the twenty-seventh draft. Let her
cook you wonderful meals and light candles for your
dinner. Let her get everything ready to make you happy
and then see the look on your stone face when you come
in at night and sit down at the table. A surprise for dinner? Oh, my dear girl, that is merely his due for a miserable day of bad writing. *That* gets no rise out of him. And
candles in the old pewter holders? Candles, after all
these years? How poignant of her, he thinks, how vulgar,
what a wistful souvenir of yesterday's tearooms. Yes,
have her run hot baths for your poor back twice a
day, and then go a week without being talked to—
let alone being touched in bed. Ask him in bed, 'What
is it, dear, what's the matter?' But of course you know all
too well what the matter is—you know why he won't
hold you, why he doesn't even know you're *there*. The
fiftieth draft!"

"That is enough," said Lonoff. "Quite thorough, very accurate, and enough."

"Fondling those papers of yours! Oh, she'll see! I got
fondled more by strangers on the rush-hour subway during two months in 1935 than I have up here in the last

twenty years! Take off your coat, Amy—you're staying. The classroom daydream has come true! You get the creative writer—and I get to go!"

"She's not staying," Lonoff said, softly again. "You're staying."

"Not for thirty-five more years of this!"

"Oh, Hopie." He put a hand out to her face, where the tears were still falling.

"I'm going to Boston! I'm going to Europe! It's too late to touch me now! I'm taking a trip around the world and never coming back! And you," she said, looking down at Amy in her chair, "*you* won't go anywhere. *You* won't see anything. If you even go out to dinner, if once in six months you get him to accept an invitation to somebody's home, then it'll be even worse—then for the hour before you go your life will be misery from his kvetching about what it's going to be like when those people start in with their *ideas*. If you dare to change the *pepper* mill, he'll ask what's the matter, what was wrong with the old one? It takes three months for him just to get used to a new brand of *soap*. Change the soap and he goes around the house *sniffing*, as though something dead is on the bathroom sink instead of just a bar of Palmolive. Nothing can be touched, nothing can be changed, everybody must be quiet, the children must shut up, their friends must stay away until four— There is his religion of art, my young successor: rejecting life! *Not* living is what he makes his beautiful fiction *out* of! And you will now be the person he is not living with!"

Amy pushed herself up out of her chair and put on the childish hat with the ball on the end of the tassel. Looking past Hope, she said to Lonoff, "I'm going."

"*I'm* going," Hope cried.

To me Amy said, "I'm leaving now, if you'd like a ride to town."

"*I'm* leaving now," Hope told her. "Take that silly hat off! School is over! You are twenty-seven! This is officially your house!"

"It's not, Hope," Amy said, beginning at last to cry. "It's yours."

And so broken and pathetic did she seem in that moment of capitulation that I thought, But of course last night is not the first time she's sat cuddled up in his lap— but of course he's seen her unclothed before. They have been lovers! Yet when I tried to imagine E. I. Lonoff stripped of his suit and on his back, and Amy naked and astride his belly, I couldn't, no more than any son can.

I don't think I could keep my wits about me, teaching such beautiful and gifted and fetching girls.

Then you shouldn't do it.

Oh, Father, is this so, were you the lover of this lovesick, worshipful, displaced daughter half your age? Knowing full well you'd never leave Hope? You succumbed too? Can that be? *You?*

The bed? I had the bed.

Convinced now that that wasn't so—that nobody, nobody, has ever really *had* the bed—I persisted nonetheless in believing that it was.

"You do as I say!" Hope again, ordering Amy. "You stay and look after him! He cannot stay here alone!"

"But I won't be alone," Lonoff explained to her. "You know that I won't be alone. Enough, enough now, for your sake, too. This is all because we've had visitors. This is all because somebody new stayed the night. There was company, we all had breakfast, and you got excited. Now everybody's going away—and this came over you. You got lonely. You got frightened. Everybody understands."

"Look, Manny, *she* is the child—don't you treat *me* like the child! She is now the child-bride here—"

But before Hope could describe her in further detail, Amy was past her and out the front door.

"Oh, the little bitch!" cried Hope.

"Hope," said Lonoff. "Don't. Not that routine."

But he did not move to stop her as she too ran from the house, carrying her bag.

I said, "Do you want me—to do anything?"

"No, no. Let it run its course."

"Okay."

"Calm down, Nathan. One at a time we are about to calm down."

Then we heard Hope scream.

I followed him to the front window, expecting to see

blood on the snow. Instead, there was Hope, seated in a drift only a few feet from the house, while Amy's car was slowly backing out of the car shed. But for the billowing exhaust fumes everything out of doors was gleaming. It was as though not one but two suns had risen that morning.

Hope watched, we watched. The car turned in the driveway. Then it was out onto the road and gone.

"Mrs. Lonoff's fallen down."

"I see that," he said sadly.

We watched her struggle to her feet. Lonoff rapped on the frosted window with his knuckles. Without bothering to look back up to the house, Hope retrieved the overnight bag from where it lay on the path and proceeded with cautious tiny steps to the car shed, where she got into the Lonoffs' Ford. But the car only whined when she tried to start it; effort after effort produced only that most disheartening of winter sounds.

"The battery," he explained.

"Maybe she flooded it."

Again she tried: same results.

"No, the battery," he said. "It's been happening all month. You charge it up and it makes no difference."

"You may need a new one," I said, since that was what he wanted to talk about.

"I shouldn't. The car is practically brand-new. Where does it go but into town?"

We waited, and finally Hope got out of the car.

"Well, good thing you got a lemon," I said.

"From whose point of view, Nathan?" He walked around to the hallway and opened the front door. I continued to watch from the window.

"Hope," he called. "Come in now. That's it."

"No!"

"But how can I live alone?"

"The boy can live with you."

"Don't be silly. The boy is going. Come inside now. If you slip again, you're going to get hurt. Darling, it's slippery, it's cold as hell—"

"I'm going to Boston."

"How will you do that?"

"I'll walk if I have to."

"Hope, it's twenty degrees. Come back in and get warm and calm down. Have some tea with me. Then we'll talk about moving to Boston."

Here, with her two hands, she hurled the overnight bag into the snow at her feet. "Oh, Manny, you wouldn't move into Stockbridge because the streets are paved, so how could I ever get you to Boston? And what difference would it be in Boston anyway? You'd be just the same—you'd be worse. How could you concentrate in Boston, with all those people swarming around? There, somebody might even ask you something about your work!"

"Then maybe the best bet is to stay here."

"Even here you can't think if I so much as make toast in

the kitchen—I have to catch my toast before it pops up so you won't be disturbed in the study!"

"Oh, Hopie," he said, laughing a little, "that's overdoing things. For the next thirty-five years just make your toast and forget about me."

"I *can't.*"

"Learn," he said sternly.

"No!" Picking up the bag, she turned and started down the driveway. Lonoff closed the door. I watched from the window to see that she stayed on her feet. The snow had been banked so high by the town plow the night before that when she turned into the road she immediately passed out of sight. But then, of course, she wasn't very big to begin with.

Lonoff was at the hall closet, wrestling with his over-shoes.

"Would you like me to come along? To help?" I asked.

"No, no. I can use the exercise after that egg." He stamped his feet on the floor in an attempt to save himself from having to bend over again to get the boots on right. "And you must have things to write down. There's paper on my desk."

"Paper for what?"

"Your feverish notes." He pulled a large, dark, belted coat—not *quite* a caftan—from the closet and I helped him into it. Pressing a dark hat over his bald head, he completed the picture of the chief rabbi, the archdeacon, the magisterial high priest of perpetual sorrows. I handed him his scarf, which had fallen out of a coat sleeve onto the floor. "You had an earful this morning."

I shrugged. "It wasn't so much."

"So much as what, last night?"

"Last night?" Then does he know all I know? But what *do* I know, other than what I can imagine?

"I'll be curious to see how we all come out someday. It could be an interesting story. You're not so nice and polite in your fiction," he said. "You're a different person."

"Am I?"

"I should hope so." Then, as though having concluded administering my rites of confirmation, he gravely shook my hand. "Which way did she go on the road? To the left?"

"Yes. Down the mountain."

He found his gloves in his pocket and after a quick glance at his watch opened the front door. "It's like being married to Tolstoy," he said, and left me to make my feverish notes while he started off after the runaway spouse, some five minutes now into her doomed journey in search of a less noble calling.

Zuckerman
Unbound

"Let Nathan see what it is to be
lifted from obscurity. Let him not
come hammering at our door to tell us
that he wasn't warned."

E. I. LONOFF
to his wife
December 10, 1956

1 "I'm Alvin Pepler"

Whd what the hell are you doing on a bus, with your dough?"

It was a small, husky young fellow with a short haircut and a new business suit who wanted to know; he had been daydreaming over an automotive magazine until he saw who was sitting next to him. That was all it took to charge him up.

Undaunted by Zuckerman's unobliging reply—on a bus to be transported through space—he happily offered his advice. These days everybody did, if they could find him. "You should buy a helicopter. That's how I'd do it. Rent the landing rights up on apartment buildings and fly straight over the dog-poop. Hey, see this guy?" This second question was for a man standing in the aisle reading his *Times*.

The bus was traveling south on Fifth Avenue, downtown from Zuckerman's new Upper East Side address. He was off to see an investment specialist on Fifty-second Street, a meeting arranged by his agent, André Schevitz, to get him to diversify his capital. Gone were the days when Zuckerman had only to worry about Zuckerman making money: henceforth he would have to worry about his money making money. "Where do you have it right now?" the investment specialist had asked when Zuckerman finally phoned. "In my shoe," Zuckerman told him. The investment specialist laughed. "You intend to keep it there?" Though the answer was yes, it was easier for the moment to say no. Zuckerman had privately declared a one-year moratorium on all serious decisions arising out of the smashing success. When he could think straight again, he would act again. All this, this luck—what did it mean? Coming so suddenly, and on such a scale, it was as baffling as a misfortune.

Because Zuckerman was not ordinarily going anywhere at the morning rush hour—except into his study with his coffee cup to reread the paragraphs from the day before—

he hadn't realized until too late that it was a bad time to be taking a bus. But then he still refused to believe that he was any less free than he'd been six weeks before to come and go as he liked, when he liked, without having to remember beforehand who he was. Ordinary everyday thoughts on the subject of who one was were lavish enough without an extra hump of narcissism to carry around.

"Hey. *Hey*." Zuckerman's excited neighbor was trying again to distract the man in the aisle from his *Times*. "See this guy next to me?"

"I do now," came the stern, affronted reply.

"He's the guy who wrote *Carnovsky*. Didn't you read about it in the papers? He just made a million bucks and he's taking a bus."

Upon hearing that a millionaire was on board, two girls in identical gray uniforms—two frail, sweet-looking children, undoubtedly well-bred little sisters on their way downtown to convent school—turned to look at him.

"Veronica," said the smaller of the two, "it's the man who wrote the book that Mummy's reading. It's Carnovsky."

The children kneeled on their seats so as to face him. A middle-aged couple in the row across from the children also turned to get a look.

"Go on, girls," said Zuckerman lightly. "Back to your homework."

"Our mother," said the older child, taking charge, "is reading your book, Mr. Carnovsky."

"Fine. But Mummy wouldn't want you to stare on the bus."

No luck. Must be phrenology they were studying at St. Mary's.

Zuckerman's companion had meanwhile turned to the seat directly behind to explain to the woman there the big goings-on. Make her a part of it. The family of man. "I'm sitting next to a guy who just made a million bucks. Probably two."

"Well," said a gentle, ladylike voice, "I hope all that money doesn't change him."

Fifteen blocks north of the investment specialist's office, Zuckerman pulled the cord and got off. Surely here, in the garden spot of anomie, it was still possible to be nobody on the rush-hour streets. If not, try a mustache. This may be far from life as you feel, see, know, and wish to know it, but if all it takes is a mustache, then, for Christ's sake, grow one. You are not Paul Newman, but you're no longer who you used to be either. A mustache. Contact lenses. Maybe a colorful costume would help. Try looking the way everybody does today instead of the way everybody looked twenty years ago in Humanities 2. Less like Albert Einstein, more like Jimi Hendrix, and you won't stick out so much. And what about your gait while you're at it? He was always meaning to work on that anyway. Zuckerman moved with his knees too close together and at a much too hurried pace. A man six feet tall should *amble* more. But he could never remember about ambling after the first dozen steps—twenty, thirty paces and he was lost in his thoughts instead of thinking about his stride. Well, now was the time to get on with it, especially with his sex credentials coming under scrutiny in the press. As aggressive in the walk as in the work. You're a millionaire, walk like one. People are watching.

The joke was on him. Someone was—the woman who'd had to be told on the bus why everyone else was agog. A tall, thin, elderly woman, her face heavily powdered . . . only why was she running after him? And undoing the latch on her purse? Suddenly his adrenalin advised Zuckerman to run too.

You see, not everybody was delighted by this book that was making Zuckerman a fortune. Plenty of people had already written to tell him off. "For depicting Jews in a peep-show atmosphere of total perversion, for depicting Jews in acts of adultery, exhibitionism, masturbation, sodomy, fetishism, and whoremongery," somebody with letterhead stationery as impressive as the President's had even suggested that he "ought to be shot." And in the spring of 1969 this was no longer just an expression. Vietnam was a slaughterhouse, and off the battlefield as well as on, many Americans had gone berserk. Just about a year before, Martin Luther King and Robert Kennedy had been gunned down by assassins. Closer to home, a former teacher of Zuckerman's was still hiding out because a rifle had been fired at him through his kitchen window as he'd been sitting at his table one night with a glass of warm milk and a Wodehouse novel. The retired bachelor had taught Middle English at the University of Chicago for thirty-five years. The course had been hard, though not that hard. But a bloody nose wasn't enough anymore. Blowing people apart seemed to have replaced the roundhouse punch in the daydreams of the aggrieved: only annihilation gave satisfaction that lasted. At the Democratic convention the summer before, hundreds had been beaten with clubs and trampled by horses and thrown through plate-glass windows for offenses against order and decency less grave than Zuckerman's were thought to be by any number of his correspondents. It didn't strike Zuckerman as at all unlikely that in a seedy room somewhere the *Life* cover featuring his face (unmustached) had been tacked up within dart-throwing distance of the bed of some "loner." Those cover stories were enough of a trial for a writer's writer friends, let alone for a semi-literate psychopath who might not know about all the good deeds he did at the PEN Club. Oh, Madam, if only you knew the real me! Don't shoot! I am a serious writer as well as one of the boys!

But it was too late to plead his cause. Behind her rimless spectacles, the powdered zealot's pale green eyes were glazed with conviction; at point-blank range she had hold of his arm. "Don't"—she was not young, and it was a struggle for her to catch her breath—"don't let all that money change you, whoever you may be. Money never made anybody happy. Only He can do that." And from her Luger-sized purse she removed a picture post-card of Jesus and pressed it into his hand. " 'There is not a just man upon earth,' " she reminded him, " 'that doeth good and sinneth not. If we say that we have no sin, we deceive ourselves, and the truth is not in us.' "

He was sipping coffee later that morning at a counter around the corner from the office of the investment specialist—studying, for the first time in his life, the business page of the morning paper—when a smiling middle-aged woman came up to tell him that from reading about his sexual liberation in *Carnovsky*, she was less "uptight" now herself. In the bank at Rockefeller Plaza where he went to cash a check, the long-haired guard asked in a whisper if he could touch Mr. Zuckerman's coat: he wanted to tell his wife about it when he got home that night. While he was walking through the park, a nicely dressed young East Side mother out with her baby and her dog stepped into his path and said, "You need love, and you need it all the time. I feel sorry for you." In the periodical room of the Public Library an elderly gentleman tapped him on the shoulder and in heavily accented English— Zuckerman's grandfather's English—told him how sorry he felt for his parents. "You didn't put in your whole life," he said sadly. "There's much more to your life than that. But you just leave it out. To get even." And then, at last, at home, a large jovial black man from Con Ed who was waiting in the hall to read his meter. "Hey, you do all that stuff in that book? With all those chicks? You are something else, man." The meter reader. But people didn't just read meters anymore, they also read that book.

Zuckerman was tall, but not as tall as Wilt Chamberlain. He was thin, but not as thin as Mahatma Gandhi. In his customary getup of tan corduroy coat, gray turtleneck sweater, and cotton khaki trousers he was neatly attired, but hardly Rubirosa. Nor was dark hair and a prominent nose the distinguishing mark in New York that it would have been in Reykjavik or Helsinki. But two, three, four times a week, they spotted him anyway. "It's Carnovsky!" "Hey, careful, Carnovsky, they arrest people for that!" "Hey, want to see my underwear, Gil?" In the beginning, when he heard someone call after him out on the street, he would wave hello to show what a good sport he was. It was the easiest thing to do, so he did it. Then the easiest thing was to pretend not to hear and keep going. Then the easiest thing was to pretend that he was hearing things, to realize that it was happening in a world that didn't exist. They had mistaken impersonation for confession and were calling out to a character who lived in a book. Zuckerman tried taking it as praise—he had made real people believe Carnovsky real too—but in the end he pretended he was only himself, and with his quick, small steps hurried on.

At the end of the day he walked out of his new neighborhood and over to Yorkville, and on Second Avenue found the haven he was looking for. Just the place to be left to himself with the evening paper, or so he thought when he peered between the salamis strung up in the window: a sixty-year-old waitress in runny eye shadow and crumbling house slippers, and behind the sandwich counter, wearing an apron about as fresh as a Manhattan snowdrift, a colossus with a carving knife. It was a few minutes after six. He could grab a sandwich and be off the streets by seven.

"Pardon me."

Zuckerman looked up from the fraying menu at a man in a dark raincoat who was standing beside his table. The dozen or so other tables were empty. The stranger was carrying a hat in his hands in a way that restored to that expression its original metaphorical luster.

"Pardon me. I only want to say thank you."

He was a large man, chesty, with big sloping shoulders and a heavy neck. A single strand of hair looped over his bald head, but otherwise his face was a boy's: shining smooth cheeks, emotional brown eyes, an impudent owlish little beak.

"Thank me? For what?" The first time in the six weeks

that it had occurred to Zuckerman to pretend that he was another person entirely. He was learning.

His admirer took it for humility. The lively, lachrymose eyes deepened with feeling. "God! For everything. The humor. The compassion. The understanding of our deepest drives. For all you have reminded us about the human comedy."

Compassion? Understanding? Only hours earlier the old man in the library had told him how sorry he felt for his family. They had him coming and going today.

"Well," said Zuckerman, "that's very kind."

The stranger pointed to the menu in Zuckerman's hand. "Please, order. I didn't mean to obtrude. I was in the washroom, and when I came out I couldn't believe my eyes. To see you in a place like this. I just had to come up and say thanks before I left."

"Quite all right."

"What makes it unbelievable is that I'm a Newarker myself."

"Are you?"

"Born and bred. You got out in forty-nine, right? Well, it's a different city today. You wouldn't recognize it. You wouldn't want to."

"So I hear."

"Me, I'm still over there, pounding away."

Zuckerman nodded, and signaled for the waitress.

"I don't think people can appreciate what you're doing for the old Newark unless they're from there themselves."

Zuckerman ordered his sandwich and some tea. How does he know I left in forty-nine? I suppose from *Life*.

He smiled and waited for the fellow to be on his way back across the river.

"You're our Marcel Proust, Mr. Zuckerman."

Zuckerman laughed. It wasn't exactly how he saw it.

"I mean it. It's not a put-on. God forbid. In my estimation you are up there with Stephen Crane. You are the two great Newark writers."

"Well, that's kind of you."

"There's Mary Mapes Dodge, but however much you may admire *Hans Brinker,* it's still only a book for children. I would have to place her third. Then there is LeRoi Jones, but him I have no trouble placing fourth. I say this without racial prejudice, and not as a result of the tragedy that has happened to the city in recent years, but what he writes is not literature. In my estimation it is black propaganda. No, in literature we have got you and Stephen Crane, in acting we have got Rod Steiger and Vivian Blaine, in playwrighting we have got Dore Schary, in singing we have got Sarah Vaughan, and in sports we have got Gene Hermanski and Herb Krautblatt. Not that you can mention sports and what you have accomplished in the same breath. In years to come I honestly see school-children visiting the city of Newark—"

"Oh," said Zuckerman, amused again, but uncertain as to what might be feeding such effusiveness, "oh, I think it's going to take more than me to bring the schoolchildren in. Especially with the Empire shut down." The Empire was the Washington Street burlesque house, long defunct, where many a New Jersey boy had in the half light seen his first G-string. Zuckerman was one, Gilbert Carnovsky another.

The fellow raised his arms—and his hat: gesture of helpless surrender. "Well, you have got the great sense of humor in life too. No comeback from me could equal that. But you'll see. It'll be you they turn to in the future when they want to remember what it was like in the old days. In *Carnovsky* you have pinned down for all time growing up in that town as a Jew."

"Well, thanks again. Thank you, really, for all the kind remarks."

The waitress appeared with his sandwich. That should end it. On a pleasant note, actually. Behind the effusiveness lay nothing but somebody who had enjoyed a book. Fine. "Thank you," said Zuckerman—the fourth time— and ceremoniously lifted half of his sandwich.

"I went to South Side. Class of forty-three."

South Side High, at the decaying heart of the old industrial city, had been almost half black even in Zuckerman's day, when Newark was still mostly white. His own school district, at the far edge of a newer residential Newark, had been populated in the twenties and thirties by Jews leaving the rundown immigrant enclaves in the central wards to rear children bound for college and the professions and, in time, for the Orange suburbs, where

Zuckerman's own brother, Henry, now owned a big house.

"You're Weequahic forty-nine."

"Look," said Zuckerman apologetically, "I have to eat and run. I'm sorry."

"Forgive me, please. I only wanted to say—well, I said it, didn't I?" He smiled regretfully at his own insistence. "Thank you, thank you again. For everything. It's been a pleasure. It's been a thrill. I didn't mean to bug you, God knows."

Zuckerman watched him move off to the register to pay for his meal. Younger than he seemed from the dark clothes and the beefy build and the vanquished air, but more ungainly, and, with his heavy splayfooted walk, more pathetic than Zuckerman had realized.

"Excuse me. I'm sorry."

Hat in hand again. Zuckerman was sure he had seen him go out the door with it on his head.

"Yes?"

"This is probably going to make you laugh. But I'm trying to write myself. You don't have to worry about the competition, I assure you. When you try your hand at it, then you really admire the stupendous accomplishment of somebody like yourself. The patience alone is phenomenal. Day in and day out facing that white piece of paper."

Zuckerman had been thinking that he should have had the good grace to ask him to sit and chat, if only for a moment. He had even begun to feel a sentimental connection, remembering him standing beside the table, announcing, "I'm a Newarker myself." He was feeling less sentimental with the Newarker standing back beside the table announcing that he was a writer too.

"I was wondering if you could recommend an editor or an agent who might be able to help someone like me."

"No."

"Okay. Fine. No problem. Just asking. I already have a producer, you see, who wants to make a musical out of my life. My own feeling is that it should come out first in public as a serious book. With all the facts."

Silence.

"That sounds preposterous to you, I know, even if you're too polite to say so. But it's true. It has nothing to do with me being anybody who matters. I ain't and I don't. One look and you know that. It's what happened to me that'll make the musical."

Silence.

"I'm Alvin Pepler."

Well, he wasn't Houdini. For a moment that had seemed in the cards.

Alvin Pepler waited to hear what Nathan Zuckerman made of meeting Alvin Pepler. When he heard nothing, he quickly came to Zuckerman's aid. And his own. "Of course to people like you the name can't mean a thing. You have better things to do with your time than waste it on TV. But I thought, as we're *landsmen,* that maybe your family might have mentioned me to you. I didn't say this earlier, I didn't think it was in order, but your father's cousin, Essie Slifer, happened to go to Central with my mother's sister Lottie way back when. They were one year apart. I don't know if this helps, but I'm the one they called in the papers 'Pepler the Man of the People.' I'm 'Alvin the Jewish Marine.' "

"Why then," said Zuckerman, relieved at last to have something to say, "you're the quiz contestant, no? You were on one of those shows."

Oh, there was more to it than that. The syrupy brown eyes went mournful and angry, filling up not with tears, but what was worse, with *truth*. "Mr. Zuckerman, for three consecutive weeks I was the winner on the biggest of them all. Bigger than 'Twenty-One.' In terms of dollars given away bigger than 'The $64,000 Question.' I was the winner on 'Smart Money.' "

Zuckerman couldn't remember ever seeing any of those quiz shows back in the late fifties, and didn't know one from another; he and his first wife, Betsy, hadn't even owned a television set. Still, he thought he could remember somebody in his family—more than likely Cousin Essie—once mentioning a Pepler family from Newark, and their oddball son, the quiz contestant and ex-Marine.

"It was Alvin Pepler they cut down to make way for the great Hewlett Lincoln. That is the subject of my book. The fraud perpetrated on the American public.

The manipulation of the trust of tens of millions of innocent people. And how for admitting it I have been turned into a pariah until this day. They made me and then they destroyed me, and, Mr. Zuckerman, they haven't finished with me yet. The others involved have all gone on, onward and upward in corporate America, and nobody cares a good goddamn what thieves and liars they were. But because I wouldn't lie for those miserable crooks, I have spent ten years as a marked man. A McCarthy victim is better off than I am. The whole country rose up against that bastard, and vindicated the innocent and so on, till at least some justice was restored. But Alvin Pepler, to this day, is a dirty name throughout the American broadcasting industry."

Zuckerman was remembering more clearly now the stir those quiz shows had made, remembering not so much Pepler but Hewlett Lincoln, the philosophical young country newspaperman and son of the Republican governor of Maine, and, while he was a contestant, the most famous television celebrity in America, admired by schoolchildren, their teachers, their parents, their grandparents —until the scandal broke, and the schoolchildren learned that the answers that came trippingly off the tongue of Hewlett Lincoln in the contestants' isolation booth had been slipped to him days earlier by the show's producers. There were front-page stories in the papers, and as Zuckerman recalled, the ludicrous finale had been a Congressional investigation.

"I wouldn't dream," Pepler was saying, "of comparing the two of us. An educated artist like yourself and a person who happens to be born with a photographic memory are two different things entirely. But while I was on 'Smart Money,' deservedly or not I had the respect of the entire nation. If I have to say so myself, I don't think it did the Jewish people any harm having a Marine veteran of two wars representing them on prime-time national television for three consecutive weeks. You may have contempt for quiz programs, even the honest ones. You have a right to—you more than anybody. But the average person didn't see it that way in those days. That's why when I was on top for those three great weeks, I made no bones about my religion. I said it right out. I wanted the country to know that a Jew in the Marine Corps could be as tough on the battlefield as anyone. I never claimed I was a war hero. Far from it. I shook like the next guy in a foxhole, but I never ran, even under fire. Of course there were a lot of Jews in combat, and braver men than me. But I was the one who got that point across to the great mass of the American people, and if I did it by way of a quiz show—well, that was the way that was given to me. Then, of course, *Variety* started calling me names, calling me 'quizling' and so on, and that was the beginning of the end. Quizling, with a *z*. When I was the only one who didn't want their answers to begin with! When all I wanted was for them to give me the subject, to let me study and memorize, and then to fight it out fair and square! I could fill volumes about those people and what they did to me. That's why running into you, coming upon Newark's great writer out of the blue—well, it strikes me as practically a miracle at this point in my life. Because if I could write a publishable book, I honestly think that people would read it and that they would believe it. My name would be restored to what it was. That little bit of good I did would not be wiped away forever, as it is now. Whoever innocent I harmed and left besmirched, all the millions I let down, Jews particularly—well, they would finally understand the truth of what happened. They would forgive me."

His own aria had not left him unmoved. The deep brown irises were cups of ore fresh from the furnace—as though a drop of Pepler's eyes could burn a hole right through you.

"Well, if that's the case," said Zuckerman, "you should work at it."

"I have." Pepler smiled the best he could. "Ten years of my life. May I?" He pointed to the empty chair across the table.

"Why not?" said Zuckerman, and tried not to think of all the reasons.

"I've worked at nothing else," said Pepler, plunging excitedly onto the seat. "I've worked at nothing else every night *for ten years*. But I don't have the gift. That's what they tell me anyway. I have sent my book to twenty-two publishers. I have rewritten it five times. I pay a young teacher from Columbia High in South Orange, which is still an A-rated school—I pay her by the hour to correct my grammar and punctuation wherever it's wrong. I wouldn't dream of submitting a single page of this book without her going over it beforehand for my errors. It's all too important for that. But if in their estimation you don't have the great gift—well, that's it. You may chalk this up to bitterness. I would too, in your shoes. But Miss Diamond, this teacher working with me, she agrees: by now all they have to see is that Alvin Pepler is the author and they throw it in the pile marked trash. I don't think they read past my name. By now I'm one big laugh, even to the lowliest editor on Publishers' Row." The speech was fervent, yet the gaze, now that he was at the level of the table, seemed drawn to what was uneaten on Zuckerman's plate. "That's why I asked you about an agent, an editor—somebody fresh who wouldn't be prejudiced right off. Who would understand that this is *serious*."

Zuckerman, sucker though he was for seriousness, was still not going to be drawn into a discussion about agents and editors. If ever there was a reason for an American writer to seek asylum in Red China, it would be to put ten thousand miles between himself and those discussions.

"There's still the musical," Zuckerman reminded him.

"A serious book is one thing, and a Broadway musical is something else."

Another discussion Zuckerman would as soon avoid. Sounded like the premise for a course at the New School.

"If," said Pepler weakly, "it even gets made."

Optimistic Zuckerman: "Well, if you've got a producer . . ."

"Yes, but so far it's only a gentlemen's agreement. No money has changed hands, nobody's signed anything. The work is supposed to start when he gets back. That's when we make the real deal."

"Well, *that's* something."

"It's why I'm in New York. I'm living over at his place, talking into a tape machine. That's all I'm supposed to do. He doesn't want to read what I wrote any more than the moguls on Publishers' Row. Just talk into the machine till he gets back. And leave out the thoughts. Just the stories. Well, beggars can't be choosers."

As good a note as any to leave on.

"But," said Pepler, when he saw Zuckerman get to his feet, "but you've eaten only half a sandwich!"

"Can't." He indicated the hour on his watch. "Someone waiting. Meeting."

"Oh, forgive me, Mr. Zuckerman, I'm sorry."

"Good luck with the musical." He reached down and shook Pepler's hand. "Good luck all around." Pepler was unable to hide the disappointment. Pepler was unable to hide *anything*. Or was that hiding everything? Impossible to tell, and another reason to go.

"Thanks a million." Then, with resignation, "Look, to switch from the sublime . . ."

What now?

"You don't mind, do you, if I eat your pickle?"

Was this a joke? Was this satire?

"I can't stay away from this stuff," he explained. "Childhood hang-up."

"Please," said Zuckerman, "go right ahead."

"Sure you don't—?"

"No, no."

He was also eyeing the uneaten half of Zuckerman's sandwich. And it was no joke. Too driven for that. "While I'm at it—" he said, with a self-deprecating smile.

"Sure, why not."

"See, there's no food in their refrigerator. I talk into that tape machine with all those stories and I get starved. I wake up in the night with something I forgot for the machine, and there's nothing to eat." He began wrapping the half sandwich in a napkin from the dispenser on the table. "Everything is send-out."

But Zuckerman was well on his way. At the register he put down a five and kept going.

Pepler popped up two blocks to the west, while Zuckerman waited for a light on Lexington. "One last thing—"

"Look—"

"Don't worry," said Pepler, "I'm not going to ask you to read my book. Nuts I am"—the admission registered in Zuckerman's chest with a light thud—"but not that nuts. You don't ask Einstein to check your bank statements."

The novelist's apprehension was hardly mitigated by the flattery. "Mr. Pepler, what do you want from me?"

"I just wonder if you think this project is right for a producer like Marty Paté. Because that's who's after it. I didn't want to bandy names around, but, okay, that's who it is. My worry isn't even the money. I don't intend to get screwed—not again—but the hell with the money for now. What I'm wondering to myself is if I can trust him to do justice to my life, to what I have been put through in this country *all my life*."

Scorn, betrayal, humiliation—the eyes disclosed for Zuckerman everything Pepler had been put through, and without "thoughts."

Zuckerman looked for a taxi. "Couldn't say."

"But you know Paté."

"Never heard of him."

"Marty Paté. The Broadway producer."

"Nope."

"But—" He looked like some large animal just batted on the head at the abattoir, badly stunned but not quite out. He looked in agony. "But—he knows *you*. He met you—through Miss O'Shea. When you were all in Ireland. For her birthday."

According to the columnists, the movie star Caesara O'Shea and the novelist Nathan Zuckerman were an "item." Actually, off the screen, Zuckerman had met with her but once in his life, as her dinner partner at the Schevitzes' some ten days before.

"Hey, how is Miss O'Shea, by the way? I wish," said Pepler, now suddenly wistful, "I could tell her—I wish you could tell her *for* me—what a great lady she is. To the public. To my mind she is the only real lady left in the movies today. Nothing they say could besmirch Miss O'Shea. I mean that."

"I'll tell her." The easiest way. Short of running for it.

"I stayed up Tuesday to watch her—she was on the Late Show. *Divine Mission.* Another incredible coincidence. Watching that and then meeting you. I watched with Paté's father. You remember Marty's old man? From Ireland? Mr. Perlmutter?"

"Vaguely." Why not, if it brought this fellow's fever down?

By now the light had changed several times. When Zuckerman crossed, Pepler did too.

"He lives with Paté. In the town house. You ought to get a load of the layout over there," Pepler said. "Offices downstairs on the main floor. Autographed photos all along the hallway coming in. You should see of who. Victor Hugo, Sarah Bernhardt, Enrico Caruso. Marty has a dealer who gets them for him. Names like that, and by the yard. There's a fourteen-carat chandelier, there's an oil painting of Napoleon, there's velvet drapes right to the floor. And this is only the office. There's a harp in the hallway, just sitting there. Mr. Perlmutter says Marty directed all the decoration himself. From pictures of Versailles. He has a valuable collection from the Napoleonic era. The drinking glasses even have gold rims, like Napoleon had. Then upstairs, where Marty actually lives, resides, completely done up in modern design. Red leather, recessed lights, pitch-black walls. Plants like in an oasis. You should see the bathroom. Cut flowers *in the bathroom*. The floral bill is a thousand a month. Toilets like dolphins and the handles on everything gold-plate. And the food is all send-out, down to salt and pepper. Nobody prepares anything. Nobody washes a dish. He's got a million-dollar kitchen in there and I don't think anybody's ever used it except to get water for an aspirin. A line on the phone direct to the restaurant next door. The old man calls down and the next thing, shish kebab. In flames. You know who else is living there right now? Of course she comes and she goes, but she was the one who let me in with my suitcase when I got here Monday. She showed me to my room. She found me my towels. Gayle Gibraltar."

The name meant nothing to Zuckerman. All he could think was that if he kept walking, he was going to have Pepler with him all the way home, and if he hailed a cab, Pepler would hop in.

"I wouldn't want to take you out of your way," Zuckerman said.

"No problem. Paté's on Sixty-second and Madison. We're almost neighbors."

How did he know that?

"You're a very approachable guy, really, aren't you? I was terrified even to come up to you. My heart was pounding. I didn't think I had the nerve. I read in the *Star-Ledger* where fans bugged you so much you went around in a limousine with drawn shutters and two gorillas for bodyguards." The *Star-Ledger* was Newark's morning paper.

"That's Sinatra."

Pepler enjoyed that one. "Well, it's like the critics say, nobody can top you with the one-liner. Of course, Sinatra's from Jersey too. Hoboken's own. He still comes back to see his mother. People don't realize how many of us there are."

"Us?"

"Boys from Jersey who became household words. You wouldn't be offended, would you, if I eat the sandwich now? It can get pretty greasy carrying around."

"Suit yourself."

"I don't want to embarrass you. The hick from home. This is your town, and you being you—"

"Mr. Pepler, it means nothing to me either way."

Gently undoing the paper napkin like a surgical dressing, leaning forward so as not to soil himself, Pepler prepared for the first bite. "I shouldn't eat this stuff," he told

Zuckerman. "Not anymore. In the service I was the guy who could eat anything. I was a joke. Pepler the human garbage can. I was famous for it. Under fire in Korea I survived on stuff you wouldn't feed a dog. Washed down with snow. You wouldn't believe what I had to eat. But then those bastards made me lose to Lincoln on only my third week—a three-part question on Americana I could have answered in my sleep—and my stomach trouble dates from that night. *All* my trouble dates from that night. That's a fact. That was the night that did me in. I can document it with doctors' reports. It's all in the book." That said, he bit into the sandwich. A quick second bite. A third. Gone. No sense prolonging the agony.

Zuckerman offered his handkerchief.

"Thanks," said Pepler. "My God, look at me, wiping my mouth with Nathan Zuckerman's hankie."

Zuckerman raised a hand to indicate that he should take it in stride. Pepler laughed uproariously.

"But," he said, carefully cleaning his fingers, "getting back to Paté, what you're saying, Nathan—"

Nathan.

"—is that by and large I shouldn't have much worry with a producer of his caliber, and the kind of outfit he runs."

"I didn't say anything of the sort."

"But"—alarmed! again the abattoir!—"you know him, you met him in Ireland. You said so!"

"Briefly."

"Ah, but that's how Marty meets everybody. He wouldn't get everything in otherwise. The phone rings and you hear the secretary over the intercom telling the old man to pick up, and you can't believe your ears."

"Victor Hugo on the line."

Pepler's laughter was uncontrollable. "Not far from it, Nathan." He was having an awfully good time now. And, Zuckerman had to admit it, so was he. Once you relaxed with this guy, he wasn't unentertaining. You could pick up worse on the way home from the delicatessen.

Except how does he know we're almost neighbors? And how do you shake him off?

"It's a Who's Who of International Entertainment, the calls coming into that place. I tell you what gives me the greatest faith in this project getting off the ground, and that's where Marty happens to be right now. On business. Take a guess."

"No idea."

"Take a guess. You especially will be impressed."

"I especially."

"Absolutely."

"You've got me, Alvin." Alvin.

"Israel," announced Pepler. "With Moshe Dayan."

"Well, well."

"He's got an option on the Six-Day War, for a musical. Yul Brynner is already as good as signed to star as Dayan. With Brynner it could be something for the Jews."

"And for Paté, too, no?"

"Christ, how can he miss? He'll rake it in. They're all but sold out the first year on theater parties alone. This is without even a script. Mr. Perlmutter has sounded them out. They're ecstatic from just the idea. I tell you something else. Highly classified. When he gets back next week from Israel, I wouldn't be surprised if he approaches Nathan Zuckerman to do the adaptation of the war for the stage."

"They're thinking of me."

"You, Herman Wouk, and Harold Pinter. Those are the three names they're kicking around."

"Mr. Pepler."

" 'Alvin' is fine."

"Alvin, who told you all this?"

"Gayle. Gibraltar."

"How does she come by such classified information?"

"Oh, well, God. For one thing, she's a terrific business brain. People don't realize, because the beauty is all they see. But before she became a Playmate, she used to work as a guide at the United Nations. She speaks four languages. It was Playmate of the Month that launched her, of course."

"Into?"

"You name it. She and Paté literally don't stop. Those two are the secret of perpetual motion. Marty found out before he left that it was Dayan's son's birthday and so Gayle went out and got him a present: a solid-chocolate chess set. And the boy loved it. Last night she went up to Massachusetts to jump from an airplane today for UNESCO. It was a benefit. And in the Sardinian film they just finished, she did her own stunts on the horse."

"So she's an actress too. In Sardinian films."

"Well, it was a Sardinian corporation. The film was international. Look"—suddenly shyness overcame him—"she's not Miss O'Shea, not by a long shot. Miss O'Shea has style. Miss O'Shea has class. Gayle is somebody . . . without hang-ups. That's what she projects, you see. When you're with her."

Pepler turned a bright red speaking about what was projected by Gayle Gibraltar when you were with her.

"Which are her four languages?" asked Zuckerman.

"I'm not sure. English, of course, is one. I haven't had a chance to check out the others."

"I would, in your shoes."

"Well, okay, I will. Good idea. Latvian must be another. That's where she was born."

"And Paté's father. Which four languages does he speak?"

Pepler saw he was being needled. But then, not by just anybody; he took it, after a moment, with another hearty, appreciative laugh. "Oh, don't worry. It's all straight from the shoulder with that guy. You couldn't meet a finer old-timer. Shakes your hand whenever you come in. Beautifully turned out, but in a sedate manner, always. Always with this nice, respectful, soft-spoken air. No, the one who gives me the confidence, frankly, is this lovely, dignified old gentleman. He keeps the books, he signs the checks, and when the decisions are made, I tell you, in his own quiet, respectful way, he makes them. He hasn't got Marty's go-go razzle-dazzle, but this is the rock, the foundation."

"I hope so."

"Please, don't worry about me. I learned my lesson. They wiped me out worse than you can begin to imagine back when they wiped me out. I haven't been the same person since. I start back after the war, and then there's Korea. I start back again after that, fight my way to the absolute top, and whammo. This actually is the best week I have had in ten years, being here in New York City with finally, *finally,* some kind of door to the future opening up. My good name, my robust health, my Marine record, and then my lovely, loyal fiancée, who took to the hills. I never saw her again. I became a walking disgrace because of those crooked bastards, and I'm not about to lay myself open like that ever again. I understand what you're trying to warn me about in your own humorous way. Well, don't worry, the one-liners aren't wasted on me. I'm warned. I'm not the wide-eyed little yokel I was back in fifty-nine. I don't think I'm with a great man anymore just because a guy has got a hundred pair of shoes in the closet and a Jacuzzi bathtub ten feet long. They were going to make me a sportscaster on the Sunday night news, did you know that? I was supposed to be Stan Lomax by now. I was supposed to be Bill Stern."

"But they didn't do it," said Zuckerman.

"May I speak frankly, Nathan? I would give anything to sit down with you for one evening, any night you wanted, and tell you what was going on in this country in the reign of Ike the Great. In my opinion the beginning of the end of what's good in this country were those quiz shows and the crooks that ran them and the public that swallowed it like so many dopes. There is where it began, and where it has ended is with another war again, and one this time that makes you want to scream. And a liar like Nixon as President of the United States. Eisenhower's gift to America. That schmegeggy in his golf shoes—this is what he leaves for posterity. But this is all in my book, spelled out in detail, step by step, the decline of every decent American thing into liars and lies. You can well understand why I have my own reasons for being nervous about throwing my lot in with anybody, Marty Paté included. After all, mine is not the kind of criticism of a country that you are used to finding in a Broadway musical. Do you agree? Can such a thing even be made into a musical without watering down the condemnation I make of the system?"

"I don't know."

"They promised me a job as a sportscaster if I didn't

admit to the D.A. about how the thing was rigged from the day it started, how even that little girl they had on, age eleven and in pigtails, they gave her the answers and didn't even tell her mother. They were going to put me on TV every Sunday night with the sports results. It was all arranged. So they told me. 'Al Pepler and the Weekend Round-up.' And from there to broadcasting the Yankee home games. What it came down to was that they couldn't afford to let a Jew be a big winner too long on 'Smart Money.' Especially a Jew who made no bones about it. They were afraid about the ratings. They were terrified they would rub the country the wrong way. Bateman and Schachtman, the producers, would have meetings about things like this and talk about it together till all hours. They would talk about whether to have an armed guard come on the stage with the questions, or the president of a bank. They would talk about whether the isolation booth should be waiting on the stage at the beginning or whether it should be rolled out by a squad of Eagle Scouts. They would talk all night long, two grown men, about what kind of tie I should wear. This is all true, Nathan. But my point is that if you study the programs the way I have, you'll see that my theory about the Jews is borne out. There were twenty quiz shows on three networks, seven of them in action five days a week. On an average week they gave away half a million bucks. I'm talking about true quiz shows, exclusive of panel shows and stunt shows and those do-good shows, where you could only get on if you had palsy or no feet. Half a million bucks a week, and yet over the bonanza period from nineteen fifty-five to fifty-eight, you won't find a single Jew who won over a hundred thousand. That was the limit for a Jew to win, and this is on programs where the producers, nearly every single one, were Jews themselves. To break the bank you had to be a goy like Hewlett. The bigger the goy, the bigger the haul. This is on programs *run* by Jews. This is what still drives me crazy. 'I will study and get ready, and maybe the chance will come.' You know who said that? Abraham Lincoln. The real Lincoln. That was who I quoted from on nationwide TV my first night on the show, before I got into the booth. Little did I know that because my father wasn't governor of Maine and I didn't go to Dartmouth College, my chance wasn't going to be the same as the next guy's, that three weeks later I'd be as good as dead. Because I didn't commune with nature, you see, up there in the Maine woods. Because while Hewlett was sitting on his ass studying to lie at Dartmouth College, I was serving this country in *two* wars. Two years in World War II and then I get called back for Korea! But this is all in my book. Whether it's all going to get in the musical, well, how could it? Face facts. You know this country better than anybody. There are people that, as soon as word gets out that I'm working on what I'm working on with Marty

Paté, who are going to put the pressure on him to drop me like a hot potato. I wouldn't even rule out payoffs from the networks. I wouldn't rule out the F.C.C. taking him aside. I can see Nixon himself getting involved to quash it. I'm supposed to be a disturbed and unstable person, you see. That's what they'll tell Marty to scare him off. That's what they told everybody, including me, including the parents of my stupid fiancée, including finally a special subcommittee from the United States House of Representatives. That was the story when I refused to go along with being dethroned for no reason after only three weeks. Bateman was practically in tears from worrying about my mental stability. 'If you knew the discussions we have had about your character, Alvin. If you knew the surprise it has been to us, that you have not turned out to be the trustworthy fellow we all so believed in. We're so worried about you,' he tells me, 'we've decided to pay for a psychiatrist for you. We want you to see Dr. Eisenberg until you have gotten over your neurosis and are yourself again.' 'Absolutely,' Schachtman says, 'I see Dr. Eisenberg, why shouldn't Alvin see Dr. Eisenberg? This organization is not going to save a few lousy dollars at the expense of Alvin's mental stability.' This is how they were going to discredit me, by setting me up as a nut. Well, that tune changed fast. Because, one, I wasn't going in for any psychiatric treatment, and two, what I wanted was a written agreement from them, guaranteeing that first Hewlett and I fight to a draw for three consecutive weeks and *then* I leave. And one month later, by popular request, a rematch, which he would win by a hair in the last second. But not on the subject of Americana. I was not going to let a goy beat a Jew again on that, not while the entire country was watching. Let him beat me on a subject like Trees, I said, which is their specialty and doesn't mean anything to anybody anyway. But I refuse to let the Jewish people go down on prime-time TV as not knowing their Americana. Either I had all that in writing, I said, or I would go to the press with the truth, including the stuff about the little girl with the braids and how they set her up too, first with the answers and then to take a dive. You should have heard Bateman then, and how much he was worried about my mental condition. 'Do you want to destroy my career, Alvin? Why? Why me? Why Schachtman and Bateman, after all we've done for you? Didn't we get your teeth cleaned? Sharp new suits? A dermatologist? Is this the way you plan to pay us back, by going up to people in the street and telling them Hewlett is a fake? Alvin, all these threats, all this blackmail. Alvin, we are not hardened criminals— we are in show business. You cannot ask random questions of people and have a show. We want 'Smart Money' to be something the people of America can look forward to every week with excitement. But if you just ask random questions, you know you would have nobody knowing the answer two times in a row. You would have just failure, and failure does not make entertainment. You have to have a plot, like in *Hamlet* or anything else first-class. To the audience, Alvin, maybe you are only contestants. But to us you are far more. You are performers. You are artists. Artists making art for America, just the way Shakespeare made it in his day for England. And that is with a plot, and conflict, and suspense, and a resolution. And the resolution is that you should lose to Hewlett, and we have a new face on the show. Does Hamlet get up from the stage and say I don't want to die at the end of the play? No, his part is over and he lies there. That is the difference, in point of fact, between schlock and art. Schlock goes every which way and couldn't care less about anything but the buck, and art is *controlled,* art is *managed,* art is *always* rigged. That is how it takes hold of the human heart.' And this is where Schachtman pipes up and tells me that they are going to make a sportscaster out of me, as a reward, if I keep my mouth shut and go down for the count. So I did. But did they, *did they,* after telling me that *I* wasn't the one to be trusted?"

"No," said Zuckerman.

"You can say that again. Three weeks, and that was it. They cleaned my teeth and they kissed my ass, and for three weeks I was their hero. The mayor had me into his office. Did I tell you that? 'You have placed the name of the city of Newark before the whole country.' He said this to me in front of the City Council, who clapped. I went to Lindy's and signed a picture of myself for their wall. Milton Berle came up to my table and asked me some questions, as a gag. One week they're taking me for cheesecake to Lindy's and the next week they tell me I'm washed up. And call me names, into the bargain. 'Alvin,' Schachtman says to me, 'is this what you're going to turn out to be, you who has done so much good for Newark and your family and the Marines and the Jews? Just another exhibitionist who has no motive but greed?' I was furious. 'What is your motive, Schachtman? What is Bateman's motive? What is the sponsor's motive? What is the network's motive?' And the truth is that greed had nothing to do with it. It was by this time my self-respect. As a man! As a war veteran! As a war veteran twice over! As a Newarker! As a Jew! What they were saying, you understand, was that all these things that made up Alvin Pepler and his pride in himself were unadulterated crap next to a Hewlett Lincoln. One hundred and seventy-three thousand dollars, that's what he wound up with, that fake. Thirty thousand fan letters. Interviewed by more than five hundred newsmen from around the world. Another face? Another *religion,* that's the ugly truth of it! This hurt me, Nathan. I am hurt still, and it isn't just egotistically either, I swear to you. This is why I'm fighting them, why I'll fight them right to the end, until my true story is before the American public. If Paté is my chance, then don't you see, I *have* to jump for it. If it has to be a musical first and *then* the book, then that's the way it has to be until my name is cleared!"

Perspiration streamed from beneath his dark rain hat, and with the handkerchief Zuckerman had given him earlier, he reached up to wipe it off—enabling Zuckerman to step away from the street-corner mailbox where Pepler had him pinned. In fifteen minutes, the two Newarkers had traveled one block.

Across the street from where they stood was a Baskin-Robbins ice-cream parlor. The evening was cool, yet customers walked in and out as though it were already summertime. Inside the lighted store there was a small crowd waiting at the counter to be served.

Because he didn't know how to begin to reply, and probably because Pepler was perspiring so, Zuckerman heard himself ask, "What about an ice cream?" Of course, what Pepler would have preferred from Zuckerman was this: *You were robbed, ruined, brutally betrayed —Carnovsky's author commits his strength to the redress of Pepler's grievance.* But the best Zuckerman could do was to offer an ice-cream snack. He doubted if anyone could do better.

"Oh, forgive me," said Pepler. "I'm sorry for this. Of course you've got to be starving, with me talking your ear off and then eating half your dinner in the bargain. Forgive me, please, if I got carried away on this subject. Meeting you has just thrown me for a loop. I don't usually go off half-cocked like this, telling everybody my troubles out on the street. I'm so quiet with people, their first impression is I'm death warmed over. Someone like Miss Gibraltar," he said, reddening, "thinks I'm practically a deaf-mute. Hey, let *me* buy *you*."

"No, no, not necessary."

But as they crossed the street, Pepler insisted. "After the pleasure you've given to me as a reader? After the earful I just gave you?" Refusing even to let Zuckerman enter the store with his money, Pepler cried, "Yes, yes, my treat, absolutely. For our great Newark writer who has cast his spell over the entire country! For that great magician who has pulled a living, breathing Carnovsky out of his artistic hat! Who has hypnotized the U.S.A.! Here's to the author of that wonderful best-selling book!" And then, suddenly, he was looking at Zuckerman as tenderly as a father on an outing with his darling baby boy. "Do you want jimmies on top, Nathan?"

"Sure."

"And flavor?"

"Chocolate is fine."

"Both dips?"

"Fine."

Comically tapping at his skull to indicate that the order was tucked safely away in the photographic memory that was once the pride of Newark, the nation, and the Jews, Pepler hurried into the store. Zuckerman waited out on the pavement alone.

But for what?

Would Mary Mapes Dodge wait like this for an ice-cream cone?

Would Frank Sinatra?

Would a ten-year-old child with any brains?

As though passing the time on a pleasant evening, he practiced ambling toward the corner. Then he ran. Down the side street, unpursued.

2 "You're Nathan Zuckerman"

Though his new number was unlisted, Zuckerman paid a service thirty dollars a month to answer for him and find out who was calling. "How's our gorgeous writer?" asked Rochelle, when later that evening he phoned for the day's messages. She was the manager of the service and treated customers she'd never laid eyes on like old friends. "When are you going to drop around and give the girls a thrill?" Zuckerman replied that he gave them enough thrills when they listened in on his line. Good-natured banter, yet he also believed it was true. But

better their eavesdropping than him having to fend off
the unlikely people who seemed to have no trouble getting his unlisted number. There was supposed to be an
outfit supplying the unlisted numbers of celebrities for
twenty-five bucks a great name. Could even be in cahoots
with his answering service. Could even be his answering
service.

"The Rollmops King called. He's gone on you, hon.
You're the Jewish Charles Dickens. Those were his words.
You've hurt his feelings, Mr. Zuckerman, by not calling
back." The Rollmops King thought Zuckerman should
endorse appetizer snacks on a television commercial—an
actress could play Mrs. Zuckerman if his own mother was
unavailable for the job. "I can't help him out. Next message." "But you like herring—it's in the book." "Everybody likes herring, Rochelle." "Why not do it then?"
"Next message." "The Italian. Twice in the morning,
twice in the afternoon." If Zuckerman did not grant him
an interview, the Italian, a Rome journalist, was going to
be out of a job. "Do you think that's true, doll?" "I hope
so." "He says he doesn't understand why you should
treat him like this. He got very emotional when I told
him I was only the service. You know what I'm afraid of?
That he is going to make it up, a personal interview with
Nathan Zuckerman, and they'll pass it off in Rome as the
real thing." "Is that something he suggested as a possibility?" "He suggested a lot of possibilities. You know
when an Italian gets going." "Anyone else ring?" "He

left a question, Mr. Zuckerman. One question." "I've answered my last question. Who else?"

Laura's was the name he was waiting for.

"Melanie. Three times." "No last name?" "No. Just tell him Melanie collect from Rhode Island. He'll know." "It's a big state—I don't." "You would if you accepted the charges. You'd know everything then," said Rochelle, turning throaty, "for only a dollar. After, you could deduct it." "I'd rather bank it." She liked that. "I don't blame you. You know how to accumulate it, Mr. Zuckerman. I'll bet the I.R.S. doesn't take it from you like they do from me." "They take what they can get." "But what about tax shelters? Are you by any chance on to macadamia nuts?" "No." "How about cattle?" "Rochelle, I can't help the Rollmops King or the Italian or Melanie, and much as I'd like to, I can't help you. I don't know anything about these shelters." "No shelters? In your bracket? You must be paying seventy cents back on your top dollar. What do you do, take 'em to the cleaners on entertainment?" "My entertaining is a grave disappointment to my accountant." "What *do* you do then? No shelters, no entertainment, and on top of your ordinary tax, Johnson's surcharge. Pardon my saying it, but if this is really so, Mr. Zuckerman, Uncle Sam should get down on his knees and kiss your ass."

More or less what the investment specialist had told him earlier that day. He was a trim, tall, cultivated gentleman not much older than Zuckerman, who had a painting by

Picasso hanging on his office wall. Mary Schevitz, sparring partner and wife to Zuckerman's agent, André, and would-be mother to André's clientele, had been hoping that Bill Wallace would influence Nathan by talking to him about money in his Brahmin accent. Wallace too had written a best-selling book, a witty attack on the securities establishment by a card-carrying Racquet Club member. According to Mary, a copy of Wallace's exposé, *Profits Without Honor,* could do wonders for the conscience pangs of all those well-heeled Jewish investors who liked to consider themselves skeptical of the system.

You couldn't put anything over on Mary; not even on upper Park Avenue was she out of touch with the lower depths. Her mother had been an Irish washerwoman in the Bronx—*the* Irish washerwoman, to hear her tell it— and she had Zuckerman pegged as someone whose secret desire was to make it big with the genteel WASPs. That Laura's family were genteel WASPs, by washerwoman standards, was only the beginning. "You think," Mary told him, "that if you pretend not to care about money, nobody will mistake you for a Newark Yid." "I'm afraid there are other distinguishing features." "Don't cloud the issue with Jewish jokes. You know what I mean. A kike."

The Brahmin investment counselor couldn't have been more charming, Zuckerman couldn't have been more Brahmin, and the Blue Period Picasso couldn't have cared less: Hear no money, see no money, think no money.

The painting's theme of tragic suffering absolutely puri-
fied the air. Mary had a point. You couldn't imagine they
were talking about what people begged for, lied for, murdered for, or even just worked for, nine to five. It was as
though they were talking about nothing.

"André says you're more conservative in financial affairs than in your fiction."

Though Zuckerman was not so well-dressed as the investment counselor, he was, for the occasion, no less soft-
spoken. "In the books I've got nothing to lose."

"No, no. You're just a sensible man, behaving as any
sensible man would. You know nothing about money,
you know you know nothing about money, and understandably you're reluctant to act."

For the next hour, as though it were opening day at
the Harvard Business School, Wallace told Zuckerman
about the fundamentals of capital investment and what
happens to money when it is left too long in a shoe.

When Zuckerman got up to go, Wallace said mildly,
"If you should ever want any help . . ." An afterthought.

"I will indeed . . ."

They shook hands, to signify that they understood not
only each other but how to bend the world their way. It
wasn't like this in Zuckerman's study.

"It may not seem so to look at me, but I'm familiar
by now with the sort of goals artists set for themselves.
I've tried to help out several of you people over the years."

Self-effacement. You people were three of the biggest names in American painting.

Wallace smiled. "None of them knew anything about stocks and bonds, but today they're all financially secure. So will their heirs be tomorrow. And not just from selling pictures. They no more want to worry about peddling than you do. Why should you? You should get on with your work, totally indifferent to the marketplace, and for as long as the work requires. 'When I think that I have gathered my fruit I shall not refuse to sell it, nor shall I forfeit hand-clapping if it is good. In the meantime I do not wish to fleece the public. That's all there is to it.' Flaubert."

Not bad. Especially if the Schevitzes hadn't tipped Wallace off beforehand to the millionaire's soft spot.

"If we begin swapping great quotations disavowing everything but the integrity of my singularly pure vocation," said Zuckerman, "we'll be here till midnight tomorrow. Let me go home and talk it over with the shoe."

Of course the one he wanted to talk it over with was Laura. There was everything to talk over with Laura, but her good sense he had lost, just when his was being challenged as never before. If he had consulted first with levelheaded Laura about leaving her, he might never have left. If they had sat down in his study, each with a yellow pad and a pencil, they could have laid out together in their usual orderly and practical way the utterly predictable consequences of starting life anew on the eve of the publication of *Carnovsky*. But he had left for the new life because, among other things, he could not bear to sit down anymore with a pad and a pencil to lay things out with her in their usual way.

It was more than two months since the movers had carried away from the downtown Bank Street floor-through his typewriter, his worktable, his orthopedic typing chair, and four file cabinets crammed with abandoned manuscripts, forgotten journals, reading notes, news clippings, and with hefty folders of correspondence dating back to college. They also carried away, by their estimate, nearly half a ton of books. While fair-minded Laura insisted that Nathan take with him half of everything they had accumulated together—down to towels, silverware, and blankets—he insisted on taking nothing but the furnishings from his study. They were both in tears and holding hands while the issue was debated.

Carrying his books from one life into the next was nothing new to Zuckerman. He had left his family for Chicago in 1949 carrying in his suitcase the annotated works of Thomas Wolfe and *Roget's Thesaurus*. Four years later, age twenty, he left Chicago with five cartons of the classics, bought secondhand out of his spending money, to be stored in his parents' attic while he served two years in the Army. In 1960, when he was divorced from Betsy, there were thirty cartons to be packed from shelves no longer his; in 1965, when he was divorced from Virginia, there were just under sixty to cart away; in 1969, he left

Bank Street with eighty-one boxes of books. To house them, new shelves twelve feet high had been built to his specifications along three walls of his new study; but though two months had passed, and though books were generally the first possession to find their proper place in his home, they remained this time in their boxes. Half a million pages untouched, unturned. The only book that seemed to exist was his own. And whenever he tried to forget it, someone reminded him.

Zuckerman had contracted for the carpentry, bought a color TV and an Oriental rug, all on the day he moved uptown. He was determined, despite the farewell tears, to be determined. But the Oriental rug constituted his first and his last stab at "decor." Purchases since had fallen way off: a pot, a pan, a dish, a towel for the dish, a shower curtain, a canvas chair, a Parsons table, a garbage pail— one thing at a time, and only when it became a necessity. After weeks on the fold-up cot from his old study, after weeks of wondering if leaving Laura hadn't been a terrible mistake, he gathered his strength and bought a real bed. At Bloomingdale's, while he stretched out on his back to see which brand was the firmest—while word traveled round the floor that Carnovsky, in person, could be seen trying out mattresses for God only knew who else or how many—Zuckerman told himself, Never mind, nothing lost, this hasn't changed a thing: if the day ever comes for the movers to truck the books back downtown, they'll take the new double bed too. Laura and he could use it to replace the one on which they had been sleeping together, or not sleeping together, for nearly three years.

Oh, how Laura was loved and admired! Heartbroken mothers, thwarted fathers, desperate girlfriends, all regularly sent her presents out of gratitude for the support she was giving their dear ones hiding in Canada from the draft. The homemade preserves, she and Zuckerman ate at breakfast; the boxes of chocolate, she circulated among the neighborhood children; the touching items of knitted apparel, she took to the Quakers who ran the Peace and Reconciliation Thrift Shop on MacDougal Street. And the cards sent with the presents, the moving, anguished notes and letters, she kept as cherished memorabilia in her files. For safety's sake, against the possibility of an F.B.I. break-in, the files were stored with Rosemary Ditson, the elderly retired schoolteacher who lived alone in the basement apartment next door and who also loved her. Rosemary's health and general welfare Laura took as her responsibility only days after she and Zuckerman moved onto the block, when Laura observed the frail, disheveled woman trying to descend the steep cement stairwell without dropping her groceries or breaking a hip.

How could you *not* love generous, devoted, thoughtful, kindhearted Laura? How could *he* not? Yet during their last months together in the Bank Street floor-through, virtually all they had left in common was the rented Xerox machine at the foot of their tub in the big tiled bathroom.

Laura's law office was in the parlor at the front of the apartment, his study in the spare room on the quiet court-yard at the back. During an ordinary productive day he sometimes had to wait his turn at the bathroom door while Laura rushed to photocopy pages going out in the next mail. If Zuckerman had to copy something especially long, he would try to hold off until she took her late-night bath, so they could chat together while the pages dropped. One afternoon they even had intercourse on the bath mat beside the Xerox machine, but that was back when it was first installed. To be running into each other during the course of the day, manuscript pages in hand, was still something of a novelty then; many things were a novelty then. But by their last year they hardly even had intercourse in bed. Laura's face was as sweet as ever, her breasts were as full as ever, and who could question that her heart was in the right place? Who could question her virtue, her rectitude, her purpose? But by the third year he had come to wonder whether Laura's purpose wasn't the shield behind which he was still hiding his own, even from himself.

Though looking after her war resisters, deserters, and conscientious objectors kept her working days, nights, and weekends, she managed nonetheless to note in her calendar book the birthday of every child living on Bank Street, and would slip a little present into the family mail-box on the morning of the event: "From Laura and Nathan Z." The same for their friends, whose anniversaries and birthdays she also recorded there along with the dates she was to fly to Toronto or appear at the courthouse in Foley Square. Any child that she encountered in the supermarket or on the bus was invariably taken aside and taught by Laura how to make an origami flying horse. Once Zuckerman watched her negotiate the length of a crowded subway car to point out to a straphanger that his billfold was protruding from his back pocket—protruding, Zuckerman observed, because he was a drunk in rags and most likely had found it in somebody's leavings or lifted it off another drunk. Though Laura wore not a trace of makeup, though her only adornment was a tiny enamel dove pinned to her trench coat, the drunk seemed to take her for a sassy prostitute on the prowl, and clutching at his trousers, he told her to piss off. Zuckerman said afterward that maybe he'd had a point. Surely she could leave the drunks to the Salvation Army. They argued about her do-goodism. Zuckerman suggested there might be limits. "Why?" asked Laura flatly. This was in January, just three months before the publication of *Carnovsky*.

The following week, with nothing to keep him locked behind the study door where usually he spent his days complicating life for himself on paper, he packed a suitcase and began again to complicate his life in the world. With his page proofs and his suitcase, he moved into a hotel. His feeling for Laura was dead. Writing this book had finished it off. Or maybe finishing the book had given him time to look up at last and see what had died; that was the way it usually worked with his wives. The woman's too good for you, he told himself, reading page proofs on the bed in his hotel room. She is the reputable face that you turn toward the reputable, the face you have been turning toward them all your life. It isn't even Laura's virtue that bores you to tears—it's the reputable, responsible, drearily virtuous face that's your own. It should bore you. It is a goddamn disgrace. Coldhearted betrayer of the most intimate confessions, cutthroat caricaturist of your own loving parents, graphic reporter of encounters with women to whom you have been deeply bound by trust, by sex, by love—no, the virtue racket ill becomes you. It is simply weakness—childish, shame-ridden, indefensible weakness—that condemns you to prove about yourself a point that you only subvert by everything that enlivens your writing, *so stop trying to prove it*. Hers is the cause of righteousness, yours the art of depiction. It really shouldn't take half a lifetime for someone with your brains to figure out the difference.

In March he moved into the new apartment in the East Eighties, thereby separating himself by much of Manhattan from Laura's missionary zeal and moral reputation.

*   *   *

After finishing with the answering service, and before starting on his mail, Zuckerman got out the telephone book to look up "Paté, Martin." There was no such listing. Couldn't find a "Paté Productions" either, not in the regular directory or in the Yellow Pages.

He dialed the answering service again.

"Rochelle, I'm trying to locate the actress Gayle Gibraltar."

"Lucky girl."

"Do you have some kind of show-business directory there?"

"Got all a man could want here, Mr. Zuckerman. I'll take a look." When she came back on the line, she said, "No Gayle Gibraltar, Mr. Zuckerman. Closest I've got is a Roberta Plymouth. You sure that's her professional and not her real name?"

"It doesn't sound real to me. But not much does lately. She was just in some Sardinian film."

"One minute, Mr. Zuckerman." But when she came back on, there was still nothing to report. "I can't find her anywhere. How did you meet her? Party?"

"I haven't met her. She's the friend of a friend."

"I get it."

"He tells me she was once Playmate of the Month."

"Okay, let's try that." But she couldn't find a Gibraltar in any of the model listings either. "Describe her to me, Mr. Zuckerman, physically."

"No need," he said, and hung up.

He opened the directory to "Perlmutter." No "Martin" listed. And of sixteen other assorted Perlmutters, none residing on East Sixty-second Street.

The mail. On to the mail. You are getting stirred up over nothing. Undoubtedly listed as "Sardinian Enterprises." Not that there is any reason to go see. No more reason than to run away. Stop running away. From what in God's name are you in flight? Stop taking every attention as an intrusion on your privacy, as an insult to your dignity—even worse, as a threat to life and limb. You are not even that big a celebrity. Let's not forget that most of the country, most of the *city,* wouldn't care if you walked around with your name and your unlisted number on a sandwich board. Even among writers, even among writers of some pretensions to seriousness, you are still no titan. I am not saying that you should be any less confounded by a change like this, I am only saying that being known, even being known for the moment as mildly notorious— mildly, for sure, by comparison with Charles Manson, or even with Mick Jagger or Jean Genet—

The mail.

He had decided that it would be better to end rather than to begin the day with his mail if he was ever going to get back to work; best to ignore the mail completely if he was ever going to get back to work. But how much more could he ignore, dismiss, or try to elude, before he became one with the stiffs at the undertaker's down the street?

The phone! Laura! He had left three messages in three days and heard nothing. But he was sure it was Laura, it had to be Laura, she was no less lonely or lost than he was. Yet, to be on the safe side, he waited for the service to pick up before quietly lifting the receiver.

Rochelle had to ask the caller several times to make himself more intelligible. Zuckerman, silently listening, couldn't understand him either. The Italian in pursuit of his interview? The Rollmops King hungry for his commercial? A man trying to speak like an animal, or an animal trying to speak like a man? Hard to tell.

"Again, *please*," said Rochelle.

In touch with Zuckerman. Urgent. Put him on.

Rochelle asked him to leave a name and number.

Put him on.

Again she asked for a name and the connection was broken.

Zuckerman spoke up. "Hello, I'm on the line. What was that all about?"

"Oh, hello, Mr. Zuckerman."

"What *was* that? Do you have any idea?"

"It could just be a pervert, Mr. Zuckerman. I wouldn't worry."

She worked nights, she should know. "Don't you think it was somebody trying to disguise his voice?"

"Could be. Or on drugs. I wouldn't worry, Mr. Zuckerman."

The mail.

Eleven letters tonight—one from André's West Coast office and ten (still pretty much the daily average) forwarded to him in a large envelope from his publisher. Of these, six were addressed to Nathan Zuckerman, three to Gilbert Carnovsky; one, sent in care of the publishing house, was addressed simply to "The Enemy of the Jews" and had been forwarded to him unopened. They were awfully smart down in that mailroom.

The only letters at all tempting were those marked "Photo Do Not Bend," and there was none in this batch. He had received five so far, the most intriguing still the first, from a young New Jersey secretary who had enclosed a color snapshot of herself, reclining in black underwear on her back lawn in Livingston, reading a novel by John Updike. An overturned tricycle in the corner of the picture seemed to belie the single status she claimed for herself in the attached curriculum vitae. However, investigation with his Compact Oxford English Dictionary magnifying glass revealed no sign on the body that it had borne a child, or the least little care in the world. Could it be that the owner of the tricycle had just happened to be pedaling by and dismounted in haste when summoned to snap the picture? Zuckerman studied the photograph on and off for the better part of a morning, before forwarding it to Massachusetts, along with a note asking if Updike would be good enough to reroute photographs of Zuckerman readers mistakenly sent to him.

From André's office a column clipped out of *Variety,* initialed by the West Coast secretary, whose admiration for his work led her to send Zuckerman items from the show-business press that he might otherwise miss. The latest was underlined in red. ". . . Independent Bob 'Sleepy' Lagoon paid close to a million for Nathan Zuckerman's unfinished sequel to the smasheroo . . ."

Oh, did he? What sequel? Who is Lagoon? Friend of Paté and Gibraltar? Why does she send me this stuff!

"—unfinished sequel—"

Oh, throw it away, laugh it off, you keep ducking when you should be smiling.

Dear Gilbert Carnovsky:

Forget about satisfaction. The question is not is Carnovsky happy, or even, does Carnovsky have the right to happiness? The question to ask yourself is this: Have I achieved all that could be done by me? A man must live independent of the barometer of happiness, or fail. A man must . . .

Dear Mr. Zuckerman:

Il faut laver son linge sale en famille!

Dear Mr. Zuckerman:

This letter is written in memory of those who suffered the horror of the Concentration Camps . . .

Dear Mr. Zuckerman:

It is hardly possible to write of Jews with more bile and contempt and hatred . . .

The phone.

He reached for it this time without thinking—the way he used to get on the bus and go out for his dinner and walk by himself through the park. "Lorelei!" he cried into the receiver. As if that would summon her forth, and all their wonderful Bank Street boredom. His life back under control. His reputable face toward the world.

"Don't hang up, Zuckerman. Don't hang up unless you're looking for bad trouble."

The character he'd overheard with Rochelle. The hoarse, high-pitched voice, with the vaguely imbecilic intonation. Sounded like some large barking animal, yes, like some up-and-coming seal who had broken into human speech. It was the speech, supposedly, of the thickheaded.

"I have an important message for you, Zuckerman. You better listen carefully."

"Who is this?"

"I want some of the money."

"Which money?"

"Come off it. You're Nathan Zuckerman, Zuckerman. Your money."

"Look, this isn't entertaining, whoever you are. You can get in trouble like this, you know, even if the imitation is meant to be humorous. What is it you're supposed to be, some punch-drunk palooka or Marlon Brando?" It was all getting much too ridiculous. Hang up. Say nothing more and hang up.

But he couldn't—not after he heard the voice saying, "Your mother lives at 1167 Silver Crescent Drive in Miami Beach. She lives in a condominium across the hall from your old cousin Essie and her husband, Mr. Metz, the bridge player. They live in 402, your mother lives in 401. A cleaning woman named Olivia comes in on Tuesdays. Friday nights your mother has dinner with Essie and her crowd at the Century Beach. Sunday mornings she goes to the Temple to help with the bazaar. Thursday afternoons there is her club. They sit by the pool and play canasta: Bea Wirth, Sylvia Adlerstein, Lily Sobol, Lily's sister-in-law Flora, and your mother. Otherwise she is visiting your old man in the nursing home. If you don't want her to disappear, you'll listen to what I have to say, and you won't waste time with cracks about my voice. This happens to be the voice that I was born with. Not everybody is perfect like you."

"Who is this?"

"I'm a fan. I admit it, despite the insults. I'm an admirer, Zuckerman. I'm somebody who has been following your career for years now. I've been waiting for a long time for you to hit it big with the public. I knew it would happen one day. It had to. You have a real talent. You make things come alive for people. Though frankly I don't think this is your best book."

"Oh, don't you?"

"Go ahead, put me down, but the depth isn't there.

Flash, yes; depth, no. This is something you had to write to make a new beginning. So it's incomplete, it's raw, it's pyrotechnics. But I understand that. I even admire it. To try things a new way is the only way to grow. I see you growing enormously as a writer, if you don't lose your guts."

"And you'll grow with me, is that the idea?"

The mirthless laugh of the stage villain. "Haw. Haw. Haw."

Zuckerman hung up. Should have as soon as he heard who it was and was not. More of what he simply must become inured to. Trivial, meaningless, only to be expected—he hadn't, after all, written *Tom Swift*. Yes, Rochelle had the right idea. "Only some pervert, Mr. Zuckerman. I wouldn't worry."

Yet he wondered if he shouldn't dial the police. What *was* worrying was all that his caller had said about his mother in Florida. But since the *Life* cover story, and the attention she subsequently got from the Miami papers, details on Nathan Zuckerman's mother were not so hard to come by, really, if you happened to be looking. She had herself successfully resisted all the determined efforts to flatter, beguile, and bully her into an "exclusive" interview; it was lonely Flora Sobol, Lily's recently widowed sister-in-law, who'd been unable to hold out against the onslaught. Though afterward Flora insisted she had spoken with the newspaperwoman for only a few minutes on the phone, a half-page article had nonetheless appeared in the weekend amusement section of the *Miami Herald,* under the title, "I Play Canasta with Carnovsky's Mother." Accompanying the article, a picture of lonely, pretty, aging Flora and her two Pekinese.

Some six weeks before publication—when he could begin to see the size of the success that was coming, and had intimations that the Hallelujah Chorus might not be entirely a pleasure from beginning to end—Zuckerman had flown down to Miami to prepare his mother for the reporters. As a result of what he told her over dinner, she was unable to get to sleep that night and had to cross the hall to Essie's apartment finally and ask if she could come in for a tranquilizer and a serious talk.

I am very proud of my son and that's all I have to say. Thank you so much and goodbye.

This was the line that she might be wisest to take when the journalists began phoning her. Of course, if she didn't mind the personal publicity, if she *wanted* her name in the papers—

"Darling, it's me you're talking to, not Elizabeth Taylor."

Whereupon, over their seafood dinner, he pretended that he was a newspaper reporter who had nothing better to do than call her up to ask about Nathan's toilet training. She in turn had to pretend that some such thing was going to be happening every day once his new novel appeared in the bookstores.

" 'But what about being Carnovsky's mother? Let's face it, Mrs. Zuckerman, this is who you are now.' "

" 'I have two fine sons I'm very proud of.' "

"That's good, Ma. If you want to put it that way, that's all right. Though you don't even have to say that much if you don't want to. You can just laugh, if you like."

"In his face?"

"No, no—no need to insult anyone. That wouldn't be a good idea either. I mean, just lightly laugh it off. Or say nothing at all. Silence is fine, and most effective."

"All right."

" 'Mrs. Zuckerman?' "

" 'Yes?' "

" 'The whole world wants to know. They've read in your boy's book all about Gilbert Carnovsky and his mother, and now they want to know from you, how does it feel to be so famous?' "

" 'I couldn't tell you. Thank you for your interest in my son.' "

"Ma, good enough. But the point I'm making is that you can say goodbye any time. They never quit, these people, so all you have to do is say goodbye and hang up."

" 'Goodbye.' "

" 'But wait a minute, not yet, please, Mrs. Zuckerman! I've got to come back with this assignment. I've got a new baby, a new house, I have bills to pay—a story about Nathan could mean a big raise.' "

" 'Oh, I'm sure you'll get one anyway.' "

"Mother, that is excellent. Keep going."

" 'Thank you for calling. Goodbye.' "

" 'Mrs. Zuckerman, just two minutes off the record?' "

" 'Thank you, goodbye.' "

" '*One* minute. One *line*. Won't you please, Mrs. Z., one little line for my article about your remarkable son?' "

" 'Goodbye, goodbye now.' "

"Ma, the truth is, you don't even have to keep saying goodbye. That's hard for a courteous person to understand. But by this time you could go ahead and hang up without feeling that you've slighted anyone."

Over dessert he put her through it again, just to be sure she was ready. Any wonder that by midnight she needed a Valium?

He knew nothing about how disturbing a visit it had been until his last trip to Miami just three weeks ago. First they went to visit his father in the nursing home. Dr. Zuckerman could not really speak comprehensibly since the last stroke—just half-formed words and truncated syllables—and there were times when he didn't know at first who she was. He looked at her and moved his mouth to say "Molly," the name of his dead sister. That you could no longer tell just how much of anything he knew was what made her daily visits such hell. Nonetheless, she seemed that day to be looking better than she had in years, if not quite the curly-headed young madonna cuddling her somber first-born son in the 1935 seaside photograph framed on his father's bed table, certainly not so done-in as to frighten you about *her* health. Ever since the trial of caring for his father had begun for her four years back—four years during which he wouldn't let her out of his sight—she had been looking far less like the energetic and indomitable mother from whom Nathan had inherited the lively burnish of his eyes (and the mild comedy of his profile) than like his gaunt, silent, defeated grandmother, the spectral widow of the tyrannical shopkeeper, her father.

When they got home, she had to lie down on the sofa with a cold cloth on her forehead.

"You look better, though, Ma."

"It's easier with him there. I hate to say it, Nathan. But I'm just beginning to feel a little like myself." He had been in the nursing home now for some twelve weeks.

"Of course it's easier," said her son. "That was the idea."

"Today was not a good day for him. I'm sorry you saw him like this."

"That's all right."

"But he knew who you were, I'm sure."

Zuckerman wasn't so sure, but said, "I know he did."

"I only wish he knew how wonderful you're doing. All this success. But it's really too much, dear, to explain in his condition."

"And it's all right too if he doesn't know. The best thing is to let him rest comfortably."

Here she lowered the cloth over her eyes. She was beginning to weep, and didn't want him to see.

"What is it, Ma?"

"It's that I'm so relieved, really, about you. I never told you, I kept it to myself, but the day you flew down to tell me all that was going to happen because of the book, I thought—well, I thought you were headed for a terrible fall. I thought maybe it was because you didn't have Daddy now as somebody who was always there behind you—that you didn't on your own know which way to turn. And then Mr. Metz"—the new husband of Dr. Zuckerman's old cousin Essie—"he said it sounded to him like 'delusions of grandeur.' He doesn't mean any harm, Mr. Metz—he goes every week to read Daddy 'The News in Review' from the Sunday paper. He's a wonderful man, but that was his opinion. And then Essie started in. She said that all his life your daddy has had delusions of grandeur—that even when they were children together he wasn't happy unless he was telling everybody how to live and butting in on what was none of his business. This is Essie, mind you, with that mouth she has on her. I said to her, 'Essie, let's leave your argument with Victor out of this. Since the man can't even talk anymore to make himself understood, maybe that should put a stop to it.' But what they said scared the daylights out of me, sweetheart. I thought, Maybe it's true—something in his makeup that he got from his father. But I should have known better. My big boy is nobody's fool. The way you are taking all this is just wonderful. People down here ask me, 'What is he like now with his picture in all the papers?' And I tell them that you are somebody who never put on airs and never will."

"But, Ma, you mustn't let them get you down with this business about Carnovsky's mother."

All at once she was like a child at whose bedside he was sitting, a child who'd been cruelly teased at school and had come home in tears, running a fever.

Smiling bravely, removing the cloth and showing him the burnish of his eyes in her head, she said, "I try not to."

"But it's hard."

"But sometimes it's hard, darling, I have to admit it. The newspapers I can deal with, thanks to you. You would be proud of me."

To the end of her sentence he silently affixed the word "Papa." He had known her papa, and how he'd made her and her sisters toe the line. First the domineering father, then the domineering, father-dominated husband. For parents Zuckerman could claim the world's most obedient daughter and son.

"Oh, you should hear me, Nathan. I'm courteous, of course, but I cut them dead, exactly the way you said. But with people I meet socially it's different. People say to me—and right out, without a second thought—'I didn't know you were crazy like that, Selma.' I tell them I'm not. I tell them what you told me: that it's a story, that she is a character in a book. So they say, 'Why does he write a story like that, unless it's true?' And then really what can I say—that they'll believe?"

"Silence, Ma. Don't say anything."

"But you can't, Nathan. If you say nothing, it doesn't work. Then they're sure they're right."

"Then tell them your boy is a madman. Tell them you're not responsible for the things that come into his head. Tell them you're lucky he doesn't make up things even worse. That's not far from the truth. Mother, you know you are yourself and not Mrs. Carnovsky, and I know you are yourself and not Mrs. Carnovsky. You and I know that it was very nearly heaven thirty years ago."

"Oh, darling, is that true?"

"Absolutely."

"But that isn't what the book says. I mean, that isn't what people think, who read it. They think it even if they *don't* read it."

"There's nothing to do about what people think, except to pay as little attention as possible."

"At the pool, when I'm not there, they say you won't have anything to do with me. Can you believe that? They tell this to Essie. Some of them say you won't have anything to do with me, some of them say I won't have anything to do with you, and the others say I'm living on

Easy Street because of all the money you send me. I'm supposed to have a Cadillac, courtesy of my millionaire son. What do you think of that? Essie tells them that I don't even drive, but that doesn't stop them. The Cadillac has a colored driver."

"Next they'll be saying he's your lover."

"I wouldn't be surprised if they say it already. They say everything. Every day I hear another story. Some I wouldn't even repeat. Thank God your father isn't able to hear them."

"Maybe Essie shouldn't pass on to you what people say. If you want, I'll tell her that."

"There was a discussion of your book at our Jewish Center."

"Was there?"

"Darling, Essie says it is already the main topic of discussion at every Jewish wedding, bar mitzvah, social club, women's club, sisterhood meeting, and closing luncheon in America. I don't know the details about everywhere else, but at our Center it wound up a discussion of you. Essie and Mr. Metz went. I thought I was better off minding my own business at home. Somebody named Posner gave the lecture. Then there was the discussion. Do you know him, Nathan? Essie says he's a boy your age."

"I don't know him, no."

"Afterward Essie went up and gave him a piece of her mind. You know Essie, when she gets going. She's driven

Daddy crazy all his life, but she is your biggest defender. Of course she's never read a book in her life, but that wouldn't stop Essie. She says you are just like her, and you were even when you wrote about her and Meema Chaya's will. You say what's on your mind and the hell with everybody else."

"That's Essie and me, Mama."

She smiled. "Always a joke." Whether the joke had eased her of her burden was something else. "Nathan, Mr. Metz's daughter was down here last week to see him, and she did the sweetest thing. She's a schoolteacher in Philadelphia, pretty as a picture, and she took me aside in the sweetest way to tell me that I shouldn't listen to what people say about the subject matter, that she and her husband think the book is beautifully written. And he is a lawyer. She told me that you are one of the most important living writers, not just in America, but the entire world. What do you think of that?"

"It's very nice."

"Oh, I love you, my darling. You are my darling boy, and whatever you do is right. I only wish Daddy was well enough to enjoy all your fame."

"It might have distressed him some, you know."

"He always defended you, always."

"If so, it couldn't have been easy for him."

"But he defended you."

"Good."

"When you were beginning, he was unhappy about some of the things you wrote—involving Cousin Sidney and the friends he had. He wasn't used to it, so he made mistakes. I would never dare to say it to him or he would chop my head off, but I can say it to you: your father was a doer, your father had a mission in life for which everybody loved and respected him, but sometimes, I know it, in his excitement to do right he mistakenly did the wrong thing. But whether you realize it or not, you made him understand. This is true. Behind your back he repeated the very words you used, even if with you he got upset sometimes and argued. That was just a habit. From being your father. But to other people he was behind you like a wall until the day he got sick." He could hear her voice beginning to weaken again. "Of course, you know and I know, once he got into the wheelchair he was unfortunately a different person."

"What is it, Ma?"

"Oh, just everything at once."

"You mean Laura?" He had finally told her—weeks after leaving Bank Street—that he and Laura were no longer together. He had waited until she was over the immediate shock of having a husband move into a nursing home from which he would never return to live with her. One thing at a time, he had thought, though as it turned out, to her it was still everything at once. Of course, it was just as well that his father wasn't in any shape to get the news; all of them, including Laura, agreed he needn't know, especially as in the past, each time Zuckerman left a wife, his father brooded and suffered and grieved, and then, utterly cast down, got on the phone in the middle of the night to apologize to the "poor girl" for his son. There had been scenes about those calls, scenes that summoned up the worst of the son's adolescence.

"You're sure she's all right?" his mother asked.

"She's fine. She's got her work. You don't have to worry about Laura."

"And you'll get divorced, Nathan? Again?"

"Ma, I'm sorry for everyone that I'm compiling such a bad marital record. On dark days I too put myself down for not being an ideal member of my sex. But I just don't have the aptitude for a binding, sentimental attachment to one woman for life. I lose interest and I have to go. Maybe my aptitude is for changing partners—one lovely new woman every five years. Try to see it that way. They're all wonderful, beautiful, devoted girls, you know. There's that to be said for me. I don't bring anything home but the best."

"But I never said you had a bad record—oh, my darling, not me, never, never, never in a million years. You are my son and whatever you decide is right. However you live is right. As long as you know what you're doing."

"I do."

"And as long as you know that it is right."

"It is."

"Then we are behind you. We have been behind you from the very beginning. As Daddy always says, What is a family if they don't stick together?"

Needless to say, he wasn't the best person to ask.

Dear Mr. Zuckerman:

I read my first erotic book seven years ago when I was thirteen. Then there was a lapse in sexy (and emotionally stimulating) reading as I had the real thing (seven years with the same putz). When that ended last winter it was back to books to forget, to remember, to escape. It was heavy for a while, so I read your book for a laugh. And now I feel as if I'm in love. Well, maybe not love but something as intense. Mr. Zuckerman (dare I call you Nathan?), you are just a definite up emotionally for me— as well as an excellent way to increase my vocabulary. Call me crazy (my friends call me Crazy Julia), call me a literary groupie, but you are truly getting through. You are as therapeutic as my shrink—and only eight ninety-five per session. In these times when a lot of what people communicate to each other is nothing but grief, guilt, hate, and the like, I thought I'd express my gratitude, appreciation, and love for you, your great wit, your fine mind, and everything you stand for.

Oh yes, and one last motive for writing you. Would you consider doing something as impulsive as accompanying me to Europe, say during semester break? I'm somewhat familiar with Switzerland (I have a secret

numbered account in the largest Swiss bank) and would
love to turn you on to some of the most surreal and moving experiences to be had in that country. We can visit
the house in which Thomas Mann spent his last years.
His widow and son still live there, in a town called Kilch-
berg in the canton of Zurich. We can visit the famous
chocolate factories, the sound Swiss banking institutions,
the mountains, the lakes, the waterfall at which Sherlock
Holmes met his destiny—need I go on?

> Not-so-crazy Julia
> Numbered Acc't 776043

Dear Julia:

I am not so crazy either and will have to say no to
your invitation. I'm sure you are a completely harmless
person, but these are strange times, in America if not
Switzerland. I wish I could be friendlier, since you sound
friendly and affectionate yourself, not to mention playful
and rich. But I'm afraid you'll have to go to the chocolate
factories without me.

> Yours,
> Nathan Zuckerman
> Bankers Trust 4863589

Dear Nathan,

I was so sad to leave without saying goodbye. But when
Fate changes horses the rider is carried along.

But this was a real letter, from someone he knew.
Signed "C." He found the envelope in his wastebasket.
It had been mailed several days earlier in Havana.

Dear Nathan,

I was so sad to leave without saying goodbye. But when Fate changes horses the rider is carried along. And so I am here. Mary had always wanted us to meet, and I shall always feel that my life has been enriched by the moment—however brief—of knowing you.

Vague memories, nothing but memories.

C.

"Vague memories, nothing but memories" was Yeats. "Fate changes horses" was Byron. Otherwise, he thought uncharitably, it looked to be the form letter. Even the intimate "C." That stood for Caesara O'Shea, keeper of the screen's softest, most inviting lilt, of a languishing air so sad and so seductive that a Warner Brothers wit had accounted for the box-office magic thus: "All the sorrow of her race and then those splendid tits." Two weeks earlier Caesara had come to New York from her home in Connemara, and on the phone Zuckerman had been summoned by his agent to be her dinner partner. More *Carnovsky* booty. She had asked specifically for him.

"You'll know most of the people," said André.

"And Caesara you should know," Mary told him. "It's about time."

"Why?" asked Zuckerman.

"Oh, Nathan," said Mary, "don't look down your nose because she's a sex symbol to the hordes. So are you to the hordes, in case you haven't heard."

"Don't be intimidated by the beauty," said André. "Or the press. Everybody gets nasty or shy, and she's nobody to be afraid of. She's a very unassuming, gentle, and intelligent woman. When she's in Ireland all she does is cook and garden and sit at night and read in front of the fire. In New York she's content to walk in the park or just go out to a movie."

"And she's had terrible luck with men," said Mary, "men I'd like to murder, really. Listen to me about you and women, Nathan, because you're as bad as she is. I've watched you mismated three times now. You married the fey elfin dancer who you could crush with one finger, you had the neurotic society girl betraying her class, and as far as I could tell, this last one was actually a certified public saint. Frankly, how you picked that Mother Superior I'll never know. But then there's a little Mother Superior in you too, isn't there? Or maybe that's part of the act. Keeping the Kike at Bay. More Goyish than the Puritan Fathers."

"Right to the heart of my mystery. Can't fool Mary."

"I don't think you fool yourself. For God's sake, come out from behind all that disgusting highbrow disapproval of the fallen people having fun. What's the sense of it after that book? You've thrown all that professor-shit precisely where it belongs—now enjoy a real man's life. And this time with a certified *woman*. Do you really not know what you're getting in Caesara O'Shea? Aside from the most beautiful thing in creation? Dignity, Nathan. Bravery. Strength. Poetry. My God, it's the very heart of Ireland you're getting!"

"Mary, I read the movie magazines too. From the sound of it, her grandfather cut the turf to warm the hut of Mary Magdalene. I may be a comedown from all that."

"Nathan," said André, "I promise you, she'll be as unsure of herself as you are."

"Who isn't," replied Zuckerman, "aside from Mary and Muhammad Ali?"

"He means," said Mary, "that you can be yourself with her."

"And who's that?"

"You'll come up with something," André assured him.

Her gown was a spectacular composition of flame-colored veils and painted wooden beads and cockatoo feathers; her hair hung in a heavy black braid down her back; and her eyes were her eyes. Serving herself the haddock mousse at dinner, she dropped a bit on the floor, making it easier for him to look directly into the celebrated Irish eyes and say things that made sense. Easier until he realized that maybe that was why she'd dropped it. Every time he turned her way, there was that face from those movies.

Not until after dinner, when they were able to move away from the other guests, and from the presumptuous intimacy of place cards inches apart, could they manage to speak intimately. It lasted only five minutes, but did not lack for fervor on either side. They had both read Ellmann's biography of Joyce and, from the sound of it, had never dared to confess the depths of their admiration for the book to anyone before; from the hushed tones, you might have thought that to do so was a criminal offense. Zuckerman revealed that he had once met Professor Ellmann up at Yale. They had actually met at a literary ceremony in New York where each had been awarded a prize, but he didn't want to appear to be trying to impress, given how hard he was trying.

His meeting Ellmann did the trick. He couldn't have come off better had it been Joyce himself. Zuckerman's temples were damp with perspiration, and Caesara had two hands drawn emotionally to her breasts. It was then that he asked if he could see her home later. She whispered yes, twice, mistily, then sailed in her veils across the room —she didn't want to appear oblivious to all the other guests she had been utterly oblivious to. So she put it.

Unsure of herself? A case could be made against that.

On the street, while Zuckerman waved to attract a cab a block away, a limousine pulled up. "Take me home in this?" Caesara asked.

Curled down beside him in the back seat, she explained that she could call day or night from Ireland and Mary was there to buck her up and tell her whom to hate and revile. He said he got much the same service in New York. She told him about all that the Schevitzes had done for her three children, and he told her about convalescing at their Southampton guest house after having nearly died of a burst appendix. He knew it sounded as though he had almost died of wounds incurred at Byron's side during the struggle for Greek independence, but talking to Caesara O'Shea in the velvety back seat of a dark limousine, you came out sounding a little like Caesara O'Shea in the velvety back seat of a dark limousine. Appendicitis as a passionate, poetic drama. He heard himself being awfully sensitive about the "slant of light" on the Southampton beach during his convalescent morning walks. On and on about the slant of light, when, according to an item in that day's paper, a certain scene in his book was considered responsible for the fifty percent increase in the sale of black silk underwear at smart New York department stores.

You'll come up with something, André had said. And this was it: the slant of light and my operation.

He asked whom she was named for, if anyone. Who was Caesara the First?

In the softest voice imaginable, she told him. ". . . for a Hebrew woman, the niece of Noah. She sought refuge in Ireland from the universal flood. My people," she said, her white hand to her white throat, "were the first to be interred there. The first of the Irish ghosts."

"You believe in ghosts?" And why not? What better

question to ask? How the Movement should respond if Nixon mines Haiphong harbor? Haven't you been over that enough with Laura? Just look at her.

"Let's say the ghosts believe in me," she replied.

"I can understand why they would," said Zuckerman. And why not? Fun was fun. A real man's life.

Still, he made no attempt to embrace her, neither while she was curled girlishly in the back seat feeding him her gentle, harmless, hypnotic blarney, nor when she stood nobly before him at the doorway of the Pierre, a woman nearly his height, with her black braid and her heavy gold earrings and her gown of veils and beads and feathers, looking in all like the pagan goddess they made the sacrifices for in a movie of hers he'd seen at college. Perhaps he might have drawn her to him had he not noticed, on entering the car, a copy of *Carnovsky* lying on the seat beside the driver. The mustached young man must have been reading to pass the time while Miss O'Shea was at dinner. A hip Smilin' Jack in sunglasses and full livery, his nose in Zuckerman's book. No, he wasn't about to impersonate his own hungering hero for the further entertainment of the fans.

Under the lights of the hotel portico, with Smilin' Jack watching sideways from the car, he settled for shaking her hand. Mustn't confuse the driver about the hypothetical nature of fiction. Important to have that straight for the seminars back at the garage.

Zuckerman felt precisely the highbrow fool that Mary

Schevitz had him down for. "After all you've been through," he heard himself telling her, "you must be a little suspicious of men."

With her free hand, she drew her silk shawl to her throat. "On the contrary," she assured him, "I admire men. I wish I could have been one."

"That seems an unlikely wish coming from you."

"If I were a man, I could have protected my mother. I could have stood up for her against my father. He drank whiskey and he beat her."

To which Zuckerman could only think to reply, "Good night, Caesara." He kissed her lightly. Staggering to see that face coming up at his. It was like kissing a billboard.

He watched her disappear into the hotel. If only he *were* Carnovsky. Instead, he would go home and write it all down. Instead of having Caesara, he would have his notes.

"Look—" he called, rushing after her into the lobby.

She turned and smiled. "I thought you were hurrying away to see Professor Ellmann."

"I have a proposal. Suppose we cut the crap, as best we can, and have a nightcap."

"Both would be nice."

"Where shall we try it?"

"Why not where all the writers go."

"The New York Public Library? At this hour?"

She was close to him now, on his arm, heading back

out the door to where the car was still waiting. The driver knew more than Zuckerman did about Zuckerman. Or about the lure of Miss O'Shea.

"No," she said, "that place they all love so on Second Avenue."

"Elaine's? Oh, I may not be the best person to show you Elaine's. The time I was there with my wife"—he had gone for dinner one evening with Laura, to see what it was all about—"we were seated as close to the lavatory as was possible without actually having the hand-towel concession. You're better off going with Salinger when he gets to town."

"Salinger, Nathan, won't be seen anywhere but El Morocco."

Couples filled the doorway waiting to get in, customers were lined up four deep at the bar waiting for a table, but this time the Zuckerman party was seated with a flourish of the manager's arms, and so far from the toilet that had he needed it in a hurry he might have been at a serious disadvantage.

"Your star has risen," whispered Caesara.

Everyone looked at her while she pretended that they were still talking alone in the car. "People in line out on the street. You'd think it was a Sadeian brothel," she said, "instead of just somewhere where they stir up the mud. How I hate these places."

"You do? Why did we come, then?"

"I thought it would be interesting watching you hate it too."

"Hate this? To me it's a great night out."

"I see that by the grinding jaws."

"Sitting here with you," Zuckerman told her, "I can feel my face actually blurring out. I feel like the out-of-focus signpost in a news photo of a head-on collision. Does this happen wherever you go?"

"No, not in the rain in Connemara."

Though they hadn't yet ordered, a waiter arrived with champagne. It was from a smiling gentleman at a corner table.

"For you?" Zuckerman asked Caesara, "or me?" and meanwhile rose half out of his chair to acknowledge the generosity.

"Either way," said Caesara, "you'd better go over—they can turn on you if you don't."

Zuckerman crossed between the tables to shake his hand: a happy, heavyset man, deeply tanned, who introduced the deeply tanned woman with him as his wife.

"Kind of you," said Zuckerman.

"My pleasure. I just want to tell you what a great job you've done with Miss O'Shea."

"Thank you."

"She only has to come on in that dress and she's got the room in the palm of her hand. She looks great. She's still got it. The tragic empress of sex. After all this time. You've done a wonderful job with her."

"Who?" asked Caesara, when Zuckerman returned.

"You."

"What were you talking about?"

"The great job I've done with you. I'm either your hairdresser or your agent."

The waiter uncorked the champagne and they raised their glasses to the corner table. "Now tell me, Nathan, who are the other famous people, aside from yourself? Who's that famous person?"

He knew she knew—everybody in the world knew—but they might as well start having a good time. It's why they were there instead of at the Public Library.

"That," he said, "is a novelist. The establishment roughneck."

"And the man drinking with him?"

"That's a tough journalist with a tender heart. The novelist's loyal second, O'Platitudo."

"Ah, I knew," said Caesara, with the lilt, "I knew there would be more to Zuckerman than nice manners and clean shoes. Go on."

"That is the *auteur,* the half-wits' intellectual. The guileless girl is his leading lady, the intellectuals' half-wit. That's the editor, the Gentiles' Jew, and that man who is looking at you devouringly is the Mayor of New York, the Jews' Gentile."

"And I had better tell you," said Caesara, "in case he makes a scene, the man at the table behind him, looking furtively at you, is the father of my last child."

"Is it really?"

"I know him by the sinking of my stomach."

"Why? How is he looking at *you*?"

"He isn't. He won't. I was his 'woman.' I gave myself to him and he'll never forgive me for it. He's not merely a monster, he's a great moralist too. Son of a sainted peasant mother who can't thank Jesus enough for all her suffering. I conceived a child by him and refused to allow him to acknowledge it. He waited outside the delivery room with a lawyer. He had papers demanding that the child bear his family's honored name. I would rather have strangled it in the crib. They had to call the police to get him to stop shouting and throw him out. All in the *Los Angeles Times*."

"I didn't recognize him with the heavy glasses and the banker's suit. The Latin life force."

She corrected him. "The Latin shit. The Latin devious lunatic and liar."

"How did you get involved with him?"

"How do I get involved with the devious lunatics and liars? I work with the he-men in the movies, that's how. Lonely on location, in some ghastly hotel, in some strange place where you can't speak the language—in this case, from my window the view was of two garbage cans and three rats crawling around. Then it starts to rain, and you wait on call for days, and if the he-man wants to charm you and see that you have a good time, and if you don't want to sit reading in your room for sixteen hours a day, and if you want somebody to have dinner with in this ghastly provincial hotel . . ."

"You could have gotten rid of the child."

"I could have. I could have gotten rid of three children by now. But I wasn't raised to get rid of children. I was raised to be their mother. Either that or a nun. Irish girls aren't raised for any of this."

"You seem to the world to do all right."

"So do you. This fame is a very crude thing, Nathan. You have to have more insolence than I do to pull it off. You have to be one of the great devious lunatics for that."

"You never like to see your face on all the posters?"

"When I was twenty, I did. You can't imagine all the pleasure I got at twenty just looking in the mirror. I used to look at myself and think that it wasn't possible that somebody should have such a perfect face."

"And now?"

"I'm a little tired of my face. I'm a little tired of what it seems to do to men."

"What is that?"

"Well, it gets them to interviewing me like this, doesn't it? They treat me like a sacred object. Everyone is terrified to lay a finger on me. Probably even the author of *Carnovsky*."

"But there must be those who can't wait to lay a finger on you just because you are a sacred object."

"True. And my children are their offspring. First they sleep with your image, and after they've had that, they sleep with your makeup girl. As soon as it gets through to them that your you isn't the world's you, it's a grave disappointment to the poor fellows. I understand. How often can you get a thrill out of deflowering the kneeling nineteen-year-old novice of that touching first film, when she's thirty-five and the mother of three? Oh, the truth is that I'm really not childish enough any longer. It was exciting at twenty, but I don't see much point to it now. Do you? I may have reached the end of my wonderful future. I don't even enjoy anymore observing the despicable absurdities. It was a bad idea, coming here. My bad idea. We should go. Unless you're enjoying yourself too much."

"Oh, being here has delighted me enough already."

"I should say hello to my child's father. Before we go. Shouldn't I?"

"I don't know how those things work."

"Do you think all present are waiting to see if I can do it?"

"I suppose it's the sort of thing some of them might wait up for."

The confidence so dazzling to him at the Schevitzes' had all but disappeared; she looked less certain of herself now than any of the young models waiting out on the sidewalk with their boyfriends to get in and catch a glimpse of the likes of Caesara O'Shea. Still, she got up and walked across the restaurant to say hello to her child's father, while Zuckerman remained behind and sipped the champagne intended for her hairdresser. He admired that walk. Under the gaze of all those stargazers it was a true dramatic achievement. He admired the whole savory mixture, sauce and stew: the self-satirizing blarney, the deep-rooted vanity, the levelheaded hatred, the playfulness, the gameness, the recklessness, the cleverness. And the relentless beauty. And the charm. And the eyes. Yes, enough to keep a man on his toes and away from his work for a lifetime.

On the way out he asked, "How was he?"

"Very cold. Very withdrawn. Very polite. He falls back on the perfidious courtliness. Out of his depth, it's either that or the cruelty. Besides, it's not only the new young mistress he's with; there's also Jessica, Our Sacred Virgin of Radcliffe College. Daughter of the first lucky masochist who made a film in his arms. The innocent child isn't supposed to know yet what a twisted, disgusting, maggoty creature Father is."

When they were back in the limousine she drew herself up straight inside the flame-colored veils and looked out the window.

"How did you get into all this?" he asked as they drove along. "If you were raised to be a nun or a mother."

"'All this,' meaning what?" she said sharply. "Show

biz? Masochism? Whoredom? How did I get into all this? You sound like a man in bed with a prostitute."

"Another twisted, disgusting, maggoty creature."

"Oh, Nathan, I'm sorry." She gripped his arm and held it as though they had been together all their lives. "Oh, I got into all this as innocently as any girl could. Playing Anne Frank at the Gate Theatre. I was nineteen years old. I had half of Dublin in tears."

"I didn't know that," said Zuckerman.

They were back at the Pierre. "Would you like to come up? Oh, of course you would," said Caesara. No false modesty about her magic, but on the other hand, no swagger either: a fact was a fact. He followed her into the lobby, his face blurring out again as hers now caught the gaze of people leaving the hotel. He was thinking of Caesara starting at nineteen as the enchanting Anne Frank, and of the photographs of film stars like the enchanting Caesara which Anne Frank pinned up beside that attic bed. That Anne Frank should come to him in this guise. That he should meet her at his agent's house, in a dress of veils and beads and cockatoo feathers. That he should take her to Elaine's to be gaped at. That she should invite him up to her penthouse suite. Yes, he thought, life has its own flippant ideas about how to handle serious fellows like Zuckerman. All you have to do is wait and it teaches you all there is to know about the art of mockery.

The first thing he saw in her drawing room was a pile of brand-new books on the dresser; three were by him —paperback copies of *Higher Education, Mixed Emotions,* and *Reversed Intentions.* Beside the books was a vase holding two dozen yellow roses. He wondered who they were from, and when she put down her shawl and went off to the bathroom he sidled over to the dresser and read the card. "To my Irish rose, Love and love and love, F." When she came back into the room, he was in the wing chair that looked across the park to the towers on Central Park West, leafing through the book that had been open on the table beside the chair. It was by Søren Kierkegaard, of all people. Called *The Crisis in the Life of an Actress.*

"And what is the crisis in the life of an actress?" he asked.

She made a sad face and dropped into the settee across from him. "Getting older."

"According to Kierkegaard or according to you?"

"Both of us." She reached across and he handed her the book. She flipped through to find the right page. " 'When,' " she read, " 'she'—the actress—'is only thirty years old she is essentially passé.' "

"In Denmark maybe, in 1850. I wouldn't take it to heart if I were you. Why are you reading this?"

He wondered if it had come from "F." along with the roses.

"Why shouldn't I?" asked Caesara.

"No reason. I suppose everybody should. What else have you underlined?"

"What everybody underlines," she said. "Everything that says 'me.' "

"May I see?" He leaned over to take the book back.

"Would you like a drink?" said Caesara.

"No, thanks. I'd like to see the book."

"You can look across the park from here up to where Mike Nichols lives. That's his triplex where the lights are. Do you know him?"

"Caesara, everybody knows Mike Nichols," Zuckerman said. "Knowing Mike Nichols is considered nothing in this town. Come on, let me see the book. I never heard of it before."

"You're making fun of me," she said. "For leaving Kierkegaard out to impress you. But I also left your books out to impress you."

"Come on, let me see what interests you so much."

Finally she passed it back to him. "Well, *I* want a drink," she said, and got up and poured herself some wine from an open bottle near the flowers. Lafite-Rothschild—also from F.? "I should have known I was to be graded."

" 'And she,' " Zuckerman read aloud, " 'who as a woman is sensitive regarding her name—as only a woman is sensitive—she knows that her name is on everyone's lips, even when they wipe their mouths with their hand-kerchiefs!' Do you know that?"

"I know that, I know things even less enchanting than that, needless to say."

"Say it anyway."

"No need. Except it isn't quite what my mother had in mind when she took me down from Dublin in my Peter Pan collar to audition for my scholarship at RADA."

The phone rang, but she ignored it. F.? or G.? or H.?

" 'She knows that she is the subject of everyone's admir-ing conversation,' " Zuckerman read to her, " 'including those who are in the utmost distress for something to chatter about. She lives on in this way year after year. That seems just splendid; it looks as though that would really be something. But if in a higher sense she had to live on the rich nourishment of their admiration, take encouragement from it, receive strength and inspiration for renewed exertions—and since even the most highly talented person, and particularly a woman, can become despondent in a weak moment for want of some expres-sion of genuine appreciation—at such a time she will really feel what she has doubtless realized often enough, just how fatuous all this is, and what a mistake it is to envy her this burdensome splendor.' The hardships," said Zuckerman, "of the idolized woman." He began turn-ing pages again, looking for her markings.

"You're welcome to borrow it, Nathan. Of course you're

also welcome to stay here and just proceed right on through."

Zuckerman laughed. "And what will you do?"

"What I always do when I invite a man to my room and he sits down and starts reading. I'll throw myself from the window."

"Your problem is this taste of yours, Caesara. If you just had Harold Robbins around, like the other actresses, it would be easier to pay attention to you."

"I thought I would impress you with my brains and instead it's Kierkegaard's brain you're impressed with."

"There's always that danger," he said.

This time, when the phone began ringing, she lifted the receiver, then quickly put it back down. Then she picked it up again and dialed the hotel operator. "Please, no more calls until noon . . . Fine. I know. I *know*. I have the message. Please, I'd just appreciate it if you'd do as I say. I have all the messages, *thank you*."

"Would you like me to leave?" asked Zuckerman.

"Would you like to?"

"Of course not."

"Okay," she said, "where are we? Oh. You tell me. What is the crisis in the life of a writer? What obstacles must *he* overcome in his relation to the public?"

"First, their indifference; then, when he's lucky, their attention. It's your profession having people look you over, but I can't get used to the gaping. I prefer my exhibitionism at several removes."

"Mary says you won't even go out of the house any-more."

"Tell Mary I never went out of the house much before. Look, I didn't go into this line of work so as to stir the masses to a frenzy."

"What then?"

"What I set out to do? Oh, I was a good boy too in my Peter Pan collar, and believed everything Aristotle taught me about literature. Tragedy exhausts pity and fear by arousing those emotions to the utmost, and comedy promotes a carefree, lighthearted state of mind in the audience by showing them that it would be absurd to take seriously the action being imitated. Well, Aristotle let me down. He didn't mention anything about the theater of the ridiculous in which I am now a leading character—because of literature."

"Oh, it's not all ridiculous. It seems that way to you only because you're so intensity-afflicted."

"And whose epithet is that? Mary's too?"

"No, mine. I've got the same disease."

"In that dress?"

"In this dress. Don't be fooled by the dress."

The phone began its ringing again.

"Seems like he's slipped past the guard," said Zuckerman and opened the book to pass the time while she decided whether or not to answer. *So now for the metamorphosis,* he read. *This actress was constituted by feminine youthfulness, though not in the usual sense of the*

*term. What is normally called youthfulness falls prey to
the years; for the grip of time may be most loving and
careful, but it seizes everything finite just the same. But in
this actress there has been an essential genius which corre-
sponds to the very idea: feminine youthfulness. This is
an idea, and an idea is something quite different—*

"Is the point you're making, reading in my little book,
that you are nothing like the notorious character in your
own? Or," she asked, once the phone had stopped ringing,
"is it that I'm not desirable?"

"To the contrary," said Zuckerman. "Your allure is
staggering and you can't imagine how depraved I
am."

"Then borrow the book and read it at home."

He came down into the deserted lobby at close to four,
carrying the Kierkegaard. The moment he stepped out
of the revolving door, Caesara's limousine pulled up in
front of the hotel, and there was Caesara's driver,
the dude who'd been reading *Carnovsky*, saluting him
through the open window. "Drop you somewhere, Mr.
Zuckerman?"

This too? Had he been instructed to wait until four?
Or all night if need be? Caesara had awakened Zucker-
man and said, "I'd rather face the dawn alone, I think."
"Painters coming early?" "No. But all the brushing of
teeth and flushing of toilets is more than I'm ready for."
Sweet surprise. First faint touch of the girl in the Peter

Pan collar. He had to admit he was feeling swamped himself.

"Sure," he told her driver. "You can take me home."

"Hop in." But he didn't hop out to open the door as he did when Miss O'Shea was along. Well, thought Zuckerman, maybe he's finished the book.

They drove slowly up Madison, Zuckerman reading her Kierkegaard under the lamp in the soft back seat . . . *She knows that her name is on everyone's lips, even when they wipe their mouths with their handkerchiefs!* He didn't know if it was just the excitement of a new woman, the thrill of all that unknownness—and of all that glamour—or if it could possibly be that in just eight hours he had fallen in love, but he devoured the paragraph as though she *had* inspired it. He couldn't believe his luck. And it didn't seem such a misfortune, either. "No, not entirely ridiculous. Much to be said for stirring the masses, if that's what stirred you too. I'm not going to sneer at how I got here." To her, and silently, he said this, then wiped his mouth, a little stupefied. All from literature. Imagine that. He would not like to have to tell Dr. Leavis, but he didn't feel the least sacrilegious.

When they got to his house, the driver refused his ten dollars. "No, no, Mr. Z. My privilege." Then he took a business card from his billfold and handed it out the window. "If we can ever put your mind at ease, sir," and sped away while Zuckerman stepped under the streetlight to read the card:

RATE SCHEDULE

Per Hour

Armed Driver and Limousine 27.50
Unarmed Driver and Armed Escort
   with Limousine 32.50
Armed Driver and Armed Escort
   with Limousine 36.00
Additional Armed Escorts 14.50
Five Hour Minimum
Major Credit Cards Honoured
(212) 555-8830

He read for the rest of the night—her book—and then at nine he phoned the hotel and was reminded that Miss O'Shea wasn't taking calls until noon. He left his name, wondering what he would do with himself and his exultation until they met at two for their walk through the park—she'd said it would be happiness enough just doing that. He couldn't look at *The Crisis in the Life of an Actress* again, or the two essays on drama that filled out the little volume. He'd been through them all twice already—the second time at six a.m., making notes in the journal he kept for his reading. He couldn't stop thinking about her, but that was an improvement over trying to take in what people were thinking, saying, and writing about him—there is such a thing as self-satiation. "You would imagine," he said to the empty bookshelves when he came in, "that after wine at dinner, champagne at Elaine's, and intercourse with Caesara, I could put the homework off until morning and get some rest." But at least sitting at his desk with a pen and a pad and a book, he had felt a little less goofy than lying in bed with her name on his lips like the rest of the fans. It didn't, of course, feel anything like a good night's work; he hadn't felt the excitement of working straight through the night since his last weeks finishing *Carnovsky*. Nor could he lay claim to some lively new idea about what book to write next. All lively new ideas were packed away like the volumes in the eighty-one cartons. But at least he'd been able to focus on something other than himself being stuffed to bursting at the trough of inanities. He was bursting now with her.

He called the Pierre, couldn't get through, and then didn't know what to do with himself. Begin to unpack the half ton of books, that's what! Bank Street is over! Laura is over! Uncarton all the boxed-in brains! Then uncarton your own!

But he had an even better idea. André's tailor! Hold the books and buy a suit! For when we fly to Venice—for checking in at the Cipriani! (Caesara had allowed, as he was leaving, that the only hotel in the world where she truly enjoyed awakening in the morning was the Cipriani.)

In his wallet he found André's tailor's card, his shirt-maker's card, his wine merchant's card, and his Jaguar dealer's card; these had been ceremoniously presented to Zuckerman over lunch at the Oak Room the day André had completed the sale to Paramount of the film rights to *Carnovsky*, bringing Zuckerman's income for 1969 to just over a million, or approximately nine hundred and eighty-five thousand dollars more than he had previously earned in any year of his life. Placing André's cards in his wallet, Zuckerman had withdrawn a card he had prepared the night before for André and handed it across to him—a large index card on which he had typed a line from the letters of Henry James. *All this is far from being life as I feel it, as I see it, as I know it, as I wish to know it.* But his agent was neither edified nor amused. "The world is yours, Nathan, don't hide from it behind Henry James. It's bad enough that that's what he hid behind. Go see Mr. White, tell him who sent you, and get him to fit you out the way he does Governor Rockefeller. It's time to stop looking like some kid at Harvard and assume your role in history."

Well, at Mr. White's that morning—waiting for Caesara to get up—he ordered six suits. If you're in a sweat over one, why *not* six? But why in a sweat? He had the dough. All he needed now was the calling.

On which side did he dress? asked Mr. White. It took a moment to fathom the meaning, and then to realize that he didn't know. If *Carnovsky* was any indication, he had for thirty-six years given more thought than most to the fate of his genitals, but whither they inclined while he went about the day's uncarnal business, he had no idea.

"Neither, really," he said.

"Thank you, sir," said Mr. White, and made a note.

On the new fly he was to have buttons. As he remembered, it was a big day in a little boy's life when he was old enough to be trusted not to get himself caught in a zipper and so bid farewell to the buttoned-up fly. But when Mr. White, an Englishman of impeccable grooming and manners, wondered aloud if Mr. Zuckerman might not prefer to change over to buttons, Zuckerman caught the tone and, mopping his face, replied, "Oh, absolutely." Whatever the Governor has, he thought. And Dean Acheson. His picture also hung among the notables on Mr. White's paneled walls.

When the taking of the measurements was over, Mr. White and an elderly assistant helped Zuckerman back into his jacket without giving any sign that they were handling rags. Even the assistant was dressed for a board meeting of A.T.&T.

Here, as though retiring to the rare-book room at the Bodleian, the three turned to where the bolts of cloth were stored. Fabrics that would serve Mr. Zuckerman for the city and his club; for the country and his weekends; for the theater, for the opera, for dining out. Each was removed from its shelf by the assistant so that Mr. Zuckerman might appreciate the cloth between his fingers. In North America, he was told, with its extremes of climate, a dozen suits would be best to cover every contingency, but Mr. Zuckerman stuck at six. He was drenched already.

Then the linings. Lavender for the gray suit. Gold for the tan suit. A daring floral pattern for the country twill

. . . Then the styling. Two-piece or three-piece? Double-breasted or single-breasted? Two-button front or three-button front? Lapels this wide or this wide? Center vents or side vents? The inside coat pocket—one or two, and how deep? Back trouser pockets—button on the left or the right? And will you be wearing suspenders, sir?

Would he, at the Cipriani, for checking in?

They were attending to the styling of his trousers—Mr. White, most respectfully, making his case for a modest flare at the cuff of the twill—when Zuckerman saw that finally it was noon. Urgent phone call, he announced. "Of course, sir," and he was left to himself, amid the bolts of cloth, to dial the Pierre.

But she was gone. Checked out. Any message for Mr. Zuckerman? None. Had she received *his* message? She had. But where had she gone? The desk had no idea—though suddenly Zuckerman did. To move in with André and Mary! She'd left the hotel to shake the unwanted suitor. She had made her choice and it was him!

He was wrong. It was the other guy.

"*Nathan*," said Mary Schevitz. "I've been trying all morning to reach *you*."

"I'm at the tailor's, Mary, suiting up for every contingency. Where is she if she's not with you two?"

"Nathan, you must understand—she left in tears. I've never seen her so distraught. It killed *me*. She said, 'Nathan Zuckerman is the best thing that's happened to me in a year.'"

"So where is she then? Why did she go?"

"She flew to Mexico City. She's flying from there to Havana. Nathan dear, I didn't know anything. Nobody's known anything. It's the best-kept secret in the world. She only told me to try to explain to me how badly she felt about you."

"Told you what?"

"She's been having an affair. Since March. With Fidel Castro. Nathan, you mustn't tell anyone. She wants to end it with him, she knows there's no future there. She's sorry it ever began. But he won't take no for an answer."

"As the world knows."

"He had his UN Ambassador phoning her every five minutes since she arrived. And this morning the Ambassador came to the hotel and insisted on taking her to breakfast. And then she called me to say she was going, that she had to. Oh, Nathan, I do feel responsible."

"Don't, Mary. Kennedy couldn't stop him, Johnson couldn't stop him, Nixon won't stop him. So how can you? Or I?"

"And you looked so charming together. Have you seen the *Post*?"

"I haven't been out of the fitting room."

"Well, it's in Leonard Lyons, about the two of you at Elaine's."

Later that day his mother phoned to tell him that it had been on the air as well; in fact, she was phoning to find out if it could possibly be true that he had flown to Ireland, without even calling her to say goodbye.

"Of course I would have called," he assured her.

"Then you're not going."

"No."

"Bea Wirth phoned me just a minute ago to say that she heard it on the television. Nathan Zuckerman is off to Ireland to stay at the palatial country estate of Caesara O'Shea. It was on Virginia Graham. I didn't even know she was a friend of yours."

"She's not, really."

"I didn't think so. She's so much older than you."

"She's not, but that isn't the point."

"She is, darling. Daddy and I saw Caesara O'Shea years ago already, playing a nun."

"Playing a novice. She was practically a child then."

"It never sounded from the papers as though she was a child."

"Well, maybe not."

"But everything is all right? You feel well?"

"I'm fine. How's Dad?"

"He's a little better. I'm not saying that just to make myself feel good, either. Mr. Metz has been going every afternoon now to read him the *Times*. He says Daddy seems to follow perfectly. He can tell by how angry he gets whenever he hears Nixon's name."

"Well, that's terrific, isn't it?"

"But you going away without calling—I told Bea it

just couldn't be. Nathan wouldn't dream of going that far without telling me, in case God forbid I had to get hold of him about his father."

"That's true."

"But why did Virginia Graham say you did? And on TV?"

"Someone must have told her an untruth, Ma."

"They did? But why?"

Dear Mr. Zuckerman:

For a number of years I have been planning to film a series of half-hour television shows (in color) to be called "A Day in the Life of . . ." The format, which is no more than a carbon of the ancient Greek Tragedy, is a recitation of the hour-by-hour activities of a well-known person, and offers an intimate personal look at someone who, in the normal course of events, the audience would not see or meet. My company, Renowned Productions, is fully financed and ready to embark upon its opening show. Briefly, it involves filming one complete day, from breakfast to bedtime, of a celebrity who will excite the interest of millions of onlookers. To achieve one day without dull spots, we will average four days of filming candid unrehearsed material.

I selected you as our first celebrity because I think your day will be as interesting as any I can envision. Also, there is broad public interest in you and your "offstage" life. Everyone, I think, would profit by watching a candid portrayal of you at work and you at play. My guess is that such a production will enhance your career—and mine too.

Please let me know your feelings, and if we agree, I will send a couple of reporters to start the initial research.

Sincerely,

Gary Wyman

President

Dear Mr. Wyman:

I think you underestimate how many days, weeks, and years of filming it would take to achieve "A Day in the Life of . . ." of me that would be without dull spots. A candid portrayal of my offstage life would probably put millions of viewers to sleep and, far from enhancing your career, destroy it forever. Better start with somebody else. Sorry.

Sincerely,

Nathan Zuckerman

Dear Mr. Zuckerman:

I have written a short novel of approximately 50,000 words. It is a romance with college characters and explicit sex but has humor and other interest as well, and an original plot. As in your latest book, the sexual activity is an integral part of the plot, so is essential.

I intended to send it to Playboy Press but have backed down because there could be repercussions. My wife and I are retired, living very happily in a retirement village in Tampa. If the book turned out to be successful and the people here found out that I wrote it, we would lose our friends at once and would probably have to sell our home and leave.

I hate to do nothing about the book because I believe it would be entertaining for readers who like explicit sex and also those who don't mind it as long as there is something worthwhile accompanying it. You are an established author and can publish such a book, as you already have, without worrying about adverse opinion.

Please let me know if I may send you the manuscript, and also the address I should use. Then if you like it, you may wish to buy it outright from me as an investment and publish it under another name than your own.

Sincerely,

Harry Nicholson

The phone.

"All right then," cried Zuckerman, "who *is* this?"

"Right now we are asking for only fifty thousand. That's because we haven't had to do the job. Kidnapping is an expensive operation. It takes planning, it takes thought, it takes highly trained personnel. If we have to go ahead and get to work, fifty thousand won't begin to cover costs. If I am going to keep my head above water, you won't get out of a kidnapping like this for under three hundred thousand. In a kidnapping like this, with nationwide coverage, we run a tremendous risk and everybody involved has to be compensated accordingly. Not to mention equipment. Not to mention time. But if you want us to go ahead, we will. Hang up on me again and you'll see how fast. My people are poised."

"Poised where, palooka?" For it was still with something like the caricatured voice of a punch-drunk pug that the caller was endeavoring to disguise his own—and threatening to kidnap Zuckerman's mother. "Look," said Zuckerman, "this isn't funny."

"I want fifty thousand bucks in cash. Otherwise we proceed with the full-scale operation and then you will be out three hundred thousand at least. Not to mention the wear and tear on your old lady. Have a heart, Zuck. Haven't you given her enough misery with that book? Don't make it any worse than it already is. Don't make it so that she regrets the day you were born, sonny."

"Look, this is call number three and has by now become a disgusting sadistic psychopathic little joke—"

"Oh, don't you tell me about disgusting jokes! Don't you call me names, you highbrow fuck! You fake! Not after what you do to your family, you heartless bastard—and in the name of Great Art! In my daily life I am a better man than you are a hundred times over, shitface. Everybody who knows me personally knows that. I detest violence. I detest suffering. What goes on in this country today makes me sick. We had a great leader in Robert Kennedy, and that crazy Arab bastard shot him. Robert Kennedy, who could have turned this country around! But what people know me to be as a human being is none of your business. God knows I don't have to prove myself to a faker like you. Right now we are talking strictly money, and it is no more disgusting than when you talk on the phone to the accountant. You have got fifty thousand dollars, I want it. It's as simple as that. I don't know a son in your financial position who would think twice about laying out fifty thousand to spare his mother some terrible tragic experience. Suppose it was cancer, would you think that was a disgusting joke too, would you make her go through that too, rather than dig into the margin account? Christ, you have just got close to another million on the sequel. How much more do you need in one year? The way the world gets the story, you're so pure you hold your nose when you have to handle change from the taxicab. You fraud, you hypocrite! Your talent I can't take away from you, but as a human being exploiting other human beings you haven't got the greatest record, you know, so don't get high and mighty with me. Because if it was my mother, let me tell you, there wouldn't be that much to debate about. I'd act, and fast. But then I would never have gotten her into this to begin with. I wouldn't have the talent for it. I wouldn't have the talent to exploit my family and make them a laughingstock the way you have. I'm not gifted enough to do that."

"So you do this," said Zuckerman, wondering meanwhile what *he* should do. What would Joseph Conrad do? Leo Tolstoy? Anton Chekhov? When first starting out as a young writer in college he was always putting things to himself that way. But that didn't seem much help now. Probably better to ask what Al Capone would do.

"Correct," he was told, "so I do this. But I don't do it with violence and I don't do it where the traffic can't bear the freight. I do research. And given operating expenses, I am by no means exorbitant in my demands. I am not interested in causing suffering. I hate suffering. I have seen enough suffering in my personal life to last forever. All I care about is making a reasonable profit on my investment and the man-hours involved. And to do what I do with responsibility. I assure you, not everybody goes about it the responsible way that I do. Not everybody thinks these things through. They kidnap like madmen, they kidnap like school kids, and that is when the shit hits the fan. My pride won't permit that. My compunctions won't permit that. I try like hell to avoid just that. And I do, when I am met on the other side by a person with compunctions like my own. I've been in this business many years now, and nobody has been hurt yet who wasn't asking for it by being greedy."

"Where did you hear that I just made a million on 'the sequel'?" If only he had a tape recorder. But the little Sony was down on Bank Street in Laura's office. Everything was that he needed.

"I didn't 'hear' it. I don't operate that way. I've got it right in front of me in your file. I'm reading it right now. *Variety,* out Wednesday. 'Independent Bob "Sleepy" Lagoon paid close to a million—' "

"But that is a lie. That is Independent Lagoon puffing himself up without paying a dime. There is no sequel."

Wasn't this the right approach, the one they recommended in the papers? To level with the kidnapper, to take him seriously, to make him your friend and equal?

"That isn't what Mr. Lagoon tells my staff, however. Funny, but I tend to trust my staff on this more than I trust you."

"My good man, Lagoon is promoting himself, period." It's Pepler, he thought. It's Alvin Pepler, the Jewish Marine!

"Haw, haw, haw. Very funny. No less than I expected from the savage satirist of American letters."

"Look, who is this?"

"I want fifty thousand in United States currency. I want it in hundred-dollar bills. Unmarked, please."

"And how would I get you the fifty thousand unmarked dollars?"

"Ah, now we are talking, now we are making some progress. You just go to your bank in Rockefeller Plaza and you get it out. We'll tell you when, at the time. Then you start walking. Easy as that. Doesn't even require a college degree. Put the money in your briefcase, go back out on the street, and just start walking. We take care of everything from there. No police, Nathan. If you smell of police, it'll get ugly. I detest violence. My kids can't watch TV because of the violence. Jack Ruby, Jack Idiot Ruby, has become the patron saint of America! I can hardly live in this country anymore because of the violence. You aren't the only one who is against this stinking war. It's a nightmare, it's a national disgrace. I will do everything in my power to avoid violence. But if I smell police, I am going to feel threatened and I am going to have to act like a threatened man. That means police stinking up Miami Beach and police stinking up New York."

"Friend," said Zuckerman, changing tactics, "too many grade-B movies. The lingo, the laugh, everything. Unoriginal. Unconvincing. Bad art."

"Haw, haw, haw. Could be, Zuck. Haw, haw, haw. Also real life. We'll be in touch to set the hour."

This time it wasn't the novelist who hung up.

3 Oswald, Ruby, et al.

Out of the front windows of his new apartment, Zuckerman could see down to the corner of his street to Frank E. Campbell, the Madison Avenue funeral parlor where they process for disposal the richest, most glamorous, and most celebrated of New York's deceased. On display in the chapel, the morning after Alvin Pepler and the threatening phone calls, lay a gangland figure, Nick "the Prince" Seratelli, who had died the day before from a cerebral hemorrhage—instead of in a spray of bullets—at a spaghetti house downtown. By nine in the morning a few bystanders had already collected around Campbell's doors to identify the entertainers, athletes, politicians, and criminals who would be arriving to get a last look at the Prince. Through the slats of his shutters, Zuckerman watched two mounted cops talking to three armed foot patrolmen guarding the funeral parlor's side door down the way from him on Eighty-first. There would be more out at the main entrance on Madison, and easily a dozen plainclothesmen moseying around the neighborhood. Here was the kind of police protection he had been thinking about all night for his mother.

This was only the third or fourth gala staged at Campbell's since Zuckerman had moved uptown. Ordinary, unnoteworthy funerals occurred every day, however, so that he had almost learned by now to ignore the cluster of mourners and the hearse by the side door across the street when he came out of the house in the morning. It wasn't easy, though, especially on mornings when the sun rolling over the East Side caught them full in the face like so many lucky vacationers on a Caribbean cruise ship; nor was it easy on mornings when the rain drummed down on their umbrellas as they waited for the funeral procession to begin, nor even on gray run-of-the-mill days, when it neither rains nor shines. No weather he'd come across yet made seeing somebody sealed up in a box something he could easily forget.

The caskets were trucked in during the day, unloaded with a forklift, then lowered in the freight elevator to the mortuary basement. Down, and down again, the first test-run. Flowers that had dropped off the wreaths going on to the cemetery or the crematorium were swept up by the uniformed black porter after the cortege bearing the body had moved out of sight. The dead petals the porter didn't get, the city sanitation machine caught among the curbside debris on the following Tuesday or Thursday. As for the dead bodies, they arrived on narrow stretchers, in dark sacks, generally after the streetlights came on. An ambulance, sometimes a station wagon, pulled into Campbell's reserved parking spot and the sack was whisked in through the side door. Over in seconds—yet during his first months uptown, it seemed to Zuckerman that he was always passing by in time to see it. Lights stayed on in the upper stories of the funeral home at all hours. No matter how late he went into the living room to turn off his own lamps, he saw theirs burning. And not because anyone was up reading or couldn't sleep. Lights that kept no one awake, except Zuckerman in his bed, remembering them.

At times, amid the crowd of mourners awaiting the pallbearers and the coffin, somebody would stare across at Zuckerman as he passed by. Because he was Zuckerman, or because he was staring at them? Couldn't tell, but as he preferred not to distract anyone at a time like that with either himself or his book, he learned within only weeks to master the shock of coming upon such a gathering virtually across from his front door the first thing each day, and, as though death left him cold, hurried on about the business of buying the morning paper and his onion roll.

He had been up all night, not only because of the lights burning at Campbell's. He was waiting to see if the kidnapper would call again or if the joke was over. At three a.m. he had nearly reached out from his bed and telephoned Laura. At four he nearly telephoned the police. At six he nearly called Miami Beach. At eight he got up and looked out the front window, and when he saw the cop on horseback outside the funeral home he thought of his father in the nursing home. He had been thinking of his father at three and four and six as well. He often did when he saw the lights burning all night at Campbell's. He was unable to get a song called "Tzena, Tzena" out of his head. They were a great family for whistling while they worked, and "Tzena, Tzena" his father had whistled for years, after putting in a decade with "Bei Mir Bist Du Schoen." "This song," Dr. Zuckerman told his family, "is going to win more hearts to the Jewish cause than anything before in the history of the world." The chiropodist even ran out to get it, maybe the fifth record he had bought in his life. Zuckerman was home for the Christmas vacation of his sophomore year, and "Tzena, Tzena" was played every night before dinner. "This is the song," Dr. Zuckerman said, "that will put the State of Israel on the map." Unfortunately, Nathan was beginning to learn about counterpoint in his humanities course, so when the father made the mistake at dinner of genially asking his older son's musical opinion, he was told that Israel's future would be determined by international power politics and not by feeding Gentiles "Jewish kitsch." Causing Dr. Zuckerman to pound the table: "That is where you are wrong! There is exactly where you fail to understand the feelings of the ordinary man!" They had disagreed all that Christmas, not only about the value of "Tzena, Tzena." But by the mid-sixties, when he played for Nathan the Barry Sisters singing the songs from *Fiddler on the Roof,* the struggle was about over. By then the father was in a wheelchair in Miami Beach, the older son a recognized writer long out of school, and after sitting down to listen to the show tunes straight through, Nathan told him they were terrific. "At the Temple," said his mother, "after the services last week, the cantor sang the title song for us. You could have heard a pin drop." Since Dr. Zuckerman's first stroke, he had begun attending Friday-night religious services with Zuckerman's mother. The first time in their lives. So that the rabbi who buried him wouldn't be a total stranger. Not that anybody had to say as much. "These Barry Sisters," his father announced, "and this record are going to do more for the Jews than anything since 'Tzena, Tzena.'" "You could be right," said Nathan. And why not? He was no longer a student in Humanities 2, the damage that he had done the Jewish cause by writing his first book was no longer one of his father's unshakable obsessions, and *Carnovsky* was still three years off.

Instead of calling Laura, the police, or Florida, he used

his head and at ten decided to phone André, who would know what to make of these threats. His gallant continental manner, his rippling silver hair, his Old World accent—all had earned him ages ago the mildly derisive *nom de guerre* "the Headwaiter"; but to those he did the business for, rather than those he gave it to, André Schevitz was more estimable than that. In addition to ministering to his international roster of novelists, André looked after the megalomania, alcoholism, satyriasis, and tax tragedies of fifteen world-famous film stars. He flew off at a moment's notice to hold their hands on location, and once every few months made it a point to call on little children around the country with mamas away making sagas in Spain or papas off in Liechtenstein tending to their dummy corporations. During the summer any child all but orphaned because of a domestic cataclysm headlined in the *National Enquirer* wound up spending school vacation with André and Mary in Southampton; on a hot August day it wasn't unusual to see two or three miniature replicas of the cinema's most photographed faces gobbling watermelon at the edge of the Schevitz pool. Zuckerman's first painful divorce, the one from Betsy nine years earlier, had been painlessly engineered for him at five-and-dime-store rates by André's (and Mrs. Rockefeller's) lawyer; two years back his life had been saved by André's society surgeon; and the scene of his convalescence from the burst appendix and peritonitis had been the Schevitz Southampton guest house: with a Schevitz maid and cook in attendance—and on weekends, his own Laura—he had snoozed on the sun deck, lolled in the pool, and regained the twenty pounds he'd lost during the month in the hospital. And had begun writing *Carnovsky.*

Oh, but those threats, those threats were just more ridiculousness—and he didn't need his agent to remind him. Zuckerman found a fresh composition book and, instead of phoning André, began to record what he could still recall of the previous day's business. Because this *was* his business: not buying and selling, but seeing and believing. Oppressive perhaps from a personal point of view, but from the point of view of business? My God, from the point of view of business, yesterday was wonderful! He should do business like that every day. *Didn't we get your teeth cleaned? Sharp new suits? A dermatologist? Alvin, we are not hardened criminals—we are in show business. We're so worried about you, he tells me, we've decided to pay for a psychiatrist for you. We want you to see Dr. Eisenberg until you have gotten over your neurosis and are yourself again. Absolutely, Schachtman says, I see Dr. Eisenberg, why shouldn't Alvin see Dr. Eisenberg?*

He wrote steadily for over an hour, every irate word of Pepler's deposition, and then, suddenly, broke into a sweat and telephoned André at his office to recount to him the details of the phone calls, right down to the haw, haw, haws.

"To resist all the temptations I strew in your path, this

I understand. To fight the way your life is going," said André, capitalizing, for the sake of the satire, on the Mitteleuropa inflections, "to be unable to accept what has happened to you, this I also understand. Even if it is you yourself who has kicked over your traces, what happens when you kick over your traces can take anybody by surprise. Especially a boy with your background. What with Papa telling you to be good, and Mama telling you to be nice, and the University of Chicago training you four years in Advanced Humanistic Decisions, well, what chance did you ever have to lead a decent life? To take you away to that place at sixteen! It's like stealing a wild little baby baboon from the branches of the trees, feeding him in the kitchen, letting him sleep in your bed and play with the light switch and wear little shirts and pants with pockets, and then, when he is big and hairy and full of himself, giving him his degree in Western Civilization and sending him back to the bush. I can just imagine what an enchanting little baboon you were at the University of Chicago. Pounding the seminar table, writing English on the blackboard, screaming at the class that they had it all wrong—you must have been all over the place. Rather like in this abrasive little book."

"What's your point, André? Someone is threatening to kidnap my mother."

"My point is that to turn a jungle baboon into a seminar baboon is a cruel, irreversible process. I understand why you won't ever be happy around the waterhole again.

But paranoia is something else. And my point for you, my question to you, is how far are you going to let paranoia take you before it takes you where it goes?"

"The question is how far the abrasive little book is going to take *them*."

"Nathan, who are 'they'? Nathan, you must do me a favor and stop going nuts."

"I had three phone calls last night from some madman threatening to kidnap my mother. Nuts it sounds, *but it happened*. What I am now trying to figure out is what to do in response that isn't nuts. I thought a worldly fellow with your admirable cynicism might have had some experience with this sort of thing."

"I can only tell you that I haven't. Among my clients are the richest and best-known stars in the world, but as far as I know, nothing like this has ever 'happened' to any of them."

"Nothing like this ever happened to me, either. That may account for why I sound the way I do."

"I understand that. But you have been sounding this way for some time. You have been sounding this way from the day it began. In all my years of experience with high-strung prima donnas, I have never seen anyone make such a fiasco of fame and fortune. I have seen all sorts of crazy indulgence, but never before indulgence in anything like this. To be chagrined by such good fortune. Why?"

"Because of the madmen who call me on the phone, for one."

"Then don't answer the phone. Don't sit there waiting by the phone, and that takes care of the phone. To take care of the bus, don't ride the bus. And while you're at it, stop eating in those filthy delicatessens. You are a rich man."

"Who says I eat in filthy delicatessens? The *News* or the *Post*?"

"I say so. And isn't it true? You buy greasy takeout chickens at these foul little barbecue holes and you eat them with your hands in that barren apartment. You hide out in Shloimie's Pastrami Haven, pretending to be harmless Mr. Nobody from Nowhere. And by now it is all beginning to lose its eccentric charm, Nathan, and is taking on a decidedly paranoiac aroma. What are you up to, anyway? Are you out to appease the gods? Are you trying to show them up in heaven and over at *Commentary* that you are only a humble, self-effacing yeshiva *bucher* and not the obstreperous author of such an indecent book? I know about all those index cards you carry around in your wallet: fortifying quotations from the great literary snobs about fame giving satisfaction only to mediocre vanities. Well, don't you believe it. There's a lot to be had out of life by a writer in your position, and not at Shloimie's, either. Those buses. To begin with, you should have a car with a driver, Nathan. Thomas Mann had a car with a driver."

"Where'd you hear that?"

"I didn't. I rode in it with him. You should have a girl

to answer your mail and run your errands for you. You should have somebody to carry your dirty things down Madison Avenue in a pillowcase—somebody instead of yourself. At least treat yourself to a laundry that picks up sackcloth and delivers."

"They lean on the bell when they pick up—it interrupts my concentration."

"A housekeeper should answer the bell. You should have someone to cook your meals and to shop for your groceries and to deal with the tradesmen at the door. You don't have to push a cart around Gristede's ever again."

"I do if I want to know what a pound of butter costs."

"Why would you want to know that?"

"André, Gristede's is where we poor writers go to lead a real life—don't take Gristede's away from me too. It's how I keep my finger on the pulse of the nation."

"You want to succeed at that, get to know what I know: the price of a pound of flesh. I am being serious. You should have a driver, a housekeeper, a cook, a secretary—"

"And where do I hide in that crowd? Where do I type?"

"Get a bigger place."

"I just got a bigger place. André, that is *more* ridiculousness, not less. I just moved in here. It's quiet, it's plenty big for me, and on East Eighty-first at five hundred a month, it's no slum."

"You should have a duplex at the United Nations Plaza."

"I don't *want* one."

"Nathan, you are no longer the egghead kid I plucked out of the pages of *Esquire*. You have achieved a success as only a handful of writers ever do—so stop acting like those who don't. First you lock yourself away in order to stir up your imagination, now you lock yourself away because you've stirred up theirs. Meanwhile, everybody in the world is dying to meet you. Trudeau was here and he wanted to meet you. Abba Eban was here and mentioned your name to me. Yves Saint Laurent is giving a big party and his office called for your number. But do I dare to give it? And would you even go?"

"Look, I already met Caesara. That should hold me for a while. By the way, tell Mary I received my Dear Juan letter from Havana. She can phone in the news to *Women's Wear Daily*. I'll send them a Xerox by messenger."

"At least Caesara got you out of that cell for one night. I wish I had another lovely lure like her. My dear boy, you live in that apartment, as far as I can tell, thinking about nothing but yourself from one day to the next. And when you even dare to go out into the street, you're worse. Everybody looks at you, everybody sidles up to you, everybody wants either to tie you to a bed or to spit in your eye. Everybody has you pegged for Gilbert Carnovsky, when what anybody with an ounce of brains should know is that you are really you. But if you recall, Nathan dear, being really you was what was driving you

crazy only a few short years ago. You told me so yourself. You felt stultified writing 'proper, responsible' novels.
You felt stultified living behind your 'drearily virtuous
face.' You felt stultified sitting in your chair every night
making notes for your files on another Great Book. 'How
much more life can I spend preparing for my final exam?
I'm too old to be writing term papers.' You felt stultified
calling Florida every Sunday like the good son, you felt
stultified signing stop-the-war petitions like the good citizen, you felt stultified most of all living with a do-gooder
like your wife. The whole country was going haywire
and you were still in your chair doing your homework.
Well, you have successfully conducted your novelistic
experiment and now that you are famous all over the
haywire country for being haywire yourself, you're
even more stultified than before. What is more, you are
outraged that everybody doesn't know how proper, responsible, and drearily virtuous you really are, and what a
great achievement it is for mankind that such a model of
Mature Adult Behavior could have given the reading
public a Gilbert Carnovsky. You set out to sabotage your
own moralizing nature, you set out to humiliate all your
dignified, high-minded gravity, and now that you've done
it, and done it with the relish of a real saboteur, now
you're humiliated, you idiot, because nobody aside from
you seems to see it as a profoundly moral and high-minded
act! 'They' misunderstand you. And as for those who do
understand you, people who've known you for five and

ten and fifteen years, you'll have nothing to do with them, either. As far as I can tell, you don't see a single one of your friends. People call me to ask what's happened to you. Your closest friends think you're out of town. Somebody called me up the other day to ask if it was true that you were in Payne Whitney."

"Oh, am I supposed to be in the bin now too?"

"Nathan, you are the decade's latest celebrity—people are going to say everything. The question I am asking is why you won't at least see old friends."

Simple. Because he couldn't sit complaining to them about becoming the decade's latest celebrity. Because being a poor misunderstood millionaire is not really a topic that intelligent people can discuss for very long. Not even friends. Least of all friends, and especially when they're writers. He didn't want them talking about him talking about his morning with the investment counselor and his night with Caesara O'Shea and how she jilted him for the Revolution. And that was all he could talk about, at least to himself. He was not fit company for anyone he considered a friend. He would get started on all the places where he no longer could show his face without causing a sensation, and soon enough he would make them into enemies. He would get started on the Rollmops King and the gossip columns and the dozen crazy letters a day, and who *could* listen? He would start talking to them about those suits. Six suits. Three thousand dollars' worth of suits to sit at home and write in. When he could

write naked, if need be; when he could sit there as he always had, in work shirt and chinos, perfectly content. With
three thousand dollars he could have bought one hundred
pairs of chinos and four hundred work shirts (he'd
worked it out). He could buy sixty pairs of Brooks
Brothers suede walking shoes of the kind he'd been wearing since he went off to Chicago. He could buy twelve
hundred pairs of Interwoven socks (four hundred blue,
four hundred brown, four hundred gray). With three
thousand dollars he could have clothed himself for life.
But instead there were now fittings with Mr. White twice
a week, discussions with Mr. White about padding the
shoulders and nipping the waist, and who could possibly listen to Zuckerman carrying on about such stuff?
He could hardly listen—but, alas, alone with himself, he
couldn't shut up. Better they should think he was in Payne
Whitney. Maybe he ought to be. Because there was also
the television—couldn't stop watching. Downtown on
Bank Street, all they saw regularly was the news. At seven
and again at eleven he and Laura used to sit together in
the living room to watch the fires in Vietnam: villages on
fire, jungles on fire, Vietnamese on fire. Then they went
back to their work on the night shift, she to her draft
dodgers, he to his Great Books. During his weeks alone,
however, Zuckerman had probably spent more hours by
the TV set than in all the years since they had begun to
broadcast test patterns back when he was finishing high
school. There was little else he could concentrate on, and

then there was the strangeness of sitting in your bathrobe on your Oriental rug eating a takeout barbecued chicken and hearing someone suddenly talking about *you*. He couldn't get over it. One night a pretty rock singer whom he'd never seen before told Johnny Carson about her one and "Thank God" only date with Nathan Zuckerman. She brought the house down describing the "gear" Zuckerman advised her to wear to dinner if she wanted "to turn him on." And just the previous Sunday he had watched three therapists sitting in lounge chairs on Channel 5 analyzing his castration complex with the program host. They all agreed that Zuckerman had a lulu. The following morning André's lawyer had gently to tell him that he couldn't sue for slander. "Your nuts, Nathan, are now in the public domain."

They were right in their way—he *was* in the bin.

"The threats, the threats, the *threats*. André," cried Zuckerman, "what about those threats? That is the subject here."

"Delivered as you described them the threats don't seem to me very serious, frankly. But then I am not you, with this sense you have that everything suddenly is beyond your control. If you are feeling the way you sound, then telephone the police and see what they say."

"But you think it's all a joke."

"I wouldn't be surprised."

"And if it isn't? If my mother winds up in the trunk of a car in the Everglades?"

"If this and if that. Do as I say. You want advice, I'm advising you. Phone the police."

"And what can they do? That's the next question."

"I have no idea what they can do when nothing actually has happened to anyone. My concern is defusing the persecution mania, Nathan. That is the job of a literary agent. I should like to restore in you some peace of mind."

"Which calling the police isn't likely to do. Call the police and it's as good as calling the city desk. Call the police and it'll be in Leonard Lyons by tomorrow, if not headlined on page one. PUG THREATENS PORN MOM. The kidnapping of Mrs. Carnovsky—that would really top off the sixties for them. Susskind will have to have three specialists in to think it through with him. 'Who in Our Sick Society Is Responsible?' Sevareid will tell us what it means to the Future of the Free World. Reston will write a column on the Breakdown of Values. If this thing happens, the torment to my mother will be nothing next to what the rest of the country is going to have to put up with."

"Ah, and this is a little more like your old amused self."

"Is it? My old amused self? Wouldn't recognize him. Who is Sleepy Lagoon, while we're at it? What is this in *Variety* about a million dollars for the sequel?"

"Bob Lagoon. I would wait before spending his million."

"But he exists."

"Off and on."

"And Marty Paté? Who is he?"

"Don't know."

"Never heard of a producer on East Sixty-second Street named Marty Paté?"

"As in *'de foie gras'*? Not yet. Why do you ask?"

No, best not to go into that. "What about Gayle Gibraltar?"

André laughed. "Sounds like you're writing a sequel right now. Sounds like some figment of Carnovsky's imagination."

"No, not Carnovsky's. What I ought to do is get a bodyguard. For my mother. Don't you think?"

"Well, if that's what's necessary for your sense of security—"

"Only it's not going to give her much of one, is it? I hate to think of her sitting across from him when he takes off his coat to eat his lunch and she sees the shoulder holster."

"Then why not restrain yourself, Nathan? Why not wait to see if this character phones again? If there is, in fact, no call to make arrangements about extortion money, so much for that. It was somebody's idea of a good time. If there is such a call—"

"Then I notify the police, the F.B.I., and whatever the papers print—"

"Exactly."

"If and when it turns out to be nothing, she'll have been protected just the same."

"And you'll feel that you did the right thing by her."

"Only there it'll be in the papers. Then the bright idea will dawn on some maniac to take a crack at it himself."

"You worry too much about maniacs."

"But they live. The maniacs live better than we do. They flourish. It's their world, André. You should read my mail."

"Nathan, you take everything too seriously, starting with your mail and ending with yourself. Maybe it's starting with yourself and ending with the mail. Maybe that's all the kidnapper is trying to tell you."

"Doing it for my education, is he? You make it sound as though it might even be you."

"I'd like to say that it was. I wish I were clever enough to have thought of it."

"I wish you were too. I wish somebody were, other than whoever it is."

"Or isn't."

As soon as he hung up, Zuckerman began searching for the card presented him by Caesara O'Shea's chauffeur. He should call to ask them to recommend an armed guard in Miami. He should fly to Miami himself. He should telephone the Miami field office of the F.B.I. He should stop eating in delicatessens. He should furnish his apartment. He should unpack his books. He should take his money out of his shoe and give it to Wallace to invest. He should forget about Caesara and get a new girl. There were hundreds of not-so-crazy Julias out there just waiting to take him to Switzerland and show him the chocolate factories. He should stop buying chickens from takeout counters. He should meet U Thant. He should stop taking seriously all the talk-show de Tocquevilles. He should stop taking seriously the cranks on the phone. He should stop taking his mail seriously. He should stop taking himself seriously. He should stop taking buses. And he should call André back and tell him for God's sake not to tell Mary anything about the kidnapper—otherwise it would end up in "Suzy Says"!

But instead he sat back down at his desk and for another hour recorded in his composition book everything the kidnapper had said. In spite of his worries, he was smiling to himself as he saw on paper what he'd heard the night before on the phone. He was reminded of a story about Flaubert coming out of his study one day and seeing a cousin of his, a young married woman, tending to her children, and Flaubert saying, ruefully, *"Ils sont dans le vrai."* A working title, Zuckerman thought, and recorded in the white window of the composition book cover the words *Dans le Vrai*. These composition books Zuckerman used for his notes were bound in the stiff covers of marbled black-and-white design that generations of Americans envision still in bad dreams about lessons unlearned. On the inside of the front cover, facing the blue ruled lines of the first page, was the chart where the student is to enter his class program, period by period, for the school week. Here Zuckerman composed his subtitle, printing in block letters across the rows of rectangles provided for the subject, room, and instructor: "Or, How I Made a Fiasco of Fame and Fortune in My Spare Time."

" 'Tzena, Tzena,' 1950."

Zuckerman was waiting for the light to change on the corner across from Campbell's. The title had been announced from just behind him. Unknown to himself, he had been whistling, and not only out on the street but through much of the morning. That same little song, again and again.

"Adapted from an Israeli popular tune, English lyrics by Mitchell Parish, Decca record by Gordon Jenkins and the Weavers."

There to inform him was Alvin Pepler. The day was fresh and bright, but Pepler was still in black raincoat and hat. Dark glasses, however, to top things off this morning. Had somebody poked him in the eye since last night, some shorter-fused celebrity than Zuckerman? Or were the dark glasses to make him look like a celebrity to himself? Or was the new pitch that he was, also, unfortunately, blind? SIGHTLESS QUIZ CONTESTANT. PLEASE GIVE.

"Good morning," said Zuckerman, backing away.

"Up early for the great event?"

One-liner, delivered with comic grin. Zuckerman chose not to reply.

"Imagine, you go out for a coffee break and run smack into Prince Seratelli lying in state."

You go for a coffee break on Sixty-second Street and run into Seratelli on Eighty-first?

"That's why I envy you New Yorkers," said Pepler. "You get into an elevator—this actually happened to me, my first day over here—and there, sharp as a tack, Victor Borge! You run out for the late paper, and who jumps from a taxi right at your feet? At midnight? Twiggy! You walk out of the bathroom in a little delicatessen, and sitting there eating is you! Victor Borge, Twiggy, and you—just in my first forty-eight hours. The cop on the horse told me that Sonny Liston is supposed to show." He pointed to the police and the onlookers gathered at the main entrance to the funeral home. Also on hand was a TV camera and crew. "But so far," said Pepler, "you haven't missed a thing."

Not a word about Zuckerman's disappearance outside Baskin-Robbins the previous evening. Or about the phone calls.

Zuckerman assumed Pepler had followed him. Dark glasses for dark intrigue. The possibility had crossed his mind before he'd even left the house: Pepler in a doorway along the street, hiding and ready to pounce. But he couldn't sit there waiting for the phone to ring just because the kidnapper had told him to. That *was* nuts. Especially if the kidnapper was this crackpot.

"What else do you know from 1950?"

"Pardon?"

"What other songs," Pepler asked him, "from 1950? Can you name me the Top Fifteen?"

Followed or not, Zuckerman had to smile. "You got me there. From 1950 I couldn't name the Top Ten."

"Want to hear which they were? All fifteen?"

"I have to be going."

"To begin with, that's the year there are three with 'cake' in the title. 'Candy and Cake.' 'If I Knew You Were Comin' I'd 'Ave Baked a Cake.' And 'Sunshine Cake.' Then, alphabetically"—for this he planted both feet firmly on the pavement—" 'Autumn Leaves,' 'A Bushel and a Peck,' 'C'est Si Bon,' 'It's a Lovely Day Today,' 'Music, Music, Music,' 'My Heart Cries for You,' 'Rag Mop,' 'Sam's Song,' 'The Thing,' 'Tzena, Tzena'—which I began with—'Wilhelmina,' and 'You, Wonderful You.' Fifteen. And Hewlett Lincoln couldn't have named you five. Without the answers in his pocket, he couldn't have named *one*. No, with the All-Time American Hit Parade, it was Alvin Pepler who was Mr. Unstoppable. Until they stopped me to get the goy on."

"I'd forgotten 'Rag Mop,' " said Zuckerman.

Pepler laughed his hearty appreciative laugh. God, he certainly seemed harmless enough. Dark glasses? A tourist indulgence. Going native. "Whistle something else," Pepler said. "Anything. As far back in time as you want."

"I really have to be off."

"Please, Nathan. Just to test me out. To prove to you I'm on the level. That I am Pepler in the flesh!"

Well, the war was on, the sirens had sounded, and his father, the street's chief air-raid warden, was out of the house in the prescribed sixty seconds. Henry, Nathan, and their mother sat at the rickety bridge table in the basement, playing casino by candlelight. Only a drill, not the real thing, never the real thing in America, but of course, if you were a ten-year-old American you never knew. They could miss Newark Airport and hit the Zuckerman house. But soon the All Clear sounded and Dr. Zuckerman came whistling down the cellar stairs in his warden hat, playfully shining his flashlight into the boys' eyes. No plane had been sighted, no bombs had been dropped, the decrepit Sonnenfelds down the street had pulled their blackout shades on their own, and neither of his sons had as yet written a book or touched a girl, let alone divorced one. So why shouldn't he be whistling? He turned on the lights and kissed them each in turn. "Deal me in," he said.

The song his father whistled descending their cellar stairs Nathan whistled now for Pepler. Instead of running.

Three notes was all he had to deliver. " 'I'll Be Seeing You,' 1943. Twenty-four appearances on the Hit Parade," said Pepler, "ten in the Number One spot. Records by

Frank Sinatra and by Hildegarde. The Top Fifteen, 1943—ready, Nathan?"

Oh, was he ready. *Dans le vrai,* and it's about time too. André was right to give it to him: you lock yourself away to stir up your imagination, then you lock yourself away because you've stirred up theirs. What kind of novels is that going to get you? If the high life with Caesara hadn't worked out, then what about the low? Where is your curiosity? Where is your old amused self? Against whom have you committed what punishable offense that you should go skulking around like a fugitive from justice? You are not in the virtue racket! Never were! Great mistake ever to think so! That is what you have escaped—into the stupendous *vrai!* "Shoot, Alvin." Reckless locution, but Zuckerman didn't care. Reckless deliberately. Enough taking cover from his own eruption. Receive what has been given! Accept what you inspire! Welcome the genies released by that book! That goes for the money, that goes for the fame, and that goes for this Angel of Manic Delights!

Who was off and running anyway:

" 'Comin' in on a Wing and a Prayer.' 'I Couldn't Sleep a Wink Last Night.' 'I'll Be Seeing You.' 'It's Love, Love, Love.' 'I've Heard That Song Before.' 'A Lovely Way to Spend an Evening.' 'Mairzy Doats.' 'Oh, What a Beautiful Mornin'.' 'Mornin',' by the way, not 'Morning,' as most people think—Hewlett Lincoln being Number One.

Though nobody of course called him on it. Not on that show. 'People Will Say We're in Love.' 'Pistol Packin' Mama.' 'Sunday, Monday or Always.' 'They're Either Too Young or Too Old.' 'Tico Tico.' 'You Keep Coming Back Like a Song.' 'You'll Never Know.' Fifteen." He relaxed, sagged a little, in fact, remembering what Hewlett had gotten away with on that show.

"How do you do it, Alvin?"

Pepler removed his dark glasses, and rolling his dark eyes (which no one had yet blackened), made a joke. " 'It's Magic,' " he confessed.

Zuckerman obliged. "Doris Day. Nineteen—forty-six."

"Close," cried Pepler gaily, "close, but forty-eight is the correct answer. Awfully sorry, Nathan. Better luck next time. Words by Sammy Cahn, music by Jule Styne. Introduced in the movie *Romance on the High Seas*. Warner Brothers. With Jack Carson, and of course the Divine Dodo, Miss Doris Day."

He had Zuckerman laughing away now. "Alvin, you're amazing."

To which Pepler rapidly replied, " 'You're Sensational.' 'You're Devastating.' 'You're My Everything.' 'You're Nobody Till Somebody Loves You.' 'You're Breaking My Heart.' 'You're Getting to Be a Habit with Me.' 'You're—' "

"This, this is quite a show. Oh, this is heaven, really." He couldn't stop laughing. Not that Pepler seemed to mind.

" '—a Grand Old Flag.' 'You're a Million Miles from

Nowhere (When You're One Little Mile from Home).'
'You're My Thrill.' Do I stop?" Agleam with perspiration, about as happy as any adrenalin addict could ever
be, he asked, "Do I stop, kid, or do you want more?"

"No," groaned Zuckerman, "no more," but oh, was it
lovely to be having a good time. And out-of-doors! In
public! Sprung! Free! Released from his captivity by
Pepler! "Take it easy on me. Please, please," Zuckerman
whispered, "there's a funeral across the street."

"Street," announced Pepler. " 'The Streets of New
York.' Across. 'Across the Alley from the Alamo.' Funeral.
Let me think that through. Please. 'Please Don't Talk
About Me When I'm Gone.' More. 'The More I See You.'
No. 'No Other Love.' Now funeral. No, I stake my repu-
tation on it. There is no song in the history of American
popular songs with the word 'funeral' in it. For obvious
reasons."

Priceless. The *vrai*. You can't beat it. Even richer in
pointless detail than the great James Joyce.

"Correction," said Pepler. " 'The More I See *of* You.'
From the motion picture *Diamond Horseshoe*. Twentieth
Century-Fox. 1945. Sung by Dick Haymes."

No stopping him now. But why should anyone want to?
No, you don't run away from phenomena like Alvin Pep-
ler, not if you're a novelist with any brains you don't.
Think how far Hemingway went to look for a lion.
Whereas Zuckerman had just stepped out the door. Yes,
sir, box up the books! Out of the study and into the streets!

At one with the decade at last! Oh, what a novel this guy would make! All that flies, sticks. He's glue, mental fly-paper, can't forget a thing. All the interfering static, he collects. What a *novelist* this guy would make! Already is one! Paté, Gibraltar, Perlmutter, Moshe Dayan—that is the novel of which he is the hero! From the daily papers and the dregs of memory, that is the novel that he conjures up! Can't say it lacks conviction, whatever may be missing in the way of finesse. Look at him go!

" 'You'll Never Know,' Decca, 1943. 'Little White Lies,' Decca, 1948." Dick Haymes's two best-selling records, according to Pepler. Whom Zuckerman saw no reason not to believe.

"Perry Como," Zuckerman asked. "*His* best-sellers."

" 'Temptation.' 'A Hubba Hubba Hubba.' 'Till the End of Time.' All RCA Victor, 1945. 1946, 'Prisoner of Love.' 1947, 'When You Were Sweet Sixteen.' 1949—"

Zuckerman had forgotten the kidnapper completely. For the moment he forgot everything, all his cares and woes. They were imaginary anyway, no?

Pepler was on to Nat "King" Cole—" 'Darling, Je Vous Aime Beaucoup,' 1955; 'Ramblin' Rose,' 1962"—when Zuckerman discovered the microphone an inch from his mouth. Then the portable camera aimed from atop somebody's shoulder.

"Mr. Zuckerman, you're here to pay your respects this morning to Prince Seratelli—"

"I am?"

The dark-haired reporter, a handsome and powerful-looking fellow, Zuckerman now recognized from one of the local news shows. "Is it," asked the reporter, "as a friend of the deceased or of the family?"

The comedy was too much. Oh, what a morning. "Oh, What a Beautiful Mornin'!" *Oklahoma!* Rodgers and Hammerstein. Even he knew that one.

Laughing, waving a hand in the air to call them off, Zuckerman said, "No, no, just passing by." He gestured toward Pepler. "With a friend."

All too distinctly he heard the friend clear his throat. The dark glasses were off, the chest had expanded, and he looked ready to remind the world of all it had caused him to suffer. Zuckerman saw the crowd at Campbell's turning in their direction.

A voice from across the way. *"Who?"*

"Koufax! Koufax!"

"Mistake, mistake." Zuckerman was a little on the fervent side now, but the aggressive reporter seemed at last to have realized his error himself and signaled to the cameraman to stop.

"Sorry, sir," he said to Zuckerman.

"That ain't Koufax, idiot."

"Who is it?"

"Nobody."

"Awfully sorry," said the reporter, apologetically smiling to Pepler now as the crew moved swiftly back to where the real action was getting underway. A limousine had arrived across the street. Everyone by the doorway tried to see if it was Sonny Liston inside.

"That," said Pepler, pointing after the TV reporter, "was J. K. Cranford. The All-American from Rutgers."

A mounted policeman had by now approached the two of them, and was leaning down from his horse to get a good look. "Hey, Mac," he said to Zuckerman, "who are you?"

"Nobody to worry about." Zuckerman patted the breast pocket of his corduroy jacket to show that he wasn't packing a gat.

The cop was willing to be amused; not nearly so much as Zuckerman's sidekick. "I mean, who are you famous?" he asked. "You were just on the TV, right?"

"No, no," explained Zuckerman. "They had the wrong guy."

"You weren't on Dinah Shore last week?"

"Not me, officer. I was home in bed."

Pepler just couldn't let this big tough cop up on a horse make any more of a fool of himself. "You don't know who this guy is? This is Nathan Zuckerman!"

The cop looked down with bemused boredom at the man in the dark glasses and the black rain gear.

"The *writer*," Pepler informed him.

"Oh, yeah?" said the cop. "What'd he write?"

"You serious? What did Nathan Zuckerman write?" With such triumph did Pepler announce the title of

Zuckerman's fourth book that the powerful sleek horse, trained though it was for civil disorder, reared sharply back and had to be reined in.

"Never heard of it," the cop replied and, swinging around, crossed handsomely back to Campbell's with the light.

Pepler, with disdain: "It's the horses they must mean are New York's finest."

Together they looked across to where All-American J. K. Cranford was interviewing a little man who had just popped out of a taxi. Manuel Somebody, Pepler said. The jockey. Pepler was surprised that he had arrived without his glamorous wife, the dancer.

After the jockey, a silver-haired gentleman, staidly dressed in a dark suit and vest. To Cranford's questions, he mournfully shook his head. Wasn't talking. "Who's he?" Zuckerman asked.

A Mob lawyer, he was told, recently released from a federal penitentiary. He looked to Zuckerman, what with the deep tan, to have recently been released from the Bahamas.

For the next few minutes Pepler identified the mourners as each was accosted by Cranford and his crew.

"You are something, Alvin."

"You think so—from *this?* You should have seen me on 'Smart Money.' This is just a *sample.* Hewlett *needed* the fix, the fake. When Schachtman came around on Sundays to deliver the answers, half the time I had to correct him, where they had something wrong. If I see a face, that's it. I know the face of anybody in the world who has ever been in the papers, whether it's a cardinal who ran for Pope or some stewardess from Belgium who went down in a crash. With my memory, it's indelible, it's there forever. I can't forget it even if I wanted to. You should have seen me at my height, Nathan, what I was like for those three weeks. I lived from Thursday to Thursday. 'He's terrifying, he knows everything.' That's how they would introduce me on the show. To them it was just more crapola to feed the idiot audience. The tragedy is that it happened to be true. And what I didn't know, I could learn. You only had to show it to me, you just had to push the right button and out came a flood of information. I could tell you, for example, everything in history that ever happened with the number 98 in it. I still can. Everybody knows 1066, but do they know 1098? Everybody knows 1492, but do they know 1498? Savonarola burned at the stake in Florence, first German pawnshop established at Nuremberg, Vasco da Gama discovers sea route to India. But why go on? What good did it do me in the end? 1598: Shakespeare writes *Much Ado about Nothing,* Korean Admiral Visunsin invents ironclad warships. 1698: Paper manufacturing begins in North America, Leopold of Anhalt-Dessau introduces goose-stepping and iron ramrods in the Prussian army. 1798: Casanova dies, Battle of Pyramids makes Napoleon master of Egypt. I could go on all day. All night. But what will it get me?

What good is all the learning if it only goes to waste? At last people in New Jersey were beginning to have a respect for knowledge, for history, for the real facts of life instead of their own stupid, narrow, prejudiced opinions. Because of me! And now, now? You know where I should be now, by all rights? Across the street. I should be J. K. Cranford!"

So hungrily did he look to Zuckerman for confirmation that there was nothing to say in reply but "I don't see why not."

"You *don't?*"

And to that impassioned plea? "Why not?" replied Zuckerman.

"Oh, Jesus, would you do me a favor, Nathan? Would you spend one minute reading something I wrote? Would you give me your candid opinion? It would mean the world to me. Not my book, something else. Something new."

"What?"

"Well, literary criticism, actually."

Gently. "You didn't tell me you were a literary critic too."

Another Zuckerman one-liner, which Pepler accorded its due. Dared even to counter with one of his own. "I thought you already knew. I thought that's why last night you took it on the lam." But then added, when Zuckerman remained sternly silent, "I'm only kidding you back, Nathan. I realized when I came out, you had business, your meeting, you had to run. So you know me: I ate your ice cream too. And paid for it all night. No, don't worry, I'm no critic. I have my likes and dislikes, I have my ulcer, but I'm no critic, not in the official sense. However, I did hear yesterday about the big shake-up at the *Times*. This is ancient history to you, but I only found out late last night."

"What shake-up?"

"The drama critic is going to get the boot, and probably the book reviewer too. It's been a long time coming."

"Yes?"

"You didn't know?"

"No."

"*Really?* Well, I heard from Mr. Perlmutter. He's in with Sulzberger, the owner. He knows the whole family. They belong to the same congregation."

Perlmutter? Mythical gentlemanly father of the mythical producer Paté? Knows Sulzberger too? This novel is some novel.

"So you're going to try for the job," said Zuckerman.

Pepler colored. "No, no, not at all. It just got me thinking. To see if I could do it. 'I'll study and get ready, and maybe the chance will come.' Strange, even to me, that I haven't become a cynic after all I've been through, that I am still this sucker for the Land of Opportunity. But how could I feel otherwise? I know this country inside out. I served this country in two wars. It isn't just popular songs —it's everything. It's sports, it's old-time radio, it's slang, proverbs, commercials, famous ships, the Constitution, great battles, longitudes and latitudes—you name it, and if it's Americana, I know it cold. And *without* the answers in my pocket. With them in my *head*. I believe in this country. I believe in it because for one thing it is a country where a man can fight back from the most ignominious defeat, if only he perseveres. If only he doesn't lose faith in himself. Look at history. Look at Nixon. Isn't that something, that survival story? I have fifteen pages on that fake in my book. Likewise the great shit slinger, Johnson. Now, where would Lyndon Johnson have been without Lee Harvey Oswald? Peddling real estate in the Senate cloakroom."

Oswald? Had Alvin Pepler just mentioned Lee Harvey Oswald? On the phone last night, hadn't his caller referred in passing to Ruby, "Jack Idiot Ruby," as America's new patron saint? And alluded to Sirhan Sirhan? *We had a great leader in Robert Kennedy and that crazy Arab bastard shot him.* It was all in Zuckerman's notes.

Time to go.

But what danger was there? Weren't there cops everywhere? But weren't they also there in Dallas, for all the good that did the President?

Oh, and was his position in America now commensurate with the Presidency, the author of *Carnovsky?*

"—my book review."

"Yes?" He'd lost the thread. His heartbeat had quickened too.

"I only began writing at midnight last night."

After your last phone call, thought Zuckerman. Yes, yes, the man before me is my mother's kidnapper. Who else?

"I haven't had time to get to the novel itself. These are simply first impressions. If they sound too cerebral, well, I realize that. It's just that I'm bending over backward while I'm writing not to say in print what of course is no great secret, at least to me. That in many ways that book is the story of my life no less than yours."

So the review was of Zuckerman's book, of all books. Time to go, all right. Forget Oswald and Ruby. When the lion comes up to Hemingway with his review of "The Short Happy Life of Francis Macomber," time to leave the jungle for home.

"I don't mean Newark alone. It goes without saying how much that meant personally to me. I mean . . . the hang-ups. The psychological ones," he said, flushing, "of a nice Jewish boy. I guess everybody has identified with that book in his own way. That's what has made it such a smash. What I mean is that if I ever had the talent to write a novel, well, *Carnovsky* would have been it."

Zuckerman looked at his watch. "Alvin, I've got to be off."

"But my review."

"Send it, why don't you." Out of the streets and into the study. Time to unbox the books.

"But here, it's here." Pepler extracted the small spiral

notebook from an inside breast pocket. Instantly he found the page and handed it to Zuckerman to read.

There was a mailbox at Zuckerman's back. Pepler had pinned him up against the mailbox, just as he had the evening before. The evening before! *The man is mad. And fixed on me. Who is he behind those dark glasses? Me! He thinks he's me!*

Suppressing the impulse to drop the notebook into the mailbox and just walk off, a free celebrity, he looked down and he read. Been reading all his life. Really, what danger was there?

"The Marcel Proust of New Jersey" was the title of Pepler's review.

"All I have so far is my opening paragraph," he explained. "But if in your opinion I am off on the right foot, then tonight I'll finish it up at Paté's. Friday Perlmutter can show it to Sulzberger."

"I see."

Pepler saw too—Zuckerman's incredulity. And rushed to reassure him. "Bigger jerks than me review books, Nathan."

Well, on that he was not going to get an argument. Pepler's one-liner made Zuckerman laugh aloud. And Zuckerman was no enemy of laughs, as the fans would attest. So, up against the mailbox, he plunged in. One more page wouldn't kill him.

The handwriting was minute, fussy, meticulous, anything but seething. Nor was the style the man, either.

Fiction is not autobiography, yet all fiction, I am convinced, is in some sense rooted in autobiography, though the connection to actual events may be tenuous indeed, even nonexistent. We are, after all, the total of our experiences, and experience includes not only what we in fact do but what we privately imagine. An author cannot write about what he does not know and the reader must grant him his material, yet there are dangers in writing so closely on the heels of one's own immediate experience: a lack of toughness, perhaps; a tendency to indulgence; an urge to justify the author's ways to men. Distance, on the other hand, either blurs experience or heightens it. For most of us it is mercifully blurred; but for writers, if they can be restrained from spilling the beans before they are digested, it is heightened.

Before Zuckerman could even speak—not that he was in any hurry to—Pepler was explaining his methodology. "I discuss the autobiographical problem before I get to the contents of the book. That I'll do tonight. It's all worked out in my mind. What I am trying is to begin with my literary theory, to create a mini-version of my own of *What Is Art?* by Leo Tolstoy, first published in English translation in 1898. What's wrong?" he said, when Zuckerman handed the notebook back to him.

"Nothing. It's fine. Good beginning."

"You don't believe that." He opened the notebook and looked at his own handwriting, so neat, so readable, so determinedly everything that Teacher could least expect from the big ungainly boy at the back of the room. "What's wrong with it? You've got to tell me. I don't want Sulzberger to read it if it stinks. I want the truth. I have been fighting and suffering for the truth all my life. Please, no sweet talk and no crapola, either. What's wrong? So I can learn, so I can improve myself and recover my rightful place!"

No, he hadn't plagiarized it. Not that it made any difference, but evidently he had cooked up this porridge all by himself, one eye on *The New York Times,* the other on Leo Tolstoy. At midnight, after the last villainous haw, haw, haw. *I will do everything in my power to avoid violence, but if I feel threatened I am going to have to act like a threatened man.* That was what was down in *Zuckerman's* notebook.

"As I say, it's not bad, not at all."

"It is! You know it is! Only tell me *why*. How will I learn if you don't tell me why!"

"Well," said Zuckerman, relenting, "I suppose I wouldn't call the writing laconic, Alvin."

"You wouldn't?"

He shook his head.

"Is that bad?"

Zuckerman tried to sound thoughtful. "No, of course it's not 'bad' . . . "

"But it's not good. Okay. All right. What about my

ideas, what I want to communicate. The writing I can polish in the next draft, when I have the time. The writing I can get Miss Diamond to fix, if you say that's what it needs. But surely the ideas, the ideas themselves . . ."

"The ideas," said Zuckerman somberly, as the notebook was handed to him again. Across the street an elderly woman was being interviewed by J. K. Cranford instead of by Alvin Pepler. Gaunt, handsome, supported by a cane. Seratelli's widow? Seratelli's mother? Would that I were that old lady, thought Zuckerman. Anything but to have to discuss these "ideas."

Fiction, Zuckerman silently read, *is not autobiography, yet all fiction, I am convinced, is in some sense rooted in autobiography, though the connection to actual events . . .*

"Forget the writing for now," Pepler told him. "This time just read it through for the thoughts."

Zuckerman looked blindly at the page. Heard the lion saying to Hemingway, "Just read it through for the thoughts."

"I read it for both already." He put a hand on Pepler's chest and gently pushed him back. Not the best idea, he knew, but what else could he do? This enabled him to step away from the mailbox. He handed back the notebook yet again. Pepler looked as though he'd been pole-axed.

"And?"

"And what?" said Zuckerman.

"The truth! This is my *life* we're talking about, my chance at a second chance. I must have the truth!"

"Well, the truth is"—but seeing the perspiration coursing down Pepler's face, he thought better of it, and concluded—"it's probably fine for the papers."

"But? There's a big but in your voice, Nathan. But *what?*"

Zuckerman counted the cops with pistols outside Frank Campbell's. On foot, four. On horseback, two. "Well, I don't think you have to go into the desert and stand on a pillar to come up with these 'thoughts.' In my opinion. Since you ask for it."

"Whooff." Feverishly he began tapping the notebook against his open palm. "You shoot from the hip all right. Whew. That book of yours doesn't come from nowhere, that's for sure. The satire, I mean. Wow."

"Alvin, listen to me. Sulzberger could be crazy about it. I'm sure he and I have different criteria entirely. This shouldn't discourage you from letting Perlmutter try him."

"Nah," he said despondently. "When it comes to writing, it's you who's the authority." As though plunging a knife into his chest, he shoved the notebook back in his pocket.

"Not everybody would agree there."

"Nah, nah, don't pull the little-me stuff. Don't give me the humble crap. We know who's tops in his field and who isn't." Whereupon he drew the notebook out again and began fiercely slapping at it with his free hand.

"What about when I say the writer should be restrained from spilling the beans before they are digested? What about *that*?"

Zuckerman the satirist remained silent.

"That stinks too?" asked Pepler. "Don't condescend to me, *tell* me!"

"Of course it doesn't 'stink.' "

"But?"

"But it's straining, isn't it, for an effect?" As serious and uncondescending a man of letters as there could ever be, Zuckerman said, "I wonder if it's worth the effort."

"There's where you're wrong. It was no strain at all. It just came to me. In those words. It's the only line here that *isn't* erased, not one word."

"Then maybe that's the problem."

"I see." Pepler nodded vigorously because of what he saw. "For me, if it comes easy it's no good, and if it comes hard it's also no good."

"I'm only talking about this line."

"I see-ee-ee-eee," he said, ominously. "But that's definitely the worst, the bottom, the limit, this line about spilling the beans."

"Sulzberger could see it differently."

"Fuck Sulzberger! I'm not asking Sulzberger! I'm asking you! And what you have told me is the following. One, the writing stinks. Two, the thoughts stink. Three, my best line stinks worst of all. What you have told me is that ordinary mortals like me shouldn't even dare to write about your book to begin with. Isn't that what it adds up to, *on the basis of one paragraph of a first draft?*"

"Why, no."

"Why, no." Pepler was mimicking him. He had removed his dark glasses to make a prissy face to show to Zuckerman. "Why, no."

"Don't turn nasty, Alvin. You wanted the truth, after all."

"After all. After all."

"Look," said Zuckerman, "you want the *whole* truth?"

"Yes!" Eyes big, eyes bulging, eyes asizzle in a glowing red face. "Yes! But the truth *unbiased,* that's what I want! Unbiased by the fact that you only wrote that book because you could! Because of having every break in life there is! While the ones who didn't obviously couldn't! Unbiased by the fact that those hang-ups you wrote about happen to be mine, and that you knew it—that you stole it!"

"I did what? Stole what?"

"From what my Aunt Lottie told your cousin Essie that she told to your mother that she told to you. About me. About my past."

Oh, was it time to go!

The light was red. Would it never be green again when he needed it? With no further criticism to make or instruction to give, Zuckerman turned to leave.

"Newark!" Pepler, behind him, delivered the word straight to the eardrum. "What do you know about

Newark, Mama's Boy! I read that fucking book! To you it's Sunday chop suey downtown at the Chink's! To you it's being Leni-Lenape Indians at school in the play! To you it's Uncle Max in his undershirt, watering the radishes at night! And Nick Etten at first for the Bears! Nick Etten! Moron! *Moron!* Newark is a nigger with a knife! Newark is a whore with the syph! Newark is junkies shitting in your hallway and everything burned to the ground! Newark is dago vigilantes hunting jigs with tire irons! Newark is bankruptcy! Newark is ashes! Newark is rubble and filth! Own a car in Newark and then you'll find out what Newark's all about! Then you can write *ten* books about Newark! They slit your throat for your radial tires! They cut off both balls for a Bulova watch! And your dick for the fun of it, if it's white!"

The light went green. Zuckerman made for the mounted policeman. "You! Whining about Mama back in Newark and how she wouldn't wipe your ass for you three times a day! Newark is finished, idiot! Newark is barbarian hordes and the Fall of Rome! But what the hell would you know up on the hoity-toity East Side of Manhattan? You fuck up Newark and you steal my life—"

Past the prancing horse, the gaping crowd, past J. K. Cranford and his camera crew ("Hi, there, Nathan"), past the uniformed porter, and into the funeral parlor.

The large foyer looked like a Broadway theater at open-ing-night intermission: backers and burghers in their finest, and conversation bubbling, as though the first act had been a million laughs and the show on its way to being a hit.

He made for an empty corner, and one of the young funeral directors immediately started toward him through the crowd. Zuckerman had seen the fellow around, usually outside in the afternoon, talking through the cab window of a truck with the casket deliveryman. One evening he'd caught sight of him, dragging on a cigarette and with his tie undone, holding open the side door for the arrival of a corpse. When the lead stretcher-bearer stumbled on the doorsill, the body stirred slightly in its sack and Zuckerman had thought of his father.

For the lying-in-state of Prince Seratelli, the young funeral director wore a carnation and a morning coat. Strong jaw, athletic build, the voice a countertenor's. "Mr. Zuckerman?"

"Yes?"

"Anything I can do for you, sir?"

"No, no, thank you. Just paying my respects."

He nodded. Whether he bought it was another matter. Zuckerman unshaven didn't look that respectful.

"If you prefer, sir, when you're ready to leave, you can depart through the rear."

"No, no. Only collecting myself. I'll be fine."

Eyeing the door, Zuckerman waited it out with the mobsters and the ex-cons and the other celebrities. You

would think he actually *was* being stalked by an Oswald.
That he *was* a Kennedy, or a Martin Luther King. But
wasn't he just that to Pepler? And what was Oswald,
before he pulled the trigger and made it big in the papers?
And not on the book page, either. Any less affronted, or
benighted, or aggrieved? Any less batty or more impressive? Motivated any more "meaningfully"? No! Bang
bang, you're dead. There was all the meaning the act was
ever meant to have. You're you, I'm me, and for that and
that alone you die. Even the professional killers with
whom he now was rubbing elbows were less to be feared.
Not that it was necessarily in his interest to hang around
them much longer, either. Unshaven, in a worn corduroy suit and a turtleneck sweater and battered suede
shoes, he could easily be taken for a nosy newsman rather
than someone still studying for his final exam. Especially
as he was busily taking notes on the back of a Frank E.
Campbell brochure, while waiting for the coast to clear.
Another writer with his urgent "thoughts."

> Remembrance of Hits Past. My pickle his madeleine. Why
> isn't P. Proust of the Pops instead of a file cabinet? The
> uneventfulness of writing, he couldn't put up with it.
> Who can? Maniacal memory without maniacal desire for
> comprehension. Drowning without detachment. Memory
> coheres around nothing (except Dostoevskian despair over
> fame). With him no things past. All now. P. memory of
> what hasn't happened to him, Proust of all that has.

Knowledge of people out of "People" page in *Time*. Another contending personality for ringside at Elaine's. But:
the bullying ego, the personal audacity, the natural coarseness, the taste for exhausting encounters—what gifts! Mix
with talent the unstoppable energy, the flypaper brain . . .
but he knows that too. It's the talentlessness that's driving
him nuts. The brute strength, the crazy tenacity, the
desperate hunger—producers figured right he'd scare the
country to death. The Jew You Can't Permit in the Parlor.
How Johnny Carson America now thinks of me. This
Peplerian barrage is what? Zeitgeist overspill? Newark
poltergeist? Tribal retribution? Secret sharer? P. as my
pop self? Not far from how P. sees it. He who's made
fantasy of others now fantasy of others. Book: *The Vrai's
Revenge*—the forms their fascination takes, the counter-
spell cast over me.

When he spotted the young funeral director, he signaled by raising one hand. Not too high, however.

He would take the rear exit, no matter how dark or
dank the subterranean corridors he had to escape through.

But it was only a bright carpeted hallway into which
he was led, with cubicle doors on both sides. No ghoul
emerged to take his measurements. It could have been an
office of the I.R.S.

His young guide pointed to the cubicle that was his.
"Could you wait, sir, just one second? Something from my
desk." He returned carrying a copy of *Carnovsky*. "If you

would . . . 'For John P. Driscoll' . . . Oh, that's awfully
kind."

On Fifth he found a taxi. "Bank Street. Step on it." The
driver, an elderly black man, was amused by the gangster
locution and, for the fun of it seemingly, drove him to
the Village in record time. Time enough, however, for
Zuckerman to gauge what he'd be up against with
Laura. *I don't want to be beaten over the head with how
boring I was for three years.* You weren't boring for three
years. *I don't please you anymore, Nathan. It's as simple
as that.* Are we talking about sex? Let's then. *There's
nothing to say about it. I can do it and you can do it. I'm
sure there are people both of us could call in to verify
that. The rest I refuse to hear. Your present state has
made you forget just how much I bored you. My affectless manner, as it is called, bored you. The way I tell a
story bored you. My conversation and my ideas bored you.
My work bored you. My friends bored you. My taste in
clothes bored you. The way I make love bored you. Not
making love to me bored you more.* The way you make
love did not bore me. Far from it. *But then it did. Something did, Nathan. You have a way of making things like
that very clear. When you're dissatisfied, your manner is
by no means affectless, to use the word.* It was the wrong
word. I'm sorry about that word. *Don't be. It's what you
meant. Nathan, stop pretending. You were bored to tears
and you need a new life.* I was wrong. I need you. I

thrived on you. I love you. *Oh, please don't try to break me down by saying reckless things. I've had a rough time too. I'd like to think that the hardest part is over. It has to be. I couldn't take those first few weeks again.* Well, I couldn't take those, I can't take these, and the ones looming ahead I don't intend to take. *You'll have to. I beg of you, don't try to kiss me, don't try to hold me, don't ever again tell me you love me. If you try to break me down that way I'll have to cut you out of my life completely.* But that's the answer, isn't it? Maybe what you call "broken down," Laura— *Once is enough, thank you. Once is enough to be told you won't do. You may finally be suffering from the fallout of leaving, but I haven't changed. I am still the same person who won't do. I am relentlessly reasonable and emotionally unflappable, if not seriously repressed. I still have my executive mind and my deadpan delivery and my do-good Christianity, all of which won't do. I am still in the "virtue racket."* That was the wrong word too. I was cursing myself more than you. *It amounts to the same thing, doesn't it? It amounts to why I became so "boring."* And that was the wrong word. Laura, I have made a terrible mistake. The words were brutally wrong. *No, they were brutally right, and you know it. After the clinging, quivering wives, I was just perfect. No tears, no fits, no euphoria, no crises in restaurants or at parties. You could get your work done with me. You could concentrate and live within yourself all you wanted. I didn't even care about having children. I had work of my own to accomplish. I never needed to be entertained, and I didn't have to entertain you, beyond a few minutes in the morning, playing wake-up games in bed. Which I loved. I loved being Lorelei, Nathan. I loved it all, and even longer than you did. But that's behind us. Now you need another dramatic personality. I need no such thing. I need you. Let me finish. You bawl me out for being an affectless goody-good Pollyanna WASP, and never saying all that's on my mind. Let me, and then it'll never have to be said again. You want to be renewed, it's what your work requires now. Whatever is finished for you there has finished it for you with someone like me. You don't want our life anymore. You think you do today because nothing has come along to take its place, except all this flap about your book. But when something does, you'll see that I'm right to refuse to let you come back. That you were perfectly right to go: having written a book like that, you had to go. That's what writing it was all about.*

And how was he going to argue with that? Everything she would say sounded so honest and persuasive, and everything he would say sounded so disingenuous and feeble. He could only hope that she wouldn't be able to make the case against him as well as he himself could. But knowing her, there wasn't much chance of that. Oh, his brave, lucid, serious, good-hearted Lorelei! But he had thrown her away. By writing a book ostensibly about someone else attempting to break free from his accustomed constraints.

At Bank Street he tipped the cabbie five dollars for valor on the West Side Highway. He could as easily have given him a hundred. He was home.

But Laura wasn't. He rang and rang, then ran next door and down the concrete stairwell to the basement apartment. He rapped loudly on the door. Rosemary, the retired schoolteacher, looked a long time through the peephole before she began unspringing locks.

Laura was in Pennsylvania at Allenwood, seeing Douglas Muller about his parole. She told him this with one chain still on. Then, reluctantly, she undid that.

Allenwood was the minimum-security prison where the federal government interned nonviolent criminals. Douglas, one of Laura's clients, was a young Jesuit who had left the priesthood to oppose the draft without the shield of clerical status. The year before, when Zuckerman went down with Laura to visit him at the prison, Douglas confided to Nathan another reason for leaving: at Harvard, where the order had sent him to study Middle Eastern languages, he had lost his virginity. "That can happen," he said, "when you walk around Cambridge without your collar." Douglas wore the collar only when he was demonstrating for Cesar Chavez or against the war; otherwise he dressed in work shirts and jeans. He was a shy, thoughtful Midwesterner in his mid-twenties, the magnitude of whose devotion to the large self-denying cause was all in the ice-like clarity of his pale blue eyes.

Douglas knew something from Laura about the novel Zuckerman was finishing and had amused the novelist, during his visit, with anecdotes about the hapless struggle he had waged as a high-school student against the sin of self-abuse. Grinning and blushing, he recalled for Zuckerman the days in Milwaukee when, having confessed first thing in the morning to the excesses of the night before, he was back in an hour to confess again. There was nothing in this world or the other that could help him, either; not the contemplation of Christ's passion, or the promise of the Resurrection, or the sympathetic priest at the Jesuit school who had in the end to refuse to give him absolution more than once every twenty-four hours. Recycled and fused with Nathan's own recollections, some of Douglas's best stories made their way into the life of Carnovsky, a budding soul no less bedeviled by onanism in Jewish New Jersey than Douglas growing up in Catholic Wisconsin. The inscribed first-edition copy of the book that the author sent to Allenwood had been acknowledged by the prisoner with a brief, compassionate note: "Tell poor Carnovsky that I pray for his strength. Fr. Douglas Muller."

"She'll be back tomorrow," Rosemary said and waited by the door for Nathan to leave. She was acting as if he had bullied his way as far as the foyer and she intended him to trespass no farther.

In Rosemary's hall closet Laura kept her correspondence files. Guarding them from an F.B.I. break-in had given the lonely woman something to live for. So had Laura. For three years Laura had been mothering Rosemary like a daughter: accompanied her to the optometrist, took her to the hairdresser, weaned her from sleeping pills, baked the big cake for her seventieth birthday . . .

Zuckerman found he had to sit down, thinking of that endless list and the good woman who'd drawn it up.

Rosemary sat too, though she wasn't happy about it. Her chair was the Danish chair from his study, the old reading chair he had left behind. The battered Moroccan ottoman at her feet had also been his before the move uptown.

"How is your new apartment, Nathan?"

"Lonely. Very lonely."

She nodded as though he'd said "Fine." "And your work?"

"Work? Terrible. Nonexistent. Haven't worked in months."

"And how is your lovely mother?"

"God only knows."

Rosemary's hands had always trembled, and Zuckerman's answers weren't helping. She still looked like she could use a good meal. Sometimes Laura had come to sit with her when she had dinner, just to be sure she ate something.

"How's Laura, Rosemary?"

"Well, she's worried about young Douglas. She went again to Congressman Koch about his parole, but it doesn't look hopeful. His mood down there in the prison is not good."

"I wouldn't think so."

"This war is criminal. Unforgivable. I want to cry when I see what it is doing to the very best of our young men."

Laura had radicalized Rosemary—no mean job, either. Under the influence of her late bachelor brother, an Air Force colonel, Rosemary used to receive in her mailbox the publications of the John Birch Society; now she harbored Laura's files and worried about the welfare of her war resisters. And thought of Zuckerman as . . . as what? Did that matter to him too, Rosemary Ditson's judgment?

"How's Laura," he asked, "when she's not worrying about Douglas? How is she managing otherwise?"

Rumor had reached him that three Movement higher-ups were pursuing Laura with great determination: a handsome philanthropist with an enormous social conscience, only recently divorced; a bearded civil-rights lawyer who could walk unaccompanied anywhere in Harlem, also recently divorced; and a burly, outspoken pacifist just back with Dave Dellinger from Hanoi, not yet married.

"You do her harm by telephoning her."

"Do I?"

She was holding the arms of her chair—his chair—to stop her hands from shaking. She wore two sweaters to keep herself warm and even in this mild May weather had a small electric heater burning by her side. Zuckerman remembered when Laura had gone out to buy it.

What she had to say wasn't easy for her, but she braced herself and got it out. "Why don't you realize that every time you leave your voice on her message machine it puts that poor girl back another two months!"

The uncharacteristic vehemence took him by surprise. "Does it? How?"

"You must not do this, Nathan. Please. You abandoned her, that was your business. But now you must stop tormenting her and let her get on with her life. You call, after what you have done—please, let me finish—"

"Go ahead," he said, though he had made no effort to stop her.

"I don't want to go into it. I am only a neighbor. It's not my affair. Never mind."

"What isn't your affair?"

"Well—what you write in your books. Nor would you, with all your renown, listen to someone like me . . . But that you could do what you have done to Laura . . ."

"What is that?"

"The things you wrote about her in that book."

"About Laura? You don't mean Carnovsky's girlfriend, do you?"

"Don't hide behind that 'Carnovsky' business. Please don't compound it with that."

"I must say, Rosemary, I'm shocked to find that a

woman who taught English in the New York school system for over thirty years cannot distinguish between the
illusionist and the illusion. Maybe you're confusing the
dictating ventriloquist with the demonic dummy."

"Don't hide behind sarcasm, either. I am old, but I am
still a person."

"But do you really believe, you of all people, that the
Laura we both know has anything in common with that
woman portrayed in my book? Do you really believe
that was what was going on next door between the two
of us and the Xerox machine? That's exactly what *wasn't*
going on."

Her head began to tremble a little, but she would not
be put off. "I have no idea what you may have led her
into. You are seven years her senior and an experienced
man who has been married three times. You are a man
who does not lack for imagination."

"Really, this is pretty foolish of you. Isn't it? It isn't
as if you didn't know me too during these three years."

"I don't think I did, not now. I knew the polite you,
the suave you, that's who I knew, Nathan. The charmer."

"The snake charmer."

"As you wish. I have read your book, if you want to
know. As much as I could until my stomach turned. I
am sure with all the publicity and all the money you can
now find plenty of women of the kind you like. But
Laura is out from under your spell, and you have no right
to try to lure her back."

"You make me sound more like Svengali than Carnovsky."

"You plead on the phone, 'Laura, Laura, call me back,' and then she goes and reads the paper and finds this."

"Finds what?"

She handed him two clippings. They were right there on the table beside her chair.

I know, I know, actually you only want to know who's doing what to whom. Well, NATHAN ZUCKERMAN and CAESARA O'SHEA are still Manhattan's most delectable twosome. They were very together at the little dinner that agent ANDRE SCHEVITZ and wife MARY gave where KAY GRAHAM talked to WILLIAM STYRON and TONY RANDALL talked to LEONARD BERNSTEIN and LAUREN BACALL talked to GORE VIDAL and Nathan and Caesara talked to one another.

The second was groovier, if further from the circumstances as he remembered them.

Dancin' to Duchin at the Maisonette: Naughty Novelist Zuckerman, Sexy Superstar O'Shea . . .

"Is that the whole dossier?" he asked her. "Who was thoughtful enough to clip these out for Laura? You, Rosemary? I don't remember Laura herself taking an inordinate interest in the swinish press."

"With your education, with your lovely parents, with

your wonderful talent for writing, with all that, to do what you have done to Laura—"

He got up to go. This was ridiculous. It was all ridiculous. Manhattan could as well have been another part of the forest, and his dignity handed over to Oberon and Puck. And handed to them by himself! To be taking to task this helpless old lady, to cast her as stand-in for everything driving him mad . . . surely, surely there was no need for him to go on.

"I assure you," he went on, "I have done absolutely nothing to harm Laura."

"Even you might speak differently if you still lived on this street and heard what I have to hear about that wonderful girl."

"Is that it? The gossips? Who? The florist? The grocer? The nice ladies in the pastry shop? Ignore 'em," he advised her, "just the way Laura does." He was surer of Laura than of himself. "I can't believe that I was born, even to my lovely parents, to provide moral reassurance to the grocer. Laura would agree."

"So that's how you do it," she said angrily. "You actually tell yourself that a young woman as fine as Laura has no feelings!"

Their conversation grew louder and more shameful and went on for another ten minutes. His world was getting stupider by the hour, and so was he.

* * *

She came to the window to watch him disappear forever from Laura's life. He mounted the concrete stairs and hurried away toward Abingdon Square. Then, at the corner, he doubled back and let himself into Laura's apartment. Their apartment. Five months, and he was still carrying the keys.

"Home!" he cried and raced for the bedroom.

Exactly as he'd left it! The anti-war posters, the post-impressionist posters, Laura's grandmother's patchwork quilt on the bed. That bed! All he had made of his indifference to her in that bed! As though he *were* Carnovsky with Carnovsky's obsession! As though, of all the readers infected by that book, the writer had had to go first. As though Rosemary were right and there'd been no illusion at all.

Next, the bathroom. There it was, the Xerox machine, third member in their ménage à trois. Taking a sheet of wastepaper from the trash basket beside the tub, he wrote on the clean side with his pen and ran off ten copies. "I LOVE YOU. PEACE NOW." But when he went with his leaflets into what once had been his study, he found a sleeping bag neatly laid out on the floor and a knapsack beside it stenciled "W.K." He had been expecting nothing, just the large barren room to which one day soon he would ship back his desk and his chair, and the four walls of empty shelves onto which he would realphabetize his books. But the shelves weren't entirely empty. Stacked

on the shelf beside the sleeping bag were a dozen paper-
backs. He picked through them, one by one: Dietrich
Bonhoeffer, Simone Weil, Danilo Dolci, Albert Camus
. . . He opened the closet where he used to store his
reams of typing paper and hang his clothes. Empty, but
for an unpressed gray jacket and a white shirt. He didn't
notice the Roman collar until he took the shirt out and
held it up to the light, ostensibly to see the size of his successor's neck.

A priest had taken his place. Father W.K.

He went into Laura's office to look at her perfectly ordered desk and her perfectly shelved books, and to see
if he was wrong about the priest and if by chance his own
photograph was still framed beside the phone. No. He
tore up the leaflets intended for her "in" box and stuffed
the pieces into his pocket. He would never have to worry
about being bored by her again. A fallen man like himself he could perhaps have challenged, but he was no
match for some saintly priest, undoubtedly yet another
boy struggling against the forces of evil like Douglas
Muller. Nor did he want to be around when Laura returned with Father W.K. from visiting Douglas at Allenwood Prison. How could they take seriously someone with
his troubles? How could he?

He used her phone to call his answering service. The
two of them had always to assume Laura's phone was
tapped, but he for one had no secrets anymore: read all
about it in Leonard Lyons. He just wanted to see if the

kidnapper had called about the money, or if this time round Pepler had dropped the disguise.

Only one message, from his cousin Essie. *Urgent. Call me in Miami Beach at once.*

So it had happened, that morning, while he was out forgetting about it. While he was out pretending it was all some nutty prank of Alvin Pepler's! He couldn't stay in to wait for the kidnapper's phone call, he couldn't hang around, a man of his eminence, to be made a fool of yet again—and so instead it had happened. And to her. And because of him and his eminence and that character in that book!

And to *her*. Not to Carnovsky's mother, but to his own! And who was she, what was she, that such a thing should happen to *her?* Terrified of her tyrannical father, devoted to her lonely mother, the most loyal of wives to her demanding husband—oh, to her husband far more than that. Fidelity was nothing, fidelity she could give him with both hands tied behind her back. (He saw her hands bound with ropes, her mouth stuffed with a rag, her bare legs shackled to a stake in the ground.) How many nights had she sat through those stories of his impoverished childhood and never yawned, or groaned, or cried out, "Not you and Papa and the hat factory, not again." No, she knitted sweaters, she polished silver, she turned collars, and uncomplainingly, she heard about her husband's narrow escape from the hat factory for the hundredth time. Once a year they quarreled. When the heavy winter rugs were taken up he tried to tell her how to roll them in the tar paper and the scene ended in shouting and tears. The husband shouting, the wife in tears. Otherwise, she never opposed him; however he did things was right.

That was the woman to whom this had happened.

Back when Henry was still in his carriage—this would be 1937—a truckdriver had whistled at her. It was summertime. She was sitting out front on the steps with the children. The truck slowed down, the driver whistled, and Zuckerman never forgot the milky smell of Henry's bottle wafting his way as he looked up from his tricycle to see her pulling her sundress over her knees and compressing her lips so as not to smile. At dinner that evening, when she told her husband the story, he leaned back in his chair and laughed. His wife a desirable woman? He was flattered. Men admiring her legs? Why not? They were legs to be proud of. Nathan, not quite five, was stunned; but not Dr. Zuckerman: any girl he'd married couldn't know the meaning of "to stray."

And to her, of all people, this had happened.

Once his mother went to a party with a flower in her hair. He must have been six or seven. It had taken him weeks to get over it.

And what else had she done to deserve this victimization?

Her youngest sister, Celia, had died in their house. She had come to recover from an operation. His mother walked Aunt Celia around the living room—he could to this day still see Celia, a frightening scarecrow in bathrobe and slippers, leaning feebly on his mother's arm. Aunt Celia had just graduated from normal school and was to be a music teacher in the Newark system. That, at any rate, was everyone's dream; she was the gifted girl in the family. But after the operation she couldn't even feed herself, let alone find strength in her hands to play chords on the piano. She couldn't make it from the breakfront to the radio without stopping to lean on the sofa, then the love seat, then his father's easy chair. But if they didn't drag her around the living room, she'd get pneumonia and die of that. "One more time, Celia dear, and that's it. A little bit every day," his mother told her, "and soon you'll be stronger. Soon you'll be yourself again." After her walk Celia went listing back to the bed and his mother locked herself in the bathroom and cried. On weekends it was his father who walked her. "That's movin' along very nicely, Celia. That-a-girl." Softly, jauntily, with his dying young sister-in-law on his arm, Dr. Zuckerman whistled "I Can't Give You Anything but Love, Baby." He told everyone that at the funeral his wife "bore up like a soldier."

What did this woman understand of the savagery in people? How could she possibly endure it? Slice. Beat. Chop. Grind. Nowhere but in the kitchen did she run across such ideas. What violence she practiced went into making dinner. Otherwise, peace.

Her parents' daughter, her sister's sister, her husband's

wife, her children's mother. What else was there? She would be the first to say "nothing." That was more than enough. Had taken all her *kayech,* her strength.

What strength would she have for this?

But she hadn't been kidnapped. It was his father: a coronary. "This is it," Essie told him. "You better hurry." When he got back to Eighty-first Street—to pack a bag before heading to Newark to meet his brother for the four o'clock Miami flight—a large manila envelope was dangling halfway out of his mailbox in the entryway. Weeks ago, after extracting an envelope, hand-delivered, addressed to "Kike, Apt. 2B," he had removed his nameplate from the box. In its place he had substituted a nameplate with his initials. Lately he had considered removing his initials and leaving the space blank, but he didn't because—because he refused to.

Across the envelope someone had scrawled with a red felt-tip pen, "Prestige Paté International." Inside was a damp matted handkerchief. It was the very one he'd given Pepler to dry his hands with the evening before, after Pepler had finished eating Zuckerman's sandwich. There was no note. Only, by way of a message, a stale acrid odor he had no difficulty identifying. Evidence, if evidence there need be, of the "hang-up" that Pepler shared with Gilbert Carnovsky, and that Zuckerman had stolen from him for that book.

4 Look Homeward, Angel

On the table beside the bed were five-cent Xerox copies of every page of every protest letter Dr. Zuckerman had mailed to Lyndon Johnson while he was President. In contrast to his collected letters to Hubert Humphrey, the Johnson folder, bound with a wide rubber band, was nearly as fat as *War and Peace*. The sparsity and brevity of the Humphrey letters—also their sarcasm, their abusive bitterness—showed how far he had sunk in Dr. Zuckerman's esteem since he'd been the darling of the A.D.A.

Most days Humphrey had gotten no more than one line of contempt and three exclamation marks. And on a post-card, so that anybody who picked it up could learn what a coward the Vice-President had become. But with the President of the United States, arrogant pig-headed bastard though he was, Dr. Zuckerman had tried to be reasonable on letterhead stationery, invoking the name of F.D.R. at every opportunity, and elucidating his argument against the war with wisdom, not always assigned with the utmost scrupulosity, from either the Talmud or a long-deceased spinster named Helen Mac-Murphy. Miss MacMurphy, as all the family knew (as all the world knew, from the title story of *Higher Education,* Nathan Zuckerman, 1959), had been his eighth-grade teacher. In 1912 she had gone to Dr. Zuckerman's father, a sweatshop worker, to demand that bright little Victor be sent to high school instead of into the local hat factory, where an older brother was already crippling his fingers working as a blocker fourteen hours a day. And as all the world knew, she had prevailed.

Though Lyndon Johnson turned out to have neither the time nor—in Mrs. Zuckerman's phrase—"the common decency" to respond to the letters he received from the lifelong Democrat ailing in Florida, Dr. Zuckerman went on dictating some three or four pages to his wife just about every other day, lecturing the President on American history, Jewish history, and his own personal philosophy. After the stroke that had wrung all coherence from his speech, he seemed not to have any idea what was going on in his room, let alone in the Oval Office, where his arch-enemy Nixon was now ruining things; but then slow improvement began once again—his will, the doctors told Mrs. Zuckerman, was a wonder to them. Mr. Metz came to visit and to read aloud to him from *The New York Times,* and then one afternoon Dr. Zuckerman managed to communicate to his wife that he wanted his correspondence folders brought to him from the table beside the wheelchair at home. She would, after this, sit there by his side and turn the sheets of paper, so he could see all he had once written and would live to write again. At his request, she began to show the letters to the doctors and nurses who stopped by his bed to attend him. He was regaining his clarity, he was even beginning to demonstrate some of his old "fire," when one day, only moments after Mr. Metz had left, just as Mrs. Zuckerman had arrived to take up the afternoon shift, he dropped into unconsciousness and had to be rushed to the hospital. Mrs. Zuckerman found herself inside the ambulance with the correspondence folders in her hands. "Anything, anything," she said, explaining her state of mind to Nathan later, "anything to give him the will to go on." Zuckerman wondered if to herself, at least, she was able to say, "Enough, let it be over. I can't endure his enduring like this anymore."

But then, she was the wife whose every thought the man had been thinking for her since she was twenty years old, not the son who'd been fighting his every thought since he was younger even than that. In the plane flying down, Zuckerman had been remembering the summer just twenty years ago, that August before he'd left for college, when he read three thousand pages of Thomas Wolfe straight through on the screened-in back porch of his family's stifling home—stifling that August as much because of the father as of the weather. "He believed himself thus at the center of life; he believed the mountains rimmed the heart of the world; he believed that from all the chaos of accident the inevitable event came at the inexorable moment to add to the sum of his life." Inevitable. Inexorable. "Oh yes!" noted stifled Nathan in the margin of his copy of *Look Homeward, Angel,* unaware that the resounding privative clang of the Latinate adjectives wasn't necessarily so stirring when you ran into the inevitable and the inexorable at the center of your life instead of on the back porch. All he wanted at sixteen was to become a romantic genius like Thomas Wolfe and leave little New Jersey and all the shallow provincials therein for the deep emancipating world of Art. As it turned out, he had taken them all with him.

Zuckerman's father got "better" and then worse again all through the first night Nathan was there, and most of the following day. Sometimes when he came to, he seemed to his wife to be inclining his head toward the letters in the folder beside the bed; she took this to mean that he had something in mind to tell the new President. Inasmuch, thought Zuckerman, as he still had a mind. She wasn't making much sense anymore herself—she'd had no sleep for over twenty-four hours, and little during the four preceding years—and finally it was easier than not for Zuckerman to pretend that she might be right. He drew a yellow pad out of his briefcase and printed in large letters "STOP THE WAR"; below it, in his own hand, he signed "Dr. Victor Zuckerman." But when he showed the page to his father it evoked no response. Dr. Zuckerman made sounds from time to time, but they were barely distinguishable as words. They were more like the squeals of a mouse. It was awful.

At dusk, after Dr. Zuckerman had again been unconscious for several hours, the resident took Nathan aside and told him it would be over in a few hours. He would silently slip away, the doctor said, but then the doctor didn't know Nathan's father the way the family did. In fact, near the end, as sometimes happens to you if you're lucky—or unlucky—the dying man opened his eyes and seemed suddenly to see them all and to see them together, and to understand as well as anyone in that room exactly what was up. This was awful too, another way. It was more awful. His soft, misty gaze somehow grew enormous, bending their images and drawing them to him like a convex mirror. His chin was quivering—not from the frustrated effort of speech but from the recognition that all effort was pointless now. And it had been the most effortful life. Being Victor Zuckerman was no job you took lightly. Day shifts, night shifts, weekends, evenings, vacations—for sheer man-hours, not so different from being his son.

Gathered around him, when he came to, were Henry, Nathan, their mother, Cousin Essie, and the newcomer to the family, Essie's kindly, genial husband Mr. Metz, a retired accountant of seventy-five, who stood benignly apart from their ancient entanglements, reproaching no one for anything and thinking mostly about playing bridge. Each was only to have stayed with Dr. Zuckerman for five minutes, but because Nathan was Nathan, hospital rules had been suspended by the physician in charge.

They all closed in to look down at that terrified, imploring gaze. Essie, at seventy-four still nobody to tamper with, took hold of his hand and began reminiscing about the winepress in the cellar of the house on Mercer Street, and how all the cousins used to love to watch Dr. Zuckerman's father crush the Concord grapes there in the fall. She had as big and commanding a voice as ever, and when she moved on from Victor's father's winepress to Victor's mother's mandel bread, a nurse came to the open door with a finger to her lips to remind Essie that people were sick.

Tucked way down into the bed sheets, Dr. Zuckerman could have been a frightened four-year-old listening to a story to put him to sleep, but for his mustache, and what three strokes and a coronary had done to his face. His gray, imploring eyes looked steadily back at Essie as she recalled how the century had begun for the new family in America. Was it getting through to him—the old wine-press, the new American children, the sweet-smelling cellar, the crunchy mandel bread, and the mother, the revered and simple mother who baked the mandel bread? Suppose he could remember it all, every cherished sensation that had been his in the life he was leaving—was that necessarily the easiest way to go? Having buried her share, maybe Essie knew what she was doing. Not that not knowing had ever worried her before. Precious time was passing, but Essie wasn't one to stint on details, nor did Nathan see any way to stop her now that she had the floor. Besides, he couldn't hold anyone in check anymore—he couldn't hold himself in check anymore. After a day and a half, he was finally in tears. There were tubes to deliver oxygen to his father's lungs, tubes to drain the urine from his bladder, tubes to drip dextrose into his veins, and none of them would make the least difference. For several minutes it was he who felt like the four-year-old, discovering for the first time how utterly helpless his protector could be.

"Remember Uncle Markish, Victor?"

From Essie's vantage point, the homeless rascal Markish had been the family character; from Dr. Zuckerman's (and his older son's—cf. "Higher Education"), it had been Essie. Uncle Markish painted their houses and slept on their stairwells, and then picked up and went off one day in his coveralls to Shanghai, China. "You'll wind up like

Markish," was what they would tell the children in that clan who came home from school with any grade lower than B. If you wanted to leave Jersey for China, you did it through the Oriental Studies Department of a top-flight school and not with nothing to your name but a paint bucket and brush. In their family either you did things right, preferably as a D.D.S. or an M.D. or an L.L.B. or a Ph.D., or you might as well not do them at all. Law laid down by the son of the toiling, uncomplaining mother who made the mandel bread and the driven, impregnable father who pressed the wine.

On the airplane down, Zuckerman had read through an illustrated paperback for laymen about the creation of the universe and the evolution of life. The author was a NASA scientist who had lately achieved celebrity by explaining elementary astronomy once a week on public television. Zuckerman bought the book off a rack at Newark Airport after meeting Henry for the flight to Miami. There were books from his boxes that might have meant more to him on his way to see his father die, but he couldn't get at them and so left the apartment for Newark empty-handed. What did those books have to do with his father anyway? If they'd ever meant to his father what the discovery of them had meant at school to him, it would have been another household, another childhood, another life. So, instead of thinking the thoughts of the great thinkers on the subject of death, he thought his own. There were more than enough for a three-hour flight: plans for his mother's future, memories of his father's life, the origin of his own mixed emotions. *Mixed Emotions* had been the title of his second book. It had confused his father no less than *Higher Education,* his first. Why should emotions be mixed? They weren't when he was a boy.

Zuckerman had reached Henry just as he'd gotten back to the office from a conference in Montreal. He hadn't heard the news, and when Zuckerman gave it to him— "This looks like it"—Henry emitted the most wrenching sob. Another reason Zuckerman wouldn't be needing anything inspirational to read on the flight down. He had a kid brother to tend to, emotionally more fragile than he liked to let on.

But Henry arrived at the airport looking nothing like a kid, in a dark pinstriped suit and carrying in his monogrammed briefcase the back issues of a dental journal he meant to catch up on. And so Zuckerman, a little let down at not having to buck him up, and a little amused at feeling a little let down—stunned a little, too, that he should have been expecting a ten-year-old child to be in his charge flying south—Zuckerman wound up reading about the origin of everything.

As a result, when it was his turn to say goodbye to his father, he did not hark back to Grandma's mandel bread. Grandma's mandel bread had been wonderful enough, but Essie had covered it as thoroughly as anyone ever could, and so instead Zuckerman explained to him the big-bang theory, as he'd come to understand it the day before. He would try to get through to him how long things had been burning up and burning out: maybe it would get through to the family as well. It wasn't just a father who was dying, or a son, or a cousin, or a husband: it was the whole creation, whatever comfort that gave.

Back before Grandma's mandel bread then. Before even Grandma.

"I was reading on the plane about the beginning of the universe. Dad, do you hear me?"

"He hears, don't worry," said Essie. "He hears everything now. He's never missed a trick in his life. Right, Victor?"

"Not the world," said Nathan, to his father's searching eyes, "but the universe. Scientists now believe it began between ten and twenty billion years ago."

His hand rested lightly on his father's arm. It seemed impossible—there was nothing to that arm anymore. As little children the Zuckerman boys would watch with delight while their father pretended to inflate his biceps by blowing air in through his thumbs. Well, they were gone now, Papa's Popeye biceps, vanished like the primordial egg of hydrogen energy in which the universe was conceived . . . Yes, in spite of a growing sense that he was engaged in a flagrant act of pretentious, useless, professorial foolishness, Zuckerman lectured on: the original egg that one fine day, reaching a temperature of thousands of billions of degrees, blew itself wide open, and like an erupting furnace forged on the spot all the elements that would ever be. "All of this," he informed his father, "in the first half hour of that very first day."

Dr. Zuckerman registered no surprise. Why should he? What was the first half hour of the first day of Creation to the last half hour of the last day of his life?

Oh, the mandel bread was a much better idea. Homely, tangible, and to the point of Victor Zuckerman's real life and a Jewish family deathbed scene. But the oration on mandel bread was Essie being Essie, and this, however foolish, was himself being himself. Proceed, Nathan, to father the father. Last chance to tell the man what he still doesn't know. Last chance ever to make him see it all another way. You'll change him yet.

"—the universe expanding outward ever since, the galaxies all rushing away, out into space, from the impact of that first big bang. And it will go on like this, the universe blowing outward and outward, for fifty billion years."

No response here, either.

"Go on, he's listening." Essie, giving instructions.

"I'm afraid," he told her softly, "it's hard enough to grasp when you're on top of the world—"

"Don't worry about it. Go on. This family has always been smarter than you think."

"I grant that, Esther. It's my stupidity I was thinking about."

"Talk to *him,* Nathan." It was his mother, in tears. "Essie, I beg you, let sleeping dogs lie, at least tonight."

Nathan looked across the bed to Henry. His brother had a tight hold on one of his father's hands, but he too was running with tears and didn't look in any shape to say anything by way of farewell. The inexpressible love breaking out, or the blockaded hatred? Henry was the good son, but it didn't come cheap, or so Zuckerman was inclined to believe. Henry was the tallest, darkest, and handsomest by far of all the Zuckerman men, a swarthy, virile, desert Zuckerman whose genes, uniquely for their clan, seemed to have traveled straight from Judea to New Jersey without the Diaspora detour. He had a light, mellifluous voice, and the most kindly, gentle, doctorly manner, and invariably his patients fell in love with him. And he fell in love with some of his patients. Zuckerman alone knew this. Some two years earlier Henry had driven to New York in the middle of the night prepared to sleep in Nathan's study in Nathan's pajamas because he could not bear any longer to sleep in the same bed with his wife. Watching Carol undress for bed had caused him to remember (not that he had reason to forget) the body of the patient whom he had himself undressed only a few hours earlier in a north Jersey motel, and he fled to New York at two a.m., without even taking time to pull socks on under his loafers. He sat up all night telling his big brother about his mistress, sounding to Zuckerman like some miserable, yearning, tenderized lover out of the great nineteenth-century literature of adultery.

Henry was still talking at seven a.m. when Carol had phoned. She didn't know what she'd done wrong and begged him to come home. Zuckerman picked up the extension to listen in. Henry was crying and Carol was pleading. "—you wanted plants like your grandmother had in her living room, I gave you plants. One day you said something about having had eggs in an eggcup as a kid on a vacation in Lakewood—the next morning I presented your boiled egg to you in an eggcup. And you were *like* a kid, so sweet, so delighted, so content from such a little thing. You couldn't wait until Leslie was old enough so you could begin to call him 'son.' You *didn't* wait. You used to lie on the floor with him and let him chew on your ear and you were in seventh heaven. You used to call out the door when dinner was ready, 'Son, come on home, time to eat.' You did it with Ruthie. You still do it with Ellen. You rush to do it when I say the food is ready. 'Little girl, come on, supper.' Ruthie plays 'Twinkle, Twinkle, Little Star' on her violin, and you, you fool, you're in tears, you're so happy. Leslie tells you that everything is made out of molecules, and you're so proud you're repeating it all night to anybody who calls. Oh, Henry, you are the softest, gentlest, kindest, most touching man there is, in your heart you are really the simplest man in the world to satisfy—"

So Henry went home.

Softest, gentlest, kindest. Responsibility. Generosity. Devotion. That's how everybody spoke of Henry. I suppose if I were Henry with his heart I wouldn't jeopardize it, either. It probably feels very good being so good. Except when it doesn't. And that probably feels good in the end too. Self-sacrifice.

They were no longer the brothers they'd once been.

A hand came gently down on Nathan's shoulder—Essie's dapper, tanned, well-meaning husband. "Finish the story," said Mr. Metz softly. "You're telling it beautiful."

He had stopped to watch his emotional brother, but now he smiled and assured Mr. Metz that he would go on. It was the first time that Mr. Metz had ever referred to anything of Zuckerman's as a "story." Zuckerman's short stories he called articles. "Your mother showed me your article in the magazine. Excellent, excellent." He was famous for buttering everyone up, Essie for tearing them down. They were an act Zuckerman always tried to take in when he flew to see his parents in Florida. With his father as a third they could have gone on tour: Dr. Zuckerman was famous for fanatical devotion. F.D.R. topped the list, followed by Mrs. Roosevelt, Harry Truman, David Ben-Gurion, and the authors of *Fiddler on the Roof*.

"You are their wordsmith," Mr. Metz whispered. "You

are their mouthpiece. You can say for everyone what is in their hearts."

He turned back to his father: no closer to death, though just as far from life. "Dad, listen to me, if you can." For whatever it was worth, Nathan smiled at him too. Last smile. "Dad, there's now a theory . . . if you can follow me."

Essie: "He can follow you."

"There is now a theory that when the fifty billion years are up, instead of everything coming to an end, instead of all the light going out because of all the energy fizzling away, gravity will take over. The force of gravity," he repeated, as though it were the familiar name of one of the beloved grandchildren up in South Orange. "Just at the edge of the end, the whole thing will begin to contract, will begin to rush back toward the center. Do you follow me? This too will take fifty billion years, until it's all pulled down inside that original egg, into this compressed droplet that it all began with. And there, you see, heat and energy build up again, and bang, another stupendous explosion, and out it'll all go flying, a brand-new roll of the dice, a brand-new creation unlike any that's been. If the theory is correct, the universe will go on like this forever. If it's correct—and I want you to hear this, this is what I want you to listen to very carefully, this is what we all want to tell you—"

"That's the ticket," said Mr. Metz.

"If it's correct, the universe *has* been going on forever: fifty billion years out, fifty billion years back. Imagine it. A universe being reborn and reborn and reborn, without end."

He did not, at this point, report to his father the objection to this theory as he had understood it on the plane ride down, a considerable objection, a crushing objection really, having to do with the density of matter in the universe being marginally insufficient for the friendly, dependable force of gravity to take over and halt the expansion before the last of the fires went out. If not for this insufficiency, the whole thing might indeed oscillate to and fro without end. But according to the paperback still in his coat pocket, right now they couldn't find what they needed anywhere, and the chances for no ending didn't look good.

But this information his father could live without. Of all that Dr. Zuckerman had so far lived without, and that Nathan would have preferred for him to live *with,* knowledge of the missing density factor was the least of it. Enough for now of what is and isn't so. Enough science, enough art, enough of fathers and sons.

A major new development in the life of Nathan and Victor Zuckerman, but then the coronary-care unit of Miami Biscayne Hospital isn't the Goddard Institute for Space Studies, as anyone who's ever been there doesn't have to be told.

Though Dr. Zuckerman didn't officially expire until the next morning, it was here that he uttered his last words. Word. Barely audible, but painstakingly pronounced. "Bastard," he said.

Meaning who? Lyndon Johnson? Hubert Humphrey? Richard Nixon? Meaning He who had not seen fit to bestow upon His own universe that measly bit of missing matter, that one lousy little hydrogen atom for each volume of ten cubic feet? Or to bestow upon Dr. Zuckerman, ardent moralist from grade school on, the simple reward of a healthy old age and a longer life? But then, when he spoke his last, it wasn't to his correspondence folders that he was looking, or upward at the face of his invisible God, but into the eyes of the apostate son.

The funeral was a tremendous strain. There was the heat, for one thing. Over the Miami cemetery, the sun made its presence known to Zuckerman as no Yahweh ever had; had it been the sun they were all addressing, he might have entered into the death rites of his people with something more than just respect for his mother's feelings. The two sons had to support her between them from the moment they left the air-conditioned limousine and started down between a row of twirling sprinklers to the burial plot. Dr. Zuckerman had bought two plots, for himself and for his wife, six years earlier, the same week he'd bought their condominium in Harbor Beach Retirement

Village. Her knees gave way by the grave, but as she had
been worn down by her husband's illness to little more
than a hundred pounds, it was no problem for Henry and
Nathan to keep her on her feet until the coffin was lowered
and they could take refuge from the heat. Behind him,
Zuckerman heard Essie tell Mr. Metz, "All the words, all
the sermons, all the quotations, and no matter what they
say, it's still final." Earlier, stepping from the limousine,
she had turned to Zuckerman to give her assessment of the
journey out for the man in the hearse. "You take a ride
and you don't get to see the scenery." Yes, Essie and
he were the ones who'd say anything.

Zuckerman, his brother, and the rabbi were, by decades,
the youngest men present. The rest of them wilting there
were either his parents' elderly neighbors from Harbor
Beach or Newark cronies of his father's who'd also retired to Florida. A few had even been boys with Dr.
Zuckerman in the Central Ward before the First World
War. Most of them Zuckerman hadn't seen since his childhood, when they'd been men not much older than he was
now. He listened to the familiar voices coming out of the
lined and jowled and fallen faces, thinking, If only I were
still writing *Carnovsky*. What memories those tones
touched off—the Charlton Street baths and the Lakewood
vacations, the fishing expeditions to the Shark River inlet
down the shore! Before the funeral everybody had come
up to put their arms around him. Nobody mentioned the
book; probably none of them had read it. Of all the

obstacles in life that these retired salesmen and merchants and manufacturers had struggled with and overcome, reading through a book was not yet one. Just as well. Not even the young rabbi made mention of *Carnovsky* to the author. Perhaps out of respect for the dead. All the better. He was not there as "the author"—the author was back in Manhattan. Here he was Nathan. Sometimes life offers no more powerful experience than just such a divestment.

He recited the Mourners' Kaddish. Over a sinking coffin, even a nonbeliever needs some words to chant, and "*Yisgadal v'yiskadash . . .*" made more sense to him than "Rage against the dying of the light." If ever there was a man to bury as a Jew it was his father. Nathan would probably wind up letting them bury him as one too. Better as that than as a bohemian.

"My two boys," said his mother, as they lifted her along the path back to the car. "My two tall strong handsome boys."

Returning through Miami to the apartment, the limousine stopped for a light just by a supermarket; the women shoppers, most of them middle-aged and Cuban, were wearing halters and shorts, and high-heeled sandals. A lot of protoplasm to take in straight from the post-retirement village of the dead. He saw Henry looking too. A halter had always seemed to Zuckerman a particularly provocative piece of attire—cloth not quite clothing—but the only thought inspired by these women oozing flesh was of his father decomposing. He'd been unable to think of much else since earlier in the day when the family had taken seats together in the first row at the Temple and the young rabbi—bearded very like Che Guevara—began to extol from the altar the virtues of the deceased. The rabbi praised him not simply as father, husband, and family man, but as "a political being engaged by all of life and anguished by the suffering of mankind." He spoke of the many magazines and newspapers Dr. Zuckerman had subscribed to and studied, the countless letters of protest he had painstakingly composed, he spoke of his enthusiasm for American democracy, his passion for Israel's survival, his revulsion against the carnage in Vietnam, his fears for the Jews in the Soviet Union, and meanwhile all Zuckerman was thinking was the word "extinguished." All that respectable moralizing, all that repressive sermonizing, all those superfluous prohibitions, that furnace of pieties, that Lucifer of rectitude, that Hercules of misunderstanding, extinguished.

Strange. It was supposed to be just the opposite. But never had he contemplated his father's life with less sentiment. It was as though they were burying the father of some other sons. As for the character being depicted by the rabbi, well, nobody had ever gotten Dr. Zuckerman quite so wrong. Maybe the rabbi was only trying to distance him from the father in *Carnovsky,* but from the portrait he painted you would have thought Dr. Zuckerman was Schweitzer. All that was missing was the organ and the lepers. But why not? Whom did it harm? It was a funeral, not a novel, let alone the Last Judgment.

What made it such a strain? Aside from the unrelenting heat and their lost, defenseless, seemingly legless mother? Aside from the pitiful sight of those old family friends, looking down into the slot where they too must be deposited, thirty, sixty, ninety days hence—the kibitzing giants out of his earliest memories, so frail now, some of them, that despite the healthy suntans, you could have pushed them in with his father and they couldn't have crawled out . . . ? Aside from all this, there were his emotions. The strain of feeling no grief. The surprise. The shame. The exultation. The shame of that. But all the grieving over his father's body had taken place when Nathan was twelve and fifteen and twenty-one: the grief over all his father had been dead to while living. From that grief the death was a release.

By the time he boarded the Newark plane with Henry, it felt like a release from even more. He couldn't entirely explain—or manage to control—this tide of euphoria sweeping him away from all inane distractions. It was very likely the same heady feeling of untrammeled freedom that people like Mary and André had been expecting him to enjoy from becoming a household name. In fact it had rather more to do with the four-day strain of Florida, with the wholly un-inane exigencies of arranging for the burial of one parent and the survival of

the other, that had put the household name and the Hallelujah Chorus behind him. He had become himself again—
though with something unknowable added: he was no
longer any man's son. Forget fathers, he told himself.
Plural.

Forget kidnappers too. During the four days away, his
answering service had taken no message from either an
ominous palooka or an addled Alvin Pepler. Had his *lands-
man* spent into Zuckerman's handkerchief the last of his
enraged and hate-filled adoration? Was that the end of
this barrage? Or would Zuckerman's imagination beget
still other Peplers conjuring up novels out of his—novels
disguising themselves as actuality itself, as nothing less
than real? Zuckerman the stupendous sublimator spawn-
ing Zuckermaniacs! A book, a piece of fiction bound between two covers, breeding living fiction exempt from all
the subjugations of the page, breeding fiction unwritten,
unreadable, unaccountable and uncontainable, instead of
doing what Aristotle promised from art in Humanities 2
and offering moral perceptions to supply us with the
knowledge of what is good or bad. Oh, if only Alvin had
studied Aristotle with him at Chicago! If only he could
understand that it is the writers who are supposed to move
the readers to pity and fear, not the other way around!

He had never so enjoyed a takeoff in his life. He
let his knees fall open and, as the plane went gunning
like a hot rod down the runway, felt the driving level
force of the fuselage as though it were his own. And

when it lifted off—lifted like some splendid, ostentatious afterthought—Zuckerman suddenly pictured Mussolini hanging by his heels. He'd never forgotten that photograph on the front page of the papers. Who could, of his generation of American youngsters? But to remember the vengeful undoing of that vile tyrant after the death of your own law-abiding, anti-Fascist, nonviolent father, chief air-raid warden of Keer Avenue and lifetime champion of the B'nai B'rith Anti-Defamation League? Reminder to the outer man of the inner man he's dealing with.

Of course for some seventy-two hours now he had been wondering if his father's last word could really have been "Bastard." Under the strain of that long vigil his hearing may not have been too subtle. Bastard? To mean what? *You were never my real son.* But was this father equal to such unillusioned thought, ever? Though maybe that's what he read in my eyes: *Henry's your boy, Papa, not me.* But from my two eyes? No, no, some things I'm not unillusioned enough for either, out of the safety of the study. Maybe he just said "Faster." Telling Death his job the way he told his wife how to roll the winter rugs and Henry how to do homework when he dawdled. "Vaster"? Unlikely. Nathan's cosmology lecture notwithstanding, for his father, in dying as in living, there were still but two points of reference in all the vastness: the family and Hitler. You could do worse, but you could also do better. Better. Of course! Not "Bastard" but "Better." First principle, final precept. Not more light but more virtue. He had only been reminding them to be better boys. "Bastard" was the writer's wishful thinking, if not quite the son's. Better scene, stronger medicine, a final repudiation by Father. Still, when Zuckerman wasn't writing he was also only human, and he'd just as soon the scene wasn't so wonderful. Kafka once wrote, "I believe that we should read only those books that bite and sting us. If a book we are reading does not rouse us with a blow to the head, then why read it?" Agreed, as to books. But as for life, why invent a blow to the head where none was intended? Up with art, but down with mythomania.

Mythomania? Alvin Pepler. The very word is like a bell that tolls thee back to me.

That Pepler's credentials were in order—if nothing else—Essie had confirmed for Zuckerman the night after the funeral, when everyone else had gone to sleep. The two were in her kitchen eating the remains of the cinnamon cake served the guests earlier in the day. For as long as Zuckerman could remember, Essie was supposed to be eating herself into an early grave. Also smoking herself to death. She was one of many his father could always find time to lecture about the right way to live. "He used to sit at the window," Essie told Nathan, "sit there in that wheelchair and call down to the people parking their cars. They didn't park right to suit him. Just yesterday I ran into a woman who your mother is still afraid to talk to because of your old man. Old Mrs. Oxburg. She is from

Cincinnati, a multimillionairess ten times over. When your little mother spots her coming, she runs the other way. One day Victor saw Mrs. Oxburg sitting in the lobby by an air conditioner, minding her own business, and he told her to move, she was going to give herself pneumonia. She said to him, 'Please, Dr. Zuckerman, where I sit is none of your business.' But, no, he wouldn't accept that for an answer. Instead he started telling her how our little cousin Sylvia died in 1918 of influenza, and how beautiful and smart she was, and what it did to Aunt Gracie. Your mother couldn't stop him. Whenever she tried just wheeling him away, he threw a fit. She had to go to the doctor to get Valium, and the Valium I had to keep for her here because if he found it he would start shouting at her about becoming a drug addict."

"He went a little over the top in that chair, Essie. We all know that."

"Poor Hubert Humphrey. I pity that poor bastard, if he read your father's postal cards. What the hell could Humphrey do, Nathan? He wasn't President, Vietnam wasn't his idea. He was as flummoxed as the next guy. But you couldn't tell that to Victor."

"Well, Humphrey's torment's over now."

"So is Victor's."

"That too."

"Okay, Nathan—let's move on. You and me are not lilies of the valley. This is my chance to get the dirt, and without your mother in between, making believe you still use your little putz just to run water through. I want to hear about you and the movie star. What happened? You dropped her or she dropped you?"

"I'll tell you all about the movie star, first tell me about the Peplers."

"From Newark? With the son, you mean? Alvin?"

"Right. Alvin from Newark. What do you have on him?"

"Well, he was on television. They had those quiz programs, remember? I think he won twenty-five grand. He had a big write-up in the *Star-Ledger*. This is years ago already. He was in the Marines before that. Didn't they award him a Purple Heart? I think he got it in the head. Maybe it was the foot. Anyway, when he came on they used to play 'From the Halls of Montezuma' in his honor. What do you want to know about him for?"

"I ran into him in New York. He introduced himself on the street. I would say from our meeting that it was the head, not the foot."

"Oh yeah? A screwball? Well, he was supposed to know his Americana inside out—that's how he won the dough. But of course they gave them the answers anyway. That was the big scandal. For a while he was all anybody in Newark talked about. I went to high school with his Aunt Lottie back in the year one, so I followed every week how he came out. Look, everybody did. Then he lost and that was that. Now he's nuts?"

"A little, I thought."

"Well, that's what they tell me about you, you know. And not just a little."

"What do you tell them?"

"I say it's true. I say he has to wear a straitjacket all the way to the bank. That shuts them up. How about the movie star? Who dumped who?"

"I dumped her."

"Idiot. She's gorgeous and must be worth a fortune. For Christ's sake, why?"

"She's gorgeous and worth a fortune, but not of our faith, Esther."

"I don't remember that stopping you before. I thought, myself, it egged you on. So who are you driving wild now?"

"Golda Meir."

"Oh, you're a sly little fox, Nathan, behind those harmless professor's glasses. You were always taking it in, even as a kid. There was your brother, the goody-good patrol boy who never stayed up past his bedtime, and there was you, thinking to yourself what a bunch of stupid bastards we all were. Still, I have to hand it to you, you have put something over on the public with this book. If I were you, I wouldn't listen to one goddamn thing they say."

The seat-belt sign had flashed off, and Henry had tilted his seat back and was sipping the martini he'd ordered at takeoff. He was hardly what you'd call a drinking man, and in fact was taking down the martini like a slightly noxious medicinal preparation. His complexion seemed somehow darkly sickish that morning—rather than darkly romantic—as though cinders had been ground into his skin. Zuckerman couldn't remember seeing his brother so emotionally done in since a weekend thirteen years before, when he'd come down from Cornell as a sophomore and announced he was giving up chemistry to become a "drama major." He was fresh from appearing as the Ragpicker in *The Madwoman of Chaillot*. Henry had gotten the lead role in the first college production he'd tried out for, and now he spoke with reverence at the dinner table of the two new influences on his life: John Carradine, who had played the Ragpicker on Broadway, and whom he hoped to emulate on the stage (in appearance as well—he'd already lost ten pounds trying), and Timmy, the young student director of the Cornell *Madwoman*. Timmy had painted flats the summer before in Provincetown, where his parents had a vacation house. Timmy was sure he could get Henry work there too, "in stock." "And when is this?" asked Mrs. Zuckerman, who was still abashed at why he'd gotten so thin. "Timmy says next summer," answered Henry. "Next June." "And what about the Chernicks?" his father asked. The previous two summers Henry had worked as a waterfront counselor for two Newark gym-teacher brothers who owned a camp for Jewish children in the Adirondacks. The job had come to someone as young as Henry as a special favor from the Chernicks to his father. "What about your responsibility to Lou and Buddy Chernick?" he was asked. In the way of vulnerable, ceremonious, intelligent children who all their lives have been delivering obedience in the form of streaming emotion, Henry couldn't give his father the kind of answer he might have come up with in a course in ethics—he ran from the table instead. Because all the way down from Ithaca he'd been expecting the worst—because for three days he'd been unable to eat, in dread of this very meal—he collapsed before it even got half as bad as he'd predicted it would to Timmy. The two boys had for days rehearsed the scene together in their dorm, Timmy playing Dr. Zuckerman like a miniature Lear, and Henry as a rather outspoken version of himself—Henry playing at being Nathan.

Only three hours into the visit, and Nathan had to be phoned in Manhattan—secretly, and tearfully, by his mother—and told to come right home to make peace between the Ragpicker and his father. Carrying messages back and forth between Henry—locked in his bedroom quoting Timmy and Sinclair Lewis's *Babbitt*—and his father—in the living room enumerating the opportunities denied to him in 1918 that life was now offering to Henry on a silver platter—Nathan was able to negotiate a settlement by three a.m. All decisions about Henry's career were to be postponed for twelve months. He could continue to act in student plays but at the same time he must continue to carry on as a chemistry major and to fulfill his "obligation," if only for one more summer, to the Chernicks. Then, next year, they would all sit down together to reassess the situation . . . a meeting that never took place, because by the following fall Henry was engaged to Carol Goff, a girl judged by Henry's father to have "a head on her shoulders," and no more was heard of John Carradine or of Timmy, either. *Timmy!* The young drama student's Christian name couldn't have sounded more Christian, or more seditious, as enunciated by their father in the heat of the fray. During that memorable Friday-night family battle back in 1956, Nathan had himself dared to counter at one point with the sacred name of Paul Muni, but *"Timmy!"* his father cried, like a war whoop, *"Timmy!"* and Nathan saw that not even Paul Muni as wily Clarence Darrow, not even Paul Muni live in their living room as patient Louis Pasteur could have persuaded Dr. Zuckerman that a Jew in pancake makeup on the stage was probably no more or less ridiculous in the eyes of God than a Jew in a dental smock drilling a tooth. Then Henry met sweet and studious Carol Goff, a scholarship girl, and gave her his ZBT pin—and so the argument ended for good. Zuckerman figured that was why he'd given her the pin, though officially, he knew, it was to commemorate the loss of Carol's virginity earlier that night. When Henry tried the next semester to get the pin back, it so upset Carol and her family that two weeks later Henry changed his mind and got engaged to Carol instead. And, in their senior year, the upshot of Henry gently trying to break the engagement was their marriage the month after graduation. No, Henry simply couldn't bear to see this kindly, thoughtful, devoted, harmless, self-sacrificing creature suffering so, and suffering so over him. He couldn't bear to make anybody who loved him suffer. He couldn't be that selfish or that cruel.

In the days after the funeral, Henry had several times simply begun to sob in the middle of a conversation—in the middle of a sentence having nothing even to do with the death of their father—and in order to collect himself, went out to take a long walk alone. One morning only minutes after Henry had fled the apartment, unshaven and again close to tears, Zuckerman called Essie in to keep his mother company at breakfast and ran downstairs after his brother. Henry seemed so disturbed, so in need of consolation. But when Zuckerman came out of the lobby onto the sunny esplanade beside the pool, he saw Henry already out on the street, making a call in a phone booth. So, another love affair. That torment too. *The Crisis,* thought Zuckerman, *in the Life of a Husband*.

In Miami Beach, Zuckerman had refrained from bringing up the deathbed scene with his brother. For one thing, their mother was nearly always within earshot, and when he and Henry were alone, either Henry was too unhappy to talk to or they were making plans for their mother's future. To their dismay, she had refused to come up with them to Jersey to stay awhile with Henry and Carol and the kids. Maybe later, but for now she insisted on remaining "close" to her husband. Essie was going to sleep on the living-room sofa bed so that their mother wouldn't be alone at night, and her canasta-club friends had volunteered to take turns staying with the grieving widow during the day. Zuckerman told Essie it might be wise if Flora Sobol was excused from duty. None of them was going to relish a piece in the *Miami Herald* entitled "I Sat Shiva with Carnovsky's Mother."

On the plane he had his first chance to learn what Henry thought about what he still couldn't puzzle out for himself. "Tell me something. What was Dad's last word that night? Did he say 'Better'?"

" 'Better'? Could be. I thought he said 'Batter.' "

Zuckerman smiled. As in "Batter my heart, three-person'd God," or "Batter up!"? "You sure?"

"Sure? No. But I thought it was because of Essie talking about the old days and Grandma. I thought he was all the way back, seeing Grandma over the mandel bread."

Well, there was Tolstoy, thought Zuckerman, to support Henry's conjecture. "To become a tiny boy, close to mother." What Tolstoy had written only days before his own death. "Mama, hold me, baby me . . ."

"I thought he said 'Bastard,' " Zuckerman told him.

Now Henry smiled. The smile his patients fell in love with. "No, I didn't hear that."

"I thought he might be writing one last letter to Lyndon Johnson."

"Oh, Christ," said Henry. "The letters," and went back unsmilingly to sipping his drink. Henry had received his share: after the near-defection at Cornell, a letter a week beginning "Dear Son."

Minutes later Henry said, "Even little Leslie, age seven, became a correspondent of Dad's, you know."

"I didn't."

"Poor kid. He's never gotten another, before or since. He thinks he should get mail all the time now, because of his three letters from Miami."

"What'd they say?"

" 'Dear Grandson. Be nicer to your sisters.' "

"Well, from now on he can be as cruel to them as he likes. Now," Zuckerman added, remembering his brother dashing down to the outdoor phone booth, "we can all be as cruel as we like."

Zuckerman ordered a martini too. First time in his life he'd had a drink only an hour after his eggs. The same was certainly true for Henry. But the inner man was having his day.

Each finished the first drink and ordered a second.

"You know all I could think at the funeral?" Henry said. "How can he be in that box?"

"That's mostly what everybody thinks," Zuckerman assured him.

"The top is screwed on and he'll never get out."

They were flying over Carolina farmland. Clear from thirty-five thousand feet where Mondrian got the idea. The tons of tilled soil, the fibrous net of rooted vegetation, and his father under it all. Not only the lid, not only the few cubic feet of floury Florida loam and the dignified slab of marble to come, but the whole outer wrapping of this seven-sextillion-ton planet.

"Do you know why I married her?" Henry suddenly said.

Ah, so that's who's boxed in and will never get out. Dear Son. Screwed down beneath the tonnage of those two little words.

"Why?" asked Zuckerman.

Henry closed his eyes. "You won't believe this."

"I'll believe anything," Zuckerman told him. "Professional deformity."

"I don't want to believe it myself." He sounded sick with self-recrimination, as though he were sorry now that he'd planted a bomb in his luggage. He was unhinged, all over again. He shouldn't be drinking, Zuckerman thought. There would be worse recriminations later, if he went ahead and spilled some humiliating secret. But Zuckerman made no attempt to save his brother from himself. He had a powerful taste for such secrets. Professional deformity.

"Know why I married Carol?" This time he used her name, as though deliberately to make what he was about to confess more brutishly indiscreet. But it wasn't Henry's savagery, really; it was the savagery of his conscience, overtaking him before he'd even begun to violate its tenets.

"No," replied Zuckerman, to whom Carol had always seemed pretty but dull, "not really."

"It wasn't because she cried. It wasn't because she'd been pinned with the pin and then engaged with the ring. It wasn't even everybody's parents expecting us to . . . I loaned her a book. I loaned her a book, and knew if I didn't marry her I'd never see it again."

"What book?"

"*An Actor Prepares*. A book by Stanislavsky."

"Couldn't you buy another?"

"My notes were in it—from when I was rehearsing the Ragpicker. Do you remember when I was in that play?"

"Oh, I remember it."

"You remember that weekend I came home?"

"I sure do, Henry. Why didn't you go and ask her for the book?"

"It was in her room in the women's dorm. I thought of getting her best friend to steal it for me. This is true. I thought of breaking in there and stealing it myself. I just couldn't bring myself to say that I wanted it back. I didn't want her to know that we were about to break up. I didn't want her to think afterward that all I could think about at a time like that was my book."

"Why did you give it to her in the first place?"

"I was a kid, Nate. She was my 'girl.' I loaned it to her after our first date. For her to see my notes. I was showing off, I suppose. Oh, you know how you loan somebody a book. It's the most natural thing in the world. You get excited and you loan it to them. I was full of a friend I'd made—"

"Timmy."

"God, yes. Timmy. You remember. The Provincetown Players and Timmy. Not that I had an ounce of talent. I thought acting was seething and sobbing. No, nothing would have come of it. And it isn't that I don't love my own work. I do, and I'm goddamn good at it. But the book meant something to me. I wanted Carol to understand. 'Just read this,' I told her. And the next thing I knew, we were married."

"At least you got the book back."

He finished off the second drink. "A lot of good it did me."

Then do him some good, thought Zuckerman. It's why he's made you his confessor. Help him raise this lid still holding him down. Lend a hand. As their father used to say, "He's your brother—*treat* him like a brother."

"Did you ever act in Chekhov that year at Cornell?"

"I had a career of two plays at Cornell. Neither was Chekhov."

"Do you know what Chekhov said as a grown man about his youth? He said he'd had to squeeze the serf out of himself drop by drop. Maybe what you ought to start squeezing out of yourself is the obedient son."

No response. He had closed his eyes again—he might not even be listening.

"You're not a kid, Henry, beholden to narrow conventional people whose idea of life you're obliged to fulfill. He's dead, Henry. Aside from being in that box with the lid screwed down, he is also dead. You loved him and he loved you—but he tried to make you somebody who would never do anything or be anything that couldn't be written up in the *Jewish News* under your graduation picture. The Jewish slice of the American piety—it's what we both fed on for years. He'd come out of the slums, he'd lived with the roughnecks—it must have terrified him to think we'd grow up bums like Sidney. Cousin Sidney, collecting the quarters from the kids who sold the football pools. But to Daddy he was Longy Zwillman's right arm. To Dad he was Lepke."

"To Dad, becoming a drama major at Cornell made you Lepke." His eyes were still shut, and the smile was sardonic.

"Well, a little of Lepke wouldn't kill you at this point."

"It isn't me I'm worried about killing."

"Come on, you're a bigger character than this. An actor prepares. Well, you've been preparing for thirty-two years. Now deliver. You don't have to play the person you were cast as, not if it's what's driving you mad."

Inventing people. Benign enough when you were typing away in the quiet study, but was this his job in the unwritten world? If Henry could perform otherwise, wouldn't he have done so long ago? You shouldn't put such ideas in Henry's head, especially when he's already reeling. But reeling was when somebody could catch you right on the jaw. And besides, Zuckerman was by now a little drunk, as was his kid brother, and somehow a little drunk, it seemed to him idiotic that his kid brother shouldn't have what he wanted. To whom was he closer? Probably more corresponding genes in Henry than in any other animal in the species. More corresponding memories, too. Bedrooms, bathrooms, duties, diseases, remedies, refrigerators, taboos, toys, trips, teachers, neighbors, relatives, yards, stoops, stairwells, jokes, names, places, cars, girls, boys, bus lines . . .

Batter. The mixture time had beaten together for making Zuckermans. Suppose their father had closed things out with that: Boys, you are what I baked. Very different loaves, but God bless you both. There's room for all types.

Neither the Father of Virtue nor the Father of Vice, but the Father of Rational Pleasures and Reasonable Alternatives. Oh, that would have been very nice indeed. But the way it works, you get what you get and the rest you have to do yourself.

"How unhappy are you at home, Henry?"

He answered with his eyes pressed tightly shut. "It's murder."

"Then, for Christ's sake, start squeezing."

At Newark Airport Zuckerman's limousine was waiting. He had phoned early that morning from Miami to arrange to be met by a car with an armed driver. It was from the same outfit that drove Caesara around in New York. He'd found their card where he'd left it—his bookmark in Caesara's Kierkegaard. Before leaving for Miami, he'd pocketed the card, just in case. The book he still meant to return, but several times had restrained himself from sending it, in care of Castro, to Cuba.

He'd slept poorly the night before, thinking of his return to Manhattan and the possibility that the ravishing of his handkerchief by Pepler was not the end of his defilement but only the beginning. What if the wanton ex-Marine was packing a gun? What if he should be hiding in the elevator and try strangling Zuckerman to death? Zuckerman could not only envision the scene—by four a.m., he could smell it. Pepler weighed a ton and reeked of Aqua Velva. He was freshly shaved. For the murder or for the TV interview afterward? *You stole it, Nathan! My hang-up! My secret! My money! My fame!* JERK-OFF ARTIST KILLS BARD OF JERKING-OFF; ZUCKERMAN DEAD BY ONANIST'S HAND.

Most disappointing to be gripped once again by such elemental fears—fears that by dawn had all but vanished; nonetheless, before leaving, he had phoned ahead to hire somebody at least to protect him during the initial stage of reentry. But when he saw the limousine, he thought, *I should have taken the bus. Forget retribution. That's over too. There are no avengers.*

He walked up to the limousine. It was Caesara's young driver, in full livery and dark glasses. "I'll bet you never thought you'd see me again," said Zuckerman.

"Oh, yes I did."

He came back to his brother. Henry was waiting to say goodbye before going to pick his car up in the parking lot.

"I'm all alone," Zuckerman said. "If you should need a place to sleep."

Henry recoiled a little at the suggestion. "I have to get to work, Nathan."

"You'll call me if you need me?"

"I'm all right," Henry said.

He's angry, Zuckerman thought. Now he has to go home knowing he doesn't have to. I should have let him be. You can leave her if you want to. Only he doesn't want to.

They shook hands in front of the terminal. Nobody watching would ever have imagined that once upon a time they had eaten ten thousand meals together, or that only an hour earlier they were momentarily as close as they had been back before either had written a book or touched a girl. A plane took off from Newark, roaring in Nathan's ears.

"He did say 'Bastard,' Nathan. He called you a bastard."

"What?"

Suddenly Henry was furious—and weeping. "You *are* a bastard. A heartless conscienceless bastard. What does loyalty mean to you? What does responsibility mean to you? What does self-denial mean, *restraint*—anything at all? To you everything is disposable! Everything is *ex*posable! Jewish morality, Jewish endurance, Jewish wisdom, Jewish families—everything is grist for your fun-machine. Even your shiksas go down the drain when they don't tickle your fancy anymore. Love, marriage, children, what the hell do you care? To you it's all fun and games. *But that isn't the way it is to the rest of us.* And the worst is how we protect you from knowing what you really are! And what you've done! You killed him, Nathan. Nobody will tell you—they're too frightened of you to say it. They think you're too famous to criticize—that you're far beyond the reach now of ordinary human beings. But you killed him, Nathan. With that book. *Of course* he said 'Bastard.' He'd seen it! He'd seen what you had done to him and Mother in that book!"

"How could he see? Henry, what are you talking about?"

But he knew, he knew, he knew, he'd known it all along. He'd known it when Essie, over their midnight snack, had told him, "If I were you, I wouldn't listen to one goddamn thing they say." He'd known during the rabbi's eulogy. And he'd known before that. He'd known when he was writing the book. But he'd written it anyway. Then, like a blessing, his father had the stroke that sent him into the nursing home, and by the time *Carnovsky* appeared he was too far gone to read it. Zuckerman thought he had beaten the risk. And beaten the rap. He hadn't.

"How could he see it, Henry?"

"Mr. Metz. Stupid, well-meaning Mr. Metz. Daddy made him bring it to him. Made him sit there and read it aloud. You don't believe me, do you? You can't believe that what you write about people has *real consequences*. To you this is probably funny too—your readers will die laughing when they hear this one! *But Dad didn't die laughing*. He died in misery. He died in the most terrible disappointment. It's one thing, God damn you, to entrust your imagination to your instincts, it's another, Nathan, to entrust *your own family!* Poor Mother! Begging us all not to tell you! Our mother, taking the shit she's taking down there because of you—and smiling through it! And still protecting you from the truth of what you've done! You and your superiority! You and your hijinks! You and your 'liberating' book! Do you really think that conscience is a Jewish invention from which you are immune? Do you really think you can just go have a good time with the rest of the swingers without troubling yourself about conscience? Without troubling about anything but seeing how funny you can be about the people who have loved you most in the world? The origin of the universe! When all he was waiting to hear was 'I love you!' 'Dad, I love you'—that was all that was required! Oh, you miserable bastard, don't you tell me about fathers and sons! I *have* a son! I know what it is to love a son, and you don't, you selfish bastard, and you never will!"

Until the spring of 1941, when the boys were eight and four and the Zuckermans moved into the one-family brick house on the tree-lined street up the hill from the park, they had lived at the less desirable end of their Jewish neighborhood, in a small apartment building at the corner of Lyons and Leslie. The plumbing and the heating and the elevator and the drains were never working all at the same time, the Ukrainian superintendent's daughter was Thea the Tease, an older girl with a big bust and a bad reputation, and not everybody in the building had a kitchen floor like the Zuckermans' that you could eat off if worse came to worst. But because of the low rent, and because of the bus stop out front, it was an ideal place for the office of a young chiropodist. In those days Dr. Zuckerman's office was still in the front room where the family listened to the radio at night.

Across the street from the boys' back bedroom, on the

other side of a high wire fence, was a Catholic orphanage with a small truck farm where the orphans worked when they weren't being taught—and, as Nathan and his little friends understood it, being beaten with a stick—by the priests in the Catholic school. Two old dray horses also worked on the farm, a most unexpected sight in their neighborhood; but then the sight of a priest buying a pack of Luckies in the candy store downstairs, or driving by in a Buick with the radio on, was more unexpected still. What he knew about horses he knew from *Black Beauty;* about priests and nuns he knew even less—only that they hated the Jews. One of Zuckerman's first short stories, written in his freshman year of high school and called "Orphans," was about a small Jewish boy with a bedroom window overlooking a Catholic orphanage, who wonders what it would be like to live behind their fence rather than his. Once a dark heavyset nun had come over from the orphanage to have his father cut away an ingrown toenail. After she left, Nathan had waited (in vain) for his mother to go into his father's office with a pail and a rag to clean the door handles the nun had touched coming and going. He had never been more curious about anything in his life than about the nun's unshod feet, but his father said nothing that evening within hearing distance of the children, and at six, Nathan was neither young enough nor old enough to go ahead and ask what they looked like. Seven years later the nun's visit became the centerpiece of "Orphans," a short-short story sent out to the editors of *Liberty,* then *Collier's,* then *The Saturday Evening Post,* under the ersatz name Nicholas Zack, and for which he received his first set of rejection slips.

Instead of going directly back to New York, he instructed the driver to follow the sign that said "Newark," postponing for just a while longer the life of the Nathan Zuckerman whom the mute inglorious little Zack had rather surprisingly become. He guided him along the highway and up the ramp to Frelinghuysen Avenue; then past the park and the tip of the lake where he and Henry had learned to ice-skate, and up the long Lyons Avenue hill; past the hospital where he had been born and circumcised, and on toward that fence that had been his first subject. His driver was armed. The only way, according to Pepler, to enter this city anymore.

Zuckerman pushed the button that lowered the glass partition. "What sort of weapon do you carry?" he asked the driver.

"A .38, sir."

"Where do you carry it?"

He slapped his right hip. "Like to see it, Mr. Z.?"

Yes, he should see it. Seeing is believing and believing is knowing and knowing beats unknowing and the unknown.

"Yes."

The driver hiked up his jacket and unsnapped a holster

hooked to his belt, a holster not much larger than an eyeglass case. When they stopped for a light, he held up in his right hand a tiny handgun with a snub black barrel.

What is Art? thought Zuckerman.

"Anybody comes within ten feet of this baby is in for a big surprise."

The pistol smelled of oil. "Freshly cleaned," said Zuckerman.

"Yes, sir."

"Freshly fired?"

"On the range, sir, last night."

"You can put it away now."

Predictably the two-story apartment building where he'd first lived struck him as a lilliputian replica of the red-brick canopied fortress he'd have described from memory. Had there been a canopy? If so, it was gone. The building's front door was also gone, torn from its hinges, and, to either side of the missing door, the large windows looking into the foyer had lost their glass and were boarded over. There was exposed wiring where once there had been two lamps to light your way in, and the entryway itself was unswept and littered with trash. The building had become a slum.

Across the street, the tailor shop had become a store for idol worshippers—holy statuary on display in the window, along with other "Spiritual Supplies." The corner storefront, once a grocery, was now owned and occupied by the Calvary Evangelistic Assembly, Inc. Four stout black women with shopping bags were standing and talking at the bus stop. In his early childhood, four black women at the bus stop would have been domestics up from Springfield Avenue to clean for the Jewish women in the Weequahic neighborhood. Now they left the neighborhood, where they themselves lived, to clean for the Jewish women in the suburbs. Except for the elderly trapped in nearby housing projects, the Jews had all vanished. So had almost everyone white, including the Catholic orphans. The orphanage appeared to have been converted into some sort of city school, and there was a small new nondescript building on the corner where the truck farm had been. A bank. Looking around, he wondered who banked there. But for candles, incense, and holy statuary, nothing seemed to be for sale any longer on Lyons Avenue. There didn't seem to be anywhere to buy a loaf of bread or a pound of meat or a pint of ice cream or a bottle of aspirin, let alone a dress or a watch or a chair. Their little thoroughfare of shops and shopkeepers was dead.

Just what he wanted to see. "Over," he thought. All his lyrical feeling for the neighborhood had gone into *Carnovsky*. It had to—there was no other place for it. "Over. Over. Over. Over. Over. I've served my time."

He had the driver cruise slowly down the block toward Chancellor Avenue, the way he'd walked each morning to school. "Stop," he said, and looked up an alleyway between two houses to the garage where the superintendent's wayward daughter, Thea, and the grocer's daughter,

Doris, had enticed him one day by telling him how pretty he was. 1939? 1940? When they shut the garage doors he feared the worst—his mother had warned him that Thea was too "developed" for her age, and no one had to remind him that she was Christian. But all Thea made him do was stand beside a big black grease spot and repeat everything she said. The words meant little to him but a great deal obviously to Thea and the grocer's daughter, who couldn't stop giggling and hugging each other. It was his first strong experience of the power of language and of the power of girls; as the orphanage fence beyond his bedroom window was the first momentous encounter with caste and chance, with the mystery of a destiny.

A young black man, his head completely shaved, stepped out of one of the houses with a German shepherd and stared down from the stoop at the chauffeur-driven limousine in front of his alleyway, and at the white man in the back seat who was looking his place up and down. A chain fence surrounded the three-story house and the little garden of weeds out front. Had the fellow cared to ask, Zuckerman could without any trouble have told him the names of the three families who lived in the flats on each floor before World War II. But that wasn't what this black man wished to know. "Who you supposed to be?" he said.

"No one," replied Zuckerman, and that was the end of that. You are no longer any man's son, you are no longer some good woman's husband, you are no longer your brother's brother, and you don't come from anywhere anymore, either. They skipped the grade school and the playground and the hot-dog joint and headed back to New York, passing on the way out to the Parkway the synagogue where he'd taken Hebrew lessons after school until he was thirteen. It was now an African Methodist Episcopal Church.

The Anatomy
Lesson

The chief obstacle to correct diagnosis in painful conditions is the fact that the symptom is often felt at a distance from its source.

—*Textbook of Orthopaedic Medicine*
JAMES CYRIAX, M.D.

1 The Collar

When he is sick, every man wants his mother; if
she's not around, other women must do. Zuckerman was
making do with four other women. He'd never had so
many women at one time, or so many doctors, or drunk
so much vodka, or done so little work, or known despair
of such wild proportions. Yet he didn't seem to have a
disease that anybody could take seriously. Only the pain—
in his neck, arms, and shoulders, pain that made it difficult to walk for more than a few city blocks or even to
stand very long in one place. Just having a neck, arms,
and shoulders was like carrying another person around.

409

Ten minutes out getting the groceries and he had to hurry home and lie down. Nor could he bring back more than one light bagful per trip, and even then he had to hold it cradled up against his chest like somebody eighty years old. Holding the bag down at his side only worsened the pain. It was painful to bend over and make his bed. To stand at the stove was painful, holding nothing heavier than a spatula and waiting for an egg to fry. He couldn't throw open a window, not one that required any strength. Consequently, it was the women who opened the windows for him: opened his windows, fried his egg, made his bed, shopped for his food, and effortlessly, manfully, toted home his bundles. One woman on her own could have done what was needed in an hour or two a day, but Zuckerman didn't have one woman any longer. That was how he came to have four.

To sit up in a chair and read he wore an orthopedic collar, a spongy lozenge in a white ribbed sleeve that he fastened around his neck to keep the cervical vertebrae aligned and to prevent him from turning his head unsupported. The support and the restriction of movement were supposed to diminish the hot line of pain that ran from behind his right ear into his neck, then branched downward beneath the scapula like a menorah held bottom side up. Sometimes the collar helped, sometimes not, but just wearing it was as maddening as the pain itself. He couldn't concentrate on anything other than himself in his collar.

The text in hand was from his college days, *The Oxford Book of Seventeenth Century Verse*. Inside the front cover, above his name and the date inscribed in blue ink, was a single penciled notation in his 1949 script, a freshman aperçu that read, "Metaphysical poets pass easily from trivial to sublime." For the first time in twenty-four years he turned to the poems of George Herbert. He'd got the book down to read "The Collar," hoping to find something there to help him wear his own. That was commonly believed to be a function of great literature: antidote to suffering through depiction of our common fate. As Zuckerman was learning, pain could make you awfully primitive if not counteracted by steady, regular doses of philosophical thinking. Maybe he could pick up some hints from Herbert.

> ... Shall I be still in suit?
> Have I no harvest but a thorn
> To let me blood, and not restore
> What I have lost with cordiall fruit?
> Sure there was wine
> Before my sighs did drie it: there was corn
> Before my tears did drown it.
> Is the yeare only lost to me?
> Have I no bayes to crown it?
> No flowers, no garlands gay? all blasted?
> All wasted?
> ... But as I rav'd and grew more fierce and wilde
> At every word

> Me thought I heard one calling, *Childe*:
> And I reply'd, *My Lord*.

As best he could with his aching arm, he threw the
volume across the room. Absolutely not! He refused to
make of his collar, or of the affliction it was designed to
assuage, a metaphor for anything grandiose. Metaphysical
poets may pass easily from trivial to sublime, but on the
strength of the experience of the past eighteen months,
Zuckerman's impression was of proceeding, if at all, in the
opposite direction.

Writing the last page of a book was as close as he'd
ever come to sublimity, and that hadn't happened in four
years. He couldn't remember when he'd written a *readable* page. Even while he was wearing the collar, the
spasm in the upper trapezius and the aching soreness to
either side of the dorsal spine made it difficult to type just
the address on an envelope. When a Mount Sinai orthopedist had ascribed his troubles to twenty years of hammering away at a manual portable, he at once went
off to buy an IBM Selectric II; however, when he tried at
home to get to work, he found that he ached as much
over the new, unfamiliar IBM keyboard as he had over the
last of his little Olivettis. Just a glimpse of the Olivetti
stowed away in its battered traveling case at the back of
his bedroom closet and the depression came rolling in—the
way Bojangles Robinson must have felt looking at his old
dancing shoes. How simple, back when he was still

healthy, to give it a shove and make room on his desk for
his lunch or his notes or his reading or his mail. How he'd
loved to push them around, those silent uncomplaining
sparring partners—the pounding he'd been giving them
since he was twenty! There when he paid his alimony and
answered his fans, there to lay his head beside when overcome by the beauty or ugliness of what he'd just composed, there for every page of every draft of the four
published novels, of the three buried alive—if Olivettis could talk, you'd get the novelist naked. While from
the IBM prescribed by the first orthopedist, you'd get
nothing—only the smug, puritanical, workmanlike hum
telling of itself and all its virtues: I am a Correcting Selectric II. I never do anything wrong. Who this man is I
have no idea. And from the look of things neither does
he.

Writing manually was no better. Even in the good old
days, pushing his left hand across the paper, he looked like
some brave determined soul learning to use an artificial
limb. Nor were the results that easy to decipher. Writing by hand was the clumsiest thing he did. He danced the
rumba better than he wrote by hand. He held the pen too
tight. He clenched his teeth and made agonized faces. He
stuck his elbow out from his side as though beginning the
breast stroke, then hooked his hand down and around
from his forearm so as to form the letters from above
rather than below—the contortionist technique by which
many a left-handed child had taught himself how not to

smear his words as he proceeded across the page from left to right back in the era of the inkwell. A highly recommended osteopath had even concluded that the cause of Zuckerman's problems was just this: the earnest left-handed schoolboy, straining to overcome the impediment of wet ink, who had begun microscopically to twist the writer's spine off the vertical axis and screw it down cockeyed into his sacrum. His rib cage was askew. His clavicle was crooked. His left scapula winged out at its lower angle like a chicken's. Even his humerus was too tightly packed into the shoulder capsule and inserted in the joint on the bias. Though to the untrained eye he might appear more or less symmetrical and decently proportioned, within he was as misshapen as Richard III. According to the osteopath, he'd been warping at a steady rate since he was seven. Began with his homework. Began with the first of his reports on life in New Jersey. "In 1666 Governor Carteret provided an interpreter for Robert Treat and also a guide up the Hackensack River to meet with a representative of Oraton, the aged chief of the Hackensacks. Robert Treat wanted Oraton to know that the white settlers wished only peace." Began at ten with Newark's Robert Treat and the euphonious elegance of *interpreter* and *representative*, ended with Newark's Gilbert Carnovsky and the blunt monosyllables *cock* and *cunt*. Such was the Hackensack up which the writer had paddled, only to dock at the port of pain.

When sitting upright at the typewriter became too painful, he tried leaning back in an easy chair and doing the best he could with his imperfect longhand. He had the collar to brace his neck, the firm, uncushioned, back of the upholstered chair to support his spine, and a piece of beaverboard, cut to his specifications, laid across the arms of the chair to serve as a portable desk for his composition books. His place was certainly quiet enough for total concentration. He'd had his big study windows double-glazed so that nobody's television or phonograph would blare through from the building backing onto his brownstone apartment, and the ceiling had been soundproofed so he wouldn't be disturbed by the scratching of his upstairs neighbor's two Pekinese. The study was carpeted, a deep copper-brown wool, and the windows were hung to the floor with creamy velvet curtains. It was a cozy, quiet, book-lined room. He'd spent half his life sealed off in rooms just like it. Atop the small cabinet where he kept his vodka bottle and his glass were favorite old photographs in Plexiglas frames: his dead parents as newlyweds in his grandparents' backyard; ex-wives blooming with health on Nantucket; his estranged brother leaving Cornell in 1957, a magna cum laude (and a tabula rasa) in a cap and gown. If during the day he spoke at all, it was only small talk to those pictures; otherwise, enough silence even to satisfy Proust. He had silence, comfort, time, money, but composing in longhand set off a throbbing pain in his upper arm that in no time at all made him sick to his stomach. He kneaded the muscle with his right hand while he continued to write with the left. He tried not thinking about it. He pretended that it wasn't *his* upper arm hurting but somebody else's. He tried to outwit it by stopping and starting. Stopping long enough helped the pain but hurt the writing; by the tenth time he'd stopped he had nothing left to write, and with nothing to write, no reason to be. When he tore off the neck collar and threw himself to the floor, the ripping sound of the Velcro fastener coming undone could have been emitted by his guts. Every thought and feeling, ensnared by the selfness of pain.

In a children's furniture store on Fifty-seventh Street he had bought a soft red plastic-covered playmat that was permanently laid out in his study now, between his desk and his easy chair. When he could no longer bear sitting up, he stretched supine upon the playmat, his head supported by *Roget's Thesaurus*. He'd come to conduct most of the business of his waking life on the playmat. From there, no longer laden with an upper torso or saddled with fifteen pounds of head, he made phone calls, received visitors, and followed Watergate on TV. Instead of his own spectacles, he wore a pair of prism glasses that enabled him to see at right angles. They were designed for the bedridden by a downtown optical firm to which he'd been referred by his physiotherapist. Through his prism glasses he followed our President's chicanery—the dummy gestures, the satanic sweating, the screwy dazzling lies. He almost felt for him, the only other American he saw daily who seemed to be in as much trouble as he was. Flat out on the floor, Zuckerman could also see whichever of his women was seated upright on the sofa. What the woman in attendance saw were the rectangular opaque undersides of the protruding glasses and Zuckerman explaining Nixon to the ceiling.

He tried from the playmat to dictate fiction to a secretary, but he hadn't the fluency for it and sometimes went as long as an hour without a word to say. He couldn't write without seeing the writing; though he could picture what the sentences pictured, he couldn't picture the sentences unless he saw them unfold and fasten one to the other. The secretary was only twenty and, during the first few weeks particularly, got too easily caught up in his anguish. The sessions were torture for both of them, and generally ended with the secretary down on the playmat. Intercourse, fellatio, and cunnilingus Zuckerman could endure more or less without pain, provided he was supine and kept the thesaurus beneath his head for support. The thesaurus was just the right thickness to prevent the back of his skull falling below the line of his shoulders and setting off the pain in his neck. Its inside cover was inscribed "From Dad—You have my every confidence," and dated "June 24, 1946." A book to enrich his vocabulary upon graduation from grade school.

To lie with him on the playmat came the four women. They were all the vibrant life he had: secretary-confidante-cook-housekeeper-companion—aside from the doses of Nixon's suffering, they were the entertainment. On his

back he felt like their whore, paying in sex for someone
to bring him the milk and the paper. They told him their
troubles and took off their clothes and lowered the orifices
for Zuckerman to fill. Without a taxing vocation or a
hopeful prognosis, he was theirs to do with as they wished;
the more conspicuous his helplessness, the more forthright their desire. Then they ran. Washed up, downed a
coffee, kneeled to kiss him goodbye, and ran off to disappear in real lives. Leaving Zuckerman on his back for
whoever rang the bell next.

Well and working, he'd never had time for liaisons like
these, not even when he'd been tempted. Too many wives
in too few years to allow for a consortium of mistresses.
Marriage had been his bulwark against the tremendous
distraction of women. He'd married for the order, the
intimacy, the dependable comradery, for the routine and
regularity of monogamous living; he'd married so as never
to waste himself on another affair, or go crazy with boredom at another party, or wind up alone in the living room
at night after a day alone in his study. To sit alone each
night doing the reading that he required to concentrate
himself for the next day's solitary writing was too much
even for Zuckerman's single-mindedness, and so into the
voluptuous austerity he had enticed a woman, one woman
at a time, a quiet, thoughtful, serious, literate, self-sufficient woman who didn't require to be taken places, who
was content instead to sit after dinner and read in silence
across from him and his book.

Following each divorce, he discovered anew that unmarried a man had to take women places: out to restaurants, for walks in the park, to museums and the opera
and the movies—not only had to go to the movies but
afterwards had to discuss them. If they became lovers,
there was the problem of getting away in the morning
while his mind was still fresh for his work. Some women
expected him to eat breakfast with them, even to talk to
them over breakfast like other human beings. Sometimes
they wanted to go back to bed. *He* wanted to go back to
bed. It was certainly going to be more eventful in bed
than back at the typewriter with the book. Much less frus-
trating too. You actually could complete what you set out
to accomplish without ten false starts and sixteen drafts
and all that pacing around the room. So he dropped his
guard—and the morning was shot.

No such temptations with the wives, not as time went
by.

But pain had changed it all. Whoever spent the night
was not only invited to breakfast but asked to stay on for
lunch if she had the time (and if no one else was to turn
up till dinner). He'd slip a wet washcloth and a bulging ice pack under his terry-cloth robe, and while the ice
anesthetized his upper trapezius (and the orthopedic
collar supported his neck), he'd lean back and listen in his
red velvet chair. He'd had a fatal weakness for high-
minded mates back when all he ever thought about was
toiling away; excellent opportunity, immobilization, to

sound out less predictably upright women than his three ex-wives. Maybe he'd learn something and maybe he wouldn't, but at least they would help to distract him, and according to the rheumatologist at NYU, distraction, pursued by the patient with real persistence, could reduce even the worst pain to tolerable levels.

The psychoanalyst whom he consulted took a contrary position: he wondered aloud if Zuckerman hadn't given up fighting the illness to *retain* (with a fairly untroubled conscience) his "harem of Florence Nightingales." Zuckerman so resented the crack he nearly walked out. Given up? What could he do that he hadn't—what was left that he was unwilling to try? Since the pains had begun in earnest eighteen months before, he'd waited his turn in the offices of three orthopedists, two neurologists, a physiotherapist, a rheumatologist, a radiologist, an osteopath, a vitamin doctor, an acupuncturist, and now the analyst. The acupuncturist had stuck twelve needles into him on fifteen different occasions, a hundred and eighty needles in all, not one of which had done a thing. Zuckerman sat shirtless in one of the acupuncturist's eight treatment cubicles, the needles hanging from him, and reading *The New York Times*—sat obediently for fifteen minutes, then paid his twenty-five dollars and rode back uptown, jangling with pain each time the cab took a pothole. The vitamin doctor gave him a series of five vitamin B-12 shots. The osteopath yanked his rib cage upward, pulled his arms outward, and cracked his neck sharply to either side. The physiotherapist gave him hot packs, ultrasound, and massage. One orthopedist gave him "trigger-point" injections and told him to throw out the Olivetti and buy the IBM; the next, having informed Zuckerman that he was an author too, though not of "best-sellers," examined him lying down and standing up and bending over, and, after Zuckerman had dressed, ushered him out of his office, announcing to his receptionist that he had no more time that week to waste on hypochondriacs. The third orthopedist prescribed a hot bath for twenty minutes every morning, after which Zuckerman was to perform a series of stretching exercises. The baths were pleasant enough—Zuckerman listened to Mahler through the open doorway—but the exercises, simple as they were, so exacerbated all his pains that within the week he rushed back to the first orthopedist, who gave him a second series of trigger-point injections that did no good. The radiologist X-rayed his chest, back, neck, cranium, shoulders, and arms. The first neurologist who saw the X-rays said he wished his own spine was in such good shape; the second prescribed hospitalization, two weeks of neck traction to alleviate pressure on a cervical disc—if not the worst experience of Zuckerman's life, easily the most humbling. He didn't even want to think about it, and generally there was nothing that happened to him, no matter how bad, that he didn't want to think about. But he was stunned by his cowardice. Even the sedation, far from helping, made the powerlessness that much more frightening and oppressive. He knew he would go berserk from the moment they fastened the weights to the harness holding his head. On the eighth morning, though there was no one in the room to hear him, he began to shout from where he was pinned to the bed, "Let me up! Let me go!" and within fifteen minutes was back in his clothes and down at the cashier's cage settling his bill. Only when he was safely out onto the street, hailing a cab, did he think, "And what if something really terrible were happening to you? What then?"

Jenny had come down from the country to help him through what was to have been the two weeks of traction. She made the round of the galleries and museums in the morning, then after lunch came to the hospital and read to him for two hours from *The Magic Mountain*. It had seemed the appropriate great tome for the occasion, but strapped inert upon his narrow bed, Zuckerman grew increasingly irritated by Hans Castorp and the dynamic opportunities for growth provided him by TB. Nor could life in New York Hospital's room 611 be said to measure up to the deluxe splendors of a Swiss sanatorium before the First World War, not even at $1,500 a week. "Sounds to me," he told Jenny, "like a cross between the Salzburg Seminars and the stately old *Queen Mary*. Five great meals a day and then tedious lectures by European intellectuals, complete with erudite jests. All that philosophy. All that snow. Reminds me of the University of Chicago."

He'd first met Jenny while visiting the retreat of some friends on a wooded mountainside in a village up the Hudson called Bearsville. The daughter of a local school-teacher, she'd been down to art school at Cooper Union and then three years on her own with a knapsack in Europe, and now, back where she'd begun, was living alone in a wood shack with a cat and her paints and a Franklin stove. She was twenty-eight, robust, lonely, blunt, pink-complexioned, with a healthy set of largish white teeth, baby-fine carrot-colored hair, and impressive muscles in her arms. No long temptress fingers like his secretary Diana—she had *hands*. "Someday, if you like," she said to Zuckerman, "I'll tell you stories about my jobs—'My Biceps and How I Got Them.'" Before leaving for Manhattan, he'd stopped off at her cabin unannounced, ostensibly to look at her landscapes. Skies, trees, hills, and roads just as blunt as she was. Van Gogh without the vibrating sun. Quotations from Van Gogh's letters to his brother were tacked up beside the easel, and a scarred copy of the French edition of the letters, the one she'd lugged around Europe in her knapsack, lay in the pile of art books by the daybed. On the fiberboard walls were pencil drawings: cows, horses, pigs, nests, flowers, vegetables—all announcing with the same forthright charm, "Here I am and I am real."

They strolled through a ravaged orchard out behind the cabin, sampling the crop of gnarled fruit. Jenny asked him, "Why does your hand keep stealing up to your shoulder?" Zuckerman hadn't even realized what he was doing; the pain, at this point, had only cornered about a quarter of his existence, and he still thought of it as something like a spot on his coat that had only to be brushed away. Yet no matter how hard he brushed, nothing happened. "Some sort of strain," he replied. "From stiff-arming the critics?" she asked. "More likely stiff-arming myself. What's it like alone up here?" "A lot of painting, a lot of gardening, a lot of masturbating. It must be nice to have money and buy things. What's the most extravagant thing you've ever done?" The most extravagant, the most foolish, the most vile, the most thrilling—he told her, then she told him. Hours of questions and answers, but for a while no further than that. "Our great sexless rapport," she called it, when they spoke for long stretches on the phone at night. "Tough luck for me, maybe, but I don't want to be one of your girls. I'm better off with my hammer, building a new floor." "How'd you learn to build a floor?" "It's easy."

One midnight she'd called to say she'd been out in the garden bringing in the vegetables by moonlight. "The natives up here tell me it's going to freeze in a few hours. I'm coming down to Lemnos to watch you lick your wounds." "Lemnos? I don't remember Lemnos." "Where the Greeks put Philoctetes and his foot."

She'd stayed for three days on Lemnos. She squirted the base of his neck with anesthetizing ethyl chloride; she sat unclothed astride his knotted back and massaged between his shoulder blades; she cooked them dinner, coq au vin and cassoulet—dishes tasting strongly of bacon—and the vegetables she'd harvested before the frost; she told him about France and her adventures there with men and women. Coming from the bathroom at bedtime, he caught her by the desk looking into his datebook. "Oddly furtive," he said, "for someone so open." She merely laughed and said, "You couldn't write if you didn't do worse. Who's 'D'? Who's 'G'? How many do we come to all together?" "Why? Like to meet some of the others?" "No thanks. I don't think I want to get into that. That's what I thought I was phasing myself out of up on my mountaintop." On the last morning of that first visit he wanted to give her something—something other than a book. He'd been giving women books (and the lectures that went with them) all his life. He gave Jenny ten $100 bills. "What's this for" she said. "You just told me that you couldn't stand coming down here looking like a yokel. Then there's the curiosity about extravagance. Van Gogh had his brother, you have me. Take it." She returned three hours later with a scarlet cashmere cloak, burgundy boots, and a big bottle of Bal à Versailles. "I went to Bergdorf's," she said rather shyly, but proudly—"here's your change," and handed him two quarters, a dime, and three pennies. She took off all her yokel clothes and put on just the cloak and the boots. "Know what?" she said, looking in the mirror. "I feel like I'm pretty." "You *are* pretty." She opened the bottle and dabbed at herself with the stopper; she perfumed the tip of her tongue. Then again to the mirror. A long look. "I feel tall." That she wasn't and wouldn't be. She phoned from the country that evening to tell him about her mother's reaction when she stopped by the house, wearing the cloak and smelling of Bal à Versailles, and explained it was a gift from a man. "She said, 'I wonder what your grandmother will say about that coat.'" Well, a harem's a harem, Zuckerman thought. "Ask your grandmother's size and I'll get her one too."

The two weeks of hospital traction began with Jenny reading to him in the afternoons from *The Magic Mountain*, then back at his apartment at night drawing pictures in her sketchbook of his desk, his chair, his bookshelves, and his clothes, pictures that she taped to the wall of his room the next time she came to visit. Each day she made a drawing of an old American sampler with an uplifting adage stitched in the center, and this too she taped to the wall he could see. "To deepen your outlook," she told him.

The only antidote to mental suffering
is physical pain.
KARL MARX

One does not love a place the less for having
suffered in it.
JANE AUSTEN

If one is strong enough to resist certain shocks,
to solve more or less complicated physical diffi-
culties, then from forty to fifty one is again in
a new relatively normal tideway.

V. VAN GOGH

She devised a chart to trace the progress of the treatment on his outlook. At the end of seven days it looked
like this:

DAY	Elan	Humor	Sanity	Appetite	Congeniality	Stoicism	Libido	Pettiness (lack of)	Pissing and Moaning	Courtesy to Jenny
1	A	A	A	A	A	A	F	A	A	A
2	B	A	B	A	A	A	F	C	C	A
3	A	A	A	A	A	A	F	B	B	A
4	C	B	C	A	C	B	A	C	C	A
5	C	B	A	C	B	A	F	B	B	B
6	C	C	C	C	C	C	C	C	B	A
7	F	D	F	F	C	D	F	D	B	F
8										
9										
10										
11										
12										
13										
14										

On the eighth afternoon, when she arrived with her drawing pad at room 611, Zuckerman was gone; she found him at home, on the playmat, half drunk. "Too much inlook for the outlook," he told her. "Too all-encompassing. Too isolating. Broke down."

"Oh," she said lightly, "I don't think this constitutes much of a breakdown. I couldn't have lasted an hour."

"Life smaller and smaller and smaller. Wake up thinking about my neck. Go to sleep thinking about my neck. Only thought, which doctor to turn to when this doesn't help the neck. There to get well and knew I was getting worse. Hans Castorp better at all this than I am, Jennifer. Nothing in that bed but me. Nothing but a neck thinking neck-thoughts. No Settembrini, no Naphta, no snow. No glamorous intellectual voyage. Trying to find my way out and I only work my way further in. Defeated. Ashamed." He was also angry enough to scream.

"No, the problem was me." She poured him another drink. "I wish I were more of an entertainer. I only wish I weren't this tough lump. Well, forget it. We tried—it didn't work."

He sat at the kitchen table rubbing his neck and finishing the vodka while she made her bacony lamb stew. He didn't want her out of his sight. Levelheaded Jenny, let's make the underside of domesticity the whole thing—live with me and be my sweet tough lump. He was about ready to ask her to move in. "I said to myself in bed, 'Come what may, when I get out of here I throw myself back into

work. If it hurts it hurts and the hell with it. Muster all
your understanding and just overcome it.' "

"And?"

"Too elementary for understanding. Understanding
doesn't touch it. Worrying about it, wondering about it,
fighting it, treating it, trying to ignore it, trying to figure
out what it is—it makes my ordinary inwardness look like
New Year's Eve in Times Square. When you're in pain all
you think about is not being in pain. Back and back and
back to the one obsession. I should never have asked you
to come down. I should have done it alone. But even this
way I was too weak. You, a witness to this."

"Witness to what? Come on, for *my* outlook it was just
fine. You don't know how I've loved running around here
wearing a skirt. I've been taking care of myself a long
time now in my earnest, blustery way. Well, for you I can
be softer, gentler, calmer—you've provided a chance for
me to provide in a womanly way. No need for anybody to
feel bad about that. It's guilt-free time, Nathan, for both
of us. I'll be of use to you, you be of use to me, and let's
neither of us worry about the consequences. Let my
grandmother do that."

Choose Jenny? Tempting if she'd have it. Her spunk,
her health, her independence, the Van Gogh quotations,
the unwavering will—how all that quieted the invalid
frenzy. But what would happen when he was well?
Choose Jenny because of the ways in which she approxi-
mates Mrs. Zuckermans I, II, and III? The best reason not

to choose her. Choose like a patient in need of a nurse? A wife as a Band-Aid? In a fix like this, the only choice is not to choose. Wait it out, as is.

It was the severe depression brought on by the eight days imprisoned in traction—and by the thought of waiting it out as is—that sent him running to the psychoanalyst. But they didn't get on at all. He spoke of the appeal of illness, the returns on sickness, he told Zuckerman about the psychic payoff for the patient. Zuckerman allowed that there might well be profits to be reckoned in similarly enigmatic cases, but as for himself, he hated being sick: there was no payoff that could possibly compensate for his disabling physical pain. The "secondary gains" the analyst identified couldn't begin to make up for the primary loss. But perhaps, the analyst suggested, the Zuckerman who was getting paid off wasn't the self he perceived as himself but the ineradicable infant, the atoning penitent, the guilty pariah—perhaps it was the remorseful son of the dead parents, the author of *Carnovsky*.

It had taken three weeks for the doctor to say this out loud. It might be months before he broke the news of the hysterical conversion symptom.

"Expiation through suffering?" Zuckerman said. "The pain being my judgment on myself and that book?"

"Is it?" the analyst asked.

"No," Zuckerman replied, and three weeks after it had begun, he terminated the therapy by walking out.

One doctor prescribed a regimen of twelve aspirin per day, another prescribed Butazolidin, another Robaxin, another Percodan, another Valium, another Prednisone; another told him to throw all the pills down the toilet, the poisonous Prednisone first, and "learn to live with it." Untreatable pain of unknown origins is one of the vicissitudes of life—however much it impaired physical movement, it was still wholly compatible with a perfect state of health. Zuckerman was simply a well man who suffered pain. "And I make it a habit," continued the no-nonsense doctor, "never to treat anybody who isn't ill. Furthermore," he advised, "after you leave here, steer clear of the psychosomologists. You don't need any more of that." "What's a psychosomologist?" "A baffled little physician. The Freudian personalization of every ache and pain is the crudest weapon to have been bequeathed to these guys since the leech pot. If pain were only the expression of something else, it would all be hunky-dory. But unhappily life isn't organized as logically as that. Pain is in addition to everything else. There are hysterics, of course, who can mime any disease, but they constitute a far more exotic species of chameleon than the psychosomologists lead all you gullible sufferers to believe. You are no such reptile. Case dismissed."

It was only days after the psychoanalyst had accused him, for the first time, of giving up the fight that Diana, his part-time secretary, took Zuckerman—who was able still to drive in forward gear but could no longer turn his

head to back up—took him out in a rent-a-car to the Long
Island laboratory where an electronic pain suppressor had
just been invented. He'd read an item in the business section of the Sunday *Times* announcing the laboratory's
acquisition of a patent on the device, and the next morning at nine phoned to arrange an appointment. The director and the chief engineer were in the parking lot to welcome him when he and Diana arrived; they were thrilled
that Nathan Zuckerman should be their first "pain patient" and snapped a Polaroid picture of him at the front
entrance. The chief engineer explained that he had developed the idea to relieve the director's wife of sinus
headaches. They were very much in the experimental
stages, still discovering refinements of technique by which
to alleviate the most recalcitrant forms of chronic pain.
He got Zuckerman out of his shirt and showed him how
to use the machine. After the demonstration session,
Zuckerman felt neither better nor worse, but the director
assured him that his wife was a new woman and insisted
that Zuckerman take a pain suppressor home on approval
and keep it for as long as he liked.

Isherwood is a camera with his shutter open, I am the
experiment in chronic pain.

The machine was about the size of an alarm clock. He
set the timer, put two moistened electrode pads above and
below the site of the pain, and six times a day gave himself
a low-voltage shock for five minutes. And six times a day
he waited for the pain to go away—actually he waited for

it to go away a hundred times a day. Having waited long enough, he then took Valium or aspirin or Butazolidin or Percodan or Robaxin; at five in the evening he said the hell with it and began taking the vodka. And as tens of millions of Russians have known for hundreds of years, that is the best pain suppressor of all.

By December 1973, he'd run out of hope of finding a treatment, drug, doctor, or cure—certainly of finding an honest disease. He was living with it, but not because he'd learned to. What he'd learned was that something decisive had happened to him, and whatever the unfathomable reason, he and his existence weren't remotely what they'd been between 1933 and 1971. He knew about solitary confinement from writing alone in a room virtually every day since his early twenties; he'd served nearly twenty years of that sentence, obediently and on his best behavior. But this was confinement without the writing and he was taking it only a little better than the eight days harnessed to room 611. Indeed, he had never left off upbraiding himself with the question that had followed him from the hospital after his escape: What if what was happening to you were really terrible?

Yet, even if this didn't register terrible on the scale of global misery, it felt terrible to him. He felt pointless, worthless, meaningless, stunned that it should *seem* so terrible and undo him so completely, bewildered by defeat on a front where he hadn't even known himself to be at war. He had shaken free at an early age from the sentimental claims of a conventional, protective, worshipful family, he had surmounted a great university's beguiling purity, he had torn loose from the puzzle of passionless marriages to three exemplary women and from the moral propriety of his own early books; he had worked hard for his place as a writer—eager for recognition in his striving twenties, desperate for serenity in his celebrated thirties—only at forty to be vanquished by a causeless, nameless, untreatable phantom disease. It wasn't leukemia or lupus or diabetes, it wasn't multiple sclerosis or muscular dystrophy or even rheumatoid arthritis—it was nothing. Yet to nothing he was losing his confidence, his sanity, and his self-respect.

He was also losing his hair. Either from all the worrying or all the drugs. He saw hair on the thesaurus when he rose from a session on the playmat. Hair came away by the combful as he prepared himself at the bathroom mirror for his next empty day. Shampooing in the shower, he found the strands of hair looped in the palms of his hands doubling and tripling with every rinse—he expected to see things getting better and with each successive rinsing they got worse.

In the Yellow Pages he found "Anton Associates Trichological Clinic"—the least outlandish ad under "Scalp Care"—and went off to the basement of the Commodore Hotel to see if they could make good on their modest promise to "control all controllable hair problems." He had the time, he had the hair problem, and it would be something like an adventure voyaging from the playmat to midtown one afternoon a week. The treatments couldn't be less effective than what he'd been getting at Manhattan's finest medical facilities for his neck, arms, and shoulders. In happier times he might have resigned himself with little more than a pang to the dismaying change in his appearance, but with so much else giving way in life, he decided "No, no further": vocationally obstructed, physically disabled, sexually mindless, intellectually inert, spiritually depressed—but not bald overnight, not that too.

The initial consultation took place in a sanitary white office with diplomas on the wall. The sight of Anton, a vegetarian and a yoga practitioner as well as a scalp specialist, made Zuckerman feel a hundred and lucky even to have retained his teeth. Anton was a small and vibrant man in his sixties who looked to be still in his forties; his own hair, gleaming like a black polished helmet, stopped just short of cheekbone and brow. As a boy in Budapest, he told Zuckerman, he had been a champion gymnast and ever since had devoted himself to the preservation of physical well-being through exercise, diet, and ethical living. He was particularly chagrined, while taking Zuckerman's history, to learn of the heavy drinking. He asked if Zuckerman was under any undue pressure: pressure was a leading cause of premature hair loss. "I'm under pressure," Zuckerman replied, "from prematurely losing hair." He wouldn't go into the pain, couldn't narrate that enigma to yet another expert with a wallful of diplomas. He wished, in fact, that he'd stayed at home. His hair at the center of his life! His receding hairline where his fiction used to be! Anton turned a lamp on Zuckerman's scalp and lightly combed the thinning hair from one side to the other. Then he extracted from the teeth of the comb the hairs that had come loose during the examination and piled them carefully onto a tissue for analysis in the lab.

Zuckerman felt no bigger than his topmost bald spot as he was led along a narrow white corridor into the clinic— a dozen curtained cubicles with plumbing, each just large enough to hold a trained trichological technician and a man losing his hair. Zuckerman was introduced to a small, delicate young woman in a white unbelted smock reaching to below her knees and a white bandanna that gave her the look of a stern and dedicated nun, a novice in a nursing order. Jaga was from Poland; her name, explained Anton, was pronounced with a "Y" but spelled with an initial "J." Mr. Zuckerman, he told Jaga—"the well-known American writer"—was suffering premature hair loss.

Zuckerman sat down before the mirror and contemplated his hair loss, while Anton elaborated on the treatment: white menthol ointment to strengthen the follicles, dark tar ointment to cleanse and disinfect, steamer to stimulate circulation, then fingertip massage, followed by Swedish electric massage and two minutes under the ultraviolet rays. To finish off, No. 7 dressing and fifteen

drops of the special hormone solution, five to the hairline at each of the temples, five where it was thinnest
at the crown. Zuckerman was to apply the drops himself every morning at home: the drops to promote growth
and then, sparingly, the pink dressing to prevent splitting and breaking of the hair ends he had left. Jaga
nodded, Anton bounded off to the lab with his pile of
specimens, and in the cubicle his treatment began, re-
calling to Zuckerman a second Mann protagonist with
whom he now shared a dubious affinity: Herr von Aschen-
bach, tinting his locks and rouging his cheeks in a Vene-
tian barbershop.

At the end of the hour session, Anton returned to
guide Zuckerman back to the office. Facing each other
across Anton's desk, they discussed the laboratory results.
"I have completed the microscopical examination of
your hair and scalp scrapings. There is a condition which
we call folliculitis simplex, which means there is clogging
of the hair follicles. Over a period of time it has led to
some loss of hair. Also, by robbing the hair of its natural
sebum flow it has created dryness of the hair, with con-
sequent breakage and splitting—which could lead to further loss of hair. I am afraid," said Anton, attempting in
no way to soften the blow, "that there are quite a lot of
follicles of the scalp which are devoid of hair. I am hoping
that with some at least the papilla is only impaired and
not destroyed. In this case regrowth can take place to
some extent, in those areas. But only time will give us the

answer to this. However, apart from the empty follicles, I feel that the prognosis in your case is good and that, with correct regular treatment and your help, your hair and scalp should respond and be restored to a healthy condition. We should be able to stop the clogging, obtain a freer flow of sebum, and restore the elasticity to the hair; then it will grow strong once again, making the overall appearance quite a bit thicker. The most important thing is that the loss of hair must not be allowed to continue."

It was the longest, most serious, most detailed and thoughtful diagnosis that Zuckerman had ever got from anyone for anything he had suffered in his life. Certainly the most optimistic he had heard in the last eighteen months. He couldn't remember ever having had a book reviewer who'd given a novel of his as full, precise, and accurate a reading as Anton had given his scalp. "Thank you, Anton," Zuckerman said.

"But."

"Yes?"

"There is a but," said Anton gravely.

"What is it?"

"What you do at home is just as important as what we do when you attend here for treatment. Number one, you must not drink to excess. You must stop this immediately. Number two, whatever is causing you undue pressure you must come to terms with. That there is undue pressure, I need no microscope to discover; I have only to look at you with my two eyes. Whatever it may be, you must eliminate it from your life. And quickly. Otherwise, Mr. Zuckerman, I must be honest with you: we are fighting a losing battle."

In the full-length mirror on his bathroom door, he saw at the start of each day a skinny old man holding Nathan's pajamas: denuded scalp, fleshy hips, bony frame, softening belly. Eighteen months without his regular morning exercises and his long afternoon walks and his body had aged twenty years. Awakening as always promptly at eight, he worked now—worked with the same stubborn resolve with which formerly he could mount a morning-long assault on a single recalcitrant page—to fall back to sleep until noon. Steady, dogged, driven Zuckerman, unable ordinarily to go half an hour without reaching for a pad to write on or a book to underline, now with a bed sheet pulled over his head to shorten the time until evening, when he could hit the bottle. Self-regulating Zuckerman emptying another fifth, self-controlled Zuckerman sucking the last of a roach, self-sufficient Zuckerman helplessly clinging to his harem (enlarged to include his trichological technician). Anything to cheer him up or put him out.

His comforters told him it was only tension and he should learn to relax. It was only loneliness and would disappear once he was back reading after dinner across from another worthy wife. They suggested that he was always finding new ways to be unhappy and didn't know how to enjoy himself unless he was suffering. They agreed with the psychoanalyst that the pain was self-inflicted: penance for the popularity of *Carnovsky*, comeuppance for the financial bonanza—the enviable, comfortable American success story wrecked by the wrathful cells. Zuckerman was taking "pain" back to its root in *poena*, the Latin word for punishment: poena for the family portrait the whole country had assumed to be his, for the tastelessness that had affronted millions and the shamelessness that had enraged his tribe. The crippling of his upper torso was, transparently, the punishment called forth by his crime: mutilation as primitive justice. If the writing arm offend thee, cut it off and cast it from thee. Beneath the ironic carapace of a tolerant soul, he was the most unforgiving Yahweh of them all. Who else could have written so blasphemously of Jewish moral suffocation but a self-suffocating Jew like Nathan? Yes, your illness is your necessity—that was the gist of it—and what prevents your recovery is you, you choosing to be incurable, you bullying into submission your own inbuilt will to be well. Unconsciously, Zuckerman was frightened of everything—another assumption generally accepted among his diagnosticians: frightened of success and frightened of failure; frightened of being known and frightened of being forgotten; frightened of being bizarre and frightened of being ordinary; frightened of being admired and frightened of being despised; frightened of being alone and frightened of being among people; frightened, after *Carnovsky*, of himself and his instincts, and frightened of being frightened. Cowardly betrayer of his verbal life—collaborator with the enemies of his filthy mouth. Unconsciously suppressing his talent for fear of what it'd do next.

But Zuckerman wasn't buying it. His unconscious wasn't that unconscious. Wasn't that conventional. His unconscious, living with a published writer since 1953, understood what the job entailed. He had great faith in his unconscious—he could never have come this far without it. If anything, it was tougher and smarter than he was, probably what *protected* him against the envy of rivals, or the contempt of mandarins, or the outrage of Jews, or the charge by his brother Henry that what had shocked their ailing father into his fatal coronary in 1969 was Zuckerman's hate-filled, mocking best-seller. If the Morse code of the psyche was indeed being tapped out along the wires of physical pain, the message had to be more original than "Don't ever write that stuff again."

Of course one could always interpret a difficulty like this as a test of character. But what was twenty years of writing fiction? He didn't need his character tested. He already had enough obstinacy to last a lifetime. Artistic principles? Up to his ears in them. If the idea was to marshal still more grim determination in the face of prolonged literary labors, then his pain was sadly misinformed. He could accomplish that on his own. Doomed to it by the mere passage of time. The resolute patience he already possessed made life more excruciating by the year. Another twenty like the last twenty and there'd be no frustration to challenge him.

No, if the pain intended to accomplish something truly worthwhile, it would not be to strengthen his adamancy but to *undo* the stranglehold. Suppose there was the message flashing forth from a buried Nathan along the fibers of his nerves: Let the others write the books. Leave the fate of literature in their good hands and relinquish life alone in your room. It isn't life and it isn't you. It's ten talons clawing at twenty-six letters. Some animal carrying on in the zoo like that and you'd think it was horrifying. "But surely they could hang a tire for him to swing on—at least bring in a little mate to roll around with him on the floor." If you were to watch some certified madman groaning over a table in his little cell, observe him trying to make something sensible out of qwertyuiop, asdfghjkl, and zxcvbnm, see him engrossed to the exclusion of all else by three such nonsensical words, you'd be appalled, you'd clutch his keeper's arm and ask, "Is there nothing to be done? No anti-hallucinogen? No surgical procedure?" But before the keeper could even reply, "Nothing—it's hopeless," the lunatic would be up on his feet, out of his mind, and shrieking at you through his bars: "Stop this infernal interference! Stop this shouting in my ears! How do I complete my life's great work with all these gaping visitors and their noise!"

Suppose pain had come, then, not to cut him down to size like Herbert's "Lord," or to teach him civility like

Tom Sawyer's Aunt Polly, or to make him into a Jew like Job, but to rescue Zuckerman from the wrong calling. What if pain was offering Zuckerman the best deal he'd ever had, a way out of what he should never have got into? The right to be stupid. The right to be lazy. The right to be no one and nothing. Instead of solitude, company; instead of silence, voices; instead of projects, escapades; instead of twenty, thirty, forty years more of relentless doubt-ridden concentration, a future of diversity, of idleness, of abandon. To leave what is given untransformed. To capitulate to qwertyuiop, asdfghjkl, and zxcvbnm, to let those three words say it all.

Pain to bring Nathan purposeless pleasure. Maybe a good dose of agony is what it took to debauch him. Drink? Dope? The intellectual sin of light amusement, of senselessness self-induced? Well, if he must. And so many women? Women arriving and departing in shifts, one barely more than a child, another the wife of his financial adviser? Usually it's the accountant who cheats the client, not the other way around. But what could he do if pain required it? He himself had been removed from command, released from all scruple by the helpless need. Zuckerman was to shut up and do what he was told—leave off rationing out the hours, stop suppressing urges and super-supervising every affair, and from here on, *drift*, just drift, carried along by whatever gives succor, lying beneath and watching as solace is delivered from above. Surrender to surrender, it's the time.

Yet if that really was the psyche's enjoinder, to what

end? To *no* end? To the end of ends? To escape completely the clutches of self-justification? To learn to lead a wholly indefensible, unjustified life—and to learn to like it? If so, thought Zuckerman, if that is the future that my pain has in mind, then this is going to be the character test to top them all.

2 Gone

Zuckerman had lost his subject. His health, his hair, and his subject. Just as well he couldn't find a posture for writing. What he'd made his fiction from was gone—his birthplace the burnt-out landscape of a racial war and the people who'd been giants to him dead. The great Jewish struggle was with the Arab states; here it was over, the Jersey side of the Hudson, his West Bank, occupied now by an alien tribe. No new Newark was going to spring up again for Zuckerman, not like the first one: no fathers like those pioneering Jewish fathers bursting with taboos, no sons like their sons boiling with temptations, no loyalties, no ambitions, no rebellions, no capitulations, no clashes quite so convulsive again. Never again to feel such tender emotion and such a desire to escape. Without a father and a mother and a homeland, he was no longer a novelist. No longer a son, no longer a writer. Everything that galvanized him had been extinguished, leaving nothing unmistakably his and nobody else's to claim, exploit, enlarge, and reconstruct.

These were his distressing thoughts, reclining on the playmat unemployed.

His brother's charge—that *Carnovsky* had precipitated their father's fatal coronary—hadn't been easy to forget. Memories of his father's last years, of the strain between them, the bitterness, the bewildering estrangement, gnawed away at him along with Henry's dubious accusation; so did the curse his father had fastened upon him with his dying breath; so did the idea that he had written what he had, as he had, simply to be odious, that his work embodied little more than stubborn defiance toward a respectable chiropodist. Having completed not a page worth keeping since that deathbed rebuke, he had half begun to believe that if it hadn't been for his father's frazzled nerves and rigid principles and narrow understanding he'd never have been a writer at all. A first-generation American father possessed by the Jewish demons, a second-generation American son possessed by their exorcism: that was his whole story.

Zuckerman's mother, a quiet, simple woman, dutiful and inoffensive though she was, always seemed to him a slightly more carefree and emancipated spirit. Redressing historical grievances, righting intolerable wrongs, changing the tragic course of Jewish history—all this she gladly left for her husband to accomplish during dinner. He made the noise and had the opinions, she contented herself with preparing their meal and feeding the children and enjoying, while it lasted, the harmonious family life. A year after his death she developed a brain tumor. For months she'd been complaining of episodes of dizziness, of headache, of little memory lapses. Her first time in the hospital, the doctors diagnosed a minor stroke, nothing to leave her seriously impaired; four months later, when they admitted her again, she was able to recognize her neurologist when he came by the room, but when he asked if she would write her name for him on a piece of paper, she took the pen from his hand and instead of "Selma" wrote the word "Holocaust," perfectly spelled. This was in Miami Beach in 1970, inscribed by a woman whose writings otherwise consisted of recipes on index cards, several thousand thank-you notes, and a voluminous file of knitting instructions. Zuckerman was pretty sure that before that morning she'd never even spoken the word aloud. Her responsibility wasn't brooding on horrors but sitting at night getting the knitting done and planning the next day's chores. But she had a tumor in her head the size of a lemon, and it seemed to have forced out everything except the one word. That it couldn't dislodge. It must have been there all the time without their even knowing.

Three years this month. December 21. In 1970 it had been a Monday. The neurologist told him on the phone that the brain tumor could take anywhere from two to four weeks to kill her, but when Zuckerman reached her room from the airport the bed was already empty. His brother, who'd arrived separately by plane an hour before, was in a chair by the window, jaw fixed, face a blank, looking, for all his size and strength, as though he were made of plaster. One good whack and he'd just be pieces on the floor. "Mother's gone," he said.

Of all the words that Zuckerman had read, written, spoken, or heard, there were none he could think of whose rhetorical effectiveness could ever measure up to those two. Not she's going, not she will go, but *she's gone*.

Zuckerman hadn't seen the inside of a synagogue since the early sixties, when he used to ride forth each month to defend *Higher Education* on the temple lecture trail. The nonbeliever wondered nonetheless if his mother oughtn't to be buried in the Orthodox manner—washed with water, wrapped in a shroud, and laid in a plain wood box. Even before she'd begun to be troubled by the first disabling signs of her fatal illness, four years of tending to an invalid husband had already reduced her to a replica of her own late mother in advanced old age, and it was in the hospital morgue, blankly staring at the prominent ancestral nose set in the small, childlike family skull, that curving sickle from which the sloping wedge of the care-worn face sharply dropped away, that he thought of an Orthodox burial. But Henry wanted her wearing the soft gray crepe dress she'd looked so pretty in the night he and Carol had taken her over to Lincoln Center to hear Theodore Bikel, and Zuckerman saw no reason to argue. He was trying really to *place* this corpse, to connect what had happened to his mother with what had happened to her mother, whose funeral he'd witnessed as a child. He was trying to figure out where, in life, they were. As for the attire in which she should molder away, let Henry have what he wished. All that mattered was to get this last job done as unbruisingly as possible; then he and Henry needn't agree on anything or speak to each other ever again. Her welfare was all that had kept them in touch anyway; over her empty hospital bed they'd met for the first time since their father's Florida funeral the year before.

Yes, she was all Henry's now. The angry edge to his organizational efficiency made it unmistakable to every-one that inquiries relating to her burial were to be ad-dressed to the younger son. When the rabbi came around to their mother's apartment to plan the chapel service—the same softly bearded young rabbi who'd officiated at their father's graveside—Nathan sat off by himself saying nothing, while Henry, who'd just gotten back from the mortician's, questioned the rabbi about the arrangements. "I thought I'd read a little poetry," the rabbi told him, "something about growing things. I know how she loved her plants." They all looked over at the plants as though they were Mrs. Zuckerman's orphaned babies. It was far too soon to see anything straight—not the plants on the windowsill, or the noodle casserole in the refrigerator, or the dry-cleaning ticket in her purse. "Then I'll read some psalms," the rabbi said. "I'd like to conclude, if you wouldn't mind, with some personal observations of my own. I knew your parents from the Temple. I knew them well. I know how much they enjoyed together as a husband and wife. I know how they loved their family." "Good," said Henry. "And you, Mr. Zuckerman?" the rabbi asked Nathan. "Any memories you'd like to share? I'll be glad to include them in my remarks." He took a pad and pencil from his jacket to note down whatever the writer had to tell him, but Nathan merely shook his head. "The memories," said Zuckerman, "come in their own time." "Rabbi," said Henry, "*I'll* deliver the eulogy." Earlier he'd said that he didn't think he'd have the emotional wherewithal to get through it. "If you could," said the rabbi, "despite your grief, that would be wonderful." "And if I cry," replied Henry, "that won't hurt either. She was the best mother in the world."

So: the historical record was to be set straight at last. Henry would cleanse from the minds of her Florida friends the libelous portrait in *Carnovsky*. Life and art are distinct, thought Zuckerman; what could be clearer? Yet the distinction is wholly elusive. That writing is an act of imagination seems to perplex and infuriate everyone.

Carol arrived on an evening plane with their two oldest kids and Henry put them up with him at a hotel over on Collins Avenue. Zuckerman slept at his mother's alone. He didn't bother making the bed up anew but, between the sheets that had covered her only two nights before, planted his face in her pillow. "Mama, where are you?" He knew where she was, at the mortician's wearing her gray crepe dress; nonetheless, he couldn't stop asking. His little mother, five feet two, had disappeared into the enormity of death. Probably the biggest thing she'd ever entered before was L. Bamberger's department store on Market Street in Newark.

Till that night Zuckerman hadn't known who the dead were or just how far away. She murmured into his dreams, but no matter how hard he strained to hear, he could not understand. An inch separated them, nothing separated them, they were indivisible—yet no message could make it through. He seemed to be dreaming that he was deaf. In the dream he thought, "Not gone; beyond gone," and awoke in the dark, bubbling saliva, her pillow soaked with his spittle. "Poor child," he said, feeling for her as though *she* were the child, his child, as though she'd died at ten instead of sixty-six. He felt a pain in his head the size of a lemon. It was her brain tumor.

Coming out of sleep that morning, struggling to be freed from a final dream of a nearby object at a dreadful distance, he began readying himself to find her beside him. Mustn't be frightened. The last thing she'd ever do would be to come back to frighten Nathan. But when he opened his eyes to the daylight and rolled over on his side there was no dead woman on the other half of the bed. There was no way to see her beside him again.

He got up to brush his teeth, then came back into the bedroom and, still in his pajamas, stepped into the closet among her clothes. He put his hand in the pocket of a poplin raincoat that looked hardly ever to have been worn, and found a freshly opened packet of Kleenex. One of the tissues lay folded in the pocket's seam. He touched it to his nose, but it smelled only of itself.

From a square plastic case down in the pocket he extracted a transparent rain bonnet. It was no bigger than a Band-Aid, folded up to about a quarter-inch thickness, but that it was tucked away so neatly didn't necessarily mean that she had never used it. The case was pale blue, stamped "Compliments of SYLVIA's, Distinctive Fashions, Boca Raton." The "S" in Sylvia's was entwined in a rose, something she would have appreciated. Little flowers always bordered her thank-you notes. Sometimes his wives had got the flowered thank-you notes for as little as a thoughtful long-distance call.

In her other pocket, something soft and gauzy. Withdrawing the unseen thing gave him a bad moment. It wasn't exactly like his mother to be carrying her underwear in her pocket like a drunk. Had the tumor impaired her thinking in pitiful little ways none of them had even known? But it wasn't a bra or her underpants, only a stocking-colored chiffon hood, something to wear home from the beauty parlor. Newly set hair, hers, or so he was ready to believe, holding the hood up to his nose and searching for some fragrance he remembered. The sharp smells, the decisive noises, the American ideals, the Zionist zeal, the Jewish indignation, all that to a boy was vivid and inspiring, almost superhuman, had belonged to his father; the mother who'd been so enormous to him for the first ten years of his life was as diaphanous in recollection as the chiffon hood. A breast, then a lap, then a fading voice calling after him, "Be careful." Then a long gap when there is nothing of her to remember, just the invisible somebody, anxious to please, reporting to him on the phone the weather in New Jersey. Then the Florida retirement and the blond hair. Neatly dressed for the tropics in pink cotton slacks and a monogrammed white blouse (wearing the pearl pin he'd bought years before in Orly Airport and brought home for her from his first summer in France), a little brown-skinned blond-haired woman waiting down at the end of the corridor when he gets off the elevator with his bag: the unconstrained grin, the encompassing dark eyes, the sad clinging embrace, instantly followed by the gratitude. Such gratitude! It was as though the President of the United States had arrived at the condominium to call upon some lucky citizen whose name and address had been drawn from a hat.

The last thing he found in her pocket was an item scissored out of *The New York Times*. Must have been sent to her by someone back home. She'd slipped it out of the envelope down by the mailbox, then put it into her pocket on the way to the beauty parlor or to Sylvia's in Boca Raton. The headaches and the dizziness still incorrectly diagnosed, she'd driven off with a friend on a rainy afternoon to look at a dress. When it got to be 4 p.m., the two widows would have decided on a restaurant for the early-bird dinner. Looking down the menu, she would have thought: "This is what Victor would order. This is what Nathan would order. This is what Henry would order." Only then would she choose for herself. "My husband," she would tell the waitress, "loved ocean scallops. If they're fresh, and the nice big ones, I'll have the ocean scallops, please."

One short paragraph in the *Times* clipping had been squared off with rough pencil markings. Not by her. Any frame she drew would have been finely made with a freshly sharpened point. The paragraph was from an article in the "New Jersey Section" dated Sunday, December 6, 1970. She died fifteen days later.

> Similarly, Newark has produced many famous people, ranging from Nathan Zuckerman, the author, to Jerry Lewis, the comedian. Elizabeth's most famous offspring are military men: General Winfield Scott, a 19th-century Army man, and Adm. William "Bull" Halsey, a World War II hero.

In a kitchen cabinet he found a yellow plastic watering can decorated with white daisies and held it under the tap. He went into the living room to sprinkle her wilting plants. So sick and lost and forgetful that last week, she'd not even tended her garden. Zuckerman turned on the FM station she'd had the dial tuned to and, listening to her favorite music—famous show tunes smothered in strings—proceeded with the watering can along the windowsill. He believed he recognized plants from New Jersey and his high-school days. Could that be? So many years as her companions? He raised the blind. Out past the new condominium that had gone up next door, he saw a wide slice of the bay. So long as her husband was alive, they used to look at the bay ritually from the bedroom balcony every evening after dinner and the TV news. "Oh, Nathan, you should have seen the colors last night at sunset—only you would have the words to describe it." But after Dr. Zuckerman's death, she couldn't face all that ineffable beauty alone and just kept watching television, no matter what was on.

There was no one out sailing yet. It wasn't even seven. But two stories below, in the parking lot between the two buildings, a very old man in bright green slacks and a bright green cap and a canary-yellow sweater was taking his constitutional, walking uncertainly back and forth between the rows of shining cars. Stopping to lean on the hood of a new two-toned Cadillac, his own perhaps, he looked up to where Zuckerman was standing in his pajamas at the picture window. He waved, Zuckerman waved back and for some reason showed him the watering can. The man called out but too weakly to be heard above the radio. On her FM station they were playing an uninterrupted medley of the tunes from *Finian's Rainbow*. "How are things in Glocca Morra, this fine day . . . ?" A spasm of emotion went through him: this fine day in Glocca Morra, where was she? Next they'd play "All the Things You Are" and break him down completely. That was the record to which she'd taught him the box step so that he could dance at his bar mitzvah reception. After he'd finished all his homework they would practice on the rugless floor between the dining- and living-room Orientals, while Henry, with an imaginary clarinet between his fingers, pretended to be Artie Shaw. Henry would mouth the words as Helen Forrest sang—anything to get into the act, even half asleep in his pajamas and slippers. At the evening reception, catered in a Bergen Street hall several rungs down from the Schary Manor, everybody in the family applauded (and all his young friends mockingly cheered) as Nathan and Mrs. Zuckerman stepped out under the rainbow lighting and began to fox-trot. When the boy bandleader lowered his sax and started to croon the lyrics—"You are/The promised kiss of springtime"— she looked proudly into the eyes of her thirteen-year-old partner—his hand placed inches away from where he imagined that even inadvertently he might touch the strap of her brassiere—and softly confided into his ear, "You *are,* darling."

The apartment, purchased ten years earlier by his father, had been decorated with the help of daughter-in-law Carol. On the longest wall hung two large reproductions framed in faded wormwood, a white Paris street by Utrillo and the hills of a lilac-colored island by Gauguin. The bright linen chosen by the women for the cushions of the bamboo living-room set showed branches of trees bearing lemons and limes. Tropical Eden, that was the idea, even as the strokes hammered her husband down into his grave. She'd done her best, but the organic opposition did better, and she'd lost.

There was nothing to do for her sadness. If ever there had been, the chance was gone.

While he was still watching the old man down in the parking lot totter from one row of cars back to the other, a key turned in the door. Despite the unequivocal gleam off the bay—that dancing of light in which the living exult, proclaiming, "Sunny existence knows nothing of death!"—the likelihood of her reappearance seemed suddenly as strong as it had while he lay on the bed dazed from the hours of dreaming on her pillow. Maybe he was still dazed up on his feet.

There was nothing to fear from her ghost. She'd return only to get a look at him, to see that he hadn't lost weight in the three months since his last visit, she'd return only to sit with him at the table and listen to him talk. He remembered when he'd first come home from college, the Wednesday evening of his first Thanksgiving vacation— how, with a great unforeseen gush of feeling, he'd told her about the books he was absorbed in at school. This was after they'd cleaned up the dinner dishes; his brother had left even before dessert for the AZA basketball game down at the Y, and his father was back in the office, dealing with the last of the day's paperwork. Zuckerman remembered her apron, her housedress, the dark graying hair, remembered the old Newark sofa re-covered—the year he went off to Chicago—in a sober, utilitarian, stain-resistant "Scotch plaid." She was stretched out on the living-room sofa, smiling faintly at all he was explaining to her, and imperceptibly falling asleep. He put her right out discussing Hobbes and the social contract. But how she loved that he knew it all. What a sedative that was, the most powerful she'd ever dared to take until, after her husband's death, they got her on phenobarbital.

All this sentiment. He wondered if it was only to compensate for the damage that he was reputed to have done her with the portrait of the mother in *Carnovsky*, if that was the origin of these tender memories softening him up while he watered her plants. He wondered if watering the plants wasn't itself willed, artificial, a bit of heart-pleasing Broadway business as contrived as his crying over her favorite kitsch show tune. Is this what writing has done? All that self-conscious self-mining—and now I can't even be allowed to take purely the shock of my own mother's death. Not even when I'm in tears am I sure what gives.

He had to smile when he saw who came in: no, it

wasn't the specter of his mother returned from the dead with a key to the door so as to hear from him now about Locke and Rousseau but a small, bottom-heavy, earth-bound stranger, the color of bittersweet chocolate. She was dressed in a roomy turquoise slacks suit and wore a wig of shiny black curls. This would be Olivia, the eighty-three-year-old cleaning woman. Who he was, this man in pajamas humming to Mrs. Zuckerman's music and watering her plants with her flowered can, she was not so quick to figure out.

"Who you!" she shouted and, stamping her foot, showed him the way out.

"You're Olivia. Take it easy, Olivia. I'm Mrs. Zuckerman's son. I'm Nathan. From New York. I slept here last night. You can close the door and come in." He extended his hand. "I'm Nathan Zuckerman."

"My God, you like t' scared me to death. My heart just flutterin.' You say you Nathan?"

"Yes."

"What you do for a livin'?"

"I'm the writer."

She walked straight up to shake his hand. "Well, you a good-lookin' man, ain't you?"

"You're a good-looking woman. How do you do?"

"Where's your mamma?"

He told her and she dropped backwards onto the sofa. "My Miz Zuckerman? My Miz Zuckerman? My beautiful Miz Zuckerman? That cain't be! I seen her last Thursday. All dressed up—goin' out. Wearin' that white coat with the big collar. I say to her, 'Oh, Miz Zuckerman, how beautiful you looks.' She *cain't* be dead, not my Miz Zuckerman!"

He sat beside her on the sofa, holding and stroking her hand until finally she was able to be consoled.

"You wants me to clean up anyway?" Olivia asked.

"If you feel you can, why not?"

"You wants me to fix you a egg?"

"No, I'm all right, thanks. You always come this early?"

"Most usually I gets here six-thirty sharp. Me and Miz Zuckerman, we likes a early start. Oh, I cain't believe that woman is dead. People always dyin', but you never gets used to it. The nicest woman in the world."

"She went quickly, Olivia. Without any pain."

"I say to Miz Zuckerman, 'Miz Zuckerman, your place so clean it hard for me to *make* it clean.'"

"I understand."

"I tells her all the time, 'You wastin' your money on me. Everything so sparklin' here, I just rubs around to make it more sparklin' but I cain't.' I never comes in here we don't hug and kiss soon as we sees each other. That woman she kind to everybody. They comes in here, the other ladies, and she sit in her chair, that one, and they start peskerin' her to give 'em some advice. The widow mens, they's no different. She go downstairs with them and she stand there and she show them how to fold up their laundry out of the dryin' machine. They wants to marry

her practically the day your father pass. The man upstairs want to take her on a fancy cruise, and some other
ones down in the lobby, they's linin' up like little boys to
takes her Sunday afternoon to the movie. But she love
your daddy too much for any monkey business. Not her.
She don't play that. She always sayin' to me, after Dr.
Zuckerman pass, 'I was lucky all my life, Olivia. I had
the three best mens in the world.' She tell me all the tales
from when you and the dentist was little boys. What you
write them books about?"

"Good question," he said.

"Okay, you can go right back to what you was doin'. I
gon' get myself along now." And as though she'd just
stopped by to chew the fat, she got up and went off to the
bathroom with her shopping bag. She came out wearing a
red cotton beret and, over her slacks, a long red apron.
"Wants me to spray the shoe closet?"

"Whatever you usually do."

"Most usually I sprays. Keep the shoes good."

"Then do it."

Henry's eulogy lasted nearly an hour. Nathan kept count
as Henry slipped each page beneath the last. Seventeen—
some five thousand words. It would have taken him a
week to write five thousand words, but Henry had done it
overnight, and in a hotel suite with three young children
and a wife. Zuckerman couldn't write if there was a cat in
the room. That was one of the differences between them.

A hundred mourners were gathered in the mortuary chapel, mostly lonely widowed Jewish women in their sixties and seventies who'd been transplanted South after a lifetime in New York and New Jersey. By the time Henry had finished, they all wished they'd had such a son, and not only because of his height, posture, profile, and lucrative practice: it was the depth of the filial devotion. Zuckerman thought, If sons were like that, I'd have had one myself. Not that Henry was out to put something over on them; it was by no means a ludicrously idealized portrait—the virtues were all hers. Yet they were virtues of the kind that make life happy for a little boy. Chekhov, drawing on material resembling Henry's, had written a story one-third that length called "The Darling." However, Chekhov wasn't undoing the damage of *Carnovsky*.

From the cemetery they went back to their cousin Essie's apartment, across the hall from their mother's, to receive and feed the mourners. Some of the women asked Henry if they might have his eulogy. He promised to oblige as soon as he got back to his office, where his receptionist would make photocopies and mail them off. "He's the dentist," Zuckerman overheard one of the widows saying, "and he writes better than the writer." Zuckerman learned from several of her friends how his mother taught the widowers to fold their laundry when they took it out of the dryer. A vigorous-looking man with a white fringe of hair and a tanned face came over to shake his hand. "Maltz is my name—sorry about your

mother." "Thank you." "You left New York when?"
"Yesterday morning." "How was the weather? Very
cold?" "Not too bad." "I should never have come here,"
Maltz said. "I'll stay till the lease runs out. Two more
years. If I live, I'll be eighty-five. Then I go home. I
have fourteen grandchildren in north Jersey. Somebody'll
take me in." While Mr. Maltz spoke, a woman wearing
dark glasses stood to the side and listened. Zuckerman
wasn't sure if she could see, though she appeared to be
by herself. He said, "I'm Nathan, how do you do?" "Oh, I
know who you are. Your mother talked about you all the
time." "Did she?" "I told her, 'Next time he comes, Selma,
bring him around—I could give him plenty of stories to
write.' My brother owns a nursing home in Lakewood,
New Jersey, and the things he sees you could make a book
out of. If somebody wrote it, it might do the world some
good." "What does he see?" Zuckerman asked. "What
doesn't he see. An old lady there sits by the door, by the
entrance to the home, all day long. When he asks her
what she's doing, she says, 'I'm waiting for my son.' Next
time the son visits, my brother says to him, 'Your mother
sits by the door waiting for you every day. Why don't you
come to visit her a little more often?' And you know what
he says? I don't even have to tell you what he says. He
says, 'Do you know what the traffic is like getting over to
Jersey from Brooklyn?'"

They stayed for hours. They talked to him, to Henry, to
each other, and though nobody asked for a drink, they ate

up most of the food, and Zuckerman thought, No, it can't be easy on these people down here when somebody in the building dies—everybody wonders if he's going to be next. And somebody is.

Henry flew back with the children to New Jersey and his patients, leaving Carol behind with Nathan to go through the apartment and decide what to give away to the Jewish charities—Carol, so that there'd be no fights. She never fought with anyone—"the sweetest disposition in the world," by the in-laws' reports. She was a peppy, youthful thirty-four, a girlishly pretty woman who cut her hair short and fancied woolen knee socks and about whom Zuckerman could say very little more, though she'd been his brother's wife for almost fifteen years. She always pretended when he was around to know nothing, to have read nothing, to have no thoughts on any subject; if he was in the same room, she wouldn't even dare to recount an anecdote, though Zuckerman often heard from his mother how "thoroughly delightful" she could be when she and Henry entertained the family. But Carol herself, in order to reveal nothing he could criticize or ridicule, revealed to him nothing at all. All he knew for sure about Carol was that she didn't want to wind up in a book.

They emptied the two shallow drawers at the top of his mother's dresser and spread her little boxes between them on the dining table. They opened them one at a time. Carol offered Nathan a ring bearing a tag that read

"Grandma Shechner's wedding band." He remembered from childhood how it had astounded him to hear of her taking it from her mother's finger moments after she had died: his mother had touched a corpse and then come home and made their dinner. "You keep it," said Nathan—"the jewelry should go to the girls someday. Or to Leslie's wife." Carol smiled—Leslie, her son, was ten. "But you must have something of hers," she pleaded. "It isn't right, our taking it all." She didn't know what he had already—the white piece of paper with the word "Holocaust" on it. "I didn't want to throw it away," the neurologist had said to him; "not until you'd seen it." Nathan had thanked him and put it in his wallet; now *he* couldn't throw it away.

In one of the boxes Carol came upon the round gold pin his mother had received for being president of the PTA back when he and Henry were in grade school: on the face, the name of their school engraved above a flowering tree; on the reverse side, the inscription "Selma Zuckerman, 1944–45." I'd be better off, he thought, carrying that around in my wallet. He told Carol to take it for Henry, however. In his eulogy, Henry had gone on for nearly a page about her PTA presidency and what a proud child that had made him.

Opening a tortoiseshell box Zuckerman found a stack of knitting instructions. The handwriting was hers, so were the precision and the practical thinking. "1 row sc all around, held in to keep flat . . . front same as back up to armhole ... sleeve 46 sts K 2 P 2 for 2½ /add 1 st each end every 5 rows ..." Each sheet of instructions was folded in half and bore on the outside the name of the grand-child, the niece, the nephew, the daughter-in-law for whom she was preparing her gift. He read the names of each of his wives in his mother's writing. "Vest for Betsy." "Raglan cardigan—Virginia." "Laura's navy sweater." "Suppose I take this," Zuckerman said. He tied the bundle with a five-inch snippet of pinkish-white yarn that he found at the bottom of the tortoiseshell box—a sample, he thought, to be matched up at the yarn shop for some project being planned only the day before yester-day. There was a snapshot at the bottom of the box, a picture of himself. Severe unsmiling face, dark low hair-line, clean polo shirt, khaki Bermudas, white sweat socks, suitably dirtied white tennis sneakers, and clutched in his hand, a Modern Library Giant. His tall skinny frame looked to him tense with impatience for the whole enor-mously unknown future. On the back of the snapshot his mother had written, "N., Labor Day 1949. On his way to college." It had been taken on the rear lawn of the Newark house by his father. He remembered the brand-new Brownie box camera and how his father was absolutely certain that the sun was supposed to shine into the cam-era. He remembered the Modern Library Giant: *Das Kapital*.

He waited for Carol to say it: "And this is the woman the world will remember as Mrs. Carnovsky, this woman who adored you." But having seen how his mother had identified the picture, she made no accusations. All she did was put one hand over her eyes as though the radiance off the bay was momentarily too much. She'd been up all night too, Nathan realized, helping Henry compose his seventeen pages. Perhaps she'd written them. She was supposed to have written wonderfully exhaustive letters to her in-laws, itemizing all she and Henry had seen and eaten when they were off on their vacation trips. She read prodigiously too, and not the books he might have imagined from the mask of innocuous niceness that she invariably showed him. Once, while using the upstairs phone in South Orange, Zuckerman had gone through the pile of books on the table at her side of the bed: a note-covered pad thrust into the second volume of a history of the Crusades, a heavily underlined paperback copy of Huizinga on the Middle Ages, and at least six books on Charlemagne borrowed from the Seton Hall University library, historical works written in French. Back in 1964, when Henry drove to Manhattan and stayed up all night in Nathan's apartment trying to decide whether he had the right to leave Carol and the children for the patient with whom he was then having an affair, he had positively rhapsodized over her "brilliance," calling her, in an exceptional outburst of lyricism, "my brain, my eyes, my understanding." When they were traveling abroad on Henry's vacation, her fluent French enabled them to see everything, go everywhere, to have a really wonderful

time; when he'd made his first small investments, Carol
had read up on stocks and bonds and given him more
good practical advice than the guy at Merrill Lynch; her
backyard full of flowers, a spectacular success written up
and photographed for the local weekly, had been planted
only after a winter of patient planning on graph paper
and studying landscape gardening books. Henry spoke
movingly of the strength she'd given her parents when
her twin brother died of meningitis in his second year of
law school. "If only she'd gone on for her Ph.D." He said
this mournfully a dozen times. "She was *made* for a
Ph.D."—as though, had the wife as well as her husband
(had the wife *instead* of the husband) proceeded after
their early student marriage to do three years of post-
graduate work, Henry would somehow be free to disregard the claims of loyalty, habit, duty, and conscience—
and his forebodings of social censure and eternal doom
—and run away with the mistress whose brilliance seemed
to reside largely in her sexual allure.

Zuckerman waited for Carol to look up at him and say,
"This woman, this touching, harmless woman who saved
this picture in this box, who wrote 'N. on his way to college,' that was her reward." But Carol, who after all these
years had still not spoken with Nathan, in English or
French, about her brother's tragic death, or the waning of
the Middle Ages, or stocks, or bonds, or landscape gardening, was not about to open her heart about his short-
comings as a son, not to a trigger-happy novelist like him.

But then Carol, as everyone knew, wouldn't fight with anyone, which was why Henry had left her behind to settle the touchy business of who should take home what from their mother's dresser. Perhaps Henry had also left her behind because of the touchier business of the mistress—either another mistress, or maybe still the same one—whom he could more readily arrange to see with a wife away in Florida a few more days. It had been an exemplary eulogy, deserving of all the praise it received— nor did Zuckerman mean to cast doubt upon the sincerity of his brother's grief; still, Henry was only human, however heroically he tried not to show it. Indeed, a son of Henry's filial devotion might even find in the hollow aftermath of such a sudden loss the need for dizzying, obliterating raptures categorically beyond the means of any wife, with or without a Ph.D.

Two hours later Zuckerman was out the door with his overnight bag and his knitting instructions. In his free hand he carried a cardboard-covered book about the size of the school composition books he used for taking notes. Carol had found it at the bottom of the lingerie drawer under some boxes of winter gloves still in their original store wrappings. Reproduced on the cover was a pinkish pastel drawing of a sleeping infant, angelically blond and endowed with regulation ringlets, lashes, and globular cheeks; an empty bottle lay to the side of the billowing coverlet, and one of the infant's little fists rested half open beside its cherry-red tiny bow lips. The book was called

Your Baby's Care. Printed near the bottom of the cover was the name of the hospital where he'd been born. *Your Baby's Care* must have been presented to her in her room shortly after his delivery. Use had weakened the binding and she had fastened the covers back together with transparent tape—two old strips of tape that had gone brownish-yellow over the decades and that cracked at the spine when Zuckerman opened the book and saw on the reverse of the cover the footprint he'd left there in the first week of life. On the first page, in her symmetrical handwriting, his mother had recorded the details of his birth—day, hour, name of parents and attending physician; on the next page, beneath the title "Notes on Development of the Baby," was recorded his weekly weight throughout his first year, then the day he held up his head, the day he sat up, crept, stood alone, spoke his first word, walked, and cut his first and second teeth. Then the contents—a hundred pages of "rules" for raising and training a newborn child. "Baby care is a great art," the new mother was told; ". . . these rules have resulted from the experience of physicians over many years . . ." Zuckerman put his suitcase on the floor of the elevator and began to turn the pages. "Let the baby sleep in the sun all morning . . . To weigh the baby, undress him completely . . . After the bath, dry him gently with soft, warm towels, patting the skin gently . . . The best stockings for a baby are cotton . . . There are two kinds of croup . . . The morning is the best time for play . . ."

The elevator stopped, the door opened, but Zuckerman's attention was fixed on a small colorless blot halfway down the page headed "Feeding." "It is important that each breast be emptied completely every 24 hours in order to keep up the supply of milk. To empty the breast by hand . . ."

His mother's milk had stained the page. He had no hard evidence to prove it, but then he was not an archaeologist presenting a paper: he was the son who had learned to live on her body, and that body was now in a box underground, and he didn't need hard evidence. If he who had spoken his first word in her presence on March 3, 1934—and his last word on the phone to her the previous Sunday—if he should choose to believe that a drop of her milk had fallen just there while she followed the paragraph instructing a young mother in how to empty her breasts, what was to stop him? Closing his eyes, he put his tongue to the page, and when he opened them again saw that he was being watched through the elevator door by an emaciated old woman across the lobby, leaning in exhaustion on her aluminum walker. Well, if she knew what she'd just seen she could now tell everyone in the building that she'd seen everything.

In the lobby there was a sign up for an Israel Bond Rally at a Bal Harbour Hotel, and hanging beside it a crayoned notice, now out of date, for a Hanukkah festival party in the condominium lobby sponsored by the building's Social Committee. He passed the bank of mailboxes and then came back and looked for hers. "Zuckerman S./414." He set down his suitcase, placed the baby book beside it, and touched the raised letters of the nameplate with his fingers. When World War I began, she was ten. When it ended, she was fourteen. When the stock market crashed, she was twenty-five. She was twenty-nine when I was born and thirty-seven on December 7, 1941. When Eisenhower invaded Europe, she was just my age . . . But none of this answered the cradle-question of where Mama had gone.

The day before, Henry had left instructions for the post office to forward her mail to South Orange. There was a plain white envelope, however, down in the box, probably a condolence note dropped through the slot by a neighbor that morning. In his jacket pocket Nathan had her extra set of house keys; one of her little tags was still attached, labeling them "Extra set of house keys." With the tiniest of the keys he opened the box. The envelope was not addressed. Inside was a pale green index card on which someone who preferred remaining anonymous had printed with a fountain pen

MAY YOUR MOTHER SUCK

COCKS IN HELL—

AND YOU SOON

JOIN HER!

YOU DESERVE IT.

ONE OF YOUR

MANY FOES

In hell no less. An act she never even committed on earth, you stupid son of a bitch. Who'd written him this? The fastest way to find out was to go back upstairs and ask Esther. She knew everybody's business. She also had no aversion to reprisals; her success in life was founded on them. They'd check together through the building directory until Essie had figured out who it was, who living in which apartment, then he'd walk over to Meyer Lansky's hotel to find out from the bell captain who could be hired to do a little job. Why not that for a change, instead of flying back to New York to file the green index card under "Mother's Death"? You could not be a nothing writer fellow forever, doing nothing with the strongest feelings but turning them over to characters to deal with in books. It'd be worth a couple thousand to have the ten fingers that wrote those twenty words smashed beneath some moron's boot. You could probably do it down here on your Diners Club card.

Only whose maimed fingers would they turn out to be? What would the comedy come up with this time—one of the widowers she'd taught how to fold laundry, or the old guy tottering around the parking lot who'd waved to Zuckerman up by the window while he was watering her plants?

A nothing fellow, he flew home to his files. A nasty, nothing fellow, surreptitiously vindictive, covertly malicious, who behind the mask of fiction had punished his adoring mother for no reason. True or false? In a school debate, he could have argued persuasively for either proposition.

Gone. Mother, father, brother, birthplace, subject, health, hair—according to the critic Milton Appel, his talent too. According to Appel, there hadn't been much talent to lose. In *Inquiry*, the Jewish cultural monthly that fifteen years earlier had published Zuckerman's first stories, Milton Appel had unleashed an attack upon Zuckerman's career that made Macduff's assault upon Macbeth look almost lackadaisical. Zuckerman should have been so lucky as to come away with decapitation. A head wasn't enough for Appel; he tore you limb from limb.

Zuckerman didn't know Appel. They'd met only twice —one August out in the Springs on Long Island, strolling by each other at the Barnes Hole beach, then briefly at a big college arts festival where each was sitting on a different panel. These meetings came some years after Appel's review of Zuckerman's first book had appeared in the Sunday *Times*. That review had thrilled him. In the *Times* in 1959, the twenty-six-year-old author had looked to Appel like a wunderkind, the stories in *Higher Education* "fresh, authoritative, exact"—for Appel, almost too pointed in their portraiture of American Jews clamoring to enter Pig Heaven: because the world Zuckerman knew still remained insufficiently transformed by the young writer's imagination, the book, for all its freshness, seemed to Appel more like social documentation, finally, than a work of art.

Fourteen years on, following the success of *Carnovsky*, Appel reconsidered what he called Zuckerman's "case": now the Jews represented in *Higher Education* had been twisted out of human recognition by a willful vulgar imagination largely indifferent to social accuracy and the tenets of realistic fiction. Except for a single readable story, that first collection was tendentious junk, the by-product of a pervasive and unfocused hostility. The three books that followed had nothing to redeem them at all— mean, joyless, patronizing little novels, contemptuously dismissive of the complex depths. No Jews like Zucker-man's had ever existed other than as caricature; as litera-ture that could interest grown people, none of the books could be said to exist at all, but were contrived as a species of sub-literature for the newly "liberated" middle class, for an "audience," as distinguished from serious readers. Though probably himself not an outright anti-Semite, Zuckerman was certainly no friend of the Jews: *Carnovsky*'s ugly animus proved that.

Since Zuckerman had heard most of this before—and usually in *Inquiry*, whose editorial admiration he'd lost long ago—he tried being reasonable for fifteen minutes. *He doesn't find me funny. Well, no sense writing to tell him to laugh. He thinks I depict Jewish lives for the sake of belittling them. He thinks I lower the tone to please the crowd. To him it's vulgar desecration. Horse-*

play as heresy. He thinks I'm "superior" and "nasty" and no more. Well, he's under no obligation to think otherwise. I never set myself up as Elie Wiesel.

But long after the reasonable quarter hour had passed, he remained shocked and outraged and hurt, not so much by Appel's reconsidered judgment as by the polemical overkill, the exhaustive reprimand that just asked for a fight. This set Zuckerman's teeth on edge. It couldn't miss. What hurt most was that Milton Appel had been a leading wunderkind of the Jewish generation preceding his own, a contributing editor to Rahv's *Partisan Review*, a fellow at Ransom's Indiana School of Letters, already publishing essays on European modernism and analyses of the exploding American mass culture while Zuckerman was still in high school taking insurgency training from Philip Wylie and his Finnley Wren. In the early fifties, during a two-year stint at Fort Dix, Zuckerman composed a fifteen-page "Letter from the Army," describing the bristling class resentment between black cadre just back from Korea, white commanding officers recalled to active duty, and the young college-educated draftees like himself. Though rejected by *Partisan*, the manuscript was returned with a note which, when he read it, excited him nearly as much as if it had been a letter of acceptance: "Study more Orwell and try us again. M.A."

One of Appel's own early *Partisan* essays, written when he was just back from World War II, had been cherished reading among Zuckerman's friends at the University of

Chicago circa 1950. No one, as far as they knew, had ever written so unapologetically about the gulf between the coarse-grained Jewish fathers whose values had developed in an embattled American immigrant milieu and their bookish, nervous American sons. Appel pushed his subject beyond moralizing into deterministic drama. It could not be otherwise on either side—a conflict of integrities. Each time Zuckerman returned to school from a bruising vacation in New Jersey, he took his copy of the essay out of its file folder ("Appel, Milton, 1918- ") and, to regain some perspective on his falling out with his family, read it through again. He wasn't alone . . . He was a social type . . . His fight with his father was a tragic necessity . . .

In truth, the type of intellectual Jewish boy whom Appel had portrayed, and whose struggles he illustrated with painful incidents from his own early life, had sounded to Zuckerman far worse off than himself. Maybe because these were boys more deeply and exclusively intellectual, maybe because their fathers were more benighted. Either way, Appel didn't minimize the suffering. *Alienated, rootless, anguished, bewildered, brooding, tortured, powerless*—he could have been describing the inner life of a convict on a Mississippi chain gang instead of the predicament of a son who worshipped books that his unschooled father was too ignorant to care about or understand. Certainly Zuckerman at twenty didn't feel tortured *plus* powerless *plus* anguished—he really just wanted his father to lay off. Despite all the solace that essay had given him, Zuckerman wondered if there might not be more comedy in the conflict than Appel was willing to grant.

Then again, Appel's might well have been a more dispiriting upbringing than his own, and the young Appel what he himself would later have labeled a "case." According to Appel, it was a source of the deepest shame to him during his adolescence that his father, whose livelihood was earned from the seat of a horse-drawn wagon, could speak to him easily only in Yiddish. When, in his twenties, the time came for the son to break away from the impoverished immigrant household and take a room of his own for himself and his books, the father couldn't begin to understand where he was going or why. They shouted, they screamed, they wept, the table was struck, the door was slammed, and only then did young Milton leave home. Zuckerman, on the other hand, had a father who spoke in English and practiced chiropody in a downtown Newark office building that overlooked the plane trees in Washington Park; a father who'd read William Shirer's *Berlin Diary* and Wendell Willkie's *One World* and took pride in keeping up; civic-minded, well-informed, a member admittedly of one of the lesser medical orders, but a professional, and in that family the first. Four older brothers were shopkeepers and salesmen; Dr. Zuckerman was the first of the line even to have gone beyond an American grade school. Zuckerman's problem was that his father *half* understood. They shouted and screamed, but in addition they sat down to reason together, and to that there is no end. Talk about torture. For the son to butcher the father with a carving knife, then step across his guts and out the door, may be a more merciful solution all around than to sit down religiously to reason together when there is nothing to reason about.

Appel's anthology of Yiddish fiction, in his own translations, appeared when Zuckerman was at Fort Dix. It was the last thing Zuckerman expected after the pained, dramatic diction of that essay proclaiming the depths of alienation from a Jewish past. There were also the critical essays that had, since then, made Appel's reputation in the quarterlies and earned him, without benefit of an advanced degree, first a lectureship at the New School and then a teaching job up the Hudson at Bard. He wrote about Camus and Koestler and Verga and Gorky, about Melville and Whitman and Dreiser, about the soul revealed in the Eisenhower press conference and the mind of Alger Hiss—about practically everything except the language in which his father had hollered for old junk from his wagon. But this was hardly because the Jew was in hiding. The disputatious stance, the aggressively marginal sensibility, the disavowal of community ties, the taste for scrutinizing a social event as though it were a dream or a work of art—to Zuckerman this was the very mark of the intellectual Jews in their thirties and forties on whom he was modeling his own style of thought.

Reading the quarterlies for the essays and fiction of Appel and his generation—Jewish sons born into immigrant families a decade or more after his own father—only corroborated what he'd first sensed as a teenage undergraduate at Chicago: to be raised as a post-immigrant Jew in America was to be given a ticket out of the ghetto into a wholly unconstrained world of thought. Without an Old Country link and a strangling church like the Italians, or the Irish, or the Poles, without generations of American forebears to bind you to American life, or blind you by your loyalty to its deformities, you could read whatever you wanted and write however and whatever you pleased. Alienated? Just another way to say "Set free!" A Jew set free even from Jews—yet only by steadily maintaining self-consciousness as a Jew. That was the thrillingly paradoxical kicker.

Though Appel's initial motive for compiling his Yiddish anthology was, more than likely, the sheer excitement of discovering a language whose range he could never have guessed from the coarseness of his father's speech, there seemed a deliberately provocative intention too. Far from signaling anything so comforting and inauthentic as a prodigal son's return to the fold, it seemed, in fact, a stand *against*: to Zuckerman, if to no one else, a stand against the secret shame of the assimilationists, against the distortions of the Jewish nostalgists, against the boring, bloodless faith of the prospering new suburbs—best of all, an exhilarating stand against the

snobbish condescension of those famous departments of
English literature from whose impeccable Christian ranks
the literary Jew, with his mongrelized speech and cater-
wauling inflections, had until just yesterday been pointedly
excluded. To Appel's restless, half-formed young admirer,
there was the dynamic feel of a rebellious act in the resurrection of those Yiddish writers, a rebellion all the more
savory for undercutting the anthologist's own early rebellion. The Jew set free, an animal so ravished and agitated
by his inexhaustible new hunger that he rears up suddenly
and bites his tail, relishing the intriguing taste of himself
even while screaming anguished sentences about the
agonies inflicted by his teeth.

After reading Appel's Yiddish anthology, Zuckerman
went up to New York on his next overnight pass, and
on lower Fourth Avenue, on booksellers' row, where
he normally loaded up with used Modern Library books
for a quarter apiece, searched the stores until he found
secondhand copies of a Yiddish grammar and an English–Yiddish dictionary. He bought them, took them
back to Fort Dix, and after supper in the mess hall, returned to the quiet empty office where during the day he
wrote press releases for the Public Information Officer.
There at his desk he sat studying Yiddish. Just one lesson
each night and by the time he was discharged he would
be reading his literary forefathers in their original tongue.
He managed to stick with it for six weeks.

Zuckerman had retained only a very dim sense of

Appel's appearance from the mid-sixties. Round-faced, bespectacled, tallish, balding—that's all he came up with. Maybe the looks weren't as memorable as the opinions. A more vivid recollection was of a striking wife. Was he still married to the pretty, delicate, dark woman who'd been walking hand in hand with him along the Barnes Hole beach? Zuckerman recalled rumors of an adulterous passion. Which had she been, the discard or the prize? According to *Inquiry*'s biographical note, Milton Appel was at Harvard for the year, on leave from his Distinguished Professorship at NYU. When literary Manhattan spoke of Appel, it seemed to Zuckerman that the name Milton was intoned with unusual warmth and respect. He couldn't turn up anyone who had it in for the bastard. He fished and found nothing. In Manhattan. Incredible. There *was* talk of a counterculture daughter, a dropout from Swarthmore who took drugs. Good. That might eat his guts out. Then word went around that Milton was in a Boston hospital with kidney stones. Zuckerman would have liked to witness their passing. Someone said that a friend had seen him walking in Cambridge with a cane. From kidney stones? Hooray. That satisfied the ill will a little. Ill will? He was furious, especially when he learned that before publishing "The Case of Nathan Zuckerman" Appel had tried it out on the road, traveled the college lecture circuit telling students and their professors just how awful a writer he was. Then Zuckerman heard that over at *Inquiry* they had received a single letter in his defense. The letter, which Appel had dismissed in a one-line rebuttal, turned out to have been written by a young woman Zuckerman had slept with during a summer on the Bread Loaf staff. Well, he'd had a good time too, but where were the rest of his supporters, all the influential allies? Writers shouldn't—and not only do they tell themselves they shouldn't, but everybody who is not a writer reminds them time and again—writers of course shouldn't, but still they do sometimes take these things to heart. Appel's attack—no, Appel in and of himself, the infuriating fact of his corporeal existence—was all he could think about (except for his pain and his harem).

The comfort that idiot had given the fatheads! Those xenophobes, those sentimental, chauvinist, philistine Jews, vindicated in their judgment of Zuckerman by the cultivated verdict of unassailable Appel, Jews whose political discussions and cultural pleasures and social arrangements, whose simple dinner conversation, the Distinguished Professor couldn't have borne for ten seconds. Their kitsch alone made Appel's gorge rise; their taste in Jewish entertainment was the subject of short scalding pieces he still dutifully published in the back pages of the intellectual journals. Nor could they have borne Appel for long either. His stern moral dissection of their harmless leisure pursuits—had the remarks been delivered around the card table at the Y, instead of in magazines they'd never heard of—would have struck them as cracked. His condemnation of their favorite hit shows would have seemed to them nothing less than anti-Semitic. Oh, he was tough on all those successful Jews for liking that cheap middlebrow crap. Beside Milton Appel, Zuckerman would have begun to look good to these people. That was the real joke. Zuckerman had been raised in the class that *loved* that crap, had known them all his life as family and family friends, visited with them, eaten with them, joked with them, had listened for hours to their opinions even while Appel was arguing in his editorial office with Philip Rahv and acting the gent to John Crowe Ransom. Zuckerman knew them still. He also knew that nowhere, not even in the most satiric of his juvenilia, was there anything to match Appel's disgust at contemplating this audience authenticating their "Jewishness" on Broadway. How did Zuckerman know? Ah, this is what you know about someone you have to hate: he charges you with his crime and castigates himself in you. Appel's disgust for the happy millions who worship at the shrine of the delicatessen and cherish *Fiddler on the Roof* was far beyond anything in Zuckerman's nastiest pages. How could Zuckerman be sure? He hated Appel, that's how. He hated Appel and would never forgive or forget that attack.

Sooner or later there comes to every writer the two-thousand-, three-thousand-, five-thousand-word lashing that doesn't just sting for the regulation seventy-two hours but rankles all his life. Zuckerman now had his: to treasure in his quotable storehouse till he died, the unkindest review of all, embedded as indelibly (and just about as useful) as "Abou Ben Adhem" and "Annabel Lee," the first two poems he'd had to memorize for a high-school English class.

Inquiry's publication of Appel's essay—and the outbreak of Zuckerman's hatred—took place in May 1973. In October, five thousand Egyptian and Syrian tanks attacked Israel on Yom Kippur afternoon. Caught off guard, the Israelis took three weeks this time to destroy the Arab armies and approach the suburbs of Damascus and Cairo. But after the rallying to victory, the Israeli defeat: in the Security Council, the European press, even in the U.S. Congress, condemnation of Jewish aggression. Of all things, in the desperate search for allies, Milton Appel turned to the worst of Jewish writers for an article in support of the Jewish state.

The appeal wasn't put directly, but through their mutual acquaintance Ivan Felt, who had once been Appel's graduate assistant at NYU. Zuckerman, who knew Felt from the artist's colony at Quahsay, had introduced him to his own publisher the year before, and Felt's first novel, soon to be published, would carry a paragraph of appreciation by Zuckerman on the jacket. The contemptuous destructive rage of the sixties was Felt's subject, the insolent anarchy and gleeful debauchery that had overturned even the most unlikely American lives while Johnson was devastating Vietnam for the networks. The book was as raw as Felt but, alas, only half as overbearing; Zuckerman's guess was that if he could get *all* that overbearing nature coursing through the prose, abandon his halfhearted objectivity and strange lingering respect for the great moral theme, Ivan Felt might yet become a real artist in the demonic, spiteful Céline line. Surely his letters, Zuckerman wrote to Felt, if not his fiction, would live forever in the annals of paranoia. As for the brash, presumptuous overconfidence and ostentatious egoism, it remained to be seen how much protection they would offer for the long-drawn-out brawl: Felt was twenty-seven and the literary career yet to begin.

Syracuse—12/1/73

Nathan—

Xerox paragraph (enclosed) from correspondence between M. Appel and myself concerning NZ. (Rest about B.U. vacancy I asked him, and now you, to support me for.) I stopped at his Harvard pulpit when in Boston ten days back. Hadn't heard any echo since galleys went off to him weeks ago. Told me he'd read a chapter but wasn't "responsive" to "what that sort of humor represents." Only trying to strip everything I fear of its "prestige." I said what's wrong with that, but he wasn't interested, said he didn't have strong impressions any longer of my book, his mind far away from fiction. On Israel's enemies. "They'd kill us all gladly," he told me. I told him that's how I saw *everything*. When later I said of Israel, "Who isn't worried?" he thought I was assuming a profitable role—took it for playacting. So out I lashed at the tirade on you. He said I should have written the magazine if I wanted to debate. He didn't have the energy or inclination now—"Other things on my mind." On leaving I added that one Jew worried about Israel was you. His paragraph follow-up to that parting shot. Civilized world knows how celebrated paranoid would rush to respond. Wait to learn what invitation to clear your conscience whips up in loving soul like you.

Your public toilet,
I.F.

"Buried anger, troves of it"; this was young Dr. Felt on the origins of Zuckerman's affliction. When news had reached him the year before that Zuckerman was hospitalized for a week, he phoned from Syracuse to find out what was wrong, and stopped by when he was next in New York. Out in the hallway, in his hooded high-school windbreaker, he'd taken his comrade by the arms —arms whose strength was ebbing by the day—and, only half mockingly, pronounced judgment.

Felt was constructed like a dockworker, strutted about like a circus strong man, piled layers of clothes on like a peasant, and had the plain ungraspable face of a successful felon. Compact neck, thick back, shock-absorbent legs —roll him up and you could shoot him from a cannon. There were those in the Syracuse English Department waiting in line with matches and powder. Not that Ivan cared. He'd already ascertained the proper relationship of Ivan Felt to his fellow man. So had Zuckerman, at twenty-seven: Stand alone. Like Swift and Dostoevsky and Joyce and Flaubert. Obstinate independence. Unshakable defiance. Perilous freedom. No, in thunder.

It was the first time they'd met on Eighty-first Street. No sooner had Felt entered the living room and begun pulling off his jacket, his cap, and the assortment of old sweaters that he was wearing under the windbreaker and over the T-shirt, than he was appraising aloud all he saw: "Velvet curtains. Persian carpet. Period mantelpiece. Overhead the ornamented plaster, below the gleaming parquet floor. Ah, but properly ascetic all the same. Not a hint of hedonism yet somehow—*cushy*. Very elegantly underfurnished, Nathan. The pad of a well-heeled monk."

But how Felt sardonically sized up the decor interested Zuckerman less than the new diagnosis. They just kept coming, these diagnoses. Everybody had a slant. The illness with a thousand meanings. They read the pain as his fifth book.

"Buried anger?" Zuckerman asked him. "Where'd you get that idea?"

"*Carnovsky*. Incomparable vehicle for the expression of your inadmissible loathings. Your hatred flows at flood level—so much hatred the heap of flesh can't contain it. Yet, outside the books, you act like you ain't even here. Moderation itself. Altogether, your books give off a greater sense of reality than you do. The first time I saw you, the night you came down into the dining room at Quahsay, the Glittering Guest of the Month, I said to little

Gina, the lesbian poet, 'I'll bet that fellow never gets mad outside of those best-sellers.' Do you? Do you know how to?"

"You're tougher than I am, Ivan."

"That's a flattering way of saying I'm nastier than you are."

"When do *you* get angry outside of the writing?"

"I get angry when I want to get rid of somebody. They're in my way. Anger is a gun. I point it and I fire, and I keep firing till they disappear. I'm like you are in the writing outside the writing *and* in the writing. You button your lip. I'll say anything."

By now, with all Felt's layers of clothes unpeeled and strewn across the floor, the pad of the well-heeled monk looked as if it had just been sacked.

"And," Zuckerman asked, "you believe what you're saying when you say anything?"

Felt looked over at him from the sofa as though Zuckerman were demented. "It doesn't matter whether *I* believe it. You're such a good soldier you don't even understand. The thing is to make *them* believe it. You are a good soldier. You seriously entertain the opposition point of view. You do all that *the right way*. You have to. You're always astonished how you provoke people by pouring out the secrets of your disgraceful inner life. You get stunned. You get *sad*. It's a wonder to you that you're such a scandal. The wonder to me is that you can possibly care. You, down with a case of the Bad-Taste Blues! To require the respect of men and women's tender caresses. Poppa's approval and Momma's love. Nathan Zuckerman! Who'd believe it?"

"And you require nothing? You believe *that*?"

"I sure don't let guilt enter everything, not the way you good soldiers do. It's nothing, guilt—it's self-indulgence. They despise me? They call me names? They don't approve? All the better. A girl tried to commit suicide at my place last week. Dropped by with her pills for a glass of my water. Swallowed them while I was off teaching my afternoon dopes. I was furious when I found her. I phoned for an ambulance, but I'd be damned if I'd go with her. If she had died? Fine with me. Let her die if that's what she wants. I don't stand in their way and nobody stands in mine. I say, 'No, I don't want any more of this—it's not for me.' And I start firing until it's gone. All you need from them is money—the rest you take care of yourself."

"Thanks for the lesson."

"Don't thank me," said Felt. "I learned it in high school, reading you. Anger. Point it and fire it and just keep firing until they disappear. You'll be a healthy novelist in no time."

Appel's paragraph, xeroxed by Felt and sent on to Zuckerman in New York:

Truth to tell, I don't know that there's much we can do—first the Jews were destroyed by gas, and now it may be in oil. Too many around New York are shameful on this matter: it's as if their circumcisions were acquired for other reasons. The people who raised hell about Vietnam are not saying much on Israel (but for a few souls). However, insofar as public opinion matters, or the tiny fraction of it we can reach, let me offer a suggestion that may irritate you, but which I'll make nonetheless. Why don't you ask your friend Nate Zuckerman to write something in behalf of Israel for the Times Op Ed page? He could surely get in there. If I come out in support of Israel there, that's not exactly news; it's expected. But if Zuckerman came out with a forthright statement, that would be news of a kind, since he has prestige with segments of the public that don't care for the rest of us. Maybe he has spoken up on this, but if so I haven't seen it. Or does he still feel that, as his Carnovsky says, the Jews can stick their historical suffering up their ass? (And yes, I know that there's a difference between characters and authors; but I also know that grown-ups should not pretend that it's quite the difference they tell their students it is.) Anyway, brushing aside my evident hostility to his view on these matters, which is neither here nor there, I honestly believe that if he were to come out publicly, it would be of some interest. I think we're at the point where the whole world is getting ready to screw the Jews. At such points even the most independent of souls might find it worth saying a word.

Well, now he was angry outside of the books. Moderation? Never heard of it. He got down a copy of *Carnov-*

sky. Had it really been proposed in these pages that Jews can stick their suffering quote unquote? A sentiment so scathing just dropped like a shoe? He looked in his book for the source of Appel's repugnance and found it a third of the way through: penultimate line of two thousand words of semi-hysterical protest against a family's obsession with their minority plight—declaration of independence delivered by Carnovsky to his older sister from the sanctuary of his bedroom at the age of fourteen.

So: undeluded by what grown-ups were pretending to their students, Appel had attributed to the author the rebellious outcry of a claustrophobic fourteen-year-old boy. This was a licensed literary critic? No, no—an overwrought polemicist for endangered Jewry. The letter could have come from the father in *Carnovsky*. It could have come from his own real father. Written in Yiddish, it could have come from Appel's, from that ignorant immigrant junkman who, if he hadn't driven young Milton even crazier than Carnovsky, had clearly broken his heart.

He pored over the paragraph like a professional litigant, drawn back in a fury to what galled him most. Then he called Diana at school. Needed her to type. Had to see her right away. Anger was a gun and he was opening fire.

Diana Rutherford was a student at Finch, the rich girls' college around the corner where the Nixons had sent Tricia. Zuckerman was out mailing a letter the first time they met. She wore the standard cowpoke denims, jeans and jacket beaten senseless on the sun-bleached stones of the Rio Grande, then shipped north to Bonwit's. "Mr. Zuckerman," she'd said, tapping him on his shoulder as he dropped the envelope in the box, "can I interview you for the school paper?" Only yards away, two roommates were in stitches over her brashness. This was obviously the college character. "Do you write for the school paper?" he asked her. "No." Confessed with a large guileless smile. Guileless, really? Twenty is the age of guile. "Walk me home," he said; "we'll talk about it." "Great," the character replied. "What's a smart girl like you doing at a place like Finch?" "My family thought I ought to learn how to cross my legs in a skirt." But when they got to his door fifty feet down the block, and he asked if she'd like to come up, the brashness gave out and she sashayed back to her friends.

The next afternoon, when the buzzer rang, he asked who it was through the intercom. "The girl who's not on the school paper." Her hands were trembling when he let her in. She lit a cigarette, then removed her coat, and without waiting to be invited, set about examining the books and the pictures. She took everything in room by room. Zuckerman followed.

In the study she asked, "Don't you have anything out of place here?"

"Only you."

"Look, it'll be no contest if you start off hypersardonic." Her voice quivering, she still spoke her mind. "Nobody like you should have to be afraid of anybody like me."

In the living room again, he took her coat from the sofa and, before hanging it in the closet, looked at the label. Bought in Milano. Setting somebody back many many hundreds of thousands of lire.

"You always this reckless?" he asked.

"I'm writing a paper on you." From the edge of the sofa she lit the next cigarette. "That's a lie. That's not true."

"You're here on a dare."

"I thought you were somebody I could talk to."

"About what?"

"Men. I can't take much more of them."

He made them coffee and she began with her boy-friend, a law student. He neglected her and she didn't understand why. He phoned in tears in the middle of the night to say that he didn't want to see her but he didn't want to lose her either. Finally she'd written a letter asking him what was going on. "I'm young," she told Zuckerman, "and I want to fuck. It makes me feel ugly when he won't do it."

Diana was a long, narrow girl with a minute behind, small conical breasts, and boyishly clipped dark curls. Her chin was round like a child's, and so were her dark Red Indian eyes. She was straight and circular, soft and angular, and certainly wasn't ugly, except for the pout, the Dead End Kid look around the mouth whenever she began to complain. Her clothes were a child's: tiny suede skirt over a black leotard and, pinched from Momma's closet to amaze the other girls, high-heeled black shoes with open toes and a sequined strap. The face was really a baby's too, until she smiled—that was big and captivating. Laughing she looked like someone who'd seen it all and emerged unscathed, a woman of fifty who'd been lucky.

What she'd seen and survived were the men. They'd been in pursuit since she was ten.

"Half your life," he said. "What have you learned?"

"Everything. They want to come in your hair, they want to beat your ass, they want to call you on the phone from work and get you to finger yourself while you're doing your homework. I'm without illusions, Mr. Zuckerman. Ever since I was in seventh grade a friend of my father's has been calling every month. He couldn't be sweeter to his wife and his kids, but me he's been calling since I'm twelve. He disguises his voice and every time it's the same damn thing: 'How would you like to straddle my cock?' "

"What do you do about it?"

"I didn't know what to do in the beginning except listen. I got frightened. I bought a whistle. To blow into the mouthpiece. To burst his eardrum. But when I blew it finally, he just laughed. It turned him on *more*. This is eight years now. He calls me at school once a month. 'How would you like to straddle my cock?' I say to him, 'Is that it? Is that the whole thing?' He doesn't answer. He doesn't have to. Because it is. Not even to do it. Just to say it. To me."

"Every month, for eight years, and you've done nothing about it except buy a whistle?"

"What am I supposed to do, call the cops?"

"What happened when you were ten?"

"The chauffeur used to play with me when he drove me to school."

"Is that true?"

"The author of *Carnovsky* asks me if that's true?"

"Well, you might be making yourself interesting by making it up. People do that."

"I assure you, it's writers who have to make things up, not girls."

After an hour he felt as if Temple Drake had hitched up from Memphis to talk about Popeye with Nathaniel Hawthorne. He was stunned. It was a little hard to believe in all she said she'd seen—in all she seemed to be saying she was. "And your parents?" he asked her. "What do they say to these chilling adventures with all the terrible men?"

"Parents?" She came catapulting up onto her feet, sprung by that one word alone from the cushioned nest she'd dug down in the sofa pillows. The length of the leotarded legs, the speed and aggression of the delicate fingers, that mocking, cocky beat she took before driving in her point—a budding female matador, Zuckerman decided. She'd certainly look great in the gear. Might be frightened out of her wits to begin with, but he could also see her going in there and doing it. *Come and get me.* She's breaking free and being brave—or trying hard, by tempting fate, to learn. Sure there's a side of her that wants and invites this erotic attention—along with the side that gets angry and confused; but all in all there is something more intriguing here than mere teenage chance-taking. There's a kind of perverse autonomy covering up a very interesting, highly strung girl (and woman, and child, and kid). He could remember what it was like saying, "Come and get me." That of course was before they'd got him. It got him. Whatever you wanted to call it, something had got him.

"Where have *you* been?" she asked. "There *are* no more parents. Parents are over. Look, I've tried to make a go of it with the law student. I thought he'd help me concentrate on this silly school. He studies, he jogs, he doesn't do too much dope, and he's only twenty-three— and for me that's young. I've worked hard on him, damn it, him *and* his hang-ups, and now, now he doesn't want to do it at all. I don't know what the matter is with that boy. I look at him cockeyed and he turns into a baby. Fear, I guess. The sane ones bore you practically to death, and the ones who fascinate you turn out to be nuts. Know what I've been pushed to? What I'm just about ready for? To be married. To be married and to get knocked up, and to say to the contractor, 'Put the pool in over there.' "

Twenty minutes after receiving Zuckerman's call, Diana was sitting in the study with the pages to be typed and mailed to Appel. He'd filled four long yellow pages before

sliding from his chair to the playmat. Back on his
back he tried to get the throbbing to subside in his upper
arm by kneading the muscle with his fingers. The base
of his neck was on fire too, the toll for the longest sus-
tained piece of prose he'd composed sitting upright in
over a year. And there were more bullets left in the
chamber. Suppose through careful analysis of those early
essays I demonstrate how Appel harshly denounces
Zuckerman because of a distressing conflict with Poppa
insufficiently settled in himself—show that it's not only
the menace of Islam that's provoked this reappraisal of
my "case" but Ocean Hill–Brownsville and black anti-
Semitism, the condemnation of Israel in the Security
Council, even the New York teachers' strike; that it's the
media dada of loud Jewish Yippies whose playpen goals
he ludicrously associates with me. Now for *my* reappraisal of him. It isn't that Appel thinks he was wrong
about Zuckerman in 1959. Or wrong about his own root-
lessness in 1946. Right then, and now that he's changed his
mind, right again. The "mind" may change, or appear to,
but never the inquisitor's passion for punishing verdicts.
Behind the admirable flexibility of judicious reappraisal
the theoretical substructure is still blast-proof concrete:
none of us as *seriozny* as Appel. "The Irrefutable Rethink-
ings of Milton Appel." "Right and Rigid in Every Decade:
The Polemical Spasms of a Hanging Judge." He came up
with titles by the dozen.

"I've never heard anybody like you on the phone,"

Diana said. She sat submerged in her secretarial camou-
flage: shapeless overalls and a bulky sweater intended
originally to help him dictate his fiction. When she
showed up in the child's skirt, little dictation was ever
taken. The skirt was another reason to give up. "You
should see yourself," she said. "Those prism glasses, that
contorted face. You should see what you look like. You
let something like this get inside you and it builds and
builds until your head comes off. And with your hair in it.
That's exactly why you're losing your hair. It's why you
have all this pain. *Look* at you. Have you looked in a
mirror?"

"Don't you get angry about things? I'm angry."

"Yes, sure, of course I do. There's always somebody in
the background of anybody's life driving you mad and
giving you cystitis. But I *think* about them. I do my yoga.
I run around the block and I play tennis and I try to get
rid of it. I can't live like that. I'd have an upset stomach
for the rest of my life."

"You don't understand."

"Well, I think I do. You have it at school."

"You can't equate this with school."

"Well, you can. You get the same kind of knocks at
college. And they're damn hard to get over. Especially
when they seem to you totally unjust."

"Type the letter."

"I'd better read it first."

"Not necessary."

Through the prism glasses he impatiently watched her reading it, meanwhile kneading away at his upper arm to try to subdue the pain. What helped sometimes with the deltoid muscle was the electronic pain suppressor. But would the neurons even register that low-voltage shock, what with this supercharge of indignation lighting up his brain?

"I'm not typing this letter. Not if this is what it says."

"What the hell business is it of yours what it says?"

"I refuse to type this letter, Nathan. You're a crazy man when you start on these things, and this letter is crazy. 'If the Arabs were undone tomorrow by a plague of cheap solar power, you wouldn't give my books a second thought.' You're off your head. That makes no sense. He wrote what he wrote about your books because that is what he thinks. Period. Why even *care* what these people think, when you are you and they are nobody? *Look* at you. What a vulnerable, resentful mouth! Your hair is actually standing on end. Who is this little squirt anyway? Who is Milton Appel? I never read any books by him. They don't teach him at school. I can't fathom this in a man like you. You're an extremely sophisticated, civilized man—how can you be caught in a trap by these people and let them upset you to such a degree?"

"You're a twenty-year-old girl from an ultraprivileged Christian–Connecticut background, and I accept that you have no idea what this is all about."

"Well, a lot of people who aren't twenty and don't

have ultraprivileged Christian–Connecticut backgrounds wouldn't understand either, not if they saw you looking like this. 'Why those Jews in *Higher Education*, all too authentic to you in 1959, are suddenly the excreta of a vulgar imagination is because the sole Jewish aggression sanctioned in 1973 is against Egypt, Syria, and the PLO.' Nathan, you can't believe the PLO is why he wrote that piece."

"But it *is*. If it wasn't for Yasir Arafat he'd never be on my ass. You don't know what frazzled Jewish nerves are like."

"I'm learning. Please, take a Percodan. Smoke some pot. Have a vodka. But *calm down*."

"You get over to that desk and type. I pay you to type for me."

"Well, not that much. Not enough for this." Again she read aloud from his letter. " 'In your view, it really isn't deranged Islam or debilitated Christianity that's going to deal us the death blow anyway, but Jewish shits who write books like mine, carrying the hereditary curse of self-hate. And all to make a dollar. Six million dead—six million sold. Isn't that the way you really see it?' Nathan, this is all ludicrous and overstated. You're a man of forty and you're flailing out like a schoolboy who's been made to stand in the corner."

"Go home. I greatly admire your self-possession in telling me off like this, but I want you to go away."

"I'll stay till you calm down."

"I'm not calming down. I've been calm long enough. Go."

"Do you really think it's intelligent to be so unforgiving about this great wrong that's been committed against you? This enormous wrong?"

"Oh, should I forgive him?"

"Yes. You see, I *am* a Christian. I do believe in Christ. And in people like Gandhi. And *you're* going back to that dreadful dreadful Old Testament. That stonelike book. Eye for eye and teeth for teeth and never forgive anybody. Yes, I'm saying that I believe in forgiving my enemies. I can't believe in the end that it isn't healthier for everybody."

"Please don't prescribe peace and love. Don't make me a member of your generation."

"Gandhi wasn't a member of my generation. Jesus isn't a member of my generation. St. Francis of Assisi wasn't a member of my generation. As you God damn well know, *I'm* not even a member of my generation."

"But I'm not Jesus, Gandhi, St. Francis, or you. I'm a petty, raging, vengeful, unforgiving Jew, and I have been insulted one time too many by another petty, raging, vengeful, unforgiving Jew, and if you intend to stay, then type what I've written, because it cost me bloody hell in my aching joints to write it."

"Okay. If you're such a Jew, and these Jews are all so central to your thinking—and that they have this hold *is* unfathomable to me, really—but if you really are stuck on Jews like this, and if Israel does mean something to you, then sure I'll type—but only if you dictate an essay about Israel for *The New York Times*."

"You don't understand. That request from him, after what he's published in *Inquiry*, is the final insult. In *Inquiry*, run by the kind of people he used to attack before he began attacking people like me!"

"Only it is not an insult. He's asked you what he's asked because people know who you are, because you can be so easily *identified* with American Jews. What I can't understand is what you're in such a state about. Either do it or don't do it, but don't take it as an insult when it wasn't meant as one."

"What *was* it meant as? He wants me to write an article that says I'm not an anti-Semite anymore and that I love Israel with all my heart—and that he *can* stick up his ass."

"I can't believe that's what he wants you to write."

"Diana, when somebody who has said about me and my work and the Jews what this guy has, then turns around and says why don't you write something nice about us for a change—well, how can you fail to understand that this is particularly *galling* to me? 'Write something in behalf of Israel.' But what about the hostility to Jews that's at the heart of every word I publish? To propagate that caricature in *Inquiry*, publicly to damn *me* as the caricaturist, and then in private to suggest this piece—and with some expectation at least of the crypto anti-

Semite's acquiescence! 'He has prestige with segments of the public that don't care for the rest of us.' Right—the scum, the scum whom his novels are fashioned to please. If Zuckerman, a Jew adored by the scum for finding Jews no less embarrassing and distasteful than they do, were to make the argument *for* the Jews *to* the scum, 'it would be of some interest.' You bet! Like a case of schizophrenia is of interest! On the other hand, when Appel speaks up in a Jewish crisis, 'it's expected.' Sign of deep human engagement and predictably superior compassion. Sign of nothing less than the good, the best, the most responsible Jewish son of them all. These Jews, these Jews and their responsible sons! First he says I vilify Jews under the guise of fiction, now he wants me to lobby for them in *The New York Times*! The comedy is that the real visceral haters of the bourgeois Jews, with the *real* contempt for their everyday lives, are these complex intellectual giants. They *loathe* them, and don't particularly care for the smell of the Jewish proletariat either. All of them full of sympathy suddenly for the ghetto world of their traditional fathers now that the traditional fathers are filed for safekeeping in Beth Moses Memorial Park. When they were alive they wanted to strangle the immigrant bastards to death because they dared to think they could actually be of consequence without ever having read Proust past *Swann's Way*. And the ghetto—what the ghetto saw of these guys was their heels: out, out, screaming for air, to write about great Jews like Ralph Waldo Emerson and William Dean Howells. But now that the Weathermen are around, and me and my friends Jerry Rubin and Herbert Marcuse and H. Rap Brown, it's where oh where's the inspired orderliness of those good old Hebrew school days? Where's the linoleum? Where's Aunt Rose? Where is all the wonderful inflexible patriarchal authority into which they wanted to stick a knife? Look, I obviously don't want to see Jews destroyed. That wouldn't make too much sense. But I am not an authority on Israel. I'm an authority on Newark. Not even on Newark. On the Weequahic section of Newark. If the truth be known, not even on the whole of the Weequahic section. I don't even go below Bergen Street."

"But it's not a matter of whether you're an authority. It's a matter of people reading what you say because at the moment you're very famous."

"So is Sammy Davis. So is Elizabeth Taylor. They're even more famous. And they're real Jews who haven't ruined their credentials writing vulgar books. They haven't set loose the illicit forces that are now corrupting the culture. Why doesn't he ask them, if he wants somebody famous? They'd jump at the chance. Besides, that I'm famous for what I'm famous for is precisely what makes me reprehensible to Appel. *That's* what he's scolding me about. He actually seems to have read that book as a manifesto for the instinctual life. As if he'd never heard of obsession. Or repression. Or repressed obsessive Jews. As if he isn't one himself, the fucking regressive nut! Diana, I have nothing to say, at Appel's request, about Israel. I can write an essay about a novelist, and even that takes six months, but I can't write an essay about international politics, not for anyone. I don't do it, I never have. I am not Joan Baez. I am not a great thinker like Leonard Bernstein. I am not a political figure—he flatters me to suggest that I am."

"But you're a Jewish figure. Whether you want to be or not. And as you seem to want to be, you might as well do it. Why are you making it so difficult? Just state your opinion. It's as simple as that. Where you stand."

"I will not make atonement on the Op Ed page for the books he's accused me of writing! I cracked a few jokes about playing stinky-pinky in Newark and you'd think I'd blown up the Knesset. Don't start confusing me with your Wasp clarity—'there is no problem.' There is! This is not my maiden appearance in the pages of *Foreskin* as their Self-Hating Jew of the Month."

"But that is a petty little ghetto quarrel of no interest to *anyone*. How many Jews can dance on the head of a pin? *No one cares*. You can't really remember what some silly magazine has said about you—your mind would just be muck. If the magazine is as awful as you say, why should you even bother to worry? Besides, the one subject is so big and the other is so tiny, and the two have come together for you in a very strange way that I *cannot* understand, no matter how many ways you explain it. To me it seems like you're balancing a very large mountain against a very tiny molehill, and, truthfully, if anybody had told me you were like this before I met you . . . or that Jews were like this. I just thought they were immigrants—period. No, I *don't* understand. Maybe I'm only twenty, but you're forty years old. Is this really what happens when people hit forty?"

"You bet. They've had it up to fucking here. This is *exactly* what happens. Twenty years into your livelihood, and whether you know how to do it, whether you should be doing it at all, still a matter of public debate! And still in doubt yourself. How do I even know that Appel isn't right? What if my writing's as bad as he says? I hate his guts, and obviously the sixties have driven him batty, but that doesn't make him a fool, you know. He's one of the few of them around who make any sense at all. Let's face it, even the worst criticism contains some truth. They always see something you're trying to hide."

"But he *exaggerates* it. It's all out of proportion. He doesn't see the good things. He won't even acknowledge that you're funny. That's ridiculous. He only sees crudely what you fail at. Well, everybody has failings."

"But suppose he's right. Suppose nobody needs my books. Suppose I don't even need them. Am I funny? And if I am, so what? So are the Ritz Brothers. Probably funnier. Suppose what he implies is true and I've poisoned their sense of the Jewish reality with my vulgar imagination. Suppose it's even half true. What if twenty years of writing has just been so much helplessness before a compulsion—submission to a lowly, inconsequential compulsion that I've dignified with all my principles, a compulsion probably not all that different from what made my mother clean the house for five hours every day. Where am I then? Look, I'm going to medical school."

"Pardon?"

"Medical school. I'm pretty sure I've got the grades. I want to be a doctor. I'm going back to the University of Chicago."

"Oh, shut up. So far, this conversation has just been depressing. Now it's idiotic."

"No, I've been thinking about this for a long time. I want to be an obstetrician."

"At your age? Really? In ten years you'll be fifty. Pardon me, but that's an old man."

"And in sixty years I'll be a hundred. But I'll worry about that then. Why don't you come with me? You can transfer your credits from Finch. We'll do our homework together."

"Do you want to write the piece about Israel or not?"

"No. I want to forget Israel. I want to forget Jews. I should have the day I left home. Take your penis out in public and of course the squad car comes around—but, really, this has gone on now a little too long. The way I found to spring myself from everything that held me captive as a boy, and it's simply extended the imprisonment to my fortieth year. Enough of my writing, enough of their scolding. Rebellion, obedience—discipline, explosion—injunction, resistance—accusation, denial—defiance, shame —no, the whole God damn thing has been a colossal mistake. This is not the position in life that I had hoped to fill. I want to be an obstetrician. Who quarrels with an obstetrician? Even the obstetrician who delivered Bugsy Siegel goes to bed at night with a clear conscience. He catches what comes out and everybody loves him. When the baby appears they don't start shouting, 'You call that a baby? That's not a baby!' No, whatever he hands them, they take it home. They're grateful for his just having been there. Imagine those butter-covered babies, Diana, with their little Chinese eyes, imagine what seeing that does to the spirit, *that* every morning, as opposed to grinding out another two dubious pages. Conception? Gestation? Gruesome laborious labor? The mother's business. You just wash your hands and hold out the net. Twenty years up here in the literary spheres is enough— now for the fun of the flowing guttter. The bilge, the ooze, the gooey drip. The stuff. No words, just stuff. Everything the word's in place of. The lowest of genres—life itself. Damn right I'll be fifty next time I look. No more words! On to the delivery room before it's too late. Headlong into the Cloaca Maxima and all the effusions thereof. Leave Finch and fly out to Chicago with me. You can go to school at my alma mater."

"Leave Finch and I lose my trust fund. You don't want

me anyway. You want a nursemaid. You want a governess."

"Would it make any difference if I said I'd marry you?"

"Don't fuck with me."

"But would it?"

"Yes, it would, of course it would. Do it. Do it now. Let's get married tonight. Then we'll run away from your life and you'll become a doctor and I'll become a doctor's wife. I'll take the phone calls. I'll make the appointments. I'll boil your instruments. The hell with my trust fund. Let's do it now. Let's go out tonight and get the license and the blood tests."

"My neck hurts too much tonight."

"That's what I figured. You're full of shit, Nathan. There's only one thing for you to do and that's *to get on with it*. WRITE ANOTHER BOOK. *Carnovsky* is not the end of the world. You cannot make yourself a life of misery out of a book that just happened to have been a roaring success. It cannot stop you in your tracks like this. Get up off the floor, get your hair back, straighten out your neck, and write a book that isn't *about* these Jews. *And then the Jews won't bug you.* Oh, what a pity you can't shake free. That you should still be aroused and hurt by this! Are you *always* fighting your father? I know it may sound like a cliché, probably it would be with somebody else, but in your case I happen to think that it's true. I look through these books on your shelves, your

Freud, your Erikson, your Bettelheim, your Reich, and every single line about a father is underlined. Yet when you describe your father to me, he doesn't sound like a creature of any stature at all. He may have been Newark's greatest chiropodist, but he sure doesn't sound like much of a challenge otherwise. That a man of your breadth of intelligence and your total freedom in the world . . . that *this* should beat you down. That you should be so broken down from these *Jews*. You hate this critic Appel? You don't ever want to stop hating him? He's done you such a grievous injury? Okay, the hell with this crazy little four-page letter—go bonk him on the nose. Are Jews scared of physical confrontations? My father would go and punch him in the nose if he thought he'd been insulted the way you do. But you aren't man enough to do that, and you aren't man enough just to forget it—you aren't even man enough to write for the Op Ed page of *The New York Times*. Instead you lie there in your prism glasses and make up fairy tales about medical school, and having a doctor's office with a picture on the desk of a doctor's wife, and coming home FROM work and going out TO RELAX, and when someone on a plane faints and a stewardess asks if anybody here is a doctor, you can stand up and say I am."

"Why the hell not? They never come around when someone faints and ask if anybody here is a writer."

"More of your black-and-blue humor. Go back to

school again, to study, to be the professor's pet and make the Dean's List and get an ID card for the library and all the student activities. At forty. You know why I wouldn't marry you? I would say no anyway, because I couldn't marry anybody so weak."

3 The Ward

One morning only a few days later, one very depressing morning in December 1973, after he'd been up much of the night vainly trying to compose into his tape recorder a more reasonable reply to Milton Appel, Zuckerman came down to the mailbox in his orthopedic collar to see why the postman had rung. He wished he'd brought a coat along: he was thinking of continuing out into the cold and on to the corner to jump from the roof of the Stanhope Hotel. He no longer seemed worth preserving. From 1 to 4 a.m., with the noose of a narrow electric heating pad encircling his cervical spine, he'd gone another fifteen rounds with Appel. And now the new day: what equally useful function could he perform through the interminable hours awake? Cunnilingus was about it. Step right up, sit right down. It was all he was good for. Blotted out everything else. That and hating Appel. Smothered with mothers and shouting at Jews. Yes, illness had done it: Zuckerman had become Carnovsky. The journalists had known it all along.

The problem with jumping is smashing your skull. That can't be pleasant. And if he wound up merely severing his spinal cord on the hotel canopy—well, he'd be bedridden for life, a fate hundreds of thousands of times worse than what already was making him miserable. On the other hand, a failed suicide that didn't completely cripple him might provide a new subject—more than could be said so far for success. But what if the pain vanished halfway down, went the way it came, leaped from his body as he sailed from the roof—what then? What if he saw in every salient detail a next book, a new start? Halfway down is probably just where that happens. Suppose he walked to the Stanhope simply as an experiment. Either the pain disappears before I reach the corner or I enter the hotel and wait for the elevator. Either it disappears before I get into the elevator or I go up to the top floor and out through the fire exit onto the roof. I walk straight to the parapet and look sixteen floors down to the traffic, and this pain comes to realize that I'm not kidding, that six-

teen floors is a very respectable distance, that after a year
and a half *it is time to leave me alone*. I lean out toward
the street and I say to the pain—and I mean what I say—
"One minute more and I jump!" I'll *scare* it out of me.

But all he scared with such thoughts was himself.

Two manila envelopes in the mailbox, so tightly
wedged together that he skinned his knuckles in the excitement of prying them out. The medical-school catalogue, his application forms! What he hadn't dared to
tell Diana was that already, weeks before, he'd sent off
his inquiry to the University of Chicago. From his seat in
the doctors' waiting rooms, watching the patients come
and go, he'd begun to think: Why not? Four decades,
four novels, two dead parents, and a brother I'll never
speak to again—looks from the evidence like my exorcism's done. Why *not* this as a second life? They talk in
earnest to fifty needy people every day. From morning to
night, bombarded by stories, and none of their own devis-
ing. Stories intending to lead to a definite, useful, authoritative conclusion. Stories with a clear and practical purpose: *Cure me*. They follow carefully all the details, then
they go to work. And either the job is doable or undoable,
while mine is both at best and mostly not.

Tearing open the bigger of the two envelopes—well, he
hadn't known a thrill quite like it since the fall of 1948,
when the first of the college mail began to arrive. Each
day he raced home after his last class and, over his quart
of milk, madly read about the life to come; not even the

delivery of the first bound edition of his first published book had promised such complete emancipation as those college catalogues. On the cover of the catalogue now in his hand, a light-and-shadow study of a university tower, stark, soaring, academic Gibraltar, the very symbol of the unassailable solidity of a medical vocation. Inside the front cover, the university calendar. *Jan. 4–5: Registration for Winter quarter . . . Jan. 4: Classes meet . . .* He quickly turned to find "Requirements for Admission" and read until he reached "Selection Policy" and the words that would change everything.

> The Committee on Admissions strives to make its decision on the basis of the ability, achievement, personality, character, and motivation of the candidates. Questions of race, color, religion, sex, marital status, age, national or ethnic origin, or geographic location have no bearing in the consideration of any application for the Pritzker School of Medicine.

They didn't care that he was forty. He was in.

But one page back, bad news. Sixteen hours of chemistry, twelve of biology, eight of physics—merely to qualify, twice as much coursework as he'd been expecting. In science. Well, the sooner the better When classes meet on January 4, I'll be there to ignite my Bunsen burner. I'll pack a bag and fly out to Chicago—over my microscope in a month! Lots of women his age were doing it—what was to stop him? A year's grind as an undergraduate, four of medical studies, three of residency, and at forty-eight he'd be ready to open an office. That would give him twenty-five years in practice—if he could depend on his health. It was the change of professions that would *restore* his health. The pain would just dwindle away; if not, he'd cure himself: it would be within his power. But never again to give himself over to doctors who weren't interested enough or patient enough or simply curious enough to see a puzzle like his through to the end.

That's where the writing years would be of use. A doctor thinks, "Everybody ends badly, nothing I can do. He's just dying and I can't cure life." But a good writer can't abandon his character's suffering, not to narcotics or to death. Nor can he just leave a character to his fate by insinuating that his pain is somehow deserved for being self-induced. A writer learns to stay around, has to, in order to make sense of incurable life, in order to chart the turnings of the punishing unknown even where there's no sense to be made. His experience with all the doctors who had misdiagnosed the early stages of his mother's tumor and then failed him had convinced Zuckerman that, even if he was washed up as a writer, he couldn't do their job any worse than they did.

He was still in the hallway removing sheaves of application blanks from the university envelope when a UPS deliveryman opened the street door and announced a package for him. Yes, it appeared to be happening: once the worst is over, even the parcels are yours. Everything is yours. The suicide threat had forced fate's hand—an essentially unintelligent idea that he found himself believing.

The box contained a rectangular urethane pillow about a foot and a half long and a foot wide. Promised to him a week before and forgotten by him since. Everything was forgotten in the workless monotony of his empty five hundred days. The evening's marijuana didn't help either. His mental activity had come to focus on managing his pain and managing his women: either he was figuring out what pills to take or scheduling arrivals and departures to minimize the likelihood of collision.

He'd been put on to the pillow at his bank. Waiting in line to cash a check—cash for Diana's connection—trying to be patient despite the burning sensation running along the rim of his winged left scapula, he'd been tapped lightly from behind by a pint-sized white-haired gentleman with an evenly tanned sympathetic face. He wore a smart double-breasted dove-gray coat. A dove-gray hat was in the gloved hand at his side. Gloves of dove-gray suede. "I know how you can get rid of that thing," he told Zuckerman, pointing to his orthopedic collar. The mildest Old Country accent. A helpful smile.

"How?"

"Dr. Kotler's pillow. Eliminates chronic pain acquired during sleep. Based on research done by Dr. Kotler. A scientifically designed pillow made expressly for sufferers like yourself. With your wide shoulders and long neck, what you're doing on an ordinary pillow is pinching nerves and causing pain. Shoulders too?" he asked. "Extend into the arms?"

Zuckerman nodded. Pain everywhere.

"And X-rays show nothing? No history of whiplash, no accident, no fall? Just on you like that, unexplained?"

"Exactly."

"All acquired during sleep. That's what Dr. Kotler discovered and how he came up with his pillow. His pillow will restore you to a pain-free life. Twenty dollars plus postage. Comes with a satin pillowcase. In blue only."

"You don't happen to be Dr. Kotler's father?"

"Never married. Whose father I am, we'll never know." He handed Zuckerman a blank envelope out of his pocket. "Write on this: name, along with mailing address. I'll see they send one tomorrow, C.O.D."

Well, he'd tried everything else, and this playful old character clearly meant no harm. With his white wavy hair and nut-colored face, in his woolens and skins of soft dove-gray, he seemed to Zuckerman like somebody out of a children's tale, one of those elfin elderly Jews, with large heart-shaped ears and dangling Buddha lobes, and dark earholes that looked as though they'd been dug to a burrow by a mouse; a nose of impressive length for a man barely reaching Zuckerman's chest, a nose that broadened as it descended, so that the nostrils, each a sizable crescent, were just about hidden by the wide, weighted tip; and eyes that were ageless, polished brown protruding eyes such as you see in photographs taken of prodigious little fiddlers at the age of three.

Watching Zuckerman write his name, the old man asked, "N. as in Nathan?"

"No," replied Zuckerman. "As in Neck."

"Of course. You are the young fellow who has handed me those laughs. I thought I recognized you but I wasn't sure—you've lost quite a number of hairs since I saw your last photo." He removed one glove and extended his hand. "I am Dr. Kotler. I don't make a production out of it with strangers. But you are no stranger, N. Zuckerman. I practiced in Newark for many, many years, began there long before you were born. Had my office in the Hotel Riviera down on Clinton and High before it was purchased by Father Divine."

"The Riviera?" Zuckerman laughed and forgot for the moment about his scapula. N. as in Nostalgia. This *was* a character out of a child's tale: his own. "The Riviera is where my parents spent their honeymoon weekend."

"Lucky couple. It was a grand hotel in those days. My first office was on Academy Street near the *Newark Ledger*. I started with the lumbago of the boys from the paper and an examining table I bought secondhand. The fire commissioner's girl friend had a lingerie shop just down the street. Mike Shumlin, brother of theatrical producer Herman, owned the Japtex shops. So you're our writer. I was expecting from the way you hit and run you'd be a little bantamweight like me. I read that book. Frankly the penis I had almost enough of by the five hundredth time, but what a floodgate of memories you opened up to those early, youthful days. A kick for me on every page. You mention Laurel Garden on Springfield Avenue. I attended Max Schmeling's third fight in the U.S., staged by Nick Kline at Laurel Garden. January 1929. His opponent, an Italian, Corri, was KO'd in one and a half minutes of the first round. Every German in Newark was there—you should have heard them. Saw Willie La Morte beat Corporal Izzie Schwartz that summer—flyweight championship, fifteen rounds. You mention the Empire Burlesque on Washington, near Market. I knew the old guy who managed it, grizzled old guy named Sutherland. Hinda Wassau, the blond Polish striptease queen—knew her personally. One of my patients. Knew producer Rube Bernstein, who Hinda married. You mention the old Newark Bears. I treated young Charlie Keller for his knee. Manager George Selkirk, one of my dearest friends. You mention the Newark Airport. When it opened up, Jerome Congleton was mayor. I attended the dedication. One hangar in those days. There the morning they cut the ribbon on the Pulaski Skyway. What a sight— a viaduct from ancient Rome rising out of the Jersey marshes. You mention the Branford Theater. Favorite place of mine. Saw the first stage shows, featuring Charley Melson and his band. Joe Penner and his 'Wanna Buy a Duck' routine. Oh, Newark was my turf then. Roast beef at Murray's. Lobsters at Dietsch's. The tube station, gateway to New York. The locust trees along the street with their skinny twisted pods. WJZ with Vincent Lopez.

WOR with John B. Gambling. Jascha Heifetz at the
Mosque. The B. F. Keith theater—the old Proctor's—featuring acts direct from the Palace on Broadway. Kitty
Doner, with her sister Rose and her brother Ted. Ted
sang, Rose danced. Mae Murray making a grand personal
appearance. Alexander Moissi, the great Austrian actor, at
the Shubert on Broad Street. George Arliss. Leslie How-
ard. Ethel Barrymore. A great place in those days, our
dear Newark. Large enough to be big-time, small enough
to walk down the street and greet people you knew. Vanished now. Everything that mattered to me down the
twentieth-century drain. My birthplace, Vilna, decimated
by Hitler, then stolen by Stalin. Newark, my America, abandoned by the whites and destroyed by the
colored. That's what I thought the night they set the
fires in 1968. First the Second World War, then the Iron
Curtain, now the Newark Fire. I cried when that riot
broke out. My beautiful Newark. I loved that city."

"So did we all, Dr. Kotler. What are you doing in New
York?"

"Good practical question. Living. Eight years now.
Man in exile. Child of the times. I gave up my wonderful practice, my cherished friends, took my books and my
mementos, packed the last of my pillows, and established
myself here at the age of seventy. Life anew in my eighth
decade on earth. Now on my way to the Metropolitan
Museum. I go for the great Rembrandt. I'm studying his
masterpieces a foot at a time. Quite a discipline. Very
rewarding. The man was a magician. Also studying Holy

Scriptures. Delving into all the translations. Amazing what's in there. Yet the writing I don't like. The Jews in the Bible were always involved in highly dramatic moments, but they never learned to write good drama. Not like the Greeks, in my estimation. The Greeks heard a sneeze and they took off. The sneezer becomes the hero, the one who reported the sneeze becomes the messenger, the ones who overheard the sneeze, they became the chorus. Lots of pity, lots of terror, lots of cliff-hanging and suspense. You don't get that with the Jews in the Bible. There it's all round-the-clock negotiation with God."

"You sound like you know how to keep going."

Wish I could say the same for myself; I wish, he thought childishly, you could teach me.

"Do as I like, Nathan. Always have. Never denied myself what counted. And I believe I know what counted. I've been some use to others too. Kept a balance, you might say. I want to send you a pillow. Free of charge. For the wonderful memories you brought back to life. No reason for you to be in this pain. You don't sleep on your stomach, I trust."

"On my side and on my back, as far as I know."

"Heard this story a thousand times. I'm sending a pillow and a case."

And here they were. Also, tucked in the box, a typewritten note on the doctor's stationery: "Remember, don't place Dr. Kotler's Pillow on top of an ordinary pillow. It does the job by itself. If there is no significant improvement in two weeks, phone me at RE 4–4482. With long-standing problems, manipulation could be required at the outset. For recalcitrant cases there are hypnotic techniques." The letter was signed "Dr. Charles L. Kotler, Dolorologist."

And if, by itself, the pillow worked and the pain completely vanished? He couldn't wait for night to fall so he could take it to sleep. He couldn't wait for it to be January 4 and the first day of class. He couldn't wait for 1981—that was when he'd be opening his office. 1982 at the latest. He'd pack the dolorologist's pillow for Chicago —and he'd leave the harem behind. With Gloria Galanter he'd gone too far, even for a man as disabled as himself. With *Roget's Thesaurus* under his head and Gloria sitting on his face, Zuckerman understood just how little one can depend upon human suffering to produce ennobling effects. She was the wife, the coddled and irreplaceable wife, of the genial wizard who'd weaned Zuckerman reluctantly away from his triple-A bonds and nearly doubled his capital in three years. Marvin Galanter was such a fan of *Carnovsky* that in the beginning he'd refused even to bill Zuckerman for his services; at their first meeting the accountant told Nathan that he would pay any penalties out of his own pocket, should the IRS challenge the shelters. *Carnovsky*, Marvin claimed, was his own life story; for the author of that book, there was nothing whatsoever that he wouldn't do.

Yes, he must divest himself at least of Gloria—only he couldn't resist her breasts. Alone on the playmat, following the rheumatologist's suggestion to try to find some means to distract himself from his pain, he sometimes thought of nothing but her breasts. Of the four women in the harem, it was with Gloria that his helplessness hit bottom—while Gloria herself seemed the happiest, in a strange and delightful way seemed the most playfully independent, tethered though she was to his wretched needs. She distracted him with her breasts and delivered his food: Greenberg's chocolate cakes, Mrs. Herbst's strudel, Zabar's pumpernickel, beluga in pots from the Caviarteria, the lemon chicken from Pearl's Chinese Restaurant, hot lasagna from "21." She sent the chauffeur all the way down to Allen Street for the stuffed peppers from Seymour's Parkway, and then came over in the car to heat them up for his dinner. She rushed into the little kitchenette in her red-fox Russian cossack coat and, when she came out with the steaming pot, was wearing only her heels. Gloria was nearing forty, a firm, hefty brunette with protruding circular breasts like targets, and electrifying growths of hair. Her face could have been a Spanish mulatto's: almond eyes, a wide, imposing jaw, and full rounded lips with peculiarly raised edges. There were bruises on her behind. He wasn't the only primitive she babied and he didn't care. He ate the food and he tasted the breasts. He ate the food off the breasts. There was nothing Gloria didn't remember to carry in her bag: nippleless bra, crotchless panties, Polaroid camera, vibrating dildo, K-Y jelly, Gucci blindfold, a length of braided velvet rope—for a treat, on his birthday, a gram of cocaine. "Times have changed," said Zuckerman, "since all you needed was a condom." "A child is sick," she said, "you bring toys." True, and Dionysian rites were once believed to have a therapeutic effect on the physically afflicted. There was also the ancient treatment known as the imposition of hands. Gloria had classical history on her side. His own mother's means for effecting a cure were to play casino on the edge of the bed with him when he was home with a fever. So as not to fall behind in her housework, she'd set her ironing board up in his bedroom while they gossiped about school and his friends. He loved the smell of ironing still. Gloria, lubricating a finger and slipping it in his anus, talked about her marriage to Marvin.

Zuckerman said to her, "Gloria, you're the dirtiest woman I've ever met."

"If I'm the dirtiest woman you've ever met, you're in trouble. I fuck Marvin twice a week. I put down my book, put out my cigarette, turn out the light, and roll over."

"On your back?"

"What else? And then he puts it in and I know just what to do to make him come. And then he mumbles something about tits and love and he comes. Then I put on the light and roll on my side and light up a cigarette and get on with my book. I'm reading the one you told me about. Jean Rhys."

"What do you do to make him come?"

"I make three circles this way, and three circles the other way, and I draw my fingernail down his spine like this—and he comes."

"So you do seven things."

"Right. Seven things. And then he says something about my tits and love, and he comes. And then he falls asleep and I can turn on the light again and read. This Jean Rhys terrifies me. The other night after reading her book about that shit-on woman and no money, I rolled over and kissed him and said, 'I love you, sweetheart.' But it's hard fucking him, Nathan. And getting harder. You always think in a marriage, 'This is as bad as it can be'— and next year it's worse. It's the most odious duty I've ever had to perform. He says to me sometimes when he's straining to come, 'Gloria, Gloria, say something dirty.' I have to think hard, but I do it. He's a wonderful father and a wonderful husband, and he deserves all the help he can get. But still, one night I really thought I couldn't take it anymore. I put down my book and I put out the light and finally I said it to him. I said, 'Marv, something's gone out of our marriage.' But he was almost snoring by then. 'Quiet,' he mumbles. 'Shhhhh, go to sleep.' I don't know what to do. There's nothing I *can* do. The odd thing and the terrible thing and the thing that's most confusing is that without a doubt Marvin was the real love of my life and beyond a doubt I was the love of Marvin's life and although we were never never happy, for about ten years we had a passionate marriage and all the trimmings, health, money, kids, Mercedes, a double sink and summer houses and everything. And so miserable and so attached. It makes no sense. And now I have these night monsters, three enormous night monsters: no money, death, and getting old. I can't leave him. I'd fall apart. He'd fall apart. The kids would go nuts and they're screwy as it is. But I need excitement. I'm thirty-eight. I need extra attention."

"So, have your affairs."

"They're murder too, you know. You can't always control your feelings in those things. You can't control the other person's feelings either. I have one now who wants to run away with me to British Columbia. He says we can live off the land. He's handsome. He's young. Bushy hair. Very savage. He came up to the house to restore some antiques and he started by restoring me. He lives in a terrible loft. He says, 'I can't believe I'm fucking you.' When he's fucking me. That excites me, Nathan. We take baths together. It's fun. But is that any reason to run out on being Adam and Toby's mother and Marvin's wife? When the kids lose something, who's going to find it for them if I'm in British Columbia? 'Mommy, where is my eraser?' 'Just a second, dear, I'm in the bathroom. Wait. I'll look for it.' Somebody's looking for something, I help—that's mothers. You lost something, I *have* to look. 'Mommy, I found it.' 'I'm glad you found it, dear.' And I am—when they find the eraser, Nathan, I'm happy.

That's how I fell in love with Marvin. The very first time I was in his apartment, and within five minutes, he looked at me and said, 'Where's my cigarette lighter, Gloria, my good lighter?' And I got up and looked around, and I found it. 'Here it is, Marvin.' 'Oh, good.' I was hooked. That was it. Look, I *live* for the baths I take with my Italian bambino and his bushy hair and his iron biceps—but how can I leave these people and expect that they'll find what they lose on their own? With you it's okay—with you it's like a brother. You need and I need and that's it. Besides, you know what a good girl you've got in Cos Cob's cunning little whore." She'd accidentally met Diana when she stopped by unannounced one afternoon and the chauffeur dragged in a potted palm tree to liven up the sickroom. "She's perfect for you. Underage, upper-class, and really slutty in that little toy skirt—juicy, like when you bite into a fresh apple or a good pear. I like the gun-moll mouth. Clever contrast to the high IQ. While we were debating where to put the tree I saw her down the corridor—in the bathroom, making herself up. A bomb could have gone off in there and she wouldn't have known it. I wouldn't drop her."

"I'm in no position," said Zuckerman, impaled upon Gloria's knuckle, "to drop anyone."

"That's good. Some women might see you as prey. That's all some women want—a suffering male who's otherwise well off. All the slow curing, the taking credit for it, and if God forbid he doesn't survive the cure, owning his life after death. Show me a woman who wouldn't love to be the widow of a famous man. To own it *all*."

"Talking about all the women, or are we talking about you?"

"If it's God's blessing, Nathan, that it happens, I can't think of a single woman who wouldn't put up with it. Luckily this kid's too young and snotty to know the fundamentals yet. Fine. Let her be fresh to you when you start to whine. You're better off. No Jewish mother like me would ever minimize the importance of a morbid affliction. Read this book *Carnovsky* if you don't believe it. Jewish mothers know how to own their suffering boys. If I were in your shoes I'd keep my eye out for that."

Jaga, during his opening hour at Anton's Trichological Clinic, had looked to him first, in white bandanna and long white smock, like a novice in a nursing order; then she spoke, and the Slavic accent—along with the clinician's get-up and the dutiful weary professionalism with which she worked her fingers across his scalp—reminded him of the women physicians in *Cancer Ward,* another of the works from which he'd taken stern instruction during his week in traction. His was the last appointment of the day, and after his second session, as he was leaving the Commodore and heading home, he caught sight of her ahead of him out on Vanderbilt Place. She was in a weatherworn black felt coat whose red embroidered hem was coming loose at the back. The shoddy look of a coat once stylish somewhere else subverted somewhat that aura of detached superiority that she affected alone in a cubicle with a balding man. The hurried agitated gait made her look like someone on the run. Maybe she was: running from more of the questions he'd begun to ask during the pleasant fingertip massage. She was small and fragile, with a complexion the color of skim milk and a tiny, pointed, bony, tired face, a face a little ratlike until, at the end of the session, she undid the bandanna and disclosed the corn-silk sheen of her ash-blond hair, and with it a delicacy otherwise obscured in that mask so tiny and taut with strain. The undecipherable violet eyes were suddenly startling. Still, he made no effort on the street to catch up. He couldn't run because of the pain, and when he remembered the heavy sarcasm with which she'd spit on his few amiable questions, he decided against calling her name. "Helping people," she'd replied, when he asked how she got into trichology. "I love helping anyone with a problem." Why had she emigrated to America? "I dreamed all my life of America." What did she make of it here? "Everybody so nice. Everybody wishing you to have a good day. We do not have such nice people in Warsaw."

The next week, to his invitation for a drink, she said yes—curtly, as though she'd said no. She was in a hurry, could stay for no more than a quick glass of wine. In the booth at the bar she drank three quick glasses, and then explained her American sojourn without his having even inquired. "I was bored in Warsaw. I had ennui. I wanted a change." The next week she again said yes as though it were no, and this time she had five glasses of wine. "Hard to believe you left simply because you were bored." "Don't be banal," she told him. "I don't want your sympathy. The client needs sympathy, not the technician with her full head of hair." The following week she came to his apartment, and through the prism glasses he watched as by herself she finished off the bottle he'd given her to open. Because of the pain he could no longer uncork a wine bottle. He was sipping vodka through a bent glass straw.

"Why do you lie on the floor?" she asked.

"Too tedious to go into."

"Were you in an accident?"

"Not that I remember. Were you, Jaga?"

"You must live more through people," she told him.

"How do you know how I should live?"

Drunkenly she tried to pursue her theme. "You must learn to live through other people." Because of the wine and because of her accent, two-thirds of what she was saying was incomprehensible to him.

At the door he helped her into the coat. She had stitched up the hem since he'd first spotted her hurrying along Vanderbilt Place, but what the coat needed was a new lining. Jaga seemed herself to have no lining at all. She looked like something that had been peeled of its rind, exposing a wan semi-transparent whiteness that wasn't even an inner membrane but the bare, pallid pulp of her being. He thought that if he touched her the sensation would make her scream.

"There's something corrupt about both of us," she said.

"What are you talking about?"

"Monomaniacs like you and me. I must never come here again."

Soon she was stopping by every evening on her way home. She began wearing eye shadow and to smell of a peppery perfume, and the face tightened up like a little rat's only when he persisted in asking the stupidest of his questions. She arrived in a new silk blouse the same pale violet as her eyes; though the topmost button was left carelessly undone, she made no move toward the playmat. She stretched instead across the sofa, snuggled cozily there under the afghan and poured out glass after glass of red wine—and then ran off to the Bronx. She climbed the library ladder in her stocking feet and browsed through the shelves. She asked from the topmost rung if she could borrow a book, and then forgot to take it home. Each day another nineteenth-century American classic was added to the stack left behind on his desk. Half contemptuously, satirizing herself, him, his library, his ladder, deriding seemingly every human dream and aspiration, she labeled where she piled the books "My spot."

"Why not take them with you?" Zuckerman asked.

"No, no, not with great novels. I am too old for this

form of seduction. Why do you allow me to come here anyway, to the sacred sanctuary of art? I am not an 'interesting character.'"

"What did you do in Warsaw?"

"I did in Warsaw the same as I do here."

"Jaga, why not give me a break? Why not a straight answer to one lousy question?"

"Please, if you are looking for somebody interesting to write about, invite from the clinic one of Anton's other girls. They are younger and prettier and sillier, they will be flattered that you ask lousy question. They have more adventures to tell than I do. You can get into their pants and they can get into your books. But if you are looking at me for sex, I am not interested. I hate lust. It's a nuisance. I don't like the smells, I don't like the sounds. Once, twice with somebody is fine—beyond that, it's a partnership in dirt."

"Are you married?"

"I am married. I have a daughter of thirteen. She lives with her grandmother in Warsaw. Now do you know everything about me?"

"What does your husband do?"

"What does he 'do'? He is not a graphomaniac like you. Why does an intelligent man ask stupid questions about what people 'do'? Because you are an American or because you are this graphomaniac? If you are writing a book and you want me to help you with my answers, I cannot. I am too dull. I am just Jaga with her upskis and downskis. And if you are trying to write a book by the answers that you get, then you are too dull."

"I ask you questions to pass the time. Is that sufficiently cynical to suit you?"

"I don't know about politics, I am not interested in politics, I don't want to answer questions about Poland. I don't *care* about Poland. To hell with all those things. I came here to get away from all that and I will appreciate it if you will leave me be about things that are the past."

On a windy November evening, with rain and hail blowing up against the windows, and the temperature down below freezing, Zuckerman offered Jaga ten dollars for a cab. She threw the money at him and left. Minutes later she was back, the black felt coat already sopping wet. "When do you want to see me again?"

"Up to you. Whenever you're feeling resentful enough."

As though to bite, she lunged for his lips. The next afternoon she said, "The first time I kissed anyone in two years."

"What about your husband?"

"We don't even do that anymore."

The man with whom she'd defected wasn't her husband. This was revealed to him the first time Jaga undid the remaining buttons of the new silk blouse and knelt beside him on the playmat.

"Why did you defect with him?"

"You see, I should not have told you even that much. I say 'defect' and you are excited. An interesting character.

You are more excited by the word 'defect' than you are by my body. My body is too skinny." She removed her blouse and bra and threw them onto the desk, by the pile of un-borrowed books. "My breasts are not the right size for an American man. I know that. They are not the right American shape. You did not know that I would look this old."

"On the contrary, it's a child's body."

"Yes, a child. She suffered from the Communists, poor child—I'll put her in a book. Why must you be so banal?"

"Why must you be so difficult?"

"It's you who is difficult. Why don't you just let me come here and drink your wine and pretend with borrowing books and kiss you, if I feel like it. Any man with half of a heart would do this. At moments you should be forgetting about writing books all the time. Here"—and after undoing her skirt and raising her slip, she turned around on her knees and leaned her weight forward onto the palms of her hands. "Here, you can see my ass. Men like that. You can do it to me from behind. The first time and you can do anything you want to me, anything at all that pleases you, *except to ask me more of your questions.*"

"Why do you hate it so much here?"

"Because I am left out here! Stupid man, of course I hate it here! I live with a man who is left out. What can he do here? It's all right that I work in a hair clinic. But not for a man. He would take a job like that and he would crumble up in a year. But I begged him to run away with me, to save me from that madness, and so I cannot ask him to start to sweep floors in New York City."

"What did he work at before coming here?"

"You would misunderstand if I told you. You would think it was 'interesting.'"

"Maybe I misunderstand less than you think."

"He saved me from the people who were poisoning my life. Now I must save him from exile. He saved me from my husband. He saved me from my lover. He saved me from the people destroying everything I love. Here I am his eyes, his voice, his source of survival. If I left, it would kill him. It isn't a matter of being loved, it's a matter of loving somebody—whether you can believe that or not."

"Nobody asked you to leave him."

Jaga uncorked a second bottle of wine and, seated naked on the floor beside him, quickly drank half of it down. "But I want to," she said.

"Who is he?"

"A boy. A boy who did not use his head. That is what my lover asked him in Warsaw. He saw us in a café and he came up to him and he was furious. 'Who are you?' he shouted at the boy."

"What did the boy answer?"

"He answered, 'None of your business.' To you that does not sound so heroic. But it is, when one man is half the age of the other."

"He ran away with you to be a hero, and you ran away with him to run away."

"And now you think you understand why I love my spot on your desk. Now you think you understand why I get myself drunk on your expensive claret. 'She is plotting to trade him for me.' Only that is not so. Even with my émigré vulnerability, I will not fall in love with you."

"Good."

"I will let you do anything you want to me, but I will not fall in love."

"Fine."

"Only good, only fine? No, in my case it is excellent. Because I am the best woman in the world for falling in love with the wrong man. I have the record in the Communist countries. Either they are married, or they are murderers, or they are like you, men finished with love. Gentle, sympathetic, kind with money and wine, but interested in you mainly as a subject. Warm ice. I know writers."

"I won't ask how. But go on."

"I know writers. Beautiful feelings. They sweep you away with their beautiful feelings. But the feelings disappear quickly once you are no longer posing for them. Once they've got you figured out and written down, you go. All they give is their attention."

"You could do worse."

"Oh yes, all that attention. It's lovely for the model while it lasts."

"What were you in Poland?"

"I told you. Champion woman to fall in love with the

wrong man." And again she offered to assume any posture for penetration that would please and excite him. "Come however you like and don't wait for me. That is better for a writer than more questions."

And what is better for you? It was difficult to do her the kindness of not asking. Jaga was right about writers—all along, Zuckerman had been thinking that if only she told him enough, he might find in what she said something to start him writing. She insulted him, she berated him, when it was time to go she sometimes grew so angry that she had all she could do not to reach out and strike him. She wanted to collapse and be rescued, and she wanted to be heroic and prevail, and she seemed to hate him most for reminding her, merely by taking it all in, that she could manage neither. A writer on the wane, Zuckerman did his best to remain unfazed. Mustn't confuse pleasure with work. He was there to listen. Listening was the only treatment he could give. They come, he thought, and tell me things, and I listen, and occasionally I say, "Maybe I understand more than you think," but there's no treatment I can offer to cure the woes of all the outpatients crossing my path, bent beneath their burdens and their separate griefs. Monstrous that all the world's suffering is good to me inasmuch as it's grist to my mill—that all I can do, when confronted with anyone's story, is to wish to turn it into *material*, but if that's the way one is possessed, that is the way one is possessed. There's a demonic side to this business that the Nobel Prize committee doesn't talk much about. It would be nice, particularly in the presence of the needy, to have pure disinterested motives like everybody else, but, alas, that isn't the job. The only patient being treated by the writer is himself.

After she'd gone, and after Gloria had stopped by with his dinner, and some hours before he resumed composing into his tape recorder another rejoinder to Appel, he told himself, "Start tonight. Get on with it tonight," and began by transcribing every word he could still remember of the protracted tirade delivered that afternoon by Jaga while he lay beneath her on the playmat. Her pelvis rose and fell like something ticking, an instrument as automatic as a metronome. Light, regular, tireless thrusts, thrusting distinct as a pulsebeat, thrusting excruciatingly minute, and all the while she spoke without stopping, spoke like she fucked, steady voluptuous coldness, as though he was a man and this was an act that she didn't yet *entirely* despise. He felt like a convict digging a tunnel with a spoon.

"I hate America," she told him. "I hate New York. I hate the Bronx. I hate Bruckner Boulevard. In a village in Poland there are at least two Renaissance buildings. Here it is just ugly houses, one after another, and Americans asking you their direct questions. You cannot have a spiritual conversation with anyone. You cannot be poor here and I hate it." Tick tock. Tick tock. Tick tock. "You think I'm morbid and psychopathic. Crazy Jaga. You think I should be like an American girl—typical American: energetic, positive, talented. Like all these intelligent American girls with their thinking, 'I can be an actress, I can be a poet, I can be a good teacher. I'm positive, I'm growing—I hadn't been growing when I was growing, but now I'm growing.' You think I should be one of those good good boring American girls with their naïveté that goodness does it, that energy does it, that talent does it. 'How can a man like Nathan Zuckerman fall in love with me for two weeks, and then abandon me? I am so good and energetic and positive and talented and growing—how can that be?' But I am not so naïve, so don't worry. I have some darkness to go back to. Whatever darkness was behind them, it was explained to them by the psychiatrist. And now for them it's all recovery. Make my life meaningful. Growth. They buy this. Some of them, the smart ones, they sell it. 'The relationship I had, I learned something from it. It's good for my growth.' If they have a darkness, it's a nice darkness. When you sleep with them, they smile. They make it wonderful." Tick tock. "They make it beautiful." Tick tock. "They make it warm and tender." Tick tock. "They make it *loving*. But I do not have this good American optimism. I cannot stand to lose people. I cannot *stand* it. And I am not smiling. And I am not growing. I am disappearing!" Tick tock. Tick tock. "Did I tell you, Nathan, that I was raped? When I left here that day in the rain?" "No, you didn't tell me that." "I was walking to the subway in that rain. I was drunk. And I thought I couldn't make it—I was too drunk to walk. And I waved for a taxi, to take me to the station. And this limousine stopped. I don't remember very much. It was the limousine driver. He had a Polish name, too— that's what I remember. I think I had a blackout when I was in the limousine. I don't even know whether I did something provocative. He drove me and drove me and drove me. I thought I was going to the subway, and then he stopped and he said that I owed him twenty dollars. And I didn't have twenty dollars. And I said, 'Well, I can only write you a check.' And he said, 'How can I know the check is good?' And I said, 'You can call my husband.' That is the last thing I wanted to do, but I was so drunk, and so I didn't know what I was doing. And I gave him your number." "Where were you at this point?" "Somewhere. I think on the West Side. So he said, 'Okay, let's call your husband on the telephone. Here's a restaurant and we can go inside and we can call.' And I went inside and it wasn't a restaurant—it was some stairway. And there he pushed me down and raped me. And after that he drove me to the station." "And was it horrible or was it nothing?" "Ah, you want 'material.' It was nothing. I was too drunk to feel anything. He was afraid after I would call the police. Because I told him that I would. I told him, 'You have raped me and I'm going to do something about it. I didn't leave Poland to come to America to be raped by a Pole.' And he said, 'Well, you could have slept with hundreds of men—nobody's going to believe you.' And I didn't even mean to go to the police. He was right—they *wouldn't* believe me. I just wanted to tell him that he had done something dreadful. He was white, he had a Polish name, he was good-looking, young—why? Why a man feels like raping a drunken woman? What kind of pleasure can that be? He drives me to the station, asking me if I'm okay, if I can make the train. Even walks me down to the platform and buys me a token." "Very generous." "And he never called you?" "No." "I'm sorry I gave him your number, Nathan." "It hardly matters." "That rape itself—it didn't mean anything. I went home and washed myself. And there waiting for me is a post-card. From my lover in Warsaw. And that's when I began to cry. *That* had meaning. Me, a postcard! Finally he writes me—and it's a postcard! I had a vision, after his postcard, of my parents' house before the war—a vision of all that went. Your country is ethically maybe a better country than Poland, but even we, even *we*—you want to come now?" "Even we what?" "Even we deserved a little better than that. I never had a normal life almost from right after I was born. I'm not a very normal person. I once had a little child to tell me that I smell good and that my meatballs are the best in the world. That's gone too. Now I don't even have half-home. Now what I have is no-home. All I'm saying is, after you get tired of fucking me, I'll understand—but, please," she said, just as his body, playing yet another trick, erupted without so much as a warning, "please, don't just drop me as a friend."

Bucking as best he could what he'd had to drink with

Jaga and to smoke with Gloria, he got himself upright in his chair and with his notebook open on the lapboard and the collar fixed around his neck, tried to invent what he still didn't know. He thought of his little exile next to hers. Hers next to Dr. Kotler's. Exile like theirs is an illness, too; either it goes away in two or three years or it's chronic and you've got it for good. He tried to imagine a Poland, a past, a daughter, a lover, a postcard, as though his cure would follow if only he began anew as a writer of stories wholly unlike his own. *The Sorrows of Jaga.* But he couldn't get anywhere. Though people are weeping in every corner of the earth from torture and ruin and cruelty and loss, that didn't mean that he could make their stories his, no matter how passionate and powerful they seemed beside his trivialities. One can be overcome by a story the way a reader is, but a reader isn't a writer. Desperation doesn't help either: it takes longer than one night to make a story, even when it's written in a sitting. Besides, if Zuckerman wrote about what he didn't know, who then would write about what he did know?

Only what did he know? The story he could dominate and to which his feelings had been enslaved had ended. Her stories weren't his stories and his stories were no longer his stories either.

To prepare himself to leave his playmat and travel eight hundred miles to Chicago—when the farthest he'd been in a year was to get a pain suppressor out on Long Island—he first spent fifteen minutes under the new hundred-dollar shower head guaranteed by Hammacher Schlemmer to pummel you into health with hot water. All that came out was a fainthearted drizzle. Some neighbor in the old brownstone running a dishwasher or filling the tub. He emerged looking sufficiently boiled but feeling no better than when he'd gone under. He frequently emerged feeling no better even when the pressure was way up and the water gushed forth as prescribed. He smeared the steam from the medicine-chest mirror and contemplated his reddened physique. No invidious organic enemy visible, no stigmata at all; only the upper torso, once a point of pride, looking just as frail as it had after the regular morning shower, the one to offset the stiffness of sleep. On the advice of the physiotherapist, he stood under scalding showers three times a day. The heat, coupled with the pounding of the water, was supposed to unglue the spasm and serve as a counterirritant to the pain. "Hyperstimulation analgesia"—principle of the acupuncture needles, and of the ice packs that he applied between scalding showers, and of jumping off the roof of the Stanhope Hotel.

While drying himself, he probed with his fingertips until he'd located the worst of the muscular soreness midway along the upper left trapezius, the burning tenderness over the processes and to the right of the third cervical vertebra, and the movement pain at the insertion of the

long head of the left biceps tendon. The intercostals between the eighth and ninth ribs were only moderately
sore, a little improved really since he'd last checked back
there two hours before, and the aching heaviness in the
left deltoid was manageable, more or less—what a pitcher
might feel having thrown nine innings on a cold September night. If it were only the deltoid that hurt, he'd go
through life a happy man; if he could somehow contract
with the Source of All Pain to take upon himself, even
unto death, the trapezial soreness, *or* the cervical raw-
ness—any *one* of his multitude of symptoms in exchange
for permanent relief from everything else . . .

He sprayed the base of his neck and the shoulder girdle
with the morning's second frosting of ethyl chloride (gift
of his last osteopath). He refastened the collar (fitted by
the neurologist) to support his neck. At breakfast he'd
taken a Percodan (rheumatologist's grudging prescription) and debated with himself—craven sufferer vs. responsible adult—about popping a second so soon. Over the
months he'd tried keeping himself to four Percodan pills
on alternate days to avoid getting hooked. Codeine con-
stipated him and made him drowsy, while Percodan not
only halved the pain but provided a nice gentle invigorat-
ing wallop to a woefully enfeebled sense of well-being.
Percodan was to Zuckerman what sucking stones were to
Molloy—without 'em couldn't go on.

Despite dire warnings about the early hour from his
former self, he wouldn't have minded a drag on a joint:

eight hundred miles of traveling too nerve-racking to contemplate otherwise. He kept a dozen handy in the egg compartment of the refrigerator, and a loose ounce (obtained by Diana from the Finch pharmacopoeia) in a plastic bag in the butter compartment. One long drag in case he hailed a taxi with no shocks: all he seemed to ride in with his neck brace were cars shipped secondhand from Brazzaville Yellow Cab. Though he couldn't depend upon marijuana to cool things down like Percodan, a few puffs did manage to detach him, sometimes for as long as half an hour, from engrossment with the pain and nothing else. By the time he got to the airport the second Percodan (precipitously swallowed despite all the hemming and hawing) would have begun its percolation, and he'd have the rest of the joint for further assistance on the flight. Two quick puffs—after the first long drag—and then, carefully, he pinched out the joint and dropped it for safekeeping into a matchbox in his jacket pocket.

He packed his bag: gray suit, black shoes, black socks. From inside his closet door he chose one of his sober foulards, then from the dresser one of his blue button-down shirts. Uniform for medical-school interview—for all public outings going on twenty-five years. To fight baldness he packed the hormone drops, the pink No. 7 dressing, a jar of Anton's specially prepared conditioner, and a bottle of his shampoo. To fight pain he packed the electronic suppressor, three brands of pills, a sealed new spray-cap bottle of ethyl chloride, his large ice bag, two electric heating pads (the narrow, nooselike pad that wrapped around his throat, the long, heavy pad that draped over his shoulders), the eleven joints left in the refrigerator, and a monogrammed Tiffany's silver flask (gift of Gloria Galanter) that he filled to the lip with hundred-proof Russian vodka (gift of husband Marvin's firm: case of Stolichnaya and case of champagne for his fortieth birthday). Last he packed Dr. Kotler's pillow. He used to travel to Chicago with a pen and a pad and a book to read.

He wouldn't phone to say where he was going until he got out to LaGuardia. He wouldn't even bother then. It wasn't going to require very much teasing from any of his women to deter him, not if he thought of the Brazzaville taxis and the East River Drive potholes and the inevitable delay at the airport. Suppose he had to stand in a line. Suppose he had to carry his suitcase into the terminal. He had trouble only that morning carrying his toothbrush up to his mouth. And of all he couldn't handle, the suitcase would be just the beginning. Sixteen hours of organic chemistry? twelve of biology? eight of physics? He couldn't follow an article in *Scientific American*. With his math he couldn't even understand the industrial bookkeeping in *Business Week*. A science student? He wasn't serious.

There was also some question as to whether he was sane, or was entering that stage of chronic ailing known as the Hysterical Search for the Miraculous Cure. That might be all that Chicago was about: purifying pilgrimage to a sacred place. If so, beware—astrology lies just around the corner. Worse, Christianity. Yield to the hunger for medical magic and you will be carried to the ultimate limit of human foolishness, to the most preposterous of all the great pipe dreams devised by ailing mankind—to the Gospels, to the pillow of our leading dolorologist, the voodoo healer Dr. Jesus Christ.

To give his muscles a rest from the effort of packing his bag, and to recover the courage to fly to Chicago—or, alternatively, to undo the grip of the cracked idea that would really send him flying (off the Stanhope roof)—he stretched across the unmade sheets in the dark cube of his bedroom. The room jutted off the parlor-floor apartment into the enclosed well of the rear courtyard. In an otherwise handsome, comfortable flat, it was the one gloomy room, undersized, underheated, only a shade more sunlight than a crypt. The two unwashable windows were permanently grated against burglars. The side window was further obscured by the trunk of the courtyard's dying tree, and the rear window half-blinded by an air conditioner. A tangle of extension cords lay coiled on the carpet—for the pain suppressor and the heating pads. Half the kitchen glasses had accumulated on the bedside table—water to wash down his pills—along with a cigarette-rolling machine and a packet of cigarette papers. On a piece of paper toweling were scattered stray green flecks of cannabis weed. The two open books, one atop the other, had been bought secondhand at the Strand: a 1920 English text on orthopedic medicine, with horrific surgical photography, and the fourteen hundred pages of Gray's *Anatomy*, a copy of the 1930 edition. He'd been studying medical books for months, and not so as to bone up for any admissions committee. The jailhouse lawyer stores his well-thumbed library under the bed and along the cell walls; so does the patient serving a stretch to which he thinks himself illegally sentenced.

The cassette tape recorder was on the unoccupied half of the double bed, just where he'd fallen asleep with it at 4 a.m. So was his file folder on Milton Appel, which he'd spent his night clutching instead of Diana. He'd phoned and begged her to stay with him after Gloria had gone back to Marvin and Jaga had left in tears for the Bronx, and after he'd flailed about between his chair and the floor trying to dream up, from Jaga's clues, some story that was hers and not his. Hopeless—and not only because of the grass and the vodka. If you get out of yourself you can't be a writer because the personal ingredient is what gets you going, and if you hang on to the personal ingredient any longer you'll disappear right up your asshole. Dante got out of hell easier than you'll escape Zuckerman-Carnovsky. You don't want to represent her Warsaw— it's what her Warsaw represents that you want: suffering that isn't semi-comical, the world of massive historical pain instead of this pain in the neck. War, destruction, anti-Semitism, totalitarianism, literature on which the fate

of a culture hinges, writing at the very heart of the up-
heaval, a martyrdom more to the point—some point, *any*
point—than bearing the cocktail-party chitchat as a guest
on Dick Cavett. Chained to self-consciousness. Chained
to retrospection. Chained to my dwarf drama till I die.
Stories now about Milton Appel? Fiction about losing my
hair? I can't face it. Anybody's hair but mine. "Diana,
come over, spend the night." "No." "Why no? Why not?"
"Because I'm not going to suck you off for ten consecutive
hours on your playmat and then listen to you for ten
hours more screaming about this Milton Appel." "But
that's all over." But she'd hung up: he'd become another
of her terrible men.

He flipped on the tape recorder and rewound the side.
Then he pushed "Play." When he heard his voice, spooky
and lugubrious because of a defect in the audio mech-
anism, he thought: I might as well have depressed "Re-
gress." This is where I came in.

"Dear Professor Appel," intoned his warbling ghost,
"my friend Ivan Felt sent on to me your odd request for
him to ask me to write an Op Ed piece on behalf of Israel.
Maybe it wasn't so odd. Maybe you've changed your mind
about me and the Jews since you distinguished for Elsa
Stromberg between anti-Semites like Goebbels (to whose
writings she compared my own in the letters column of
Inquiry) and those like Zuckerman who just don't like us.
It was a most gracious concession."

He pushed "Stop," then "Fast Forward," and then tried

"Play" again. He couldn't be so stupid as he sounded. The problem was the speed of the tape.

"You write to Felt that we 'grown-ups' should not kid ourselves (it's okay if we kid students) about 'the differences between characters and authors.' However, would this not seem to contradict—"

He lay there listening till the reel ended. Anybody who says "Would this not seem to contradict" should be shot. You said I said. He said you said. She said I said he said you said. All in this syrupy, pedantic, ghostly drone. My life in art.

No, it wasn't a fight he needed; what he desperately needed was a reconciliation, and not with Milton Appel. He still couldn't imagine having fallen out with his brother. Certainly it happens, yet when you hear about families in which brothers don't speak it's so awful, so stupid, it seems so impossible. He couldn't believe that a book could seem no more to Henry than a murder weapon. It was too dull a point of view for a man of Henry's intelligence to sustain for four years. Perhaps he was only waiting for Nathan, as the elder, to write him a letter or give him a ring. Zuckerman could not believe that Henry, the sweetest and most thoughtful kid, burdened always with too big, too kind a heart, could really continue hating him year after year.

Without any evidence, Zuckerman located his true enemy in Carol. Yes, they were the ones who knew how to hate and keep hating, the mice who couldn't look you straight in the eye. Don't touch him, she'd told Henry, or you'll wind up a caricature in a book—so will I, so will the children. Or maybe it was the money: when families split apart like this, it's usually not literature that does it. Carol resented that Nathan had been left half of Henry's parents' estate, Nathan, who'd made a million by *defaming* his benefactors, left a hundred thousand bucks after taxes. Oh, but that wasn't Carol. Carol was a liberal, responsible, well-meaning woman whose enlightened tolerance was her pride. Yet if nothing was holding Henry back, why no message even on Nathan's birthday? He'd been getting birthday calls from Henry since his first year at college. "Well, how does it feel, Natey, to be seventeen?" To be twenty-five. To be thirty. "Forty?" Zuckerman would have said—"It would feel better, Hesh, if we cut the crap and had lunch." But the biggest of birthdays came and went, and no call or card or telegram from the remaining member of his family; just Marvin's champagne in the morning and Marvin's wife in the afternoon, and in the early evening, drunken Jaga, her cheek crushed to the playmat and her rear raised to face him, and crying out, "Nail me, nail me, crucify me with your Jewish prick!" even while Zuckerman wondered who had been more foolish, Henry for failing to seize the occasion of the milestone to declare a truce or himself for expecting that his turning forty should automatically unburden Henry of what it meant having Nathan Zuckerman as his brother.

He picked up the bedside phone but couldn't dial even

a single digit of the area code, so overtaken was he by fatigue. This had happened before on the brink of phoning Henry. As weary of his sentimentality as of their righteousness. He could not have both that brother and that book.

The number he dialed was Jenny's. Somebody to whom, as yet, he owed no explanations.

He let it ring. She would be out back with her pad, drawing snowdrifts in the orchard, or in the shed with her ax, splitting wood. He'd received a long letter from Bearsville only the day before, a long, captivating letter in which she'd written, "I feel you're on the verge of something nuts," and he'd kept picking it up and looking to be sure she'd said on the verge of something nuts and not already going nuts. Fighting back from a *real* breakdown would be terrible. It could take as long as medical school. Longer. Even after the dissolution of his marriages— wreckage he still couldn't square with an orderly personality like his—he'd neither gone nuts nor gone under. However bad it was, always he'd pushed sanely on until a new alliance came along to help restore the old proportions. Only during the last half year had gloomy, frightening bouts of confusion seriously begun to erode the talent for steady living, and that wasn't from the pain alone: it was also from living without nursing a book that nursed him. In his former life he could never have imagined lasting a week without writing. He used to wonder how all the billions who didn't write could take the daily blizzard —all that beset them, such a saturation of the brain, and so little of it known or named. If he wasn't cultivating hypothetical Zuckermans he really had no more means than a fire hydrant to decipher his existence. But either there was no existence left to decipher or he was without sufficient imaginative power to convert into his fiction of seeming self-exposure what existence had now become. There was no rhetorical overlay left: he was bound and gagged by the real raw thing, ground down to his own unhypothetical nub. He could no longer pretend to be anyone else, and as a medium for his books he had ceased to be.

Breathless from running, Jenny answered the phone on the fifteenth ring and Zuckerman immediately hung up. If he told her where he was going she'd try like Diana to stop him. They would all try to stop him, just as lucidity was breaking through. Jaga in her murky accent would shower him with Polish despair: "You want to be like people with real hot ordinary pursuits inside. You want to have fine feelings like the middle class. You want to be a doctor the way some people admit to uncommitted crimes. Hallo Dostoevsky. Don't be so banal." Gloria would laugh and say something ludicrous: "Maybe you need a child. I'll become a bigamist and we'll have one. Marvin wouldn't mind—he loves you more than I do." But Jenny's real wisdom would stop him. He didn't even understand why she continued to bother with him. Why any of them did. For Gloria, he supposed, coming to his place to loll around in her G-string was something to do a couple afternoons a week; Diana, the budding matador,

would try anything once; and Jaga needed a haven somewhere between the home that was no-home and Anton's
clinic, and his playmat, alas, was the best she could do.
But why did Jenny bother? Jenny was in the long line of
levelheaded wives, writers' wives as skillful as explosive
experts at defusing a writer's dreadful paranoia and
brooding indignation, at regularly hacking back the in-
compatible desires that burgeon in the study, lovely
women not likely to bite your balls off, lovely, clear-
headed, dependable women, the dutiful daughters of their
own troubled families, perfect women whom in the end
he divorced. What do you prove by going it alone when
there's Jenny's colossal willingness and her undespairing
heart?

Bearsville, N.Y.
Early Pleistocene Epoch

Dear Nathan,
    I'm feeling strong and optimistic and whistling march-
ing tunes as I often do when I feel this way, and you are
getting more desperate. There is something across your
face these days that disappears only after sex and then only
for about five minutes. Lately I feel you're on the verge of
something nuts. I know this because there is something
in me that is bent to your shape (which sounds more
obscene than it is). There's a great deal that you don't
have to do to please me. My grandmother (who asks me
to tell you she wears a size 16 coat) used to say, "All I
want is for you to be happy" and it used to gall me. Happiness wasn't all I wanted. How vapid! Eventually I've

come to see more depth in that and in simple good nature generally. You have found a girl you could make happy. I am that kind, if that interests you.

I never told you that I went to a psychoanalyst when I came back so confused from France. He told me that men and women whose sexual instincts are particularly unruly are often drawn to styles of extreme repression; with weaker instincts, they might feel free to let the beast in them free. By way of explaining further what I mean about something in me that is bent to your shape. (Erotically speaking, we—women—decide very young that we'll be either priestesses or sacrifices. And we stick to it. And then midway into your career you long to switch and that is just the opportunity you gave me with the grand that I blew at Bergdorf's. By way of explaining still further.)

Snowed in. 10 inches fell atop 12 from the night before. Expected high today on this mountain: zero. There is a nice new ice age on the way. I'm painting it. Strange and lunar. Expect to look in the mirror and see I've grown saber-teeth. Are you alive and well and still living in New York? I didn't think so when we spoke on Monday. I hung up and began thinking of you as someone I used to know. Is Milton Appel's really the final word? Let us name him Tevye and see if you are still upset. He thinks you do what you do for the sadistic joy of it? I thought your book was one genial trick after another. I'm astonished at your doubt. In my view a good novelist is less like a high priest of secular culture than he is like an intelligent dog. Extraordinary sensitivity to some stimuli, like a dog's sense of smell, and selective impoverishment in the communication of them. The combination produces not talking but barking, whining, frantic burrowing, pointing, howling, groveling, anything. Good dog good book. And you are a good dog. Isn't that enough? You once wrote a novel called *Mixed Emotions*. Why don't you read it? At least read the title. In someone who has made his work and his destiny out of mixed emotions, toward his family, toward his country, toward his religion and his education and even his own sex—skip it. To my point. I can't say nothing and saying it to myself isn't the same. There's a little house for rent up here that you would like. Not primitive like mine but warm and cozy. And nearby. I could see that you were all right. I could introduce you to the people around to talk to. I could introduce you to nature. There's no beating nature: *the most abstract art uses colors that occur in nature.* You are forty, the halfway point, and you are exhausted. No punning diagnosis intended, but you are sick of yourself, sick of serving your imagination's purposes, sick of fighting the alien purposes of the Jewish Appels. Up here you can get past all that. If you won't get past your pain, maybe you'll at least lay down the burden of your fiendish dignity and the search for motives, good or bad. I'm not proposing my magic white mountain for the Castorpian seven-year cure. But why not see what happens in seven months? I can't imagine anyone thinking of New York as home. I don't think you do or did, ever. You certainly don't live there that way. You don't live there at all. You're locked up on a closed ward. Here in the woods it's only rarely crushing isolation. Mostly it's useful solitude. Out here it makes *sense* living apart from people. And I live here. If worst comes to worst, you can talk to me. It's beginning to throw me off balance to have only myself and a cat to care about.

More quotations for your outlook. (Intelligent people are corny too.)

> Nel mezzo del cammin di nostra vita
> mi ritrovai per una selva oscura,
> che la diritta via era smarrita.
> —Dante

> It is a good thing in the winter to be deep in the snow, in the autumn deep in the yellow leaves, in the summer among the ripe corn, in spring amid the grass; it is a good thing to be always with the mowers and the peasant girls, in summer with a big sky overhead, in winter by the fireside, and to feel that it always has been and always will be so. One may sleep on straw, eat black bread, well, one will only be the healthier for it.
> —Van Gogh

> Love,
> A Peasant Girl

P.S. I am sorry that your shoulder is still bad, but I don't think it's going to stop you. If I were a devil, plotting with my minions how to shut Zuckerman up, and some minion said, "How about plaguing shoulder pain?" I would say, "No, sorry, I just don't think that will do it." I hope the pain subsides, and think that if you came up here, in time you'd feel the inner clench loosening. But if it didn't, you would just live with it and write with it. Life really is stronger than death. If you don't believe me, come look at my fat new picture book (32 smackers) of seventeenth-century Dutch realism. Jan Steen couldn't paint an upholstery tack without proclaiming just that.

No, he wouldn't tell her what he was planning and he wouldn't rent the house nearby. It's my vitality I long for, not a deeper retreat; the job is to make sense back among people, not to take a higher degree in surviving alone. Even with you to talk to, winter by the fireside and the big summer sky overhead are not going to produce a potent new man—they're going to give us a little boy. Our son will be *me*. No, I cannot be mothered in that warm cozy house. I will not abet that analyst's inanities about "returning to the infantile mode." Now to renounce renunciation—to reunite with the race!

Yet what if Jenny's black bread is my cure? *There's a great deal that you don't have to do to please me. You have found a girl you could make happy. It's beginning to throw me off balance to have only myself and a cat to care about. You'd feel the inner clench unloosening.*

Yes, and after the novelty of healing me wore off? No doubt Gloria is right and the suffering male (who is otherwise well) is to some women the great temptation, but what happens when the slow curing fails to take place and the tender rewards are not forthcoming? Every morning, nine on the button, she's off to the studio and shows up next only for lunch—stained with paint and full of painting problems, anxious to bolt a sandwich and get back to work. I know that absorption. So do my ex-wives. If I were healthy and nailed to a book, I might go ahead and make the move, buy a parka and snow boots and turn peasant with Jennifer. Separate by day for deep concentration, toil alone like slaves of the earth over the obstinate brainchild, then coming uncoiled together at night to share food and wine and talk and feeling and sex. But it's easier to share sex than to share pain. That would dawn on her soon enough, and I'd wind up reading *ARTnews* from under my ice bag and learning to hate Hilton Kramer, while nights as well as days she slugged it out in the studio with Van Gogh. No, he couldn't go from being an artist to being an artist's chick. He had to be rid of all the women. If there wasn't something suspect about someone hanging around somebody like him, it was surely wrong for him to be hanging on to all of them. They all, with their benevolence, with their indulgence, with their compliance to my need, make off with what I most need to climb out of this pit. Diana is smarter, Jenny's the artist, and Jaga *really* suffers. And with Gloria I mostly feel like Gregor Samsa waiting on the floor beneath the cupboard for his sister to bring him his bowl of slops. All these voices, this insistent chorus, reminding me, as though I could forget, how unreasonable I am, how idle and helpless and overprivileged, how fortunate even in my misfortune. If one more woman preaches to me, I'll be ready for the padded cell.

He phoned Dr. Kotler.

"This is Nathan Zuckerman. What do you mean by 'dolorologist'?"

"Hello there, Nathan. So my pillow arrived. You're on your way."

"It's here, yes, thank you. You sign yourself 'dolorologist.' I'm lying on the pillow at this very moment and thought I'd phone for a definition."

But he'd phoned to find out about the hypnotic procedures employed in recalcitrant cases; he'd phoned because the orthodox techniques of the highly esteemed doctors had alleviated nothing, because he could hardly afford to reject the prospect of a cure on account of the age or eccentricity of the physician, or because the physician happened to be a nostalgic exile from the same pile of rubble as himself. Everybody comes from somewhere, reaches an age, and speaks with some accent or other. Cure was not going to come either from God or from Mount Sinai Hospital, that much was clear by now. Hypnosis seemed a terrible comedown after years of making the hypnotic phenomena himself, yet if someone actually could talk to the pain *directly*, without his looking for meaning, without all the interfering ego static . . .

"Is dolorology a coinage of Kotler's or a real medical specialty you can study?"

"It's something every doctor studies every day when the patient walks in and says, 'Doctor, it hurts.' But I happen to consider dolorology my particular specialty because of my approach: anti-prescription, anti-machine. I date back to the stethoscope, the thermometer, and the forceps. For the rest you had two eyes, two ears, two hands, a mouth, and the instrument most important of all, clinical intuition. Pain is like a baby crying. What it wants it can't name. The dolorologist unearths what that is. Chronic pain is a puzzle for which few of my colleagues have time. Most of them are frightened by it. Most doctors are frightened of death and the dying. People need an incredible amount of support when they die. And the doctor who is frightened can't give it to them."

"Are you free this afternoon?"

"For Nathan Zuckerman I am free day and night."

"I'd like to come by, I'd like to talk about what we'll do if the pillow doesn't help."

"You sound distraught, my boy. Come first and have lunch. I overlook the East River. When I moved in I thought I would stand staring at the river four and five hours a day. Now I'm so busy weeks go by and I don't even know the river is here."

"I'm interested in discussing hypnosis. Hypnosis, you say in your note, is sometimes useful for what I have."

"Without minimizing what you have, for far worse than you have. Asthma, migraines, colitis, dermatitis—I have seen a man suicidal from trigeminal neuralgia, a most nightmarish pain that attacks the face, reclaim his life through hypnosis. I've seen the people in my practice that everybody else has written off, and now I can't answer my mail from these patients, given up as incurable, whom I have hypnotized back to health. My secretary needs a secretary, that's how heavy my mail runs."

"I'll be there in an hour."

But an hour later he was on the unmade bed in the little room dialing Cambridge, Mass. Enough cowering before the attack. *But I'm not cowering and it's not the first attack. And will he sit up and listen, no matter how generous the amplitude with which I patiently spell out his hundred mistakes? You expect him to suffer remorse? You figure you'll win his blessing by phoning long distance to tell him he can't read? He expresses the right thoughts about Jews and you express the wrong thoughts about Jews, and nothing you shout is going to change that.* But it's these Appels who've whammied my muscles with their Jewish evil eye. They push in the pins and I yell ouch and swallow a dozen Percodans. But what you do with the evil eye is poke it out with a burning stick! *But he is not my father's deputy, let alone the great warrior chieftain that young Nathan longed to please and couldn't help antagonizing. I am not young Nathan. I am a forty-year-old client at Anton's Trichological Clinic. To be "understood" is no longer necessary once you seriously begin losing your hair. The father who called you a bastard from his deathbed is dead, and the allegiance known as "Jewishness" beyond their moralizing judgment. It's from Milton Appel that I found that out, in one of his own incarnations. And you needn't bother to tell him.*

Too late for reason: he had Harvard on the phone and

was waiting to be connected to the English Department. The real shitside of literature, these inspired exchanges, but into the bitter shit I go if churning up shit is what it takes to get better. Nothing to lose but my pain. *Only Appel has nothing to do with the pain. The pain pre-dates that essay by a year. There are no Jewish evil eyes or double Jewish whammies. Illness is an organic condition. Illness is as natural as health. The motive is not revenge. There is no motive. There are only nerve cells, twelve thousand million nerve cells, any one of which can drive you mad without the help of a book review. Go get hypnotized. Even that's less primitive than this. Let the oracular little dolorologist be your fairy godfather, if it's a regressive solution you're after. Go and let him feed you lunch. Tell Gloria to come over and you can blindfold each other. Move to the mountains. Marry Jenny. But no further appeals to the Court of Appels.*

The English Department secretary rang through to Appel's office, where a graduate student came on the line to tell him that the Distinguished Professor wasn't there.

"Is he home?"

"Can't say."

"Have you his home number?"

"Can't be reached."

Disciple, undoubtedly, holding sacred all of the Distinguished Professor's opinions, including those on me.

"This is Nathan Zuckerman."

Zuckerman imagined the smirking disciple passing a cryptic comic note to another smirking disciple. Must have them up there by the dozens. Used to be one myself.

"It's about a piece Appel asked me to write. I'm calling from New York."

"He hasn't been well," the disciple offered. "You'll have to wait till he gets back."

"Can't," Zuckerman told him. "Haven't been well either," and promptly called Boston information. While the operator searched the suburbs for a listing, Zuckerman spread the contents of Appel's file folder on the bed. He pushed his medical books onto the carpet, and arranged on the bedside table all the unfinished draft letters that he'd eked out in longhand. He couldn't trust himself to extemporize, not while worked up like this; yet if he waited till he could think straight and talk sensibly, he wouldn't make the call.

A woman answered at the Appel residence in Newton. The pretty dark wife from the Barnes Hole beach? She must be white-haired by now. *Everybody moving on to wisdom but me. All you do on the phone is document his original insight. All you are doing on the phone is becoming one of the crazies of the kind who phone you. When you saw him strolling by you on the beach, were you that impressed by his narrow shoulders and his soft white waist? Of course he hates your work. All that semen underfoot is no longer to his taste. Never was—not in books at least. You two are a perfect mismatch. You draw stories from your vices, dream up doubles for your demons—he finds criticism a voice for virtue, the pulpit to berate us for our failings. Virtue comes with the franchise. Virtue is the* goal. *He teaches, he judges, he corrects— rightness is all. And to rightness you are acting out indefensible desires by spurious pseudo-literary means, committing the culture crime of desublimation. There's the quarrel, as banal as that: you shouldn't make a Jewish comedy out of genital life. Leave the spurting hard-on to goyim like Genet. Sublimate, my child, sublimate, like the physicists who gave us the atomic bomb.*

"This is Nathan Zuckerman. May I speak with Milton Appel?"

"He's resting right now."

"It's pretty urgent business." She didn't answer, and so somberly he added, "About Israel."

He was shuffling meanwhile through the letters on the table, looking for an opening shot. He chose (for their adversarial pithiness), then rejected (for lack of tact and want of respect), then reconsidered (for just the sake of those deficiencies) three sentences written the night before, after he'd given up on writing about Jaga; about Jaga he'd been unable to write even three words. *Professor Appel, I am convinced that the quality about a man or a group that most invites the violence of neurotic guilt is public righteousness and innocence. The roots of anti-Semitism are deep and twisted and not easily sterilized. However, to the extent that published statements by Jews have any effect at all, one way or another, on Gentile opinion and prejudice, the words "Jews jerk off daily" on lavatory walls would do us all more good than what you want me to write on the Op Ed page.*

"This is Milton Appel."

"This is Nathan Zuckerman. I'm sorry to bother you when you're resting."

"What is it you want?"

"Do you have a few minutes to talk?"

"Please, what is it?"

How sick is he? Sicker than I am? Sounds strained. Burdened. Maybe he always does, or maybe there's something worse in his kidney than stones. Maybe the evil eye works both ways and I've given him a malignancy. I can't say the hatred hasn't been on that scale.

"My friend Ivan Felt has sent on to me your letter requesting him to ask me to write a piece on Israel."

"Felt sent that letter on to you? He had no right to do that."

"Well, he did it. Xeroxed your paragraph about his friend Nate Zuckerman. I have it in front of me. 'Why don't you ask your friend Nate Zuckerman to write, etc. . . . unless he feels the Jews can stick their historical suffering up their ass.' Odd request. Very odd. To me in that context, infuriatingly odd." Zuckerman had begun to read now from one of his unfinished letters. "Though since you so regularly change your opinion about my 'case,' for all I know you've had yet another flexibility spasm since you

distinguished in *Inquiry* between anti-Semites like Goebbels and people like Zuckerman who 'just don't like us.' "

His voice was already out of control, quivering so with
rage that he even thought to turn on the tape from the
night before and let that double for him over the phone
until he recovered the modulations of a mature, confident,
reasonable, authoritative adult. But no—purgation requires
more turbulence than that, otherwise you might as well lie
back on Dr. Kotler's pillow to take your bottle. No—drive
pain out with your battering heart the way a clapper
knocks sound from a bell. He tried to envision how this
would happen. Pain waves springing longitudinally from
his silhouetted torso, snaking along the floor, spreading
over the furniture, slithering through the blinds, and then
throughout his apartment, throughout the whole building, rattling every window in its frame—the roar of his
discharged affliction echoing out over all Manhattan, and
the evening *Post* hitting the street headlined: ZUCKERMAN
PAIN-FREE AT LAST, *18 Month Ordeal Ends with Sonic
Boom*. "If I correctly understand your letter to Felt asking
him to ask me what apparently you'd rather not ask
me directly yourself, you seem to suspect (privately, of
course, and not in print or on the lecture circuit) that far
from disliking Jews 'for being Jews,' and pathologically
reviling them in my work, there's a possibility that I
might actually be troubled by their troubles—"

"Look, hold on. You have every right to be angry, but
not primarily with me. This paragraph that Felt so kindly

sent to you was written in a letter privately addressed to him. He never asked me whether it was okay to forward it. When he did so he must surely have known it could only inflame your feelings, since what I wrote was certainly not civil and obviously represented an eruption of personal feelings. But that seems to me just the sort of thing that would be done by that character in that book he's written with his two club feet. I regard it as hostile, provocative, and nasty—toward both of us. Whatever you may think of my essay on your work or my general opinions, you probably will grant that if I were writing directly to you and asking you to do a piece on Israel for the Op Ed page, I'd be more civil about it and not do it so as to enrage you, rightly or wrongly."

"Because you would be more 'civil' in a letter written directly to me, despite having written about my work as you did in that piece—" Feeble quibbling. Pedantry. Must not extemporize and lose your way.

He looked everywhere on the bed for his three stinging lines from the night before. The page must have slipped to the floor. He reached to retrieve it without bending his neck or turning his head and, only after rushing to resume the attack, discovered that he was reading Appel the wrong page. "It's one thing to think you're pretending to your students when you tell them there's a difference between characters and the author, if that's the way you see it these days—but to strip the book of its tone, the plot of its circumstances, the action of its momentum, to disregard totally the context that gives to a theme its spirit, its flavor, its life—"

"Look, I haven't the energy for Literature 101."

"Don't flatter yourself. I was talking about Remedial Reading. And don't hang up—I have more to say."

"I'm sorry but I can't listen to much more. I didn't expect that you'd like what I wrote about your work any more than I like bad reviews of what I write. In these situations, strain is unavoidable. But I really do feel that both of us might have been spared this exacerbation had Felt shown some manners. I wrote him a personal letter in response to a visit he paid. I had a right to assume that a personal letter wouldn't be circulated unless I gave permission. He never asked for it."

"First you scold me, now you scold Felt." And that's why *he's* sick, Zuckerman realized. The addiction to scolding. He's overdosed on scolding. All the verdicts, all the judgments—what's good for the culture, what's bad for the culture—and finally it's poisoning him to death. Let's hope.

"Let me finish," said Appel. "I was given reason by Felt to suppose that you did indeed feel some strong concern about Israel. It won't strike you as any less irritating if you know why I wrote it, but at least you should understand that my suggestion wasn't a mere gratuitous provocation. That I leave to our friend Ivan, whose talent as far as I can tell lies solely in that direction. My letter was for his eyes. If he had behaved decently—"

"Like you. Of course. Mannerly, decently, courteously, decorously, uprightly, civil—oh, what a gorgeous Torah cloth you throw over your meat hooks! How *clean* you are!"

"And your Torah cloth? No more abuse, please. What is this phone call about, except your Torah cloth? If Felt had behaved decently, he'd have written you: 'Appel thinks it would be useful if you did a piece for Op Ed on Israel, since things look black and since he feels you, Zuckerman, would reach kinds of people that he can't.'"

"And what kinds of people are they? People like me who don't like Jews? Or people like Goebbels who gas them? Or the kind of people I pander to by choosing—as you put it so civilly and decently and decorously in *Inquiry*—by choosing an 'audience' instead of choosing readers the way you and Flaubert do. My calculating sub-literary shenanigans and your unsullied critical heart! And you call Felt hostile and nasty! What's disgusting in Felt, in Appel is virtue—in you it's all virtue, even the ascribing of dishonorable motives. Then in that blood-thirsty essay you have the fucking gall to call *my* moral stance 'superior'! You call my sin 'distortion,' then distort my book to show how distorted it is! You pervert my intentions, then call me perverse! You lay hold of my comedy with your ten-ton gravity and turn it into a travesty! My coarse, vindictive fantasies, your honorable, idealistic humanist concerns! I'm a sellout to the pop-porno culture, you're the Defender of the Faith! Western Civilization! The Great Tradition! The Serious Viewpoint! As though seriousness can't be as stupid as anything else! You sententious bastard, have you ever in your life taken a mental position that isn't a moral judgment? I doubt you'd even know how. All you unstained, undegenerate, unselfish, loyal, responsible, high-minded Jews, good responsible citizen Jews, taking on the burdens of the Jewish people and worrying about the future of the State of Israel —and chinning yourselves like muscle-builders on your virtue! Milton Appel, the Charles Atlas of Goodness! Oh, the comforts of that difficult role! And how you play it! Even a mask of modesty to throw us dodos off the track! I'm 'fashionable,' you're for the ages. I fuck around, you *think*. My shitty books are cast in concrete, you make judicious reappraisals. I'm a 'case,' I have a 'career,' you of course have a calling. Oh, I'll tell you your calling—President of the Rabbinical Society for the Suppression of Laughter in the Interest of Loftier Values! Minister of the Official Style for Jewish Books Other than the Manual for Circumcision. Regulation number one: Do not mention your cock. You dumb prick! What if I trotted out your youthful essay about being insufficiently Jewish for Poppa and the Jews—written before you got frozen stiff in your militant grown-upism! I wonder what the kosher butchers over at *Inquisition* would have to say about that. Awfully strange to me that you should no longer care to remember your great *cri de coeur*, written before your self became so legitimate and your heart so pure, while my first stories you can't forget!"

"Mr. Zuckerman, you're entitled to think anything you

want of me, and I'll have to try to live with that, as you've managed obviously to live with what I said about your books. What is strange to *me* is that you don't seem to have anything to say about the suggestion itself, regardless of your anger against the person who made it. But what may lie in store for the Jews is a much larger matter than what I think of your books, early or late, or what you think of my thinking."

Oh, if only he were fourteen and Gilbert Carnovsky, he'd tell him to take what may lie in store for the Jews and stick it up his ass. But he was forty and Zuckerman, and so, demonstrating to himself if to no one else the difference between character and author, he hung up the receiver, and found of course that he wasn't anything like pain-free. Standing atop the paper-strewn bed, his hands clutched into fists and raised to the ceiling of that dark tiny room, he cried out, he screamed, to find that from phoning Appel and venting his rage, he was only worse.

4 Burning

A double vodka on takeoff, then over some waterway in Pennsylvania three drags on a joint in the airplane toilet, and Zuckerman was managing well enough. Not much more pain than he would have felt at home doing nothing but tending pain. And every time his determination began to crumble and he told himself that he was running away on a ridiculous impulse, running away to nothing that made sense or promised relief, running away from what it was impossible to escape, he opened the medical-school catalogue and reread the chart on page 42 that laid out the daily course load for a medical student's first year.

You start at eight-thirty, five mornings a week, with Biology 310/311. From nine-thirty to noon, Clinics 300 and 390. An hour for lunch, and from one to five every afternoon, Anatomy 301. Then the evening's homework. Days and nights, filled not by him with what little he knew but by them with all he didn't. He turned to the description of Clinics 390.

> INTRODUCTION TO THE PATIENT. This course is offered in the first year of training . . . Each student will interview a patient before the group, focusing on the present complaint, the illness onset, reaction to the illness and hospitalization, life changes related, personality characteristics, coping styles, etc. . . .

Sounds familiar. Sounds like the art of fiction, except that the coping style and the personality characteristics belong to a patient in off the street. Other people. Somebody should have told me about them a long time ago.

> 360. FETAL-MATERNAL MEDICINE. The student will work full-time in the labor-delivery floor. He will be required to review the bibliography related to methods and techniques of recording maternal and fetal physiologic parameters during labor and delivery . . .
>
> 361. OBSTETRICS: BIRTH ROOMS. This elective will primarily encompass inpatient obstetrics, especially birth-room experience. Some continuity of care can be achieved by postpartum follow-up on selected patients . . .

Not until Michigan did Zuckerman discover that if you take obstetrics as your specialty you specialize in gynecology too. Tumor formations. Infected reproductive organs. Well, it'd bestow a new perspective on an old obsession. What's more, he owed it to women after *Carnovsky*. From what he'd read of the reviews in the feminist press, he could expect a picture of himself up in the post office, alongside the mug shot of the Marquis de Sade, once the militants took Washington and began guillotining the thousand top misogynists in the arts. He came off no better there than with the disapproving Jews. Worse. They had put him on the cover of one of their magazines. WHY DOES THIS MAN HATE WOMEN? Those girls meant business—wanted blood. Well, he'd turn the tables and tend to abnormalities in the discharge of theirs. Relieving menstrual disorders beats he said she said I said you said on anyone's scale of values. In memory of the mother to whom he'd intended no harm. In the name of ex-wives who had done their damnedest. For his ministering harem. Where I have fornicated, there shall I diagnose, prescribe, operate, and cure. Up with colposcopy, down with Carnovsky.

Going to medical school is nuts, a sick man's delusion about healing himself. And Jenny saw it coming: I should have gone to Bearsville.

But he was *not* a sick man—he was *fighting* the idea of himself as sick. Every thought and feeling ensnared by the selfness of pain, pain endlessly circling back on itself, diminishing everything except isolation—first it's the pain that empties the world, then it's the effort to overcome it. He refused to endure one day more.

Other people. So busy diagnosing everybody else there's no time to overdiagnose yourself. The unexamined life—the only one worth living.

The man beside him in the aisle seat was filing into his attaché case the papers that had been absorbing his attention since they'd come on board. As the plane began its descent, he turned to Zuckerman and, in a neighborly way, he asked, "Going out on business?"

"That's right."

"What line you in?"

"Pornography," Zuckerman said.

He looked to be amused by the novel reply. "Selling it or buying it?"

"Publish it. Out to Chicago to see Hefner. Hugh Hefner. *Playboy.*"

"Oh, everyone knows who Hefner is. I read the other day in *The Wall Street Journal* where he grosses a hundred and fifty million a year."

"Don't rub it in," Zuckerman said.

The man laughed amiably and seemed ready to leave it at that. Until curiosity got the better of him. "What exactly do you publish?"

"*Lickety Split,*" said Zuckerman.

"That's the publication?"

"You never see *Lickety Split*? On your newsstand?"

"No, afraid I haven't."

"But you see *Playboy*, don't you?"

"I see it occasionally."

"Open it up to look at, right?"

"From time to time."

"Well, personally I find *Playboy* boring. That's why I don't gross a hundred and fifty million: my magazine isn't as boring as his. Okay, I admit it, I'm extremely envious of Hefner's money. He has much more respectability, he has entrée, he has national distribution, and *Lickety Split* is still in the porno ghetto. I'm not surprised you haven't seen it. *Lickety Split* is not a mass-distribution publication because it's too dirty. It doesn't have Jean-Paul Sartre in it to make it kosher for a guy like you to buy at a news-stand and go home and jerk off to the tits. I don't believe in that. Hefner is basically a businessman. I don't think that describes me. Sure it's a high-profit business—but with me money is not the paramount issue."

It wasn't clear how much the "guy like you" had been offended by the allusion. He was dressed in a gray double-breasted chalk-stripe suit and a maroon silk tie, a tall, fit gray-haired man in his fifties who, though perhaps not accustomed to such a casual insult, was not about to take too seriously the provocations of a social inferior. Zuckerman imagined Diana's father looking rather like this. He asked Zuckerman, "What's your name, sir—may I ask?"

"Milton Appel. A-p-p-e-l. Accent on the second syllable. Je m'appelle Appel."

"Well, I'll keep an eye out for your journal."

Putting me down. "You do that," Zuckerman said. His neck was hurting and he got up and went off to the toilet to finish the joint.

They were high over the lake, still way above the rippling gray water and the zigzag slabs of floating ice, when he got back to his seat. Wide stretches of the lake were frozen over completely and strewn with shards of ice, a vast waste of slivers looking like the wreckage of millions of frosted light bulbs jettisoned from the sky. He'd expected that they'd already be passing over the Gold Coast towers and buckling their belts to land. Maybe the descent he'd imagined hadn't been the plane's but his own. Probably he should have tolerated this resurgence of pain instead of piling more grass on top of the pills and the vodka. But his plan wasn't to lie on his back for the rest of the day after they had landed. Flipping through the faculty register in the medical-school catalogue, he'd come upon the name of one of his oldest friends, Bobby Freytag. In their freshman year, they'd been thrown together as roommates just across the Midway in Burton Judson Hall. Now Bobby was a professor of anesthesiology in the School of Medicine and on the staff at Billings Hospital. Knowing Bobby was going to expedite everything. His first lucky break in a year and a half. Nothing now was going to stop him. He'd give up New York and move back to Chicago. It was more than twenty years since his graduation. How he'd loved it out there then! Eight hundred miles between him and home: Pennsylvania, Ohio, Indiana—the best friends a boy ever had. He figured he'd live in Chicago forever, after only his first day. He felt as though he'd come out from the East by covered wagon, a removal that immense, that final. He became a large, hearty American six-footer and a contemptuous bohemian all at once, and returned home twelve pounds heavier for his first Christmas vacation, ready to pick a fight with the nearest philistine. In his first year at Chicago he'd go down to the lake and make noises there alone on starry nights—the Gantian goat cry he'd read about in *Of Time and the River*. He carried *The Waste Land* with him on the El, reading away until Clark Street, where girls no older than himself were taking their clothes off in the striptease bars. If you bought them a drink when they came down off the runway, they did you a favor and put a hand on your cock. He wrote people letters about this. He was seventeen and thought continuously about his courses, his cock, and his pals Pennsylvania, Indiana, and Ohio. Talk to him about medical school in those days and he would have laughed in your face: he wasn't about to spend his life writing out prescriptions. His life was too big for that. Inspiring teachers, impenetrable texts, neurotic classmates, embattled causes, semantic hairsplitting—"What do you *mean* by 'mean'?"—his life was *enormous*. He met people his age who were brilliant but terrifically depressed, couldn't get up in the morning, didn't go to class or finish courses. He met geniuses sixteen years old who'd placed out of the college in two quarters and were already beginning law school. He met girls who never changed their clothes, who wore black makeup around their eyes and the same Left Bank outfit every day, bold, brash, talkative girls with hair halfway down to their black stockings. He had a roommate who wore a cape. He wore a field jacket and khaki trousers, like the last of the ex-GIs. In Stineway's Drugstore he saw people with white hair who'd begun in the college long before the war and were still hanging around contemplating their incompletes and trying to get laid. He joined the Film Society and saw *Bicycle Thief* and *Open City* and *Les Enfants du Paradis*. They were a revelation to him. So was Professor Mackauer's "History of Western Civilization"—so was the wallowing in ass-wiping throughout Rabelais and all the ripened turds dotting Luther's Table Talk. He'd study from six till ten every night, then head off to Jimmy's, where he waited with his friends for the racier members of the faculty to show up. A sociologist of pop culture who'd once worked in the fallen world for *Fortune* would drink with them some nights until closing time. Even more glamorous was his teacher in Humanities 3, "a published poet" who'd parachuted into occupied Italy for the OSS and still wore a trench coat. He had a broken nose and read Shakespeare aloud in class and all the girls were in love with him, and so was young Zuckerman. He taught them *The Poetics, The Oresteia, Passage to India, The Alchemist, Portrait of the Artist, King Lear,*

The Autobiography of Benvenuto Cellini—taught them all like holy books. Enrico Fermi gave a lecture in their physical-science survey course and did the ingratiating number up at the blackboard about needing help with the math. When the students clustered around after to ask the usual dumb celebrity questions, he had dared to inquire of the theoretician of The Bomb what he was doing now. Fermi laughed. "Nothing very important," he told him; "after all, I was trained in pre-Fermi physics." It was the cleverest remark that he had ever heard. He was becoming clever in conversation himself, droll, quick, deliciously self-effacing—and full of disgust for the country and its values. The worst days of the Cold War and they were studying *The Communist Manifesto* in the social-science course. On top of being a Jew in Christian America, he was becoming a member of yet another unloved, suspect minority, the "eggheads" ridiculed by the *Chicago Tribune*, the cultural Fifth Column of the commercial society. For weeks he mooned after a tall blond girl in a plaid flannel shirt who painted abstract pictures. He was floored when he found out she was a lesbian. He was rapidly growing sophisticated—Manischewitz and Velveeta had by now been superseded by "wine and cheese," Taystee Bread by "French" bread when he could afford to eat out —but a lesbian? It never occurred to him. He did, however, have a girl friend, very briefly, who was mulatto. Fondling madly beneath her sweater in the basement of Ida Noyes Hall, he was still sufficiently analytical to think,

"This is real life," though nothing in life had ever seemed stranger. He made a friend a few years older than himself, a Stineway's regular, who was in psychoanalysis, smoked marijuana, knew about jazz, and was a self-proclaimed Trotskyist. To a kid in 1950 this was hot stuff. They went to a jazz club up on Forty-sixth Street, two white Jewish students studiously listening to the music, surrounded on every side by dark, unfriendly, very unstudious faces. One thrilling night he listened to Nelson Algren talk about the prizefights at Jimmy's. Thomas Mann came to Chicago during his first term; *he* spoke at Rockefeller Chapel. Great event: the Goethe Bicentennial. In a German accent Mann spoke the richest English he had ever heard; he spoke *prose*, elegant and powerful and clear— with withering urbanity, pungent phrases intimately describing the genius of Bismarck, Erasmus, and Voltaire as though they were colleagues who'd been to dine at his house the evening before. Goethe was "a miracle," he said, but the real miracle was to be two rows down from the podium, learning from the Good European how to speak your own tongue. Mann said "greatness" fifty times that afternoon: Greatness, Mighty, Sublime. He phoned home that night in ecstasy from all the erudition, but nobody in New Jersey knew who Thomas Mann was, or even Nelson Algren. "Sorry," he said aloud, after hanging up, "sorry it wasn't Sam Levenson." He learned German. He read Galileo, St. Augustine, Freud. He protested the underpaying of the Negroes who worked at the university hospital. The Korean War began and he and his closest friend declared themselves enemies of Syngman Rhee. He read Croce, he ordered onion soup, he put a candle in a Chianti bottle and threw a party. He discovered Charlie Chaplin and W. C. Fields and documentary films and the dirtiest shows in Calumet City. He went up to the Near North Side to look down his nose at the advertising types and the tourists. He swam off the Point with a logical positivist, he savagely reviewed beat novels for *The Maroon*, he bought his first classical records—the Budapest String Quartet—from a homosexual salesman at the co-op whom he called by his first name. He began in conversation to call himself "one." Oh, everything was wonderful, as big and exciting a life as could be imagined, and then he made his first mistake. He published a short story while still an undergraduate, an "Atlantic First"—ten pages about a family of Newark Jews clashing with a family of Syrian Jews in a rooming house at the Jersey shore, the conflict loosely modeled on a battle provoked by a hotheaded uncle and narrated to him (disapprovingly) by his father on a visit home. An Atlantic First. It looked as though life had become bigger yet. Writing would intensify everything even further. Writing, as Mann had testified—not least by his own example—was the only worthwhile attainment, the surpassing experience, the exalted struggle, and there was no way to write other than like a fanatic. Without fanaticism, nothing great in fiction could ever be achieved. He had the highest possible con-

ception of the gigantic capacities of literature to engulf
and purify life. He would write more, publish more,
and life would become colossal.

But what became colossal was the next page. He
thought he had chosen life but what he had chosen was
the next page. Stealing time to write stories, he never
thought to wonder what time might be stealing from him.
Only gradually did the perfecting of a writer's iron will
begin to feel like the evasion of experience, and the means
to imaginative release, to the exposure, revelation, and
invention of life, like the sternest form of incarceration.
He thought he'd chosen the intensification of everything
and he'd chosen monasticism and retreat instead. Inherent
in this choice was a paradox that he had never foreseen.
When, some years later, he went to see a production of
Waiting for Godot, he said afterwards to the woman who
was then his lonely wife, "What's so harrowing? It's any
writer's ordinary day. Except you don't get Pozzo and
Lucky."

Chicago had sprung him from Jewish New Jersey, then
fiction took over and boomeranged him right back. He
wasn't the first: they fled Newark, New Jersey, and Cam-
den, Ohio, and Sauk Centre, Minnesota, and Asheville,
North Carolina; they couldn't stand the ignorance, the
feuds, the boredom, the righteousness, the bigotry, the
repetitious narrow-minded types; they couldn't endure the
smallness; and then they spent the rest of their lives thinking about nothing else. Of all the tens of thousands who

flee, those setting the pace for the exodus are the exiles who fail to get away. Not getting away becomes their job—it's what they do all day.

Of course he now wanted to become a doctor instead— to escape not only the never-ending retrospection but all the quarrels he'd provoked by drawing his last novel from the original quarrel. After the popular triumph of his devilish act of aggression, the penitential act of submission. Now that his parents were gone he could go ahead and make them happy: from filial outcast to Jewish internist, concluding the quarrel and the scandal. Five years down the line, he'd take a residency in leprosy and be forgiven by all. Like Nathan Leopold. Like Macbeth, after ordering the last innocent carcass to be dumped in a ditch, joining Amnesty International.

Won't do, thought Zuckerman. No, won't work. A seriously sentimental illusion. If you kill a king, kill a king—then either break down and ruin yourself or, better still, step up to be crowned. And if it's lay on MacAppel, then so be it.

"You know why I can't get national distribution?" he said, turning to the man in the seat beside him. "Because my magazine isn't as boring as his."

"You mentioned that."

"His is just an obsession with big-titted women. That and Hefner shooting off his mouth about the First Amendment. In *Lickety Split, everything's* in it. I don't believe in censorship anywhere. My magazine is a mirror and we reflect it *all*. I want my readers to know that they shouldn't feel self-hatred if they want to get laid. If they jerk off it doesn't make them beneath contempt. And they don't need Sartre to make it legit. I'm not gay, but we're starting to run a lot of stuff on it. We help out married men who are looking for quick sex. Today most of the blow jobs are being given by guys who are married. You married?"

"Yes, I happen to be married. Happen to have three children."

"And you didn't know that?"

"No, I didn't."

"Well, you wouldn't know it from *Playboy*. Not for Hefner's readers, not that stuff. Not for *The Wall Street Journal* either. But in the back of movie theaters, in the washrooms of bars, outside the diners where the truck drivers stop—most of the blow jobs in America, being given right there. Sex is changing in America—people are swinging, eating pussy, women are fucking more, married men suck cocks, so *Lickety Split* reflects that. What are we supposed to do—lie? I see the statistics. These are real fundamental changes. As a revolutionary it's never enough for me. I feel it's so slow. Still, over the last decade semen production is up in America by at least two hundred percent. Only you're not going to find that out reading *Business Week*. You talk about *Playboy*. The married guy like you who looks at *Playboy*, he looks at those bunnies and the woman is inaccessible, it's the girl you can never get. Fine. Beats off and gets back in bed with his wife. But in *Lickety Split*, if you look at the broads, you know you can have them for a phone call and fifty bucks. It's the difference between infantile fantasy and reality."

"Well," replied the man beside him, turning away again to file the last of his papers, "I'll keep my eye out for it."

"You do that," Zuckerman said. Yet he didn't feel like stopping, not even if this guy had had it. It was starting to be real fun being the pornographer Milton Appel. A little holiday from Zuckerman.

Well, not quite—but why quit? "Know how I began *Lickety Split*?"

No reply. No, he obviously didn't care to know how Appel had begun *Lickety Split*. But Nathan did.

"I used to own a swinging club," Zuckerman said. "Eighty-first Street. Milton's Millennia. You never heard of that either. It was a membership club. No prostitution, no one paying for sex, and there was no law they could bust me on. Consensual sex, and in New York that's legal. They just harassed me to death, that's all. My fire extinguisher is twelve inches off the ground and not six inches off the ground. I lose my liquor license. Suddenly there's a broken main and no running water in the showers. The time wasn't ripe for it, that's all. Well, I had a manager there who's now in jail for forgery. He got six years. A

very sweet guy named Horowitz. Mortimer Horowitz."
Mortimer Horowitz was *Inquiry*'s editor in chief. "Another Jew," said Zuckerman. "There are a lot of Jews in
the business. Jews gravitate to pornography like to the
rest of the media. You Jewish?" he asked.

"No."

"Well, most of the pornographers who are successful
are Jews. And Catholics too. You Catholic?"

"Yes," he said, no longer making the effort to disguise
his annoyance, "I am Roman Catholic."

"Well, a lot are Roman Catholics. Who are rebelling.
Anyway, Horowitz was sort of fat"—indeed he was,
the son of a bitch—"and he sweats, and I liked Horowitz.
He's not very deep, but he's a sweet sort of schmuck. A
nice man. Well, sexually Horowitz was very boastful, so I
bet him a thousand dollars, somebody else bet him two
thousand dollars, somebody else bet him five thousand
dollars, how many orgasms he could have. He said he
could come fifteen times in eighteen hours. He came fifteen times in *fourteen* hours. We had a medical student
there who checked the ejaculation. He'd have to pull out
so we could check each time. This is in a dark room at the
back of Milton's Millennia. 1969. He's fucking a woman,
then he'd be yelling I'm coming, the medical student
would run over with a flashlight, and we'd see the come.
I remember standing there and saying, 'This is my life,
and it's not perverse, it's fascinating.' I remember thinking, 'When they do *The Milton Appel Story* this'll be

a great scene.' But what really got me was this fascination. I thought, 'We keep records about everything. Assists. Hits. Batting averages. Why not cock? Here's Horowitz and this great record that should be on the front page of *The New York Times*, and nobody knows about it.' That was my cover story in the first issue of *Lickety Split*. Four years ago. Changed my life. Look, I wouldn't *want* a magazine like *Playboy*, not if I was guaranteed five *hundred* million—"

The plane banged down on the runway. Zuckerman was back. Chicago! But he couldn't stop. What fun this was! And how long since he'd had any. How long before he'd have any again. Back to school for four more years.

"Some guy calls the other day and says, 'Appel, how much would you give to publish pictures of Hugh Hefner fucking?' He says he can get his hands on a dozen pictures of Hefner fucking his bunnies. I told him I wouldn't give him a dime. 'You think it's news that Hugh Hefner fucks? Get me pictures of the Pope fucking—then we can do business.' "

"Look here," said the man beside him, "that is quite enough!" and suddenly he had undone his seat belt and, though the plane was still careening down the runway, jumped across the aisle to an empty seat. "Sir!" called the stewardess. "Remain where you are till we reach the gate, *please*."

Before even waiting for the luggage to appear, Zuckerman found a pay phone and called Billings Hospital. He had to feed a second dime into the phone while waiting for the secretary to find Bobby. Couldn't hang up to be called back later, he told her; he was an old friend just arrived in town and he had to speak to Dr. Freytag right away. "Well, he's stepped down the corridor . . ." "Try to get him. Tell him it's Nathan Zuckerman. Tell him it's very important."

"Zuck!" said Bobby, when he came to the phone. "Zuck, this is terrific. Where are you?"

"I'm at the airport. O'Hare. Just landed."

"Well, great. You out here to lecture?"

"I'm out here to go back to school. As a student. I'm sick and tired of writing, Bob. I've made a big success and I made a pile of dough and I hate the whole God damn thing. I don't want to do it anymore. I really want to quit. And the only thing I can think of that would satisfy me would be becoming a doctor. I want to go to medical school. I flew out to see if I can enroll in the college for the winter quarter and finish up my science requirements. Bobby, I have to see you right away. I have the applications. I want to sit down and talk to you and see how I can get it done. What do you make of all this? Will they have me, age forty and a scientific ignoramus? On my transcript I'll show nearly straight A's. And they were hard-earned A's, Bob. They're hard-earned 1950s A's—they're like 1950 dollars."

Bobby was laughing—Nathan had been one of their dormitory's big-name late-night entertainers and this must be more of the same, mini-performance over the phone whipped up for old times' sake. Bobby had always been the softest touch. They'd had to live apart in their second year because laughing was murder on Bobby's asthma— out of control, it could bring on an attack. When Bobby saw Nathan heading toward him from across the quadrangle, he'd raise a hand and plead, "Don't, don't. I have a class." Oh, it had been great fun being funny in those days. Everybody had told him he was crazy if he didn't write the stuff down and get it published. So he had. Now he wanted to be a doctor.

"Bob, can I come by to see you this afternoon?"

"I'm tied up till five."

"Driving in will take till five."

"At six I've got a meeting, Zuck."

"Just for the hour then, to say hello. Look, my bag's here—see you soon."

Back in Chicago and feeling exactly as he had the first time around. A new existence. This was the way to do it: defiant, resolute, fearless, instead of tentative, doubt-ridden, and perpetually dismayed. Before leaving the phone booth, rather than hazard a third Percodan in eight hours, he took a swig of vodka from his flask. Aside from the raw stinging line of pain threading down behind the right ear through the base of the neck and into the meat of the upper back, he felt relatively little serious discomfort. But that was the pain he particularly didn't like. If he hadn't been feeling defiant, resolute, and fearless he might even have begun to feel a little dismayed. The muscle soreness he could manage, the tenderness, the tautness, the spasm, all of that he could take, even over the long haul; but not this steadily burning thread of fire that went white-hot with the minutest bob or flick of the head. It didn't always go out overnight. The previous summer he'd had it for nine weeks. After a twelve-day course of Butazolidin it had subsided somewhat, but by then the Butazolidin had so badly irritated his stomach that he couldn't digest anything heavier than rice pudding. Gloria baked rice pudding for him whenever she could stay for two hours. Every thirty minutes, when the timer rang in the kitchen, she'd jump up from the playmat and in garter belt and heels run off to open the oven and stir the rice. After a month of Gloria's rice pudding and little more, when there was still no improvement, he was sent to Mount Sinai for barium X-rays of his digestive tract. They found no hole in the lining anywhere along his gut, but he was warned by the gastroenterologist never again to wash down Butazolidin with champagne. That's how he'd done it: a bottle from the case that Marvin had sent him for his fortieth birthday, whenever Diana came by after school and he tried and failed at dictating a single page—a single paragraph. Didn't see why he shouldn't celebrate: his career was over, Diana's was just beginning, and it was vintage Dom Pérignon.

He hired a limousine. A limousine would be the fastest and smoothest way in, and the driver would be there to carry his suitcase. He'd keep the car till he'd found a hotel for the night.

His driver turned out to be a woman, a very fair young woman, shortish, stocky, about thirty, with fine white teeth, a slender neck, and a snappy, efficient way about her that was gentlemanly in the manner of the gentleman's gentleman. Her dark green worsted uniform was cut like a riding habit, and she wore high black leather boots. A blond braid hung down from the back of her cap.

"The South Side. Billings Hospital. I'll be about an hour. You'll wait."

"Right, sir."

The car began to move. Back! "Shall I comment on the fact that you're not the man I was expecting?"

"Up to you, sir," she said with a lively, bright laugh.

"This a sideline or this your work?"

"Oh, this is it, this is the work, all right. What about you?" Perky girl.

"Pornography. I publish a magazine, I own a swinging club, and I make films. I'm out here to see Hugh Hefner."

"Staying over at the Playboy Mansion?"

"That place makes me sick. I'm not interested in Hefner and his entourage. That to me is like his magazine: cold and boring and elitist."

That he was a pornographer hadn't disturbed her at all.

"My loyalty is to the common man," he told her. "My loyalty is to the guys on the street corner I grew up with and the guys I served with in the merchant marine. That's why I'm in this. It's the hypocrisy I can't stand. The sham. The denial of our cocks. The disparity between life as I lived it on the street corner, which was sexual and jerking off and constantly thinking about pussy, and the people who say it shouldn't be like that. How to get it—that was the question. That was the only question. That was the biggest question there was. It still is. It's frightening it's so big—and yet if you say this out loud you're a monster. There's an anti-humanity there that I can't stand. There's a lie there that makes me sick. You understand what I mean?"

"I think I do, sir."

"I know you do. You wouldn't be driving a limousine if you didn't. You're like me. I don't do well with discipline or authority. I don't want a white line drawn that says that I can't cross it. Because I'll cross it. When I was a kid, whenever I got into a fistfight, most every one was because I didn't want people to say no to me. It makes me crazy. The rebellious part of me says, Fuck 'em, no one's gonna tell me what to do."

"Yes, sir."

"That doesn't mean I've got to oppose every rule just because it's there. Violence I don't do. Children being exploited I find repugnant. Rape is not what I'm in favor of. I'm not into peeing and shit. There are some stories in my magazine I find disgusting. 'Grandma's Lollypop Hour'—I hated that story. It was vulgar and vile and I hated it. But I got a good bright staff, and as long as

they're not pissing on the walls and they're doing their
job, I let them do what they want. Either they're free or
they're not free. I'm not like Sulzberger at *The New York
Times*. I don't worry what they think up in the board
rooms of corporate America. That's why you don't see my
magazine out here. That's why I can't get national distribution like Hefner. That's why I'm paying him a call.
He's a First Amendment absolutist? Then let him put his
power where his mouth is in the state of Illinois. With
me money is not the paramount issue the way it is with
him. You know what is?"

"What?"

"The defiance is. The hatred is. The outrage is. The
hatred is endless. The outrage is huge. What's your
name?"

"Ricky."

"I'm Appel, Milton Appel. Rhymes with 'lapel' like
in zoot suit. Everybody is so fucking serious out there
about sex, Ricky—and there are so many fucking lies.
There's the paramount issue. When I was in school I believed in Civics class that America was special. I couldn't
understand the first time I was arrested that I was being
arrested for being free. People used to say to me when I
first went into sleaze, How long are they going to let you
do this? That's crazy. What are they letting me do?
They're letting me be an American. I'm breaking the law?
I don't want to sound like Hefner but I thought the First
Amendment was the law. Didn't you?"

"It is, Mr. Appel."

"And the ACLU, do they help? They think I give freedom a bad name. Freedom's *supposed* to have a bad name. What I do is what freedom's about. Freedom isn't making room for Hefner—it's making room for *me*. For *Lickety Split* and Milton's Millennia and Supercarnal Productions. I admit it, ninety percent of pornography is dull and trivial and boring. But so are the lives of most human beings, and we don't tell them they can't exist. For most people it's real reality that's boring and trivial. Reality is taking a crap. Or waiting for a cab. And being stuck in the rain. Just doing nothing is real reality. Reading *Time* magazine. But when people fuck they close their eyes and fantasize about something else, something that's absent, something that's elusive. Well, I fight for that, and I give them that, and I think what I do is good most of the time. I look in the mirror and I feel that I'm not a shit. I've never sold out my people, never. I like to fly first-class to Honolulu, I like to wear a fourteen-thousand-dollar watch, but I never let my money bulldoze me and manipulate me. I make more money than anybody who works for me because I get the grief and I get the indictments and they don't. They get their rocks off, at my office, calling me an acquisitive capitalist dog—they're all pro-Fidel and anti-Appel, and write graffiti on my door that their professors taught them at Harvard. 'The Management Sucks.' '*Lickety Split* is too intellectual.' Anarchists from nine to five, with me footing the bill. But I don't live in an anarchy. I live in a corrupt society. I've

got a world of John Mitchells and Richard Nixons to face
out there, plus an analyst, plus death, plus a fourth wife
who's talking divorce, plus a seven-year-old kid I don't
want to lay my trip on because that isn't the way I want
it. That's not freedom for him. You follow me?"

"Yes, sir."

"About a year ago, when my wife started talking divorce, before I agreed to analysis, she took on a lover, the
first in her life, and I felt myself destroyed. Couldn't handle it. I got crazed. Very insecure. I fuck hundreds of
women and she fucked one guy, and I was wigged out.
And he was nothing. She picked a guy who was older
than me, who was impotent—I mean she didn't pick a
twenty-five-year-old stud, and still I was wigged out. The
guy was a checkers champion. Mortimer Horowitz. Always sitting there looking at his board. 'King me.' That's
what she wanted. We had a reconciliation and I told her,
'Sweetheart, at least pick a guy next time who's a threat to
me, pick a California surfer.' But she picks a Jewish
nebish—the checkers champion of Washington Square
Park. But that's the pressure I'm under, Ricky: to play
games, to sit still, to talk soft, to be nice. But I have never
softened my stand so as to be nice and get the rewards
that the nice boys get, like staying out of jail and owning
legal guns and not having to wear a bulletproof vest every
time I go out for a meal. I have never softened my stand
to protect my money. There's a part of me that says, Fuck
all that money. I like that part of me. When Nixon came

in, I could have softened the magazine and avoided a lot. After they closed down Milton's Millennia, I could have got the message and quit. But I came back with Millennia Two, bigger and better and swankier than the old place, with its own fifty-foot swimming pool and a transvestite stripper for entertainment, a beautiful girl with a big dong, and let Nixon go fuck himself. I see the way blacks are treated in this country. I see the inequities and it makes me sick. But do they fight the inequities? No. They fight kike-pornographer. Well, kike-pornographer is gonna fight back. Because I believe deep down in what I'm doing, Ricky. My staff laughs: it's become a polemic in my life that Milton Appel believes what he's doing. It's like Marilyn Monroe saying, 'I'm an actress I'm an actress.' She was also tits. I can tell people a thousand times that I'm a serious person, but it's hard for them to take at face value when the prosecution holds up *Lickety Split* and on the cover is a white girl sucking a big black cock and simultaneously fucking a broom. It's an unforgiving world we live in, Ricky. Those who transgress are truly hated as scum. Well, that's fine with me. But don't tell me scum has no right to exist along with everybody who's nice. Nobody should tell me that *ever*. Because scum is human too. *That's* what's paramount to me: not the money but the anti-humanity that calls itself nice. Nice. I don't care what my kid grows up to be, I don't care if he grows up wearing pantyhose as long as he doesn't turn out *nice*. You know what terrifies me more than jail? That he'll rebel against a father like me, and that's what I'll get. Decent society's fucking revenge: a kid who's very very very nice—another frightened soul, tamed by inhibition, suppressing madness, and wanting only to live with the rulers in harmonious peace."

"I want a second life. It's as ordinary as that."

"But what are you assuming?" Bobby asked. "That you're somehow going to be a completely erased tablet too? I don't believe in that, Zuck. If you're really going to do it, why pick a profession that's the most difficult and tedious to prepare for? At least choose an easier one so you don't lose so much."

"What's easier doesn't answer the need for something difficult."

"Go climb Mount Everest."

"That's like writing. You're alone with the mountain and an ax. You're all by yourself and it's practically undoable. It *is* writing."

"You're by yourself when you're a doctor too. When you're leaning over a patient in a bed, you've entered into a highly complicated, specialized relationship that you develop over the years through training and experience, but you're still back there somewhere by yourself, you know."

"That's not what 'by yourself' means to me. Any skilled worker's by himself like that. When I'm by myself what I'm examining isn't the patient in the bed. I'm leaning over a bed, all right, but I'm in it. There are writers who start from the other direction, but the thing that I grow grows on me. I listen, I listen carefully, but all I've got to go on, really, is my inner life—and I can't take any more of my inner life. Not even that little that's left. Subjectivity's the subject, and I've had it."

"That's all you're running out on?"

Do I tell him? Can Bobby cure me? I didn't come here to be treated but to learn to give the treatment, not to be reabsorbed in the pain but to make a new world to absorb myself in, not passively to receive somebody's care and attention but to master the profession that provides it. He'll put me in the hospital if I tell him, and I came out for the school.

"My life as cud, that's what I'm running out on. Swallow as experience, then up from the gut for a second go as art. Chewing on everything, seeking connections—too much inward-dwelling, Bob, too much burrowing back. Too much doubt if it's even worth the effort. Am I wrong to assume that in anesthesiology doubt isn't half of your life? I look at you and I see a big, confident, bearded fellow without the slightest doubt that what he's doing is worthwhile and that he does it well. That yours is a valuable service is undebatable fact. The surgeon hacks open his patient to remove something rotten and the patient doesn't feel a thing—because of you. It's clear, it's straightforward, it's unarguably useful and right to the point. I envy that."

"Yes? You want to be an anesthesiologist? Since when?"

"Since I laid eyes on you. You look like a million bucks. It must be great. You go up to them the night before the operation, you say, 'I'm Bobby Freytag and I'm going to put you to sleep tomorrow with a little sodium pentothal. I'm going to stay with you throughout the operation to be sure all your systems are okay, and when you come out of it, I'll be right there to hold your hand and see that you're comfortable. Here, swallow one of these and you'll sleep like a baby. I'm Bobby Freytag and I've been studying and training and working all my life just to be sure you're all right.' Yes, absolutely—I want to be an anesthesiologist like you."

"Come on, what's this all about, Zuck? You look like hell. You stink of gin."

"Vodka. On the plane. Fear of flying."

"You look worse than that. Your eyes. Your color. What the hell is going on?"

No. He would not let this pain poison another connection. Hadn't even worn the collar, fearing they wouldn't begin to consider him for medical school if they were to discover that he was not only forty and a scientific ignoramus but sick besides. Repetitious pain's clamorous needs were back on the playmat with his prism glasses. No more looking from the floor at everybody gigantically up on their feet. Percodan if required, Kotler's pillow for that chance in a million, but otherwise, to all he met in Chicago—to Bobby and the admissions committee certainly—another indestructible mortal, happy and healthy as the day he was born. Must suppress every temptation to describe it (from the meaningless first twinge through the disabling affliction) to your enviable old roommate, dedicated pain-killer though he may be. No more to be done for my pain, no more to be said. Either the medicines are still too primitive or the doctors aren't yet up to it or I'm incurable. When he felt pain, he'd pretend instead that it was pleasure. Every time the fire flares up, just say to yourself, "Ah, that's good—makes me glad to be alive." Think of it not as unreasonable punishment but as gratuitous reward. Think of it as chronic rapture, irksome only inasmuch as one can have too much even of a good thing. Think of it as the ticket to a second life. Imagine you owe it everything. Imagine anything you like. Forget those fictionalized book-bound Zuckermans and invent a real one now for the world. That's how the others do it. Your next work of art—*you*.

"Tell me about anesthesiology. I'll bet it's beautifully clear. You give them something to sleep, they sleep. You want to raise their blood pressure—you give them a drug, you raise their blood pressure. You want to raise it this much, you get this much—you want that much, you get that much. Isn't that true? You wouldn't look like you look if it wasn't. A leads to B and B leads to C. You know when you're right and you know when you're wrong. Am I idealizing it? You don't even have to answer. I see it on you, in you, all over you."

It was the Percodan he'd swallowed on the hospital steps, his third of the day (at least he was hoping it was his third and not his fourth), that had him talking away like this. Percodan could do that: first that lovely opening wallop and then for two hours you didn't shut up. In addition there was the excitement of seeing earnest, shy, amiable Bobby as a large full-grown physician: a pitch-black chin beard to cover his acne scars, a corner office in Billings overlooking the Midway lawn where once they'd played their Sunday softball, and rows of shelves bearing hundreds of books not one of which the novelist could recognize. It was thrilling just seeing Bobby weigh two hundred pounds. Bobby had been even skinnier than Nathan, a studious bean-pole with asthma, bad skin, and the kindest disposition in the history of adolescence. He was the only grateful seventeen-year-old that Nathan had ever met. Zuckerman was suddenly so proud of him he felt like his father, like Bobby's father, like the owner of the ladies' handbag store on Seventy-first Street where Bobby used to go to help on Wednesday nights and Saturday afternoons. A strong weepy feeling started to heat up his eyes, but no, he'd never get Bobby's backing by lowering his head to the desk and sobbing his heart out. This wasn't the place or the moment, even if both were urging everything so long held back to come forth in one big purgative gush. Look, it would be nice to shoot somebody too. Whoever had disabled him like this. Only no one was responsible—and unlike the pornographer he didn't own a gun.

The tears he suppressed, but he couldn't stop talking.

Aside from the Percodan buoying him up, there was the decisive landmark decision made only the minute before —to have no pain even when he had it, to treat it like pleasure instead. He didn't mean masochistic pleasure either. It was bunk, at least in his case, that the payoff for being in pain was morbid secret gratifications. Everybody wants to make pain interesting—first the religions, then the poets, then, not to be left behind, even the doctors getting in on the act with their psychosomatic obsession. They want to give it *significance*. What does it mean? What are you hiding? What are you showing? What are you betraying? It's impossible just to suffer the pain, you have to suffer its meaning. But it's not interesting and it has no meaning—it's just plain stupid pain, it's the *opposite* of interesting, and nothing, *nothing* made it worth it unless you were mad to begin with. Nothing made it worth the doctors' offices and the hospitals and the drugstores and the clinics and the contradictory diagnoses. Nothing made it worth the depression and the humiliation and the helplessness, being robbed of work and walks and exercise and every last shred of independence. Nothing made it worth not being able to make your own bed in the morning without crawling back in immediately afterwards, nothing, not even a harem of a hundred in only their garter belts cooking rice pudding all at the same time. Nobody could make him believe that he'd had this pain for a year and a half because he believed he deserved it. What made him so resentful was that he didn't. He wasn't relieving guilt feelings—he didn't *have* guilt feelings. If he agreed with the Appels and their admonitions, he wouldn't have written those books in the first place. He wouldn't have been able to. He wouldn't have wanted to. Sure he was weary of the fight, but it didn't follow that his illness represented capitulation to their verdict. It wasn't punishment or guilt that he was expiating. He had not been four years to this great university having rational humanism drummed into his skull in order to wind up expiating irrational guilt through organic pain. He hadn't been writing for twenty years, writing principally *about* irrational guilt, to wind up irrationally guilty. Nor was he in need of a sickness to gain attention. Losing attention was what he was after—masked and gowned in the operating room, *that* was the objective. He did not wish to be a suffering person for any banal, romantic, ingenious, poetical, theological, or psychoanalytical reason, and certainly not to satisfy Mortimer Horowitz. Mortimer Horowitz was the best reason in the world to stay well. There was nothing in it and he wouldn't do it. He refused.

Three (or four) Percodan, two-thirds of a gram of marijuana, six ounces of vodka, and he saw everything clearly and couldn't stop talking. It was over. The eighteen months were over. He'd made up his mind and that was that. *I am well*.

"I can't get over it. I was the great performer, glib and satiric and worldly, and you were this earnest, dutiful, asthmatic kid helping his father in the handbag shop. I saw your name in the catalogue and I thought, 'So that's where Bobby's found to hide. Behind the surgeon.' But what I see is somebody hiding from nothing. Somebody who knows when he's right and knows when he's wrong. Somebody who doesn't have time in the operating room to sit around wondering what to do next and whether it'll work or not. Somebody who knows *how* to be right— how to be right *quickly*. No errors allowed. The stakes never in doubt. Life vs. Death. Health vs. Disease. Anesthesia vs. Pain. What that must do for a man!"

Bobby leaned back and laughed. Big hearty laugh, no oxygen shortage in those lungs anymore. He's the size of Falstaff. And not from booze but from this usefulness. He's the size of his worth.

"When you know how to do it, Zuck, it's very easy. It's like riding a bike."

"No, no, people tend to devalue the sophistication of their own special field. It's easy only because of all you know."

"Speaking of specialties, in *Time* they say you've had four wives."

"In life only three. And you?"

"One. One wife," said Bobby, "one child, one divorce."

"How's your father?"

"Not so good. My mom just died. Forty-five years of marriage. He's in a bad way. In the best of times he's not your most unemotional Jew—he can't even tell you it's

Wednesday without tears coming to his eyes. So it's pretty rough right now. He's staying at my place for the time being. And your folks?"

"My father died in '69. Half out of it with a stroke, and then a coronary. My mother went a year later. Brain tumor. Very sudden."

"So you're orphaned. And right now no wife. Is that the problem? Abandonment?"

"I've got some girls looking after me."

"What drug you on, Zuck?"

"None, nothing. Just beat, that's all. The wives, the books, the girls, the funerals. The death of my folks was strong medicine. I'd been rehearsing it for years in my fiction, but I still never got the idea. But mostly I'm dead tired of the job. It's not the elevating experience they promised in Humanities 3. Starving myself of experience and eating only words. It brought out the drudge in me, Bob, this ritual that it takes to write. It may look to outsiders like the life of freedom—not on a schedule, in command of yourself, singled out for glory, the choice apparently to write about anything. But once one's writing, it's *all* limits. Bound to a subject. Bound to make sense of it. Bound to make a book of it. If you want to be reminded of your limitations virtually every minute, there's no better occupation to choose. Your memory, your diction, your intelligence, your sympathies, your observations, your sensations, your understanding—never enough. You find out more about what's missing in you than you really ought to know. All of you an enclosure you keep trying to break out of. And all the obligations more ferocious for being self-imposed."

"Every construction that helps anybody is also a boundary. I hate to tell you, but that's true even in medicine. Everybody's trapped in the thing he does best."

"Look, it's simple: I'm sick of raiding my memory and feeding on the past. There's nothing more to see from my angle; if it ever was the thing I did best, it isn't anymore. I want an active connection to life and I want it now. I want an active connection to *myself*. I'm sick of channeling everything into writing. I want the real thing, the thing *in the raw*, and not for the writing but for itself. Too long living out of the suitcase of myself. I want to start again for ten hundred different reasons."

But Bobby shook his bearded head: didn't get it, wouldn't buy it. "If you were a penniless failure as a writer, and nothing you wrote got published, and nobody knew your name, and if you were going into social work, say, which only took two years more of study, well, okay. If during all these years as the writer you are you'd been hanging around hospitals and doctors, if for the last twenty years you'd been reading medical books and the medical journals on the side—but as you say yourself, you're just as stupid about science as you were in 1950. If you really had been living some kind of secret life all these years—but have you? When did you get this great idea?"

"Two, three months ago."

"I think you've got another problem."

"What's that?"

"I don't know. Maybe you *are* just tired. Maybe you want to hang a sign on your door, 'Gone Fishin,' and take off to Tahiti for a year. Maybe you just need your second wind as a writer. You tell me. Maybe you've got to get screwed more or something."

"No help. Tried it. All the outward trappings of pleasure, but the result is the inverse of pleasure. Getting screwed, climbing Mount Everest, writing books—not enough companionship. Mailer ran for Mayor of New York. Kafka talked about becoming a waiter in a Tel Aviv café. I want to be a doctor. The dream of breaking out isn't that rare. It happens to the most hardened writers. The work draws on you and draws on you and you begin to wonder how much of you there is to draw on. Some turn to the bottle, others the shotgun. I prefer medical school."

"Except, whatever problems are plaguing you in writing, they're going to be right there, you know, when you're a doctor. You can grow sick and tired of the real thing too. Tired of the cancers, tired of the strokes, tired of the families taking the bad news. You can get just as tired of malignant tumors as you can of anything else. Look, I've had experience right up to here, and it doesn't pay off as greatly as you might think. You get so involved in experience, you lose the opportunity to grasp what you're going through. You pay your money, Zuck, and you take your choice. I happen to think you're going to be Zuckerman the doctor just the way you're Zuckerman the writer, no different."

"But the isolation won't be there, the solitude won't be there—it *can't* be there. The physical differences are too great. There are a thousand people walking around this hospital. Know who walks around my study, who I palpate and tell to say 'Ahhh'? Writing is not a very sociable business."

"I don't even agree with that. Your solitude is of your own making. Working with people is obviously alien to your nature. Your temperament's your temperament, and it'll still be yourself you're telling to say 'Ahhh.' "

"Bob, remember me out here? You don't remember an isolate, damn it. I was a lively, gregarious, outgoing kid. Laughing. Self-confident. I was practically crazy with intellectual excitement. Your old pal Zuck was not a remote personality. I was somebody burning to begin."

"And now you're burning to end. That's the impression I get anyway, underneath what you say."

"No, no, no—burning to begin *again*. Look, I want to take a crack at med school. What the hell is so wrong with that?"

"Because it isn't like you're taking a six-month sabbatical. It's a big investment of time and money. For a man of forty without real demonstrable qualifications, with an unscientific mind, it's just going to be too arduous."

"I can do it."

"Okay—let's say you even manage to, which I doubt. By the time you're worth anything you're going to be damn near fifty. You'll have plenty of companionship, but you'll have no recognition, and how the hell are you going to like that when you're fifty?"

"I'll love it."

"Bullshit."

"You're wrong. I had the recognition. I had the public. In the end it doesn't do anything to the public, but to me it did plenty. I sentenced myself to house arrest. Bobby, I have no desire to confess or to be taken for a confessor, and that was mostly where their interest got stuck. It wasn't literary fame, it was sexual fame, and sexual fame stinks. No, I'll be content to give that up. The most enviable genius in literary history is the guy who invented alphabet soup: nobody knows who he is. There's nothing more wearing than having to go around pretending to be the author of one's own books—except pretending not to be."

"What about money, if you think you don't need recognition?"

"I made money. Plenty of money. A lot of money and a lot of embarrassment, and I don't need any more of either."

"Well, you'll have plenty of money, minus what it's going to cost you to go to medical school and to live for ten years. You haven't sold me on the idea that you want to be a doctor or ought to be a doctor, and you're not going to sell the admissions committee."

"What about my grades? All those A's, damn it. Nineteen-fifties A's!"

"Zuck, as a faculty member of this institution I'm quite touched to learn that you're still hung up on bringing home all those A's. But I have to tell you, we don't even look at anything that isn't an A. The problem is which A we take. And we're not going to take an A just because we've got a writer who doesn't want to be alone anymore with his typewriter and is sick of screwing his girlfriends. This might be a nice out for you from what you're doing, but we've got a doctor shortage in this country and only so many medical-school openings, et cetera and so forth. If I were the dean that's what I'd tell you. I wouldn't want to have to be the one to explain your case to the board of trustees. Not the way you've explained it, and not with you looking like this. Have you had a good physical lately?"

"I've been traveling, that's all."

"For more than three hours, from the sound of it."

Bobby's phone rang. "Dr. Freytag . . . What's the matter? . . . Come on, pull yourself together. Calm down. Nothing has happened to him . . . Dad, I don't know where he is either . . . He's not dead—he's out . . . Look, come to the hospital and wait in my office. We can go to the Chinese place . . . Then watch TV and I'll be home at eight and make us some spaghetti . . . I don't care what Gregory eats . . . I know he's a beautiful, wonderful boy, but I happen not to care any longer whether he eats or not. Don't sit there waiting for Gregory. You're driving yourself nuts with Gregory. Look, you know who's here, sitting across from my desk? My old roommate Zuck . . . Nathan. Nathan Zuckerman . . . Here, I'll put him on." He handed the phone across the desk. "My old man. Say hello."

"Mr. Freytag—it's Nathan Zuckerman. How are you?"

"Oh, not so good today. Not good at all. I lost my wife. I lost my Julie." He began to cry.

"I heard that. I'm terribly sorry. Bobby told me."

"Forty-five years, wonderful years, and now my Julie's gone. She's in the cemetery. How can that be? A cemetery where you can't even leave a flower or someone will steal it. Look, tell Bobby—is he still there? Did he go out?"

"He's here."

"Tell him, please, I forgot to tell him—I have to go there tomorrow. I must go out to the cemetery before it snows."

Zuckerman passed the phone over to Bobby.

"What is it? . . . No, Gregory can't take you out. Dad, Gregory can't take the garbage out. We're lucky we got him to give up a morning for the funeral . . . I know he's a wonderful boy, but you can't . . . What? . . . Sure, just a minute." To Zuckerman he said, "He wants to say something to you."

"Yes? Mr. Freytag?"

"Zuck, Zuck—it just now dawned on me. I'm sorry, I'm in a terrible state of confusion. Joel Kupperman—remember? I used to call you Joel Kupperman, the Quiz Kid."

"That's right."

"Sure, you had all the answers."

"I'll bet I did."

"Sure, you and Bobby with your studies. What students you boys were! I was telling Gregory just this morning how his father used to sit at that table and study. He's a good boy, Zuck. He just needs direction. We are not losing that boy! We made a Bobby, we can make another Bobby. And if I have to do it singlehanded I will. Zuck, quick, Bob again, before I forget."

The phone back over to Bobby.

"Yes, Dad . . . Dad, tell him one more time how much I loved my homework and the kid'll knife us both . . . You'll get to the cemetery . . . I understand that. I'll take care of it . . . I'll be home around eight . . . Dad, live with it—he is not coming home for dinner just because you'd like him to . . . Because he *often* doesn't come home for dinner . . . I don't know where, but he'll eat something, I'm sure. I'll be home at eight. Just watch the TV till I get there. I'll see you in a few hours . . ."

Bobby had been through it lately. Divorce from a depressive wife, contempt from a recalcitrant eighteen-year-old son, responsibility for a bereaved seventy-two-year-old father who filled him with infinite tenderness and infinite exasperation; also, since the divorce, sole responsibility for the son. Because of a severe case of mumps in late adolescence, Bobby could father no children, and Gregory had been adopted while Bobby was still a medical student. To raise an infant then had been an enormous burden, but his young wife was impatient to begin a family, and Bobby had been an earnest and dutiful young man. Of course his parents doted on Gregory from the moment the newborn child arrived. "Everybody doted on him—and what's come of him? Nothing."

The voice, weary with loathing, attested more to Bobby's suffering than to the hardening of his heart. It clearly wasn't easy to kill the last of his love for the thoughtless brat. Zuckerman's own father had had to feel himself leaving life before *he* could finally face disowning a son. "He's ignorant, he's lazy, he's selfish. A shitty little American consumer. His friends are nobodies, nothings, the kids they make the car commercials for. All they talk about is how to be millionaires before they're twenty-five—without working, of course. Imagine, when we were in the college, somebody saying 'millionaire' with awe. I hear him rattling off the names of the titans in the rock business and I want to wring his neck. I didn't think it could happen, but with his feet up and his bottle of Bud, watching a doubleheader on TV, he's even made me hate the White Sox. If I didn't see Gregory for another twenty years I'd be perfectly happy. But he's a fucking freeloader and it looks like I'll have him forever. He's supposed to be enrolled at some college downtown and I don't even think he knows which one. He tells me he doesn't go because he can't find a place to park. I ask him to do something and he tells me to eat shit and that he's leaving to live with his mother and never coming back because I'm such a demanding prick. 'Go, Greg,' I say, 'drive up tonight and I'll pay for the gas.' But she's in freezing Wisconsin and sort of screwy, and the louts he knows all hang out down here, and so next thing I know is that instead of leaving home and never coming back he's screwing some little twat in his room. He's a honey, Gregory. The morning after my mother died, when I told him his grandfather was coming to stay with us until he was better, he hit the ceiling. 'Grandpa *here*? How can Grandpa come here? If Grandpa moves in here, where am I going to fuck Marie? I'm asking a serious question. *Tell* me. Her house? With her whole family watching?' This is twelve hours after my mother had dropped dead. I'd been at their place all night with my old man. They'd set up the card table in the living room and were starting their game of gin, just the two of them. Suddenly my mother puts down her hand. 'I don't want to play anymore,' she says. Her head goes back, and that's it. Massive coronary. Now he's with us until the worst is over. Gregory goes out to start the night just when my father's in his pajamas watching the ten o'clock news. 'Where's he going at this hour? Where are you going, bubeleh, at ten o'clock at night?'

The kid thinks he's hearing Swahili. I say, 'Dad, forget it.' 'But if he's first going out ten at night, what time is he coming home?' I tell him that those are questions that exceed all understanding—you have to have the brain of an Ann Landers to answer those questions. Sad business. He's facing the truth about bubeleh, and just when he's least prepared. Bubeleh turns out to be a con man and a bullshit artist who can't even be bothered to go out to the corner to get a quart of milk for Grandpa's cornflakes. It's been rough to watch. We've been together these last three weeks the way we were when I was a kid working in the store. Only now he's the kid. The mother dies, the old father becomes the son's son. We watch the Watergate news together. We eat dinner together. I make breakfast for him in the morning before I go to the hospital. I stop on the way home to get the chocolate-covered cookies that he likes. Before he goes to bed, I give him two with a Valium and a warm glass of milk. The night my mother died I stayed there and slept with him in their bed. During the day, during the first week, he came and sat at my desk while I was down in surgery. He told my secretary about the handbag business. Every day he sat in my office and read the paper for four hours until I came up from the operating room and took him down to the cafeteria for lunch. Nothing like a father's defenselessness to bring you to your knees. It's why I can't forgive that fucking kid. The vulnerability of this old guy and it leaves him absolutely cold. I know he's only eighteen. But *so* callous? *So* blind? Even at eight it would stink. But that's how it worked out, and there we are. I've been so busy with my old man I haven't even had time to think about my mother. That'll come later, I suppose. What's it like for you, without them? I still remember your folks and your kid brother when they all came out to visit on the train."

The differences in their family predicament Zuckerman preferred not discussing right then—it could only promote further dismissive interpretations of his motives. Zuckerman was still stunned by how matter-of-factly Bobby had opposed him. His plan to change his life had seemed as absurd to Bobby as it had to Diana when he'd invited her to come out with him to Chicago and go to school.

"What's it like," Bobby asked him, "three, four years after they're gone?"

"I miss them." To miss. To feel the absence of. Also, to fail to do, as to miss an opportunity.

"What'd they make of *Carnovsky*?"

In the old days he would have told him the truth— back then Zuckerman would have kept Bobby up half the night telling him the truth. But to explain that his father had never forgiven the mockery that he saw in *Carnovsky*, of both the Zuckermans and the Jews; to describe his acquiescent mother's discomposure, the wounded pride, the confused emotions, the social embarrassment during the last year of her life, all because of the mother in *Carnovsky*; to tell him that his brother had gone so far as to claim that what he'd committed wasn't mockery but murder ... well, he didn't consider it seemly, twenty years on, still to be complaining to his roommate that nobody from New Jersey knew how to read.

Up the Outer Drive with Ricky at the wheel. Chicago by night, said the Percodan, visit the new Picasso, the old El, see how the dingy bars you wrote up in your diary as "real" have now become far-out boutiques— "First a room where I can lie down. My neck. Must get my collar out of the suitcase." But the Percodan wouldn't hear of it: Your collar's a crutch. You're not going to medical school in that collar. "What's Percodan then?" True, but one crutch to be discarded at a time. You're back, but it's only Chicago, not Lourdes.

On the Outer Drive it seemed more like Chartres he'd returned to: away while they were hauling up the spires, he was seeing a wonder and an era all complete, a legend knocked together in twenty years. They'd built Rome, Athens, Angkor Wat, and Machu Picchu all while he was writing (and defending—stupidly defending!) his four books. He could have been seeing electric lighting for the first time too. Broken bands of illumination, starred, squared, braided, climbing light, then a ghost wall of lakeshore, and of this day and age, nothing more. And to confound the enigma of all that light encoding all that black—and of the four books, the thousand pages, the three hundred thousand words that had made him what he was today—there was all the synthetic opium lacing his blood and steeping his brain.

Oxycodone. That was the ingredient doing the confounding. What egg whites had been to his mother's angel-food cake, oxycodone was to Percodan. He'd learned about oxycodone from the *Physicians' Desk Reference to Pharmaceuticals and Biologicals*, the big blue 25th edition, a full fifteen hundred pages to select from at bedtime, three hundred more even than his bedside copy of Gray's *Anatomy*. Thirty pages showed color photographs, in actual size, of a thousand prescription drugs. He would swallow 500 milligrams of Placidyl—a rubbery reddish sleeping capsule exuding a faintly stinging aftertaste and odor—and, while waiting to discover if just one would work, lay alone in the lamplight with his *PDR*, boning up on side effects and contraindications, and feeling (if he could manage to) like the sleepy boy who used to take his stamp album into his bed with him back when inspecting watermarks under his magnifying lens was all it took to put him out—and not for thirty minutes, but ten hours.

Most of the pills looked banal enough, like M&Ms, like the pharmacopoeia's counterpart of the multicolored sets of boring stamps portraying impregnable monarchs and founding fathers. But waiting on sleep he had all the time in the world, and like the young philatelist of years ago scanned the thousand pictures to find the most delicately decorated, the whimsical, the inspired: to subdue nausea,

Wans, suppositories looking like pastel torpedoes out of a toy war game; a pill called Naqua, to treat edema, fashioned like a fragile snowflake; Quaalude pills, marketed for sedation, initialed like a signet ring. For steroid therapy, Decadron, modeled after the party hat, and to soften the stool, Colace capsules as radiant as rubies. Paral capsules, another sedative, looked like garnet-shaped bottles of burgundy wine, and to combat severe infection, V-Cillin K, tiny white ostrich eggs stamped, as though for a birthday child, "Lilly." Antivert they marked with a fossil arrowhead, Ethaquin with a fossil insect, and scratched upon the Theokin was a character identified by Zuckerman as runic. To alleviate pain there were dollhouse lipsticks called Darvon capsules, Phenaphen pills disguised as raspberry mints, and the die from which they cast the Urplacebo, the little pink Talwin pill. But none of these— and he'd tried enormous doses of all three—alleviated Zuckerman's pain like the oxycodone that the master chef at Endo Laboratories, Inc., mixed with a little aspirin, a little caffeine, a little phenacetin, then lightly sprinkled with a dash of homatropine terephthalate, to make mellow, soft, and cheering Percodan. Where would he be without it? Praying at the pillow of Dr. Kotler, instead of out on the town with midnight still hours away.

To cease upon the midnight with no pain. Keats studied medicine (was also said to have died of a review). Keats, Conan Doyle, Smollett, Rabelais, Walker Percy, Sir Thomas Browne. The affinity between vocations was real

—and that wasn't Percodan sweet talk, that was weighty biographical fact. Chekhov. Céline. A. J. Cronin. Carlo Levi. W. C. Williams of Rutherford, N.J. . . .

He should have recited that list for Bobby. But they were all doctors first, Bobby would have replied. No, other doctors won't trust me because I chose first to be an artiste. Nobody'll believe I can do it. Or mean it. I'll be as suspect a physician as I was a writer. And what about the poor patients? This new doctor wrote *Carnovsky*—he doesn't want to cure me, he just wants to get my story and put it in a book.

"You a feminist, Ricky?"

"I just drive a car, sir."

"Don't get me wrong. I like the feminists actually because they're so fucking stupid. They talk about exploitation. To them exploitation in most cases is if a guy has sex with a woman. When I do the TV shows, when they invite me there to fight the feminists and those women start carrying on, I say to them, 'You know, I've got the place for you: no pornography, no prostitution, no perversion. It's called the Soviet Union. Why don't you go?' It generally shuts them up for a while. Wherever I am, there seems to be controversy. Always suing and fighting. It's a constant being at war. I am an endangered species, under attack. That's because I'm threatening. The most threatening. Physically I'm constantly aware of being hurt. That's not just dramatizing. There are people who can hurt me. I get death threats, Ricky. If I showed you some of my death mail, half of it deals with 'Only a Jew could do this. Only a kike could crawl so low.' It's like the body count in Vietnam. If you're defined as not being human, somebody can justify your execution. One guy with a bullet can end it all. He can do it to me tomorrow. He can do it tonight. I want a gun permit. I want it now. I have many guns, but I'd like to have them legal, you know. In New York the Mayor still makes me fight to get a gun permit, and then he asks me to endorse his opponent. Never directly, no, not like that—but somebody comes down to the club and says, 'The Mayor would appreciate blah blah blah,' and so I do it. Otherwise City Hall would make it even worse than it is. I'm very frightened of kidnapping. In all my interviews and public statements I never touch on my wife and my son. I've got kidnapping insurance with Lloyds of London. But that doesn't mean they're going to get me to stop. I'll never be the good acceptable pornographer like Hefner, with an acceptable bullshit 'philosophy.' I'll never be the good acceptable Jew, never. What's your religion?"

"Lutheran."

"I never wanted to be Protestant. Jews do, plenty of them. Not me. To be assimilated, to be respectable, to be detached like the Wasps, I understand the desire, but I knew never to try. I see all those distinguished Wasps with the beautiful gray hair and the pinstripe suits who don't have pimples on their ass. They're my lawyers. That's who I send into court for me. I don't send in Jews. Jews are too crazy. They're like me. Volatile extremes. Jews sweat. These guys are in control, there's a coolness there that I respect. These guys are *quiet*. I don't want to be that way. I couldn't begin to be that way. I'm the wild Jew of the pampas. I am the Golem of the U.S.A. But I love these guys—they keep me out of prison. Though a lot of them are crazy too, you know. They're alcoholics, their wives stick their heads in ovens, their kids drop LSD and jump out of windows to see if they can fly. Wasps have troubles, I know that. What they don't have is my enemies. I've cornered the market. Everybody hates me. Everybody. There's a theatrical club in New York where I'd love to be a member. The Inquiry Club. I love show business, slapstick, the old comics. But they won't let me in. They'll take Mafia hit men, they'll accept Shylocks, but the Jewish businessmen who run it won't let me in. I've got more enemies than Nixon. The police. The mob. Crazy, fucking, paranoid Nixon himself. I've got Chief Justice Warren Burger. Justice Lewis Powell. Justice Harry Blackmun. Justice William Rehnquist. Justice 'Whizzer' All-American White. My *wife* is my enemy. My *child* is my enemy. I've got an analyst who gets *paid* to be my enemy. Either they're out to bust me, to indict me, to usurp me, or they want to change me into somebody else. I started psychoanalysis three months ago. You ever been in psychoanalysis?"

"No, sir."

"It's very scary, Ricky. There's no product. I was just

complaining to the shrink this morning that it's an endless process. Sometimes I don't know from one session to another if I'm getting my money's worth. It's a hundred bucks a session. It's over sixteen hundred dollars a month. It's expensive. But my wife is a very conservative woman and she wants it and I'm doing it. This is my fourth wife. She's conservative and we fight all the time. She thinks pornography is juvenile. I tell her, 'Yes, it's true, so what?' She thinks it's beneath me. She tells me that I'm boxed in with a persona that doesn't fit. What a grand human being I would be if only I would be somebody else. That's what she and the analyst have in mind. I can't say I'm not a little sick of pornography. There's a lot of compulsivity in all this—I know that. I'm to some degree bored with talking about eating pussy and sucking cock and whose dick is larger than whose. A lot of times I'm tired of the lawsuits. I'm tired of the debates. It's getting harder for me to wage a fervent battle about letting people watch other people fuck—but for those who want it, why 'no'? Every other kind of shit is accessible, why not this? The analyst says to me, 'Why do you go to such lengths to be unacceptable?' Do I? I'm not unacceptable to the readers of *Lickety Split*. I'm not unacceptable to the poor bastards who want to go to a good porno film and jerk off. I'm not unacceptable to the people who come to Milton's Millennia Two. I'm not saying you can come to my place and throw the women down on the floor and fuck them. I never said you can fuck everybody you

want. Those are words that have been put into my mouth
by all those fucking fascistic feminists who hated their
fathers and now hate me. But that is not my position.
Everything's by mutual consent and every woman comes
with a man to escort her inside. But immediately you
eliminate the ninety percent of the people who say, 'Oh, I
don't do that.' You're immediately in the ball park. Whoever *wants* you to fuck 'em, you fuck 'em. It's the best buy
in New York. For a couple it's thirty-five dollars. That
includes dinner, dancing, and staying till 4 a.m. You go to
a disco in New York, you pay twenty-five dollars just to
get in. At Milton's for thirty-five bucks you've got your
hotel room, you got your food, and you got your whole
evening. And you're *safe*. I reopened a year and a half
ago and there hasn't been a fight yet. Name a bar in Chicago without a fight in the last eighteen months. To fight
over a woman there, you have to be off the fucking wall
to do it. You fight when there's repression, when you're
denied. At Milton's, you're obviously with a woman,
you're in there *because* you're with a woman—so you can
either watch and jerk off, or you fuck the woman you
brought, or you can swing with another couple, if each
person finds the other one compatible. We've got small
rooms if you want to fuck alone and we've got a big orgy
room with mirrors and a bar. Sure, to some degree it's
boring—a hundred people fucking, so what? I'm not saying it's classy. These are people who live in Jersey and
Queens. The pretty people aren't going to Milton's, other

than to look. The real swingers who are very attractive
swing privately at parties, California-style. At Milton's
it's nice people, schleppy people—it's sort of middle-class.
You know how many come there who actually fuck?"

"No, sir."

"Take a guess."

"Better if I concentrate on my driving, sir. Heavy
traffic."

"Twenty percent. Tops. Eighty percent watch. Like
television. Spectator stuff. But it's not like Hefner's mansion and the champagne parties for his entourage. I see
him and Barbi on television and I want to throw up. I
provide a service for the common man. I give entertainment, information—I legitimize feelings in people as real
as anybody else. They need it dirty to get turned on? So
what? They're still human beings, you know, and there
are millions of them out there. All the men's magazines
taken together have thirty million readers. That's more
people than voted for McGovern. If the men's magazines
had got together and held a convention and put up a can-
didate, he would have beaten George McGovern. That's
more men buying magazines to jerk off with than there
are people living in Holland, Belgium, Sweden, Finland,
and Norway combined. Still, the analyst tells me that all
I've done is institutionalized my neurosis. So did Napoleon. So did Sigmund Freud! This is the problem with
analysis for me. Sure I want to be a better father. I have to
deal with a seven-year-old son who is very bright, very

precious to me, and very difficult. He's a ball-breaking, bright kid, who's constantly interrogating everything I do. Do I give my little Nathan values where he's to challenge authority or to accept authority? I don't have a glimmer. I don't like the job of forbidding something—it's not my way. But here I am, grossing seven million a year, the most wanted terrorist of the sexual revolution, and I don't have a fucking glimmer what to teach him. I want to learn to share with him. I want him to feel my strength and who I am, and to enjoy him. I'm concerned about Nathan. In some ways people are going to treat him badly because of me. But must I change my entire life for him? Right now he's only seven and he doesn't quite know who I am. He knows that sometimes people ask me for my autograph, but he doesn't know what the business is. I tell him I make movies and I own a nightclub and I publish a magazine. He once wanted to look at *Lickety Split*. I tell him, 'It's not for you, it's for grown-ups.' He says, 'Well, what's in it?' I say, 'People making love.' He says, 'Oh.' 'What do you think making love is?' I ask him. So he says, 'How should I know?'—very indignant. But when he knows, it's going to be difficult for him. When I pick him up at school, the twelve-year-olds know who I am—and I'm concerned about that. But analysis is complicated for someone like me. I've gotten such payoffs from being repulsive. I hear the analyst talking about monogamy and making a commitment to marriage, and these ideas are sort of goofy to me. That's what he holds up to me as health. I don't know—am I defending a stupid entrenched neurosis, or am I paying a hundred dollars an hour to get myself brainwashed by a professional bourgeois? I have a lot of girl friends. I'm supposed to get rid of them. I do group sex. I'm supposed to cut it out. I get blow jobs from my receptionist. I'm supposed to stop. My wife is sort of tuned-out—she's detached and innocent and good, and she doesn't know. People can't believe she doesn't know, but that's the kind of woman she is, and I'm careful. So there's *The Milton Appel Story*: the most notorious pornographer in America, and I live the dishonest life of most Americans about my sexuality. Ridiculous. The wildest antisocial desperado of them all, the embodiment of crudity, the Castro of cock, the personification of orgasmic mania, commander in chief of the American pornocracy—"

He couldn't have stopped if he'd wanted to. *Let him speak.*

5   The Corpus

He had registered as a man grossing seven million a year. He remembered, some time earlier, trying a sentimental walk around the Loop as himself. When that didn't work he got back in the car, and they drove on to the Ambassador East. They drank in the bar. As best he remembered, he'd brought tremendous pressure on her to come back with him to New York to drive his Rolls. When men like that want something, they don't stop till they get it. He'd offered an enormous future as chauffeur to Milton Appel. She laughed, a good-natured girl of twenty-seven, only a few years out of rural Minnesota, cheery, polite, not at all so simple as she'd first sounded, with remarkable turquoise eyes and a blond braid and the chunky arms of a healthy child. She laughed and said no, but he wouldn't let up. The well-known pornographical paradox: one has to esteem innocence highly to enjoy its violation. He was taking her to the Pump Room, he told her, to negotiate further over dinner, but when he came up to his room to wash and to change, he'd dropped onto the bed to assuage the flesh, and now it was a dim winter morning.

Back in 1949, when the dangers of night stalking were still all metaphorical, he'd circle the Loop three and four times after dark. Starting at Orchestra Hall, where the unmusical boy raised on "Make-Believe Ballroom" and "Your Hit Parade" had first heard Beethoven's Fifth, he would cut across to LaSalle (seething with hatred for the Stock Exchange) and on up to Randolph and the garish downtown that reminded him always of home, of Market Street back in Newark, of the chop-suey joints and cheap specialty shops, the saloon grills, the shoe stores, the penny arcades, all battened down beneath rooftop billboards and fastened in by the movie palaces. At State and Lake he'd pass under the El and, resting against a pillar, wait for the thrill of the first vibrations. That he who had been born in New Jersey should hear an elevated train pounding overhead in Illinois seemed to him as dark and exalting as any of the impenetrable mysteries tormenting

Eugene Gant in *Of Time and the River. If this can happen, anything can happen.* Meaning by "anything" nothing at all like the pain in the neck that in 1973 forced him back to the limousine after just a few blocks, and on to the hotel where he'd slept for ten hours in his clothes.

He'd dreamed all night. There was a nude woman. She was short and firm, her face obscure, her age indecipherable except for the youthful breasts, grotesquely high and spherical and hard. She was posing on a platform for an art class. It was his mother. Drenched in yearning, he dreamed again. She flew into his room, this time clearly his mother and no one else—only she flew in as a dove, a white dove with a large round white disc, toothed like a circular saw, whirling between her wings to keep her aloft. "Strife," she said, and flew out through an open window. He called after her from where he was pinned to his bed. Never had he felt so wretched. He was six and calling, "Mama, I didn't mean it, please come back."

She's with me here. At 3 a.m., in the Ambassador East, where he was doubly disguised—falsely registered under his worst enemy's name, and passing himself off as a social menace—his mother's ghost had tracked him down. He wasn't being poetic or mad. Some power of his mother's spirit had survived her body. Always he had tended to think rationally, as a rationalist, that life ends with the death of the human body. But at three that night, wide awake in the dark, he understood that this is not so. It ends and it doesn't. There is some spiritual power, some mental power, that lives after the body is dead, and that clings to those who think about the dead one, and my mother has revealed hers here in Chicago. People would say this is only more subjectivity. I would have said so myself. But subjectivity is a mystery too. Do birds have subjectivity? Subjectivity is just the name for the route she takes to reach me. It's not that I want to have this contact or that she wants to have this contact, and it's not that the contact will continue forever. It is also dying like the body is dying, this remnant of her spirit is dying too, but it's not quite gone yet. It's in this room. It's beside this bed.

"Close," he said to her, very softly, ". . . but not too close."

When she was alive she didn't want to risk antagonizing me. She wanted me to love her. She didn't want to lose my love and would never be critical or argue. Now she doesn't care if I love her or not. She doesn't need love, she doesn't need support, she is beyond all these encumbrances. All that is left is the wound I inflicted. And it was a terrible wound. "You were intelligent enough to know that literature is literature, but still, there were things that were real that Nathan had used, and you loved Nathan more than anything else in the world . . ."

He didn't know if the sound of her voice would be wonderful or terrifying. He didn't find out. He waited for what she would say, but she wasn't speaking: simply purely present.

"Mother, what do you want?"

But she was dead. She wanted nothing.

He awakened in a large penthouse suite looking out over the lake. Before even removing his clothes to shower, he called Bobby's house. But by eight Bobby's hospital day had already begun. Eight to eight, thought Zuckerman, and at night the emergency calls.

Mr. Freytag answered the phone. The old man was vacuuming carpets and had to turn off the machine in order to hear him. He said that Bobby was gone.

"The mornings aren't good," he told Zuckerman. "I cleaned out the oven, I defrosted the freezer—but my Julie, I want her back. Is that wrong, is that only selfish, to want my Julie back for myself?"

"No, it isn't."

"I've been up since five. Gregory never came home. I don't understand how Bobby accepts it. He hasn't even called to tell his father where he is. It's morning. It's starting to snow. We're going to have that storm, and big. Everybody in the world knows. The 'Today Show' says so. The papers say so. Only Gregory hasn't heard. I'm supposed to go out this morning before it really starts up, but where is Gregory?" He was beginning to sob. "To snow— to snow so soon. Zuck, I can't stand it. Two feet of snow."

"Suppose I take you. Suppose we go out in a taxi together."

"I've got my car, it runs beautiful—only Bobby would be furious if I went alone, especially in this weather.

How she loved to look out the window when it snowed. Like a little girl, whenever she saw the first snow."

"I'll take you in your car."

"Out of the question. You have a life to live. I wouldn't hear of it."

"I'll be by at ten."

"But if Gregory comes back—"

"If he's back, go. If no one's home, I'll understand that you went with him."

Under the shower he tested his torso. Nothing encouraging there. The change was that for a second consecutive day it would be him taking charge, not the pain. The best adaptation to make to pain is to make no adaptation. A year and a half to learn but now he knew. First, he would take Mr. Freytag to visit the grave before the snow buried his wife a second time. His own son was busy, his grandson still missing, but Zuckerman was free and fit enough. To so easily answer a father's need! It was a job for which he'd received an excellent education—for which he'd displayed prodigious talent even as a very small boy. Only when he was fully grown did the task for which his other talents equipped him keep getting in the way. How he went about *that* estranged him from father, mother, brother, and then from three wives—rooted more in the writing than in them, the sacrificial relationship with the books and not with the people who'd helped to inspire them. As the years passed, along with the charge of being out of reach, there were sexual complaints from the wives.

Then the pain, so persistent as to estrange him even from the writing. On the playmat every other predicament, large or small, was inconceivable: no character imaginable other than the one in pain. What prevents my recovery, what I do or what I don't do? What does this illness want with me anyway? Or is it I who want something from it? The interrogation had no useful purpose, yet the sole motif of his existence was this hourly search for the missing meaning. Had he kept a pain diary, the only entry would have been one word: Myself.

Back when he'd still been hunting for a hidden cause, he'd even come to wonder if the aim of the affliction mightn't be to provide a fresh subject, the anatomy's gift to the vanishing muse. Some gift. To pay not only a patient's fixated attention to a mystifying infirmity but an obsessional writer's as well! God only knew what his body would come up with, if physical suffering turned out to be good for his work.

No, divorce number four from the flesh and its incessant wailing. Once and for all to dissolve that misalliance and resume life as your own man. First, out to the cemetery as a stand-in son, then lunch with Bobby and, if he'll arrange it (and he will, if at lunch I insist), fifteen minutes with the medical-school dean. Didn't Bobby see how the dean could make a big thing out of this? "We believe in diversity in this medical school. We brought in this writer, and we put him here with these other students, and it's going to be a new and broadening experience for him, it's going to be a new and broadening experience for all of us. We are all going to benefit by this ingenious alchemy that I, Dr. Innovative, have wrought." Why the hell not? At least let me have my crack at him. And after lunch, the registrar, to sign on for the first quarter back in the college. By nightfall his career as a writer would be officially over and the future as a physician underway. As of yesterday, he'd officially signed off as a patient. This was as far as he'd be pushed by mindless matter. Now for the spirit to speak out. I have longings and they must be met.

He washed down a Percodan with a mouthful of vodka and from a phone beside the toilet rang for coffee to be sent up while he shaved. He'd have to watch the booze and the pills. And enough of Milton Appel. All that raw force pouring out over his life. More squeezed out of him in that limousine than in the last four years at his desk. He'd felt like some enormous tube of linguistic paste. Diatribe, alibi, anecdote, confession, expostulation, promotion, pedagogy, philosophy, assault, apologia, denunciation, a foaming confluence of passion and language, and all for an audience of one. Into his parched-out desert, that oasis of words! The more energy he spends, the more he gains. They are hypnotic, these talking nuts. They go all the way out, and not just on paper. They say it all. His humanity. His depravity. His ideals. Is this guy a charlatan, Zuckerman wondered. Doesn't seem to know himself, doesn't know whether to make himself sound worse than he is or better. Though had he really said much that we haven't already heard in *Mrs. Warren's Profession*? The language may have ripened since Shaw, but nothing much had happened to the wisdom: the madam is more moral than the sick and hypocritical society. It was still Sade, and not the publisher of *Lickety Split*, who could carry that argument to the bottom of the bottom and dispense with every moral pretext—no other claim than that pleasure justifies everything. Perhaps it was only the wife and the analyst and the kid—and you make his life much easier by giving him a son instead of a daughter—but he still couldn't get himself to go that far. Of course, he was a Jew, and anti-Semitically speaking, if a Jew wants to make money running a brothel, he'll make it sound like an adult day-care center. Philo-Semitically speaking, what poor Ricky had endured in that bar was a saint in the line of the great healer Jews going back to Freud and his circle: crusading, do-gooding Dr. Appel, easing suffering mankind of its psychic tensions. The noble cause of Milton's Millennia. Not a fistfight there in eighteen months—if the place catches on like McDonald's, it might mean the end of war. Yet, the moral stubbornness, the passionate otherness—maybe he is what makes one secretly proudest of being a Jew after all. The more he sits with me, the more I find to like.

"I'm *serious*," said Zuckerman aloud, in the bedroom now dressing for the big day ahead, "—why is it so hard for people to take that at face value? I had to apply to four private schools to get Nathan accepted. A kid with an IQ of 167 and the first three schools turned him down. Because of me. I went with him for interviews. Why shouldn't I? I asked them questions about the curriculum. I'm a dignified man. I feel myself to be a very dignified man. I have deep respect for education. I want him to have the best. I remember reading Henry Miller when I was fifteen. Pages and pages of eating pussy. I would read his description of pussies and think how limited I was. I couldn't describe a pussy in longer than six words. That's the first time in my life that it occurred to me to be ashamed of my vocabulary. If the teachers at school had told me that by building up my vocabulary I could write descriptions of pussy like Henry Miller, I would never have been left back. I would have had the motivation. That's what I want to give my son. I would do anything in the world for him. I took a bath with him just last week. It was wonderful. You can't imagine it. Then I go to Dr. Horowitz and he tells me don't do that, the male cock is threatening to a young child. The child feels inadequate. I feel terrible. Horowitz tells me I got that wrong too. But I want to share a *closeness* with Nathan. And I did. Man to man. My father was never behind me, never. I was going to change all that. My father gave me nothing. I'm a success so now he's impressed. He sees the Rolls, he sees that people work for me, that I live in a multimillion-dollar house, he sees the way my wife dresses, the school the kid goes to, and that keeps his fucking mouth shut. But the kid has got an IQ of 167, and when he starts asking me what I do, what am I supposed to tell him? You're the writer, you're the genius who has the great ideas—you tell me what it is to be a father without having the answers. I have to get through the day *without having the answers*. And you don't know them any more than I do. You don't have kids so you don't know *anything*. You would abolish, for all future Zuckermans, the maximum security of that crazy love. You would abolish all future Zuckermans! Zuckerman the Great Emancipator brings all that begetting to a stop . . . But you don't know suffering until you have children. You don't know joy. You don't know boredom, you don't know—*period*. When he's twelve, when he starts to jerk off, then I can get through to him what the business is about. But at seven? How do you explain to a child of seven the irrepressible urge to spurt?"

Well, however much pleasure was to be had from that mischief, it was time now to go. As a character he is still far from complete, but who isn't? So Zuckerman thought until down in the lobby he was told by the doorman that the car and driver were waiting. The pornographer with the protesting mouth had apparently hired her for the length of his stay.

Big white snowflakes swept lightly across the hood of the limousine as they headed back onto the Drive. The distant sky looked just about ready to bring on in from the northern plains the season's first big show. Mr. Freytag's ordeal was now to begin: a Midwestern winter—blizzards to bury her anew every night. Zuckerman's mother was stored in the sunny South, where they buried you only once. After her funeral, a muscular man in a soiled T-shirt, his bicep tattooed "USMC," had taken Zuckerman aside to say that he was Mike, the cemetery caretaker, and to ask how deep the family wanted her letters chiseled. Mike understood that both sons would be returning to New Jersey and wanted to be sure he had his instructions right. Zuckerman told him, "The same as my father's letters." "That's a half inch deep," Mike warned; "not everybody knows how to do it that deep." Zuckerman, stunned by the murderous speed of the tumor and then the swiftness of the interment, still couldn't follow. The burial had taken no time at all. He was thinking that they *ought* to do these things twice: the first time you could just stand there not knowing what's happening, while the second time you could look around, see who was in tears, hear the words being said, understand at least a little of what was going on; sentiments uttered over a grave can sometimes alter a life, and he'd heard nothing. He didn't feel like a son who'd just witnessed his mother's burial, but like an actor's understudy, the one they use in rehearsals to see how the costumes look under the lights. "Look," said Mike, "just leave it to me. I'll get somebody who won't damage the stone. I'll see you don't get rooked. I know you want your mother looked after right." Zuckerman got the message. He handed Mike all the loose bills in his pocket, and assured him he would see him the following year. But once the apartment had been emptied and sold, he never visited Florida again. Cousin Essie saw to the stone, and wrote the two boys to assure them that the cemetery sprinkled the grass daily to keep the grave site green. But that was like sprinkling Antarctica for the good it did the astonishingly intractable grief. Mother's gone. Mother is matter, too. Almost three years, yet that idea had lost no force. It could still pop up out of nowhere to shut down all other thinking. A life previously subdivided by the dates of his marriages, his divorces, and his publications had fallen into two clean-cut historical epochs: before those words and after. Mother's gone. The theme of his tortured night-long dreaming, the words that had moved his little double to cry, "Come back, I didn't mean it."

This longing for a mother he'd left behind at sixteen—would he be suffering it so if he were working and well? Would he be feeling *any* of this so keenly? All a consequence of being mysteriously ill! But if not for the longing would he have fallen ill? Of course a large, unexpected loss can undermine anyone's health—so will controversy and angry opposition. But undermining it still, three and four years on? How deep can a shock go? And how delicate can I be?

Oh, too delicate, too delicate by far for even your own contradictions. The experience of contradiction *is* the human experience; everybody's balancing that baggage—

how can you knuckle under to that? A novelist without his irreconcilable halves, quarters, eighths, and sixteenths? Someone who hasn't the means to make novels. Nor the right. He wasn't leaving voluntarily, he was being drummed out of the corps. Physically unfit for being torn apart. Hasn't the muscle for it. Hasn't the soul.

Equally pointless, he thought: trying to defend your work and trying to explain your pain. Once I've recovered, won't indulge in either ever again. *Once I've recovered.* Terrific tribute to the indomitable will to have so bracing a thought only the morning after—and about as likely as a dead woman returning to life because of a child in a dream crying out that he's sorry.

Zuckerman finally realized that his mother had been his only love. And returning to school? The dream of at least being loved again by his teachers, now that she was gone. Gone and yet more present than she'd been in thirty years. Back to school and the days of effortlessly satisfying the powers that be—and of the most passionate bond of a lifetime.

He popped a second Percodan and pushed the button lowering the partition window between the front and back seats.

"Why am I unacceptable to you, Ricky?"

"You're not. You're interesting to me."

Since their negotiating session in the bar she'd dropped the "sir."

"What interests you about me?"

"The way you see things. That would interest anyone."

"But you wouldn't work for me in New York."

"No."

"You think I exploit women, don't you? You think I debase them. A girl works at the Merchandise Mart making a hundred a week and she's not being exploited, but a girl works in a Supercarnal flick, makes five hundred in a day—in a *day*, Rick—and she's being exploited. Is that what you think?"

"I don't get paid to think."

"Oh, you know how to think, all right. Who do you fuck out here, a good-looking independent young woman like you? In your position you must get a lot of cock."

"Look, I don't understand what you mean."

"You got a boyfriend?"

"I'm just divorced."

"You a parent?"

"No."

"Why not? You don't want to bring children into the world? Why, because you feminists find motherhood a nuisance or is it because of The Bomb? I'm asking why you don't have kids, Ricky. What are you afraid of?"

"Is a childless home a sign of fear to the owner of *Lickety Split*?"

"Very sharp. But what are you sparring with me for? I'm asking you a serious question about life. I'm a serious person. Why won't you buy that? I'm not saying I'm sinless—but I am a man of values, I am a crusading person,

and so I talk about what I'm crusading for. Why is it hard
for people to take that at face value? I have been crucified
on the sexual cross—I am a martyr on the sexual cross,
and don't give me that look, it's true. Religion interests
me. Not their fucking prohibitions, but *religion*. Jesus interests me. Why shouldn't he? His suffering is something
that I can sympathize with. I tell that to people and they
look at me just like you. Egomania. Ignorance. Blas-
phemy. I say that on a talk show and the death threats
start rolling in. But he never referred to himself, you
know, as the Son of God. He insisted that he was just the
Son of Man, a member of the human race, with all that
goes with it. But the Christians made him into the Son of
God anyway, and became everything he preached against,
a new Israel in just the wrong way. But the new Israel is
me, Ricky—Milton Appel."

That got her.

"You and Jesus. My God," she said, "there really are
people who think they can get away with anything."

"Why not Jesus? They hated him too. Men of sorrows
acquainted with grief. Appel Dolorosus."

"'Grief'? What about pleasure? Power? What about
wealth?"

"That's true. I admit it. I love pleasure. I love to ejaculate. To ejaculate is a deep, wonderful feeling. My wife
and I had sex the night before I left. She had her period, I
was horny, and so she gave me a blow job. It felt great. It
felt so great that I couldn't sleep. Two hours later I jerked

off. I didn't want to let go of the feeling. I wanted to feel it again. But she woke up and saw me coming, and she started to cry. She doesn't understand. But you do, don't you, a woman of the world like you?"

She did not bother to answer. Did what she was paid to do and drove. Superhuman restraint, Zuckerman thought. Make some novelist a wonderful wife.

"So you do think I debase women. That's why whatever I would offer you, you still wouldn't come with me back to New York."

When she did not reply, Zuckerman leaned forward in his seat, the better to drop each word in her ear. "Because you are a God damn feminist."

"Look, Mr. Dolorosus, I drive who pays me. This is my car and I do what I like. I work for myself. I'm not under contract to Hefner out here—I don't want to be under contract to you there."

"Because you are a God damn feminist."

"No, because that partition between you and me in this car is there for me as well. Because the truth is I'm not interested *at all* in your life, and I certainly wouldn't go to New York and become involved in that kind of setup. It smells bad, if you want to know my opinion. And it's your honesty that stinks the most. You think because you're honest and open about it, that it's acceptable. But that doesn't make it acceptable. It only makes it worse. Even your honesty is a way of debasing things."

"Am I worse than the executives you drive around who

are screwing the American worker? Am I worse than the politicians you drive around who are screwing the American nigger?"

"I don't know. Most of them are quiet in the back. They've got their briefcases and they're writing out their little notes, and I don't know how awful they are, or if they're awful at all. But I do know about you."

"And I'm the worst person you ever met."

"Probably. I don't know you intimately. I'm sure your wife would say you were."

"The worst."

"I would think so."

"You feel sorry for my wife, do you?"

"Oh God, yes. To try to have an ordinary life, to try to bring up a child and to have a fairly decent life—and with a man like you? With a man whose life is devoted to 'cunts' and 'cocks' and 'coming,' to 'pussy' or whatever you like to call it—?"

"You feel sorry for me too, Ricky?"

"You? No. *You* want it. But *she* doesn't want that kind of life. I feel sorry for your child."

"The poor child too."

"Personally I would think your child's chances are nil, Mr. Appel. Oh, I'm sure you do love him in your ego-maniacal way—but to grow up and know that that was what your father did for a living, and that he was pretty famous for it, well, that's a tough start in life, isn't it? Of course if you want him to run your empire, he's set. But is that what you're sending him to the best private schools for? To run *Lickety Split*? I feel sorry for your wife, I feel sorry for your child, and I feel sorry for all the people who sit in the movie theaters to watch your Supercarnal productions. I'm sorry for them if that's what it takes to get them turned on. And I'm sorry for the girls in those films, if that's how they have to make a living. I wasn't trained for anything, either. I was trained to get married, and that didn't work out very well. So now I'm a chauffeur. And a good one. I wouldn't do the kind of work they do, never—and not because I'm feminist: because it would ruin my sex life, and I like sex too much to have it ruined. I'd have the scars forever. Privacy is as good a cause as pornography, you know. No, I don't find you unacceptable because I'm a God damn feminist. It's because I'm a human being. You don't just debase women. Only part of it's the exploitation of these dumb women. You debase everything. Your life is filth. On every level. And you make it all the more awful because you won't even shut up."

"Oh, but let's just stick to women, my dear human being—to those girls you feel so sorry for, who don't happen to run their own limousines. There are girls, some of them, in my pictures, that are such bubbleheads they don't even know how to brush their teeth—and I pay 'em a hundred bucks an hour. Is this debasing women? Is this scarring them for life, giving them money to pay the rent? I've been on the set where I've taken girls to the bathroom and washed their *feet* for them because they were so dirty. Is this debasing women? If someone smells bad, we show her feminine hygiene. Because some of these girls, my dear human being, some of them come in off the street stinking even worse than I do. But we go out and buy the whole kit for them and show them how to use it. Most of these girls, when they work for me, they enter idiots and leave at least *resembling* what I take to be people. Shirley Temper happens to be as bright as any actress working in the legitimate theater. Why is she doing it? She's doing it because she is pulling in *a thousand dollars a day. My money.* Is that debasing women? She's doing it because a Broadway play opens and closes in a week and she's back with the unemployed, while with me she works all the time, has the dignity of a working person, and gets the chance to play a whole variety of roles. Sure, some of them are the classic woman who is looking for a strong pimp to rob them blind. Some people are always going to be exploited and not take responsibility for their own lives. Exploiting goes on everywhere there are people will- ing to be exploited. But Shirley says fuck that. And she didn't belong to the college sorority with Jane Fonda and Gloria Steinem. Scranton PA, that was her college. Fuck that, she said, age sixteen, and got out from behind a checkout counter at the A&P—out of the Scranton slums to make fifty grand her first year in the business. At *sixteen*. The girls who are in porno films, most of them take *pride* in what they do. It turns you on to drive the big

limo and dress yourself up in a man's uniform? Well, it
turns them on to show their pussies. They enjoy the exhibitionism, and who are you in your Gestapo boots to tell
them that they shouldn't? There are guys out there jerking
off over them. They love that. That's exploitation? That's
debasement? That's *power*, sister. What you have got behind this wheel. Marilyn Monroe is dead, but kids all over
America are still flogging their dum-dums over those tits.
That's exploitation of Marilyn Monroe? That's her im-
mortality! She's nothing in the ground, but to kids who
haven't even been born yet, she'll always be this great piece
of ass. These are women who feel no shame about fucking
in public. They love it. Nobody's forcing anybody to do
anything. If the ribbon counter at Woolworth's makes
them feel liberated, let 'em work there for two bucks an
hour. There are enough bodies you can get, enough
women who want to do it for money or kicks, for cathar-
sis, that you don't have to force people. The fact is that
the women have it easier than anybody. They can fake
orgasm, but for the poor guy up in front of the lights,
it's no picnic. The guy who exhibits the greatest bravado,
who says, Hey, I'd like to do that, I got a big cock—he
can't get it up at all. Exploited? If anybody's exploited
it's the God damn *men*. Most of these girls are on a total
ego trip in front of the camera. Sure I had animals in my
last film, but nobody there forced anybody to fuck them.
Chuck Raw, my star, walked off the picture because of the
dog. He says, 'I love dogs and I won't be a party to this,

Milton. Banging women fucks up their minds—they can't handle it. Any dog who fucks a woman is finished as an animal.' I respected Chuck for that. I have the courage of my convictions, he has the courage of his. Don't you get the idea yet? Nobody is putting these people in chains! I am taking them *out* of their chains! I am a monster with something to offer! I am changing American fucking forever! I am setting this country free!"

A third Percodan and the stupor began. Suddenly no words would stick in his mind, all the words were flying apart and no two seconds would hold together. To know what he was thinking required an enormous effort. By the time he found an answer, he could no longer remember the question. Laboriously he had to begin again. Beyond the fog there was a moat and beyond the moat an airy blankness. Don't ask how, but beyond that, out of the window and above the lake, he saw a marvel of gentle inaudible movement: snow falling. There was nothing that could ever equal coming home through the snow in late afternoon from Chancellor Avenue School. That was the best life had to offer. Snow was childhood, protected, carefree, loved, obedient. Then came audacity, after audacity doubt, after doubt pain. What does chronic pain teach us? Step to the front of the class and write your answer on the board. Chronic pain teaches us: one, what well-being is; two, what cowardice is; three, a little something of what it is to be sentenced to hard labor. Pain is work. What else, Nathan, what above everything? It teaches us who is boss. Correct. Now list all the ways of confronting chronic pain. You can suffer it. You can struggle against it. You can hate it. You can attempt to understand it. You can try running. And if none of these techniques provide relief? Percodan, said Zuckerman; if nothing else works, then the hell with consciousness as the highest value: drink vodka and take drugs. To make so much of consciousness may have been my first mistake. There is much to be said for irresponsible stupefaction. That is something I never believed and am still reluctant to admit. But it's true: pain is ennobling in the long run, I'm sure, but a dose of stupefaction isn't bad either. Stupefaction can't make you a hero the way suffering can, but it certainly is merciful and sweet.

By the time the limousine drew up in front of Bobby's town house, Zuckerman had emptied the last drop from his flask and was ready for the cemetery. On the front steps, in fur hat, storm coat, and buckled black galoshes, an old man was trying to sweep away the snow. It was falling heavily now, and as soon as he got to the bottom step, he had to start again at the top. There were four steps and the old man kept going up and down them with his broom.

Zuckerman, watching from the car: "It's not called the vale of tears for nothing."

Later: "You don't want to be a doctor, you want to be a magician."

Ricky came around to open his door. As he could barely think what he was thinking, he couldn't begin to surmise what she might be thinking. But that was fine—to be dumb to all that was a blessing. Especially as what you thought they were thinking wasn't what they were thinking, but no less your invention than anything else. Oh, ironic paranoia is the worst. Usually when you're busy with your paranoia at least the irony is gone and you really want to win. But to see your roaring, righteous hatred as a supremely comical act subdues no one but yourself. "Be out in ten minutes," he told her. "Just going in to get laid."

He started toward the old man still vainly sweeping the stairs.

"Mr. Freytag?"

"Yes? Who are you? What is it?"

Even in his stupor, Zuckerman understood. Who is dead, where is the body? What savage catastrophe, the old man was asking, had overtaken which of his beloved, irreplaceable kin? They belong to another history, these old Jewish people, a history that is not ours, a way of being and loving that is not ours, that we do not want for ourselves, that would be horrible for us, and yet, because of that history, they cannot leave you unaffected when their faces show such fear.

"Nathan Zuckerman." Identifying himself required a difficult, concentrated moment of thought. "Zuck," Zuckerman said.

"My God, Zuck! But Bobby's not here. Bobby's at school. Bobby's mother died. I lost my wife."

"I know."

"Of course! My thoughts are everywhere! Except where I am! My thoughts—they're so scattered!"

"I'm taking you to the cemetery."

Mr. Freytag nearly tripped over himself backing into the stairs. Maybe he smelled the drink or maybe it was the sight of the long black car.

"The car is mine."

"Zuck, what a boat. My God."

"I hit the jackpot, Mr. Freytag."

"Bobby told me. Isn't that wonderful. Isn't that something."

"Let's," said Zuckerman. "Go. Now." If he got back into the car he wouldn't collapse.

"But I'm waiting for Gregory." He pushed up his sleeve to check the time. "He should be home any minute. I don't want him taking a fall. He runs everywhere. He doesn't *look*. If anything should happen to that boy—! I have to get salt to sprinkle—before he gets home. Ice will never form once you get the salt in under the snow. It eats from beneath. Hey, your hat! Zuck, you're standing here without a hat!"

Inside, Zuckerman made for a chair and sat. Mr. Freytag was speaking to him from the kitchen. "The thick crystal salt—the kosher salt—" A very long disquisition on salt.

Navajo carpet. Teak furniture. Noguchi lamps.

Hyde Park Shakerism.

Yet things were missing. Pale shadows at eye level of paintings that had been removed. Holes in the plaster where hooks had been. The property settlement. The wife got them. Took the records too. In the shelves beneath the phonograph only four records left, their jackets torn and tattered. The living-room bookshelves looked plundered as well. All that Bobby had got to keep intact seemed to be Gregory.

Zuckerman was working hard to see where he was—to *be* where he was—when he was somewhere else. Gregory's bedroom. Mr. Freytag was holding open the door to the boy's closet. "He is not one of those kids you see around today who isn't neat and clean. He's neat as a pin. Beautifully combed. A lovely dresser. Just look at the shirts. The blues all together, the browns all together, the striped shirts at one end, the checked shirts at the other, the solids in between. Everything perfect."

"A good boy."

"In his heart a *wonderful* boy, but Bobby is a busy man and from his mother, unfortunately, the child got no direction. She couldn't give herself any, how could she give him? But I've been working on him since I'm here, and I tell you, it's having some influence. We sat yesterday morning, just the two of us right in this room, and I told him about his father. How Bobby used to study. How he used to work in the store. And you should have seen him listening. 'Yes, Grandpa, yes, I understand.' I told him how I started out in the handbag business, how with my brother I left school and worked in the tannery to help my father support a family of eight. At fourteen years of age. After the Crash, how I got a pushcart and on weekends and at night went door-to-door, selling imperfect handbags. During the day I twisted challahs in a bakery, and at night I went out with the pushcart, and you know what he said to me, when I finished? He said to me, 'You had a rough life, Grandpa.' Bobby has got his job and I've got mine. That's what I realized sitting with that boy. I am going to be a father again. Someone has to do it and it's going to be me!" He took off his storm coat and looked again at his watch. "We'll wait," he said. "Fifteen more minutes, till it's ten on the button, and if he's not here, we go. I don't understand it. I called all his friends. He's not there. Where does he go all night? Where does he drive to? How do I know if he's all right? They drive, and where are they going, do *they* even know? That car of his: mistake number fifty-six. I told Robert, 'He must not have a car!' " Then he burst into tears. He was a strong, heavy-set man, dark-complexioned like Bobby, though now sickly gray from grief. He fought the tears with his entire torso: you could see in his shoulders, in his chest, in the meaty hands that had twisted those Depression challahs, how much he despised his weakness: he looked ready to tear things apart. He was wearing a checkered pair of slacks and a new red flannel shirt—the outfit of a man who wasn't submitting to anything if he could help it. But he couldn't help it.

They were sitting on Gregory's bed, beneath a large poster of a tattooed ten-year-old in mirrored glasses. The room was small and warm and Zuckerman wanted only to get into the bed. He was riding the waves, coasting up the crest and into the light, then down into the stupor's swell.

"We were playing cards. I said, 'Honey, watch my discards. You're not paying attention to my discards. You should never have given me that three.' A three of diamonds. A three of diamonds—and that's it. There's no way to grasp it. Urine coming out of her, out of this woman so spotless all her life. Onto her living-room rug. I saw the urine and I knew it was over. Come in here, come with me, I want to show you something beautiful."

Another closet. A woman's fur coat. "See this?"

He saw, but that too was it.

"Look how she cared for this coat. Still in mint condition. The way she looked after *everything*. You see? Black silk lining with her initials. The best bone buttons. Everything the best. The only thing she let me buy her all her life. I said to her, 'We're not poor people anymore, let me get you a diamond pin.' 'I don't need diamonds.' 'Let me get you a beautiful ring then, with your birthstone in it. You worked in the store all those years like a dog, you deserve it.' No, her wedding ring is enough. But twelve years ago this last fall, her fifty-fifth birthday, I forced her, literally *forced* her to come with me to buy the coat. During the fitting you should have seen her—white as a ghost, as though it was our last penny we were throwing away. A woman who for herself wanted *nothing*."

"Mine too."

Mr. Freytag didn't seem to hear him. Could be that Zuckerman hadn't spoken. Possible he wasn't even awake.

"I didn't want a coat like this sitting in that empty apartment where somebody could break in. She got it out of storage, Zuck, the day . . . the same day . . . the *morning* . . ."

Back in the living room he stood by the front window and looked out at the street. "We'll give him five more minutes. Ten."

"Take your time."

"I see little signs now of how ill she was. She would iron half a shirt and have to sit down for fifteen minutes. I couldn't add two and two. I thought the exhaustion was all in her head. Oh, am I angry! Am I furious! Okay, damn it, we go! We're going. I get you a hat and we go. And boots. I'll get you a pair of Bobby's boots. How does a grown man go out in this weather without a hat, without boots, without anything? All you need is to get sick!"

In the car to the cemetery, what is there to think? On the road to the cemetery, stupefied or wide awake, it's simple: what is coming. No, it stays unseen, out of sight, and you come to it. Illness is a message from the grave. Greetings: You and your body are one—it goes, you follow. His parents were gone and he was next. Out to the

cemetery in a long black car. No wonder Mr. Freytag
had fallen back in alarm: all that was missing was the
box.

The old man bent forward, his face in his hands. "She
was my *memory*."

"Mine too."

"Stop!" Mr. Freytag was hammering his fist on the
glass partition. "Pull over! Here!" To Zuckerman he
cried, "That's it, the store, my friend's store!"

The car edged to the side of a wide bleak boulevard.
Low warehouses, vacant shops, auto wreckers on three
corners.

"He used to be our janitor. A Mexican boy, a sweet
lovely boy. He bought this place with his cousin. Business
is murder. Whenever I come by, I buy something, even if
I don't need it. Three beautiful little children and the
poor wife is a double mastectomy. A girl of thirty-four.
Awful."

Ricky kept the motor idling as Mr. Freytag and Zuckerman passed across the pavement arm-in-arm. The snow
was covering everything.

"Where's Manuel?" Mr. Freytag asked the girl at the
checkout counter. She pointed through the dimness to the
rear of the store. Passing the rows of canned goods, Zuckerman became terrified: he would fall and pull everything
down.

Manuel, a roundish man with a fleshy dark Indian face,
was kneeling on the floor, stamping the price on breakfast-

cereal boxes. He greeted Mr. Freytag with a hearty laugh. "Hey, Big Man! What do you say, Big Man?"

Mr. Freytag motioned for Manuel to leave what he was doing and come close. Something he had to confide.

"What is it, Big Man?"

His lips to Manuel's ear, he whispered, "I lost my wife."

"Oh, no."

"Lost my wife of forty-five years. Twenty-three days ago."

"Oh no. That's no good. That's bad."

"I'm on my way to the cemetery. A storm is coming."

"Oh, that was such a nice lady. Such a good lady."

"I stopped to buy some salt. I need the coarse kosher salt."

Manuel led him to the salt. Mr. Freytag removed two boxes from the rack. At the register Manuel refused his money. After bagging the boxes himself he accompanied them out into the snow in his shirt sleeves.

They shook hands to part. Mr. Freytag, close to tears, said, "You'll tell Dolores."

"It's no good," said Manuel. "No good."

Back in the car, remembering something more to say, Mr. Freytag reached to roll down the window. When he couldn't find a handle anywhere on the door, he began to pound at the glass. "Open it! I can't open it!"

Ricky pushed a button and, to the old man's relief, the window slid away. "Manuel!" he called out, into the snow-fall. "Hey, Manuel—come here!"

The young grocer, turning in the doorway, wearily passed a hand back through his dark hair to brush away the snow. "Yes, sir."

"You better shovel this, Manuel. All you need on top of everything is for somebody to slip."

Mr. Freytag wept the rest of the way. In his lap he held the two boxes of coarse kosher salt, cradling the bag as though it contained Mrs. Freytag's remains. The snow whacking against the car windows, heavy whirling clots of it, caused Zuckerman to wonder if he shouldn't tell Ricky to turn back. The storm was here. But Zuckerman was feeling like a clean table, like an empty table, like a pale scrubbed wooden table, waiting to be set. No force left.

They passed beneath a railway bridge sprayed in six colors with mongoloid hieroglyphs. "Hateful bastards," said Mr. Freytag when he saw the public property defaced. The underpass was riddled with potholes, the potholes awash with black water. "Criminal," said Mr. Freytag as Ricky took the roadway at a crawl. "Funerals drive under here. Hearses, mourners, but Daley lines his pockets and everybody else can go to hell."

They passed through the tunnel, turned sharply along a steep railroad embankment littered with rusted chunks of abandoned machinery, and there, across the road, beyond a high black fence of iron palings, the gravestones began, miles and miles of treeless cemetery, ending at the far horizon in a large boxlike structure that was probably nothing but a factory, but that smoking foully away through the gray of the storm looked like something far worse.

"Here!" Mr. Freytag was rapping on the partition. "This gate!" And saw for the first time that their driver wasn't a man. He pulled at Nathan's sleeve but Nathan wasn't there. Out where everything ended, he had ended too. He was no longer even that table.

Ricky had unfurled a black umbrella and was shepherding the two passengers to the cemetery gate. A job to do and she did it. Dignity. For whomever.

"I saw the braid, a girl's braid, and it didn't even register." Mr. Freytag had struck up a conversation. "All I see is grief."

"That's all right, sir."

"A young girl. With a car this size. In weather like this."

"I began my career for a Jewish funeral home. My first position as a chauffeur."

"Is that so? But—what did you drive?"

"The relatives of the deceased."

"Amazing."

"I always used to say to my husband that there must be Jewish ESP, the way the word gets out when a Jewish person dies. The mourners come in droves, they come from everywhere to comfort the bereaved. It was my first experience of Jewish people. My respect for Jews began right there."

Mr. Freytag burst into tears. "I got three shoeboxes filled with condolence cards."

"Well," Ricky said to him, "that shows how much she was loved."

"You have children, young lady?"

"No, sir. Not yet."

"Oh, you must, you must."

Along a whitening path, alone, the two men entered the Jewish burial ground. They stood together before a mound of raw earth and a headstone bearing the family name. Now he was in a rage. "But this is not what I wanted! Why haven't they flattened it? Why hasn't this been leveled off? They left it like a garbage dump! Three whole weeks and now it's snowing and they still haven't made it *right*! Here it is—I don't get it. Julie's grave. I say the words, they have no meaning. Look how they left it!" He was leading Zuckerman by the hand from one family plot to the next. "My brother is here, my sister-in-law here, then Julie"—the pile left like a garbage dump —"and I'll be here. And there," he said, waving toward the smoking factory, "off there, the old part—her father and mother, my father, my mother, my two beautiful young sisters, one of them age sixteen years, dying in my arms . . ." They were standing again before the footstone engraved "PAUL FREYTAG 1899–1970." "You got pockets in there, Paul? My stupid brother. Made his money in gloves. Wouldn't spend a penny. Bought day-old bread all his life. All he thought about was his money. His money and his pecker. Pardon me but that's the truth. Always on his wife. No consideration. Wouldn't leave his poor wife alone, not even when she had cancer of the vagina. Little guy who looked like a candy-store owner. And she was a doll. The sweetest nature. A clever woman too. The best card player, Tilly—she could beat 'em all. What times we had, the four of us. Sold his business in 1965 for a hundred thousand and the building for another hundred. They paid him three, four thousand a year just to stay on and look after his accounts. But he wouldn't give that wonderful woman a nickel to buy a thing. For the two years he was sick wouldn't even buy himself a remote-control switch so he doesn't have to get out of bed to change the channels. Saving it right to the end. The end. The end, Paul! You got pockets in there, you tight bastard? He's gone—they're all gone. And I stand on the edge and wait to be pushed. You know how I live with death now? I go to bed at night and I say, 'I don't give a shit.' That's how you lose your fear of death—you don't give a shit anymore."

He drew Nathan back to the upturned chunks of frozen earth heaped up over his wife. "Her Bobby. Her baby. How she nursed him in that dark room. How that kid suffered with those mumps. And that's what changes a life. I don't believe it. Zuck, it's idiotic. Would Bobby have chosen that girl for a wife if he had known he was a hundred percent? Not in a million years. He actually didn't think he was good enough for anything better. That

Julie's Robert should have such a thought! Yet this, I believe, is what happened. With what that kid had to offer, with all his achievements, the respect and admiration he has in his field—and his downfall? The mumps! And a son who tells his father to eat shit! Would Bobby have produced, on his own, a boy so full of contempt? He would have had a child who has *feelings*, feelings like *we* have feelings. A child who worked and who studied and stayed home, and who wanted to excel like his father. Is that what death and dying is supposed to be about? Is that what the hardship and the struggle is for? For a piece of contempt who gets on the phone with his father and tells him to go eat shit? Who thinks to himself, 'This family, these people, I'm not even theirs and look what they do.' Who thinks, 'Watch me bend them around my finger with all their stupid Jewish love!' Because who is he? Do we even know where he comes from? She wanted a baby, right away, off the bat, had to have a baby. So they found a little orphan baby, and what in his roots that we don't know makes him behave this way to Bobby? I have a brilliant son. And all that brilliance locked in his genes! Everything we gave him, trapped like that in Bobby's genes, while everything we are *not*, everything we are *against*— How can all of this end with Gregory? Eat shit? To his *father*? I'll break his neck for what he's done to this family! I'll kill that little bastard! I *will*!"

Zuckerman, with what strength remained in his enfeebled arms, pounced upon the old man's neck. *He* would kill—and never again suppose himself better than his crime: an end to denial; of the heaviest judgment guilty as charged. "Your sacred genes! What do you see inside your head? Genes with JEW sewed on them? Is that all you see in that lunatic mind, the unstained natural virtue of Jews?"

"Stop!" Mr. Freytag began pushing him off with his thick gloved hands. "Stop this! Zuck!"

"What's he do all night long? He's out studying fucking!"

"Zuck, no—Zuck, the dead!"

"*We* are the dead! These bones in boxes are the Jewish living! These are the people running the show!"

"Help me!" He struggled free, turned to the gate, stumbled—and Zuckerman slid after him. "Hurry!" Mr. Freytag called. "Something's happened!" And wailing for help as he ran, the old man to be strangled was gone.

Just white snow whirling now, all else obliterated but the chiseled stones, and his hands frantically straining to throttle that throat. "Our genes! Our sacred little packet of Jewish sugars!" Then his legs flew off and he was sitting. From there he began his recitation, at the top of his voice read aloud the words he saw carved all around him in rock. "Honor thy Finkelstein! Do not commit Kaufman! Make no idols in the form of Levine! Thou shalt not take in vain the name of Katz!"

"He—he—snapped!"

"O Lord," cried Zuckerman, sledding inch by inch on

his palms and his knees, "who bringeth forth from the earth the urge to spurt that maketh monkeys of us all, blessed art thou!" Eyes all but blinded by the melting snow, icy water ringing his collar and freezing slush filling his socks, he continued to crawl toward the last of the fathers demanding to be pleased. "Freytag! Forbidder! Now I murder *you*!"

But the boots stopped him: two tall cavalry boots burnished with oil and shedding the snow, ominous powerful sleek splendid boots that would have prompted caution in his bearded forebears too.

"This"—Zuckerman laughed, spewing flakes of burning ice—"this is your protection, Poppa Freytag? This great respecter of the Jews?" He strained to find the power to leave the graveyard ground. "Out of my way, you innocent bitch!" But against Ricky's boots got nowhere.

He awoke in a hospital cubicle. Something was wrong with his mouth. His head was enormously large. All he was aware of was this huge echoing hole which was the inside of his head. Within the enormous head there was something barely moving that was just as enormous. This was his tongue. The whole of his mouth, from ear to ear, was just pain.

Standing beside his bed was Bobby. "You're going to be all right," he said.

Zuckerman could begin to feel his lips now, lips swelled

nearly to the size of his tongue. But below the lips, nothing.

"We're waiting for the plastic surgeon. He's going to sew up your chin. You've burst all the skin on the underside of your jaw. We don't know whether you've broken it, but the gash under your chin he can put together, and then we'll get some X-rays of your mouth and see the extent of the damage. Also of your head. I don't think the skull's fractured, but we better look. So far it seems you got off lightly: the gash and a few smashed teeth. Nothing that can't be fixed."

Zuckerman understood none of this—only that his head was getting larger and was about to roll off. Bobby repeated the story: "You were out on the heath with King Lear. You keeled over. Face forward, straight out, onto my Uncle Paul's footstone. My father says it sounded like a rock hitting the pavement. He thought you'd had a heart attack. You took the impact on the point of your chin. Burst the skin. Your two front teeth snapped just below the gum line. When they picked you up, you came around for a few seconds, completely came to, and said, 'Wait a minute, I've got to get rid of some teeth.' You spat the bits of teeth into your hand, then blacked out again. Doesn't look to be a fracture, no intracranial bleeding, but let's be sure of everything before we take the next step. It'll hurt for a while, but you're going to be fine."

The gloved fist that was Zuckerman's tongue went off in search of his front teeth. The tongue found instead their spongy gritty sockets. Otherwise, within his head, he felt giddy, echoing, black.

Patiently, Bobby tried a third explanation. "You were at the cemetery. Remember that? You took my father to visit my mother's grave. You turned up in a car about nine-thirty this morning. It's now three. You drove out to the cemetery, the driver parked by the embankment, and you and my father went in. He got a little overwrought from the sound of it. So did you. You don't remember any of this? You went a little haywire, Zuck. At first my old man thought it was a fit. The driver was a woman. Strong as a little ox. You apparently tried to knock her down. That's when you fell. She's the one who carried you out."

Zuckerman indicated, by a dim croak, that he still didn't remember a thing. All this damage had happened and he didn't know how. His jaw wouldn't come undone to allow him to speak. Also his neck had begun stiffening up. He couldn't move his head at all. Imprisonment complete.

"A little temporary amnesia, that's all. Don't panic. Not from the fall. No brain injury, I'm sure. It's from the stuff you were on. People have these blackouts, especially if there's a lot of alcohol involved. I'm not surprised to hear that you lost your manners with the lady. They went through your pockets. Three joints, about twenty Percodan tablets, and a beautiful monogrammed Tiffany flask completely emptied of NZ's booze. You've been flying for quite some time. The driver had some story you'd given her all about you and Hugh Hefner. Is this what is known as irresponsible hedonism, some sort of recreational thing, or is it a form of self-treatment for something?"

He discovered an intravenous tube in his right arm. He felt himself beginning to inch back from some black place of which he knew nothing. With the index finger of the free hand he traced the letter "P" in the air. The fingers worked, the arm worked; he tested the legs and the toes. They worked. Below his collarbone he was completely alive, but he himself had become his mouth. He had turned from a neck and shoulders and arms into a mouth. In that hole was his being.

"You were treating pain with all this stuff."

Zuckerman managed to grunt—and tasted his own blood. He'd progressed from vodka to blood.

"Show me where it hurts. I don't mean the mouth. The pain you were treating on your own, before the morning's fun began."

Zuckerman pointed.

"Diagnosis?" asked Bobby. "Write down the diagnosis. In that book."

There was a pad on the bed beside him, a large spiral note pad and a felt-tipped Magic Marker. Bobby uncapped the Magic Marker for him and put it into Zuckerman's hand. "Don't try to speak. It'll hurt too much. No talking, no yawning, no eating, no laughing, and try not to sneeze—not for a while yet. Write for me, Zuck. You know how to do that."

He wrote a word: NONE.

"No diagnosis? How long has this been going on? Write that down."

He preferred to show him the number with his fingers —to prove again that the fingers could move and that he could count and that his head hadn't rolled away.

"Eighteen," said Bobby. "Hours, days, months, or years?"

In the air, with the tip of the marker, Zuckerman formed an "M."

"That's a little too long to suit me," Bobby said. "If you've had pain for eighteen months, something's causing it."

The sensation of being brainless continued to lift. He still couldn't remember what had happened, but for the moment he didn't give a fuck: all he understood was that he was in trouble and it hurt. It had become excruciating.

Meanwhile, he gave off a harsh, growling sound: yes (the growl was intended to suggest), more than likely something is causing it.

"Well, you're not leaving here till we find what it is."

Zuckerman snorted, downing in the process a second shot of old blood.

"Oh, you've made the medical rounds, have you?"

With one finger Zuckerman indicated that he'd been round and round again. He was getting sardonic. Angry. Furious. I did *this* to myself too! Forcing the world to pay attention to my moan!

"Well, that's over. We're going to put you through a multidisciplinary examination right here in the hospital, we're going to track it down, and then we're going to get rid of it for you."

Zuckerman had a clear compound thought, his first since the morning. Since leaving New York. Maybe in eighteen months. He thought: The doctors are all confidence, the pornographers are all confidence, and, needless to say, the oxlike young women who now drive the limousines live far beyond the reach of doubt. While doubt is half a writer's life. Two-thirds. Nine-tenths. Another day, another doubt. The only thing I never doubted was the doubt.

"We're also going to get you off the medication merrygo-round. As long as you're not on it for kicks, we can break your habit easily enough. Medical addiction, no real problem. As soon as your mouth is fixed and the trauma subsides, we're going to phase you out of all your pain-killers and away from the alcohol. The grass too. That's *really* childish. You're going to stay here as my patient until you're no longer addicted. That means three weeks at least. There's to be no cheating, Zuck. The cure for alcoholism isn't two little martinis before dinner. We're going to eliminate the drugs and the drink and we're going to do our best to find the cause and eliminate the pain that causes the need to get blotto. Is this clear? I'm going to oversee your withdrawal myself. It'll be gradual and painless, and if you cooperate and don't

cheat, it'll be lasting. You'll be back where you were before it all began. I wish you'd told me you were in this
when I saw you yesterday. I'm not going to ask why you
didn't. We'll save that. I thought something was up, you
looked so God damned gaga, but you said no, and it just
didn't occur to me in my office, Zuckerman, to look you
over for needle tracks. Are you in bad pain right now?
From the mouth?"

Zuckerman indicated that he was indeed in pain.

"Well, we're just waiting for the plastic surgeon. We're
still in emergency. He'll come down and trim up the
wound and get all the grit out and stitch you up so there's
hardly a scar. I want him doing it so that afterwards it
looks right. Then we'll get some pictures. If your mouth
needs work right away, we'll get the jaw man down. He
knows you're here. If they have to wire anything together,
he's the best. He's the guy who wrote the book. I'll stay
with you all the way—but one thing at a time. I can't give
you anything for the pain right now, not after what you've
come off of. Don't want more 'fits.' Just go with it. Ride
it out. It'll end like everything else. The whole thing won't
be the shortest journey imaginable, but it won't last
forever either."

Zuckerman found the Magic Marker and, with fingers
as awkward as a first-grader's, wrote four words in the
spiral notebook: CAN'T STAY THREE WEEKS.

"No? Why not?"

CLASSES BEGIN JAN. 4.

Bobby tore out the sheet, folded it in half, and stuck it in the pocket of his smock. He rubbed the edge of his hand slowly back and forth across his bearded chin—clinical detachment—but his eyes, examining the patient, showed only exasperation. He is thinking—thought Zuckerman—"What's become of this guy?"

A doctor named Walsh appeared in Zuckerman's cubicle, how long after Bobby left Zuckerman had no way of telling. He was a tall, bony man in his fifties, with a long, pouchy, haggard face, wispy gray hair, and a smoker's hoarse catch in his voice. He sucked continuously at a cigarette as he spoke. "Well," he said to Zuckerman, with a disconcerting smile, "we see thirty thousand people a year down here, but you're the first I know of to cross the threshold in his lady chauffeur's arms."

Zuckerman wrote on a clean notebook page: WHEN HE IS SICK EVERY MAN NEEDS A MOTHER.

Walsh shrugged. "The hoi polloi generally crawl through on their knees or roll in comatose on the stretcher. Especially hopheads like yourself. The lady says you gave a real fine show before you left for the Land of Oz. Sounds like you were nice and wacky. What all were you on?"

WHAT YOU FOUND. PERCODAN VODKA POT. KILLING PAIN.

"Yep, that'll do it. If it's your maiden voyage, three or four tablets of Percodan, a couple highballs, and if you don't have much tolerance, you're out for the count. People start overtreating pain, and next thing they either set fire to the mattress or they're under the wheels of a bus.

We had a guy in here the other night, smashed like you and feelin' groovy, whammo, ass over skull down four flights. Only thing he *didn't* break was his teeth. You got off lucky. From a straight fall like yours you could have done worse. You could have brained yourself but good. You could have bitten off your God damn tongue."

HOW FAR GONE WAS I?

"Oh, you were zonked, bud. You weren't breathing very hard, you'd thrown up all over yourself, and your face was a mess. We drew some blood to see what you had in you, we passed a tube down your stomach to wash you out, we injected a narcotic antagonist, we got you breathing and hooked up to the IV. We're waiting for the surgeon to come down. We cleaned out the wound but he's going to have to stick you together if you still want to turn on the girls."

WHAT'S IT LIKE TO BE AN EMERGENCY-ROOM DOCTOR? NEVER KNOW WHAT'S COMING THROUGH THE DOOR. CALLS FOR QUICK THINKING. LOTS OF SKILLS.

The doctor laughed. "You writing a book or what?" He had a funny, honking sort of laugh and a vast array of jittery gestures. A doctor with doubts. There had to be one somewhere. You might have taken him for the orderly—or for a psychiatric patient. His eyes looked scared to death. "I never read anything, but the nurse knew who you were. Before you get out of here, she's going to get your autograph. She says we got a celebrity here."

QUESTION SERIOUS. He was trying to think of something

other than the ear-to-ear pain. ABOUT TO ENTER MEDICAL SCHOOL. EMERGENCY-ROOM MEDICINE REWARDING?

"Well, it's a God damn tough way to earn a living, if you want to know. Average guy burns out at this job in about seven years. But I don't know what you mean, entering medical school. You're the famous writer. You wrote the dirty book."

MUST SAVE LOTS OF LIVES. MUST MAKE THE HARD WORK WORTH IT.

"I suppose. Sure there are two or three cliff-hangers in a day. People come in here on the rack and you try to do something for them. I can't say everyone leaves with a smile, it doesn't work out that way. You, for instance. You come in here OD'd and three, four hours after admission, you begin to lighten up. Sometimes they *never* wake up. Look, you pulling my leg? You write these hilarious best-sellers, from what they all tell me—what are you trying, to put me in one?"

HOW DID YOU BECOME AN EMERGENCY-ROOM DOCTOR?

Another nervous honk. "Monkey on my back," he said, and then was seized by a shattering cough that seemed of itself to hurl him out of the room. A moment later Zuckerman heard him call down the corridor, "Where the hell'd they put the diabetic?"

Zuckerman had no idea how much more of the day had passed before Walsh appeared at his bedside again. He had something urgent to say, something to make clear about himself before he (or the writer) went back on duty. If he was going to wind up in a hilarious best-seller, Zuckerman might as well get it right.

A book machine is what they see when they meet me. And appalling as it is, they're right. A book machine consuming lives—including, Dr. Walsh, my own.

"Most every emergency-room doctor I know has something on his back," he said. "Alcoholism. Mental disorder. No spika dee English. Okay, with me it was Demerol. Percodan turns me off, morphine turns me off, even alcohol disagrees with me. But Demerol—it's a good thing you didn't find out about Demerol. It's a great favorite with us folks whose pain drags on and on. Gives a lot of elation. Relaxation. No more problems."

WHAT PROBLEMS WERE YOURS?

"Okay," he said, his anger raw now and undisguised. "I'll tell you, Zuckerman, since you want to know. I used to have a practice over in Elgin. A wife, a child, and a practice. Couldn't handle it. You'll understand that. You wouldn't be here if you didn't understand that. So I got through on Demerol. Ten years ago this is. The big problem for me in dealing with patients is getting someone out of a difficult situation over a period of time. Down here in emergency, we just light the fuse and run. We put our finger in the dike for a while and that's it. But if a guy gets a tough case up on the floors, a case that goes on day after day, you've got to push the right buttons over the long haul. You've got to watch them die without falling apart. I can't do that. With my history, and pushing sixty, I'm lucky I can do this. I work forty hours a week, they pay me, and I go home. That's about all Gordon Walsh can handle. Now you know."

But that sounded to Zuckerman like all a man could want, an end to the search for the release from self. After Walsh had left for the second time, he tried to imagine those forty-hour weeks in order to forget what was happening in his mouth. Car accidents. Motorcycle accidents. Falls. Burns. Strokes. Coronaries. Overdoses. Knife wounds. Bullet wounds. Dog bites. Human bites. Childbirth. Lunacy. Breakdown. Now, there's *work*. They come in on the rack and you keep them alive till the surgeon can wire them together. You get them off the rack and then you disappear. Self-oblivion. What could be less ambiguous than that? If the dean were to say to him over at the medical school, "No, no room, not with your history, not at your age, not after the stunt you pulled out here," he'd reply that he wanted only to be another emergency-room doctor with a monkey on his back and an exemplary record of doubt. Nothing in the world could make him happier.

It was dark in Chicago when the plastic surgeon arrived. He apologized for being late but he'd driven in through the blizzard from Homewood. He sewed him up right in the room, stitched him up from inside the flesh so there'd be nothing afterwards but a hairline scar. "If you want," he said—a joke to lift the patient's spirits—"we'll take another tuck right here and nip that dewlap in the bud. Keep you young for the ladies." Whether he was given a local anesthetic Zuckerman had no idea. Maybe everything just hurt too much for him to feel the stitching.

The X-rays showed a fracture of the jaw in two places, so the maxillo-facial surgeon was called down, and at about the dinner hour Zuckerman was wheeled into the operating room. The elderly surgeon explained everything beforehand—in the quietest voice, like the TV announcer at the tennis match, described for Zuckerman what was next. Two fractures, he explained: an oblique fracture at the front, a thin vertical line running from between where the teeth had broken off down to the point of the chin, and a second fracture up by the hinge. Because the fragments weren't in a very good position running down to the chin, he'd have to make a small incision just beneath the chin to go in and get them aligned, then take very fine wire, drill some holes, and wire the bone together. Up by the hinge no surgery necessary. They'd put metal bars on his upper and lower teeth, crisscross rubber bands to hold the bars fastened together, and that's all it would take to heal the second fracture and give him an even bite. He shouldn't be alarmed when he woke up if he experienced a slight choking sensation—it would only be from the rubber bands clamping his mouth "more or less shut." They would be loosening that up as soon as they could. And then, for the twentieth time that day, Zuckerman was assured that after his face was all fixed, he'd still be able to wow the girls.

"Yes, it's a clean fracture, but not quite clean enough to suit me." These words of the surgeon's were the last that he heard. Bobby, there to administer the anesthesia, patted his shoulder. "Off to Xanadu, Zuck," and off he went, to the tune of ". . . not quite clean enough . . ."

Bobby was there to put him out and was there in the recovery room to check up on him when Zuckerman came to, but when the Xylocaine wore off sometime during the night, Zuckerman was alone and at long last he found out just what pain could really do. He'd had no idea.

One of the maneuvers he adopted to get from one minute to the next was to try calling himself Mr. Zuckerman, as though from the bench. Chasing that old man around those tombstones, Mr. Zuckerman, is the dumbest thing you have ever done. You have opened the wrong windows, closed the wrong doors, you have granted jurisdiction over your conscience to the wrong court; you have been in hiding half your life and a son far too long—you, Mr. Zuckerman, have been the most improbable slave to embarrassment and shame, yet for sheer pointless inexcusable stupidity, nothing comes close to chasing across a cemetery, through a snowstorm, a retired handbag salesman understandably horrified to discover grafted upon his own family tree the goy who spoils everything. To fix all that pain and repression and exhaustion on this Katzenjammer Karamazov, this bush-league Pontifex, to smash him, like some false divinity, into smithereens . . . but of course there were Gregory's inalienable rights to defend, the liberties of a repellent mindless little shit whom you, Mr. Zuckerman, would loathe on sight. It appears, Mr. Zuckerman, that you may have lost your way since Thomas Mann last looked down from the altar and charged you to become a great man. I hereby sentence you to a mouth clamped shut.

When the lighthearted approach proved ineffective— and then the distraction of reciting to himself what he could remember from high school of the *Canterbury Tales*—he held his own hand, pretending that it was somebody else. His brother, his mother, his father, his wives—each took a turn sitting beside the bed and holding his hand in theirs. The pain was amazing. If he could have opened his mouth, he would have screamed. After five hours, if he could have got himself to the window, he would have jumped, and after ten hours the pain began to subside.

For the next few days he was nothing but a broken mouth. He sucked through a straw and he slept. That was it. Sucking would seem to be the easiest thing in the world to do, something nobody had to be taught, but because his lips were so bruised and sore and the overall swelling so bad, and because the straw only fit sideways into his mouth, he couldn't even suck right, and had to sort of draw in from down in the stomach to get the stuff to begin to trickle through him. In this way he sucked in carrot soup and mushed-up fruit, and a milky drink, banana-flavored and extolled as highly nutritious, that was so sweet it made him gag. When he wasn't sucking liquid pulp or sleeping, he went exploring his mouth with his tongue. Nothing existed but the inside of his mouth. He made all sorts of discoveries in there. Your mouth is who you are. You can't get very much closer to what you think of as yourself. The next stop up is the brain. No wonder fellatio has achieved such renown. Your tongue lives in your mouth and your tongue is you. He sent his tongue everywhere to see what was doing beyond the metal arch bars and the elastic bands. Across the raw vaulted dome of the palate, down to the tender cavernous sockets of the missing teeth, and then the plunge below the gum line. That was where they'd opened him up and wired him together. For the tongue it was like the journey up the river in "Heart of Darkness." The mysterious stillness, the miles of silence, the tongue creeping conradianly on toward Kurtz. I am the Marlow of my mouth.

Below the gum line there had been bits of jawbone and teeth smashed up, and the doctor had spent some time, before setting the fracture, picking around in there to take out all the tiny fragments. Giving him new front teeth was still to come. He couldn't imagine ever again biting into anything. The idea of anyone touching his face was horrible. He slept at one point for eighteen hours and afterwards had no recollection of having his blood pressure taken or his IV changed.

A young night nurse came by to cheer him up with the

Chicago Tribune. "Well," she said, flushed a little with excitement, "you really are somebody, aren't you?" He motioned for her to leave the paper beside his sleeping pill. In the middle of the night—some night or other—he finally picked up the copy she'd left him and looked at it under the bed light. The paper was folded back to an item in one of the columns.

> Latest from our celebrity chauffeur: How time jets! Sixties rebel, Novelist Nathan ("Carnovsky") Zuckerman recouping at Billings from cosmetic surgery. Just a nip and a tuck for the fortyish Romeo, then back to "Elaine's" and the NY scene. Nathan slipped into town incognito to party at the Pump Room on the eve of the lift . . .

A card arrived from Mr. Freytag. On the envelope's return-address sticker, where it read "Mr. and Mrs. Harry Freytag," Mr. Freytag had put a line through "and Mrs." Drawing that line would have taken some doing. The card read "Hurry and Get Well!" On the back he had hand-written a personal message.

> Dear Nathan,
>   Bobby explained about the death of your beloved parents that I did not know about. Your terrible grief as a son explains whatever happened and nothing more has to be added. The cemetery was the last place in the world for you to be. I only kick myself that I didn't know beforehand. I hope I didn't make it worse with anything I said.
>   You have made a great name in life for which all my

congratulations. But I want you to know you are still
Joel Kupperman ("The Quiz Kid") to Bobby's Dad and
always will be. Hurry and get well.

> Love from the Freytags,
> Harry, Bobby, and Greg

The last of the old-fashioned fathers. And we, thought
Zuckerman, the last of the old-fashioned sons. Who that
follows after us will understand how midway through the
twentieth century, in this huge, lax, disjointed democracy,
a father—and not even a father of learning or eminence
or demonstrable power—could still assume the stature of
a father in a Kafka story? No, the good old days are just
about over, when half the time, without even knowing it,
a father could sentence a son to punishment for his
crimes, and the love and hatred of authority could be such
a painful, tangled mess.

There was a letter from the student paper, *The Maroon*.
The editors wanted to interview him about the future of
his kind of fiction in the post-modernist era of John Barth
and Thomas Pynchon. Since they understood that because
of his surgery he might not wish to be seen, would he
please answer, at whatever length he chose, the ten questions on the sheet attached.

Well, they were kind not to show up and just grill him
on the spot; he didn't feel ready quite yet for the social
pleasures of an author's life.

*1. Why do you continue to write? 2. What purpose
does your work serve? 3. Do you feel yourself part of a*

rearguard action, in the service of a declining tradition? 4.
Has your sense of vocation altered significantly because of
the events of the last decade?

Yes, yes, said Zuckerman, very much so, and dropped
back below the gum line.

The fourth morning he got up and looked in the mirror. Until then he hadn't been interested. Very pale, very
drawn. Surgical tape under his chin. Hollow cheeks that
a movie star would envy, and around the surgical tape a
scraggly growth of beard that had come in all white.
And balder. Four days in Chicago had undone four
months of trichological treatment. The swelling had subsided, but the jaw was alarmingly lopsided and even
through the whiskers looked badly bruised. Mulberry,
like a birthmark. His cracked and spotted lips had also
turned colors. And two teeth were indeed gone. He realized that his glasses were gone. Under the snow in the
cemetery, buried till spring with Bobby's mother. All the
better: for now he didn't care to see clearly the clever
jokes that mockery plays. He'd been considered a great
mocker once himself, but never as diabolically inspired
as this. Even without the aid of his glasses, he understood
that he didn't look like he was on the ball. He thought,
Just don't make me write about it after. Not everything
has to be a book. Not that, too.

But back in bed he thought, The burden isn't that
everything has to be a book. It's that everything *can* be a
book. And doesn't count as life until it is.

Then the euphoria of convalescence—and the loosening of his rubber bands. During the weeks that followed the successful operation, in the excitement of giving up each day a little more of the narcotic support, full of the pleasure of learning for the second time in forty years to form simple monosyllabic English with his lips and his palate and his tongue and his teeth, he wandered the hospital in his robe and slippers and the new white beard. Nothing he pronounced, in his weakened voice, felt time-worn—all the words seemed rapturously clean, and the oral catastrophe behind him. He tried to forget all that had happened in the limousine, at the cemetery, on the plane; he tried to forget everything that had happened since he'd come out to go to school here the first time. *I was sixteen, intoning ". . . shantih, shantih, shantih" on the El. That's the last I remember.*

The first-year interns, young men in their mid-twenties, mustaches newly cultivated and eyes darkly circled from working days and nights, came around to his room after supper to introduce themselves and chat. They struck him as artless, innocent children. It was as though, leaving the platform with their medical-school diplomas, they'd taken a wrong turn and fallen back headlong into the second grade. They brought their copies of *Carnovsky* for him to autograph and solemnly asked if he was working on a new book. What Zuckerman wanted to know was the age of the oldest member of their medical-school class.

He began helping the post-operative patients just up out of bed, slowly wheeling along the corridor the poles slung with their IV bags. "Twelve times around," moaned a forlorn man of sixty with a freshly bandaged head; dark pigmented moles could be seen at the base of his spine where the ties to his gown had come undone. ". . . twelve times around the floor," he told Zuckerman, ". . . supposed to be a mile." "Well," said Zuckerman, through a rigid jaw, "you don't have to do the mile today." "I own a seafood restaurant. You like fish?" "Love it." "You'll come when you're better. Al's Dock. 'Where lobsters are the Maine thing.' Spelled M-a-i-n-e. You'll have dinner on me. Everything fresh that day. One thing I learned. You can't serve frozen fish. There are people who can tell the difference and you can't get away with it. You have got to serve fresh fish. The only thing we have that's frozen is the shrimp. What do you do?" Oh, God—should I now do my number? No, no, in their weakened condition too alarming for both of them. Donning that mask wasn't a joke: all the while he was enjoying it, his exuberant performance was making even more unrelenting all the ghosts and the rages. What looked like a new obsession to exorcise the old obsessions was only the old obsessions merrily driving him as far as he could go. As far? Don't bet on it. Plenty more turmoil where that came from. "Out of work," said Zuckerman. "A bright young guy like you?" Zuckerman shrugged. "Temporary setback, that's all." "Well, you ought to learn the seafood business." "Could be," said Zuckerman. "You're young—" and with those words, the restaurateur was choking back tears, suddenly fighting down the convalescent's pity for all vulnerable things, including himself now and his bandaged head. "I can't tell you what it was like," he said. "Close to death. You can't understand. How it draws you to life. You survive," he said, "and you see it all new, *everything*," and six days later he had a hemorrhage and died.

The sobbing of a woman, and Zuckerman was transfixed outside her room. He was wondering what, if anything, he should do—*What is the matter? What does she need?*—when a nurse popped out and rushed right past him, muttering only half to herself, "Some people think you're going to torture them." Zuckerman peered inside. He saw the graying hair spread across her pillow, and a paperback copy of *David Copperfield* open on the sheet that covered her chest. She was about his age and wearing a pale blue nightgown of her own; the delicate shoulder straps looked absurdly fetching. She might have been lying down to rest for a moment before rushing off to a dinner party on a summer evening. "Is there anything—?" "This cannot be!" she shouted. He came farther into the room. "What is it?" he whispered. "They're removing my larynx," she cried—"go away!"

In the lounge at the end of the ear, nose, and throat floor he checked the relatives of the surgical patients waiting for the results. He sat and waited with them. Always somebody at the card table playing solitaire. All there was to worry about, yet not one forgot to give the deck a good shuffle before dealing a new game. One afternoon Walsh, his emergency-room doctor, found him there in the lounge, on his lap a yellow pad where he'd been able to write nothing more than "Dear Jenny." Dear Diana. Dear Jaga. Dear Gloria. Mostly he sat crossing out words that were wrong in every possible way: *overwrought . . . self-contempt . . . weary of treatment . . . the mania of sickness . . . the reign of error . . . hypersensitized to all the inescapable limits . . . engrossed to the exclusion of everything else . . .* Nothing would flow with any reality—a mannered, stilted letter-voice, aping tones of great sincerity and expressing, if anything, his great reservations about writing to explain at all. He couldn't be intelligent about having failed to make good as a man on his back, and he could not be apologetic or ashamed. Wasn't emotionally persuasive any longer. Yet as soon as he sat down to write, out came another explanation, causing him to recoil from his words in disgust. The same with the books: however ingenious and elaborate the disguise, answering charges, countering allegations, angrily sharpening the conflict while earnestly striving to be understood. The endless public deposition—what a curse! The best reason of all never to write again.

While they rode the down elevator, Walsh savored the last of his cigarette—savoring, Zuckerman thought, some contempt for me too.

"Who set your jaw finally?" Walsh asked.

Zuckerman told him.

"Nothing but the best," said Walsh. "Know how he rose to the white-haired heights? Studied years ago with the big guy in France. Experimented on monkeys. Wrote it all up. Bashed in their faces with a baseball bat and then studied the fracture lines."

To then write it up? Even more barbaric than what went on in his line. "Is that true?"

"Is that how you get to the heights? Don't ask me. Gordon Walsh never got to do much bashing. How about the five-dollar habit, Mr. Zuckerman? Remove you from your Percodan yet?"

Because of his habit Zuckerman was handed a drink twice a day looking and tasting like a cherry soda—his "pain cocktail" they called it. It was delivered routinely— early morning, late afternoon—by the nurse who put the addict through his paces. Taken at fixed times and not in response to the pain, the drink furnished the opportunity to "relearn" facing his "problem." "Give us this day," she said, "our daily fix," while obedient Zuckerman emptied the glass. "Not taking anything on the sly, are we, Mr. Z.?" Though for the first several days off the pills and the vodka he'd been feeling unpleasantly jittery and nervous—at moments shaky enough to wonder who he could find in the hospital to help him break Bobby's rules —the answer was no. "Nothing surreptitious about Mr. Z.," he assured her. "That's the boy," she said, and with a conspiratorial hospital wink ended the pseudo-seductive little game. The changing proportion of active ingredients to cherry syrup was known only to the staff; the cocktail was the centerpiece of Bobby's deconditioning plan, a gradual fading process to reduce Zuckerman's medication to zero over a period of six weeks. The idea was to phase Zuckerman out of physiological dependence on pain-killers as well as the "pain behavior syndrome."

As for the investigation into the pain so conducive to the behavior, it had yet to be ordered. Bobby didn't want Zuckerman, whose morale after a year and a half required a certain tactful treatment of its own, to drop into a state of confused depression because of too many fingers of too many doctors poking around to see what was wrong. Zuckerman's energy was to be engaged for now in overcoming the long-standing addiction to the drugs and the strength-sapping trauma to the face, especially as the occlusion of the jaw wasn't exactly as it should be and there were two front teeth still to come.

"So far so good," reported Zuckerman on the subject of his habit.

"Well," Walsh replied, "we'll see when you're out from under surveillance. No armed robber breaks into a bank while still a guest of the state. That happens the week he gets sprung."

At the ground floor they left the elevator and started down the corridor to the emergency ward. "We just admitted a woman of eighty-eight. Ambulance went to get her eighty-one-year-old brother—a stroke. They took one whiff and brought her along too."

"What'd they smell?"

"You'll see."

The woman had only half a face. One cheek, up to the eye socket, and the whole side of her jaw had been eaten away by cancer. Ever since it had begun, as just a blister, four years before, she had been treating it on her own with Mercurochrome and dressing it with a bandage that she changed once a week. She lived with her brother in one room, cooked for him and cleaned for him, and no neighbor, no shopkeeper, no one who saw it had ever looked under the bandage and called a doctor. She was a slight, shy, demure, well-spoken old woman, poor but a lady, and when Zuckerman came in alongside of Walsh, she pulled her hospital nightie around her bare throat. She lowered her eyes. "How do you do, sir?"

Walsh introduced his companion. "This is Dr. Zuckerman. Our resident humanist. He'd like to take a look, Mrs. Brentford."

Zuckerman was dressed in the hospital robe and slippers and his beard was, as yet, without distinction. He lacked two front teeth and had a mouth full of metal. Yet the woman said, "Oh, yes. Thank you."

To Zuckerman, Walsh explained the case. "We've been cutting the scabs away and draining pus for an hour—all cleaned up for you, Doc." He led the resident humanist to the far side of the bed and shined a pocket light on the wound.

There was a hole in her cheek the size of a quarter.

Through it Zuckerman could see her tongue as it nervously skittered about inside her mouth. The jawbone itself was partially exposed, an inch of it as white and clean as enamel tile. The rest, up to the eye socket, was a chunk of raw flesh, something off the butcher's floor to cut up for the cat. He tried not to inhale the smell.

Out in the hallway Walsh was racked with the cough ignited by his laughter. "You look green, Doctor," he said when finally he could speak. "Maybe you're better off sticking to books."

By midmorning each day the large canvas bins along the corridor were stuffed with the night's soiled linen. Zuckerman had been eyeing these bins for weeks, each time he passed beside one tempted by the strangest yearning. It was on the morning after Walsh's caper, when there was no one anywhere nearby to ask what the hell he thought he was doing, that finally he plunged his arms down through the tangle of sheets and bed wear and towels. He never expected so much to be so damp. The strength rushed from his groin, his mouth filled with bile —it was as though he were up to his elbows in blood. It was as though the reeking flesh of Mrs. Brentford's face was there between his two hands. Down the corridor he heard a woman begin to howl, somebody's mother or sister or daughter, the cry of a survivor—"She pinched us! She hit us! The names that she called us! Then she went!" Another catastrophe—every moment, behind every wall, *right next door*, the worst ordeals that anyone could imagine, pain that was ruthless and inescapably real, crying and suffering truly worthy of all a man's defiance. He would become Mrs. Brentford's physician. He would become a maxillo-facial surgeon. He would study anesthesiology. He would run a detoxification program, setting his patients the example of his own successful withdrawal.

Until someone down the corridor shouted, "Hey, *you!* You all right?" Zuckerman remained submerged to his shoulders in the sheets of the healing, the ailing, and the dying—and of whoever had died there during the night—his hope as deep as the abiding claim of his remote but unrelinquishable home. *This is life. With real teeth in it.*

From that evening on, whenever the interns dropped by to say hello, he asked to accompany them on their rounds. In every bed the fear was different. What the doctor wanted to know the patient told him. Nobody's secret a scandal or a disgrace—everything revealed and everything at stake. And always the enemy was wicked and real. "We had to give you a little haircut to get that all cleaned out." "Oh, that's all right," the enormous baby-faced black woman replied in a small compliant voice. The intern gently turned her head. "Was it very deep, Doctor?" "We got it all," the intern told her, showing Zuckerman the long stitched-up wound under the oily dressing just behind her ear. "Nothing there to worry you anymore." "Yes? Well, that's good then." "Absolutely." "And—and am I going to see you again?" "You sure are," he said, squeezing her hand, and then he left her at peace on her pillow, with Zuckerman, the intern's intern, in tow. What a job! The paternal bond to those in duress, the urgent, immediate human exchange! All this indispensable work to be done, all this digging away at disease —and he'd given his fanatical devotion to sitting with a typewriter alone in a room!

For nearly as long as he remained a patient, Zuckerman roamed the busy corridors of the university hospital, patrolling and planning on his own by day, then out on the quiet floor with the interns at night, as though he still believed that he could unchain himself from a future as a man apart and escape the corpus that was his.

Epilogue:
The Prague Orgy

. . . from Zuckerman's notebooks

New York, Jan. 11, 1976

Your novel," he says, "is absolutely one of the five or six books of my life."

"You must assure Mr. Sisovsky," I say to his companion, "that he has flattered me enough."

"You have flattered him enough," she tells him. A woman of about forty, pale eyes, broad cheekbones, dark, severely parted hair—a distraught, arresting face. One blue vein bulges dangerously in her temple as she perches at the edge of my sofa, quite still. In black like Prince Hamlet. Signs of serious wear at the seat of the black velvet skirt of her funereal suit. Her fragrance is strong, her stockings laddered, her nerves shot.

He is younger, perhaps by ten years: thick-bodied, small, sturdy, with a broad, small-nosed face that has the ominous potency of a gloved fist. I see him lowering the brow and breaking doors down with it. Yet the longish hair is the hair of the heartthrob, heavy, silky hair of an almost Oriental darkness and sheen. He wears a gray suit, a faintly luminous fabric, the jacket tailored high under the arms and pinching a little at the shoulders. The trousers cling to a disproportionately powerful lower torso—a soccer player in long pants. His pointed white shoes are in need of repair; his white shirt is worn with the top buttons open. Something of the wastrel, something of the mobster, something too of the overprivileged boy. Where the woman's English is heavily accented, Sisovsky's is only mildly flawed, and articulated so confidently—with oddly elegant Oxonian vowels—that the occasional syntactical contusion strikes me as a form of cunning, an ironical game to remind his American host that he is, after all, only a refugee, little more than a newcomer to the tongue mastered already with so much fluency and charm. Beneath all this deference to me, I take him to be one of the strong ones, one of the stallions who has the strength of his outrage.

"Tell him to tell me about *his* book," I say to her. "What was it called?"

But on he continues about mine. "When we arrived in

Canada from Rome, yours was the first book that I bought. I have learned that it had a scandalous response here in America. When you were so kind to agree to see me, I went to the library to find out how Americans have perceived your work. The question interests me because of how Czechs perceived my own work, which also had a scandalous response."

"What was the scandal?"

"Please," he says, "I don't wish to compare our two books. Yours is a work of genius, and mine is nothing. When I studied Kafka, the fate of his books in the hands of the Kafkologists seemed to me to be more grotesque than the fate of Josef K. I feel this is true also with you. This scandalous response gives another grotesque dimension, and belongs now to your book as Kafkologine stupidities belong to Kafka. Even as the banning of my own little book creates a dimension not at all intended by me."

"Why was it banned, your book?"

"The weight of the stupidity you must carry is heavier than the weight of banning."

"Not true."

"I am afraid it is, *cher maître*. You come to belittle the meaning of your vocation. You come to believe that there is no literary culture that matters. There is a definite existential weakening of your position. This is regrettable because, in fact, you have written a masterpiece."

Yet he never says what it is about my book that he likes.

Maybe he doesn't really like it. Maybe he hasn't read it. Much subtlety in such persistence. The ruined exile will not be deflected from commiserating with the American success.

What's he want?

"But it's you," I remind him, "who's been denied the right to practice his profession. Whatever the scandal, I have been profusely—bizarrely—rewarded. Everything from an Upper East Side address to helping worthy murderers get out on parole. That's the power a scandal bestows over here. It's *you* who's been punished in the harshest way. Banning your book, prohibiting your publication, driving you from your country—what could be more burdensome and stupid than that? I'm glad you think well of my work, but don't be polite about *cher maître*'s situation, *mon cher ami*. What made what you wrote such a scandal?"

The woman says, "Zdenek, tell him."

"What is there to tell?" he says. "A satirical smile is harder for them than outright ideological fanaticism. I laughed. They are ideologues. I hate ideologues. That is what causes so much offense. It also causes my doubt."

I ask him to explain the doubt.

"I published one harmless little satire in Prague in 1967. The Russians came to visit in 1968 and I have not published anything since. There is nothing more to say. What interests me are these foolish reviews that I read in the library of your book. Not that they are foolish, that goes without saying. It is that there is not one which could be called intelligent. One reads such things in America and one is struck with terror for the future, for the world, for everything."

"Terror for the future, even for the world, I understand. But for 'everything'? Sympathize with a writer about his foolish reviews and you have a friend for life, Sisovsky, but now that this has been achieved, I'd like to hear about your doubt."

"Tell him about your *doubt*, Zdenek!"

"How can I? I don't even believe in my doubt, frankly. I don't think I have any doubt at all. But I think I should."

"Why?" I say.

"I remember the time before the invasion of Prague," he says. "I swear to you that every single review of your work could not have been published in Prague in the sixties—the level is too low. And this in spite of the fact that according to simplified notions we were a Stalinate country and the U.S.A. was the country of intellectual freedom."

"Zdenek, he wants to hear not about these reviews—he wishes to hear about your doubt!"

"Calm down," he tells her.

"The man is asking a question."

"I am answering it."

"Then do it. *Do it.* He has told you already that you have flattered him enough!" Italy, Canada, now New York—she is as sick of him as of their wandering. While he speaks her eyes momentarily close and she touches the distended vein in her temple—as though remembering yet another irreversible loss. Sisovsky drinks my whiskey, she refuses even a cup of tea. She wants to go, probably all the way back to Czechoslovakia, and probably on her own.

I intervene—before she can scream—and ask him, "Could you have stayed on in Czechoslovakia, despite the banning of your book?"

"Yes. But if I had stayed in Czechoslovakia, I am afraid I would have taken the way of resignation. I could not write, speak in public, I could not even see my friends without being taken in for interrogation. To try to do something, anything, is to endanger one's own well-being, and the well-being of one's wife and children and parents. I have a wife there. I have a child and I have an aging mother who has already been deprived of enough. You choose resignation because you realize that there is nothing to be done. There is no resistance against the Russification of my country. The fact that the occupation is hated by everyone isn't any defense in the long run. You Americans think in terms of one year or two; Russians think in centuries. They know instinctively that they live in a long time, and that the time is theirs. They know it deeply, and they are right. The truth is that as time goes by, the population slowly accepts its fate. Eight years have passed. Only writers and intellectuals continue to be persecuted, only writing and thinking are suppressed; everybody else is content, content even with their hatred of the Russians, and mostly they live better than they ever have. Modesty alone demands that we leave them be. You can't keep clamoring about being published without wondering if it is only your vanity speaking. I am not a great genius like you. People have Musil and Proust and Mann and Nathan Zuckerman to read, why should they read me? My book was a scandal not only because of my satirical smile but because in 1967 when I was published I was twenty-five. The new generation. The future. But my generation of the future has made better peace with the Russians than anyone. For me to stay in Czechoslovakia and make trouble with the Russians about my little books —why? Why is another book from me important?"

"That isn't Solzhenitsyn's point of view."

"Good for him. Why should I pay everything to try to publish another book with a satirical smile? What am I proving by fighting against them and endangering myself and everyone I know? Unfortunately, however, as much as I mistrust the way of reckless vanity, I suspect even more the way of resignation. Not for others—they do as they must—but for myself. I am not a courageous person, but I cannot be out-and-out cowardly."

"Or is that also just vanity?"

"Exactly—I am *totally* in doubt. In Czechoslovakia, if I stay there, yes, I can find some kind of work and at least live in my own country and derive some strength from that. There I can at least be a Czech—but I cannot be a writer. While in the West, I can be a writer, but not a Czech. Here, where as a writer I am totally negligible, I am *only* a writer. As I no longer have all the other things that gave meaning to life—my country, my language, friends, family, memories, et cetera—here for me making literature is everything. But the only literature I can make is so much about life there that only there can it have the effect I desire."

"So, what's even heavier than the weight of the banning is this doubt that it foments."

"In me. Only in me. Eva has no doubt. She has only hatred."

Eva is astonished. "Hatred for what?"

"For everyone who has betrayed you," he says to her. "For everyone who deserted you. You hate them and wish they were dead."

"I don't even think of them anymore."

"You wish them to be tortured in Hell."

"I have forgotten them completely."

"I should like to tell you about Eva Kalinova," he says to me. "It is too vulgar to announce such a thing, but it is too ridiculous for you not to know. It is personally humiliating that I should ask you to endure the great drama of my doubt while Eva sits here like no one."

"I am happy to be sitting like no one," she says. "This is not necessary."

"Eva," he says, "is Prague's great Chekhovian actress. Go to Prague and ask. No one there will dispute it, not even the regime. There is no Nina since hers, no Irina, no Masha."

"I don't want this," she says.

"When Eva gets on the streetcar in Prague, people still applaud. All of Prague has been in love with her since she was eighteen."

"Is that why they write on my wall 'the Jew's whore'? Because they are in love with me? Don't be stupid. That is over."

"Soon she will be acting again," he assures me.

"To be an actress in America, you must speak English that does not give people a headache!"

"Eva, sit down."

But her career is finished. She cannot sit.

"You cannot be on the stage and speak English that nobody can understand! Nobody will hire you to do that. I do not want to perform in more plays—I have had enough of being an artificial person. I am tired of imitating all the touching Irinas and Ninas and Mashas and Sashas. It confuses me and it confuses everyone else. We are people who fantasize too much to begin with. We read too much, we feel too much, we fantasize too much —we want all the wrong things! I am *glad* to be finished with all my successes. The success comes to the person anyway, not to the acting. What good does it do? What does it serve? Only egomania. Brezhnev has given me a chance to be an ordinary nobody who performs a real job. I sell dresses—and dresses are needed more by people than stupid touching Chekhovian actresses!"

"But what," I ask, "do Chekhovian actresses need?"

"To be in the life of others the way they are in a play,

and not in a play the way they are supposed to be in the life of others! They need to be rid of their selfishness and their feelings and their looks and their art!" Beginning to cry, she says, "At last I am rid of mine!"

"Eva, tell him about your Jewish demons. He is the American authority on Jewish demons. She is pursued, Mr. Zuckerman, by Jewish demons. Eva, you must tell him about the Vice-Minister of Culture and what happened with him after you left your husband. Eva was married to somebody that in America you have never heard of, but in Czechoslovakia the whole country loves him. He is a very beloved theatrical personality. You can watch him on television every week. He has all the old mothers crying when he sings Moravian folk songs. When he talks to them with that dreadful voice, the girls are all swooning. You hear him on the jukeboxes, you hear him on the radio, wherever you go you hear this dreadful voice that is supposed to be a hot-blooded gypsy. If you are that man's wife you don't have to worry. You can play all the great heroines at the National Theater. You can have plenty of room to live. You can take all the trips you want abroad. If you are that man's wife, they leave you alone."

"He leaves you alone too," she says. "Zdenek, why do you persecute me? I do not care to be an ironical Czech character in an ironical Czech story. Everything that happens in Czechoslovakia, they shrug their shoulders and say, 'Pure Schweik, pure Kafka.' I am sick of them both."

"Tell me about your Jewish demons," I say.

"I don't have them," she replies, looking furiously at Sisovsky.

"Eva fell in love with a Mr. Polak and left her husband for him. Now, if you are Mr. Polak's mistress," Sisovsky says, "they do not leave you alone. Mr. Polak has had many mistresses and they have never left any of them alone. Eva Kalinova is married to a Czechoslovak Artist of Merit, but she leaves him to take up with a Zionist agent and bourgeois enemy of the people. And this is why they write 'the Jew's whore' on the wall outside the theater, and send poems to her in the mail about her immorality, and drawings of Polak with a big Jewish nose. This is why they write letters to the Minister of Culture denouncing her and demanding that she be removed from the stage. This is why she is called in to see the Vice-Minister of Culture. Leaving a great Artist of Merit and a boring, sentimental egomaniac like Petr Kalina for a Jew and a parasite like Pavel Polak, she is no better than a Jew herself."

"Please," says Eva, "stop telling this story. All these people, they suffer for their ideas and for their banned books, and for democracy to return to Czechoslovakia— they suffer for their principles, for their humanity, for their hatred of the Russians, and in this terrible story I am still suffering for love!"

" 'Do you know,' he says to her, our enlightened Vice-Minister of Culture, 'do you know, Madam Kalinova,' " Sisovsky continues, " 'that half our countrymen believe you

really are a Jewess, by blood?' Eva says to him, very dryly
—for Eva can be a very dry, very beautiful, very intelligent
woman when she is not angry with people or frightened
out of her wits—very dryly she says, 'My dear Mr. Vice-
Minister, my family was being persecuted as Protestants in
Bohemia in the sixteenth century.' But this does not stop
him—he knows this already. He says to her, 'Tell me—why
did you play the role of the Jewess Anne Frank on the
stage when you were only nineteen years old?' Eva answers, 'I played the role because I was chosen from ten
young actresses. And all of them wanted it more than
the world.' 'Young actresses,' he asks her, 'or young
Jewesses?' "

"I beg you, Zdenek, I cannot hear my ridiculous story!
I cannot hear *your* ridiculous story! I am sick and tired
of hearing our story, I am sick and tired of *having* our
story! That was Europe, this is America! I shudder to
think I was ever that woman!"

" 'Young actresses,' he asks her, 'or young Jewesses?'
Eva says, 'What difference does that make? Some were
Jewish, I suppose. But I am not.' 'Well then,' he says to
Eva, 'why did you want to continue playing this Jewess
on the stage for two years, if you weren't, at the least, a
Zionist sympathizer even then?' Eva replies, 'I have played
a Jewess in *Ivanov* by Anton Chekhov. I have played a
Jewess in *The Merchant of Venice* by Shakespeare.' This
convinces him of nothing. That Eva had wanted to play
a Jewess even in a play by Anton Chekhov, where you

have to look for one high and low, does not, in the opinion of the vice-minister, strengthen her position. 'But everybody understands,' Eva explains to him, '. . . these are only *roles*. If half the country thinks I'm a Jew, that does not make it so. They once said I was part gypsy too; probably there are as many people who still believe that because of the ridiculous film I made with Petr. But, Mr. Vice-Minister,' Eva says, 'what everybody knows, what is true and indisputable, is that I am none of these things: *I am an actress.*' He corrects her. 'An actress, Madam Kalinova, who likes to portray Jewesses, who portrays them masterfully—*that* is what everyone knows. What everyone knows is that no one in all of our country can portray a Jewess better.' 'And if that is even true? Is that also a crime in this country now?' By then Eva is shouting and, of course, she is crying. She is shaking all over. And this makes him nice to her suddenly, certainly nicer than before. He offers brandy to calm her down. He explains that he is not talking about what is the law. He is not even speaking for himself. His heart happens to have been greatly moved in 1956 when he saw Eva playing little Anne Frank. He wept at her performance—he has never forgotten it. His confession causes Eva to become completely crazy. 'Then what are you talking about?' she asks him. 'The feelings of the people,' he replies. 'The sentiments of the great Czech people. To desert Petr Kalina, an Artist of Merit, to become the mistress of the Zionist Polak would have been damaging enough, but to the people it is unforgivable because of your long history of always playing Jewesses on the stage.' 'This makes no sense,' Eva tells him. 'It cannot be. The Czech people loved Anne Frank, they loved *me* for portraying her!' Here he removes from his file all these fake letters by all the offended members of the theatergoing public—fake, just like the writing on the theater walls. This closes the case. Eva is dismissed from the National Theater. The vice-minister is so pleased with himself that he goes around boasting how he handled Polak's whore and made that arrogant Jew bastard know just who is running this country. He believes that when the news reaches Moscow, the Russians will give him a medal for his cruelty and his anti-Semitism. They have a gold medal just for this. But instead he loses his job. The last I heard he was assistant editor of the publishing house of religious literature. Because the Czechs *did* love Anne Frank—and because somebody high up wants to be rid of the stupid vice-minister anyway—he is fired for how he has handled Eva Kalinova. Of course for Eva it would have been better if instead of firing the vice-minister they would restore her position as leading actress with the National Theater. But our system of justice is not yet so developed. It is stronger on punishment than on restitution."

"They are strong on *nothing*," says Eva. "It is that I am so weak. That I am stupid and cannot defend myself against all of these bullies! I cry, I shake, I cave in. I *deserve* what they do. In this world, still to carry on about a man! They should have cut my head off. *That* would have been justice!"

"And now," says Sisovsky, "she is with another Jew. At her age. Now Eva is ruined completely."

She erupts in Czech, he replies in English. "On Sunday," he says to her, "what will you do at home? Have a drink, Eviczka. Have some whiskey. Try to enjoy life."

Again, in Czech, she pleads with him, or berates him, or berates herself. In English, and again most gently, he says, "I understand. But *Zuckerman* is interested."

"I am going!" she tells me—"I must go!" and rushes from the living room.

"Well, I stay . . ." he mutters and empties his glass. Before I can get up to show her out, the door to my apartment is opened and slammed shut.

"Since you are curious," says Sisovsky, while I pour him another drink, "she said that she is going home and I said what will you do at home and she said, 'I am sick of your mind and I am sick of my body and I am sick to death of these boring stories!' "

"She wants to hear a new story."

"What she wants is to hear a new man. Today she is angry because she says I bring her here with me only to show her to you. What am I to do—leave her alone in our room to hang herself? On a Sunday? Wherever we go now in New York and there is a man, she accuses me of this. 'What is the function of this man?' she says. There are dramatic scenes where she calls me a pimp. I am the pimp because she wants to leave me and is afraid to leave me because in New York she is nobody and alone."

"And she can't go back to Prague?"

"It is better for her not to be Eva Kalinova here than not to be Eva Kalinova there. In Prague, Eva would go out of her mind when she saw who they had cast to play Madam Arkadina."

"But here she's out of her mind selling dresses."

"No," he says. "The problem is not dresses. It's Sundays. Sunday is not the best day in the émigré's week."

"Why did they let the two of you go?"

"The latest thing is to let people go, people who want to leave the country. Those who don't want to leave, they must keep silent. And those who don't want to leave, and who don't wish to keep silent, they finish up in jail."

"I didn't realize, Sisovsky, that on top of everything else you were Jewish."

"I resemble my mother, who was not. My father was the Jew. Not only a Jew, but like you, a Jew writing about Jews; like you, Semite-obsessed all his life. He wrote hundreds of stories about Jews, only he did not publish one. My father was an introverted man. He taught mathematics in the high school in our provincial town. The writing was for himself. Do you know Yiddish?"

"I am a Jew whose language is English."

"My father's stories were in Yiddish. To read the stories, I taught myself Yiddish. I cannot speak. I never had him to speak it to. He died in 1941. Before the Jews began even to be deported, a Nazi came to our house and shot him."

"Why him?"

"Since Eva is no longer here, I can tell you. It's another of my boring European stories. One of her favorites. In our town there was a Gestapo officer who loved to play chess. After the occupation began, he found out that my father was the chess master of the region, and so he had him to his house every night. My father was horribly shy of people, even of his students. But because he believed that my mother and my brother would be protected if he was courteous with the officer, he went whenever he was called. And they *were* protected. All the Jews in the town were huddled into the Jewish quarter. For the others things got a little worse every day, but not for my family. For more than a year nobody bothered them. My father could no longer teach at the high school, but he was now allowed to go around as a private tutor to earn some money. At night, after our dinner, he would leave the Jewish quarter and go to play chess with the Gestapo officer. Well, stationed in the town there was another Gestapo officer. He had a Jewish dentist whom *he* was protecting. The dentist was fixing all his teeth for him. His family too was left alone, and the dentist was allowed to continue with his practice. One Sunday, a Sunday probably much like today, the two Gestapo officers went out drinking together and they got drunk, much the way, thanks to your hospitality, we are getting nicely drunk here. They had an argument. They were good friends, so it must have been a terrible argument, because the one who played chess with my father was so angry that he walked over to the dentist's house and got the dentist out of bed and shot him. This enraged the other Nazi so much that the next morning he came to our house and he shot my father, and my brother also, who was eight. When he was taken before the German commandant, my father's murderer explained, 'He shot my Jew, so I shot his.' 'But why did you shoot the child?' 'That's how God-damn angry I was, sir.' They were reprimanded and told not to do it again. That was all. But even that reprimand was something. There was no law in those days against shooting Jews in their houses, or even on the street."

"And your mother?"

"My mother hid on a farm. There I was born, two months later. Neither of us looks like my father. Neither did my brother, but his short life was just bad luck. We two survived."

"And why did your father, with an Aryan wife, write stories in Yiddish? Why not in Czech? He must have spoken Czech to the students at the high school."

"Czech was for Czechs to write. He married my mother, but he never thought he was a real Czech. A Jew who marries a Jew is able at home to forget he's a Jew. A Jew who marries an Aryan like my mother has her face there always to remind him."

"He didn't ever write in German?"

"We were not Sudeten Germans, you see, and we were not Prague Jews. Of course German was less foreign to him than Czech, because of Yiddish. German he insisted on for my brother to be properly educated. He himself read Lessing, Herder, Goethe, and Schiller, but his own father had been, not even a town Jew like him, he had been a Jew in the farmlands, a village shopkeeper. To the Czechs such Jews spoke Czech, but in the family they spoke only Yiddish. All of this is in my father's stories: homelessness beyond homelessness. One story is called 'Mother Tongue.' Three pages only, about a little Jewish boy who speaks bookish German, Czech without the native flavor, and the Yiddish of people simpler than himself. Kafka's homelessness, if I may say so, was nothing beside my father's. Kafka had at least the nineteenth century in his blood—all those Prague Jews did. Kafka belonged to literature, if nothing else. My father belonged to nothing. If he had lived, I think that I would have developed a great antagonism to my father. I would have thought, 'What is this man so lonely for? Why is he so sad and withdrawn? He should join the revolution—then he would not sit with his head in his hands, wondering where he belongs.'"

"Sons are famous the world over for generous thoughts about fathers."

"When I came to New York and wrote my letter to you, I said to Eva, 'I am a relative of this great man.' I was thinking of my father and his stories. Since we have come from Europe, I have already read fifty American novels about Jews. In Prague I knew nothing about this incredible phenomenon and how vast it was. Between the wars in Czechoslovakia my father was a freak. Even had he wished to publish his stories, where would they have appeared? Even if he had published all two hundred of them, no one would have paid attention—not to that subject. But in America my father would have been a celebrated writer. Had he emigrated before I was born, had he come to New York City in his thirties, he would have been discovered by some helpful person and published in the best magazines. He would be something more now than just another murdered Jew. For years I never thought of my father, now every minute I wonder what he would make of the America I am seeing. I wonder what America would have made of him. He would be seventy-two. I am obsessed now with this great Jewish writer that might have been."

"His stories are that good?"

"I am not exaggerating his excellence. He was a deep and wonderful writer."

"Like whom? Sholem Aleichem? Isaac Babel?"

"I can tell you only that he was elliptical, humble, self-conscious, all in his own way. He could be passionate, he could be florid, he could be erudite—he could be anything. No, this is not the Yiddish of Sholem Aleichem. This is the Yiddish of Flaubert. His last work, ten little stories about Nazis and Jews, the saddest commentary I have

ever read about the worst life has to offer. They are about
the family of the Nazi commandant he played chess with
at night. About his visits to the house and how charmed
they all were. He called them 'Stories about Chess.' "

"What became of those stories?"

"They are with my books in Prague. And my books in
Prague are with my wife. And my wife does not like me
so much anymore. She has become a drunk because of me.
Our daughter has become crazy because of me and lives
with her aunt because of me. The police will not leave my
wife alone because of me. I don't think I'll ever see my
father's stories again. My mother goes to ask my wife for
her husband's stories and my wife recounts for her all of
my infidelities. She shows my mother photographs of all
my mistresses, unclothed. These too I unfortunately left
behind with my books."

"Will she destroy your father's stories?"

"No, no. She couldn't do it. Olga is a writer too. In
Czechoslovakia she is very well known for her writing,
for her drinking, and for showing everybody her cunt.
You would like Olga. She was once very beautiful, with
beautiful long legs and gray cat-eyes and her books were
once beautiful too. She is a most compliant woman. It is
I alone whom she opposes. Anything another man wants,
Olga will do it. She will do it well. If you were to visit
Prague, and you were to meet Olga and Olga were to fall
in love with you, she would even give you my father's
stories, if you were to go about it the right way. She loves

love. She does anything for love. An American writer, a famous, attractive, American genius who does not practice the American innocence to a shameless degree—if he were to ask for my father's stories, Olga would give them to him, I am sure of it. The only thing is not to lay her too soon."

Prague, Feb. 4, 1976

At Klenek's every Tuesday night, with or without Klenek in residence, there is a wonderful party to go to. Klenek is currently directing a film in France. Because he is technically still married to a German baroness, he is by Czech law allowed to leave the country half of each year, ostensibly to be with her. The Czech film industry is no longer open to him, but he continues to live in his palazzo and is permitted to associate with his old friends, many of whom the regime now honors as its leading enemies. No one is sure why he is privileged—perhaps because Klenek is useful propaganda, somebody the regime can hold up to its foreign critics as an artist who lives as he wishes. Also, by letting him work abroad, they can continue to tax his large foreign earnings. And, explains Bolotka, Klenek may well be a spy. "Probably he tells them things," says Bolotka. "Not that it matters. Nobody tells him anything, and he knows nobody tells him anything, and they know nobody tells him anything."

"What's the point then?"

"With Klenek the point is to spy not on politics but on sex. The house is bugged everywhere. The secret police listen to the tape recordings of Klenek's parties. They prowl outside and look in the windows. It's their job. Sometimes they even see something and get excited. This is a pleasant distraction from the pettiness and viciousness of their regular work. It does them good. It does everybody good. Fifteen-year-old girls come to Klenek's. They dress up like streetwalkers and come from as far away as a hundred miles. Everybody, even schoolchildren, is looking for fun. You like orgies, you come with me. Since the Russians, the best orgies in Europe are in Czechoslovakia. Less liberty, better fucks. You can do whatever you want at Klenek's. No drugs, but plenty of whiskey. You can fuck, you can masturbate, you can look at dirty pictures, you can look at yourself in the mirror, you can do nothing. All the best people are there. Also the worst. We are all comrades now. Come to the orgy, Zuckerman—you will see the final stage of the revolution."

Klenek's is a small seventeenth-century palazzo on the Kampa, a little residential island we reach by descending a long wet stairway from the Charles Bridge. Standing in the cobbled square outside of Klenek's, I hear the Vltava churning past the deep stone embankment. I've walked with Bolotka from my hotel through the maze of the ghetto, passing on the way the capsized tombstones of what he informs me is the oldest Jewish cemetery left in Europe. Within the iron grating, the jumble of crooked, eroded markers looks less like a place of eternal rest than something a cyclone has torn apart. Twelve thousand Jews buried in layers in what in New York would be a small parking lot. Drizzle dampening the tombstones, ravens in the trees.

Klenek's: large older women in dark rayon raincoats, young pretty women with jewels and long dresses, stout middle-aged men dressed in boxy suits and looking like postal clerks, elderly men with white hair, a few slight young men in American jeans—but no fifteen-year-old girls. Bolotka may be having some fun exaggerating for his visitor the depths of Prague depravity—a little cold water on free-world fantasies of virtuous political suffering.

Beside me on a sofa, Bolotka explains who is who and who likes what.

"That one was a journalist till they fired him. He loves pornography. I saw him with my eyes fucking a girl from behind and reading a dirty book at the same time. That one, he is a terrible abstract painter. The best abstract painting he did was the day the Russians came. He went out and painted over all the street signs so the tanks wouldn't know where they were. He has the longest prick in Prague. That one, the little clerk, that is Mr. Vodicka.

He is a very good writer, an excellent writer, but everything scares him. If he sees a petition, he passes out. When you bring him to life again, he says he will sign it: he has ninety-eight percent reason to sign, and only two percent reason not to sign, and he has only to think about the two percent and he will sign. By the next day the two percent has grown to one hundred percent. Just this week Mr. Vodicka told the government that if he made bad politics he is sorry. He is hoping this way they will let him write again about his perversion."

"Will they?"

"Of course not. They will tell him now to write a historical novel about Pilsen beer."

We are joined by a tall, slender woman, distinguished by a mass of hair dyed the color of a new penny and twisted down over her forehead in curls. Heavy white makeup encases her sharp, birdlike face. Her eyes are gray cat-eyes, her smile is beckoning. "I know who you are," she whispers to me.

"And you are who?"

"I don't know. I don't even feel I exist." To Bolotka: "Do I exist?"

"This one is Olga," Bolotka says. "She has the best legs in Prague. She is showing them to you. Otherwise she does not exist."

Mr. Vodicka approaches Olga, bows like a courtier, and takes her hand. He is a little, unobtrusive man of sixty, neatly dressed and wearing heavy spectacles. Olga pays him no attention.

"My lover wants to kill me," she says to me.

Mr. Vodicka is whispering in her ear. She waves him away, but passionately he presses her hand to his cheek.

"He wants to know if she has any boys for him," Bolotka explains.

"Who is she?"

"She was the most famous woman in the country. Olga wrote our love stories. A man stood her up in a restaurant and she wrote a love story, and the whole country talked about why he stood her up. She had an abortion and she told the doctor it could be one of eleven men, and the whole country debated whether it could actually be so many. She went to bed with a woman and the whole country read the story and was guessing who it was. She was seventeen, she already wrote a bestseller, *Touha.* Longing. Our Olga loves most the absent thing. She loves the Bohemian countryside. She loves her childhood. But always something is missing. Olga suffers the madness that follows after loss. And this even *before* the Russians. Klenek saw her in a café, a tall country girl, her heart full of *touha,* and he took her here to live with him. This is over twenty years ago. For seven years Olga was married. She had a child. Poor child. Now her husband runs off with the other famous woman in our country, a beautiful Czech actress who he will destroy in America, and Olga, Klenek looks after."

"Why does she need looking after?"

"Why do you need looking after?" Bolotka asks her.

"This is awful," she says. "I hear stories about myself tonight. Stories about who I fuck. I would never fuck such people."

"Why do you need looking after, Olga?" Bolotka asks again.

"Because I'm shaking. Feel me shaking. I never stop shaking. I am frightened of everything." Points to me. "I am frightened of him." She flops down onto the sofa, in the space between Bolotka and me. I feel pressing against mine the best legs in Prague. Also believe I feel the *touha*.

"You don't act frightened," I say.

"Since I am frightened of everything it is as well to go in one direction as the other. If I get into too much trouble, you will come and marry me and take me to America. I will telegram and you will come and save me." She says to Bolotka, "Do you know what Mr. Vodicka wants now? He has a boy who has never seen a woman. He wants me to show it to him. He is going into the street to get him." Then, to me: "Why are you in Prague? Are you looking for Kafka? The intellectuals all come here looking for Kafka. Kafka is dead. They should be looking for Olga. Are you planning to make love to anybody in Prague? If so, you will let me know." To Bolotka: "Kouba. There is Kouba! I cannot be in this house with that Kouba!" To me: "You want to know why I need looking after? *Because of stupid communists like Kouba!*" She points to a short man with a bald head who is animatedly entertaining a circle of friends in the center of the milling crowd. "Kouba knew what the good life was for all of us. It has taken the Koubas twenty years to learn, and they're *still* too stupid to learn. All brains and no intelligence. *None*. Kouba is one of our great communist heroes. It is surprising he is still in Prague. Not all of our great communist heroes who were in Italy with their girl friends when the Russians invaded have bothered to come back from their holiday yet. Do you know why? Because when the Russians occupied Prague, at last they were free of their wives. Some of our greatest communist heroes are now with their girl friends teaching Marxism-Leninism in New York. They are only sorry that the revolution fell into the wrong hands. Otherwise they are like Kouba—still one hundred percent sure they are right. So why do you come to Prague? You are not looking for Kafka, none of our heroes in New York sent you, and you don't want to fuck. I love this word fuck. Why don't we have this word, Rudolf?" To me again: "Teach me how to say fuck. This is a good fucking party. I was really fucked. Wonderful word. Teach me."

"Shut the fuck up."

"Beautiful word. Shut the fuck up. More."

"Fuck it all. Fuck everything."

"Yes, fuck it all. Fuck everything and fuck everybody. Fuck the world till it cannot fuck me anymore. See, I learn fast. In America I would be a famous writer like you. You are afraid to fuck me. Why is that? Why do you write this book about fucking that makes you so famous if you are afraid to fuck somebody? You hate fucking everybody or just me?"

"Everybody."

"He is kind to you, Olga," Bolotka says. "He is a gentleman, so he doesn't tell you the truth because you are so hopeless."

"Why am I hopeless?"

"Because in America the girls don't talk to him like this."

"What do they say in America? Teach me to be an American girl."

"First you would take your hand off my prick."

"I see. Okay. Now what?"

"We would talk to each other. We would try to get to know each other first."

"Why? I don't understand this. Talk about what? The Indians?"

"Yes, we would talk at length about the Indians."

"And *then* I put my hand on your prick."

"That's right."

"And then you fuck me."

"That would be the way we would do it, yes."

"It is a very strange country."

"It's one of them."

Mr. Vodicka, pink with excitement, is dragging the boy through the room. Everything excites Mr. Vodicka: Olga

dismissing him like a bothersome child, Bolotka addressing him like a whipped dog, the indifferent boy weary
already of being so cravenly desired. The stage-set splendors of Klenek's drawing room—velvet burgundy draper-
ies, massive carved antiques, threadbare Oriental carpets,
tiers of dark romantic landscapes leaning from the paneled
oak walls—evoke no more from the boy than a mean little
smirk. Been everywhere already, seen the best in brothels
by the time he was twelve.

Mr. Vodicka is fastidious with the introductions.
Bolotka translates. "He is saying to Olga that the boy has
never seen a woman. That's how Mr. Vodicka has got him
in from the street. He promised he would show him one.
He is telling Olga that she has to show it to him, otherwise the boy will go."

"What do you do now?" I ask Olga.

"What I do? I show it to him. I have you to fuck me.
Mr. Vodicka has only dreams to fuck. He is more frightened of everything than I am."

"You're doing it out of sentiment."

Placing my hands over her breasts, Olga says, "If it
weren't for sentiment, Zuckerman, one person would not
pass another person a glass of water."

Czech exchange. Bolotka translates.

Olga says to Mr. V., "First I want to see his."

The boy won't hear of it. Plump, smooth, dark, and
cruel: a very creamy caramel dessert.

Olga waves her hand. The hell with it, get out, go.

"Why do you want to see it?" I ask her.

"I don't. I have seen too many already. Mr. Vodicka wants to see it."

For five minutes she addresses the boy in the softest, most caressing Czech, until, at last, he shuffles childishly toward the sofa and, frowning at the ceiling, undoes his zipper. Olga summons him one step closer and then, with two fingers and a thumb, reaches delicately into his trousers. The boy yawns. She withdraws his penis. Mr. Vodicka looks. We all look. Light entertainment in occupied Prague.

"Now," says Olga, "they will put on television a photograph of me with his prick. Everywhere in this house there are cameras. On the street someone is always snapping my picture. Half the country is employed spying on the other half. I am a rotten degenerate bourgeois negativist pseudo-artist—and this will prove it. This is how they destroy me."

"Why do you do it then?"

"It is too silly not to." In English she says to Mr. V., "Come, I'll show it to him." She zips the boy up and leads him away, Mr. Vodicka eagerly following.

"*Are* cameras hidden here?" I ask Bolotka.

"Klenek says no, only microphones. Maybe there are cameras in the bedrooms, for the fucking. But you go on the floor and turn the light out. Don't worry. Don't be scared. You want to fuck her, fuck her on the floor. Nobody would take your picture there."

"Who is the lover who wants to kill her?"

"Don't be afraid of him; he won't kill her or you either. He doesn't even want to see her. One night Olga is drunk and angry because he is tired of her, and she finds out he has a new girl friend, so she telephones the police and she tells them that he has threatened to murder her. The police come, and by then the joke is over and he is undressed and sorry about the new girl friend. But the police are also drunk, so they take him away. The whole country is drunk. Our president must go on television for three hours to tell the people to stop drinking and go back to work. You get onto a streetcar at night when the great working class is on its way home, and the great working class smells like a brewery."

"What happened to Olga's lover?"

"He has a note from a doctor saying he is a psychiatric case."

"Is he?"

"He carries the note to be left alone. They leave you alone if you can prove you are crazy. He is a perfectly reasonable person: he is interested in fucking women and writing poems, and not in stupid politics. This proves he is *not* crazy. But the police come and they read the note and they take him to the lunatic asylum. He is still there. Olga thinks now he will kill her because of what she did. But he is happy where he is. In the lunatic asylum he is not required to be a worker all day in the railway office. There he has some peace and quiet and at last he writes something again. There he has the whole day to write poems instead of railroad tickets."

"How do you all live like this?"

"Human adaptability is a great blessing."

Olga, who has returned, sits herself on my lap.

"Where is Mr. Vodicka?" I ask her.

"He stays in the loo with the boy."

"What did you do to them, Olga?" Bolotka asks.

"I did nothing. When I showed it to him, the boy screamed. I took down my pants and he screamed, 'It's awful.' But Mr. Vodicka was bending over, with his hands on his knees, and studying me through his thick glasses. Maybe he wants to write about something new. He is studying me through his glasses, and then he says to the boy, 'Oh, I don't know, my friend—it's not our cup of tea, but from an aesthetic point of view it's not *horrible*.'"

Ten-thirty. I am to meet Hos and Hoffman in a wine bar at eleven. Everyone believes I am visiting Prague to commiserate with their proscribed writers when in fact I am here to strike a deal with the woman full of *touha* on my lap.

"You have to get up, Olga. I'm going."

"I come with you."

"You must have patience," Bolotka says to me. "Ours is a small country. We do not have so many millions of fifteen-year-old girls. But if you will have patience, she will come. And she will be worth it. The little Czech dumpling that we all like to eat. What is your hurry? What are you afraid of? You see—nothing happens. You do whatever you want in Prague and nobody cares. You cannot have such freedom in New York."

"He does not want a girl of fifteen," says Olga. "They are old whores by now, those little girls. He wants one who is forty."

I slide Olga off my lap and stand up to leave.

"Why do you act like this?" Olga asks. "You come all the way to Czechoslovakia and then you act like this. I will never see you again."

"Yes you will."

"You are lying. You will go back to those American girls and talk about Indians and fuck them. Next time you will tell me before, and I will study my Indian tribes and then we will fuck."

"Have lunch with me tomorrow, Olga. I'll pick you up here."

"But what about *tonight*? Why don't you fuck me *now*? Why are you leaving me, if you like me? I don't understand these American writers."

Neither, if they could see me, would my American readers. I am not fucking everyone, or indeed anyone, but sit quietly on the sofa being polite. I am a dignified, well-behaved, reliable spectator, secure, urbane, calm, polite, the quiet respectable one who does not take his trousers off, and *these* are the menacing writers. All the treats and blandishments, all the spoils that spoil are mine, and yet what a witty, stylish comedy of manners these have-nots of Prague make out of their unbearable condition, this crushing business of being completely balked and walking the treadmill of humiliation. They, silenced, are all mouth. I am only ears—and plans, an American gentleman abroad, with the bracing if old-fashioned illusion that he is playing a worthwhile, dignified, and honorable role.

Bolotka offers Olga a comforting explanation for why she is no longer in my lap. "He is a middle-class boy. Leave him alone."

"But this is a classless society," she says. "This is socialism. What good is socialism if when I want to nobody will fuck me? All the great international figures come to Prague to see our oppression, but none of them will ever fuck me. Why is that? Sartre was here and he would not fuck me. Simone de Beauvoir came with him and she would not fuck me. Heinrich Böll, Carlos Fuentes, Graham Greene—and none of them will fuck me. Now you, and it is the same thing. You think to sign a petition will save Czechoslovakia, *but what will save Czechoslovakia would be to fuck Olga.*"

"Olga is drunk," Bolotka says.

"She's also crying," I point out.

"Don't worry about her," Bolotka says. "This is just Olga."

"Now," says Olga, "they will interrogate me about you. For six hours they will interrogate me about you, and I won't even be able to tell them we fucked."

"Is that what happens?" I ask Bolotka.

"Their interrogations are not to be dramatized," he says. "It is routine work. Whenever someone is questioned by Czech police he is questioned about everything that he can be asked. They are interested in everything. Now they are interested in you, but it does not mean that to be in touch with you could compromise anybody and that the police could accuse people who are in touch with you. They don't need that to accuse people. If they want to accuse you, they accuse you, and they don't need anything. If they interrogate me about why you came to Czechoslovakia, I will tell them."

"Yes? What will you say?"

"I will tell them you came for the fifteen-year-old girls. I will say, 'Read his book and you will see why he came.' Olga will be all right. In a couple of weeks Klenek returns home and Olga will be fine. You don't have to bother to fuck her tonight. Someone will do it, don't worry."

"I will *not* be all right," Olga cries. "Marry me and take me away from here. Zuckerman, if you marry me, they must let me go. That is the law—even *they* obey it. You wouldn't have to fuck me. You could fuck the American girls. You wouldn't have to love me, or even give me money."

"And she would scrub your floors," says Bolotka, "and iron your beautiful shirts. Wouldn't you, Olga?"

"Yes! Yes! I would iron your shirts all day long."

"That would be the first week," Bolotka says. "Then

would begin the second week and the excitement of being Mr. Olga."

"That isn't true," she says, "I would leave him alone."

"Then would begin the vodka," Bolotka says. "Then would begin the adventures."

"Not in America," weeps Olga.

"Oh," says Bolotka, "you would not be homesick for Prague in New York City?"

"No!"

"Olga, in America you would shoot yourself."

"I will shoot myself *here*!"

"With what?" asks Bolotka.

"A tank! Tonight! I will steal a Russian tank and I will shoot myself with it tonight!"

Bolotka occupies a dank room at the top of a bleak stairwell on a street of tenements near the outskirts of Prague. I visited him there earlier in the day. He reassures me, when he observes me looking sadly around, that I shouldn't feel too bad about his standard of living—this was his hideaway from his wife long before his theater was disbanded and he was forbidden to produce his "decadent" revues. For a man of his predilections it really is the *best* place to live. "It excites young girls," Bolotka informs me, "to be fucked in squalor." He is intrigued by my herringbone tweed suit and asks to try it on to see how it feels to be a rich American writer. He is a stoop-shouldered man, large and shambling, with a wide Mongol face, badly pitted skin, and razor-blade eyes, eyes like rifts in the bone of his skull, slitted green eyes whose manifesto is "You will jam nothing bogus into this brain." He has a wife somewhere, even children; recently the wife's arm was broken when she tried to prevent the police from entering their apartment to impound her absentee husband's several thousand books.

"Why does she care so much about you?"

"She doesn't—she hates me. But she hates them more. Old married couples in Prague have something to hate now even more than each other."

A month earlier the police came to the door of Bolotka's hole at the top of the stairwell to inform him that the country's leading troublemakers were being given papers to leave. They would allow him forty-eight hours to get out.

"I said to them, 'Why don't *you* leave? That would amount to the same thing, you know. I give *you* forty-eight hours.'"

But would he *not* be better off in Paris, or across the border in Vienna, where he has a reputation as a theatrical innovator and could resume his career?

"I have sixteen girl friends in Prague," he replies. "How can I leave?"

I am handed his robe to keep myself warm while he undresses and gets into my suit. "You look even more like a gorilla," I say, when he stands to model himself in my clothes.

"And even in my disgraceful dressing gown," he says, "you look like a happy, healthy, carefree impostor."

Bolotka's story.

"I was nineteen years old, I was a student at the university. I wanted like my father to be a lawyer. But after one year I decide I must quit and enroll at the School of Fine Arts. Of course I have first to go for an interview. This is 1950. Probably I would have to go to fifty interviews, but I only got to number one. I went in and they took out my 'record.' It was a foot thick. I said to them, 'How can it be a foot thick, I haven't lived yet. I have had no life—how can you have all this information?' But they don't explain. I sit there and they look it over and they say I cannot quit. The workers' money is being spent on my education. The workers have invested a year in my future as a lawyer. The workers have not made this investment so I can change my mind and decide to become a fine artist. They tell me that I cannot matriculate at the School of Fine Arts, or anywhere ever again, and so I said okay and went home. I didn't care that much. It wasn't so bad. I didn't have to become a lawyer, I had some girl friends, I had my prick, I had books, and to talk to and to keep me company, I had my childhood friend Blecha. Only they had him to talk with too. Blecha was planning then to be a famous poet and a famous novelist and a famous playwright. One night he got drunk and he admitted to me that he was spying on me. They knew he was an old friend and they knew that he wrote, and they

knew he came to see me, so they hired him to spy on me
and to write a report once a week. But he was a terrible
writer. He is still a terrible writer. They told him that
when they read his reports they could make no sense of
them. They told him everything he wrote about me is
unbelievable. So I said, 'Blecha, don't be depressed, let me
see the reports—probably they are not as bad as they say.
What do they know?' But they *were* terrible. He missed
the point of everything I said, he got everything backwards about when I went where, and the writing was a
disgrace. Blecha was afraid they were going to fire him—
he was afraid they might even suspect him of playing
some kind of trick, out of loyalty to me. And if that
went into *his* record, he would be damaged for the rest
of his life. Besides, all the time he should be spending
on his poems and his stories and his plays, he was spending listening to me. He was getting nothing accomplished for himself. He was full of sadness over this. He
had thought he could just betray a few hours a day and
otherwise get on with being National Artist, Artist of
Merit, and winner of the State Award for Outstanding
Work. Well, it was obvious what to do. I said, 'Blecha, I
will follow myself for you. I know what I do all day better than you, and I have nothing else to keep me busy. I
will spy on myself and I will write it up, and you can
submit it to them as your own. They will wonder how
your rotten writing has improved overnight, but you just
tell them you were sick. This way you won't have any-

thing damaging on your record, and I can be rid of your company, you shitface.' Blecha was thrilled. He gave me half of what they paid him and everything was fine—until they decided that he was such a good spy and such a good writer, they promoted him. He was terrified. He came to me and said I had gotten him into this and so I had to help him. They were putting him now to spy on bigger troublemakers than me. They were even using his reports in the Ministry of Interior to teach new recruits. He said, 'You have the knack of it, Rudolf, with you it's just a technique. I am too imaginative for this work. But if I say no to them now, it will go in my record and I will be damaged by it later on. I could be seriously damaged now, if they knew you had written the reports on yourself.' So this is how I made a bit of a living when I was young. I taught our celebrated Artist of Merit and winner of the State Award for Outstanding Work how to write in plain Czech and describe a little what life is like. It was not easy. The man could not describe a shoelace. He did not know the word for anything. And he saw nothing. I would say, 'But, Blecha, was the friend sad or happy, clumsy or graceful, did he smoke, did he listen mostly or did he talk? Blecha, how will you ever become a great writer if you are such a bad spy?' This made him angry with me. He did not like my insults. He said spying was sickening to him and caused him to have writer's block. He said he could not use his creative talent while his spirit was being compromised like this. For me it was different. Yes, he had to tell me—it was different for me because I did not have high artistic ideals. I did not have any ideals. If I did I would not agree to spy on myself. I certainly would not take money for it. He had come to lose his respect for me. This is a sad irony to him, because when I left university, it was my integrity that meant so much to him and our friendship. Blecha told me this again recently. He was having lunch with Mr. Knap, another of our celebrated Artists of Merit and winner of the State Award for Outstanding Work, and secretary now of their Writers' Union. Blecha was quite drunk and always when he is quite drunk Blecha gets over-emotional and must tell you the truth. He came up to the table where I was having my lunch and he asked if everything is all right. He said he wished he could help an old friend in trouble, and then he whispered, 'Perhaps in a few months' time . . . but they do not like that you are so alienated, Rudolf. The phenomenon of alienation is not approved of from above. Still, for you I will do all that I can . . .' But then he sat suddenly down at the table and he said, 'But you must not go around Prague telling lies about me, Rudolf. Nobody believes you anyway. My books are everywhere. Schoolchildren read my poems, tens of thousands of people read my novels, on TV they perform my plays. You only make yourself look irresponsible and bitter by telling that story. And, if I may say so, a little crazy.' So I said to him, 'But, Blecha, I don't tell it. I have never told it to a soul.' And he said, 'Come now, my dear old friend

—how then does everybody know?' And so I said, 'Be-cause their children read your poems, they themselves have read your novels, and when they turn on TV, they see your plays.' "

Prague, Feb. 5, 1976

The phone awakens me at quarter to eight.

"This is your wife-to-be. Good morning. I am going to visit you. I am in the lobby of the hotel. I am coming now to visit you in your room."

"No, no. I'll come down to you. It was to be lunch, not breakfast."

"Why are you scared for me to visit you when I love you?" asks Olga.

"It's not the best idea here. You know that."

"I am coming up."

"You're going to get yourself in trouble."

"Not me," she says.

I'm still doing up my trousers when she is at the door, wearing a long suede coat that might have seen her through trench warfare, and a pair of tall leather boots that look as if she'd been farming in them. Against the worn, soiled animal skins, her white neck and white face appear dramatically vulnerable—you can see why people do things to her that she does not necessarily like: bedraggled, bold, and helpless, a deep ineradicable sexual helplessness such as once made bourgeois husbands so proud in the drawing room and so confident in bed. *Since I am frightened of everything, it is as well to go in one direction as the other.* Well, not only is she going, she's gone: she is reckless desperation incarnate.

I let her in quickly and close the door. "Prudence isn't your strong point."

"This I have never heard. Why do you say this?" she asks.

I point to the brass chandelier suspended above the bed, a favored place, Sisovsky had already told me back in New York, for the installation of a bugging device. "In your room," he warned me, "be careful about what you say. There are devices hidden everywhere. And on the phone it is best to say nothing. Don't mention the manuscript to her on the phone."

She drops into a chair beside the window while I continue to dress.

"You must understand," she says loudly, "that I am not marrying you for your money. I am marrying you," she continues, gesturing toward the light fixture, "because you tell me you love me at first sight, and because I believe this, and because at first sight I love you."

"You haven't been to sleep."

"How can I sleep? I am thinking only of my love for you, and I am happy and sad all at once. When I am

thinking of our marriage and our children I do not want
to sleep."

"Let's have breakfast somewhere. Let's get out of here."

"First tell me you love me."

"I love you."

"Is this why you marry me? For love?"

"What other reason could there be?"

"Tell me what you love most about me."

"Your sense of reality."

"But you must not love me for my sense of reality,
you must love me for myself. Tell me all the reasons you
love me."

"At breakfast."

"No. Now. I cannot marry a man who I have only just
met"—she is scribbling on a piece of paper as she speaks
—"and risk my happiness by making the wrong choice.
I must be sure. I owe it to myself. And to my aged
parents."

She hands me the note and I read it. *You cannot trust
Czech police to understand ANYTHING, even in Czech.
You must speak CLEAR and SLOW and LOUD.*

"I love your wit," I say.

"My beauty?"

"I love your beauty."

"My flesh?"

"I love your flesh."

"You love when we make love?"

"Indescribably."

Olga points to the chandelier. "What means 'indescribably,' darling?"

"More than words can say."

"It is much better fucking than with the American girls."

"It's the best."

In the hotel elevator, as we ride down along with the uniformed operator (another police agent, according to Bolotka) and three Japanese early-risers, Olga asks, "*Do you fuck anybody yet in Czechoslovakia?*"

"No, Olga, I haven't. Though a few people in Czechoslovakia may yet fuck me."

"How much is a room at this hotel?"

"I don't know."

"Of course. You're so rich you don't have to know. Do you know why they bug these big hotels, and always above the bed?"

"Why?"

"They listen in the rooms to the foreigners fucking. They want to hear how the women are coming in the different languages. Zuckerman, how are they coming in America? Teach me which words the American girls say."

In the lobby, the front-desk clerk moves out from behind the reception counter and crosses the lobby to meet us. Politely excusing himself to me, he addresses Olga in Czech.

"Speak English!" she demands. "I want him to understand! I want him to hear this insult in English!"

A stocky gray-haired man with formal manners and a heavy unsmiling face, the clerk is oblivious to her rage; he continues unemotionally in Czech.

"What is it?" I ask her.

"Tell him!" she shouts at the clerk. "Tell him what you want!"

"Sir, the lady must show her identity card. It is a regulation."

"Why is it a regulation?" she demands. "Tell him!"

"Foreign guests must register with a passport. Czech citizens must show an identity card if they go up to the rooms to make a call."

"Except if the Czech is a prostitute! Then she does not have to show anything but money! Here—I am a prostitute. Here is your fifty kroner—leave us in peace!"

He turns away from the money she is sticking into his face.

To me Olga explains, "I am sorry, Mister, I should have told you. Whipping a woman is against the law in a civilized country, even if she is being paid to be beaten. But everything is all right if you pay off the scum. Here," she cries, turning again to the clerk, "here is a hundred! I do not mean to insult you! Here is a hundred and fifty!"

"I need an identity card for Madame, please."

"You know who I am," she snarls, "everybody in this country knows who I am."

"I must record the number in my ledger, Madame."

"Tell me, please, why do you embarrass me like this in front of my prospective husband? Why do you try to make me ashamed of my nationality in front of the man I love? Look at him! Look at how he dresses! Look at his coat with a velvet collar! On his trousers he has buttons and not a little zipper like you! Why do you try to give such a man second thoughts about marrying a Czech woman?"

"I wish only to see her identity card, sir. I will return it immediately."

"Olga," I say softly, "enough."

"Do you see?" she shouts at the clerk. "Now he is disgusted. And do you know why? Because he is thinking, Where are their fine old European manners? What kind of country permits such a breach of etiquette toward a lady in the lobby of a grand hotel?"

"Madame, I will have to ask you to remain here while I report you for failing to show your identity card."

"Do that. And I will report you for your breach of etiquette toward a lady in the lobby of a grand hotel in a civilized European country. We will see which of us they put in jail. You will see which of us will go to a slave-labor camp."

I whisper, "Give him the card."

"Go!" she screams at the clerk. "Call the police, please. A man who failed to remove his hat to a lady in the elevator of the Jalta Hotel is now serving ten years in a uranium mine. A doorman who neglected to bow farewell to a lady at the Hotel Esplanade is now in solitary confinement without even toilet facilities. For what you have done you will never again see your wife or your old mother. Your children will grow up ashamed of their father's name. Go. Go! I want my husband-to-be to see what we do in this country to people without manners. I want him to see that we do not smile here upon rudeness to a Czech woman! Call the authorities—this minute! In the meantime, we are going to have our breakfast. Come, my dear one, my darling."

Taking my arm, she starts away, but not before the clerk says, "There is a message, sir," and slips me an envelope. The note is handwritten on hotel stationery.

Dear Mr. Zuckerman,

I am a Czech student with a deep interest in American writing. I have written a study of your fiction about which I would like to talk to you. "The Luxury of Self-Analysis As It Relates to American Economic Conditions." I will meet with you here at the hotel anytime, if you will be willing to receive me. Please leave word at the desk.

Yours most respectfully,
Oldrich Hrobek

The guests already taking breakfast watch over the rims of their coffee cups while Olga vigorously declines to sit at the corner table to which we have been shown by the headwaiter. She points to a table beside the glass doors to the lobby. In English the headwaiter explains to me that this table is reserved.

"For breakfast?" she replies. "That is a fucking lie."

We are seated at the table by the lobby doors. I say, "What now, Olga? Tell me what's coming next."

"Please don't ask me about these things. They are just stupidities. I want eggs, please. Poached eggs. Nothing in life is as pure as a poached egg. If I don't eat I will faint."

"Tell me what was wrong with the first table."

"Bugged. Probably this table they bug too; probably all are bugged. Fuck it, I am too weak. Fuck the whole thing. Fuck it all. Teach me another one. I need this morning one that is really good."

"Where have you been all night?"

"You would not have me so I found some people who would. Call the waiter, please, or I will faint. I am going to faint. I am feeling sick. I am going to the loo to be sick."

I follow after her as she runs from the table, but when I reach the dining-room door, my way is blocked by a young man with a tiny chin beard; he is in a toggled loden coat and carrying a heavy briefcase. "Please," he says, his face only inches from mine—a face taut with panic and dreadful concern—"I have tried to reach you just now in your room. I am Oldrich Hrobek. You have received my note?"

"Only this minute," I say, watching Olga rush through the lobby to the ladies' room.

"You must leave Prague as soon as possible. You must not stay here. If you do not leave immediately, the authorities will harm you."

"Me? How do you know this?"

"Because they are building a case. I'm at Charles University. They questioned my professor, they questioned me."

"But I just got here. *What* case?"

"They told me you were on an espionage mission and to stay away from you. They said they will put you in jail for what you are doing here."

"For espionage?"

"Plotting against the Czech people. Plotting with troublemakers against the socialist system. You are an ideological saboteur—you must leave today."

"I'm an American citizen." I touch the billfold that holds not only my passport but my membership card in the American PEN Club, signed by the president, Jerzy Kosinski.

"Recently an American got off the train in Bratislava and was immediately put into jail for two months because he was mistaken for somebody else. He wasn't even the right person and that didn't get him out. An Austrian was taken from his hotel to prison a week ago and is to stand trial for anti-Czech activities. A West German journalist they drowned in the river. They said he was fishing and fell in. There are hard-line people who want to make an impression on the country. With you they can make an impression. This is what the police have told me. Many, many arrests are going to be made."

I hear very clearly the sound of the river splashing against the steep stone embankment outside of Klenek's palazzo.

"Because of me."

"Including you."

"Maybe they are just frightening you," I say, *my* heart galloping, galloping to burst.

"Mr. Zuckerman, I should not be in here. I must not be in here—but I am afraid to miss you. There is more. If you will walk to the railway station I will meet you there in five minutes. It is at the top of the main street—just to the left. You will see it. I will pretend to run into you outside the big station café. Please, they told my girlfriend the same thing. They questioned her at her job—about you."

"About me. You sure of all this?"

The student takes my hand and begins to pump it with exaggerated vigor. "It is an honor to meet you!" He speaks up so that all in the dining room who wish to can hear. "I am sorry I interrupted but I had to meet you. I can't help it if I am a silly fan! Goodbye, sir!"

Olga returns looking even worse than when she left. She also smells. "What a country." She falls heavily into her chair. "You cannot even throw up in the loo that someone does not write a report about it. There is a man waiting outside the cubicle when I am finished. He is listening to me from there all the time. 'Did you leave it clean?' he asks me. 'Yes,' I said, 'yes, I left it clean.' 'You shout, you scream, you have no respect for anything,' he tells me. 'Someone will come in after you and see your mess and blame it on me.' 'Go in then, go check,' I told him. And he did it. A man in a suit who can reason and think! He went in and inspected."

"Has anyone else bothered you?"

"They won't. They won't dare. Not if I am having breakfast with you. You are an international writer. They do not want to make trouble in the presence of an international writer."

"Then why did he bother about your identity card?"

"Because he is afraid not to. Everybody is afraid. I want to have my breakfast now with my international writer. I am hungry."

"Why don't we go somewhere else? I want to talk to you about something serious."

"You want to marry me. When?"

"Not quite yet. Come, let's go."

"No, we must not move. You must show them always that you are not afraid." When she picks up the menu I see she is trembling. "You must not leave," she says. "You must sit here and enjoy your breakfast and drink many cups of coffee, and then you must smoke a cigar. If they see you smoking a cigar, they will leave you alone."

"You put great stock in a single cigar."

"I know these Czech police—blow a little smoke in their faces and you'll see how brave they are. Last night I was in the pub, because you would not fuck me, and I am talking to the bartender about the hockey game and two men come in and sit down and begin to buy me drinks. Outside is parked a state limousine. We drink, they make loud jokes with the bartender, and then they show me the big car. They say to me, 'How would you like to take a ride in that? Not to question you, but to have a good time. We'll drink some more vodka and have a good time.' I thought, 'Don't be afraid, don't show them you are afraid.' So they drive me to an office building and we go inside and everything is dark, and when I say I can't see where I'm going one of them says they cannot turn the lights on. 'Everything,' he says, 'is observed where the lights are on.' You see, *he* is afraid. Now I know he is afraid too. Probably they should not even have the car, it belongs to their boss—something is wrong here. They open a door and we sit in a dark room and the two of them pour vodka for me, but they cannot even wait for me to drink, one of them takes out his prick and tries to pull me down on it. I feel him with my hand and I say to him, 'But it is technically impossible with this. You could never come with something so soft. Let me try his. No, his is technically impossible even more. I want to go. There is no fun here, and I can't even see anything. I want to go!' I begin to shout . . ."

The waiter returns to take the order. Poached eggs for two—as pure a thing as life has to offer.

After my three cups of coffee, Olga orders me a Cuban cigar and, at 8:30 a.m. Central European Time, I, who smoke a cigar once every decade and afterwards always wonder why, oblige her and light up.

"You must finish the cigar, Zuckerman. When freedom returns to Czechoslovakia, you will be made an honorary citizen for finishing that cigar. They will put a plaque outside this hotel about Zuckerman and his cigar."

"I'll finish the cigar," I say, dropping my voice, "if you give me Sisovsky's father's stories. The stories in Yiddish that Sisovsky left behind. I met your husband in New York. He asked me to come here and get the stories."

"That swine! That pig!"

"Olga, I didn't want to spring it on you out of the blue, but I've been advised not to hang around this country much longer."

"You met that monster in New York!"

"Yes."

"And the aging ingenue? You have met her too? And did she tell you how much she suffers from all the men at her feet? Did he tell you how with her it is never boring love-making—with her it is always like rape! This is why you are here, not for Kafka but for *him*?"

"Lower your voice. I'm taking those stories to America."

"So he can make money out of his dead father—in New York? So he can buy jewelry for her now in New York too?"

"He wants to publish his father's stories, in translation, in America."

"What—out of love? Out of *devotion*?"

"I don't know."

"*I* know! I know! That's why he left his mother, that's why he left me, that's why he left his child—because of all of this devoted love he has. Left us all for that whore they all rape. What's *she* doing in New York? Still playing Nina in *The Seagull*?"

"I wouldn't think so."

"Why not? She did here. Our leading Czech actress who ages but never grows up. Poor little star always in tears. And how much did he flatter you to make you believe that he was a man with love and devotion who cared only for the memory of his beloved father? How much did he flatter you about your books that you cannot see through what *both* of them are? *He* is why you come to Czechoslovakia—him? Because you took pity on two homeless Czechs? Take pity on *me*. I am at home, *and it is worse!*"

"I see that."

"And of course he told you the story of his father's death."

"He did."

" 'He shot my Jew, so I shot his.' "

"Yes."

"Well, that is another lie. It happened to another writer, who didn't even write in Yiddish. Who didn't have a wife or have a child. Sisovsky's father was killed in a bus accident. Sisovsky's father hid in the bathroom of a Gentile friend, hid there through the war from the Nazis, and his friend brought him cigarettes and whores."

"I find it hard believing that."

"Of course—because it's not as horrible a story! They all say their fathers were killed by the Nazis. By now even the sixteen-year-old girls know not to believe them. Only people like you, only a shallow, sentimental, American idiot Jew who thinks there is virtue in suffering!"

"You've got the wrong Jew—I think nothing of the sort. Let me have the manuscripts. What good do they do anybody here?"

"The good of not being there, doing good for him and that terrible actress! You cannot even *hear* her if you sit ten rows back. You could *never* hear her. She is a stinking actress who has ruined Chekhov for Prague for the last hundred years with all her stinking sensitive pauses, and now she will ruin Chekhov for New York. Nina? She should be playing Firs! He wants to live off of his father? The hell with him! Let him live off of his actress! If anybody can even hear her!"

* * *

I wait for Hrobek on a long bench in the corridor outside the railway café. Either because the student has himself waited and lost hope and gone home or because he has been taken into custody or because he was not a student but a provocateur got up in a wispy chin beard and worn loden coat, he is nowhere to be seen.

On the chance that he has decided to wait inside rather than under the scrutiny of the plainclothes security agents patrolling the halls, I enter the café and look around: a big dingy room, a dirty, airless, oppressive place. Patched, fraying tablecloths set with mugs of beer, and clinging to the mugs, men with close-cropped hair wearing gray-black work clothes, swathed in cigarette smoke and saying little. Off the night shift somewhere, or maybe tanking up on their way *to* work. Their faces indicate that not everybody heard the president when he went on television for three hours to ask the people not to drink so much.

Two waiters in soiled white jackets attend the fifty or so tables, both of them elderly and in no hurry. Since half of the country, by Olga's count, is employed in spying on the other half, chances are that one at least works for the police. (Am I getting drastically paranoid or am I getting the idea?) In German I order a cup of coffee.

The workmen at their beer remind me of Bolotka, a janitor in a museum now that he no longer runs his theater. "This," Bolotka explains, "is the way we arrange things now. The menial work is done by the writers and the teachers and the construction engineers, and the construction is run by the drunks and the crooks. Half a million people have been fired from their jobs. *Everything* is run by the drunks and the crooks. They get along better with the Russians." I imagine Styron washing glasses in a Penn Station barroom, Susan Sontag wrapping buns at a Broadway bakery, Gore Vidal bicycling salamis to school lunchrooms in Queens—I look at the filthy floor and see myself sweeping it.

Someone stares at me from a nearby table while I continue sizing up the floor and with it the unforeseen consequences of art. I am remembering the actress Eva Kalinova and how they have used Anne Frank as a whip to drive her from the stage, how the ghost of the Jewish saint has returned to haunt her as a demon. Anne Frank as a curse and a stigma! No, there's nothing that can't be done to a book, no cause in which even the most innocent of all books cannot be enlisted, not only by *them*, but by you and me. Had Eva Kalinova been born in New Jersey she too would have wished that Anne Frank had never died as she did; but coming, like Anne Frank, from the wrong continent at the wrong time, she could only wish that the Jewish girl and her little diary had never even existed.

Mightier than the *sword*? This place is proof that a book isn't as mighty as the mind of its most benighted reader.

When I get up to go, the young workman who'd been staring at me gets up and follows.

I board a trolley by the river, then jump off halfway to the museum where Bolotka is expecting me to pay him a visit. On foot, and with the help of a Prague map, I proceed to lose my way but also to shake my escort. By the time I reach the museum this seems to me a city that I've known all my life. The old-time streetcars, the barren shops, the soot-blackened bridges, the tunneled alleys and medieval streets, the people in a state of impervious heaviness, their faces shut down by solemnity, faces that appear to be on strike against life—this is the city I imagined during the war's worst years, when, as a Hebrew-school student of little more than nine, I went out after supper with my blue-and-white collection can to solicit from the neighbors for the Jewish National Fund. This is the city I imagined the Jews would buy when they had accumulated enough money for a homeland. I knew about Palestine and the hearty Jewish teenagers there reclaiming the desert and draining the swamps, but I also recalled, from our vague family chronicle, shadowy, cramped streets where the innkeepers and distillery workers who were our Old World forebears had dwelled apart, as strangers, from the notorious Poles—and so, what I privately pictured the Jews able to afford with the nickels and dimes I collected was a used city, a broken city, a city so worn and grim that nobody else would even put in a bid. It would go for a song, the owner delighted to be rid of it before it completely caved in. In this used city, one would hear endless stories being told—on benches in the park, in kitchens at night, while waiting your turn at the grocery or over the clothesline in the yard, anxious tales of harassment and flight, stories of fantastic endurance and pitiful collapse. What was to betoken a Jewish homeland to an impressionable, emotional nine-year-old child, highly susceptible to the emblems of pathos, was, first, the overpowering oldness of the homes, the centuries of deterioration that had made the property so cheap, the leaky pipes and moldy walls and rotting timbers and smoking stoves and simmering cabbages souring the air of the semidark stairwells; second were the stories, all the telling and listening to be done, their infinite interest in their own existence, the fascination with their alarming plight, the mining and refining of *tons* of these stories—the national industry of the Jewish homeland, if not the sole means of production (if not the sole source of satisfaction), the construction of narrative out of the exertions of survival; third were the jokes—because beneath the ordeal of perpetual melancholia and the tremendous strain of just getting through, a joke is always lurking somewhere, a derisory portrait, a scathing crack, a joke which builds with subtle self-savaging to the uproarious punch line, "And this is what suffering does!" What you smell are centuries and what you hear are voices and what you see are Jews, wild with lament and rippling with amusement, their voices tremulous with rancor and vibrating with pain, a choral society proclaiming vehemently, "Do you believe it? Can you imagine it?" even as they affirm with every wizardly trick in the book, by a thousand acoustical fluctuations of tempo, tone, inflection, and pitch, "Yet this is exactly what happened!" That such things can happen—there's the moral of the stories—that such things happen to me, to him, to her, to you, to us. That is the national anthem of the Jewish homeland. By all rights, when you hear someone there begin telling a story—when you see the Jewish faces mastering anxiety and feigning innocence and registering astonishment at their own fortitude—you ought to stand and put your hand to your heart.

Here where the literary culture is held hostage, the art of narration flourishes by mouth. In Prague, stories aren't simply stories; it's what they have instead of life. Here they have become their stories, in lieu of being permitted to be anything else. Storytelling is the form their resistance has taken against the coercion of the powers-that-be.

I say nothing to Bolotka of the sentiments stirred up by my circuitous escape route, or the association it's inspired between my ancestors' Poland, his Prague tenement, and the Jewish Atlantis of an American childhood dream. I only explain why I'm late. "I was followed from the train station onto the trolley. I shook him before I got here. I hope I wasn't wrong to come anyway." I describe the student Hrobek and show Bolotka his note. "The note was given to me by a hotel clerk who I think is a cop."

After reading it twice he says, "Don't worry, they were only frightening him and his teacher."

"If so, they succeeded. In frightening me too."

"Whatever the reason, it is not to build a case against you. They do this to everyone. It is one of the laws of power, the spreading of general distrust. It is one of several basic techniques of *adjusting* people. But they cannot touch you. That would be pointless, even by Prague standards. A regime can only be so stupid, and then the other side comes back into power. Here *you* frighten *them*. A student should understand that. He is not enrolled in the right courses."

"Coming to the hotel then, he made things worse for himself—for his teacher too, if all this is true."

"I can't say. There is probably more about this boy that we don't know. The student and his teacher are who they are interested in, not you. You are not responsible for the boy's bad judgment."

"He was young. He wanted to help."

"Don't be tender about his martyr complex. And don't credit the secret police with so much. Of course the hotel clerk is a cop. Everybody is in that hotel. But the police are like literary critics—of what little they see, they get most wrong anyway. They *are* the literary critics. Our literary criticism is police criticism. As for the boy, he is right now back in his room with his pants off, boasting to his girl friend about saving your life."

Bolotka is padded out beneath his overalls with a scruffy,

repulsive reddish fur vest that could be the hair off his own thick hide, and consequently looks even more barbarous, more feral, at work than he did at play. He looks, in *this* enclosure, like one of the zoo's larger beasts, a bison or a bear. We are in a freezing storage room about twice as big as an ordinary clothes closet and a third the size of his living quarters. Both of us are sipping slivovitz-larded tea from his mug, I to calm down and Bolotka to warm up. The cartons stacked to the ceiling contain his cleanser, his toilet tissue, his floor polish, his lye; ranged along the walls are the janitor's buffing machine, ladder, and collection of brooms. In one corner, the corner Bolotka calls "my office," are a low stool, a gooseneck lamp, and the electric kettle to boil the water into which to dip his tea bag and pour the brandy. He reads here, writes, hides, sleeps, here on a scrap of carpet between the push broom and the buffer he entertains sixteen girls, though never, he informs me, in so tiny a space, all of them at one time. "More than two girls and there's no room for my prick."

"And there's nothing to be done about this boy's warning? I'm relying on you, Rudolf. When you come to New York I'll see you're not mugged in Central Park by going to take a leak there at 3 a.m. I expect the same consideration from you here. Am I in danger?"

"I was once briefly in jail, waiting to stand trial, Nathan. Before the trial began, they released me. It was too ridiculous even for them. They told me I had committed a crime against the state: in my theater, the heroes were always laughing when they should be crying, and this was a crime. I was an ideological saboteur. Stalinist criticism, which once existed in this country until it became a laughingstock, always reproached characters for not being moral and setting a good example. When a hero's wife died on the stage, which was often happening in my theater, he had to sob a lot to please Stalin. And Stalin of course knew quite well what it was when one's wife died. He himself killed three wives and in killing them he was always sobbing. Well, when I was in jail, you realized when you woke up where you were, and you began cursing. You could hear them cursing in their cells, all the professional criminals, all the pimps and murderers and thieves. I was only a young man, but I began cursing too. The thing I learned was not to stop cursing, never to stop cursing, not when you are in a prison. Forget this note. To hell with these people and their warnings. Anything you want to do in Prague, anything you want to see in Prague, anyone you want to fuck in Prague, you tell me and I arrange it. There is still some pleasure for a stranger in *Mitteleuropa*. I hesitate to say Prague is 'gay,' but sometimes these days it can be very amusing."

Afternoon. Olga's garret atop Klenek's palazzo. A pinnacle of Prague's castle blurrily visible through the leaded

*window. Olga in her robe on the bed. Witchy, very whit-
ish, even without the makeup. I pace, wearing my coat,
wondering why these stories must be retrieved. Why am I
forcing the issue? What's the motive here? Is this a passionate struggle for those marvelous stories or a renewal
of the struggle toward self-caricature? Still the son, still
the child, in strenuous pursuit of the father's loving response? (Even when the father is Sisovsky's?) Suppose
the stories aren't even marvelous, that I only long for that
—the form taken by* my touha. *Why am I saying to myself,* "Do not let yourself be stopped"? *Why be drawn
further along, the larger the obstacles? That's okay writing a book, that's what it* is *to write a book, but would it
be so hard to convince myself that I am stupidly endowing
these stories with a significance that they can't begin to
have? How consequential can they be? If their genius
could really astound us they would somehow have sur-
faced long ago. The author's purpose wasn't to be read
anyway, but to write for no necessity other than his own.
Why not let him have it his way, rather than yours or
Sisovsky's? Think of all that his stories will be spared if
instead of wrenching his fiction out of oblivion, you just
turn around and go . . . Yet I stay. In the old parables
about the spiritual life, the hero searches for a kind of holi-
ness, or holy object, or transcendence, boning up on magic
practices as he goes off hunting after his higher being,
getting help from crones and soothsayers, donning masks*

—well, this is the mockery of that parable, that parable the idealization of this farce. The soul sinking into ridiculousness even while it strives to be saved. Enter Zuckerman, a serious person.

O. You're afraid to marry an alcoholic? I would love you so, I wouldn't drink.

Z. And you give me the stories as your dowry.

O. Maybe.

Z. Where are the stories?

O. I don't know where.

Z. He left them with you—you must know. His mother came to you and tried to get them, and you showed her photographs of his mistresses. That's what he told me.

O. Don't be sentimental. They were pictures of their cunts. Do you think they were so different from mine? You think theirs were prettier? Here. (*Opens her robe*) Look. Theirs were exactly the same.

Z. You have all your things here?

O. I don't have *things*. In the sense that you Americans have *things*, I don't have *anything*.

Z. Do you have the stories here?

O. Let's go to the American Embassy and get married.

Z. And then you'll give me the stories.

O. More than likely. Tell me, what are you getting out of this?

Z. A headache. A terrific headache and a look at your cunt. That's about it.

O. Ah, you are doing it for idealistic reasons. You do it for literature. For altruism. You are a great American, a great humanitarian, and a great Jew.

Z. I'll give you ten thousand dollars.

O. Ten thousand dollars? I could use ten thousand dollars. But there's no amount of money you could give me. Nothing would be worth it.

Z. And you don't care about literature.

O. I care about literature. I love literature. But not as much as I love to keep these things from him. And from her. You really think I am going to give you these stories so he can keep her in jewels? You really think that in New York he's going to publish these stories under his father's name?

Z. Why shouldn't he?

O. Why should he—what's in it for *him*? He'll publish them under his own name. His beloved father is dead now ten times over. He'll publish the stories under his own name and become famous in America like all you Jews.

Z. I didn't know you were an anti-Semite.

O. Only because of Sisovsky. If you would marry me, I would change. Am I so unattractive to you that you don't want to marry me? Is his aging ingenue more attractive to you than I am?

Z. I can't really believe you mean all this. You're an impressive character, Olga. In your own way you're fighting to live.

O. Then marry me, if I am so impressive from fighting to live. You're not married to anyone else. What are you afraid of—that I'll take your millions?

Z. Look, you want a ticket out of Czechoslovakia?

O. Maybe I want you.

Z. What if I get someone to marry you. He'll come here, get you to America, and when you divorce him I'll give you ten thousand dollars.

O. Am I so revolting that I can only marry one of your queer friends?

Z. Olga, how do I wrest these stories from you? Just tell me.

O. Zuckerman, if you were such an idealist about literature as you want me to be, if you would make great sacrifices for literature as you expect me to make, we would have been married twenty minutes already.

Z. Is whatever Sisovsky did so awful that his dead father must suffer too?

O. When the stories are published in New York without the father's name, the father will suffer more, believe me.

Z. Suppose that doesn't happen. Suppose I make that impossible.

O. *You* will outtrick Zdenek?

Z. I'll contact *The New York Times*. Before seeing Zdenek, I'll tell them the whole story of these stories. They'll run an article about them. Suppose I do that as soon as I'm back.

O. So *that's* what you get out of it! *That's* your idealism! The marvelous Zuckerman brings from behind the Iron Curtain two hundred unpublished Yiddish stories written by a victim of a Nazi bullet. You will be a hero to the Jews and to literature and to all of the Free World. On top of all your millions of dollars and millions of girls, you will win the American Prize for Idealism about Literature. And what will happen to me? I will go to prison for smuggling a manuscript to the West.

Z. They won't know the stories came through you.

O. But they know already that I have them. They know everything I have. They have a list of everything that *everybody* has. You get the idealism prize, he gets the royalties, she gets the jewelry, and I get seven years. For the sake of literature.

Here she gets up from the bed, goes to the dresser, and removes from the top drawer a deep box for chocolates. I untie the ribbon on the box. Inside, hundreds of pages of unusually thick paper, rather like the heavy waxed paper that oily foodstuffs used to be wrapped in at the grocery. The ink is black, the margins perfect, the Yiddish script is sharp and neat. None of the stories seems longer than five or six pages. I can't read them.

O. (*Back in bed*) You don't have to give me money. You don't have to find me a queer to be my husband. (*Beginning to cry*) You don't even have to fuck me, if I am such an unattractive woman. To be fucked is the only freedom left in this country. To fuck and to be fucked is all we have left that they cannot stop, but you do not have to fuck me, if I am such an unattractive woman compared to the American girls. He can even print the stories in his own name, your friend Sisovsky. The hell with it. The hell with everything. In spite of the charm with which he seduced you, with which he seduces *everybody*, he can be quite vicious—do you know? There is great brutality in your Sisovsky. Did he tell you about all his doubts—his tragic doubts? What shit! Before Zdenek left Prague, we measured personal vanity here in millisisovskys. Zdenek will survive in America. He is human in the worst sense of the word. Zdenek will flourish, thanks to his dead father. So will she. And in return, I want nothing. Only that when he asks you how much did you have to give her, how much money and how many fucks, you will do me one favor: tell him you had to give me nothing. Tell *her*.

At the hotel, two plainclothes policemen come to the room and confiscate the candy box full of Yiddish manuscript within fifteen minutes of my return. They are accompanied by the hotel clerk who'd earlier in the day handed me Hrobek's note. "They wish to examine your belongings, sir," he tells me—"they say somebody has mislaid something which you may have picked up by mistake." "My belongings are none of their business." "I'm afraid you are wrong. That is precisely their business." As the police begin their search I ask him, "And you, what's your business?" "I merely work at the reception desk. It is not only the intellectual who may be sent down to the mines if he does not cooperate with the present regime, the hotel clerk can be demoted as well. As one of our famous dissidents has said, a man who speaks only the truth, 'There is always a lower rung under the feet of every citizen on the ladder of the state.'" I demand to be allowed to telephone the American Embassy, and not so as to arrange a wedding. I am told instead to pack my bags. I will be driven to the airport and put on the next plane out of Prague. I am no longer welcome as a visitor in Czechoslovakia. "I want to speak to the American ambassador. They cannot confiscate my belongings. There are no grounds on which to expel me from this country." "Sir, though it may appear to you that ardent supporters of this regime are few and far between, there are also those, like these two gentlemen, who have no trouble believing that what they do is right, correct, and necessary. Brutally necessary. I am afraid that any further delay is going to cause them to be less lenient than you would like." "What the box contains is simply manuscript—stories written by somebody who's been dead now thirty years, fiction about a world that no longer even exists. It is no possible threat to anyone." "I am grateful, sir, in times like these, still to be able to support my family. There is nothing a clerk in a Prague hotel can do for any writer, living or dead." When I demand for the third time to speak to the Embassy, I am told that if I do not immediately pack my bags and prepare to leave, I will be arrested and taken to jail. "How do I know," I ask, "that they won't take me to jail anyway?" "I suppose," the clerk replies, "that you will have to trust them."

Either Olga had a change of heart and called the cops, or else they called on her. Klenek's is bugged, everyone says so. I just cannot believe that she and the hotel clerk work for the same boss, but maybe that's because I *am* a shallow, sentimental, American idiot Jew.

At the desk the police wait while I charge my bills to the Diners Club and then I am accompanied by them to a black limousine. One policeman sits up front with the driver and the candy box, and the other in the back with me and a bulky, bespectacled, elderly man who introduces himself gruffly as Novak. Soft, fine white hair like the fluff of a dry dandelion. Otherwise a man made of meat. He is no charmer like the hotel clerk.

Out beyond the heavy city traffic I am unable to tell if we really are on the airport road. Can they be taking me to jail in a limo? I always seem to end up in these large black cars. The dashboard says this one is a Tatra 603.

"*Sie sprechen Deutsch, nicht wahr?*" Novak asks me.

"*Etwas.*"

"*Kennen sie Fraulein Betty MacDonald?*"

We continue in German. "I don't," I say.

"You *don't*?"

"No."

"You don't know Miss Betty MacDonald?"

I can't stop thinking how badly this can still turn out— or, alternatively, that I could honorably have abandoned the mission once I saw the dangers were real. Because Sisovsky claimed to be my counterpart from the world that my own fortunate family had eluded didn't mean I had to prove him right by rushing in to change places. I assume his fate and he assumes mine—wasn't that sort of his idea from the start? *When I came to New York I said to Eva, "I am a relative of this great man."*

Guilty of conspiring against the Czech people with somebody named Betty MacDonald. Thus I conclude my penance.

"Sorry," I say, "I don't know her."

"But," says Novak, "she is the author of *The Egg and I*."

"Ah. Yes. About a farm—wasn't it? I haven't read it since I was a schoolboy."

Novak is incredulous. "But it is a masterpiece."

"Well, I can't say it's considered a masterpiece in America. I'd be surprised if in America anybody under thirty has even heard of *The Egg and I*."

"I cannot believe this."

"It's true. It was popular in the forties, a bestseller, a movie, but books like that come and go. Surely you have the same thing here."

"That is a tragedy. And what has happened to Miss Betty MacDonald?"

"I have no idea."

"Why does something like this happen in America to a writer like Miss MacDonald?"

"I don't think even Miss MacDonald expected her book to endure forever."

"You have not answered me. You avoid the question. Why does this happen in America?"

"I don't know."

I search in vain for signs to the airport.

Novak is suddenly angry. "There is no paranoia here about writers."

"I didn't say there was."

"I am a writer. I am a successful writer. Nobody is paranoid about me. Ours is the most literate country in Europe. Our people love books. I have in the Writers' Union dozens of writers, poets, novelists, playwrights, and no one is paranoid about them. No, it isn't writers who fall under our suspicion in Czechoslovakia. In this small country the writers have a great burden to bear: they must not only make the country's literature, they must be the touchstone for general decency and public conscience.

They occupy a high position in our national life because they are people who live beyond reproach. Our writers are loved by their readers. The country looks to them for moral leadership. No, it is those who stand outside of the common life, that is who we all fear. And we are right to."

I can imagine what he contributes to his country's literature: *Still more humorous Novakian tales about the crooked little streets of Old Prague, stories that poke fun at all citizens, high and low, and always with spicy folk humor and mischievous fantasy. A must for the sentimental at holiday time.*

"You are with the Writers' Union?" I ask.

My ignorance ignites a glower of contempt. I dare to think of myself as an educated person and know nothing of the meaning of the Tatra 603? He says, *"Ich bin der Kulturminister."*

So he is the man who administers the culture of Czechoslovakia, whose job is to bring the aims of literature into line with the aims of society, to make literature less *inefficient*, from a social point of view. You write, if you even can here, into the teeth of this.

"Well," I say, "it's kind of you personally to see me out, Mr. Minister. This is the road to the airport? Frankly I don't recognize it."

"You should have taken the time to come to see me when you first arrived. It would have been worth your while. I would have made you realize what the common

life is in Czechoslovakia. You would understand that the
ordinary Czech citizen does not think like the sort of
people you have chosen to meet. He does not behave like
them and he does not admire them. The ordinary Czech
is repelled by such people. Who are they? Sexual perverts.
Alienated neurotics. Bitter egomaniacs. They seem to you
courageous? You find it thrilling, the price they pay for
their great art? Well, the ordinary hardworking Czech
who wants a better life for himself and his family is not
so thrilled. He considers them malcontents and parasites
and outcasts. At least their blessed Kafka knew he was a
freak, recognized that he was a misfit who could never
enter into a healthy, ordinary existence alongside his countrymen. But *these* people? Incorrigible deviants who pro-
pose to make their moral outlook the norm. The worst is
that left to themselves, left to run free to do as they
wish, these people would destroy this country. I don't
even speak of their moral degeneracy. With this they only
make themselves and their families miserable, and destroy
the lives of their children. I am thinking of their political
stupidity. Do you know what Brezhnev told Dubček when
he flew our great reform leader to the Soviet Union back
in '68? Brezhnev sent several hundred thousand troops to
Prague to get Mr. Dubček to come to his senses about his
great program of reforms. But to be on the safe side with
this genius, he had him taken one evening from his office
and flown to the Soviet Union for a little talk."

To the Soviet Union. Suppose they put me aboard Aeroflot, suppose that's the next plane out of Prague. Suppose they keep me *here. As Nathan Zuckerman awoke one morning from uneasy dreams he found himself transformed in his bed into a sweeper of floors in a railway café. There are petitions for him to sign, or not to sign; there are questions for him to answer, or not to answer; there are enemies to despise, there are friends to console, mail doesn't reach him, a phone they withhold, there are informers, breakdowns, betrayals, threats, there is for him even a strange brand of freedom—invalidated by the authorities, a superfluous person with no responsibilities and nothing to do, he has the kind of good times you have in Dante's Inferno; and finally, to really break him on the rack of farce, there is Novak squatting over the face of culture: when he awakens in the morning, realizes where he is and remembers what he's turned into, he begins to curse and doesn't stop cursing.*

I speak up. "I am an American citizen, Mr. Minister. I want to know what's going on here. Why these policemen? I have committed no crime."

"You have committed several crimes, each punishable by sentences of up to twenty years in jail."

"I demand to be taken to the American Embassy."

"Let me tell you what Brezhnev told Mr. Dubček that Mr. Bolotka neglected to say while elucidating on the size of his sexual organ. One, he would deport our Czech intelligentsia en masse to Siberia; two, he would turn Czechoslovakia into a Soviet republic; three, he would make Russian the language in the schools. In twenty years nobody would even remember that such a country as Czechoslovakia had ever existed. This is not the United States of America where every freakish thought is a fit subject for writing, where there is no such thing as propriety, decorum, or shame, nor a decent respect for the morality of the ordinary, hardworking citizen. This is a small country of fifteen million, dependent as it has always been upon the goodwill of a mighty neighbor. Those Czechs who inflame the anger of our mighty neighbor are not patriots—*they are the enemy*. There is nothing praiseworthy about them. The men to praise in this country are men like my own little father. You want to respect somebody in Czechoslovakia? Respect my father! I admire my old father and with good reason. I am *proud* of this little man."

And your father, is he proud of you and does he think you are all you should be? Certainly Novak is all he thinks he should be—perceives perfectly what *everybody* should be. One conviction seems to follow from the other.

"My father is a simple machinist, now long retired, and do you know how he has made his contribution to the survival of Czech culture and the Czech people and the Czech language—even of Czech literature? A contribution greater than your lesbian whore who when she opens her legs for an American writer represents to him the authentic Czech spirit. Do you know how my father has expressed his love of country all his life? In 1937 he praised Masaryk and the Republic, praised Masaryk as our great national hero and saviour. When Hitler came in he praised Hitler. After the war he praised Beneš when he was elected prime minister. When Stalin threw Beneš out, he praised Stalin and our great leader Gottwald. Even when Dubček came in, for a few minutes he praised Dubček. But now that Dubček and his great reform government are gone, he would not dream of praising them. Do you know what he tells me now? Do you want to hear the political philosophy of a true Czech patriot who has lived in this little country for eighty-six years, who made a decent and comfortable little home for his wife and his four children, and who lives now in dignified retirement, enjoying, as he has every right to enjoy, his pipe, and his grandchildren, and his pint of beer, and the company of his dear old friends? He says to me, 'Son, if someone called Jan Hus nothing but a dirty Jew, I would agree.' These are our people who represent the true Czech spirit—*these are our realists!* People who understand what *necessity* is. People who do not sneer at order and see only the worst in everything. People who know to distinguish between what remains possible in a little country like ours and what is a stupid, maniacal delusion—*people who know how to submit decently to their historical misfortune! These are* the people to whom we owe the survival of our beloved land, and not to alienated, degenerate, egomaniacal artistes!"

Customs a breeze—my possessions combed over so many times while still in the dresser at the hotel that my bags are put right on through at the weigh-in counter and I'm accompanied by the plainclothesmen straight to passport control. I have not been arrested, I will not be tried, convicted, and jailed; Dubček's fate isn't to be mine, nor is Bolotka's, Olga's, or Zdenek Sisovsky's. I am to be placed on board the Swissair flight bound nonstop for Geneva, and from there I'll catch a plane for New York.

Swissair. The most beautiful word in the English language.

Yet it makes you furious to be thrown out, once the fear has begun to subside. "What could entice me to this desolate country," says K., "except the wish to stay here?" —here where there's no nonsense about purity and goodness, where the division is not that easy to discern between the heroic and the perverse, where every sort of repression foments a parody of freedom and the suffering of their historical misfortune engenders in its imaginative victims these clownish forms of human despair—here where they're careful to remind the citizens (in case anybody gets any screwy ideas) "the phenomenon of alienation is not approved of from above." In this nation of narrators I'd only just begun hearing all their stories; I'd only just begun to sense myself shedding *my* story, as wordlessly as

possible snaking away from the narrative encasing me.
Worst of all, I've lost that astonishingly real candy box
stuffed with the stories I came to Prague to retrieve. Another Jewish writer who might have been is not going to
be; his imagination won't leave even the faintest imprint
and no one else's imagination will be imprinted on his,
neither the policemen practicing literary criticism nor the
meaning-mad students living only for art.

Of course my theatrical friend Olga, for whose routine
I have been playing straight man, wasn't necessarily making Prague mischief when she disclosed that the Yiddish
author's war was endured in a bathroom, surviving on
cigarettes and whores, and that when he perished it was
under a bus. And maybe it *was* Sisovsky's plan to pretend
in America that the father's achievement was his. Yet even
if Sisovsky's stories, those told to me in New York, were
tailored to exploit the listener's sentiments, a strategically
devised fiction to set me in motion, that still doesn't miti-
gate the sense of extraneous irrelevancy I now feel. Another assault upon a world of significance degenerating
into a personal fiasco, and this time in a record forty-eight
hours! No, one's story isn't a skin to be shed—it's inescapable, one's body and blood. You go on pumping it
out till you die, the story veined with the themes of your
life, the ever-recurring story that's at once your invention
and the invention of you. To be transformed into a cultural eminence elevated by the literary deeds he performs
would not seem to be my fate. A forty-minute valedictory

from the Minister of Culture on artistic deviance and filial respect is all I have been given to carry home. They must have seen me coming.

I also have to wonder if Novak's narrative is any less an invention than Sisovsky's. The true Czech patriot to whom the land owes its survival may well be another character out of mock-autobiography, yet another fabricated father manufactured to serve the purposes of a storytelling son. As if the core of existence isn't fantastic enough, still more fabulation to embellish the edges.

A sleek, well-groomed, dark-eyed man, slight, sultry, a Persian-looking fellow of about my own age, is standing back of the passport desk, alongside the on-duty army officer whose job is to process foreigners out of the country. His hourglass blue suit looks to have been styled specially for him in Paris or Rome—nothing like the suits I've seen around here, either in the streets or at the orgies. A man of European sophistication, no less a ladies' man, I would guess, than Novak's whoremaster Bolotka. Ostentatiously in English he asks to see the gentleman's papers. I pass them to the soldier, who in turn hands them to him. He reads over the biographical details—to determine, you see, if I am fiction or fact—then, sardonically, examining me as though I am now utterly transparent, comes so close that I smell the oil in his hair and the skin bracer that he's used after shaving. "Ah yes," he says, his magnitude in the scheme of things impressed upon me with that smile whose purpose is to make one uneasy, the smile of power being benign, "Zuckerman the Zionist agent," he says, and returns my American passport. "An honor," he informs me, "to have entertained you here, sir. Now back to the little world around the corner."